Blue Honor

⌘

Blue Honor
1-4392-2094-8
ISBN: 9781439220948

Cover Photo: "Cavalry Soldier"

Available as a print at www.bluehonor.com

Produced and published in conjunction with

BookSurge Publishing

7290 Investment Dr Unit B
North Charleston, SC 29418

Printed in the United States of America

Contents

⌘

I. Beginnings

Vermont Countryside, Near Montpelier
Summer, 1857

The halcyon morning gilded the simple countryside of northern Vermont. In the center of a green clearing, a white plank church starkly resided before a dirt road. Horses and carriages lined the lane impatiently waiting for absent owners. Farms and fields dotted the background of lush spring green, broken by stone fences and stands of trees, which stretched as far as the eye could reach beneath a spotted sky.

Startling the peace like a gunshot, the double doors of the church suddenly swung inward. Mass had ended. Below the straight soaring steeple, the renewed congregation slowly abandoned the dusky confines of their holy shelter. Serious or elated, they spread down the stairs and over the lawn with noise like a beehive. They drew into tight clusters, mimicking the flowers spotting the ground, not yet ready to relinquish their time. Sunday was a day to shamelessly parade in fine suits and gowns with countless trimmings.

A teenage girl sprang from the crowd jamming the doorway. She abruptly halted and blinked at the sunlight, as if disoriented by the show on the lawn. She placed a lace gloved hand at her brow, shading her scanning eyes. Her sleeves pulled and her neckline moved. She adjusted and readjusted, giving a bothered sigh. The gown she wore fit exceptionally well, but left her uneasy regardless. The pale jade and ivory of her clothes blended flawlessly with the setting, and yet she prevailed the most daring among the parishioners for its striking finery. The girl peered down her figure and saw more of herself than politely revealed in church before. Her eyes bulged and she quickly pulled up the neckline. The cap covering her mink hair slipped loose over her brow. She blew a ragged breath and pulled the ties loose to retie the blasted thing tighter. Why she decided to wear the awful costume bewildered her, especially now that she had so many eyes to see it and more of her too. The garment was meant for an older girl or a ball, not a child like her or church.

While she twisted the silk ribbon of her bonnet, her gaze continued to desperately search for the elusive. The ribbon pulled into a bow and her doll lips flattened. She scratched her head through the straw of the hat and looked thoughtful and disappointed. Only the usual women, children and old men of the local farms and town stood before her. Annoyance quickly took to her pretty face, spreading over her body until her fingers tapped on the banister. Then, her foot tapped and she set a hand on her hip.

The girl clutched her fists tight, as if she could squeeze what she looked for from the air. She swung her leg, turning to squint back into the interior behind. Several faces met her expectant eyes, none of which she looked for, but all made her realize her mistake. Blushing for her lapse, she stepped to the rail to allow them to pass with a shy apology.

In the effort to exit, none of those stalled disturbed or jostled the girl aside. Instead, they tipped hats and nodded, offering warm smiles and went around. Despite her lack of consideration, she clearly held their respect and admiration. However, piqued emotions strangled her attention. She failed to portray any bearing of a kind and adored girl.

The girl's thoughts turned to possibilities her worry produced. Usual for most girls her age, she wanted the company of a certain young man. Indeed he was someone she cared a great deal for, but not in the manner most presumed. He was a close friend or displaced brother of sorts. The idea of him home again warmed her heart and brought happiness to the bored old shadows, until a tiny smile turned the corner of her lips. A great desire to speak with him on a pressing matter had become her single thought. The blossom of a smile turned into a pain filled grimace.

While she waited to meet with her friend, the events of the past hour played in her mind, begging what kept them apart now. Sources reported his presence and he remained hidden throughout the sermon. It felt like she relived her childhood, when set far across the pews, at last they found one another and traded contorted faces for amusement until their parents hissed them still. Through the entire sermon this time, she forced her body stiff and straight, only watching ahead. The pain of her mother rapping her knuckles was not easily forgotten, not to mention that every movement could mean her dress did something deplorable.

The image of the black suited pastor floated in her mind, cast on a background of white and a single tall cross of polished wood. His mouth continually orated, but she had heard little or nothing of what he said. Devilish thoughts nagged, like nettles stuck in her shoes. She held still, hardly breathing. Her body still ached with the pain, trapped like a prisoner pinned to her own cross.

A weak explanation formed in her mind. The rumor of her friend's attendance reached her on the lips of her trustworthy father. It had not originated with him, so there was no telling the truth of it. Granted leave from school, the friend she sought would have arrived late in the evening the day before. Resulting from a long trip home, he conceded church to the notion of a visit to her home. Therefore, he never made it to church. Then she realized how very serious his family was about the Sabbath. Knowing her friend, he delayed the family, forcing them to show late, and they had to sit in the back, as not to disturb anyone. By either explanation, he could not have called out to her or joined her. He would have been first from the building and at the mercy of those on the lawn curious of his days away from their small town.

Either way, she hoped one of those stories true. Only he could help. She looked and searched, stood on tiptoes and moved fitfully on the stoop. Her eyes filled with hopeless misery. It meant more than a prized cow at the fair. She shook her fist, looking near tears. She bit her lip to keep from crying.

The girl descended the steps in leaps, stopping at the bottom to repeat the motions from before. She had to find him before they left for home.

"Good day to you, Emily Conrad," an elderly woman said, revealing the girl's name and pulling her attention from her desperate task.

Emily held her breath, recognizing the voice. She slowly turned. Her eyes went wide, seeing the short old women she feared to stand behind her. She sucked in a laughing breath and wrung her hands.

"Good morning," Emily's voice flowed worriedly, as she forced a smile.

"You are growing so lovely, dear," the woman continued.

The aged mouth rarely spoke kindly to anyone without a hook to trap a tidbit of distasteful news. Worse was her tone, cloying and nosey. Then, her watery eyes peered deeply from behind tiny wire rimmed glasses, reaching into Emily's mind for her soul, like a devil.

"What a charming smile you have," she added warmly, touching Emily's arm when the girl's attention flitted away.

Emily breathed a nervous laugh, feeling as if she would faint. Her hands trembled and she squeezed her fists tight. Her heart beat hard in her chest, as her chance to catch her friend slipped away. Now was not the time to share an idle conversation with the town gossip. She thought to ignore the woman, since it might make her leave. She stammered, trying to think of things to excuse herself with, knowing the woman trapped her, sighting her search and curious to get a clue. Nothing came to mind. Emily peered around the woman's enormous hat to see who stood along the side of the church and they danced like courting geese. The woman refused to leave or stop smiling until acknowledged. She wanted her bit of saucy news and if Emily stood there too long, she was sure to get it.

"Yes—thank you, Mrs. Handel. What a lovely hat!" Emily said breathlessly.

"Oh, you are such a dear," the woman said, adjusting the wide brim.

"Have you seen my parents?" Emily asked worriedly. "I'm afraid we've been separated. I must not delay them. They're awfully busy on the farm, as you know. Excuse me," she added, watching the woman look about and try to respond. She had finally found the words she needed.

Emily touched the woman's papery hand briefly, before continuing away from her. Leaving abruptly helped avoid further conversation or inquests, which were sure to last until her father finally approached, calling in annoyance, as they were the last to vacate the churchyard.

Free once more to study the congregation, Emily watched each smile or frown, shake or nod, while they engaged in disjointed chats. A few even laughed and some greeted her. However, each drew her farther from her intention. Anxiety twisted her features and made her insides ache with dreadful intensity. She touched her stomach and stepped slower, fighting to calm her thoughts, but panic prevailed. Emily put a hand over her heart and drew a deep breath of disappointment. After all the time they spent as children, it hurt that he did not wish to see her. His absence had been long and they were unable to keep contact, due to her mother's societal principles, but he could not have forgotten her entirely. Her lip pushed out in a pout.

Holding her silk skirts from underfoot, Emily walked the brick path from the church to the roadside. Her pace slowed, convinced he hid from her. She sniffed a little, remembering how she refused to see him off at the train. She thought he would have understood, knowing how their families tried to throw them together, and how they refused to obey.

With chin hung to chest, hardly able to refuse her father lied or the boy forgot her, she sought their carriage, the last proof of even his family's presence. Daylight darkened with her spirits, as a cloud wandered overhead. The spring breeze blew last fall's leaves across her path. She hesitated and watched them, as if she saw a terrible omen in their erratic flight. She shivered and hugged herself, wishing for a shawl for her shoulders.

Emily stepped into the road, hoping to spy the horse and carriage her friend took. There were too many to discern the Howell's. She feared her moment would not be had in time. Her hope drifted off with the leaves. Impressive determination profited nothing. Despite the crucial need for an interview, he just would not appear. Lifting her chin, she choked the frustration back, refusing to fall to tears before the town. Someone always watched from somewhere. They would put together some crazy story to spread around, surely enough.

Pivoting on her heels, she disguised her disappointment with indifference and boredom. She regained the brick path and the sunlight burst forth again, radiating warmth and hope. The wind blew again, but instead of ill omens, it felt like a whisper in her ear. Emily walked briskly back, holding the church doors in the line of her sight.

If he's here, she prayed, *God, let him appear right now.*

Every desperate thread of hope pled with the powers of fate. Then, it happened, much to her open mouthed astonishment. Withdrawing through the shadowy door, the last tenants of the church stepped onto the landing with the pastor. The first was a young man, immaculately clothed in a cadet uniform. The man next to him, older by some years, appeared comparatively threadbare. The young one's head gleamed like polished ebony and she knew instantly her prayer answered without any further delay. Her eyes held him triumphantly and she grinned and bounced on her toes like a little girl about to receive a gift.

Emily's friend looked well despite his absence from his mother's care for over a year. He smiled charmingly and bore great confidence, something West Point Academy issued with the uniform. Even his swagger was improved. She felt proud, as if she had a hand in his creation.

Emily swiftly traversed the distance, intent on reaching him before he disappeared from the stairs, as the pastor already had. The distance stretched forever with him only held in her gaze. Afraid to forget her words in her excitement, she mumbled to herself.

You need to convince him. Daddy can't.

Emily charged up the steps to the boy's side. Her porcelain features glowed in the sun and a grin split her face. A momentary glance passed, but the boy disregarded her to follow his father to the lawn. Emily's words washed from her mind with her stolen joy. She frowned at their backs. His father whispered to him and peered at her over his shoulder. Though obvious as the day in a big hoop skirt, hat and horrid lacy frills, he stepped past without a notice. She looked at them with hurt by that he forgot her. No, he did not forget. He was angry she refused to see him off, though not unusual in days gone by.

Emily cocked her head to the side and followed, stepping hard. He should have understood her reasons. She scowled deeply at her friend's back. He slipped his fingers through his brilliant raven hair. He flashed a grin at something his father said. The old man looked to her again, but said nothing. She stopped following, realizing she openly stared.

The sire lowered his head to listen to something his son said. Mr. Howell touched the graying whiskers he kept on his face for as long as she could remember. They both guarded their words and eyed the congregation warily. What did they speak of that worried them so, and kept them from acknowledging anyone but each other? She looked around and then shook her head frustrated.

Whatever it was, it was not as important as her task, nor more important than greeting an old friend.

"Evan Howell," Emily cried at the ill mannered lout. She would be just as rude, if that is what it took.

Emily's voice reached Evan's ear. He turned warily to face her. She raised her brow when he stared clueless. She crossed her arms and stared dumbly back. His eyes ran the length of her. Touching his shaven chin and squinting, she saw recognition slowly settle on his features. He smiled and then laughed. He looked to his father confused and then back to her. Mr. Howell nodded, also laughing a little.

Outraged, Emily clasped her fists to her sides, waiting before she boxed his ears. It really had not been that long. She had not changed that much in one year. She scowled a smile at him, tilting her chin to the side and stepped toward them.

"Miss Emily Conrad," Evan declared with surprise. "You look—"

"Where have you been? I was looking all over this yard for you," Emily snapped. "And when I do find you—you don't even look at me. Not at all gentlemanly, Evan." Emily watched him give her a sheepish apologetic look. He scrubbed his hand on the back of his neck unable to speak. She stood barely to his shoulder, but was capable of the presence of a mountain lion. She quickly flicked her attention to his father before he could answer. "Hello Mr. Howell. How are you and your wife today?" She smiled with a much warmer tone.

"We're fine, Em. How are you?" Mr. Howell asked in return. He appeared ready to laugh at how she handled his son so adeptly at her age. She'd make a good wife for him. Turning somber, he said, "Mrs. Howell stayed home with Davie today. He wasn't so well this morning."

"Oh—do you want me to come round? To give Mrs. Howell a rest," she said concerned.

"That won't be necessary, dear. But, thank you," he nodded to her. His weathered features grayed with pain. He removed his hat and ran a hand through his dusty hued hair and laughed off whatever bothered him. "Well—I'll leave you two young people ta catch up. Your parents still here, Em?"

"Yes, Mr. Howell. Over there," Emily answered, sorry she brought up Davie. She had hurt him.

Emily pointed to the affluent pair who stood guard by a wide oak. Discovery settled on his features when he saw her father. Together they observed them in silence.

Mr. Stuart Conrad presented himself every ounce the gentleman their town thought him. A head of white hair and muttonchops framed his laughing pink face, while he enjoyed the company of the preacher. His charisma showed in how he wore his clothing, such as the overtly held pocket watch with a narrow chain connecting it to his rich green waistcoat, not to be outdone by a splendid pewter jacket. A fine hat of matching silk topped his head. He turned his body, tucking his watch away and then his arms behind him to show his protruding belly. Emily smiled with pride at him. She loved her father more than anyone in the world.

Beside him was Emily's mother, Margaret. The story she heard told was they married twenty-three years ago, at this church, and existed under mysterious circumstances for the first four years. Since they lived at the dairy, the pair bore two children, of which Emily was the second. Some said Margaret bore other children, but they had died early on. Emily never found anything to prove such a thing.

Emily shifted on her feet, distracted by her mother's story and superior conduct. Her fine gown made Emily uncomfortable in her own again. The pastor spoke, and her mother's head bobbed beneath a cumbersome hat, fluttering in the air. If Emily knew her mother, the woman stood there knowing she looked better than any of the others, the only one of a few unrefined sides of her.

Sadly, no hat or gown could hide the lines of gray in Margaret's brown hair, or shade the developing lines around her mouth or in the corner of her eyes. Amid the desperate cling of faded youth and true loveliness of her face, Margaret usually held her thin lips pinched tight, adding severity to her expression. Her mother was not always doting, but she loved her family deeply, regardless of the secreted bitterness. This side contrasted her husband's constant warmth. Perhaps that was the clue Emily always sought, but took for granted. If Emily ever knew the secrets that soured such a woman, she would have thought it the loss of children. But, not even Mrs. Handel had figured it out, even trying for years to do so.

Margaret smiled deeply, looking at the pastor with eyes of bright blue like her daughter's. Her mannerisms were precise and polite, if not snobbish and practiced. Only on occasion she managed such a smile, when a neighbor or acquaintance bid her good day in public passing. Sometimes, she gave Emily that smile. Margaret thought custom and duty the most important tasks of a woman, and it should be done well and right. Margaret symbolized the ideal of refinement and propriety for many. Some believed it came from her upbringing in one of New York's socially mobile families. The sense of superiority was a fault of many where her mother came from.

Emily looked over her jade gown. Emily contrasted her, raised on a farm far from city life, destined to be a shy and awkward farm wife. Somehow the lace seemed tattered, and wrinkles like mountains marred the silk. Emily sighed with disgust, tired of a continually poor performance. She wished she was half as proper as her sire and dame. She must be such a disappointment to them. The adjustments to her gown began again.

"Got bugs, Em?" Evan teased.

"Now you notice me," she replied with a grimace.

With the Conrad Elders in site, Mr. Howell took leave of his son and Emily. He adjusted the worn brown bowler on his head and stopped several times to return the greetings of friends and acquaintances.

Emily lost her worry in her admiration of Evan's father, despite his roughness. Her hands stilled, thinking of how Mr. Howell struggled before her growing eyes, obtaining the little wealth he claimed. With that small bit, he carved a better future for his family, starting with Evan. Mr. Howell commanded great strength and determination in the face of harsh conditions.

Biting her bottom lip, Emily prayed for Mr. Howell's youngest son. They had enough of struggle to last a lifetime already.

Evan shifted on his feet, eagerly awaiting Emily's further words. His eyes sparkled with mischief.

With Mr. Howell out of earshot, Emily could at last speak freely with Evan. She gave him a bright aggravating smile, delaying again. He smiled back with confusion and gestured for her to let it out.

"Not here," she forced a deeper smile to disguise her words.

"It's that good?" Evan whispered, rubbing his hands together.

Emily cast a nervous glance about the crowd. It stopped at the oak where her parents stood. Mr. Howell just joined them, assuring their time. She looked back to Evan and with a light laugh took hold of his sleeve. She led him to a more secluded place, along the wall of the church. Her playful expression turned quite serious while she passed another glance over the parishioners, pushing Evan back against the church to see better. The people were busy with each other and had not noticed the pair sneak away. Her eyes went back to Evan.

"I had no idea, Miss Emily, that you felt this way," Evan teased, as she stood against him. "I missed you too, but I don't think the churchyard is the place for a cuddle and kiss."

Emily glowered at him a moment, studying his face. He had not changed at all.

"I wanted to speak to you about something serious, Evan," Emily said, stepping back. Her treasured eyes stared up at him without an ounce of affection, and she held him back at arms length.

"I thought I understood that," Evan replied.

Unlike his sisters, Emily did not make a display for no good reason. If something was wrong, everyone knew it, anyone who knew her anyway. She released him assured he would listen.

Evan fixed his cadet hat under his arm and stood up straight from the church wall. Managing a smile, he offered his elbow. Emily reluctantly looped her arm in his and they walked toward the back of the church.

"I guess now is as good a time as any," Emily said. She laughed uncomfortably as he looked down at her curiously. Her smile faded to sad worry, and she looked to the tree line ahead. "Daddy's concerned about Michael. He's refused to continue his studies," Emily told him. "He's done with basics now, you know."

"Is he?" Evan sounded unconvinced of the news. "Time does go fast," he said with wonder.

Emily looked back over their shoulders. Already eyes followed them. She pushed him behind the church to continue their walk without the town prying. Evan went dutifully where she guided.

"I wouldn't worry about Mike, Em. He's got enough smarts for better than this old place."

Emily cocked her head to the side and watched his profile, half laughing at the statement, "does he?"

Evan grimaced and his black gaze shifted over the lawn and the people on the other side of the church. They turned and walked back in the other direction. He was tense, standing alone with her. When his eyes met hers, he smiled questioningly. The longer they spent in secret conference, the more those people believed they were right about them.

"You see, that's just it," Emily continued. "He thinks he needs to stay on the farm for Daddy's sake, so he can take over the business," she told him. "Before Daddy passes on, God forbid," she groaned dramatically.

"Well that is foolish," Evan frowned. He drew his brows down and thought. "At least he must realize there's a whole world out there. Michael would just waste himself sitting here."

"That's what Daddy told him," Emily said sadly. Biting her lip, she lowered her eyes, placing her arms behind her back. Emily could feel Evan's eyes on her.

She smiled nervously under his scrutiny. No matter what, things had changed and he was nearly a stranger. "I wonder if you would talk to him, Ev. You going to school and all," Emily divulged her plan.

Evan smiled broadly, "For my favorite girl?" His tone sounded as though he meant to merely appease her and not follow through. He pinched a bit of her skirt between his gloved fingers and lifted it slightly. He laughed slightly. "You do look gorgeous. When did you grow up, Em? I'll have to marry you now for sure. Just to keep you honest from meeting me back here—alone." He pulled her to him.

"Aw, Ev," Emily blushed. "You're just flattering me to get out of it. Haven't you met any nice girls at school yet?" Emily pushed him away.

"Lotsa girls, yeah," he said, scratching his neck and reddening with embarrassment to admit it. "But, I don't think they're what you'd call nice."

"Evan Howell!" Emily gasped. "Well, now that I know this, you'd best do as I ask, before I tell your mother!"

They stared at each other and then fell to laughter.

"I know I can count on you," Emily hugged him.

"And the trap is laid," Evan squeezed her back. He kissed the side of her head. "Yeah, sure you can count on me—for what?" Evan pretended to forget. "I already told you I'm not letting them see us married."

"Talk to Michael," Emily sighed.

"Do you really think it's wise to say a thing to Mike? I mean—your mother an all," he asked nervous as a trapped cat trying to laugh away a rabid dog.

"Evan," Emily breathed. Her eyes narrowed. "I waited to see you all morning for this one tiny favor."

"All right—all right," he gave in. "Let me think it through first," he waved his hand.

"Evan," Emily said more demandingly.

"He's ornery as a badger, Em," Evan whined. "Specially if he's got his mind made up."

"You're afraid of him? A boy with less training and education than yourself?" She laughed at Evan.

Evan grimaced. He was quite capable of withstanding her manipulations, if he wanted to. He took her arm and once more escorted her, but this time toward the oak and their parents. He did not think it right to change a man's mind once made. So, he would play stubborn, not allowing their friendship to misguide him right into a family dispute.

Emily eyed him with a catty glare. She blinked her frustration away when it produced no concessions. The man was a stone, but more likely a jackass scared of a little woman and her boy. Her mouth curled from a grim line into a smile, picturing it. She choked back the giddiness it brought, covering her mouth with a fist and clearing her throat.

"I'm not afraid," Evan insisted.

"Fat baby," Emily mumbled with a smile.

Emily looked to the congregation as they went and said no more. The people smiled at them, offering glances of approval.

As much as Evan cared for her, Emily's family already caused him enough trouble. Spreading the seeds of rumor that he would marry Emily and chasing off the girls he did like was all quite enough.

Emily drooped under the pressure of the stares and anguished by the ideas she knew flew about. She quickly forgot about her task, wishing to hide under Evan's coat away from the eyes on her. From the corner of her vision, she saw Evan hold his chin high with confidence. She drew herself up, drawing strength from a place she had missed for sometime.

"If anyone can convince him," Emily said. "It's you."

Evan shook his head and laughed at her determination.

Emily rested her head against his shoulder, hugging his arm to her. She could not be angry with her hero. He would not let her down, because he never had.

At the oak tree, Mr. Howell and the Conrads watched the two young people in their fervent secretive conversation, wandering from one hiding spot to another. They each appeared much happier than previously, especially Emily's mother. She watched the pair with sparkling eyes of hope. Her tight lips curled into a tiny smile. Taking hold of her husband's arm, she made a contented sigh and even blushed a little in the apples of her pallid cheeks. Stuart looked down at her with a smile. He patted her hand rested on his arm and looked back to their daughter. They were such fools.

Emily heard what they said to each other, as they closed in on the tree and it defiled the sparkle Evan had put back in her eye.

"We may become family yet, Stuart." Mr. Howell said. He gripped his lapels and tugged, drawing up proudly.

"I believe you're right there, Jackson," Stuart agreed, also grasping his coat lapels and tugging with a grin on his cheerful face.

"Would be a wonderful good occasion," Margaret said with hope. She liked when her plans succeeded.

Would be nice to have what I want, Emily thought. *Not what you chose for me.*

Emily let them assume what passed between them. It happened every time she stood near Evan. She exhausted herself explaining the truth of their relationship long ago. Annoyed she may need to do so again, she narrowed her eyes at her parents, daring them to speak about it. Instead, they beamed proud and hopeful and ignored her churlish expression. Emily resisted a sigh of frustration and forced a smile, choosing to ignore their idiocy over picking a fight she could not win.

Releasing Evan's arm, Emily dutifully went to her father's free side. Her mother gave an approving smile and nod, but Emily returned the warmly loaded expression with an emotive stare and took her father's hand for protection. The quiet exchange provided the only means of retaliation allowed the youngest Conrad.

The pastor excused himself from them and went to other members of the flock.

With the eyes of God gone, Emily's mother only dropped her ridiculous grin to give a silent promise of punishment later for her daughter. Margaret then turned her loaded expression on Evan. That was Margaret's form of retaliation.

Frustrated, Emily watched her parents welcome her friend with enthusiastic gestures and warm words. Evan met them graciously, capably disguising his true feelings behind a smiling mask. Their parents continually meddled in their lives, a great nuisance that bothered him.

After further dull conversation, the congregation broke apart around them and soon, few families remained on the lush cool grass of the lawn. Instead, their carriages spun up dust, leaving a hazy brown cloud over the road. The haze accompanied by creaking wheels and whickering horses, stood the last hint of human presence.

"Well, now I'd best be getting on home," Jackson tipped his hat to Emily's mother and then her. He shook Stuart's hand, taking Emily's safety from her. "Good to see you again Conrads—as always. Come Evan."

Evan nodded to them, drawing Emily's eyes to his face. He looked concerned.

"Mrs. Conrad—Ma wanted to know if she could call for tea tomorrow?" Evan suddenly said, making his father pause. "She's cooped up in the house accounna Davie bein sick so much lately," he continued with a weak smile.

"Oh, of course, dear. You tell her to come right over," Mrs. Conrad said warmly She was pleasant when she desired to be or when it benefited her. "Your family is always welcome at our house." Her gaze altered between father and son. "As a matter of fact, Evan—why don't you come with her tomorrow? Michael missed you today, and you could visit with Emily some more. They do miss you so," her suggesting eye roved over Emily.

Emily's brows stitched together and she bit her lip, impatiently glaring at her mother. Her mouth popped open to protest the masked statement but closed it. She clasped and unclasped her hands, shifting on her feet, thinking of all she wanted to say. Her eyes went to the church, and she sought the only source of help not yet tried. If he didn't help, she would throttle her mother right before God and her father without remorse. She imagined a long finger wagging at her, *love thy parents.* Her mouth twisted and she thought she would be sick on the ground right then.

Evan snickered, waking Emily out of her imagination. The sentiment would prove lost on her mother, as well. She looked and it saw it so.

"I'd love to," Evan forced a smile for the woman. She beamed at him pleased. "I've missed Mike too."

Emily heard Margaret laugh lightly and saw her smile waver. He had not said he missed Emily. Emily put a finger in front of her lips to stop her joy at the deft play. Her mother raised a gloved hand to touch the bun at the back of her head. She obviously caught that meaning. Emily's eyes went to Evan, wondering if he had found a way to thwart their constant scheming.

Evan winked at Emily. Yet again, it was mistaken for loving admiration, but Emily knew he assured her request. She smiled back at him unafraid. They were together in the mess after all. She rolled her eyes and sighed at the reactions. The only sure convincing would be if one married someone else.

The Howell's then bid their final farewells for the day, while Emily guardedly watched them go. Evan's uniform drew a dark shadow with it and the sky rumbled with thunder in the distance. She wondered at the strange weather that day, having thought the bright sunshine would last. A storm hung on the western horizon, dashing that hope.

The Conrads stood left to themselves, the last family on the lawn. Even the pastor had gone into his modest house beside the church. Emily still watched the road where the Howell's had gone.

Out of the corner of her eye, Emily noticed her parents eyeing her. They probably mistook her for some mooning lovesick idiot. If they would trust when she said she felt only the love of a sister for him, then they would not find their plans disintegrating beneath them.

Placing her gaze on her family, she saw the hope in their eyes and the joy. She felt her heart quicken at the thought of destroying it, expecting their words would force her to. Emily lowered her eyes.

"Well," Margaret prompted her. "What were you two so secretive about?"

"Michael," Emily said, lifting a brow and looking dead in her mother's eye with all the defiance she felt. The time came to set them straight. "He's going to come and speak to him about going to a university."

"That's wonderful," Stuart smiled at her. "Good girl," he added, putting his arm about her and squeezing.

If he would only challenge her mother about the match they sought with Evan. He must understand how she felt. Her father would not approve a union she opposed. In the end, he stood the last pillar of hope against her mother's plot, unless fate saw fit to send something more convincing. Her body relaxed at the thought. Putting her arm about his waist, she allowed him to lead her from the churchyard to their waiting carriage with her mother close behind.

By their carriage, Emily looked to her mother and stepped aside to let her climb in first. Margaret's face pinched tight and her eyes avoided any contact with Emily. Margaret's disappointment meant something bad later, proven often.

Emily swallowed the burning knot in her throat and climbed into the seat beside her mother. Her dress pulled and she was reminded of how terrible the day had already been. Settled on the buttoned seat, she looked back to the church, seeking help. She bit back her misery with little success. She closed her eyes on her frustration.

The carriage rocked, as her father climbed into the driver's seat.

Emily just could not love Evan the way they wanted her to. Looking at the church again, she wondered if fate could possibly grant her more. Emily sighed. She sat back and spared a glance toward her mother. The woman sat with her hands folded in her lap, wearing her displeasure openly. Her chin angled high, and her lips pinched, tightly holding back the tirade of emotion filled words building in her mind. Though she kept silent, Emily could hear her say a great deal. Close in body, their opposition on Evan forced them far apart.

Emily stuck her eyes to the road, half seeing her father take up the reins. He paid no attention to what went on right behind him. Emily's body tensed. Why would he not speak on her behalf? She wanted to cry, but refused to be their victim. She feared the reprisals that would come of it. Her mother would shout and claim her mad from the books she read all day.

Had too many books taught her what she knew of her dear friend and made him so undesirable a mate?

Emily heard the reins snap and her father's sharp command. The carriage lurched forward groaning and creaking. The edge of a book poked Emily's back and she remembered the volume she had discarded there on their arrival that morning. She pulled the object to her lap, receiving an acknowledgement from her mother at last.

Margaret rolled her eyes and sighed disgustedly at her daughter.

"I don't know what you find so interesting in those stories, Em," her mother sighed, dramatic, disappointed and tired. "They're going to ruin your mind for sure."

"Father thinks they're good for me," she replied. "They have such interesting lives, mother. Forgive me if the day to day of the farm bores me," Emily said, though she knew better. She could see her father smile and her mother frown. He shook his head and tried not to make a sound. Tucking the reins about his arm, he lit his pipe and carried on. "They entertain me, I mean," Emily corrected herself. "Besides, it improves my vocabulary and grammar."

"Emily, really," her mother sighed. "There are so many inappropriate things for a girl your age in them."

"Then you should have let me go with Mrs. Murphy for the spring," Emily added.

"I'd not let you anywhere with that woman alone, especially in Europe. Silly girl," Her mother chided.

Emily held her breath, looking at the leather bound in her lap, hoping her words had not taken them away from her. She opened the cover, and found her page to resume the story. In silence they returned home.

The sky darkened over the little white church, standing lonely on its empty yard, slowly disappearing behind the green leaves and gray branches of the trees.

~

The night spread black like crude spilled over the world. Under a fierce storm full of lightening flashes, three figures ambled across a cattle field. Between them they carried a fourth member, wrapped tight in a useless wet blanket. In the distance a three story house, gray in the dark, stood with lighted windows, inviting them toward it.

"A farm," one said with a woman's voice from beneath the brim of a leaky wide brimmed hat. "Come on," she waved an arm to direct them toward it.

The mismatched pair who carried the fourth put down their bundle and stopped the woman from journeying any closer to it or its associated buildings. They pulled her back with strong thick hands. She looked to them with a question on her round ruddy face, smeared by dirt and oils. Shelter hung just out of reach and she could not understand their resistance.

"What is it?" She asked.

"Are you mad?" The smaller of the men asked with a distinctly foreign accent. "Yur gonna get us caught."

"It's a place to get out of the rain," she declared, placing chubby fists on her robust hips. She swayed threateningly. "What are you afraid of? This is Vermont."

The smaller man stepped up to her and the tall one checked on the fourth they laid in the grass. He pulled the wet blanket back to reveal the face of a dark skinned woman. Her eyes remained tightly closed, while her wrapped head rolled back and forth to find relief from the rain falling on her. Her full lips parted, speaking low words incoherently. The large man touched a brown hand to her forehead. His stony face twisted with displeasure. In a quick motion, he flipped the blanket back over her face and returned to the others arguing on the hillside.

"Her fever's worse," he said. His words prevented the fistfight about to occur between the Brit and the fat woman.

The pair quit arguing to look at him. His dark face was lost under his hat brim. In silence they stood in the rain. The sound pounded out reason.

"We have to leave her," the woman said. "She's dead fur sure."

"Zekiel," a voice breathed from the blankets.

"We can still get you outta here," she said to the taller man.

"She's not dead yet," the tall man rasped.

"We've gotta get ya cross the border, mate," the Brit said. "Bounty hunters'll catch us for sure if we wait ere—I doubt the people in tha mansion'd care."

They stood in silence again.

"Come on," the woman trudged off.

The men looked each other over.

"Dodgy business, mate," the Brit said. "But, we've still got you to worry ar hides."

The Brit grabbed the tall man's arm to urge him along, but the tall man would not move. He watched the runaway slave's face work around the dilemma. His eyes went from the body on the ground to the large one headed for the forest. He would have to go if he wanted his freedom.

One weak step after another saw the runaway's step grow stronger, until they ran through the rain, disappearing in the night.

"If I don't go—that's gonna be me layin there."

ঌ

In the early morning of the next day, Evan arrived with his mother, as promised in the churchyard. A stable hand drew away the carriage, and they stood on the Conrad lawn, staring at the Conrad door before traversing the porch steps to approach and ring the bell. All the while, Evan supported his biggest fan on his arm.

Evan's mother was a sturdier woman than her slight frame and appearance displayed. Mrs. Howell birthed five children for her husband. Among them was Evan the eldest and Davie the youngest. Between, three girls arrived, Millicent and Minerva the twins and Lauralee the second eldest. All children survived infancy, now pacing through childhood and adolescence to adulthood. Born to her last, Little Davie just reached the age of six. After having a strong constitution through the first years, he showed symptoms of an exhausting and lasting illness in the more recent ones. Despite this change, the Howells had remained optimistic of recovery. Of late though, the worn Mrs. Howell showed signs of doubt.

When the young Conrad housekeeper, Rose Benson, answered the ring, she appeared shocked to see Evan stand beside his mother. Her green eyes swept over him. She bore not just the question of his presence but also clear appreciation unspoken on her lips. The curls at the corners of her mouth curled into a smile. She breathlessly tried to speak. Then, suddenly, the joy was gone. Bad luck hung on the Howell home like ivy. Rose touched her raven hair self-consciously, forcing a laugh and begged their pardon at her gawking.

Rose's eyes went to Evan again and his mother raised her brows at the girl. During his time away, Evan undoubtedly grew into the choicest of young men their little town could offer a girl. However, that did not excuse her lascivious staring. Mrs. Howell brushed past her with a discouraging glance to cease her forwardness.

Forced from her thoughts, Rose backed away from the door to let Evan pass, as well. She blushed and smoothed her apron nervously.

"I'll call the family for you—tea will be served in the parlor in a few moments," Rose said, doing her best to keep her eyes away from Mrs. Howell's son. The pair stood in the paneled hallway, looking at her while she shut the door. She turned back and exchanged warm smiles again with Evan. "Good to see you again, Evan," she dared to say with a small curl in her lip.

Evan smiled back to her, and nodded, "Good to be seen, Miss Benson. Thank you."

Under his mother's scrutiny, Rose took Evan's hat from him and hung it on a hook of the coat bench by the door. Mrs. Howell shook her head barely amused by her son's playful tone. Though Mrs. Howell little approved, the young people held a longstanding friendship.

Once their things lay settled and they in the in the parlor, Rose excused herself from the Howells. When Rose was gone, Mrs. Howell looked at her son with a reproving glare.

"Evan really," Mrs. Howell said.

"What?" He grinned. "It's just Rose."

Mrs. Howell tsked and rolled her eyes.

When Rose's footsteps faded away, another set rang through the home from the floors above. Evan's eyes lifted to the staircase outside the arch of the parlor. He rose to his feet and slowly went to the hall, already suspecting the culprit. His gaze met Emily, rushing down the steps in one of her lovely day gowns.

Emily felt unchecked joy at seeing her old friend again. He stood in the foyer like so many days before he went to school. She leapt from the last stair into his waiting arms and listened to him warmly chuckle in her ear.

The girl felt good against him and he closed his eyes, as she hugged him back. Evan spun her around and she laughed out loud. It had been too long. Then, he suddenly set her down and stepped hurriedly back.

Emily looked at his flat and guarded expression with concern. She felt cold and strange in light of his rejection. He cleared his throat, looking past her to the parlor, coughing in his hand to prevent a smile that troubled his lips. Emily turned. She self consciously touched her minky locks, fixed up in two braided buns at the nape of her neck, to be sure they remained so.

Mrs. Howell sat on the family sofa. She smiled and nodded to Emily, eliciting a nervous twitter from the girl. Emily turned a bright face back to Evan and grabbed hold of his sleeve, relieved to see the reason for his strange behavior. Dragging him along behind her, she stopped just inside the parlor to greet his mother.

"Good afternoon, Mrs. Howell," Emily grinned to the small woman, despite the usual aggravation at being suspected of a love that did not exist. "How are you? Mind if I steal Ev for a walk with Mike?"

Mrs. Howell chuckled with a warm expression just like her sons, "not at all, Emmy. You go right ahead, my darling."

Emily nodded, a bit annoyed by how Mrs. Howell spoke to her. She saw herself as a ten year old in pigtails, getting her head patted. Tightening her grip on Evan's sleeve, she made him wince with pain. Leading him down the hall toward the back of the house, she frowned with a sour mood.

"You could have warned me," she said.

"You didn't give me time," Evan replied.

With each step, the feeling ebbed and Emily turned her attentions to more important matters, such as her brother Michael. Stopping halfway to the back door, she checked the hall for spies.

Emily leaned close to whisper, "take Michael for a walk and see what you can do. I'm going to stay here and take tea with our mothers. Mamma wants me to and you know how she is. Besides, we don't want them thinking you know what." At her last words she gave him a sorry expression. She preferred the idea of going with the boys.

"I'll try my best, Emily. I just hope I can talk sense into him. If it is sense," Evan said, somehow sounding optimistic. "You're right, at least they can't make eyes at us when we're apart," he added, laughing. "Of course, I can't make eyes at you either."

"Not amusing, Evan Howell." Emily glared at him. Turning, she continued down the hall. "Don't worry none about Michael," Emily smiled. "He's in a fine mood today."

Hearing her mother and Rose on the stairs up the hall, Emily quickly opened the back door. She hurried outside towing the cadet with her, preventing any glimpse to her mother's doubtlessly hopeful face. Everyone would watch and listen to them on the porch, but she would not worry. They only discussed Michael, not a silly secret meeting for later.

"Quiet," she whispered to him, peeking through the screen into the hall. Her mother and Rose went to the parlor without hesitation. "Mike looks up to you. That's why I asked," Emily lowered her voice and leaned toward him. Evan smiled and shook his head at her words. Emily assessed him, seeing the mirth in his features. "He's out in the milking house," Emily inspired him with a little push toward the back steps. "Take him for a walk, and if he gives you a hard time, tell him Daddy told him to take a break."

Evan stepped down the stairs however reluctant at her prompting. Turning back, he looked to her with an expression of betrayal. He had hoped Emily meant for them both to lecture her brother. He could hardly speak to Michael alone. He would need help if he was still the stubborn kid he once knew. Evan lowered his head, apprehensively standing in the same spot. Michael had the tenacity of a nasty terrier.

"Say, Em—" His voice faded. "Some help would be nice."

Emily smiled at him and quickly dashed back in the house before he could beg her to help. But then, he also knew, she could not go with him while her plan carried out. Michael would suspect and a fight he would have the whole way. After such an assured promise to his sister, he could not fail.

Exhaling deeply, Evan finally turned toward the outbuildings. Luck willing, Michael would be flexible that day and they could avoid a fight. He collected his thoughts, in preparation of exactly what he would say. He wanted to succeed, just like in class at the Point, and if it meant making Mrs. Conrad unhappy, it would prove easier to make it happen. Evan knew the scheming woman must have a hand in the kid's decision. She probably filled him with guilt for a single thought of leaving.

Evan entered the milking house and sometime later, emerged with Michael to walk the dirt lane between the house and the farm buildings. Overhung with trees and lined with a white plank fence, the track served as an aesthetic barrier between the home and the workhouses. Cresting the hill at the far western end, the young men slowly made their way to the pastures where their discussion turned serious.

Michael presented the picture of his father in his youth, golden haired with bright sapphire eyes. He also held the jovial expression innate in their bloodline. Michael's boyish features were contrary to Evan's darker more powerful appearance. However, Michael suffered nothing from his classification as a pretty man. He complained only when time ran thin for all the young women drifting his way at the dances and other social occasions. In fact, neither of them suffered for their looks. They held the favor of the local young women above all others.

The scene was reminiscent of days long past. The boys spoke easily on this and that. Then, Evan deftly brought him around to the point of the talk. Michael stood open to a discussion of his future. Again, his luck withstood. Mrs. Conrad had not yet won.

Michael appeared dispirited about his decision. From this Evan suspected for sure his mother had goaded him into it. It was Michael's decision to plan his own future, without her interference, but was he behaving any differently? Once, both young men faced a life on their respective farms, but now the future offered a chance at something else. The dairy could wait, if it ever needed him. There was little harm in guiding him that way.

"You're smart enough to go to a university, Mike," Evan said, leading him to think for himself. He clapped his friend on the back and gave him a grand smile. "At least try it before giving up."

"Giving up? Oh—I'm not giving up, Ev," Michael laughed him off, but it somehow fell short of his eyes. He would not directly meet his friend's gaze. "Pop needs someone here to help run the farm," Michael justified himself. "I wouldn't want to leave him alone or nothing."

Evan looked at Michael, searching for something to use. It sounded as if he feared leaving due to some imminent danger. The farm offered an easy life, which he could not rightly turn his back on. Perhaps, he even saw it as a means to a legacy, but his life would know little experience. He was so unlike Emily who dreamed of change. Evan hoped the dreamer would at least move on.

"I felt the same—but my father wanted me to be more than a farmer, and he saved money for a long time to send me," Evan said, offering him a chance to voice his real opinion. "I have to admit—I'm glad he did. It's not like I can't come back if I want."

"Yeah?" Michael paused to think on his words. He looked at his friend. Evan stood inches taller and many times more impressive. He picked at his vest, seemingly disappointed in his appearance. His squinting gaze went to the house in the distance, a white ghost of memories. His expression turned solemn. He could hardly imagine leaving the place he had been all his life. "What's it like, Ev—going to school far away like that?" Michael asked him.

"Damn fun, if you ask me," Evan laughed away the terror his friend could not disguise. If he meant to succeed, he had to defeat doubt. Evan took a more serious expression to assure his move. "You get used to it, and there's plenty other men round in the same position. Some are farther away than you," Evan explained. Michael appeared a little less reticent. "My friend Joe Maynard's from Frederick, Maryland. I'll have to bring him home one time. You'd all love him—real nice fellow. He's lots farther away than us and never showed a sign a homesick."

Evan watched Michael, think over what he said. Evan turned his eyes up to the blue sky spread high and far above them. He wondered how the friend he spoke of spent his carefully won time away. Neither of them went home in months. Freshmen almost never received time away. Lowering his chin, his eyes searched over the fields surrounding them.

Emily would like Joe. He was her type surer than anyone; a real gentleman, having a flare for knowing just how to persuade a woman to fall in his arms. He smiled, thinking of how smooth Joe handled women. Then again, he thought it might be wiser to keep him away. The Conrads would never forgive him, if something like Joe happened to their daughter. Evan was the one they wanted to marry their girl since long ago. He couldn't wish a man on her that never seemed to care for any of the young women hunting him. He said they could not hold his attention, that they acted the trophy and not the partner. Evan knew what he meant. They agreed with everything you said, and simpered and smiled constantly. But, Emily never did any of that. He half wondered if their parents were right, knowing no one could care for her right.

"Michael! Evan!" Emily's distinctive voice cried to them over the fields, as if she felt his thoughts.

Evan and Michael turned at the same time. Their expressions betrayed their emotions, fearful at the sound of such a desperate cry. Misfortune trailed for sure. He heard Michael breathe her name in a voice filled with concern. Together they loped toward her, as she ran to them despite her long skirts. Her face was torn by fear her brother and friend could only imagine. She called to them again, feeling her anguish, slowing her pace unable to run uphill any further. She stopped, falling to her knees on the ground exhausted and breathless. Tears flooded her eyes.

Evan passed Michael, slapping his shoulder to move him faster. The kid called to her again, exciting a lurch in Evan's heart, just like when Davie had one of his nights.

Together, the young men stomped to a halt, joining Emily where she knelt in the high grass, drawing ragged breaths. When Evan touched her arm, she looked at him, tears springing from her enlarged eyes. Whatever happened, it must be gravely serious to darken her brightness. Evan fought to speak, but Michael beat him to it.

"Is it May-Belle, Em?" Michael asked.

Emily shook her head no before speaking, "come to the stables. It's horrible—horrible," If possible, her face turned fiercely grim. "Daddy needs your help—in the stable—we need to bring som—someone in the house." She wrapped her arms about herself and cried. "It's so horrible."

"Sure, Em." Evan said, touching her back consolingly. She never looked so overwrought in her life. "Come on Mike."

Emily watched Evan and Michael run across the field, trying to gather her strength before she stood to follow. She had not prepared them for what they would find, hardly to mention what she had. It would not have helped, for nothing could protect them from the shock. The image of what lay in the barn flashed in her mind. She quickly dismissed it before it gripped her in terror again. Her body shivered with the remnants.

Emily turned from the view of the stables to the back road of the house, cradling her arms about her stomach. The guestroom needed fixing for when Michael and Evan carried the poor thing inside. There was barely time to finish the arduous task. Yet, there she stood, dawdling in the field avoiding the job, like a frightened baby.

Leaning into her step, Emily strode quickly back to the house. She refused to think anymore about what was said and all she saw. None the less, it haunted her mind until more tears ran down her cheeks. Soon, she ran along the lane between the house and outbuildings, sobbing.

Beyond Emily, Evan and Michael reached the stable door that stood open on its dark interior, trampling dirt under dusty boots. The young men exchanged a questioning glance before continuing. Neither could have answered the other's unspoken words, wholly ignorant of more than something horrible waited for them there. Though Evan looked quite dapper in his uniform and Michael rather work-worn, both appeared tight as a cork ready to pop.

Against the weathered interior, Jack the foreman waited, chewing something and holding his weathered hands in his dungaree pockets. He frowned deeply from his loose scruffy face and spat a brown liquid on the dry ground. He said nothing and squinted painfully at them. The usually cheerful old man stilled their hearts with his silence. Then their eyes took in his strangely stained clothes. The boys could only suspect what it was.

Evan guessed for himself what happened to put the family into such a twist. He did not live there, as fact, but he knew many of the workers who did, holding positions in the stable. The job included lengthy stays at the farm, intensive labor and climbing a ladder to the loft where the hay and other supplies for the animals were stored. Evan imagined one of the men had fallen. From the height he remembered, a broken limb was certain, and worse was almost definite. He saw a man fall hard at the Point once. He never got up again, twisted like a rope in knots. There was no blood, but the image terrified equally.

"We're keeping the workers away until the matter's settled—so move fast boys, Mr. Conrad's waiting on you," Jack pointed them inside.

"Yes, sir." Michael said softly with a bob of his boyish head. He rushed ahead of Evan.

Evan fought back the reticence to follow into the dark interior of the stable, but he hated to let the kid go alone. He did not want to see another twisted wreck and already his stomach felt sick. The pair tracked along the hay littered path, turned left and wandered down a wide passage, between the two rows of stalls. Random whickers and neighs added to the aura of the horror they expected. A gray black gloom grew so strong the young men hesitated to move another step.

Evan now took the lead, ashamed of himself for his childish apprehension. He cast a glance over his shoulder for Jack, hoping the old man did not watch. However, the foreman stood in the doorway, watching them and refusing to follow. Jack shook his head, hanging it like a guilty dog. Evan cleared his throat, desperate to make a sound. His throat was dry and clenched. He continued on, wishing Michael's doleful eyes off him. He looked so damned sad, a puppy with no direction. If only Emily had not asked him there today.

A few paces forward revealed Mr. Conrad. He stood near the end of the row with his broad shouldered back turned. At the sound of the boy's arrival, he turned round to face them. The older man's expression of grave seriousness distressed Evan greater than anything yet. Mr. Conrad worked up a smile, eyeing both with troubled eyes. His nostrils flared in a steadying breath. Like his foreman, Mr. Conrad was a kind man of bright spirits. This dark bearing was chillingly unlike him.

In the moment of silence, Evan noticed Mr. Conrad dressed casually that day, perhaps to work in the fields with his men. He was known to help with duties, as his health allowed. He enjoyed working and you could tell by the rough lines and creases oh his hands, accented by dirt and sometimes a wound. Despite the knowledge, it struck Evan strange to see him in a plain shirt with no collar and a rough old leather waistcoat. On his lower half, Stuart even sported a pair of work worn pants, but on his feet he wore his fine tall boots. Either way, he was still an inspiring figure, demanding the respect of all around him. It made Evan smile slightly and his fears ease.

Stuart looked over Evan in much the same manner. Embarrassed by his sudden lack of refinement, he unconfidently smoothed his waistcoat. By the lines on their faces, he saw his actions put them little at ease, worrying the worst they dared to imagine. He half smiled, but it wavered weakly, failing to assure even himself.

The young men shifted on their feet, waiting for his orders. Stuart's dithering admitted his discretion in involving them in the matter. But, then he waved them forward with no choice but to seal them in the pact.

"Help me get her inside," Stuart said. He wished he could continue, as before, but fate brought other plans. "I can't have anyone seeing this."

"Her?" Evan questioned under his breath.

Before clearly seeing, he half thought the man now hid a lame born foal. That did not explain the secrecy, but it did explain Emily's reaction. It could hardly be true either, if he meant for them to lift and carry it in the house. Those things were done in the fields and barns. He thought of the maids and his heart stilled.

Mr. Conrad looked to their faces, assessing their readiness, if he could. Then, he unlatched and opened the gate with one hand, not explaining further. His eyes remained on their faces to capture what lay there when all was revealed. What he planned to involve them in would change them absolutely and bring a sad period to those counted as Conrad and Conrad friend.

Evan indeed imagined wrong. Inside the protective dark planks of the horse stall, a woman of obvious African descent laid asleep or dead. He felt his heart break at the sight of her. Her dark face glistened with perspiration and attested to fever. He stepped inside, legs wobbling nervously. Michael entered next, startling him to look back at what came. Now, he was the nervous child, searching for reassurance. A runaway slave meant trouble for anyone who dare help them. What was right did not matter with the law.

Mr. Conrad noticed the pause and fearful reaction of the boys to the occupant of the stall. He grimaced at their gaping, but said nothing. Neither experienced the like before that moment, and neither wished the trouble they knew it could bring. He could involve his son easy enough, but another man's boy was not his to order about illegally. He would let Evan be the judge of his own fate. Hoping to keep the boys as confidantes, Stuart explained what happened.

Old Jack brought the woman from the fields where he had been working, carrying her all the way to the outbuildings, searching for help. When Stuart gained his side, the man knelt with the rickety frame of the woman in his arms, soaked through with sweat. The pair looked dire and he could not refuse them.

Accommodating the soul in need, he placed the runaway on the fresh hay of the stall and covered her with a fresh blanket, previously the property of the hand that slept there. He hoped to keep the frail thing comfortable. Then, he went to his wife and told of what was found, not sparing Mrs. Howell or Emily, who took tea with her at the moment. Once Margaret had been apprised of the situation, he returned to the stables with Jack and his daughter went to the fields to find them. As they spoke, a room on the third floor, where guest overflow and servants slept, was being arranged as a hospital.

Evan listened to the tale Mr. Conrad told. What foul individual mangled a helpless woman? He stared at her bruised and battered face, horrified at how crime went on so openly. His heart pounded in his chest. Men would look for her, to collect a reward careless of her condition. She was sick with something and helpless to whatever came.

Evan roused from his thoughts, as Mr. Conrad moved behind him. He shook from his ankles to his fingertips. What would Joe have to say of this? Now he just felt embarrassed, picturing his companion laughing at him. Joe would carry her by himself, strait to the third floor, no explanation needed. He stuck to his aim without considering cost, quite sure of his convictions.

Stuart put a hand on their shoulders, offering some comfort and drawing their attention to him, "I want to bring her inside to a real bed, and see what we can do. No woman'll die on my watch—not when something can be done." Stuart paused, eyeing them quite convincingly. "You don't have to do it, Evan. I know what trouble it could bring you."

"I'm not worried about me, Mr. Conrad. As a gentleman, I cannot deny a woman my help," Evan said, though he did worry. It was what Joe would have said. *Crazy abolitionist.*

"Good," Stuart smiled. "Pick her up. Let's get her in the house."

"Yes, sir," Michael spoke for the first time since the field, never questioning his father.

Without another lost moment, they stepped to the runaway and hoisted her into a litter. She groaned and seemed to protest the motion. She was definitely alive, but for how long?

Evan avoided her dark eyes when they rolled open, afraid of what he may see there. The pale light of day danced over her broken features, perhaps once beautiful. It was effortless to lift her and effortless to feel sorry for her. The terrible feel of her bony figure lingered in his hands and dragged his mouth down in a frown. He stood there and stared for a long moment until Michael brought him back. His mind could not work around what was going on.

"Help me lift the litter, Ev. I can't drag this outta here on my own," Michael said, bent over her feet.

"Yeah—right," Evan stammered. He looked to his gloves, stained in a mix of blood and disease.

"Ready," Michael said, grabbing his end, as Evan took the opposite.

They lifted the litter from the stall and entered the wide lane of the barn. Silence became their guardian. Moving quickly, the instance took on a sense of urgency and reality stirringly back.

Stuart shut the stall door and hurried behind, "God be with us."

In the open air, the noble Jack joined them, rushing behind on spindly legs. He joined Mr. Conrad, who nodded to him, and led the procession. His eyes continually scanned the entire expanse, unable to predict who might see. He preferred no one, but only the roll of dice assured that. Still, no bleak outlook would frighten him off the task.

Their path led them closer to the far porch stairs at the front of the main house. Each tense step filled with racing hearts and hard drawn breaths. Evan struggled with the load he and Michael shared. The woman continually grew heavier despite her state. He prayed for strength, knowing failure would not serve the stranger well, and his fear made him weak.

There was one thing to do. Evan recalled his training and tucked the weakness into the back of his mind. He watched Mr. Conrad's back, walking ahead of them, trying to focus his efforts. Then he felt Michael's eyes on him. Evan studied the front door of the house fixedly, afraid to meet his gaze.

Evan's eyes shifted to the sick woman in his arms. He adjusted his hands where he held the litter, careful not to let go and harm her further. While his hands moved, he felt the fluid sticky on his gloves, and the sweat on the inside. Panic gripped his insides and he wished them upstairs quickly, nearly ill at the thought of what may smear his skin. She scared him, for he never saw the like of her illness and never wanted to again.

Lifting his eyes from the sick woman's pained features, he saw Mr. Conrad step aside at the stairs. They were nearly there, the journey almost over. He held his gaze to the door of the home, willing it closer.

Stuart's mind turned on other concerns than the boys who carried the stranger into his home. He looked to Jack who had stepped aside like him. The man's old eyes scanned the perimeter of the house, the yards and fields beyond. He could not hide his worry. Stuart cast his eyes back to the young men. He smiled pleased to see them carry out the duty with courage. Stuart patted Michael's back and stepped past them toward the house.

"That's a good man," he added, reassuring his son.

The boys took the first two steps of the porch. Evan's legs shook nervously. At the third step, he saw the front door of the big house open. From it, Michael's mother appeared with his own mother close behind. Mrs.

Howell smiled consolingly and held the opening wide for them to pass without incident. Evan was quite thankful for the timely emergence. Looking to Mrs. Conrad, he noticed her usually pinched face soften. She tried to smile at both of them, but it faded fast with worry that forced her eyes to the road beyond the farm's fence. Evan was glad for the reprieve. He could not hold her gaze for long in any circumstance. He lowered his eyes to his hands. Gritting his teeth with determination, he mustered still more strength.

Evan and Michael cleared the opening, and brought the tragic stranger inside the Conrad farmhouse and the safety it offered. Evan looked up distracted by movement on the stairs above. Emily stood there, waiting for them. Her cheeks glistened wet with tears and her eyes were red. She no longer cried like before in the fields, adopting a gravely serious pose instead. Evan lowered his eyes to nothing in particular, wishing not to see anymore.

Apart from noisy boot steps, the air of the hall buzzed with anxious energy. Everyone cloistered in the hall and Mrs. Howell closed the door tight. Eyes flicked from face to face, memorizing the guilty parties and partners in the crime. They listened to silence press in on them.

"Do you boys need a rest before bringing her upstairs?" Margaret asked when the boys moved to tackle the steps.

Evan breathed an emphatic no, at once echoed by Michael. Evan hardly saw the point of stopping now. The climb would occur at some point and the woman could not wait for them. Jostling into position first, Evan brought them to the base of the stairs. He turned toward Emily and slowly climbed ahead of Michael, holding the slave's head at his back.

Michael watched his friend lead them up the flight without a word. He carefully placed his foot, feeling out the flat plank with his toe each time. Below him, Michael stepped the same. His eyes lowered to the feverish face before him and he could see nothing else.

The rest of the compatriots followed. Evan squeezed his eyes shut for a moment, wishing the moment quickly away. His arms could not hold on too much longer, shaking from fear and effort. His training entered his thoughts once more. He focused on the sounds of the house, blending with the terrible cadence of their step, like an army marching. Evan lost himself in the thought, pretending he worked at one of their exercises back at the Point.

The boys arrived at the second floor. Then, they turned and mounted the rise to the third. It became increasingly difficult to continue. Their arms trembled, threatening to drop the woman on the hard stairs. Breathing hard, they watched Emily lead the way, occasionally peering over her shoulder to them. An apologetic twist of her mouth, but no words comforted them. Her eyes turned forward, as they neared the top. At that moment, their grip slipped and the elder men moved to take hold of the litter, only to be refused. The boys paused, adjusting the contraption and carried on.

At the top of the flight Emily disappeared and Rose took her place. The raven haired girl encouraged them on their final approach, giving smiles and compliments to their strength. Both Michael and Evan laughed through their lost breaths, doubting the truth of her words and embarrassed she had noticed. Rose shook her head at them, pursing her lips.

Previously unrealized strength brought the young men to the final leg of their journey. In reality, the real end of the adventure was very far off. They held Rose in their sights, as the girl wriggled her finger and laughing with her demure smile, led them down the hall. At the end of the dusky passage, Rose stepped aside and indicated a small room, bare of spare furnishing and decoration. With their burden at its destination, Evan and Michael placed her carefully on a narrow bed.

Stepping back, the young men allowed Margaret to near her patient. Resting their exhausted limbs, they watched the elder Conrad woman get to work without hesitation. Margaret removed the old wool blanket. They held their breaths unsure of what to expect underneath. Expectancy turned to horror around the room. None saw the like in all their lives.

When Margaret turned back the covers, she revealed a tragic figure on the bed in an old worn dress, once possibly calico. Her own sweat and blood of unseen wounds pasted the meager garments to her starved body, disguising the design. The woman shivered from fever, a mere sack of bones, wasting to dust before their eyes.

Emily neared the bed and Michael reached out to pull her back. She put her hand up to refuse his concerns and continued to the woman's side. Evan and Michael exchanged glances, unsure of what else to do.

The slave's face turned toward the girl who came to stand at her side. Dark bleary pools opened to see her surroundings, but stood as empty as death. Emily lost her fears in those eyes. She watched the slave's mouth move around soundless words. A thin arm extended a skeletal hand to Emily. Emily blinked at that hand, hesitating but a moment. Sealing away her fears of what the woman suffered, she took hold of the bony digits and knelt by the bed. A tiny smile formed on the dry cracked lips of the slave and she murmured something, rolling her eyes closed before drifting back to sleep.

The boys looked from the scene before them, noticing the mess of their clothes. Amanda tapped her son's shoulder. He and then Michael looked to see Mrs. Howell's consoling smile. With a nod of her head, she guided them to a waiting basin of hot water and soap. She patted Evan's shoulder. Then, she gathered another basin and pile of linens to bring to the bedside.

"Thank you, boys," Margaret whispered, stepping back from the bed to look at them. "I want you to wash up quickly and leave. We need to undress the poor dear and get her bathed."

Michael nodded for both of them. He watched Evan's mother shoo Jack and his father out of the room. His eyes fell back on Evan, but the cadet busily dried his hands and ignored him, wearing a grimace of distress. The basin now stood open for his use. Michael dove in quickly, petrified of what was on his skin, and petrified to stay there any longer. When finished, he followed Evan out of the room, drying his hands. Margaret shut the door behind him, offering a last assuring smile that disappeared behind the panel. They were left to each other and the shadows.

Quarantined from the sick woman, the men stood about unsure of what to do. None of them spoke, preferring to stick with silence. Now they saw for themselves what happened hundreds of miles away, because it had come to their door and demanded they know. No longer would the horrors of the South exist in mere tales.

In the midst of personal reflections, the sound of hurried steps on the stairs reached their ears. The men lifted their eyes, thankful for a reprieve from having to say something just yet. Rose reappeared, carrying more steaming water. They had not noticed her escape ahead of them, engrossed in the moment. The men smiled graciously to her and she returned the expression with her own.

Rose entered the room past them, closing the door behind her. The light from the small room improved the hall momentarily and then the somber gray ensnared them again. Their eyes shifted warily.

Michael looked to Evan, who leaned against the wall opposite the door. The cadet wore a serious expression. His usually smiling features hung sallow and he would not hold Michael's gaze. Evan shifted his hands behind his back, pressed them to the wall and studied the floor, almost guilty.

This incident brought them indefinite change, which just began its work on each of them. Despite the insecurity obvious in everyone else, Michael found his mind free and clear of its burdens. At last, he stood prepared to decide his fate. With that helpless creature beyond the door and on the verge of death, he could no longer think of staying on the farm. He knew his purpose lay in helping others; forcing an institution he detested out of the American way of life.

"Pop," Michael said in low tones, feeling apprehensive. "I want to ask you something."

"Go ahead," Stuart said. He smiled, grateful for the distraction and grateful that he did not have to speak first.

"I've decided that you might be right—and I'd like to apply to school for the fall term —if I may, sir."

Michael saw Evan's approving smile followed by that of Jack. His father appeared shocked. It quickly faded to delight and relief. Michael shifted on his feet and smiled back at his father, now smiling very broadly at him. His father started and stopped speaking several times before he could get his words out. Michael worried he upset the older man, wondering if it the wrong decision at the wrong time.

"That's grand," Stuart stammered. "Grand—have you thought of anywhere in particular?"

"I dunno," Michael said, stuffing his hands in his pockets. "Maybe West Point like Evan," he said. "I think being a soldier would be grand. If we can pay for it, I mean."

"Pay for it? Oh, listen to him. Indeed," Stuart beamed. "Oh yes—yes of course we can boy. You wanna go to school? Then, to school you'll go," Stuart said. "Why don't you and Evan go talk about it," Stuart urged him off. "Go on—you can use my study. I'll have to go see Mr. Adams tomorrow. What do you think uh that, Jack?" He continued wistfully. "He wants to go to school."

"I'd be proud if he was my boy," Jack said, gumming his words and smiling excitedly. He saw Michael grow from infancy to maturity, and he felt nothing but pride.

The woman in the room was forgotten for a time, along with the darkness.

Michael nodded to his father's orders and smiled sheepishly. Stuffing his hands into his pockets, he looked to Evan who showed pride shamelessly. Indeed, Evan had won and gloated about it as always. Regardless, his friend's expression lit a fire of excitement in him. He wanted to be on his way right then. His mind already worked on ideas of what his life would soon be like. Shifting his feet on the plank flooring, he listened to it creak before he spoke.

"Let's go downstairs," Michael said. "You can tell me all about it, while Rose gets your jacket cleaned up," Michael added, removing his waistcoat.

"Sure," Evan said, pushing himself off the wall, once again wearing a big grin. "First thing—you need someone to appoint you to the school—I'm sure it won't be a problem with your pa's standing in the town. He got me in," Evan laughed, pointing to himself. "If you get it—oh boy, you're gonna love it there. I can't wait to introduce you to Joe—now I don't mean it's easy."

Stuart listened to Evan's voice until it faded down the hall and disappeared on the stairs. Their voices echoed back in distant indistinct tones. The matter of Michael now settled in his household, Stuart sighed, thinking of the new test of wills. The stranger had already brought much change.

Baltimore, Maryland
June 1860

Along the cobblestone streets, the citizens and visitors to the city of Baltimore tread with minds full of their own business. Unaware they passed the Front Street Theater, where a small piece of history launched. Within the ornate walls of the theater, the people that concerned themselves with the fiery politics of the day gathered to debate the issues of their political party. Having already met in Charleston, South Carolina, the United States Democratic Party adjourned to meet again in Baltimore, no more near an agreement.

Once more in session, the conventioneers sat beneath dazzling chandeliers that provided a sleepy haze of light in which to work. They prattled noisily while some of their constituents viewed the nonsense. To those watchers, it provided a needed distraction from daily toil, and came in the form of a comical trial of raucous hotheads. It also displayed a mockery of United States politics, embodied in lazy fat men, who tried desperately to complete private and exhausting agendas.

The session started with a speech from the honored Reverend of the day. Both the observers and conventioneers fell quiet and sat with their heads bowed in reverence to him, as he delivered the prayer. The respectful silence hung in the air and lasted only through the cleric's retreat. When he officially took his leave, the delegates immediately started their debate, which filled the hall with a numbing din. With all motions opposed by at least one delegate, it appeared they would never settle their issues.

"The gentleman from New York," the convention's president stood and addressed the assembly in a stoic political voice. "You wish to address the motion you placed before the convention."

"I do," the gentleman from New York said. He rose to his feet in one of the many rows of theater seats near the stage. "I wish to admit the votes of the seceding southern states—"

"Nay," a voice called from somewhere.

"They deserve to stand counted as we are, considering they were present in South Carolina," the gentleman from New York spoke over him forcibly. "They resist nominating Mr. Douglas, and it is their right to do such."

The representative from New York continued. Other delegates and the president of the convention soon interrupted his speech. It took several tries to overpower him, but his voice disappeared eventually. The delegates then turned the debate in another direction and he conceded the floor to them. Taking to his seat, he shook his head regretfully, forced from his stance like a willful upstart. A raucous outcry met his defeat.

The Democratic Party faced a gravely serious issue. Their fate strongly hinged on the vote still ahead of them. Yet, they failed to move on a presidential candidate nomination each time it presented itself. Perhaps the fear of losing power drove these men to stall the question, preferring to go on about anything else. It threatened the stability of the party and only time would tell if the northern representatives would be the only representatives. They appeared tired and thoroughly worn, but the desire for power would not let them sway.

This moment passed under the observation of a pair of Maryland natives, who watched among the rest with great disgust. Their eyes flitted from face to face. Carefully tuned ears jumped to catch all that was said.

The youngest, Joseph Maynard, appeared the most annoyed of the two. Joseph reached the age of twenty-one years a few months prior; just a man with hair still a healthy tawny and his eyes a deep russet, flecked by notes of jade. By his expression, he harbored no patience for such dealings and only attended them at the request of his father who sat at his elbow. Reaching up, he scratched his closely trimmed beard and fought back a strong yawn of boredom. He stifled it, not wanting his father to see him act so crude in public and embarrass him. He respected his sire too much to do so and had been taught better at school. Joseph tugged his cadet jacket straight and looked to the older man beside him, reminded of his presence.

John Maynard served full partner in the firm of Rhys, Maynard and Wallace, a respected Baltimore lawyer. Joseph's lineage showed visibly in his features. John sat in his seat with his noble chin held high, displaying a somber and attentive expression. His long fingered hands stretched on a carved ebony cane, topped by a silver dog head pommel. Originally, the cane belonged to his father's great grandfather. Joseph smiled at the memory of his forebear. He came from noble stock out of Scotland in the early years of the American colonies, with that stick.

John's smart black suit spoke more of his prosperous station, and his graying hair gave him a further distinguished appearance. Joseph could only hope he looked so well, sitting beside him, since he felt much less presentable inside. He ruefully smiled about it. Even his uniform failed to make him feel worthy to sit beside his father at this horrible little meeting of idiots.

Turning back to the convention, Joseph reminded himself that his father, as a lawyer, provided the sole reason for their attendance of the convention. Politics fascinated him and was his business. However, fascination excluded pure enjoyment. Joseph looked to him again. His father's gaze looked glassed over. The lids drooped like a Basset Hound.

"This doesn't surprise me," Joseph said to his father in a low Maryland drawl.

Joseph then heaved a weighted sigh of annoyance and rolled his eyes. He could think of many other ways to spend his time more usefully. None included these daylilies. He hoped his actions would release his father from any duty he felt to remain there. It felt worse than a day of lectures.

John laughed silently and smiled at his son with understanding. They held standing among the Republicans and not the Democrats. The convention merely gave heart to their plight against the opposition, and it hardly heralded the end of the world, like so many led others to believe. However, it displayed the excess and irrationality of politicians as a whole. Such could damage either party. No to mention the damage it could do to one's carefully managed temperament and wish to ever witness history created again.

"Tis the privilege of the politician, my boy." John replied dryly. He raised his brows and revealed his jest to his son. "Let us leave. I've seen enough of this foolishness," he said, displaying his own irritation.

John slowly stood under the gaze of his son. Joseph waited for his father to take up his overcoat from the back of his seat where it lay neatly folded. He put it on, appearing more tired than Joseph assumed. The garment now rested full on his father's shoulders, and he looked back to his seat for any lost possessions. Joseph then rose to his feet, seeing John's careworn features brighten slightly. He smiled, knowing he must be thankful to not sit there any longer.

Joseph gathered his uniform cloak, while his father checked his pocket watch. Joseph swung the garment onto his shoulders with a flourish. In the act, John patiently waited for him, his eyes suddenly taking on pain. Joseph's hopeful gaze turned somber. He clasped the garment with a button. Turning away, he gathered his own belongings trying to figure out what just happened. Out of the corner of his eye, he caught sight of the fluttering corner of his cloak when it came down. The garment came to him as part of a required uniform at West Point. He had grown used to wearing it since last September, and thought little on it.

Joseph drew up straight, rising to a height nearly a head taller than his father. Looking to John, he saw him force a smile of approval, fixing his gloves on his hands. They both knew where that uniform led him, and they both knew where this convention led the country. Joseph offered a weak smile of assurance and apology to his father. John returned that smile, adding a good humored nod. He then led the way from their row to the street beyond the theater doors.

Outside the day still hung in the young hours before noon. A warm breeze blew along the summer street, rustling their hair. In response, the men placed their hats on their heads. Both thought of all to do until they might return to the convention, if they went back. Neither man cared for the events in the theater. That became obvious when they walked out. It soured their stomachs to think of the pettiness in which men engaged. Such stubborn single mindedness served no one.

Joseph looked to his father, respectfully putting his hand and arm out for him to take the lead. John smiled deeply also finding the humor in his son's move. Turning up the street, John tucked his walking cane under his arm and again adjusted his gloves on his hands. Joseph never knew them to serve for laboring hands, unless putting pen to paper or gesturing proved true labor. They aged nonetheless.

"Your mother will be disappointed—we won't return for another day," John drawled desolately. He nearly always missed Joseph's mother when away on extended business trips. "We've only a few days left to have you back to school."

"It's long enough," Joseph smiled not so disappointed. "Thank you for getting me out." He wished his father would not make him feel so guilty about his choices, now that he faced only a short time before the finish of his schooling.

"Not for your mother," John said, casting his gray eyes to his son. He almost laughed, seeing the regret on Joseph's face. "But—you're welcome."

Joseph felt a pang in his heart for his mother and father. He tucked his hands behind his back and hung his head. He wished he could spend more time with his family, but he was grown and gone to school. Attending class prevented it by the university's rules. Not to mention, his wings spread years ago and he could not wait to fly on his own. The small taste of freedom he received at school left him with a relentless craving for more. It was not without regret. He had left his loved ones behind, including his younger sister. Now that he matured, Mary annoyed him very little as she had in childhood. Of course, having anyone of his family doting on him turned into more of an awkward nuisance than a welcomed event, especially his mother.

Joseph knew his thoughts selfish. To console himself, he put his arm about his father's shoulder and pulled him closer. John responded in kind and warmly chuckled. Joseph fought a wry smile filled with the elation his father's approval gave him. Despite all his growing and maturing, he only admitted to enjoying the company of his parents rarely.

"Mr. John Maynard?" They heard a deep southern accent call from a small distance ahead of them.

Joseph and John both searched out the source with questioning expressions, stepping apart. An unfamiliar man stood ahead of them. People arched a path around his bulky figure. He grinned almost madly from an ailing face edged by hoary coarse black muttonchops. With a touch to his hat, he neared, hoisting his gnarled wood walking stick into his left hand.

Joseph looked between his father and this stranger, trying to detect what would pass. His father revealed an unguarded expression. Joseph grew increasingly wary knowing his father never peered at people with such open contempt. Joseph geared himself up for a learning experience he would not soon forget. Tucking his hands in his back, he watched the stranger join them and reach for his father's hand. Though they shook hands friendly enough, Joseph could feel the ice thicken between them.

"Mr. Maynard—have you come for the convention? No matter," he waved the questions away with a dismissing hand and continued in rough tones. "It's a wonderful thing, isn't it? Meeting in a theater," he pointed out the theater with a nod of his head.

"Mr. Oates—as I recall," Joseph's father spoke with obvious loathing. He looked at Mr. Oates suspiciously. "It's been a longtime, but I see you don't forget," he continued.

Joseph's father smiled barely pleasantly though it missed Mr. Oates. The stranger stepped in to tower over his father even more than he naturally stood. Mr. Oates tried to use his size to a conversational advantage, much like the men they left behind moments ago.

"Quite a long memory," he said, grinning deviously. He stepped too close.

However, Joseph's proud father would not be intimidated. He refused to take a step back even when Oates neared too close. Joseph took his father's grand cue and closed in. He stepped to the side of both men, forming a close uncomfortable circle. Carefully, Joseph continued to note his father's manner of speech throughout their discussion. He wanted to help if he could.

"How's the practice since last I saw you?" John smiled. His eye glinted assured of his supremacy.

Joseph's father leaned in toward Oates when speaking to him. It gave a subtle but unmissed message. Oates retreated. He stepped back and disguised his submission with a laugh to the comments made. His father won an unseen battle in a single fluid maneuver. It unconditionally asserted him to be the better man. Joseph's eyes turned back to the newcomer, wearing a small smile of satisfaction.

At ease that his father handled the moment effectively, he turned his attention to other matters. His eyes studied the tall man again and again. He sensed something dark about the stranger apart from his hair. His father must have known this by experience, considering his hesitation of the chance meeting.

"Good—very good. How's your own firm faring? Have you decided to join us in politics yet, my friend?" Mr. Oates asked, adjusting the cane under his arm to fix his glove. So, he would not leave off yet. He eyed Joseph then John with a lack of sureness, despite his friendly tones. "Are you not Republicans by practice?"

"No—indeed," John chuckled at the idea. "I'm still practicing Republicanism, as you say. I've just come to see the beginnings of war."

"You don't know how prophetic your words are. If these good men elect Douglas, it's the end to Democratic solidarity, and I fear it's the end of our grand nation. We lawyers will have a bit to do. Won't we, John?"

"Yes," Joseph's father laughed. "Because of pigheadedness."

Joseph felt his skin spring up with goose bumps at Mr. Oates's words. His gaze turned away distracted and the sky darkened ominously. Joseph worriedly wondered exactly what they all faced, standing there on the street corner. He felt his uniform press in on his body.

All around their tiny group, people continued their tasks, feeling no particular threat faced their peaceful lives. His eyes saw the children who played in the streets and their parents who simply watched or heatedly reprimanded. They knew nothing of what lay ahead for them. He honestly knew nothing of it either, but he pitied them more. At least, he made his choice of his own.

Joseph's eyes lifted to the opposite side of the street, distracted by a new mess just brewing there. A wagon noisily raced along the cobble street fatally heedless of pedestrians. Joseph's eyes widened and he cursed. He could only watch helplessly. His heart pounded hard against his chest and he turned slightly toward the street.

A woman rushed desperately into the street to pull her child to the safety of the sidewalk. After a quick check, she faced the driver, yelling curses up to him. The woman shook her frail fist, but it failed to have any affect. Retreating from the horrifying scene, she disappeared behind the enormous iron buckled wheels that almost killed her boy.

With her gone, Joseph placed his attention on the swarthy red haired driver. The man jumped down, still ignoring the comments from those he offended. His coarse manner was obvious. He grinned a sneer avoiding their eyes. He dragged his heavily decorated body at a lumbering roll to the back of the high sided cart. Using his pudgy pink hands, he opened the gate and stepped back, dropping it to the road like a ramp. Then, a line of African slaves stepped down, each chained to the next. The red headed man's watery gaze showed disgust. When they stood on the street, the red headed man herded them across the dangerous gauntlet of the roadway to the side Joseph stood on. His colorful sharp words plainly held the rumble of a foreign accent.

Behind them, the angry mother reappeared one last time. She drew her son away, watching the spectacle and censuring her child. The boy swayed angrily at her words and covered his little ears. Her face was a mask of fear.

Joseph half smiled at the exchange between mother and son, remembering his own numerous reprimands. The expression quickly left his face when a small slave boy emerged from the cart with an oversized basket forced into his possession. The line of slaves continued across the street. Their master oversaw them in the middle. Joseph's eyes remained on the boy's dark face. He wore dirty rags not fit to line a puppy box and labored hard under the weight of his burden. Joseph felt himself grow angrier at the clear mistreatment of a powerless child. His jaw clenched and forced his gaze back to the stranger and his father. Unfortunately, his eyes continually went back to the boy.

The slaves entered a crossroad, disappearing one after the other behind the brick buildings. Joseph's eyes drew back just in time to see the basket fall from the boy's grip and his frail form tumble to the ground with it. He tripped on the curb and now sat himself up. He lifted his face with tears streaming down his cheeks. Though he howled and wailed, no one came to his aid. The little boy looked over his scraped hands, holding them up to the callous passersby. When his cries continued to go ignored, he lowered his gaze to his bleeding knees, and tenderly touched them. His tears became intensively worse, but his sobs were silent.

Jostling his way through the crowd and his slaves, the owner growled and cursed about the boy's stupidity. He came down on him strong, using his cane to punish him severely. The boy covered his head with his arms and curled up to protect his already injured body from the blows. His cries turned to screams, but only attracted the curiosity of watchers and no help.

Joseph saw enough. Despite what many thought of slaves, a boy should not have to carry a load that a grown man might spill and then suffer punishment when it did fall from his hands. His upbringing taught him mistreatment of so defenseless an individual must not continue unchallenged. Seething, he moved from between his father and Mr. Oates toward the fat man and child to see the abuse stopped.

Having sensed the loss of John Maynard's attention to the spectacle building behind him, Mr. Oates peered back over his shoulder to also see the ruckus. When he turned, he saw Joseph making his move and caught his arm in a strong grasp. The youngest of the Maynard pair met his reproving gaze with a hate filled stare. The boy silently clashed wills with him, as he continued to hold his arm in a tightening grip. Mr. Oates's dark gaze seared into the boy and anger ticked wildly in Joseph's cheek. Oates grinned, knowing he more than bothered the boy by his interference.

Joseph held himself still against a growing need to rip Oates's arm from its socket and continue his plan. No one dared to touch him in such a manner. They respected him too much. When Oates finally released him, Joseph straightened his jacket sharply, and brushed his sleeves with an angry grimace. He could feel the bruising grip still around his arm, not to mention his pride. Crossly driven, he hoped to see him on the battlefield when war at last broke out. Smirking at his arrogant grin, Joseph knew this slippery snake would sell any position appointed him and go into hiding from brave duty.

"It isn't your fight, boy." Mr. Oates added salt to the wound. He continued speaking, stepping into Joseph's line of sight and blocking the spectacle from him. "He belongs to that man and interfering will bring a suit on you."

"He can't jus'—" Joseph defended or tried to defend. It sounded more like a puppy whimper. Embarrassed, his rage roared higher, striking him mute.

"He can," his father said with a low dark tone, before his son moved to do more damage to a worsening event.

Joseph's father sadly lowered his eyes from the scene. Joseph looked past Oates's shoulder. A crowd formed, making it difficult to see anymore anyway. However, Joseph still tried. Between the bowlers and bonnets, trousers and skirts, the pink faced man dragged the small slave boy to his feet. Red welts from the blows of his cane now turned to purple bruises. Tears still streamed down the boy's small round face, and he carried on in agony despite his punishment. Irritably stirred, the slave owner forced the basket back into his possession and yelled at him with a strike of his stick to get him moving again. No bystander made an attempt to help, though some loudly made their opposition known. However, the owner gave no sign of caution at their warning. He ignored them instead and moved his slaves onward. With them absent, the crowd's interest in the grotesque waned. Nothing legal presented a good choice with which to repair the evil. It would have ended in a terrible and embarrassing lawsuit; one Joseph's father would most definitely not need to fight at that time.

"Let's go somewhere more befitting—respectable gentleman," Joseph said, nearly spitting the anger from his mouth. He turned an unguarded gaze ripe with scorn on Mr. Oates's face. His advantage disguised itself in youth, and its tool used unhindered arrogance.

Mr. Oates regarded him carefully a moment, perhaps beaten at the game of superiority. A slow smile split his face again. Joseph rolled his eyes, anticipating he must have thought of something else to say. He could hardly wait to hear it.

"You're old enough to go to a university now aren't you, boy?" He smiled at Joseph with scarcely masked irritation.

"He'll be going back to West Point in the fall," Joseph's father answered for him, while trying to impress on Oates their standing. Joseph could sense that his father little trusted where Oates wished to turn the conversation now. "His last term. He'll be an officer of the United States Army."

"And then, I assume you'll follow in your father's steps—be a lawyer," Oates said and then paused to eye him amused by his own words. "Perhaps when you have as many gray hairs as we do, you'll not act so quick to intervene where another's property is concerned. Laws are clear—let sense dictate your actions, young man, not your foolish sentiments."

"If my action has offended you, I do apologize," Joseph said with a wry grin. He decidedly hated this man that stood before him. "It isn't in my nature to sit and watch a child beat for no fault of his own. It is dishonorable."

Mr. Oates chuckled annoyed, "when you've ya own slaves, you'll see my point."

Oates probably never owned slaves in his life, but given the means, he surely would have bought Africans wholesale. Not to mention, he would probably go down in history a conservative supporter of the liberal whip.

"We do not own slaves," Joseph's father drew up with a dark glare at his old acquaintance. "Have you forgotten? Perhaps your memory's not so good, after all," he said, holding Oates's disgusted look at his derisive tone. Before continuing, he looked to Joseph with a warm smile. "Let's go to our rooms and rest before lunch, Joseph. I mean to send a telegram to your mother."

Joseph's father took no more notice of his colleague. He stepped forward past him without a good bye to send him off. He placed his cane just so with each step. Joseph could tell the experience enraged him. That explained why he never kept up with Mr. Oates and Joseph mercifully never met this acquaintance.

Joseph raised a mirth filled brow to Mr. Oates, and past him to follow his father away from that place. He could feel Mr. Oates watch them go, most likely with disgust a plague on his pallid features. He could not help but wonder at how a presumably intelligent man could be so ignorant. Looking back over his square broad shoulder, Joseph saw Oates duck into the theater and he snickered.

"And that is why they break our beloved country apart," Joseph murmured angered.

"Joseph—you're a good boy with a good heart, and you'll do good. I've no doubt," his father said and then paused, setting his features with worry. "But—I fear it may hurt you if not guarded—sometimes you must hold back when you feel you should act," His father said, patting his back. "No matter—it's in the past."

Together they determinedly walked toward their hotel. Joseph held a reverent silence. He kept his hands tucked in the small of his back. Clearing his throat, Joseph turned his gaze abashedly to the street and the people passing them. He hoped he was not solely to blame for acting so poorly back there and he still stood in his father's good graces. Joseph never held back in the face of duty and honor, especially when it dictated he should aid the helpless. He thought his father raised him to react in such a manner. As abolitionists, they always respected the rights of everyone. With that in mind, Joseph tried to heed his father's advice and display his respect the only way he knew how. Joseph worried he mistook his meaning.

John's cane went just so with each step, clacking against the stone.

Joseph saw his sire smile proudly once again. His father suddenly chuckled low and warm. His father sounded amused, probably by his reaction to the events, but more likely he tried to laugh it away. Joseph's gaze swept over his father's head, still concerned he embarrassed his sire.

"I think maybe we should go home," his father said, looking along the street. "I've no care to be in the same city with these men any longer. I've seen enough of what's happening."

Joseph's father looked to him, offering a weak smile. He patted Joseph on the back. By his father's features, Joseph felt the blame skitter elsewhere. His father smiled more deeply, assuring him. Joseph smiled in return, feeling his unyielding approval once again. He had done well.

II. Sealing Fate

West Point, New York
Late June 1860

"Paper says the convention elected Douglas. The party stands split over the nomination and the southern delegates plan to elect their own man. They want to separate themselves from what they term black republicanism," Stuart Conrad read aloud to his family, where they all gathered, in a rented but distinguished townhouse parlor.

Emily smiled at him from a slightly more mature face distracted from the pillow she sewed. On his nose rested a pair of rectangular gold rimmed glasses, giving him a professor like appearance. Her father loved to discuss politics if allowed and to display his unrivaled intelligence. So, they humored him nightly, while he read his paper. Besides, Emily felt that it improved her mind instead of filling it with naive nonsense. He told her that no good match would want her to be an ignoramus and he worked hard to see to her education.

Emily looked at her father with appreciation for all that he carried out. He often equally humored her by buying books for her to read and expand her knowledge safely. He now proudly sat his girth in a cushioned chair beside a lamp, ignorant that he also sat under observation of his biggest fan. Emily admired her father and often prayed for someone like him to come to the farm and sweep her away. Although, she would oblige the right man, hunting him down, however unseemly.

Emily tipped her head to the side thinking. Her eyes studied the fine needlework of her father's waistcoat, among many accomplishments her mother performed. Her mother stitched that and the snowy shirt he wore only a month ago. Emily's eyes went to her mother. She sat beside her on the hard cushion of a carved wood and green velvet sofa. The elder Conrad woman concentrated on a quilt now. Margaret made a great many things for the family, deserved recognition for her pains, but demanded it too vehemently. Emily's father rarely complained of his work, as she did.

Emily's father fumbled reflexively with a gold watch chain that stretched from one of the waistcoat's gold buttons to the pocket. Emily looked back to him hidden behind his paper from the watch fob up. Emily bought the fob for him for Christmas with her allowance, after the last broke in a fray with an unruly cow. He always wore it.

"At least some of them have come to their senses. They should have stopped yielding to the southern branch long ago," he continued, smiling in amusement. He lowered his paper to turn the page and winked at her.

Emily smiled and looked over to her mother again. Her quilting went smoothly, nearly finished in the frame. Emily lowered her gaze self consciously. She worked on her pillow and sampler for months now. For every stitch she put in, her mother made her pull three. Her mother just began teaching her and made a hard taskmistress. With her gaze lowered, Emily could see the decorative hem of her mother's fine gown, also hand stitched by her mother of course. The gown displayed her fine sophistication and solemn mood. Emily lifted her eyes to her mother's face, pinched in concentration. She carefully watched the needle, cautiously laying each stitch. Quilting impassioned her. She won awards at it and could only get better, in her own words, but it drove her to be harder on Emily. She said teaching her would prove her hardest, though finest work, both insulting and complimenting. Margaret always spoke like a double bladed knife.

At Margaret's urbane elbow, Emily felt out of place. Unlike her parents, she wore a simple gown of pumpkin cotton with an ivory and gray apron over the skirt. Emily enjoyed bright colors, but never found need to dress ostentatiously in them like her parents. Before she reduced her mood further, she returned to her little pillow and studied the sampler partially stitched to it. She finished the patch on their long voyage from Vermont to West Point in an attempt to distract her mind productively. Her mother would have it no other way.

Emily sighed heavily bored with her work. Her mother touched her head lovingly and she half smiled consolingly at her. Emily weakly smiled back and found her gaze drawn to her brother. Michael sat in a chair, facing them from the other side of the room cast in the shadows. His expression showed concern over something the others failed to notice yet. Emily studied the uniform of the military academy that dressed him. She had not grown used to it, even after three years. She watched his golden head lower until his chin nearly rested on his chest. His cheeks puffed out with a breath. Perhaps, the news filled him with hard emotions that rambled about his mind with no outlet.

Indeed, Stuart's words resonated relentlessly in Michael's mind. The news disturbed him more than his sister could ever know. Unlike her, Michael knew of something bigger than any of them suspected and it came because of what Stuart read. His professors lectured them on it daily. They stood on the eve of war. For all the threat it posed to their lives, no one showed a care.

Looking up, he saw Emily. She stared at him with a strange expression on her face. Then, he saw her elbow his mother. He sighed, knowing what that would do.

Margaret's head popped up and she looked sternly at Emily. Emily jutted her chin at her brother. Mother and daughter peered at him together. He looked desolate, resting there alone.

"Are you feeling all right, Michael?" Margaret asked, looking over her nose at him with a small but warm loving smile.

"You can't just sit here and talk about it like it isn't happening," Michael shockingly bellowed. He pushed forward in his chair and his hands clutched the arms. He gripped so tight his knuckles turned white. "For Christ sakes it's the end of the world!"

"Don't take the Lord's name in vain!" Margaret chastened him, shocked at the distasteful behavior from a young man that should be learning proper manners with his education. The academy obviously made a horrible change in him.

Emily's face turned up and she gave her brother a wry smile with a raised brow. Emily always found entertainment in his misfortune, part of their sibling rivalry. However, she loved him and feared what his mood meant. Michael changed since last they saw him. He became dark and brooding, surrounded by negative thoughts and actions.

"Watch your language round the women," Stuart reprimanded him, adjusting his spectacles and continuing to read his paper. He honestly cared little about Michael's use of profanity, having colored many of his meanings before, also. Besides, Michael turned into a man when he went to school and could make his own choices now.

"I'm sorry, Mamma—I'm just—" he stopped speaking.

Michael stood and walked around the room agitated. His demeanor matured compared to several years ago despite his last outburst. He also illustrated a measure of refinement about him like the room they stood in. But like his days on the farm, he once again could not find the words to express his emotions. He felt powerless and yet so powerful in light of what they faced. What would the split of the United States mean for them? What would war bring his home and his father? What would become of him?

"You know as well as I do what's happening here," Michael finally said.

Behind him the sound of porcelain rattling on a tray came nearer through the doorway from the hall beyond. Michael turned to see Henrietta Benson, a runaway slave who lived with them in their home since her escape from the south three years ago. She risked her existence to be with them now. However, she refused to stay at the farm for any measure of comfort when she could see him. The woman smiled warmly at him. Michael could still feel the strain in his features from what he said. His eyes lowered to the tray in her hands and he hurried to relieve her of her load. Michael felt obligated to not let her labor for their sake since she took up position in their home under the title of housekeeper. After all her suffering, someone should wait on her instead.

"Let me help you, Hettie," he rasped, trying to pull the tray from her delicate hands.

"Michael," Stuart corrected him. "Let Hettie do her job."

Hettie smiled at him, pulling the tray back and stepping around him, whispering a soft thank you. She set the tray on a small table, removing a vase from the windowsill. Returning to the tray, she poured tea for the family. The room fell silent. She continued to work, wearing a small smile on her full lips. She grew used to Michael's doting sometime ago. Turning slightly, she passed a cup to Stuart and moved to the next. They all doted on her in their own way.

"Oh—thank you, Hettie," Stuart said, drawing the cup closer. He sipped, "ahh, perfect, as usual."

Michael resumed his seat with an uncomfortable expression, marring his young handsome features embarrassed by his actions. His sheepish gaze trailed to his mother and sister. Emily sat with her pillow drawn close to her eyes to double check her work before mother got to it. Over the soft edge, she spied his smile, finding some humor in her. Before he could annoy her with sibling games of his own, a distraction stopped it. Hettie stepped between them.

"Ya'll needn't make up for what they done," her soft voice said to him. His eyes focused on the fragile cup she held out to him. Michael followed her fingers to her arm and from there to her dark eyes. "Nothing ya'll could do would ever do that."

"Sorry, Hettie." Michael apologized in a heavy sigh.

"Ya just make it worse, boy," Hettie mumbled to him warningly.

Hettie often tried to make Michael understand her point, but time and again he tried to undo her past. Hettie became frustrated by his efforts, upset that it made her wish that somehow it could all be erased and knowing it could never be. He only reminded her of a horrible past. Forgetting those thoughts, Hettie turned away and poured the next cup. Once ready, she presented it to Mrs. Conrad with a small smile.

"Thank you, Henrietta," Margaret said, taking the cup with a gracious smile in return. They both knew her son could be a handful. She sipped her tea, looking at him stew in his chair. "Perfect as usual," she smiled at Hettie. The maid smiled back with a nod. "Have you heard any news?" Margaret asked her.

"No— ma'am," Hettie stammered, losing her joy. She wiped her hands on her apron to keep them from noticing how she shook at those words. Her thoughts turned south where many friends and family were stranded. "Nothing yet."

"You soon will, I believe," Margaret said, forcing a smile to her thin lips. She could not imagine what it would feel like if she stood separated from loved ones in the same manner, but was beginning to through her son. "God doesn't desert his flock, as we well know."

"Thank you, ma'am," Hettie said, turning back to the tea tray none the better for Mrs. Conrad's encouragement.

Hettie poured the last cup for Emily and served her. Facing Margaret, Hettie asked to be excused in a much more somber voice than moments ago. Margaret easily granted the request. In the past, the request of such liberties without waiting for the master's discretion would lead to a beating or confinement in the meat cellar for days. Such behavior was considered wicked disobedience.

Stepping to the parlor door, Hettie caught sight of Michael, warily eyeing her. She turned her face from him and hung her head low. She hated him seeing her like this. It made her think again about an unchangeable past. Already, she could not forget easily with her heart still enslaved.

The shadows of the dusky hall disguised Hettie's tears. She listlessly wandered down the hall, wishing she were strong enough to handle her trials without falling to pieces before the Conrads. Her chin lifted and her steps halted. The narrow door at the end of the hall glowed entrancing gold. She stared at it reminded of the farmhouse kitchen where she felt her first sense of safety and peace. Hettie wished herself there now, missing her room where she could lament alone. The small kitchen beyond the glow could not help with that. Hettie wiped her face with her apron and continued toward the light.

"Did you bring them tea?" A woman's voice called from the kitchen's interior before she even set foot there.

Hettie hesitated in the open door. She tried to keep her eyes down, knowing the question came from Rose Benson, the other housekeeper who joined the Conrads from their home in Vermont. Hettie knew she wouldn't be alone in the kitchen. She looked reluctantly toward Rose from the shadows. The dark haired girl sat at the small table, taking dinner alone. She smiled at Hettie, tipping her little white frilly capped head to the side, oblivious of Hettie's tears.

"Yes," Hettie backed more into the shadows and flicked her eyes back and forth nervously. She wanted to hide from Rose.

"Supper's ready," the girl added with a smile, looking to her from devious green eyes. "Mr. Conrad had me make us a whole chicken—"

"I'm not hungry," Hettie answered in clipped husky tones.

"After all that work we did today? I bet you're famished—what's wrong?" Rose asked, finally noticing Hettie's change in mood.

Rose stared with a scowl, slowly chewing her dinner. Hettie would not meet her gaze. Rose looked to her plate and scratched her head through her cap. These silences made her uncomfortable, unable to think of a word to say.

"I just need some fresh air," Hettie said miserably.

Hettie pivoted on her feet and left the light of the kitchen for the back door. She could no longer wait to find somewhere quiet and lonely to cry. Tears grew thick in her eyes. Hettie pushed through the back door onto a small back porch. Voices rose in greeting the moment her foot touched the wood planks.

Jack sat with one of the other hands in a pair of rockers to either side of the backdoor. They smoked and drank their coffee in the cool evening air, after filling their bellies on a good supper. She forgot about the men until that moment.

Rubbing her hand on her apron, Hettie bobbed her head to each man and stammered hello. Hurriedly, she ran off the porch and across the yard. Disappearing behind the tall hedges beyond the yard, she worried they would say something to the Conrads. She always had more to say to them. Her sullen run from the house would excite their curiosity and cause questions.

Stepping into the inner square of the garden, Hettie spied a tall willow. Looking at it with tear filled eyes, she decided to let them gossip about her if they would. She hurt too much to care. Hettie sighed and found the bench beneath the tree. She sat and peered up at the moon.

Inside the rented townhouse, Emily drank her tea in quick swallows, knowing her mother and Michael had upset Hettie. Her eyes roved over the occupants of the room. They appeared ignorant of what happened. Despite her youth, Emily perceived a great deal of what went on around her, especially when it concerned her dearest friend.

Excusing herself, Emily set her cup on a side table. She stood and placed the pillow on the cushion where she previously sat. Without another hesitation, she walked out of the room and down the hall to the kitchen in search of Hettie. Rounding the bright narrow doorway, Emily stopped short with a worrisome expression. Rose sat alone. She smiled guardedly and returned to her meal without a word. Emily eyed the woman disappointed. It was bad enough Hettie was not there, but Rose obviously hid something regardless of friendship.

Emily clasped her hands at her waist and pursed her lips waiting. The maid looked to her again, but with guilt in her eyes this time. Her hand lifted and she pointed Emily to the backdoor, unable to hold the secret any longer. Emily whispered a thank you. Rose smiled and shook her head. Pivoting on her heels, Emily dashed from the room and out of the back door with a bang.

"Good evening, Miss Emily," Jack's voice rang out at her noisy arrival.

"Good evening," Emily replied distantly. She peered around the tiny porch, feeling a little confused. "Have you seen Hettie?" She asked, facing the old man.

"She went walking up that way," Old Jack gestured toward the garden hedge. He seemed not to care, lounging in the rocker and enjoying his pipe. Emily frowned at his scruffy face and unkempt clothes. Jack played the humble man to a fault. "Is she all right, Em?" He asked, peering at her suspiciously. His face melted into a soft concerned expression.

"Yes—she wanted to ask me about something, away from my folks. Why?" Emily asked, using a taunting voice that turned his suspicion back on him. She raised a brow at him. Then, she eyed the other man on in the other rocker to be sure they understood not to bother thinking too much on what was happening. However, they looked at her with heightened curiosity instead. They were worse than old Mrs. Handel.

"No reason," Jack drawled, settling back in his seat. His face reflected a lack of care. Emily stood there, eyeing him suspiciously. "Go on with you now, before your pa yells at me fur gettin you in trouble," Jake waved her away with a swing of his hand to strike her bottom, but purposely missed, as she turned and darted off the porch. He chased her with a cackling laugh.

"Thank you, Jack," Emily said, smiling back over her shoulder.

Emily then bent her attention on her task. She must find Hettie before she sat in the dark night alone for too long. She would find herself ill doing that. Drawing her skirts into her hands, Emily rushed along the path, which cut the lawn in two. Her booted feet clicked on the red bricks, silencing the crickets and warning anything else in her path.

Emily soon faced a blind unyielding wall of deep evergreen shrubbery. Looking left and then right, she saw the path disappear in two directions. Emily hesitated unsure of what lie on the paths in either route. However, one provided Hettie's escape and she needed to find out which. Emily bent her ears to listen. It took little time before the sound of Hettie's heartache reached her, clearly marking the left path.

Emily faced the dark. It appeared little used since well before their arrival. Even she had ignored the gardens, not thinking once of exploring them. Casting her eyes about, she would change that in the morning, and only go far enough to find Hettie then. She stepped carefully and precisely, following the path behind the hedges and into the claustrophobic dark beyond. In another turn, the darkness ended in a violet blushing sunset. Taking the last few steps, Emily faced the mirror of her passage. Both paths led to the same garden.

Annoyed at thinking her decision would be so important and finding it less than such, Emily huffed. She then stomped up the brick path to three low but ornate marble stairs, rising onto the main green of the garden. Emily lifted her chin, stepping slowly up the last stair. Her jaw dropped with sheer awe.

The entire expanse lay within the tall thick frame of an evergreen hedge. The same red brick path that led her there branched around, creating a border between the hedge and the grounds. Looking behind and to the side, she noted a brick entranceway lined by low marble walls set at intervals with flower filled urns. Emily turned back and slowly paced her way along a crushed stone pathway. Clasping her hands at her waist, she tried to take in the vast square garden. Two large flowerbeds lay to either side of her, halting at the edge of a green lawn. An enormous willow sat to the right of her view, sweeping its verdant tendrils toward a wide pond on the left. A red path wore its way along in the velvety grass and led beneath the branches of the tree. Emily stared beyond them. She could just make out the bench at the trunk base, and the curled frame of Henrietta Benson on top.

Hesitating, Emily cast her eyes over the lily pad pond, sparkling silver in the rising moonlight. Beyond it, an ornate bridge stretched a narrow part of the pond to yet another section of garden where an arbor and wrought iron gazebo stood behind a fence. Her eyes swept back to where Hettie sat.

Emily hung her head, trying to imagine what she could say, but found herself overwhelmed by the beauty of this unknown Eden. Her eyes searched Hettie, hoping the woman would spare a clue. She only sat with her knees drawn up to her chest, weeping into her hands. Hettie shook with the force of unrestrained hurt. Emily lifted her chin, as her mouth lowered with sad concern. She could not rightly stand there like an ass when Hettie needed her. Her quiet presence would at least be more than that. Tucking away her worries, she ducked beneath the low tendrils of the tree and went to her.

"Hettie," Emily called softly. She tiptoed forward, clutching her skirt in one hand and held the other out for a balance. "Hettie," she called again, standing before her friend.

Emily looked to Hettie's bent head and rounded back. The line of her dress across her shoulders revealed the tips of her scars. Emily dressed the wounds they came from many times before they healed, so infected by her rank accommodations wherever she lived before their farm. Now, they pained her in a different way. Emily felt the tears burn in her eyes, helpless to change the past and dying to try.

"Oh, Em—when'll it end?" Hettie cried hopelessly, looking toward the bleak sky.

Emily lifted her eyes to her. She could not think of a word to say. Suddenly, she recalled something Hettie told her when she faced difficulty, like when Michael left for school, as close as she would ever come to understanding the other woman's experience. Emily smiled bittersweet. Drawing a breath, she sat beside Hettie and clasped her hands in her lap, leaning against her friend.

"You once told me—with faith all trials will be overcome, and that tears are merely our doubt, trying to steal that faith," she spoke low.

"I can't stop crying—no matter how I try—I can't stop," Hettie sobbed.

Emily saw her lift her teary face to the branches, pleading for relief. The tears glistened against the light of the moon and ran down her cheeks to drip from her chin. Emily watched her pain filled eyes open to the willow canopy and cerulean patches that peeked through. Her friend's eyes sparkled like polished ebony, as if joy and not suffering filled her to bursting.

"You've been through more than I'll ever understand," Emily whispered. "I wish there were a power to take it away—but, I'm sorry Hettie—I know there's little comfort in my apology, but I am just the same."

Hettie's head lowered into her trembling hands with a groan of agony, tearing from her throat. Her tears flowed freely. Emily could not find the words to make her friend's torment end. Still she tried, searching every crevice of her memory to find some shred of comfort. Emily bit her upper lip. Nothing could reverse the reasons, but Emily could offer her friendship and care. She reached a small hand out and placed it on Hettie's shaking back. Through the cloth of her dress, dark reminders of nightmares pressed back. Without a flinch, Emily watched Hettie sob.

"Hettie," Emily spoke in a soft voice. She found something to at least distract her with. "Tell me about your husband—and son. You didn't say much about your son yet," Emily said, drawing her legs up under her skirt to rest on the bench.

Hettie lifted her sad face from her hands and looked at the tears soaking them. Her expression masked what she thought, but her eyes turned hard when she looked up to the icy moon, daring it to freeze her soul. Emily swallowed, thinking she misspoke. Hettie usually liked to mention her family, but she rarely spoke of the boy.

Hettie wiped her eyes and drew a deep breath that lifted her shoulders. Emily folded her hands in her lap and lowered her eyes to them. Hettie's hand reached and closed over hers. She squeezed and Emily felt reassured.

"I can still see their faces," Hettie breathed, staring into nothing.

Emily lifted her face to look upon the garden while she listened. Hettie sat back on the bench. Her eyes still sought something in the sky. A slow smile spread on her lips. Emily twisted her hand to hold her friend's.

"When I married Isaiah—it was the master's doin—the ceremony wen just like they do for ya white folks," Hettie gritted her teeth, as if her words cut her insides to speak them. Though she spoke of her husband with love at every chance, it sometimes appeared that was not so. Hettie half smiled and squeezed Emily's hand. "I was never so scared in all my life," She breathed nervously. The moment relived in her head. "He used to work in the fields—I never even knew his name until that day. They brought him to the back of the gardens—he was the biggest man I'd ever seen—had a mean look to em. I guess it was the circumstance," She lowered her head, guilty for describing her beloved Isaiah in such a manner. "Over time, I also learned he's the most gentle man I ever met," Hettie wistfully recalled later days they spent together on the farm. She no longer stayed in the plantation house. The owner moved them to the rickety row of white cottages with the rest of the slaves. When she became pregnant, she hid out of sight of the white guests who came to the plantation. The orders of the master provided her many days of relative peace. "Two years pass—mah boy Ezekiel was born. He was my only pride an joy. I'll ne'er forget his eyes or his face, so longs I live," Hettie looked up at the branches of the willow, picturing her son's infant face, as he looked up at her with feeble joy a sparkle in his black eyes when she held him.

A story of sorrow then unfolded that left Emily frigid. She could remember getting the willow switch when she behaved badly. A switch hurt badly enough on tender bare skin. With rising fear, she imagined a bullwhip striking her. Clutching Hettie's hand tighter, Emily moved closer to her for protection. Her mind wondered at what it could possibly be like to be someone's property, never having the choices offered to so many around you. Suffer abuse like an animal and made to do tasks that no human should endure.

Emily tucked her free arm around her waist, feeling Hettie's words speak to her nightmares. She trembled like a cold breeze blew over her, but the night air permeated warmth and stood listlessly still. Emily lowered her head to rest against Hettie's shoulder. They sat like loving sisters in mannerism, but fate had simply made them friends, united by only their emotions. Emily felt Hettie's hand reach up and caress her hair.

"I'm sorry, Em. I shouldn be tellin y'all that," Hettie said, still marked by her suffering. She often forgot Emily's age, and failed to guard her speech accordingly.

"No—I asked," Emily said, quickly excusing her. "And, I'm not a little girl anymore."

Emily looked at Hettie's hand, holding hers and noted the contrast of the darker digits in her pale ones. She wondered how merely superficial differences could make people react so dreadfully. People used nonsense to justify so many abuses she knew so little of. Emily thought she would never understand any of it, and she could not make Hettie go through explanations anymore.

"It's sumthin a girl shouldn hear," Hettie sighed. She stood and walked to the edge of the sweeping willow branches, gazing out over the pond.

"Much less endure," Emily added with a sigh. She pushed forward on the cold iron bench and gripped the edge. "Why do they do these things? Why is it all right?" She asked, crossing her legs beneath her skirts. She heard Hettie sigh and slightly turn back, looking to the ground at her side. "I'll never understand," she added hopelessly.

After a pause, Hettie looked at Emily and smiled. She searched the young woman's blue eyes for the innocence of the girl that faded away from her. Still fresh to the world, Emily sat on the cusp of womanhood at only eighteen years. Sometime ago, her education had finished meagerly. All too soon, in mind and body, her innocent Emily would be a worldly woman, the wife of some man yet unknown to them. Hettie wished she knew what it felt like to exist in the middle of so much promise. Childhood and innocence held too high a price in her world. Her life never promised anything but pain. Then, she inadvertently awoke on the Conrad Farm. Providence led her there and everything changed.

Hettie stepped back to the bench and touched Emily's face. She smiled almost bitterly. Releasing Emily's chin from her fingertips, she prayed poor Emily never knew a thing of the torment life could be. God willing, no evil would befall her and destroy what she loved Emily for.

"I hope ya ne'er have ta see such things I've seen. I don't wish it on any man," Hettie sat back beside her friend. "I jus wan mah family back. I wan what you have," she sighed, giving voice to her thoughts.

"I'd give it to you if I'd the power," Emily said, looking at the side of Hettie's face. Smiling, she turned to the back of the bench and the trunk of the tree where creeping roses wound their way up to the branches. She broke off the most perfect bloom that grew there and returned to Hettie. "I can give you this," Emily smiled, holding out the rose.

Hettie looked to the bright blossom. Her eyes glided across velvet petals and leathery leaves to the pale fingers that held the thorny stem. Hettie's gaze shifted to Emily's.

The girl lounged on the bench, offering a simple gift with no idea of meaning. Hettie saw the woman coming, sure as a storm at sea. Emily's mink brown hair once hung loose. Now, the tresses were bound in braids and wound in buns, some draping slackly, but all secured with combs and pins. Any other style would be considered unseemly in public. Only her husband could release her locks for his pleasure, if she was able to claim one. Emily fared no better than she, serving like a slave beneath a different title.

Hettie smiled at Emily and took the rose. She softly smiled, searched her blue eyes that shone to rival the moon. Hettie found comfort in those eyes. They showed a real soul, as noble as the gift she gave. By some grace, Emily had grown into a creature fine of feature and delicate, owning a heart so true it showed in inextinguishable beauty. Though she knew Emily's innocence faded like her hope, she tried to hold onto it for comfort from the raging world around them. Too soon, Hettie's one joy would be lost, as Emily went to live a life of her own with the days given her by fate.

Emily watched her dear friend spin the rose in her fingers. She gave a small smile, knowing Hettie appreciated the sentiment more than anyone was capable. The crimson petals would become a keepsake, cherished as pressed memories in a book. Much time had passed since she existed as property, having no rights and owning nothing, not even a simple flower. Emily stroked her stomach, sick at the very idea. Here with her and her family, Hettie had more than a slave could claim. It must have seemed quite strange and desperately frightening. Emily's father tried very hard to help Hettie begin her new life. She earned wages for her work, even enough to save with. Until she reunited with her family, Hettie used the third floor of their home for her own. Though she hoped a reunion would happen soon, Emily feared her leaving. She often spoke of moving to Canada, like her original plan. Then, Hettie would muse about staying at the dairy, where she would make a home near the people who helped save her life. She could not picture her life without Hettie somehow in it.

With a place to stay and ready wages, all that remained was to see Isaiah again and for him to be hired on the farm. Emily could not expect them to stay. In the end, Hettie would give in to her husband's wishes. After all, Isaiah came from the same past, and had no good experiences with which to judge her family by. Emily could not blame him if they left, but it would hurt.

Of late, Mr. Conrad urged Hettie to use some of her savings to purchase items for her future, wherever it lie. So long she fled dreams of such, and still fought against the torture of the past that existed far from her. The small flower in her hand represented how far. The Conrads would never allow her to return to the plantation, even if the master himself showed up at their door. Thus far, not a soul in Vermont reported her to the dozens of bounty hunters trying to collect rewards for runaways. She sighed to quiet the worries of her heart.

Hettie tucked the rose into her buttonhole and wiped her tired eyes. Soon perhaps, laws would secure her freedom. Mr. Conrad said so. It could not be a sand castle, waiting to topple under the force of one angry wave. Educated and determined as he was, he could not guarantee she would not stand alone, with nothing but broken dreams and empty hands in the end.

"B'fore mah scape I prayed I'd find sumwhere like I did on ya farm," she whispered, searching the sky through the tree branches. She reached to touch Emily's hand without looking again. "Now I have—an I still ain't satisfied. I wish I could have what y'all have, Em. I ain't sure I'll ever find it, but imma try anyway."

"You'll have it, Hettie," Emily sighed, knowing her friend's fears and doubts held a great deal of weight. Hettie's status as a runaway slave still afforded her no rights or promises. "You never take no for an answer."

Hettie grinned at her friend's jest and Emily put a consoling arm around her. Rubbing her back, she offered some comfort. She hung her head ashamed that Emily need feel her scars, testaments to the treachery of sin. Despite them, Emily's features remained unchanged. Hettie looked into Emily's eyes half smiling, thankful to have her at her side. She truly cared for her.

"When your family comes, will you stay with us still?" Emily asked, revealing her deepest concern. Her emotions pinched her young face a little.

"I dunno," Hettie replied, lowering her chin with a dismissing smile. "If things cud be perfect—I'd like ta stay." Smiling, she added, "I doan care for many ah your kind Emily Conrad, but I care for you and ya family. I just wonder how Isaiah's gonna take it all in."

"I don't care for many of us either," Emily said, crushing her in a hug. "Not after what happened to you," she added softly, laying her head on Hettie's shoulder. She saw her smile at her silly response. Emily giggled and let her go, pulling her hands into hers. She smiled and demanded in a bright voice, "Tell me more about Isaiah. He sounds wonderful—handsome and so tall."

Hettie cocked her head to the side, looking at the bench seat. Emily's innocence would forever be her grace. A slow smile spread on her lips again. *Isaiah.*

"Now there's a long tall story ya doan have any business hearin at your age," Hettie said. She beamed with all the love burning in her heart for him.

A short time passed, and Emily appeared on the brick path of the lawn from the gardens with Hettie held close at her side. They walked arm in arm like sisters and giggled like children. Their steps remained slow and deliberate, not wishing to end their whispery discussion of an unwanted match that turned to a loving marriage. However, when they reached the distance set in the light of the porch lamps, the scene playing out there wiped the joy from their faces and hearts. They stopped and worriedly stared.

Jack stood pressed to the door beside the other farmhand, listening to a heated argument that gusted at them from the parlor down the hall. The voices they heard belonged to Stuart Conrad and his son Michael. The like of this argument went unheard since young Michael's mother tried to forbid him to leave for West Point. Since they had arrived for their visit, it became a constant affair. Jack shook his head with disappointment.

Suddenly feeling eyes on the back of his neck, Jack turned to see the faces of the women. Hettie peered at him with narrowing eyes and he froze all over his body, except his arm with which he reached up and tapped the other man who still stared into the hall beyond. The man turned and his face bore shame and shock.

Emily was horrified and she knew her expression showed it. Her father and mother came to visit with Michael because they missed him, not to fight over matters far too late to amend. Michael made his choice, and though he may be wavering time and again, Emily knew that her brother wanted to be an officer in his country's army. He needed to defend his nation against the agitation that grew within it. If they could not respect his decision, he would never settle himself to it. Without their support, he would only fail. Tears sprang to Emily's eyes, keenly feeling the blame in her heart for bringing her family to this.

Regardless, the yelling must stop. Emily was unsure how to end it, but she meant to try, climbing the stairs with a sad but determined expression. Hettie held onto Emily's arm tightly. She wanted to keep her there for some reason. Emily looked at her solemnly and pulled free. She cast her eyes over each of them, seeing their pity and unspoken cautions.

"Em, stay out here with us," Jack said.

Emily glared at him and growled, "Get you to your rooms! This isn't any business of yours, Jack. Go on with you!"

Hettie hurried to Emily's side and shooed the old men away before the girl struck at them with her volatile tongue again. Emily was embarrassed that they witnessed the argument and meant nothing by snapping. She held her breath, hoping the men understood.

Emily glared at the hands, tears standing in her eyes. She quickly tore through the door and dashed inside.

"Ya'll bettah do what she tole ya," Hettie said gently but firm. "Ya know ya doan need ta hear any a this."

"Yes, Miss Benson," the one hand said.

"All right," Hettie touched his arm with a smile and followed after Emily. Hettie walked fast, keeping Emily in her sight. She was determined to throw herself into the battle, without even a pocketknife to defend herself with. "All this foolishness'll just rip y'all apart."

The clack of the back screen door rattled in Emily's head. Tears burned her eyes and embarrassment burned her pride. She felt anger rise in her heart and heated words banged around her mind, finding no outlet on her tongue. She had hoped Hettie would have stayed back. Now, the men would gather again at the door and listen. She could hear the gentle pad of Hettie's shoes on the hall floor. The entire dairy would be enlightened to the family problems. She wished they would mind their own business and go elsewhere for privacy's sake.

Emily listened to her father's raised voice. He rarely used anger to argue his points, which made the occasion all the more upsetting. Nearing the parlor, she discovered the argument was over the usual: Michael's choice to join the military academy. Her father had helped Michael get in and once reveled in the boy's decision to go to school. Ever since the country sat on the brink of war, their mother spoke about her fears for Michael. She could only imagine what went on in her mother's mind while the news filled the parlor. Mother wanted to keep him at home, hiding from duty and living what she planned for him. Her mother made her father fight for her despite his real convictions, manipulating his fears to carry out her agenda. Her room rested only a wall away from theirs. Many nights, they argued about their children and father never won.

Emily knew trouble would come from the papers her father read. The stories made her tremble too. She stood by as they sliced her family in twain. Michael's resolve wavered under the pecking, but it seemed Michael had now chosen to stay his course, faced with duty. It must bother her father a great deal to hear such.

Upon entering the doorway of the parlor, Emily found Rose Benson standing over her mother who lay across the couch unconscious. Her mother probably faked a swoon, as usual, to manipulate the men into doing what she desired. Still, Rose fanned Mrs. Conrad's face with her father's discarded paper and watched the men heatedly argue. Emily spun inside herself. Rose should not be witness anymore than Hettie or the farmhands. Between Rose and her father Jack, all of Vermont would know what happened.

Emily flicked her eyes from the women to the men. In the middle of the room, her father and brother stood in red faced confrontation. Michael had developed his own ideas of the world, now he lived away from home. More often than not, conversations with their father ended in terrible arguments. However, Michael's eyes held a desperate need to prove himself there. He fought against their mother's controls. Confident that what occurred could be chalked up to her mother's meddling again, Emily tried to think of a way to bring peace to their parlor once more.

"I've made my choice—and there's nothing you can say," Michael demanded, standing toe to toe with his father. Michael never flinched. Every ounce of fear left him. He was a man now.

"Think of your mother, boy!" Their father pleaded. "She came here to bring you home!"

Emily slowly stepped into the room where they could see her. She looked at them warily, her head tipped slightly down under the weight of the moment. Out of the corner of her eye, she saw Hettie's apron swing round the door edge. The maid held back to linger in the hall. Emily looked to her wide eyed. Hettie hung her head anxious with the arguing. She had told Emily she despised raised voices, for they meant an ill hand later. No amount of good treatment erased such hard lessons.

"I am—and Em too," Michael said, regaining Emily's attention to the argument. "I can't stand here and watch the world fall down around my ears. I'm going to do something if I can, and I won't run from it anymore—you can't stop me. I'll see Evan in the morning, and he'll probably speak for me. Hopefully they'll ignore my effort to leave and things'll go a bit easier." He paused, eyeing their father sulkily. "I'm supposed to report to my barracks now—good night," he said, shuffling his feet undecided and hanging his head with open guilt.

Silence fell over the room. Emily felt it press them under its weight. Her father watched Michael with an expression of hurt and anger, most likely at himself. He stood still and refused to speak. Her brother hesitated before turning to leave. Emily searched his sad angry face when he looked to her in the archway. He could not hold her gaze. His eyes lowered full of guilt. Emily felt their separation deepen. He was going for good this time.

"Michael," Emily breathed. "You just said you wanted to come home," she added, not realizing those words helped her mother. She clamped her mouth shut.

"Forgive me," Michael mumbled. Did he make the wrong decision? "I'm going to do it for you and Hettie," he added, lowering his eyes again. "You both deserve a better world than you've been offered. I can help with that."

In the hall just outside the archway, Hettie felt those words slam against her like a mule kick. Her chest felt like it collapsed and her breath failed her. She heard enough of their foolish arguing. At least they knew where each other could be found. They knew they still enjoyed the blessing of each other needed or not. Every day she survived never knowing if her family lived or if they would ever come home. A longtime would pass before she would allow a fight between them, a long time.

"Michael," Hettie heard Emily whimper. Hettie cried with guilt.

However, Hettie did not entirely credit Michael's foolishness as her responsibility. If he died, sure as the sun rose in the morning, they would blame her. They might not say so, but it would linger in their eyes and unspoken meanings. *If you never came, he'd not have gotten those notions.*

Michael's sense of right and honor linked itself unalterably to acts of foolishness. With her dark shinning eyes, Hettie told Michael he was wrong. Hettie shook her head. She feared being the reason they should let Michael kill himself. On numb legs, Hettie stepped into the room. She shook her head and pointed a sharp finger at him. Fear and anger never left her, but this time she would make it work for her.

"Doan ya'll dare blame this on me, boy!" Hettie growled at him. She surprised herself with the force of her words. "I doan ask anyone ta fight mah battles. I doan need em too, I doan need you to." Hettie looked up in his innocent face, seeing the broken ideas. "It's mah war, Michael. Not yours."

"It will be an honor to make them pay for what they did. They break our nation—state rights or no, they fight for an institution no one can abide."

With that said, Michael took up his hat from the table beside his chair and made to leave. Hettie's eyes bored through him. He almost believed himself in the wrong for his convictions, but his insides told him he was right.

"They abide," his father said gruffly, making him pause.

"Not after what I've seen!" Michael looked back over his shoulder with a sneer of anger.

Michael shared a brief exchange of glances with his father. He kept his reasons for staying at the academy, whether they liked them or not. His father's eyes sadly lowered to the floor at his feet. Michael turned away incapable of holding his gaze any longer. He suffered, making them hurt.

Michael thought of his forebears. These men existed in vague memories passed down by his grandfather and father, but he recalled something he learned of them.

They passed on the creed that each should stand by his convictions, because such strength made a good man. Michael tried to live up to the ideal, but his mother and father continually tried to make him fail. He guessed she kept her reasons and deserved to keep them, but his father he could not excuse.

"The Union will remain because of men like me," Michael said. "Great grandfather did not fight to make this country what it is for nothing, and he would not wish me to remain behind while a bunch of fools ruin it."

"Your great grandfather wasn't all you think of him," his father replied flatly, lifting his somber round face to look at him.

"I know—I want to be like you," Michael told his father. His anger ebbed and tears filled his eyes. "An honorable man. One that'll fight for what he believes. Someone who will risk everything to do right."

This time Michael turned away without looking back. He swept soundlessly from the room, gently touching Emily's shoulder, as he went. His path led him to the front door and out of the rented flat, finally free of his mother's control. He was his own man at last.

Emily stood in the arch, staring at the floor. Her face paled and she trembled with fear. Tears dripped from her chin. Michael spoke against their parents, leaving them all in shock. When the door closed behind him, she knew things were changed forever. Her ears buzzed in the eerie silence.

Emily looked at her mother draped across the couch. A frown of blame and anger knitted her finely arched brows together. Her eyes were still closed, but she was aware of what just happened.

Rose stopped fanning Mrs. Conrad's face and stood gaping with unabashed awe.

Emily turned her eyes to her father. His troubled features were deeply lined with pain. He still watched the empty archway. Then his eyes trailed to Hettie who stood somewhere behind her. Emily looked to her friend. Hettie shook her head, muttering about blame. The maid's hand shakily lifted to her forehead. She froze when she noticed them looking at her. She stared back a moment before her fears crashed on her features. She covered her mouth with trembling fingers and wept with panic. Turning quickly, she ran up the hall toward the kitchen.

Emily looked back to her father. He turned away from her bearing his teeth in an angry sneer. Emily lowered her chin and placed her ashamed gaze on the floor. They argued like churls before their housekeepers and farmhands, never thinking of recourse. Emily's vision blurred. The rug beneath her feat swirled and swam while tears filled her eyes. Quietly she wept her anger and embarrassment.

Inside, Emily's heart was proud of Michael's stand. He broke free of their mother's hand. She swore the sound of a church bell rang a death knell in the distance. His fight held a price. All fights held a price.

ঌ

Through the halls of his barracks, Michael stalked to his room with an angry bearing that kept his peers at a good distance. Some still dared to speak to him, but he stepped away and around determined to be alone. Climbing the stairs to his floor, he found a nearly empty and quiet hall. One of the other cadet's came from the washroom, eyeing him worriedly. He passed him too. Three more doors down, he found his door. Tearing it open, he went in and slammed it closed behind him, shutting everyone but his roommates out.

"Mike?" A voice called to him from the dark bunk behind.

Facing the dark room with an apology ready, he blinked at the other man.

"Sorry, Marcus," Michael said. "Go back to sleep."

"Rough night?"

"I don't want to talk about it."

Marcus yawned and flopped back, "Good, cause I don't think I could stay awake anyway."

Michael lit a candle while stewing over the fight he just shared with his father. The light illuminated the room, but not his heart. He tried to believe that he should not become a soldier with no one but his sister believing in him. He rarely saw Evan, and the man knew nothing of his accomplishments. He busied himself with his friends. Michael held back among the cadets in his class. He could hardly tell them of his concerns. They would heckle him to shame. With little or no support to find for his cause, he reasoned out his resignation to be the best possible decision.

Going to his dresser, he picked up an envelope left on the top. His commandant's name glared up at him from the outside. Looking at it for several seconds, his face took on a determined energy. Suddenly, he tore the letter into several pieces and threw them into a wastebasket. He meant to give his superior the defaming letter by the end of the week. His mother tried to make sure of it. Her damage still stood to change his life, but he meant to make it good again.

For his own sake, Michael would no longer waver on his decision. He knew the truth. The insecurity he once felt belonged to a prying mother. Without her sway, it scattered. Since his arrival at West Point, he tasted a freedom she tried to keep from him. Without her there, he became his own man. She had not planned for this. He told himself his mother merely feared for him, and never intended to cause pain.

Shaking his head, he looked into the mirror that hung above his chest of drawers. Many mornings he set a basin there and shaved his face with barely a hair to shave. After only a year, the face he saw in the reflection no longer belonged to a mere boy. He looked at the face of a man, clean shaven as it might look. His duty to defend his beliefs like a man was before him.

"I won't stand here and watch when there's work to do," he whispered to his reflection, determined to answer his honor's need. "I'm a soldier now, and this is my duty."

"Talking to yourself now?" Marcus grumbled half asleep.

Michael snickered, removing his hat and jacket. He hung them up.

"Yeah," Michael admitted.

"Did you go see that pretty sister a yours?"

"Yeah," Michael said, going to the bunks. "I won't see them anymore. I'm staying here."

"Well that's grand," Marcus said unconvinced.

"What?"

"Nothing," he said. Marcus laid back. "Do you think Miss Conrad would like a man like me? I could go with them in your place."

Michael looked at him blankly, half shocked he would ask him such. Of course Emily would not like him. She never liked men like him. When he thought more on the subject, he could not think of what men she liked, but it would not be Marcus.

"No."

"Why not?" Marcus challenged with a grin.

"I don't know," Michael sat on his bed. "She likes men like Evan Howell."

"They gonna get married like you said?"

"If my Mamma has her way," Michael sighed and looked out the box pain window beside the bed.

"Too bad," Marcus said. "Now your mother's gonna live her life."

Michael laughed.

"Evan's a lucky man anyway," Marcus said after a pause.

"You've no idea," Michael said, spying the moonlight on the tree outside.

"I think I do. He's graduating this year. I heard he's going to join the Potomac down in Virginia."

"Where did you hear that?" He asked, pulling off his boots.

"From him," Marcus said. "He says that's where his friend Maynard went. Made his captain ask for him directly. I bet he's gonna get in the practice with him—get rich too."

"Joe Maynard?" Michael sounded distracted. He unbuttoned his shirt and removed the collar, undid the cuffs.

"Yeah, the rich kid," Marcus scoffed.

"We're all rich," Michael smiled. He thought about Joe Maynard and his infallible reputation at the point. He would give anything to be like him, so resolute and so respected.

"Most, but not like him," Marcus said. "I bet Emily'd like him. All the girls liked him."

Michael laughed, "Probably, Marcus. Probably." He doubted it.

"So you're staying?"

"Yeah—I'm staying."

"Good," Marcus said. "You can sleep on that bed over there then and watch my back when this thing falls on our heads."

"Sure Marcus," Michael said, laying back on his bed. His eyes lifted to the window. He prayed for Emily. He begged their mother would not make her live the life planned for her, but allow her to find her own way and find her own love. "What did you have for dinner tonight?"

"Wasn't bad," Marcus murmured. "Roasted chicken—served with roasted potatoes. They held the side of roasted manipulation for you."

"Awe, Mark. She isn't all that bad," Michael defended his mother. "She's just scared."

"So are we," Marcus said disturbingly. "We could die soon, Mike. You know that?"

Michael remained silent.

"Rich kids or not," Marcus continued. "We could all die in this."

"It hasn't happened yet," Michael tried to dismiss the dark fears.

"It will. I can feel it," Marcus's voice shook.

Michael remained at school. His family long since returned home. They would have to face the reality of him called away to war, possibly to never return. Their family now stood torn apart.

Time passed in its meandering way. The cadets of the West Point Military Academy found themselves swept up in the greatest turmoil of the 1860's. With Lincoln's election came the forewarned secession of the South. The United States of America dissolved around its citizens, true to Marcus's feeling. The northern unionists and their allies prepared to preserve that Union, and the South readied to achieve their goal despite them. The southern states would not relinquish their direction, regardless of what such determination caused. The South planned its own republic, in its own image. All around men mobilized for war and others rallied. For southern or northern will, men would fight and die. They chose their side, Blue or Gray.

III. Findings

Vermont, Near Montpelier
Late March 1862

The rain fell like tears from gray skies that folded the earth in a somber tone. A mantle of snow hugged the ground, slowly melting in the late winter just awakening to spring. The workers of the Conrad Dairy Farm, old men left behind by the war, filtered into the workhouses and barns. When the field stood empty, the rains slowed and the first rays of the dawn sun peaked over the eastern treetops like fire.

Sitting in her cushioned window seat, having just washed her face, hands and hair, Emily watched the workers come to the dairy for a day's work. A letter lay open on the sill, discarded but not forgotten. Her expression appeared sadder since the day her brother decided to stay at the military academy. A deep worry that any happiness once gained in their day would sweep away under a single moment of chance. It took route in her heart sometime ago and soured her mind with its disease.

A heavy sigh of boredom escaped her. She watched the rain run down the windowpanes. Emily felt the painful dullness of the day like so many before. Time went slow with little incident. Since Michael was at the Point, she found little distraction to occupy her apart from chores. Her brother provided the only man able to escort her to dances. He was also the only one who offered a balance to her emotions during her trials. Michael had been a confidant and champion.

Far too interested in getting to work on time, the farmhands did not notice the young woman watching them from her window. The same play repeated every day, and would tomorrow too. They came in along the road, then the right side of the house to the back and the lane of trees that disguised the buildings from the sight of guests. From right to left came the giant barn, chicken coop, the dual milking houses, the dairy behind that, and lastly the men's quarters. Just like the fixed buildings that created it, nothing changed on the farm. The lane stood empty again, except for a few of the usual stragglers.

Emily found no distraction left to occupy her mind from the usual lamentations it went on when left alone. She looked to the morning sky. The rain was clearing with the sunrise, and the far reaches turned yellow. Keeping her eyes on the scattered clouds, she lowered her chin to her arm where it rested against the window casing. Her arm felt cold and strange, as if not part of her. She tried to dream of the things hidden within her heart, but they quickly turned to hopeless yearning. The gold rays of the sun, shot brightly across the trees and fields, but the warmth never reached her. She grew colder.

Emily realized the pains of her maturity, when the knowledge of a better future lay just out of reach. Emily's eyes glistened with unshed tears. She lifted them to the sun, rising behind the tall pines, bordering the eastern yard of the farm. The light reminded her of hope, trapped behind dark walls of doubt and insurmountable trials. The expanse of fields below reflected her grave mood, still soaked in rainy hues.

The same gray clung to the walls and air of her room. She felt surrounded by despair. It caged her like an animal. Emily cried with a deep longing for an escape that eluded her. It panged her heart when it made its presence known. Still, what she really desired was virtually unknown to her. Until she discovered it, no escape would come. Even if she would eventually fail, she wanted to try, but where could she go to find out what was in her heart?

Watching the full clouds roll one over the other in a slow meandering trek north, Emily wished she could catch the edge of one and ride it to wherever it went over the horizon. She imagined a place away from all dullness. It would be a land where no gray days existed, where she would never feel so separated and excitement was the order of the day. Maybe there she would discover the love she had yet to find. Though only whimsy, her inescapable dreaming became painful longing again.

Emily feared in her heart that such fantasies arose from her books, as her mother suggested. Her life was so meager compared to those in the volumes she read. It was not much wonder why she worried about her life never changing. Her desire to be like the unreal characters was what made her wan. She mulled too much over the things she did not have. If she stayed home doing nothing to change the course of he life, nothing would happen. Yet, without direction, how could she take a step?

Emily closed her eyes to the scene and prayed for help to bear the pain swelling in her heart. Hettie told her the difficulty would pass. She was just bored and upset by the letter she received yesterday, she thought, hearing Hettie's words at the time. However, proof of her friend's words had yet to present itself. Focusing her frustration, she willed the proof to face her, as a test of truth.

The sound of footsteps and a swishing skirt came from the hall outside her room, putting a definite end to her reflection and test of wills with fate. Emily quickly put away her frustrations in exchange for a heart racing panic. Her mother told her not to dawdle that morning. They would need her right away in the kitchen.

"Emily," Her mother's voice came from the other side of the door.

Rising to her feet, Emily looked around her room desperate to find someway to disguise the previous moments still plain on her face. If her mother found her sitting there lamenting again, another droning lecture would follow, regarding the need for her to make more friends with the girls of the town. It hardly could provide her a solution, considering they cared little for her, and it could only be likened to torture when placed among them. She pictured their nasty faces, pinched in sinisterly fake tiny smiles.

Emily's expression relaxed when her eyes settled on her hairbrush resting on the surface of her vanity. She snatched up the letter and moved quickly to pick up the brush. She stuffed the letter in her pocket and smoothed her skirts with a trembling hand to calm her thoughts and answered her mother. She looked in the mirror hesitating. The light of the room stayed dim enough to conceal her tears.

"I'm up, Mamma," she said, running the brush through her damp hair.

Emily's strife faded from her features. It passed for weariness and perhaps her mother would believe the same. The test came quick when her mother opened the door and entered studying her. Emily kept her eyes on her reflection.

Momentarily turning to close the door, Margaret then faced her daughter. She eyed her with an annoyed expression, assessing every motion. She woke before dawn and worked for nearly an hour already. Heaving a heavy sigh, she shook her head slightly at Emily and attempted to temper her mood. Emily would learn the way in her own home, under the stern hand of a good husband. She could not teach her any more than she had.

"Hurry yourself up, Emily. The eggs need collecting and the men are already at work," Margaret complained.

Emily returned her mother's gaze through the mirror, awaiting a lecture on laziness. Making a sound of agreement, Emily hurried to complete her bun and not receive her mother's temper so early that morning. By her expression the option passed. However, Emily would not give up at just that. Her mother's expression often appeared one of dismay and left those close to her guessing at her mood by the minute.

Margaret let her hand fall from the doorknob to her waist where it clasped the other, awaiting her daughter impatiently. Her features expressed a tight warning of little toleration for Emily's tardiness that morning. She could not help but wonder if her daughter sat at her vanity daydreaming again. Then, Emily faced her with a smile on her young face. Margaret felt hope her little girl may come out of her low point once and for all. She was once such a joyful presence in their home. She wished to have those days back.

In quick motions, Emily took up her cap, placed it on her head, and left the somber chamber with her mother, closing the door behind them. The hallway stood dark with no windows. Lowering her head and clasping her hands at her waist, Emily followed her mother down the hall. Her eyes wandered the dark wainscoting and wallpaper. She noticed her mother's thin silhouette and her perfect hair. Her mother always appeared perfect, even at home.

Coming to the carved banister staircase, Emily kept her mouth tightly closed. She wanted to stay clear of reprisal. Step after step, she listened to the wood creak beneath them and the clop of their feet. In the empty hall below, her mother left her at the coat rack beside the front door, continuing down the hall to the kitchen. Emily half watched her go, still assessing her mother's mood. Taking down her gray wool cloak, she swung it onto her shoulders in preparation of going outside and beginning her daily chores. After a thoughtful pause, Emily sat down on the hard wood seat of the coat rack and took up her boots from the corner, caked in mud from the previous trek in the yard only yesterday.

Emily stood and made her way toward the kitchen. Her mother emerged in the doorway at the sound of her close steps. In her hand, she expectantly held a basket to send with Emily on her way. Her mother half smiled, a rueful expression if not a warning one, which made her daughter pause. If Emily failed to guard her expressions more carefully, she would find herself attending a tea party with the girls at church. An affair that made Emily's blood run cold. Margaret lifted a brow at Emily's hesitation. Rousing herself from the image of ribbons, bows and nightmares, Emily quickly took the egg basket from her mother's waiting hand. She left the woman in the kitchen door and exited the house through the back door, situated in perfect symmetry with the front.

The move placed Emily on the back porch and facing the lane she watched only moments ago. She turned her face up to the sky. The weather struggled between rain and sunshine. The crisp air of the early morning belied any good weather that might come. Emily cast her eyes about the snow patched scene with a shiver. Spring stood weeks away, but the cold hand of winter grew feeble despite the nip it tried to give.

Adjusting her cloak on her shoulders, Emily stepped across the porch planking to the stairs. She paused only long enough to take up a pair of work gloves from a basket by the railing. Looping the egg basket on her arm, she put on the cold canvas gloves, taking each step carefully. Turning toward the enormous Dutch barn, she walked the lane to the chicken coop. Her mind thought of each monotonous day she did this task and felt her heart constrict at the idea that it would be this way for a very long time to come.

Constructed before her birth, the rude structure of the coop housed many generations of Conrad fowl. It consisted of old boards nailed together and raised up on splintering footings. At the back, a wire fence run gave the birds a safe place to exercise. The hens and roosters seldom used the run, allowed to roam free in the yard at their leisure via a small opening afforded them in the door that locked down at night. Emily kept a wary eye on the menacing little coop, tucking away angst for the sake of her pride.

Since the war with the South, a number of the hands left to join the Federal Army. Many of the chores then fell onto those left behind, including Emily's family. Mr. Conrad insisted they humble themselves to bear the increased load, during this difficult time. They each did their best to complete the vacated jobs. It little mattered how she felt about it, considering the work must be done. If it aided the beloved Union in her course, then they must produce as usual for the sake of the troops and ease their suffering. Emily often repeated the lecture to herself, as given by her father to chase away the resentment that came of doing her chores.

The first work Emily did for the day consisted of gathering eggs. The chickens, usually bad tempered to begin with, became impossibly worse with the added excitement of stealing their few possessions. Emily stared at the coop, thinking of yesterday and the beating she received at their wings. Drawing a deep breath, she shut her eyes and gave an inaudible and encouraging speech to herself.

Ducking inside, Emily saw the rooster watch her from his spot in the opening of the run. When she stood before him, he ambled out of sight. Stepping further inside, she watched the hens flutter around and balk like a fox came to dine on them. Per the usual, when she approached their nests, they turned downright spastic in an effort to drive her away. After she reached for the first egg, they realized their warnings futile. They then pecked her hands and feet, threw a fuss, batted her with their wings and propelled themselves at her person. Emily ignored them and went about her duty feeling quite sorry for herself.

The rooster attack came about in carefully planned steps and always followed the failure of the hen's to thwart her callous thievery. On the last egg, the rooster would reveal himself. She eyed the opening warily, knowing he would soon make his courageous stand. There were only a few more to collect. Thankfully, her long skirts would protect her shins from his outburst. He served the worst punishment by far. Emily thanked the good Lord that he made her a girl and she could hide in her skirts and petticoats.

Emily reached for the last egg and the last hen exited to the run fearfully. He peered in like a little spy, carefully biding his time. Emily took up the fat brown orb and placed it in the basket with the others, slowly turning her back. Out of the corner of her eye, she saw his calculating eyes peep through the opening. His head popped up and down and his little beak hung open, drawing the wintry air. Now he would wait for her retreat when her back faced him. He was quite a coward for a brave fighter.

This day proved no different. The moment Emily stepped toward the exit, he jumped into the coop and scratched with his unusually large yellow legs. With a ridiculous chicken war cry, the rooster delivered the mightiest charge a cavalryman could muster for his size. It looked rather bold with a lack of weapons and size.

Emily cursed out loud and dashed from the coop, slamming the door closed on him and locking down the chicken hatch for spite. The door jumped as the body of the bird struck it. Emily held it, not so sure he could not break through. Shaking her head at the closed door, she listened to the chickens and rooster still complaining. Emily set her jaw, mumbling the strutting nuisance would be on her plate one day for daring to use his spurs on her.

When Emily turned to the yard, she looked like the miserable looser in a pillow fight. However, she would not allow it to ruin her composure in front of the farmhands, who now waited for their breakfast on the porches of their quarters. They watched her do this every morning and thought it the best amusement in all of Vermont. Irritated and embarrassed, Emily thrust forth her chin and threw her shoulders back, stalking proudly as the rooster back to the farmhouse.

The hands watched her, gnashing their gums and loitering about. They chuckled to one another and mumbled their comments. Usually Emily ignored them, but their idiotic laughter riled her already sour mood to no end. Shooting them an angry glance, she quickly set them right. The men dropped their toothless grins and lowered their voices back to their private conversations, looking quite chastened. Emily glared at them until they took notice of her again.

"Sorry, Miss Emily," Mr. Fordder spoke for them all as Jack's second. He shifted uncomfortably on his shabby booted feet.

"Get yourselves to work—the meal's gonna take a while yet," Emily snapped at him. He should know better, having a wife and daughters. "My father doesn't pay you to stand about and laugh at me. I'm tired of you all waiting for me to get them damn eggs, like its some show every morning. Next time, you can get your own eggs for breakfast or eat at home with your families!" She added haughtily, all tones of girlhood gone from her voice.

"Yes, Miss Conrad." Several voices said.

"I'll speak to Mr. Conrad about it," she warned. "Good morning, gentlemen." With that said, Emily traversed the stairs to the porch and slammed her way back inside the farmhouse, leaving the chastised workers behind for the day. Cursing under her breath, she realized how like her mother she had become.

After kicking off her boots and hanging up her coat on the hook outside the door, Emily paused in the door of the yellow kitchen. She observed her mother diligently working at the heavy wooden table set in the center. Emily's mood softened at the sight of her, but not forgetting the near miss.

Emily entered, routing around the table to go to her mother's side. With a small smile, she kissed her cheek. Her mother smiled back, touching Emily's face with a loving hand. Emily then darted to the sink. Still smiling, she placed the basket of eggs in the basin and washed them off in an icy cold pail of water set beside it.

The smells from the oven chased off Emily's misery with their distraction while she worked. She drew a deep breath, hardly able to wait for the fresh bread. She felt absolutely famished. Placing the clean eggs in a bowl, she went to the table to help bring the morning meal to a reality.

Emily quietly watched her mother work, wondering if she should yet mention the letter. She felt Emily's stare and looked up with a smile. Her mother then slid a cutting board with a knife and slab of bacon across the table surface toward her. Emily took it without a word and sliced thin lengthwise pieces, placing them on a plate. There was always something to do, but nothing she wanted. She got to work, deciding to leave the letter for later.

Later that morning, the Conrad family sat down to breakfast in their warmly decorated dining room. The sun shone bright through the sheers hung ethereally before the tall windows, also draped with green velvet curtains. To one side, a pocket door remained still closed, partially obscuring the hall beyond. An empty chair sat at the end of the polished table beneath a crystal chandelier. The empty chair belonged to Michael when they ate their meals together, as a family. Emily eyed it sadly, waiting for her plate and trying not to think of Michael's absence. He would come home to them soon, she told herself.

Hettie made the rounds of the table, serving Emily's parents first. She offered them both her usual bright smile and received many in return. Hettie's smile became a much needed courtesy that she gave plenty of lately. Emily craved it the most that morning, but could barely look at her for all the sad feelings swimming in her head. Her eyes drew back to the chair and she fell into a somber reflective trance.

Each of the housekeeper's footsteps echoed against the ceiling from the wood floor, eventually waking Emily from her grieving. She remained unconvinced of her brother's homecoming. Life just looked too stark from where she sat now.

When Emily's head popped up, Hettie looked to her, giving a small smile. Hettie set a plate in front of the girl. Before leaving, she placed a knowing and consoling hand on her back. With everyone settled, Hettie's job stood presently completed. She faced Mr. Conrad, clasping her long fingered hands at her narrow waist.

She made to excuse herself to join Rose in the kitchen for their breakfast, until it came time to clean up.

"If y'all settled Mr. Conrad," Hettie said in a smooth drawl.

Stuart nodded with a smile, "Yes, Hettie, indeed. Thank you, dear."

After Hettie left the room, Emily found herself staring at her brother's chair once again. No matter where she turned, she felt Michael's absence poignantly. It left a great void, impossibly gaping at her side. She still enjoyed friendships with Hettie and Rose, but could only tell them little things. Hettie had her own pain to deal with and deserved better than a little girl demanding her attention all of the time. As for Rose, the maid meant no harm, but often spoke to freely with anyone.

Emily lowered her eyes to her plate. The sunny breakfast stared back up at her. A bright white fried egg lay with a pink yolk. She popped it with her fork. Gold ran to perfectly toasted bread smeared with melting butter. Sautéed red and gold striped bacon and a browned sausage link tempted. Potato hash steamed. Hettie made the hash special for her every Saturday.

The monotony began at dawn and continued. Life was predictable to the point of knowing the meals by the days of the week. She poked the egg again, dragging the runny yolk across the white. She hated the farm when it felt like this.

"How was your morning, Stuart dear?" Margaret's voice disrupted her thoughts, as it usually did in the same words every morning since her memory began. The events went like clockwork; so banal that Emily felt her mouth turn dry in panic. She picked up her sunny juice and sipped it, looking at the clock. She knew what minute it would read without having to look, about five after eight o'clock. Emily swished the nectar around her mouth, gaining a reproving glance from her mother. Emily looked away, swallowing hard. She poked her egg again, then picked up her warm toast and smeared it with a forkful of gummy yolk.

"Fine—just fine," her father typically answered, while he read the newspaper from the evening before all over again. The time stood at six after eight, dragging on like every other day.

"Michael sent me a letter," Emily said, breaking into the conversation with the loud clap of her voice. She found that she too fell in the same rut that imprisoned them all. A letter arrived once a week on a Friday evening. She handled its presence in the same manner each time. She horded it, reading it again and again, picking and choosing what she would later share with them at Saturday breakfast. The best parts stood secret between her, her brother and Hettie.

In routine, everything stopped when Emily mentioned the news. She shoved potato hash in her mouth and watched. Her father lowered his paper and looked expectantly from behind his spectacles and over his nose. Her mother waited impatiently, also. Need glowed strongly in their eyes, almost frightening.

Emily set her fork aside with a clack and swallowed her mouth full of food uneasily. Emily tried to smile, but only managed a small curl on the corners of her lips. She lifted the letter to where she could read it easily.

"He writes—Dear Em, how are you faring all by yourself at home? Has mother been keeping you busy? I know that she must since I do not hear from you all that often. Life here is very structured, as you know, so I have no time to worry about much for very long. I am glad for it. Evan wrote to tell me he would be going home on leave soon."

"Oh—the Howell's boy is coming home," Margaret said, interrupting most excitedly. "I should call on Mrs. Howell and see about a visit."

Emily blinked at her confused by the excitement her mother displayed. She should have known. These letters became a major concern. They were so desperate to hear from their sons, and even more so when one returned from the war with news. It gave a way to deny the possibility of tragedy. Emily looked to her father. He noisily folded his paper and roughly set it down on the table.

"Quiet, Marge," Stuart said. His gaze returned to Emily much softer, but hungry for more news of his son. "Go on," he urged with a smile and began to eat.

"Evan graduated a year ago and was assigned as a second lieutenant in the cavalry of the army of the Potomac. I have not received my assignment yet, but wherever it is, it will be grand. If you see Ev, send him my thanks for all that he did and continues to do for me here. Now more than ever, I know I made the right decision," Emily read aloud. She paused to turn the page, feeling the presence of her parents press on her. She continued a little nervously under their stares, "He says, ask father if it would be all right for you to visit. It has been awhile, so I will remind you that there are many young men here and we have an event at least once a month still. It would do you some good to see a new face and I'm sure it would brighten their day too."

"I don' think it's a good idea, dear. Your brother is so far away," Margaret said, returning to her meal with an air resistance. She shoveled food into her mouth, as not to explain. She hardly wanted to come out and say she did not want her daughter involved with those military men, or any other aside from the young Mr. Evan Howell. Stuart was sure to balk for hours if she dare mention it.

"It's a wonderful idea," Emily's father said most serious. He looked to his wife questioningly. "We'll all go when the weather's better. I'd like to see my son again anyway."

"Michael will be done with school by then, and commissioned to a unit somewhere else," Emily looked up from the paper she read with a confused expression.

Did her parents not receive the news of his eventual placement, as she just read? No, they denied it. Emily looked to her father. His expression showed how deeply crushed he felt. Emily lowered her gaze from him to the paper in her hands.

"He wrote me that he would stay and seek a position at the school," Stuart said distantly. His saddened eyes lowered to his plate.

"He didn't mention that to me," Emily said, sad to hurt him with the truth. "I hoped to see him sooner too—but, I guess that will not happen."

"Read on," Stuart's voice rumbled low. He forced himself to finish his breakfast despite the sick feeling rising in his stomach.

"Where was I?" Emily said now muted, lowering her eyes to the letter again. "Some of my friends have seen the family picture you sent in my package. I think they have their heart set on meeting you. If father hears, he'll never let you visit, and I don't think I want you to either, knowing their intentions," Emily smiled, looking to her father with a blush.

Stuart managed a weak smile in return for his daughter. He nodded happily. Stuart wanted his young Emily to be happy and he was sure a nice young man could help that along.

Emily continued on, "Further down he says he can't wait to join the fight and that it'll not be long now."

The letter from Michael caused more damage than help for her family's aching hearts. Against all hopes and prayers, he would not return to them any time soon, for the Army would see him an officer and he would be placed in a regiment far away from home. The family remained silent, thinking over his bright words, but feeling dark under their affects.

Emily set the letter on the table. She eyed her parents while they went back to their breakfasts and finished. They looked deeply troubled. With her inner turmoil affirmed, Emily kept silent. She wondered if her mother would now understand the reason behind her gloom.

One by one, they parted the dining room to continue their day. Last, Emily sat alone still picking at her egg, half pulled apart on the plate. A sprinkling of coarse breadcrumbs trailed over it. She hardly even noticed when Rose and Hettie entered to pick up. Instead, she stared at the letter, set out on the table like a nasty exposed secret.

Emily felt the pain surge within her. She felt her tears burn her eyes and her throat ached with unsounded sobs. If Michael never came home, they were sure to never see him again, and it was already more than a year since the last visit. She blamed herself and she knew for sure her mother blamed her. She saw it in her eyes every time she looked at her. After all, Emily begged Evan to speak to him about joining.

Hettie approached the table, carefully studying Emily's somber features. The girl looked like a statue frozen in her chair. She could tell without having to know something skulked outside the door, waiting to feed off the Conrads. Picking up Margaret's plate, she continued to watch Emily, waiting for her to speak first.

Looking over her shoulder to Rose, Hettie saw the other woman gather the silver serving dishes from the sideboard set between the twin windows and then turn to see what passed behind her. Rose must have felt the weight of her stare. The other woman shrugged her shoulders and went back to her task unmoved by Emily's appearance.

Disappointed Rose did not care to help. Hettie turned her gaze back to Emily. The girl remained still, so she cleaned around her, waiting for her to speak. Emily distanced herself for some reason and that reason must lie in the letter she stared so hard at. Hettie gave a quizzical smile. Emily would speak to her when she felt ready, but she could hold a silence for a good long time too. She sighed and decided to do something.

"Emily," Hettie said softly. "Miss Emily?" She repeated when Emily did not respond.

Emily rocked back in her seat slightly and swallowed. She blinked slowly, gathering her thoughts. She needed to tread carefully when she spoke. Things tended to find her mother's ear when she least wanted them to. Her mother could not hear what she wanted to say.

"Michael wants me to visit. I don't know if I should—but I don't know if I'll see him again," Emily finally spoke, but did not meet Hettie's eyes. "Father thinks it's a good idea."

"Y'all ask ya father that," Hettie said, rounding the edge of the table to take her plate. She reached for it and lifted it away. "It ain all that far. Right where we wen last time, right?"

"Yeah—Southern New York," Emily said with a sunken look behind her eyes. She wanted to go and she wanted to dance with his friends like last time. The state's name resounded in her head, as if it fell from somewhere other than her lips. Her mouth stilled so suddenly after saying it.

"I'd go again, if I could. He mus miss ya," Hettie paused, thinking over her next words, but bowled into them anyway. "Wus there a young man tha suit'd ya fancy there?" Hettie's eyes glinted devilishly. "Y'all had sucha good time b'fore."

"Between you and my father, I'll be married to God knows who in a week," Emily smirked annoyed by the mentioning of a made up hero to rescue her, when they all knew it unlikely. It stung to hear Hettie speak her thoughts so closely.

"Not at all darlin—you'd leave us," Rose said quite sarcastically.

"You're not funny, Rose Benson," Emily snapped. She rose up from her seat, throwing the napkin down where her plate once rested. "This day is no different than any other—just perfectly useless—and not you or anyone else can change it." With that said, Emily charged from the room leaving the housekeepers to wonder at why she reacted so tenderly.

Hettie looked to Rose and the woman shrugged as if innocent. Hettie shook her head and spoke under her breath going back to work. She tried to help Emily but Rose only upset the girl anyway. She wished something could happen to help. She missed her old friend and her bright sunny smile. Feeling her throat burn with sadness, she wiped her wrist beneath her eye. She would not cry in front of Rose. In the motion, she saw the letter on the table. Moving quickly, she grabbed it up and folded it into her pocket.

"What's that?" Rose asked.

"None yur bizzness," Hettie answered. "Get them dishes ta the kitchen, b'fore Mrs. Conrad starts hollerin."

True to Emily's prediction, the day turned out no different than the others before. She quilted with her mother, watched the maids swing about the house cleaning, and listened to the men outside working. Even the words they spoke sounded the same. Emily could box their ears, but they would never understand.

Once evening fell over the farm, the air hung about them heavy and silent, like the strange silence before a hurricane wreaks its destruction. The farm employees returned home or retired to their rooms in the houses, adding to the stillness. Soon, Hettie would bring them their evening cup of tea and the monotony continued unimpeded.

The Conrads retired to their usual places in the parlor. This time Emily refused to sit beside her mother, working on her dull needlepoint skills. Instead, she dropped into a chair on the back wall by the shelves of books. Curling her legs up under her skirts, Emily cracked open her copy of *Much Ado About Nothing.* Her father recently bought the volume for her via mail order, after she expressed interest in what her brother read away at school. Before long, Emily read several pages and found herself wholly immersed in Shakespeare's world. However, she suddenly yawned and the spell broke. She thought it time for bed, but looked up at the clock, which read only fifteen minutes after seven. She sat there for only fifteen minutes. She grew anxious and her legs twitched.

Lowering her eyes to her book, she adjusted the high cream lace collar of her dress. Reading the lines of act four and the argument of marrying Beatrice, Emily pulled a lock of hair free from its arrangement of perfect smooth curls. She sunk lower in the chair, just falling short of laying down for the night right there. Determined to continue her reading, Emily convinced herself that getting ready for bed would exhaust her beyond the energy she held right then.

Waking her from her boredom, Stuart rattled his newspaper, turning the page to go onto the next column. Emily saw Margaret look up at him from her needlework and smile warmly. Emily lowered her gaze to her book and Hettie entered with the tea. Emily's eyes flicked to the clock. Tea service entered right on time.

Emily forced herself to read. However, the line failed to sink in and she read it several times, listening to Hettie pour and then serve her parents. The housekeeper then faced her. Emily shook her head no, receiving a strange glance back. Blankly looking at Hettie, she watched her turn away with a shrug and approached her mother.

"If that's all?" Hettie said softly.

"Thank you, Hettie," Margaret replied, smiling up at her.

Emily lowered her eyes back to her book and heard Hettie pick up the tray and whisk out of the room. That ended well enough. She felt convinced her mother would question her change, but her mother surprised her again. Actually, she did not cooperate in helping Emily to add a little fun to the day. She ignored and essentially manipulated her into the usual once again. Emily resolved to make this day different, even if it meant tearing the paper and needlepoint from her parents' hands and slapping them with it.

Emily pictured her mother's reaction and almost laughed out loud. She saw the shocked face in her mind and it hung there comically. Her mother would never expect such a thing from her well bred daughter. Emily smiled to herself deviously. What child never loved thinking of fighting against the system that tied them down? However, Emily was a woman now, not a child that could play.

Widening her eyes to focus them, the lines on the page melted together and her mind lulled her to go to bed. She felt too tired to keep reading and the subject matter bothered her. Emily closed her book, drawing a deep breath. She set the book on the table next to her chair. Sliding forward on the leather upholstery, it creaked loudly in the quiet room. She would make a go at one final blow to the routine. Quickly standing, she stepped over to her mother's side.

"May I be excused, Mamma? I can't keep my eyes open," she said, gaining a loving smile from her father behind his paper.

"Of course, dear," Margaret said. She kept her eye on her work mid stitch, but smiled slightly.

Emily gave a small smile, feeling odd with her mother's words. She watched her work on the third dress hem of the day. The woman probably could not care what her daughter did right then. Emily went to her father and kissed his cheek.

"Good night, Daddy," she said.

"Good night, Emmy," he replied with a warm smile, touching her youthful face with his aged hand.

Emily quickly turned out of the room and went to the sideboard in the hall where an oil lamp awaited her. Taking the lamp in hand, she went to the stairs in pursuit of solitude. Taking the first step, she heaved a sigh and felt her body ache with weariness. Climbing the stairs to her room would take all her effort. Emily looked up at the dark hall above her, feeling a pang of dissatisfaction. She failed to make a difference that day, despite how tired she felt. She worked so hard and accomplished so little.

While Emily took the next four steps, she heard someone tear open the backdoor and rush up the hall toward the parlor. Emily paused to look, placing her hand on the polished banister and her gaze on the shining bare head of Jack Benson. The stairs creaked beneath her, attracting the attention of the old man. He looked up with an expression of desperation. Recognition set on his features, but he failed to smile like he usually did when seeing her. Instead, he met her with a rolling explanation that eluded her understanding. Emily's mouth popped open and she fumbled to hear his hurried words. A fire burned on the grounds.

Somehow, she finally understood him and pointed dumbly to the parlor where she left her parents. Jack bobbed his head with its circlet of short and coarse silver hairs. He hurried toward the parlor. Emily watched him go, clutching the banister tightly. She could not move up or down.

"The barn—Mister Conrad—the barn's on fire!" Jack hollered frantically.

Emily heard the man yell to her father and her heart stilled with the blow of what his words meant. Life just changed on the farm in one single instance. A fire was a very powerful force of change. Feeling sure she willed fate, she feared exactly what this change would bring.

Taking the first step back down, Emily watched her father and Jack emerge from the parlor, leading her panicked mother. Emily took in the scene hungrily. The three rushed up the wood floor hall to the back of the house. The sound of their footsteps raged in the silent house, just like the day they brought Hettie to safety. Emily's heart raced excitedly. What had she asked for?

Finally breaking free of her shock, Emily hurried after her parents. She stopped short, recalling the lamp and sat it back on the sideboard with a hollow roll of the metal base. Emily continued on her way, grasping the skirt of her gown to keep from tripping on it.

Emily burst out of the back door, and raced across the porch, feeling her bare feet on the cold planking. She looked down and saw her soft ivory stockings. Cursing, she ran back in the house and fetched her boots. Hopping along the hall, she quickly put them on her feet without lacing them. She hopped just inside the kitchen to grab up her wool cloak from the hook on the wall. When she swung in the yellow little room, she caught sight of both Hettie and Rose who stared out the window with fearful awe.

"God—this is terrible," Rose said. "What'll they do?"

Emily rushed out of the room, tossing her cloak on her shoulders and ignored the other women. She ripped open the door and ran out of the house to join her parents in the back lane lit orange by the firelight. When she at last reached them in the open field beside the barn, Jack spoke to her father hurriedly about some tale that left her troubled. Too much change came all at once. Indeed, what would they do now?

Before each of them, the barn blazed and smoked in devastating destruction. The sound of the flames made a loud chorus of taunting voices, hissing at them threateningly like demons of hell. Emily's body trembled, thinking her prayers answered by powers other than God. She felt the heat even at the distance she stood. What had she dared to ask for?

Emily half listened to Jack's words, shocked to numbness by the sight before her eyes. Suddenly, his speech broke through her worry and she heard him clearly. Her eyes dragged to his leathery face aglow in the fire light. She fought for each breathe, finding it increasingly difficult.

"Some young fella stopped to help pull out the cows. Seems he's ridin long and saw the smoke," Jack said. He paused to shake his little old head. "Thank God for em."

Margaret looked over her shoulder to see Emily who stared up at the flames with terrified awe. Leaving her husband, she joined her daughter, huddling close for comfort against Nature's great wrath. They held tight to each other, one awestruck and the other weeping. Her daughter tried to sooth away her fears, but it could not reverse the destruction happening just steps from them. She feared for Emily and what the loss would bring.

Margaret knew a barn fire posed an enormous threat to the stability and success of a farm. With every moment that the fire burned, her family stood to lose more than they could easily replace. If any of the stock died, it did not only mean the loss of their productivity, it meant the cost of replacing the animal too. The cost of rebuilding the barn, the housing structure for the cows and the bulls that sired the stock, would follow.

Margaret reached up and touched her daughter's hair, trying to find comfort in the locks she brushed for years. Emily rested her head on her shoulder and remained silent. Margaret squeezed her closer, wanting to draw her away to the kitchen where they could wait safely for Stuart to tell them the damages, but they were rooted to the spot.

Emily's head suddenly lifted and her face expressed shock of a new kind. Her eyes filled with tears and she gasped the words the baby and May-Belle. She thought of her cow and May-Belle's first calf. Emily felt her heart race with absolute terror. Her babies could lie dead and charred within the structure.

"Shakes," Emily breathed the bull's name.

Tears flowed out of Emily's eyes. She helped the cow give birth to her first calf a few days ago and quickly took a strong bond to the animal. He came early to them, because May-Belle came into season early last year and the bull stood more than ready to oblige. Stuart allowed for it with the modern conveniences at their beckon call to assure the result came to a success. The calf presented Emily with a symbol of her success with rearing his mother, after rescuing it from certain death and she named him after the author of her fantasies.

Panicking, Emily wondered if she saved May-Belle only to have her slaughtered in a more gruesome death by fire. The fire would only compound her pains.

One of the hands, soot covered and panting, ran straight to Emily's father. She heard him breathlessly explain that all but the new calf stood safe. Her heart skipped a beat and she felt lightening strike her stomach. Her whole body turned numb. She listened to her own breath drawing coarsely through her mouth. Emily's wide eyes observed the man, wiping his brow with an old kerchief and bent down to catch his breath. Emily's features looked as if she felt the pain of torture to the point of agony, and she cried.

Time lengthened around Emily. Her mother pulled her into her arms and held her there. Emily wept with worry for her animal and felt little comfort from her mother's consoling touch. She told herself that it must not be true. Emily dried her tears with a swipe of her hand. Her cheeks felt sticky and itchy. She lifted her head from her mother's shoulder, seeing a smile meant to comfort. Her mother kissed her forehead and whispered encouraging words. Emily nodded and smiled only half listening. She turned away to stand by herself and face the flames.

Emily looked upon the burning barn agonizingly. She had been at the birth of her cow, her calf and now at her calf's death. Emily told herself that May-Belle lived to have another, but they needed Shake's to replace the elderly one that would pass soon, perhaps that summer. Emily loved the calf the instant he took his first breath. She prayed hope would not fail her this time.

Emily's ears tuned in on the conversation Jack held with her father. He spoke of a stranger, someone who arrived in time to help. He remained unaccounted for. Despite the sadness that rose with fear, a strange feeling bubbled up. Emily bit her bottom lip, looking at Jack.

"He went back in ta get the calf," Jack said. "We lost him after that."

Perhaps somehow, the stranger managed to rescue Shake's and sat in the backfield, catching his breath before returning. Emily's heart rested in this new hope. Her eyes went to her father who ignored everyone to gape at the engulfed structure. Despair burned in the flames reflected in his eyes. Nothing could save it, she wanted to say to him, but held her tongue, unlike that morning. He worked so very hard to amass their fortune. Now, they faced ruin.

Emily lowered her chin and looked at the glinting snow. It sparkled orange and yellow, taunting colors that reminded her of her favorite party dress. She shifted her feet, feeling the cold through her boots. The warm air coming from the fire beat it back from the rest of her. Emily blinked and a tear dripped from her eye, falling to the snow and freezing. How could she think of any dress or party at a time like this? Her prayers had destroyed everything. *Poor little Shakes.*

A knot of nearby workers quarreled, until their voices carried above the sound of the fire. The argument was over the stranger that came to help. The hands stood divided about his fate. Some argued he perished in the flames, while others claimed that no earthly fury could harm such a man. Yet another demanded he was the kind of hero that suffered no such mortality. Emily's brows knitted in disgusted horror, wondering how they could argue such things. Despite their beliefs and the supposed power of any hero, they finally agreed his loss possible. Slowly their rage at each other ebbed and they each turned attention to mourn the man's loss.

Jack mumbled to himself, stealing Emily's attention to him. He drew his old felt cap from his pocket and spun it around in his hands, before he put it on his head again. His eyes lifted and he looked to her, eyes brimming with tears. He could not hold her gaze and turned away to join her father.

"He done worked the hardest of any a us—he's the finest man that ever lived," he mumbled to her father in a voice round with sorrow. "Damn shame to give is life for strangers—though it weren't in vain fur sure," Jack added. He lowered his sooty head, and Emily's father patted his shoulder, still not paying attention.

Emily looked back to the barn and prayed the man alive. If he was dead, so was the bull.

"Show me the stock, Jack." Emily heard her father speak.

Emily listened to the men's footsteps, as they walked away. No more could be done there that night, and the stock needed looking after. Another barn would be planned for in the morning, she presumed. Perhaps they could easily rebuild, having enough funds. After all, only Shakes counted a loss out of the stock and she guessed the cows would stay in the milking facilities until a new barn stood. Emily looked to the retreating figures of her father and Mr. Benson.

"It'd be the will a God to take such a man," Jack said, touching her father's shoulder.

Emily's blue eyes looked up to the fire. The flames raged just as angry. She felt so small and alone standing there. Her ears listened to the fire and she failed to hear the approach of Rose and Hettie. Her gaze shifted to the horrified faces of her friends. Hettie gave a weak smile and put her arm about her.

"It's gonna be okay, Em," she said, as tears slipped down her cheeks.

Emily whispered the news of Shakes and the man who died. She rested her head on Hettie's shoulder, feeling nauseated. Hettie's assurance slowly relaxed her worry. She trusted her friend. Hettie's experience far outweighed hers or even her mother's. Hettie knew most everything and exactly how it would turn out.

In the background, Emily heard the other maid ask her mother if she needed anything. Her mother refused and soon only the sound of the flames surrounded them. They now glowed through the cracks of the planks, taking over the second floor and closer to the back of the structure. Emily wondered why such a horrible thing must happen. Did any justice exist in this? She held tighter to Hettie, sensing something more waited to happen. She watched and listened.

"B'God's grace," Hettie murmured. "Somethins comin."

"Ain no grace, Hettie. It's dreadful," Rose replied from where she stood by Emily's mother.

In her childhood, Emily crawled around the barn, playing with Michael and Evan. With this fire, another part of her childhood passed wholly into memory. Fate demanded she relinquish the past with its vehement display of destruction. Budding softly into womanhood, she really needed to leave the child behind. From there forth, she was grown and the power of the flames sealed it with passion. Emily wondered why fate dealt her this change when she only meant to find love and go somewhere better than a farm in Vermont. What good could fire bring?

Emily lifted her head and looked to Hettie. She could see that the woman saw as deeply as she did.

"Somethins sure ta happen," Hettie whispered. Her black eyes shifted over the yard and trees. She lowered her sparkling gaze to Emily's face. The girl looked back at her questioningly. "I can feel it."

"Someone's died, Hettie. How can you feel good about this?"

"He ain dead—he could get out the back," she pointed to the back of the barn, free of flame but smoking heavily.

Hettie and Emily parted glances, turning their eyes back to the barn. With a spray of sparks that made those surprising thoughts end abruptly, the wall of the barn burst open suddenly. Black smoke billowed forth and on it a dark figure emerged. It came forward like a monster in the night. Slowly, it floated toward them definite in its direction and conscious of its actions. Emily watched him, as if the devil had come born on the flames to walk the mortal earth. Emily drew a ragged breath. Her heart raced excitedly, but the color in her cheeks drained.

Hettie pulled away, drawing Emily's attention with her. Emily watched the maids run away to the darkness of the lane and the warm house beyond. She turned back, watching the form shakily trudge along the snowy hillock toward them.

The figure drew closer and the farmhands moved toward him to relieve him of the hoofed package he carried. Emily gasped, darting toward them.

"Shakes!"

The little bull kicked in his hold, as he bent to place it on the ground. Her dear one was yet alive.

When the stranger knelt on the ground a few paces from her, Emily drew up quick and flung herself back a step. She touched her mouth when he coughed from the smoke and watched with wide eyes, as wiped his face with a dirty hand. Emily guardedly studied his figure bent there before her, horribly sooty.

At her side, the farmhands cheered him, surrounding them both. So, he survived the terrible devastation and returned to them with her prized baby bull. Emily heard his soft warm chuckle before it turned into a raspy cough. It warmed her stomach and her trembling continued for other reasons.

Emily turned her pale eyes slowly to the men, standing tall all about her and the stranger. Faces covered in oily soot smiled with untold joy. Emily could feel her face expressing only shock. It quickly turned to anger. Setting her jaw, she glared at them and each looked to her with joy turning to concern. The men stopped their celebration and excused themselves in gruff voices from her presence. Emily eyed them while they backed away, unmoved by their sheepish expressions and apologies. Emily keenly felt outrage at how they dared to celebrate right in front of her and their stupidity's victim. How could they just leave this poor man to perish in the fire for his efforts? She wanted to slap their faces for the selfish carelessness. Instead, her hands balled into fists at her sides unable to do a thing.

Emily stood alone with the stranger, hovering like a protective mother. She shook her head and lowered her chin, gathering her thoughts. She wanted to apologize to the man, but words froze in her throat. Nothing could make up for him nearly dying for the sake of the calf.

Margaret joined her daughter, announcing her presence with a small trembling hand on her shoulder. Emily snapped a strong glance back to her that eased when she saw Margaret's soft features. Emily turned her attention back to the young man who kneeled at their feet, ignoring the fire he left. Margaret looked down at him, studying his shaggy head, glowing with golden highlights in the firelight. She waited for him to speak or do something, but he just remained in a motionless crouch, breathing hard.

The glowing embers of the burning barn fell about them like red snow flurries, ending in gray black ash on the snow.

Kneeling on the ground, the stranger collected his scattered thoughts. He drew each breath carefully with eyes closed and listened. While inside, the structure began falling apart around him. He wanted to tell the people, but his head swam and words failed him. He just wanted to breathe. Suddenly, the sound drew louder from within the barn. He looked quick over his shoulder, the light sparkling brightly in his dark eyes. The barn was going to collapse and they stood too close to be left unharmed. His attention went to those people before him. Skirts.

The man got to his feet and yelled for the women to stand back, but they only shook suddenly in fear of him. He heard the whining groan of the barn structure giving in, followed by the women's surprised gasps. His eyes swept over the beautiful face of the young woman who stood before him. He hesitated, as his heart thumped another rhythm. He shook it off, realizing he could not spare a moment.

The man put his arm around the young one and took up the hand of the older. He quickly drew them to the safety of the road behind where they stood. The girl felt strangely right pressed to his side and almost too sensual. He wanted to keep her there, but he knew he must let her go. He felt her leg wrap about his to steady her body against his. His run came to a stop and he quickly set the young woman down, putting space back between them. He turned to see the roof sink with a resounding crash. Then, the barn fell in on itself.

The stranger cursed under his breath, watching a spray of sparks and flames rise like canon shot. It little affected him otherwise, as he continued to watch.

Opposite the hero, Emily stood with wide eyes pinned to the stranger. She still felt his body, running down the length of her. It filled her with sensations she never felt in her life. She smoothed her skirts and drew a ragged breath. She was shocked and dismayed a man would put his hands on her in any situation, such as he did.

Beside her, she heard her mother gasp and looked to see her clap a hand over her mouth before it stifled her outcry entirely. Her mother looked terror stricken and wavered on her feet. Emily made a move to go to her, but then she heard the stranger's coughs and stopped. She looked to him with concern on her features, feeling unusually torn between her own mother and a stranger. Somehow, he held her attention despite the affront. In fact, it was the memory of his body pressed to hers that made it impossible to think of anything else.

Lowering her eyes, Emily inwardly chided herself for such awful wantonness. What if he saw her staring at him like that? Her eyes coyly rose to him again, unable to keep away. Her eyes slid up his long legs lined with a gold stripe on his trousers. Her gaze shifted to his broad shoulders. She thought she recognized a Federal uniform.

Jack suddenly dashed in front of Emily's study. He looked utterly filled with joy and went straight to the stranger without one ounce of hesitation in his bouncing step. Emily's eyes went to the young soldier's face, as it turned in profile to look at the old man, clapping him on the back. The soldier smiled handsomely and her heart skipped.

"By God!" Jack said to him. "You're all right, boy."

"Yeah—yes, sir. I am," the man drawled between coughs.

Emily swallowed hard and felt her breath escape her. The sound of his voice spoke to her heart in ways nothing else spoke. Emily drew a ragged breath, like when she first awoke in the morning. Her body felt strangely enlivened from his simple response to Jack. For all the life she felt within herself, she could not move from the spot she stood, the spot he placed her in. Thinking of his arm strongly positioned around her waist, Emily's heart beat hard. Foreign emotions filled her again. She danced with men in much the same hold and not once felt such effects as this.

While she allowed her eyes to delve into him, she wondered if he was the product of her prayers. She could not look away from him. Each moment stood precious, not knowing when he would take his leave and if he would ever return.

The men spoke in tones to low to reach her ears over the dirge of the fire. Emily strained to pick up the tones that stole her soul moments ago. She failed, but received his return glance instead. The young man's eyes drew to her and he smiled. His expression startled her and forced her gaze to the ground at his feet, shyly avoiding him.

Having woken from the sight of her collapsing barn, Margaret saw the weak little calf lowing for attention as it brushed against her daughter's skirt. She quickly went to him when Emily failed to help and dragged him off to one of the workers. She instructed the man to take him to his mother and send her husband back to them when he finished with the head count. The man survived the fire and he would want to meet him.

Stepping back to her daughter, she noticed that Emily stared at the ground with a strange little terrified look on her face. Margaret's terror turned on another course. Her Emily reacted shyly with men only when she found them to her taste. Margaret lifted a brow at her daughter, though she would not see. Then her eyes flicked to the young man a few paces in front of her. She discerned a telling gold stripe up his dark pant leg. A Union soldier, but why this far north? Her heart stilled at the idea of the war in their backyard.

"May I bother a lady ta fetch me a drink a water?" The stranger said, turning to ask in distinctly southern tones. He placed his hard gaze on Emily.

Emily gaped, fighting to think of something to say. She could feel that gaze, reaching in under her skin and taking hold of her. Strangely, she wanted it to. Emily dumbly stood there, as he slowly smiled. She clutched her hands together at her waist, looking up at him helpless. He adjusted on his feet to better face her and her mother. Another cough escaped him, showing the affects of the smoke on his body. It shook her awake and she was relieved to have a reprieve from his attention. Her throat felt dry and she could not answer. Her feet were frozen to the ground and she could not comply with his request. She shifted her gaze about the snow.

Emily saw Jack give his approving nod and heard his low laugh. Emily's heart skipped, realizing someone saw how she looked at the man. Self consciously, she lowered her eyes to the ground, while Jack struck the hero's back to help get out the smoke.

"Thank you," he murmured to Jack.

Margaret's mouth popped open, watching this display. She grew increasingly shocked that the stranger would dare address her daughter while she stood right there. Then his eyes lifted to hers and he looked expectant of an answer. Margaret drew up beside her daughter, girding herself against the threat the man posed to her Emily.

"Certainly you may," Margaret said friendly enough. She looked at her daughter in annoyance and sighed heavy.

"Thank you, ma'am," he drawled in his accent.

The suspicion that he was a bloody Rebel hiding in the North, fleeing from rightful persecution, played out in Margaret's mind. Margaret coached herself to remain a congenial hostess for now. He stopped to help and saved their calf and stock from certain death. For this, she would afford him her hospitality. Then, she would see him off.

Turning to Emily, Margaret said, "Fetch the young man some water, dear."

Margaret looked sharply at her daughter, careful to keep her icy expression from the stranger's gaze. Her words were a command and they stood to exemplify her desire for Emily to be gone from there. Emily's large round eyes searched her face. Her emotions stood clear to her daughter by the look on the girl's face. Emily must know she would take no chances with her. Considering what happened to Hettie, how could she trust any southerner? Every one of them was an animal in her mind. Margaret turned her back on Emily, placing her body between her and the stranger. Margaret smiled widely, masking the irritation at her daughter and the southerner, but she could not hide the embers of hate in her eyes. She wanted the man to go without incident, but he appeared happy to stand there, as long as Emily gaped at him.

"Yes, Mamma," Emily said softly and darted away.

The stranger's gaze followed the girl until she disappeared in the shadows beside the house and the little stone well that stood there. He slid his eyes back to her mother when she approached him. He smiled with a nod to her. He received ample warning of this one.

"Excuse our Emily," Margaret said. "She gets distracted easily. She was so concerned about the calf. He means the world to her."

Now revealed to him, the girl's name reverberated around his mind. He smiled with delight at the memory of his friend's explanation of the Conrad's. Forgetting where he stood at the moment, he lost himself in thoughts of the girl and it made him forget how very sick he felt. He fought the urge to look toward the well, strong like a craving for one more cigarette before bed. He smiled and nodded to the mother's words, gaining an uneasy expression in return. He almost laughed, but it turned into another cough in his throat.

Margaret eyed the man, intimidated by his height. He towered over her while they waited for his cup of water.

"You know barn fires are quite common round here and we've the means to deal with the loss," Margaret said self consciously, rattling on after a too lengthy pause. "You really needn't have risked your life on our behalf, young man."

"I was passing thru—saw the fire and thought you might be needing help," he explained in a distinct accent and well educated manner. He smiled at the pinch faced woman, but not because of her. His friend was right in what he said, as usual.

Margaret now stood assured of what she heard moments ago with his response. A damnable and bloody southern Rebel! Desperate with fear, she fought to keep her features serene and think of an effective way to get him away from her home. Not only was her daughter in danger, but Hettie was now threatened too. None of them could predict what the beast may try to do. By the way he eyed Emily, his ideas looked clear. If they failed to chase him away right then, he may return to take his fill at a more opportune time and sell Hettie for a bounty later for extra measure.

"By God, could no end be reached? Did they never tire of their base debauchery? Could they find no filling of by their sins?" Margaret thought to herself.

Margaret's eyes took in the man's clothing and she tried to summon the courage and words to dismiss him from their farm. The uniform trousers of a Union soldier glared at her in the firelight, boldly twinkling gold embroidery and shinning black boots. Anger deeper than that for the South came to the front of her mind. The Federals, if that guise posed the truth, had come to steal her last baby from her. They won Michael over three years ago, and they would send him to die for his love of them. And now, they would woo her daughter to her own grave. Emily needed her protection.

"Thought with the war on and all you might not have enough hands—being its night too," The stranger spoke again, looking around and up at the sky.

At the well, Emily felt her heart race with curious wonder. In all her life, she never met such a handsome man and thought she never would again. Drawing the bucket up with the crank wheel, she smiled overly giddy. She failed to think of a great many things when praying for a change to her life. However, it felt like those prayers went answered just as she meant them. Shake's was all right and it seemed more good fortune came.

The bucket sloshed and swung heavily on its rope, full to the top with water. Emily grabbed it and tipped it out on the ground. She did not want to let this man out of her sight just yet, no matter how her mother felt about him. She drew another bucket full, and checked the terracotta pitcher and one of the cups sitting on the edge of the well. She rinsed the pitcher and a cup in the second bucket of water. Then, she dumped the water on the ground again. Drawing out her task gave her more time.

Letting the bucket fall to the bottom again, she drew her third draft of water and cranked the wheel slowly to bring it back up. She smirked deviously to herself, thinking of what her mother must think of her delay. Taking hold of the last bucket, she poured the contents into the pitcher careful not to spill a drop. Once full, she lowered the bucket down the well, remarking how cleverly she was. It made her smile even deeper. She lowered the bucket gain and released the hand crank when the bucket touched the water. Finally, she took hold of the cup and poured some water from the pitcher into it. Emily wiped the smirk from her face, setting her features in a mask of nothingness. She intended to walk slowly back to them, providing more time for her father to return. When he showed, he would insist on the stranger taking a rest in the house before he returned to wherever he came from. Emily took up the pitcher, smiling a self satisfied bow of her lips. Father would be most helpful.

Emily returned with her chipped old pitcher and cup clutched in her small hands just as the soldier's eyes came back from another glance at the fire. His features looked less grim, as he had wiped the soot from them, as best he could. However, the soldier now observed her with guarded glances. Emily preferred the appreciative but sly glances from before. Her mother's charm must have worked its magic. He looked perfectly miserable under her watch him and she looked bitterly pleased.

Emily stepped straight up to him, reaching the height of his shoulder. She offered him the cup of water with one hand, holding the jug in the other. He felt his lips curl in a smile at her, hesitating before he accepted her offering. He stood mesmerized by the beauty of her eyes, reflecting both the moon and firelight. If her overprotective mother stood aside, he would have said something, but he could not think of a thing to say that would not strike offense in the older woman's mind.

Margaret grew quite tense when the young people's eyes locked. She thought Emily removed from the threat the southerner posed. Margaret knew better than to think Emily would understand. The girl should have gone in the house for the night and sent out Rose to give him his drink. Margaret pursed her lips and narrowed her eyes. She tightened her shawl around her shoulders.

Emily blushed, but the color was promptly hidden by the orange light of the fire. Her eyes flicked to her mother and she saw the warning in the woman's. She thought to take her leave, not wanting the punishment to come, but found herself unable to move again. Recalling the wrath her mother could display, she wondered if she should have sent Rose instead. It would have been wiser to do so and not risk angering her mother further. It always only caused her problems.

Looking back to the stranger, Emily held out the cup still. This time he took it, but with the hint of an amused grin. Then his smile broke free and full, showing his embarrassment at caught staring too long. Emily flicked her eyes back to her mother and the woman regarded her with disappointment. Emily waited for him to finish and return the cup to her. She lowered the cold pitcher to her waist, cradling it with both hands and kept her eyes on the contents.

"Calf might not make it with the smoke," he said over the lip of the cup to Emily. She looked at him surprised. His eyes burned with an intense flame, searing into her core. "I'm sorry I couldn't get him out sooner," he helplessly apologized.

"Shakes, he's a strong one. He'll pull through," Emily replied resolute and excited.

Emily often grew excited when given the chance to speak about the bull. The pitiable animal was a testament to her hard work and represented all her pride. However, right then, she knew of something else that excited her aside from big doe eyes and floppy ears, something that stood right in front of her tall with broad shoulders and eyes like a warm autumn. She looked up at him and he smiled his appreciation for what she said, or maybe something more.

"I hope you're right," he said.

The sound of her mother clearing her throat broke the spell and she dropped her smile. After, exchanging apologetic glances with the stranger, Emily turned her gaze back to the pitcher in her hands, letting him finish his drink. She replied far too eagerly to his conversation, making herself look an idiot. She stood sure to hear of this from her mother when he went on his way. If it would not make matters worse, Emily would have walked straight back to the house.

The southerner returned the small cup with a smile and said, "Thank you, Miss Emily."

Emily looked up at him captured by the movement of his lips. She felt herself entranced by them. Gazing at his sensual mouth a little too long, she reluctantly took the cup back. For a quick second, their fingers touched and it startled her. With her fingers burning, she felt her heart pound a rhythm unlike any she knew. Her mouth went dry and she wished for her own drink. Instead, she licked her lips to moisten them, while her mind contemplated things it never dared before. Her thoughts were less than a breath and went undetected by everyone but him.

"You're welcome," Emily said softly.

"Are you feeling better?" Margaret asked him.

Emily's mother stepped up, forcing her to take a step back and replace some of the distance between them. The color rose in her cheeks again, but she stood safe from detection in the dark of her mother's shadow. Free of his stare, she still burned with curiosity. The reason for her brash behavior eluded her, but something about the stranger made her want to know more. She raised her eyes to him over her mother's shoulder, and trembled at the thought of him seeing what happened within her. A lighting bolt ran down her neck to the middle of her back, spreading over her like molten metal. Shadows and light danced around the snow covered yard, gray and blue like far off battlefields.

"Indeed, ma'am. Thank you," he said.

Margaret understood quite clearly what happened before her eyes. Both shock and horror swirled on her face. Her daughter wantonly participated in very visible and very inexcusably torrid exchanges with a stranger. It spoke volumes of warnings, so similar to an exchange she engaged in many years ago, the evening she met Stuart the first time. Regardless, she had failed her daughter by not keeping her from the company of Rose. That girl's influence was sure to be to blame.

This desperate situation required an immediate remedy. Evan would return from the war and pose the only respectable choice for a girl of Emily's station to marry. This upstart before them would ruin those plans. She knew his type. He only wanted to use Emily and go his merry way without further thinking of it when he finished. Margaret gathered herself for a fight.

Stuart would return soon, most likely grateful, and invite this new danger into their home. He would let him relax with some tea, until his strength came back. She could not let such a thing come to pass, if she meant to save her daughter from him. This evil could not cross the threshold of her home. Margaret's back stiffened and she adjusted the shawl on her arms. She would stand up to the gates of hell, if need arose to rid of this threat.

"Fetch a basin and some soap, Em. Our hero would probably like to clean his dirty face," Margaret said, masking her anxieties and trying to embarrass him at the same time.

Margaret tried to smile at him, but her eyes could not hold his piercing gaze. He frightened her terribly. She looked away to her daughter who sat the pitcher and cup down in the snow and went to do as asked, a dutiful daughter once more.

Emily retreated to the house in pursuit of Margaret's request for wash water. She felt the stranger's gaze follow until she vanished in the dark shadows of the lane. She smiled to herself, thinking of his handsome features, his voice and the way he held her to him, trying to keep her safe from the fire. How heroic could one man prove? He saved the cows, her bull, her ungrateful mother and her. She sighed, clasping her hands together and smiled broadly. Leaning into a run, she hurried to the house feeling like a little girl on Christmas Day.

Margaret faced the soldier again, but he peered at his feet, as if distracted by his sooty boots.

"Thank you, ma'am," the southerner nodded congenially despite her menacing undertones. He very much wanted to make a positive impression on Miss Emily, but her mother was making it impossible.

The soldier knew he discovered a rare jewel in his travels to Vermont, by the grace of fate. Shaking himself free from the bewitchment Miss Emily put upon him, he felt like he awoke to a new morning. He gave another small smile unable to not watch her retreat. No lovelier woman stood out in his mind upon first glance.

As the stranger and Margaret stood in silence, one of the farmhands ambled up with his hands full of the man's belongings, including his hat and jacket. He took them with a nod and a thank you. Then, he laid them on the ground and started to replace them on his person. The farm hand backed away reverently, thinking the young soldier an angelic apparition. No one could possibly survive such a blaze.

The stranger straightened from his redressing, hat in hand. He meticulously brushed his sleeves off and adjusted his coat. He prided himself on a neat uniform, not that he could help blemishing the wool under the circumstances. With a frown, he brushed the black Stetson with a few swipes of his hand and placed it on his head. Another hand ventured forth and offered him a pair of slightly stained chamois gloves. The soldier thanked him with a smile and took the gloves, tucking them in his belt.

The moment provided him time to think of things to say that may ease the mother's whipped up temper. However, from what he heard, it mattered little what efforts he took and the girl muddled his thoughts. He would have to ask his host more about the Conrads and learn all about the treasure they protected before he ventured further. There was no sense charging in without a plan or knowing what you faced.

The young man became keenly aware of the lengthened silence between him and the mother. She weighed and measured him, while he replaced his discarded belongings somewhere on his person. In her delving eyes, he saw her disgust. Her compressed thin lips and tight jaw lit by the firelight made her appear like a hag. He smiled at her, musing in his mind over all kinds of disrespect. He quickly reminded himself that he left the monsters behind in Virginia.

"What's your name, young man?" Margaret asked him suddenly, still unsure how to rid of the evil. "Where are you from?" She smiled deviously, trying to hide her hate behind innocent interest. She only gave a clue to a possible reason for her boorish behavior. "You sound southern, if I may say." The farmhands neared at those words. Margaret felt sure they would turn on their right good hero, once they knew he hailed from the uncivilized southern reaches of their once great nation. *"To hell with the South. Let it the filth fall away. They're wretches! There is no way their kind could ever have my daughter,"* she thought. Her eyes flicked to the workers slyly satisfied.

"My name's Lieutenant Joseph Maynard," the stranger said with a friendly expression to purposely spite her. His distaste grew for this suspicious woman. He already surmised the game she played, but his father taught him to remain a gentleman no matter. He tucked away what he would really like to say to her. "Of the Baltimore and Frederick Maynards, ma'am —but, I'm on leave now from my Potomac Cavalry platoon. I came with one of my men—he's visiting family," Joseph continued. He emphasized his relation to the Union's Virginia Calvary, having picked up on her inference of to the South.

Margaret felt shock jolt through her and she could not find words to respond. She stammered and then smiled, "Is that so? How very kind of you."

Inside the house, Rose and Hettie hid in the kitchen, watching the fire from the window behind the sink and hand pump. They kept silent until Emily entered among them. Then, Rose stepped back to allow Hettie to barrage the young woman with several nervous questions. Emily eyed her, pausing in the doorway without answer. Hettie drew nearer, twittering on and looking quite concerned. Rose flicked her eyes between them with a small smile on her lips. Hettie said she felt afraid to stay outside with everyone else. The man might be someone who shouldn't see her. Hettie could little afford such a discovery and lived in fear of it.

"Mamma wants some wash water for the man outside," Emily said over her friend to Rose.

Rose nodded and went to work on the order. Hettie continued on nervously, as she filled a kettle with some water and put it on the fire to heat. She turned back to see Emily make her way to the window, still ignoring

Hettie's questions. Rose smiled softly, knowing Emily stood lost in her own world of thoughts, and could not sense any threat this man may pose to them.

"What's he doin here?" Hettie hissed. Her face twisted with fear and misery.

"He saw the fire and stopped to help," Emily said, staring out the window over the sink, trying to see where he stood with her mother.

In loud crashing roars, the barn crushed itself again. For a moment the light intensified around the figures. The man protected her churlish mother again, ushering her back to safe ground with the farmhands. He still presented himself a gentleman, despite everything she did. Emily smiled, watching him speak with the men. She could not look away. Her mother's slight reedy figure stood out easily beside the tall one. The soldier created a stark contrast to the rest of the figures who loitered about the yard, broad of shoulder and nearly a head taller than all of them. She still could not look away, feeling pulled to him by some strange force. Suddenly, she heard Rose gasp and turned, blinking at her like she woke from a dream. Rose smiled at her blushing.

"Oh—my," Rose whispered. "It's happened."

"Emily, ave y'all heard a word I've said?" Hettie said, stepping closer. She touched her shoulder, drawing the girl's attention to her. Rose's statement went unanswered forgotten. "Em?"

"No—I'm sorry," Emily said, looking sleepy. She stepped back from the window with a regretful sheepish expression. What did Rose mean, it happened?

"I axed if ya knew where he'd come from?" Hettie repeated a little annoyed.

"He didn't say much. Mamma sent me away before he could finish," Emily said in a sigh. "I think he's soldier—probably come with Evan. Michael said he was coming home. He's the only Union man in these parts."

"A northern soldier?"

"Of course, Henrietta." Rose snapped. She avoided Hettie's gaze, moving from the table, to the fireplace with a basin. She watched the kettle, waiting for it to boil. “A Confederate couldn’t make it this far. Someone woulda killed em before now—then again, they ain’t very bright round here.”

Hettie stroked a hand over her narrow waist and swallowed, trying to fight the waves of nausea. She knew the other girl spoke the truth. She was just scared. Still, her discovery by the wrong person could mean the end of her freedom. If she went back to the farm, she would have to pay for freeing the slaves and running away all over again. That payment could be her death, a price she would not pay.

“Rose,” Emily turned to say, sensing her friend’s fears. “You just don’t understand, do you,” she eyed the raven haired girl now annoyed herself. “If Hettie’s seen by the wrong man, we could lose her and she could lose her life.”

Rose said nothing. Instead, she kept her gaze on the kettle. She spoke too soon, but she still really did not understand living in fear like Hettie did for her entire life. There must come a point when you cared little for what happened, as long as you lived the moment and you could be thankful for it.

“It’s a right, Rose. Y’all right. I’m actin like I doan know where I’m at. I’m jus bein silly,” Hettie said slowly, trying to convince herself that what she said rang true. She drew a steadying breath, and watched Emily return her attention to the stranger outside through the window. “What’s goin on with you, Miss Emily?” she asked after a moment with knitted brows.

“Hmmm?” Emily murmured not entirely hearing what Hettie said. Her dreamy expression turned to her friend.

Hettie stepped closer and peeked out of the window, the sound of the kettle boiling filled the room. The firelight gleamed in her soft brown eyes. She studied the forms, milling about the disaster. Her face suddenly changed from fear to knowing and she smiled. She could just make out the young man where he stood near Mrs. Conrad. He must look a pretty picture, so tall and broad shouldered dressed in the Federal Army uniform.

Anyone could see the bearing he held, clearly born with it. Every ounce of him spoke of a good family. Hettie imagined what went on in little Emily's mind, standing there watching him like a wildcat over its prey. She wished she stayed long enough to see him face to face. Then again, time might grant such a wish.

"What's goin on with ya, Em?"

"I don't know," she said eventually, giving a shrug of her shoulders and pursing her lips. A slow smile came to her face and she giggled.

Rose joined them at the window, peering out curiously. A silence surrounded all three, as they watched the visitor afraid to look away and miss something. Suddenly Hettie clapped her hands, startling them from the moment. The girls looked at her wide eyed, as she dashed to the cupboard and gathered some cloths and shoved them into Emily's hands. She smiled at the girl shrewdly.

"Y'all better get out there b'fore the man as ta ride home covered in dirt," she said. She hurried to get the hot water from the kettle, poured it into the basin, and emptied a pump of cold water to cool it nicely. She then forced the basin into Rose's hands. "There—y'all set," she said, turning them to the door. Hettie guided them out onto the porch, practically shoving them. "An I doan wanna hear it from Mrs. Conrad either." Hettie remained behind, letting the girls carry the water and towels to the stranger alone and looking like chastened children.

The conversation between Joseph and Margaret took another lull, and Joseph soon found himself wondering where the pretty girl went. He really did not need to clean up there, but he would like another look at the northern jewel he discovered. His host proved most correct when he promised something significant. Assured that it could not take so long to fetch a washbasin and cloth, Joseph thought she hid from him, reading her mother's directions more clearly than she let on.

Joseph's eyes searched the stretch of farmyard behind the aggravating woman beside him. She guarded her daughter from his gaze, drawing him into her instead. However, his eyes settled on a pair of distinctly feminine shadows despite her. The bell shaped figures traversed the icy road toward them from the back porch of the grand farmhouse.

Joseph reminded himself not to stare at the girl too long. His eyes lifted from their distraction to that of the immense structure just beyond. The farmhouse made a monstrous sight in the dark, which could hardly fall under the classification of farmhouse except that it stood on a farm. The firelight flickered on the siding in menacing orange, while the glass of the windows glinted at him like demon eyes. If the fire did not characterize it so ominously, it might appear more like an enormous Charleston townhouse. He could have even likened the home to a smaller copy of the great houses on his own street back in Maryland. The gables stood out impressively in their design and the detailed ginger bread, painted just so to accentuate the greater details of the scalloped siding and artful roof, made a whimsical addition that beckoned the past.

Joseph tucked away his thoughts of home with great remorse. He wanted to forget about home, as it was a place he would be kept away from for some time. Joseph's mood darkened, if possible with the company he presently held. His gaze shifted back to his inhospitable companion.

Mrs. Conrad's voice numbly buzzed in his ear with an uncaught question. The woman's sharp 'excuse me' bit into his ears, and he shook himself free of his meandering thoughts. He half smiled with a vaguely uninterested expression at the slight woman. She stood there expectantly, not unlike a harpy at the hunt.

Joseph cleared his throat and said, "I'm sorry, ma'am. I was just noticing your beautiful home. What was it you were sayin?"

"One of your men—you said before the collapse, Lieutenant? What's his name, if I may be so bold as to ask?" Margaret said edgily. Her eyes darkened with hatred and her smile was visibly forced. *"So you are a Federal soldier—well, blast you to hell too! Your kind stole my precious boy, and none of us will ever see him again, if you have it your way,"* she thought.

"Yes ma'am," he said, looking almost through her. Joseph wanted to express his lack of fear at her apparent disfavor.

Joseph lost his control with each moment that passed. He grew impatient with her lack of appreciation at how he set his own life aside for her three times, by his count at that moment. In all his life, he never met the like of such an ungrateful wretch. And, he dared to believe his friend only exaggerated about her.

"I came with Second Lieutenant Evan Howell," he said.

Evan's name uttered from the stranger's mouth hit Margaret like a runaway steam train, making her eyes bulged and her heart nearly jumped out of her throat. He spoke of their neighbor's son so familiarly. If she held any hope of never seeing this scoundrel again, Evan dashed them all.

Evan had taken Michael away, though he came by day and made use of his pretty educated words, and promises of magnificent glory. Becoming a soldier gave Michael the life he wanted and it would kill him. Margaret begged him to let his family buy him from his service, but he would not allow it, saying Evan did this and Evan did that for him. Margaret was sure if her son stood there, he would protect his sister from the threat looming over her poor little head. Then again, Evan might tell him to let it go and Michael would listen. Despite Margaret's long held desire to see her daughter joined with the Howell in marriage, she still angrily blamed Evan for Michael being all but lost to them. Her children always looked up to Evan. Michael would do anything to be like him and Emily wanted to spend all her time with him.

Foremost of all of Margaret's frustrations, things had changed so the young Howell most likely would not return to complete the plans so carefully laid by their families. Like him, her boy would die too, as so many already had. The only thing left was Emily and she would not let her go easily, even if the new threat stood there tempting as the devil. This Lieutenant Maynard intended to end the little stability Margaret gained and built upon the foundation of Emily. She looked through him and saw his evil path.

Margaret shook free of her thoughts. Lifting her eyes to the stranger, she saw his questioning expression and gave a faltering smile. Her false warmth reflected how cool she felt inside. She watched the soldier force a smile in return, simply to patronize her. She immediately discounted his heroic deeds as a means to work evil.

"Oh my, this tragedy has truly overwrought me," Margaret declared, welling her eyes in false tears. She hoped he was too stupid to pick up on her fakery. "Evan is home then? We haven't seen that boy in such a long time. Emily'll be delighted. She misses him so. They're so close," she coolly mentioned the pair, alluding to something without admitting a thing. She sniffed and wiped her eyes, pausing to view the affect her words had on the man. "So, you're a soldier?" She pretended not to have noticed until he said so. "Why I must not be paying any attention. Of course you are. You said so, and here is your uniform," She gestured at his shoulders and chest, mocking him in her tone.

Margaret looked at him with distaste. The beautiful wool jacket symbolized an organization that killed in the name of noble peace. Devils came in all disguises. She mistakenly allowed Evan to steal her son, never thinking him capable of such atrocities, slacking in her vigilance. Well she learned her lesson. She would not let this new demon take her last baby, no matter the cost. Thoughts of Hettie raised the force of her resolve higher, grasping toward his other fault. She could not forget the sounds that came from his tongue. If it must be, then the uniform belonged on the back of a northern boy who fought for freedom of the exploited, fighting to hold together the one country in the world that could provide freedom to the oppressed.

"Yes—Second Lieutenant Howell is on leave," Joseph said, a tone of mildly disguised irritation edged his voice. He looked at the woman confused by her strange thoughtfulness.

Joseph looked from her to the two women when they approached close. The snow crunched under their footsteps and the sound of their light chatter distracted him. Joseph's anger melted at the sight of Emily. The firelight cast her in a warm glow apart from the darkness surrounding them. He felt like he saw her for the first time all over again. He imagined it would always be that way.

Emily had returned and with Rose close at her side, toting a washbasin and towels between them. The two girls offered him the soap and water wordlessly and backed away once he accepted. Rose smiled at him a little too flirtatiously when he thanked them both, stepping aside to wash the greasy soot from his face and hands. She reminded him of the daisies of Baltimore ballrooms.

Emily watched him carefully, unsure of what she felt building inside her. The stranger was clearly handsome, even Rose had noticed. She pictured the specimen many times in her mind and none compared until now. His sudden appearance whispered of a hope she dare not trust.

Emily continued to watch him while he washed, unafraid he would see her at that moment and unafraid of what her panicked mother would do. She could not tear her eyes from him, even with the strength of Hercules. Running the linen through her hands, she remarked on how sweet it felt to finally find someone interesting.

Rose touched Emily's arm secretively and the girl's eyes drew to hers. Rose smiled and raised a brow. Emily placed a finger beneath her lips, smiled and thought to answer, and then nearly laughed out loud. Margaret cast them a correcting glance, wiping the grins from their faces permanently. Emily lowered her eyes to the ground and stepped closer to the man with the towel half held forward.

Joseph finished bathing and took the offered cloth from the girl. He dried his face, glad to have her back at his side. He could barely disguise his appreciation of her. He returned the linen to Emily, holding his eyes on hers and slightly smiling. Instead of Emily, Rose dashed to take the towel from him and emptied the bowl of steaming water onto the ground.

"Well there now," Rose grinned. "Will there be anything more, Mrs. Conrad?"

"No, I think that was all the Lieutenant required for now," Margaret posed it as a question. She did not care if he wanted another thing unless it was to take his leave.

"Yes, thank you, ma'am. That's all," Joseph spoke up.

The distraction made Emily forget what she thought she might learn at that moment, staring into the stranger's eyes. She stepped back, listening to the fire burn and her heart pound. With his face clear of the marring soot, she could not find the strength to look at him any longer. She pinned her eyes on the flames. Emily's stomach flipped when he spoke and twisted round when his eyes went to her.

Joseph was more handsome than she at first thought. She quickly committed his image to memory. He stood impressively tall beside her. His eyes shone like dark ebony in the firelight, sparkling like the stars that witnessed above. His face was lined by a shortly groomed beard, which accented his square jaw line and outlined his mouth. It suited him well, unlike the terrible coarse beards most men wore of late. She preferred his much better.

Emily's eyes raked his uniform, when he turned to watch the barn burn. The gold embroidery and accents emphasized his figure, only making him more striking. Emily clutched her hands into fists at her sides to keep from sticking a finger into his broad chest and be sure he really stood there. Her eyes shifted to his polished boots. He kept himself well, from head to foot, more meticulous than a tomcat. She wondered what he looked like in the light of day, so stunning by the firelight and stars. She felt the heat rise in her cheeks.

Out of the corner of her eye, Emily saw him give another startling grin. Her heart skipped a beat. He saw her make a catalog of his person. She hoped he enjoyed her appraisal, because it made her madly uncomfortable. She wondered how Rose managed such tasks with finesse and never a blush.

Joseph indeed felt Emily assess him. She eyed everything from his riding gloves and boots to his uniform jacket and face. He saw her eyes widen at the sight of the pistol, returned to him by the farm hands and hanging threateningly from his belt. He wondered if she thought the same as he and if it scared her like it did him.

"You're all very kind," Joseph said, filling the silence and turning back to them. He meant the jewel and her father's workers.

Emily's eyes trailed to Rose who returned to her side. Rose adjusted her shawl and smiled at him in that way she looked when she found a young man to her taste. She found no fear in looking at him. If she had an ounce of that confidence, Emily would have had herself married sometime ago. That would have been a shame.

"It's you who's kind, sir." Rose said, grinning greatly. "Risking your life for the Conrads."

Joseph smiled at her and lowered his chin, feeling a little embarrassed by her compliment. He shook his head in refusal. Lifting his face, he thanked her, but his eyes continued to search out the girl next to her. He could see Emily thought about something and he wished he could make her talk.

Emily hardly heard him speak, busy wondering if all the men looked so handsome in their uniforms and so dangerous with their weaponry. The last she saw of Evan, he wore a cadet uniform and was not apt to carry a gun. She wondered how time had changed her friend and grew anxious to see him again. Of course, visitations with the young Howell, now Second Lieutenant Howell, fell subject to her parents' permission. With the way her mother now reacted, she would be against it, because Lieutenant Maynard would be with him. Emily could not accept missing her childhood friend over such silliness. Her mother must allow it.

"Mother? Can't we have Evan over?" Emily asked suddenly. She looked urgently at her mother. "I haven't seen him in years."

"Of course, dear. If the boy has time, he's welcome to our home, as always," Margaret replied thankful for the implication of something between her daughter and Evan. The man was sure to turn tail and bolt now.

"I can hardly wait," Emily breathed happily.

The breath was stolen from Emily's lungs when her eyes cast back to the soldier and she saw the sadness there. Emily recalled the way her parents threw her at the feet of the Howell's son. They misconstrued the bond entirely. Evan was like another brother and she was as one of his sisters. Had her mother implied more before the stranger? They were friends in the purest sense of the word. However, no outsider would understand what that meant. Her heart beat hard in a panic. Everyone always thought them the perfect match.

Joseph felt his hope disintegrate in his core. Evan did not mention her in any detail, only saying she was a friend. He wished he could know more of her like his subordinate, but had Evan meant to keep her a secret for a reason? He thought he knew his friend, but there were often things yet to discover. It would be so unlike him to favor a girl for more than a brief passing.

"Thank you kindly for your hospitality, but I must go now," Joseph said, addressing Margaret, with a half hearted smile. He could not stand there all night, waiting for an invitation. He had to return to his hosts. Besides, he had a serious line of questioning for a certain officer under his command.

Joseph guessed his friend wondered where he kept himself by now. Knowing Evan, he was already searching for him. Sooner or later, Evan would discover him there and remove him anyway. It would be better to go of his own accord.

"If I may, I'd like to call tomorrow and see how your family's doing, ma'am." Joseph assumed she would dismiss him noncommittally.

"Oh!" Margaret uttered sharply, as if prodded by something sharp.

Margaret hoped he would stay away from her home, having dually taken her hidden meanings. Despite her desires or sensibilities, Margaret remained wary of what denying him would cause. She imagined Stuart's reaction if she told Lieutenant Maynard not to bother. The man saved their cows and she already knew Stuart would want to meet him.

"Well—well, yes of course!" Margaret stammered, feigning confusion at his request. She offered him her hand to hasten his departure. No need to draw things out.

Joseph clasped Margaret's outstretched hand, but briefly. It looked more like a claw than a human appendage. Reminding himself of his upbringing, he forced a gentlemanly humor and tipped his hat to her. He would be glad when he escaped Mrs. Conrad's eyesight.

Turning from the Vermont harpy, he faced the young woman he supposed the housekeeper. Joseph also tipped his hat to her and gave a smile and nod, appreciating the water she brought him to wash with. Placing his hat on his disheveled head, he shook hands with the present farmhands, intentionally saving the jewel of the farm's crown for last. He saw Emily step back, biting her bottom lip and looking disappointed. The men wished him well, smiled and gave hearty handshakes.

The oldest and shortest of the hands stepped to Joseph, grinning from ear to ear. Joseph smiled down at him, thinking of the girl he wanted to bid farewell to. The old man patted his back and thanked him for his efforts, the most eloquent of them all.

"We're all glad you made it," Jack told him, looking into his face with unabashed admiration. "You must have the devil's own luck, boy. We hope to see you again under finer circumstances."

"Thank you," Joseph replied to the old man. He liked this man and wished he had time to know him better. "You sure you got this from here?" He asked the old man. When the old man nodded, he smiled "tomorrow then."

Jack nodded and the men parted from Joseph.

Joseph stood just a few paces away from the girl that stole his heart with a single glance. He turned and looked at her, standing there with her heart shaped face tipped toward the ground. She ignored him, as if hurt by placing her last. If only she knew.

Joseph stepped forward, taking the gloves from his belt and put them on his hands. A gentleman would touch a lady no other way. Reaching for Emily's hand, he waited no longer to hold the delicate digits. He prayed it would prove, as sweet as he imagined. If Evan intended a life with Emily or not, then the man should have moved long ago to stake a claim. She was fair game else.

Emily froze at the soldier's advance and slightly drew her hands away in a protective manner. She looked at him with wide agate medallions. Quickly regaining her composure, Emily lowered her eyes and allowed him to take hold of her hand. She wanted him to see her completely at ease with such an exchange. She trembled regardless. Emily eyed the chamois gloved hand while it took hold of hers. Time slowed around them. Every tense moment strangled her precarious poise. His touch lit a potent fire that raced up her arm, nestling in her neck and melting her spine until it spilled down her back into the gentle curve above her hips, where it exploded.

Despite the things that passed over her, Emily forced her eyes to his face, wanting to smile, but wearing a serious expression that drew her mouth in a straight line instead. He smiled at her, dismissing the veil of uncertainty. Emily wanted to hide from all present, as they watched them carefully. A tiny shy smile curled the corners of her mouth insistently. Delight turned to alarm.

"He'll go in a moment and that'll bring the end of it," she told herself.

When he took her hand in his gloved one, Joseph gave it an appreciative and respectful squeeze. Though he could not wholly feel her fingers, kept from him by a barrier of leather and his own civility, he quite enjoyed the contact.

With hands clasped together, both Joseph and Emily looked into each other's eyes, stuck to the spots in which they stood. To the observers, they looked like a sculpture of tangible marble adoration. The moment, though brief in reality, revealed many intentions.

Joseph made his next move and Emily stood ill equipped to receive it. Her mouth opened slightly and her heart quickened. She helplessly watched his head lower and her hand lift under the guidance. He pressed his lips to her knuckles. The soft brush of his mouth on her skin held far too much intimacy to what she was ready for. She stared at him, eyes wide with fear. At that moment she could not think of a thing to say. He shattered her sensibilities. She felt her interest in him but she also felt her fears at the power of it.

Emily quickly caught the expression of shock from Rose. What could she say? Then, the moment was over. The soldier released her and straightened. Frightened she allowed something improper to happen, Emily looked to her mother. She plainly saw the disapproval and drew her hand back slowly. She reluctantly looked to the Lieutenant. Thankfully, the young man who held her hand let it go when he did. However, that did not halt the gloom taking hold. Emily's head ached with her dilemma. She forced her eyes to the ground, away from him. Emily was unsure of what exactly passed between them, though her mother's expression informed her it was inappropriate.

Joseph would not entirely let go his hold on the young lady, no matter the fight he would have with her mother. He watched her a moment longer. His heart pained him to see her fear his appreciation. Taking a step back, he flashed a hopeful grin and lifted her chin to make her look at him again. She blushed and heard her mother gasp this time.

"Thank you fur your trouble, miss," Joseph said. He looked straight into her eyes one last time and then let her go.

Emily opened her mouth to reply, stammering in the fear he meant to kiss her. His gaze pinned her words still. She could still feel his finger on her chin, though it had gone.

"You're welcome," Emily choked. She tried to smile, knowing the expression defied her mother and would deepen the cost of the contact.

The storm grew stronger. Though her emotions flailed about her like a gale, a sense of ease was at its center. The sensation was unlike any other she experienced in the presence of young men. More than his perfectly chiseled features affected her. With his intense gaze burned in her memory, she knew she should pay attention this time.

The imposing champion turned away. Emily wanted to say more to him, but the opportunity passed held in check by indecision. She watched him whistle, placing two fingers in his mouth. The shrill sound startled her from the spell he weaved about her.

Joseph stepped from the Conrads and their employees to approach the lane. He peered into the dark, waiting for something. The sound of hooves came first, followed by the ghostly form of a black satin horse. When the mount came into clear view, he was painfully reminded of his duty. The horse whickered and shook his head. It turned, loping sideways toward him. The letters U and S shone in the firelight on his rump.

Emily would be a dream until the war ended but more likely forever.

The animal came to Joseph, acting more like a dog called by its master than a horse. He swung up into the saddle, as fluid as a skater on ice. Pulling the reins, he faced Emily one last time. He gave another smile, capturing her features in his memory. Reaching up, he touched a finger to the brim of his Stetson and nodded to her. He saw her watch him curious of the beast beneath him and his manner in which they behaved.

Suddenly, Joseph snapped the reins, squeezed his knees into the flanks of his horse and voiced a sharp command. The horse quickly spun around and galloped into the shadows toward the road beyond the fence. He must return to his gracious hosts before they worry too much over him. Mrs. Howell found quite enough to worry over without him adding to it.

Amidst the fire glow that burned away the icon of Emily's past, the women and farmhands watched the hero disappear into the night. Rose lost interest first, stepping toward Emily when she wandered in the soldier's direction. Nothing would have made him stay. Emily held no power over him. The noble soldier would leave by the whim of his manhood or that of another and remain just a stranger.

Still stepping forward, Emily watched his shadow outlined in moonlight. Her heart and soul cried to go with him. Suddenly, her mother appeared before her, replacing the reason for panic with another. Emily timidly eyed the woman and halted. She felt embarrassed by her actions, as if Margaret's controlling behavior failed to sadden her lonely heart enough. Fear crept into her hopes and washed them away. Emily drew a deep breath, drawing strength from the proof of her defiance. Her eyes reached past her mother's shoulder. The soldier was gone from sight. Emily's heart beat fierce. She only need wait until tomorrow. On the new day, she could make up her mind, defy her mother or comply with her.

"Emily," Margaret warned.

Pulling her cloak tighter around her shoulders, Emily wondered what she would do and feared what her mother would do to stop it. She could not act too hastily in deciding. She knew nothing of him and did not know if she ever would know anything. Slowly, she found calm again. All the excitement of the barn burning and nearly loosing her calf had wrought her incapable of seeing the moment clearly. It presented an infatuation at best. Most certainly tomorrow would see it all a ridiculous result of the tragedy. His eyes haunted her thoughts. He would have been charming to anyone in that light.

"What were you thinking?" Her mother began.

While Emily stood there, waiting for her mother's lecture on morals, her father returned to them from the fields.

Stuart had attended his inspection and left the hands with further instructions, to assure they faired as well as he surmised. Once his employees attended to his wishes, he hurried back to meet the hero who thankfully survived the inferno. Stuart was impressed by the show of bravery and good fortune to survive. He could hardly wait to meet such a young man.

Moving as fast as he could, Stuart entered the lane and saw the man in question mount his horse and ride off. Stuart stood too far to call out. The man should not have run off so quickly. Rushing to his wife's side, Stuart assessed the situation. Touching Margaret's arm, he gently brought her attention from their daughter to him. Stuart looked into her eyes and saw all he needed to know. He grit his teeth and bit back the words he wanted to say. He would not discuss these matters before Emily or the workers.

Stuart's gaze swept over the nearby farmhands, ashamed of what he could only guess had happened. Jack nodded to him with a mash mouth grin. He trusted Jack but the others he was unsure of. Jack nodded and turned to shoo the others away, but himself stayed.

"Go on wich ya! Get summin ta put that fire out!" Jack directed, waving his arms.

Stuart's gaze shifted to Rose, but she was already picking up a basin from the snow and taking her leave.

Stuart looked to the road and sighed disappointed. He spoke to Margaret about her manner with others, but obviously she did not care. Those who laid down their lives to help strangers, in the manner the young man had, deserved better thanks for their efforts. Stuart came too late to fix things this time. His face contorted and he looked to his wife, with the question on his lips.

"You let em go?" Stuart said.

Stuart's tone told Margaret he knew. She looked to him then to Emily, not answering. Stuart followed her gaze to Emily and he knew all too clearly what had transpired. The distant look in his daughter's eye replayed the tale. Stuart's heart leapt up with joy where his wife's had lunged with fear. His little girl had noticed someone.

"For Christ sakes, Margaret! He risked his life for our cows—so, if he wants to look at a pretty face. No harm's done."

"He's calling tomorrow," Margaret replied. She looked over her bony shoulder to him.

Stuart regarded her coolly for a moment, not moving a muscle. The dark cast in her eyes warned him of her aim. He saw it when her future for Michael fell apart, because the boy decided on a career she had not chosen for him. He sighed with grave worry and wondered what the young hero had done to offend her delicate sensibilities. Given time, he would surely hear all about it, although she turned facts to her advantage and the truth became a puzzle.

"Is he?" Stuart muttered bitterly. "What did you say to him?" He asked. When his wife only looked at him blankly in response, his face reddened with anger. "Fool," he mumbled. "What bothers you about this one?" He felt disappointed in his beloved wife, missing the way she used to be. "It'll do us all a great deal of good to see someone's fresh face," Stuart told her. He knew she wanted to use her usual excuse. The man was not nice or he had an ill manner about him. She only raised her chin and watched him with a cold gaze, without even a nod. She tightened her shawl and looked to their daughter. "She's eighteen, Marge. You can't go round bemoaning the evils of every man that comes near her. Let it be." Unable to look at his wife and her self satisfied expression, Stuart looked to the distance. "I don't want her to be alone for the rest of her life—it'd be nice to have grandchildren some day," he continued distractedly, eyes flicking to his little girl.

At her father's last words, Emily quickly turned with an expression of shock. A crimson blush rose on her cheeks, reaching her ears until she was as pink as a rose. Tears filled her eyes, thinking of how obvious she acted in regard to the stranger. Emily lowered her chin mortified to the core and exhaled disgusted.

"He's a right good man, Mrs. Conrad" Jack said, reminding them he had not gone with the other hands. It seemed such a silly thing to argue over. He would love for Rose to find such a nice young man, instead of the slapdash rudiments she hung around with. "Any man thad give his life fur one a God's simple creatures—he's a right good man."

All they knew of this right good man came from that night, his deeds and the little he told them. His actions alone should prove his character, but things did not always bear out what they seemed. First Lieutenant Joseph Maynard was a mystery, born in Maryland and an officer of the Union Army on leave with their neighbor's son. Only time would reveal what manner of man this Maynard truly was and why fate brought him there.

~

Joseph watched the moonlit road stretch before him, while he wandered toward the Howell homestead. He examined the events of the night, attempting to figure out what just happened to him.

Joseph was there on leave, accompanying his constant companion Second Lieutenant Evan Howell, who wished him to visit with his family and introduce a respected companion to them. Evan insisted Joseph come with him and Joseph could not refuse. In two days, they found the farm nestled in the Vermont countryside. It was a smaller dairy farm, bordering the eastern side of the broad Conrad claim. The structures of the house and farm stood much more modest compared to the neighbors and that much friendlier, too.

Unfortunately, after only a few short hours of idleness, Joseph's mind became edgy. His thoughts grew wild, as if sodden with drink. He tried to amuse himself with the Howells and their children, but to little affect. Then, he partook of a wonderfully filling dinner. From their hospitality, he regained his energy, as in days before the war. That energy compelled him to search for something beyond their walls. He obliged the feeling with little argument, thinking a ride would run the restlessness from his body. The familiar black cavalry horse came close to accomplishing just that. However, things quickly changed.

While he rode back along the road beside a well situated farm, Joseph smelled smoke and looked to see it rise from the barn. Joseph was ignorant that offering his help would spin the night even more out of control. Seeing the blaze, he thought his duty clear.

The smell of smoke still hung thick about him. The night air felt frigid against his singed body, now that he sat far from the warmth of the devastating flames. Once again, he stood reminded of how he nearly died, trying to save a calf. Joseph often imagined his life ending on the battlefield, but never in a fire on leave. It terrified him. For some reason, this event struck deeper than any he faced before it. He wondered why, when only days ago he faced rifles by the hundreds. Joseph squeezed his eyes tightly closed and the image of the blue eyed angel stood before him with chin hung low, as if something pushed her down. He wondered about her more than he should.

Lifting his eyes, Joseph tried to forget the enrapturing face. Ahead, the moon shone brightly on the dirt road where it crested a hill bordered on both sides by fence and trees. The ruts and hoof prints from horses and carriages made deep black lines, interweaving with each other, like growing vines. Focusing on this image, Joseph attempted to quiet his numerous thoughts.

Joseph listened to the night that encircled him. At that moment, the distinct sound of horse hooves on the soft ground beyond where he rode touched his ears. Joseph looked to the horizon. Surprise widened his gaze and quickened his breath. Reining in his mount to wait for what came, he watched the crest of the hill, half expecting a unit of wayward Rebels to charge at him. Instead, his eyes saw the charge of one lonesome darkly clad rider.

The horseman came to a stop at the top of the hill, turning sideways. The moonlight etched out his frame eerily. Slowly, the dark rider moved forward again and did not stop until it stood right before Joseph. The action startled him, wondering what manner of man would roam the roads at night and act so familiarly. His hand stealthily went to the pistol at his side, while his eyes remained on the man. The man's features remained hidden in the shadow of a military cap brim and a cloak that hung from his shoulders to his mount's back. The reddish fur of the stallion reminded him of just what kind of a man. The moonlight waned as the silvery orb slid behind a knot of clouds just come in from the southern horizon beyond the trees.

"Where've you been?" a familiar voice came from the dark figure followed by a breeze through the branches of the trees. The scene came straight out of Irving's *Sleepy Hollow.*

"Evan?" Joseph breathed with relief. His eyes looked large with concern. "Damn you scared the crap outta me!" He drew a deep breath, revealing just how scared he felt.

"Did ya think a band of Rebs was running ya down, Lieutenant?" Evan laughed, flashing a grin that shown gray in the dark.

"I don't know what I was thinking," Joseph smiled.

"Let's get home before ma wakes up and misses both of us," Evan suggested, turning his horse about.

Joseph followed his friend's lead, bringing Manny up to the other horse's side. When he did, Joseph could not help but look back over his shoulder. The home of his lost jewel stood indiscernible behind the thick line of trees and the deep dark of night. He recalled the pillar of smoke. It probably still rose into the sky, but it too remained out of sight behind the arch of branches overhead. Turning back, he gave thanks for the preservation of his life and the opportunity to meet the girl who lived there. Joseph felt strangely refreshed after his experience, having once again cheated death.

"Where did you go?" Evan asked, observing Joseph's strange expression. "You smell terrible. You shouldn't smoke so much."

"For a ride," Joseph answered guardedly at first. "Your neighbor's barn was on fire when I came back, so I went to help them."

"The Conrads?" Evan exclaimed with horror. "They all right?" He added worriedly. "By God—I should go over," he said. Evan shook his head and looked back over his shoulder toward the farm they could not see. He whistled a shrill drawn out sound and made to go to their rescue.

"They're fine," Joseph said, assuring him. "They didn't lose a single cow thanks to God," Joseph added when his gaze returned to his face.

"You mean thanks to you," Evan smiled, easing off. He returned to their original course. "Me and Pa should see to them tomorrow."

Joseph only smiled, not betraying anything to Evan. However, Evan sensed much more behind his friend's story than what he said. He knew Joseph well enough to know something made him deliberate. He saw it in his face, just like when he calculated a maneuver. Having attended three years of school at West Point beside the Lieutenant and nearly one year beside him in the Army, it certainly qualified him to know better. Yet, Joseph did not speak. He knew that meant more too.

Evan looked to Joseph, hopelessly waiting for him to explain what happened. A light glimmered in the man's eyes unseen since graduation. He watched him turn his attention back to the road behind and then ahead again. Shaking his head, Evan could only laugh. How foolish was he? Without a doubt, his unsuspecting friend fell victim to Emily Conrad's notable beauty. Emily's presence alone put light in a man's eye and left him changed forever. Evan felt joy at the mere prospect of being free to pursue his vices, without the expectation of returning to her one day.

"Have you met her then?" Evan finally asked, quite assured of what else happened in light of the asinine expression his friend bore.

"Met who?" Joseph knitted his brows almost angrily. He knotted Manny's reins around his fist and scowled ahead at the dark. He recalled Emily's mentioning of Evan and worried again.

"Emily Conrad," Evan said, as if it stood more than obvious what he meant. "Good God, Joseph—I'm not stupid," he added when Joseph refused to part with the information. Pausing to smile, he sized Joseph up. Joseph and Emily would make a truly charming couple. "Look at you. A hero now, eh?" Evan whistled and then leaned in to whisper low to him, "That'll get you up her skirts. No doubt." Evan leaned with a chuckle. He cast his eyes over the dark and saw the future that lay ahead of them.

"The Conrad girl?" Joseph questioned. He rolled his eyes sideways to look at Evan with the words on his lips. He slowly smiled, noticing the way Evan looked amused by it. He wondered how long it would last if he played along or had Evan just revealed the secret of their association. "Yeah—but, I don't think saving her calf would get me near that sweet skin."

Evan's hand shot up to silence him. He shook his head and smiled derisively. It was his own fault for bringing it up, but he did not like Emily spoken of disrespectfully.

"Then don't mention it," Joseph laughed at him, thinking it took no time to defeat him.

Evan eyed him angered and continued speaking, "Your South may have its belles, but we keep the real gems up here."

Evan smiled, thinking of the girl that nearly became his wife. If his life never led him to the warpath, it may still be true. Evan felt no regrets over his choices and he never loved Emily for more than a sister. It would have wasted both their lives to follow a path their folks expected of them. Evan delighted in the idea of Joseph smitten with the girl. He was a noble man and would do well by Emily.

"I've asked to pay a call tomorrow," Joseph said unsure. He tried to feel out Evan's true position on the situation. "Should I keep my appointment—go alone? Or do you and your father want to go?" He paused, glancing at Evan's cat grin. Looking quizzically at him, he added, "You should probably go—"

"No—go. Me and Pa'll wait until after. You're their hero," Evan replied, waving off his doubts with his hand. "And don't listen to Mrs. Conrad. She's a difficult one."

"Good," Joseph smiled broadly, betraying his thoughts and eliciting another laugh from his friend. "I hoped you wouldn't mind," he added. There were still more questions to ask, but he could not bring himself to pry any further.

"Lord help her," Evan said, drawing paper and tobacco from beneath his cloak. He rolled the cigarette and lit it. "You better be good to my girl," he warned, exhaling the smoke. Noting the broad grin on his friend's face, he offered the cigarette to Joseph. "She's not just anybody, you know." He adjusted in his saddle and gazed up to the star speckled sky, when Joseph accepted. "Gah! A barn fire," he shook his head. "I suppose you'll be out there helpin ta build the new barn too, Lancelot?"

Joseph offered a half smile and shook his head, not saying a word. Evan had assured him dually that his path was clear.

IV. The Unwanted Guest

The next day arrived with gloomy clouds that masked the sun and soaked the ground. It was welcome rain to keep the fire out. The dusky light of dawn barely lit Emily's room, but she swung about with new energy, completing her morning tasks despite it. However, her energy failed to last and she soon slowed to a stop. She gazed around her room, thinking of the night before and how the flames had lit the walls with a terrible glow.

Emily stopped dressing once her corset and undergarments adorned her figure. Instead of putting on her morning dress, she sat in her window seat. It once held a view of a happy barnyard. Emily lounged, sadly watching the hands gather about the black cinders that once made a barn. She could only imagine the words they spoke over the pile of char. She watched them move on.

Snoozing lazily against the window and listening to the rain fall, Emily heard the rattles and clomps of the cows in the lane below. The men drew them out of the milking house to put them in the field while they cleared their new accommodations. Her eyes seized on the calf when it came into view beneath her window.

Emily was again thankful. The doleful infant survived the night. She sat up and managed a weak smile for Shakes, but the emotions in her threatened to tear her heart open. She saw the man who saved him when she looked in his large doe eyes. That man would not stay long, even if he did stay with Evan, like her mother told her last night.

As if the creature felt her stare like a soft call, Shakes stopped and looked towards the window snuffling the air. Emily heard May-Belle call to him, standing several yards ahead and turning to look back. The calf rushed to her instinctively. Emily followed the pair, as far as her eyes would allow.

Once they disappeared, Emily felt a strange and powerful emptiness fill her insides. She curled up on her window seat and stared at the rainy sky, imagining the stranger. The more she thought of him, the worse it felt. She thought sadness left her when she awoke rested and happy. However, the old familiar feelings soon haunted her by the stark light of day.

Frustrated by the return of the desolate emotions, Emily's heart pained. Tears filled her eyes and freely fell to her chin. Drawing her knees to her chest, she put her arms around her legs and cradled her head there, crying without effort.

Swiping the vexing tears from her face, Emily tried to blame the sad calf's devotion to its mother. If Emily ever had the benefit of such devotion, never again would the rain or a gray day bog her down. Someone would be there to remind her it was not all her fault.

Leaning her head against the corner of the wall behind her, Emily's misery deepened in view of the smoking remains of the barn. Emily wiped the rest of her tears away, angry with her depression and how it turned to longing for a man she knew nothing about. Releasing her legs, she stretched them out along the seat and released a heavy sigh. She prayed for forgiveness and an end to the terrible blame she kept for her serious actions.

Suddenly, the moment fell away to the sound of scuffing footsteps near her door. Though the start effectively brought her out of her misery, it did not erase the appearance of it on her face. She looked desperately at the door, worried her mother may find her once again in the midst of despair. Emily jumped up and went to her washbasin. She doused her reddened face with cold water to disguise the tears. While she bent over the porcelain, washing her face a second time, she heard her door open and admit someone. When she straightened to look, her mother's grave expression and sudden presence so close managed to still give her a start, despite the ample warning of her steps.

"Hurry yourself child," Margaret tsked. She pulled Emily's gray dress from her armoire. "Did you get up late again?"

"Yes, Mamma. I'm so worn out from yesterday," Emily said, drying her face. She kept her back to her mother.

Margaret looked worriedly at her, if not angrily.

"No matter. Get your dress on," she said handing the garment to her. She could see her daughter wept before she entered and she wondered why now. Perhaps the bull worried her. "Little Henry gathered the eggs already for breakfast. I'll need your help in the kitchen if we expect to have any decent meals today. Our guest will be hungry. I'm sure."

"What's the sense?" Emily heard herself ask. She felt annoyed he would come and remind her of her last night. She felt so embarrassed at herself. "I don't believe Lieutenant Maynard will come. He only behaved politely," Emily said, going to her vanity mirror and rearranging her loose locks with nervous hands. She felt like she would get sick on the floor. Why did the mere mention of him unease her so?

"Nonsense," Margaret neared her, but hoped her daughter's words would prove true. She replaced her daughter's fumbling hands with her more steady ones, and added a little stiffly, "He's a military man. He's disciplined." Emily remained quiet, sulking at her. She watched her mother in the mirror ready to cry and not caring if she saw. "Your father suggested you should wear your blue dress to dinner. It'll do you some good to have some fresh company to speak with—and I agree with him. Besides, he might bring Evan, and you want to look nice for him," Margaret said, returning her daughter's gaze back through the mirror, the lie evident in her features. After fastening Emily's hair in place, she helped to tie her corset tighter and button her dress. "Put on your shoes and hurry down stairs," Margaret said before exiting. "And try not to look so sad. Evan's home."

Emily had no strength to argue over Evan or the soldier. She placed a pair of black heeled boots on her feet at her mother's prompting. Then she turned and gazed at herself in the mirror one last time, smoothing the gray cotton dress into place. Refitting her composure, she believed her mother right and there was no sense in feeling any other way. Emily turned away and left the room and the troubles that plagued her soul behind.

Right behind Margaret, Emily hurried down the stairs and swept into the bright kitchen already filled with the smells of cooking breads and meats. Sitting at the table, Hettie worked hard on some kind of batter for their afternoon tea snack later. The housekeeper looked up and smiled sweetly to her, returning to her task without a word. Emily quietly sat across from her on a stool set there for the purpose and waited for her mother.

The kitchen became the hub of the Conrad women's daily activities two years ago when the war began. They spent most of their time cooking and cleaning within that room. In their concerted efforts, it quickly became cramped and the once ample kitchen lost its efficiency. Despite its size, they made due out of necessity. Without enough hired help to perform the tasks, they alone produced three meals a day for worker's residing there, and two for those that lived off the premises. No complaint was aired over the hospitality, finding it a fulfilling gesture on both sides and not wishing to end it.

Emily felt differently about the work. Her father's desire to make a meal courtesy part of the workers' pay, created a great deal of difficulty. He wanted assurance of their loyalty and efficiency, forgetting his family's comfort, loyalty and love. Though it existed as one of only a few policies her father continued from his grandfather's time, he held onto it because of him. He said it worked well, but Emily knew it was memories.

"Those look lovely, Henrietta," Margaret said encouragingly when she saw the batter for the cakes, sitting in their iron pans ready to bake.

Margaret turned from Hettie back to her daughter, intending to employ her in a number of other tasks and effectively distract her. Her constant dismal mood of late served only to depress the rest of the house. Margaret greatly disapproved, but her husband would not allow her to meddle and fix things. Tea with some of the girls would have had her set right in no time. Regardless, she could keep her busy at home and it turned out the most effective tool. Once the instructions and ingredients sat beside Emily, Margaret stepped aside, watching her work on the batter for corn bread for a moment. The men would enjoy the bread with their lunches in a few short hours, alongside some nice ham roasting behind her.

"We're all settled now, Hettie. Thank you," Margaret said, allowing Hettie to go and clean the front rooms before their guest arrived to a dirty house.

When Emily finished the cornbread batter and filled the skillets, she cooked them through and surrendered the bread to her mother. She then cleared the dishes into the sink that lay all over the worktable. Her stomach rumbled and her eyes went to the ticking clock on the wall by the door. The time read nearly eleven o'clock. Emily looked away gathering more dishes. She had risen late and dawdled in her room for sometime just staring out the window and crying. She would have to wait until lunch to eat. She prayed the soldier would not arrive before then and listen to her stomach growl because she had nothing to say.

Emily filled a heavy pot of water and looked out of the window. The room fell quiet as she worked the hand pump by the sink. Emily put the full pot on the open fire and left it to heat. From under the skirted sink, she pulled out the washtub and placed it on the table. Emily could feel her mother's eyes on her while she worked and met the gaze. Her mother looked away, appearing to concentrate on mixing the basting sauce for the ham. Emily half smiled, knowing better. Her mother saw her agony plain on her face. There was never any sense in trying to hide from her.

Emily turned back to the pump bringing the tub with her. She set it into the sink and filled it halfway with water. Her mother worried too much about things she could do nothing to change. With that thought in mind, Emily looked at her gray reflection in the tub water. She worried too much about things she could not change. Things looked clearer in the wash water, surrounded by silence.

"Rose went to see about hiring some of the girls from the men's families today," Margaret informed her. "I hope you won't have to do this much longer."

"It will be nice to have the company," Emily said starkly. She had nothing to say to her mother either and they fell silent.

When Emily finished the stack of dishes, she stepped outside to dump the water and returned to join her mother at the worktable again. She remained silent doing the tasks given her, attempting to hide from her mother's prying. She soon found herself wrist deep, kneading a batch of brown bread mixed early that morning, which they would serve with their lunch.

The smell of the ham baking made her stomach growl again. Her mother cast an 'I told you so' look her way. Emily had explained earlier that she was tired and slept through breakfast. Her mother knew she was a late riser and should have set something aside. The thought of the soup filled Emily with impatience for its arrival.

Molding the bread dough into its pan, Emily's thoughts turned to other matters and other hungers. A small smile bloomed on her lips. She pictured his handsome face by firelight at the exact moment he said good bye to her for the night. What would her mother have done if he had kissed her? The very idea of it made her want to laugh out loud. She bit her lip and wiped her hands on a towel, wondering when the Lieutenant would come, if he would. No one could place the time of arrival, since he had not said. However, they prepared for it to occur any moment. She thought about stealing a piece of ham from the rotisserie. The tidbit only made her hungrier. She turned from the oven and wiped her arm across her forehead.

Emily noticed her mother barely spoke even while directing the tasks. She guessed the woman was distracted by the coming events of the afternoon. Her mother often worried about entertaining guests, worse so when they were strangers.

When this Maynard man arrived, Emily imagined her mother would attempt to welcome him in a manner much like last night. The Lieutenant deserved the family's thanks for what he did and her father would be present to observe all her mother did. If the previous evening told her anything, her father would quickly quash her mother's efforts to rid of the unwanted guest.

Then there still existed the issue of Emily and her reaction to the man. The girl must accompany them while the guest visited or her mother's game would be deftly executed without any effort. Her father knew how she felt in one glance and her absence could only arise from one person. After the argument her parent's had last night out of sight of all, she felt assured her mother did not dare order or sway Emily's decision. Perhaps that was the reason her mother held her tongue.

"Good morning," a warm and deep voice entered the room.

Both women looked to its source. Stuart moved aside as Hettie reentered the room. She scooted past him, joining Emily at the table.

"Good morning, Daddy," Emily said, smiling brightly despite her inner turmoil. She often wore a mask of happiness before him, not wishing him to suffer for her.

Margaret only smiled and then turned her attention to the fireplace where the ham finished baking. She worked the handle of the rotisserie and spread the thick honey glaze over the outside.

Stuart stepped to the table with his hands clasped behind his back. He stood beside his daughter where she worked. He watched her a moment and placed an affectionate hand over the bun of her hair. His eyes lifted to his wife bent at the fire. The blue orbs still displayed all the love he felt for her, but suspicion was there too.

Stuart carefully watched her place the basting mop and bowl on the table. She turned to the oven and checked the dough rising beside it. With that done she faced him wearing a tight expression. He offered her a smile.

"What are we having for our guest?" Stuart asked. He stepped behind Hettie leaving his daughter to her chores. His gaze flicked to each of the women's faces.

Margaret looked to him, folding her hands flat on the surface of the worktable. She tried to smile, still angry with him. Stuart always affected her in a calming manner, which allowed her to forget cares. It was her simple reason for falling in love with him and the single reason they rarely fought over disagreements.

"If he arrives for dinner, we'll have the goose," she said in a relaxed tone. "If he arrives for lunch, we'll be having potato and ham cream soup with brown bread. I made the rest of the ham for the men's lunch."

"I would rather enjoy a sample of either," Stuart said, chuckling. He gripped his lapels, practically smacking his lips while maneuvering to the rotisserie.

"Not till it's finished cooking—you'll get sick," Margaret smiled warningly. She blocked his advance to the meat, swatting his hand with a wooden spoon.

"Of course, dear. Of course," he laughed, tucking his arm up. She beat him back once again. "We'll let our guest decide then," Stuart smiled down at her, failing to receive such a warm reception to his words in return. "I must go back to work," he said, turning to leave.

"Lunch will be ready soon," she crooned softly, indicating the pot of potatoes Emily placed on the fire to boil. They only need add the seasoning, ham and cream to finish up.

Turning from his inspection, Stuart chuckled and wished the women a good day. He passed Hettie on the way out, putting a warmly meant hand on her shoulder. They smiled at each other and he went on his way. When he stood only a memory in their minds, the attention moved from him to Margaret.

Margaret instructed Emily to get the ingredients ready for the soup. While her daughter hurried about her task, she listened to the door to the back yard open and close. Pulling the ham from the fire, she paid it little attention.

Now free to speak, Hettie informed Margaret of her progress. She could tell the older woman felt distressed, counting the minutes left to prepare. Hettie hoped her assurance could ease the woman's concern. However, the eventual arrival of a man, whom she despised for whatever reason, probably prevented it.

"The fron room's clean—an the hall—Mr. Conrad's study too—what else y'all need me ta do?" Hettie asked.

"Good—we need your help right here," Margaret said. She placed the ham on the table and went to find a cutting knife. "Two of us to make a horrible mess for all them men and none to help clean it up," she prattled exasperated. "The goose needs cleaning. Prepare it for roasting. If we're going to eat at a decent time, it'll take a miracle."

"Right away, Mrs. Conrad," Hettie said. She left the room to get the goose from where she hung it that morning on the back porch.

The youth of the morning faded, but enough time remained for them not to worry, as Mrs. Conrad did. With the ham complete and Emily fixing the soup, Margaret turned her attention on the dinner they faced later that day. The fire stood plenty warm for the goose and other parts of the meal could be begun.

Much more calmly than her mistress, Hettie reentered the kitchen and finished the cleaning of the goose. While she worked, her eyes raised to Emily. A small smile played on her lips, wondering what the girl thought of all this. She looked at the soup she prepared, from gathering the herbs and ingredients, to the cream and ham.

"Are ya excited?" Hettie asked, goading her knowingly.

"I don't know what I am," Emily replied, feeling a giggle inside of her. Looking up she saw her mother's disapproval and choked it back before she continued. "I can't say if he's coming or not. How can I feel either way?"

"Ya mean ya doan know if you want em ta show or not," Hettie's dark eyes sparkled with deviousness, while the girl chopped.

Emily stopped cutting to look at her friend with a raised eyebrow, the only reproachful glance she could offer. She pursed her lips similarly to her mother. Hettie struck a nerve and her mind struggled to find something to retort. Whatever she said, Hettie would know exactly how she felt and that would make it known to Emily's mother. Hettie saw right through all of Emily's cloaks and scrims and then spoke too much about things Emily wished discussed more secretly. Right then, Emily wanted her thoughts about the soldier unknown, until she at least knew what they were. Besides, he had yet to prove himself worthy or even interested.

Emily watched Hettie coolly assessing her. She probably already knew what Emily thought, without shielding words. She knew Hettie would speak the truth in a moment and Emily feared admitting to it.

"Don't give me your devil eye, Henrietta. I know what you're thinking. You're thinking he shore is handsome, Hettie. I hope he does come for dinner. I am as excited as if it's Christmas. Did I mention he looked so handsome last night, Hettie?" Emily finally spoke in a sarcastic tone, gesturing exaggeratedly.

Emily looked to Hettie, trying not to laugh despite her annoyance. Hettie shook her head laughing aloud and Emily went back to her work. It was too late to hide it from her now.

"It couldn hurt," Hettie mumbled, egging Emily on.

"Enough chatter," Margaret snapped, facing the girls with the horror of their talk plain on her face. She grabbed the paddle to put the bread in the oven, failing to find this gossip about the Lieutenant amusement in the least. "We've work to do." Her face looked white as a sheet as she shoved and yanked the loaf around. Emily jolted at the suddenness and severity of her mother's words. Her fingers jumped to her lips and she looked at her questioningly. "The meals aren't going to cook themselves."

"Yes, Mamma," Emily said in a whimper, quite chastened.

Emily returned all her concentration to the soup. Hettie grinned and winked soothing away the alarm. Her mother still obviously felt the same as the night before, unable to appreciate what took place for the good of it. It went against her plans and she never found good in such things. Emily thought of the man that worried her mother trying to figure out what possibly bothered her so much. Aside from being southern and a soldier, there was nothing her mother could take offense to. She took the potatoes off the fire and brought them to the sink to drain the water. She poured them into a bowl. The steam rose and with it so did understanding.

Hettie found no wrong with the man. Though she only saw him from afar and the idea of him had at first frightened her, she presumed he was no threat to anyone. She considered his heroic acts a testament to his honor. None of the southern men she spoke of in stories of her past would have offered his life up for strangers, unless compensation was to be gained. The Lieutenant had not asked for a thing. That was good enough for Emily.

The morning passed with no incident to disrupt it. Just before noon, Emily's mother interrupted her in her duties. The noon meal stood finished and dinner moved on its way. Taking a small break, Emily ate her soup and bread in the kitchen. When finished, she washed the potatoes and peeled them, putting them in a pot of water to wait. Then, she mixed the dough for the dinner rolls. By the fire, Hettie basted the goose with garlic and butter. Emily's mother washed the vegetables. The Conrad daughter looked away from the other women and kneaded the dough. Moments later, she placed it back in the bowl covering it with a damp towel and washed her hands at the sink. Her mother wandered over to her.

"Go upstairs and freshen up. Put on your pretty dress," her mother said, brushing a lock of hair behind her ear. She smiled warmly, guiding her away from the sink.

"Rose will come along soon—I just hope she found us some more hands to help. The good Lord knows we could use them. I haven't even done the wash yet," she added to no one in particular. She left Emily standing dumbly in the doorway, while she continued on. She faced her again with a strangely misplaced encouraging smile. "Go on, child," her mother gestured her out. "I'm sure Lieutenant Maynard will arrive very soon—look at you covered in flour. Hurry up and get cleaned up, you look like an Irish refugee."

Emily looked to Hettie with a brief glance when her friend looked to her from the goose with a big grin. Emily looked at her blankly, feeling excitement grow in her belly. She placed a steadying hand on her stomach and smiled back. Hettie shook her head and went back to work. Turning away, Emily barely breathed. It felt like a cow sat on her chest.

Emily left the room as her mother asked, stepping slowly down the hall to the carved wood staircase. She eyed the door just ahead, glowing gray with the dismal light of the rainy day. She could not begrudge her mother the right to show her off, even if her own unmentionable behavior hung over her head. Her thoughts scattered and she imagined him bursting through the door to claim her in a most indecent manner. Her heart skipped at the notion and a strange thrill ran up her back. Her step turned hesitant and the doorway of her home looked more ominous, like the mouth of a gaping monster.

Emily quickly righted her wandering mind. Back in her own boots, she reminded herself of her mother's feelings about this. She felt embarrassed all over again by the appalling ideas. She hoped he would not come. Emily knew in her heart she would be disappointed if he did not. She clasped her hands over her stomach, feeling it grow uneasy. Her heart pounded and her head went light.

Wondering at the ferocity of her new feelings, Emily tried to convince herself that they would quickly fade and prove no more than a passing fad. She forced herself forward. Her body trembled, as she faced the awful front door. Any moment he would stand right there, bidding entrance. She saw his eyes, burned in her memory, and paused. She could duck in the closet under the stairs and stay there until he went away. No one would think to look there. Emily licked her lips, telling herself she was a grown woman and not a child to hide in closets when a storm came.

Emily stared at the front door of her once safe home, as if the Devil would open it. Ever so warily, she stepped to the base of the stairs. She drew a quick breath and turned to climb. Unfortunately, she could barely move and each step took all her courage. Glancing back over her shoulder, as she mounted the first, second and then third step, she watched the dark panel door. Through the frosted glass, she could see the porch and yard beyond. If he appeared now, he would spy her retreat. Emily felt her heart skip. Her throat constricted and she fought to swallow. Her hands felt clammy, as she closed and unclosed her fists. She stilled them over the knots of her stomach, climbing up the stairs to the next floor where she would be safe from reach. Emily raced up to the top and down the hall. At the end, she dashed right, closing herself tightly in her room. For extra measure she turned her key, locking the door. Emily faced her room, searching it with her eyes. She drew a deep breath. She had never behaved so ridiculously in all her life. Her eyes trailed to her bed and from there to her windows. The rain ran down the pains in meandering strings of silver.

Carefully avoiding any further thoughts that would upset her fragile mood, Emily hurried through her preparations, even avoiding a thought too deep into them. She soon stood in a simple ivory dress with maroon pin striping. She adjusted the collar about her neck and gave her reflection a smirk. She was proud to have chosen her clothes herself and relieved to know she would not be on edge due to unsuitable garments.

Returning to her dressing table, Emily searched for a pin to adorn her collar. Frustrated by the clutter of her table, she went to her armoire and pulled out a carved box. Tipping back the lid, she found the treasure she sought and set the box back. Emily pinned the piece to her dress on the collar. Sunlight glinted in the window drawing her attention there. The rain slowed. The sound of the wind blowing against the house threatened her concentration. She turned her back to the window and continued dressing.

Checking the mirror, she saw the cameo lay crooked. Emily sat at her vanity and worked the piece until it was right. Searching her table top, she found a pair of teardrop pearl earrings. She fixed the earrings on each of her ears and then paused to look at herself again. She still needed to deal with the unruly mop of her hair. Pulling the bun loose, she took up her brush. Turning her head to run the bristles through her minky tresses, she saw a letter sticking out from the edge of her vanity. She picked up the pages and examined it. It was the letter from Michael, she read to her parents yesterday morning in the dining room at breakfast. Eyeing the folded pages, her mind worked. She had left it in the dining room, forgetting it until then. Hettie must have placed it there.

Setting the letter back on her vanity, Emily stroked her hair with the brush and watched her reflection. Thoughts wandered and Emily wondered if her brother knew the man. It made some sense in light of Evan and his bars of rank spoke of an officer's commission. Setting the brush on her vanity, she forced the idea from her mind. It would be too strange if the soldier turned out to be a friend of Michael's.

Emily braided her long hair, while the Lieutenant haunted her despite careful efforts to the contrary. Winding the braid into a bun, she pinned her hair and found the preparations for the visit completed. She drew a handkerchief from one of the vanity drawers and looked back to the mirror. Folding the smooth blue cloth, she tried to think better of the approaching prospect.

Just as Emily began fantasizing, a sudden commotion reached her ears from the lower floor. She held her breath, expecting Lieutenant Maynard had arrived. The front door closed loudly. Emily stood from her table and went to her door. Leaning against the cool wood panel, she listened to the muffled voices. Rose's distinct tones stood out among the sounds of young girls. Emily breathed with relief.

Unlocking her door, Emily forgot her concern of facing the soldier in the excitement of meeting the farmhand's children. Emily stepped down the hall quickly entering into their midst.

Prior to the outbreak of war, a great deal of life existed on the farm. However, change came and her outings and friends declined to nearly none. Then, the gloom of boredom confused her thinking until she avoided any inclination to venturing outdoors. Tossing it all aside, last night ushered her down a new path, quite possibly wrought with more risk than lose of hope.

Emily stood on the second floor landing eyeing the small handful of girls below. She sighed, a little disappointed at the majority of obvious youth. Children would be of little help. Their families most likely required the older ones at home to do the work their fathers and brothers abandoned for battle. The war with the South brought a great burden on everyone and it showed in the three children who answered the vacancies.

Another sigh escaped Emily, as she took the first step toward them. In the least it was not the Lieutenant. Their faces tipped up to her at the sound of her shoes on the stairs. She smiled, looking at the three eager faces and masked her worry. Other than their vague resemblances, she was unfamiliar with them. She hoped this would be a refreshing change. She descended the last stair and wondered aloud at their failure to come earlier.

Rose replied for the dumbstruck girls, explaining they were still too young before today. The oldest would just turn sixteen that week.

Emily welcomed each girl, introducing herself and shaking hands. She smiled warmly at all three faces. In turn, they introduced themselves and presented their references and eagerness to work. Emily's mother would most likely not turn them away without the references, but predicting her mood correctly was challenging.

Blythe Holloway spoke first and Emily hoped the girl close to her age would be another ally such as Rose. She looked just like a doll, with features consisting of tight bouncy blonde curls and pale eyes of cat green. Those eyes went deep, warning of her tendency to snoop and gossip. Blythe reminded Emily of one of the old ladies at church. Emily stared at the girl, as she prattled on quite distracted with her new surroundings.

"We've come to work for your mother, like Rose said—my references," Blythe told Emily, shoving a fistful of papers in the Conrad girl's face.

Blythe studied the pretty daughter of the Conrads, having heard much about her from her father and mother. She thought Emily almost as lovely as she heard, but something distant about the woman made her cold. Beauty aside, Blythe could not decide whether she liked her or not. It little mattered anyway, when she needed to work for the family for the sake of her own. Emily Conrad would decide for her.

Emily's eyes uncrossed from the papers flicked into her face. She focused on Blythe and laughed off the girl's actions as immaturity. Clearing her throat, Emily took hold of the papers and handed them to Rose with a quiet thank you to the new maid. Blythe stepped back, appearing censured. Emily moved onto the next candidate, clasping her hands at her waist and forgot about allies for now.

"Did you bring your references, Miss Fordder?" Emily asked the second oldest.

"MaryJane, ma'am," the girl said nervously, looking at her with large sepia eyes. She flicked her glance to Rose, displaying a lack of confidence and the woman put her arm around her consolingly. She nodded, and drew a paper from her pocket, "Yes."

"Her ma said she's a bit nervous with everyone to start, but not to fear, she's a good little helper," Rose smiled at the girl and Emily. "She wants her to socialize more, now she's eleven."

"No worries, MaryJane," Emily smiled. "We are happy you've come to us—and there's no better place to make friends."

"Thank you, miss," MaryJane's voice sounded small and doubtful.

Touching the girl's face like a loving aunt, Emily let her know she was welcome. The girl returned the warm gesture with a bright smile.

Emily moved onto the last and youngest child. The girl stood only to the height of her waist. She could not have been more than eight years, by Emily's best guess. The small girl looked absolutely adorable in her bonnet and cloak. She clutched a basket to her chest in little mittened hands. A doll peeked from beneath the cover. Emily's smiled deepened and she felt real joy for the first time in years. The child's serious demeanor made Emily fall instantly in love with her. Emily hoped one day to be a mother. That idea returned the coming threat to the forefront of her thoughts. She pushed him back for sake of duty.

"Your name, little one?"

"Jo-Hanna Fordder," she spoke in a smooth but tiny voice. "MaryJane's my sister."

"Sisters?" Emily smiled. "That's wonderful. I've a brother myself, but he's away at school now. He'll join the army when he's done."

"We've a brother in the war too," MaryJane piped up proudly.

"Then we already have something in common," Emily told them, feeling the tears build behind her eyes at being reminded of her dual dilemma.

The girls appeared fine candidates for the openings. Emily turned from introductions to instructions. Her mother's absence left her in charge of orienting them to the duties, including housecleaning and cooking. The three girls would find the chores divided among them.

"Blythe, you'll help Rose and Hettie with the cleaning and laundry," she said, receiving a nod in return.

"MaryJane, you'll help Mrs. Conrad with the cooking," the little girl smiled, obviously liking the idea. "And Jo-Hanna," Emily smiled down at the little girl. "I'll have you help me with a few of my chores and then you'll work with your sister the rest of the day."

"Yes, miss." Jo-Hanna smiled for the first time, revealing two spaces.

Emily turned to Rose, telling her that Hettie would join them shortly. Calling the other two children to follow, Emily stepped down the hall to the kitchen. Quick introductions to her mother took place and after warm welcomes, her mother appointed MaryJane some tasks, leaving Emily to care for the last girl alone.

Turning to take hold of her cloak, Emily faced the little girl, who stood in the entrance of the kitchen. Jo-Hanna waited quiet and patient. Her large brown eyes looked around with a nervous wonderment. She still clung to her basket with whitening knuckles. Emily smiled again, trying to ease her fears. She felt bad they frightened the child already. Touching her shoulder, she turned her out of the kitchen into the hallway and to the back door.

"Let's go outside and see what you'll do each morning for me," Emily said, donning her cloak. Her voice sounded soft and reassuring.

"K—" she breathed. Jo-Hanna felt sure she liked Emily Conrad. She took hold of her hand to let her know.

Emily smiled down at her, touched by the display of affection. She opened the door and led her outside into the yard. Securing her wrap against the breeze that blew in from the west, she realized things had taken a fine turn. Despite the season, the day felt unusually warm and the path they would take from the back of the house to the chickens looked thick with sticky mud from the melting ice.

"You said Mr. Fordder is your father?"

"Uh-huh," Jo-Hanna sounded, looking at Emily's smiling face.

"I know your father very well," Emily said.

Emily recalled the middle aged man who helped Jack supervise the workers. He walked with a limp since a long dead bull gored his thigh. The wound kept him from service in the war, much to his family's approval. However, his eldest son left on military duty last fall and Mr. Fordder displayed some scars for the loss.

Emily gazed towards the outbuildings, set behind leafless trees and bare bushes that lined the fence. Mr. Fordder worked inside the building there. Emily stared at the white siding, feeling sorry for the Fordders.

Jo-Hanna adjusted her grip on Emily's hand, reminding the young woman of her presence. Emily looked down at her, slightly smiling to see her little head bobbing along, as if to an unheard tune. Emily forgot her troubles, losing them in the moment. Listening, she heard the girl sing under her breath, alternating with sudden energetic gusts of sound.

Emily lifted her chin. She smiled brightly now energized by the spirit at her side. Despair washed away with the rain. The farm stilled peacefully.

Hands clasped, the pair walked along the muddy track between the outbuildings and the house toward the chicken coop. The rude little coop stood lonely at the eastern edge of the lane, ahead of the large pile of blackened timbers and heaps of ashes that used to make up a barn. Last night, some quick thinking hands wet it down before it also caught fire, effectively rescuing the creatures living inside. The gray metal bucket, which still sat on top of the slanted roof, testified to the job.

Emily looked to the little girl, despairing the long lost innocence, freedom and hope of youth. Jo-Hanna's large brown eyes swept over the remains of the barn, while her face made a telling expression of awe. She stopped her tune and squinted at the smoking rubble, walking slowly wherever Emily led. Her eyes surveyed her new surroundings with great but restrained curiosity. Her father must have told them about it.

"Henry already collected the eggs today," Emily said. "But, first thing you'll do when you come with your dad is feed the chickens and fetch the eggs to Mrs. Conrad,"

Emily continued. She watched the girl's expression. Jo-Hanna eyed the chickens, hopping about the pen, scratching at the frozen ground. "Watch the chickens though. They can get real upset," Emily explained. "Here—I'll show you the latch on the feed shed and then the coop," Emily said. Then, she showed the child how to open the latches of the two doors and how to get carefully inside the coop. She watched Jo-Hanna perform the tasks herself to feel assured her instruction worthwhile. "Careful to not let any chickens get out. They'll freeze if left in the cold or be eaten by a fox," Emily said. Jo-Hanna listened intently, but only time would reveal if she heeded the lesson.

"I will," Jo-Hanna smiled up at her.

"Come back inside," Emily said, touching the girl's cap to lead her.

With her hand on Jo-Hanna's back, Emily guided the child back to the house and away from the cold. Above their heads, the clouds thinned and a gray gold light filled the lane. Emily's gaze lifted, drawn to the road beyond the front yard. A lone rider moved toward the house, brass buttons glinting off his clothes. Emily's breath caught in her throat and her heart raced at the sight of him. She could not tear her eyes from his Stetson and rain cloak. The rhythmic clomp of horse hooves filled her ears, hypnotizing with its tempo. Emily stopped and stared, looking like a dazed frog, including her throat working to swallow.

"Miss Emily," Jo-Hanna said, distracting her. "What's wrong?"

Jo-Hanna followed her gaze and watched the stranger on the road, gaping like her companion.

Emily looked to her with worry straining her features, "Nothing, dear. S-sorry. Let's get you inside before you catch a cold."

Continuing back to the house, Emily peered toward the clearing sky. The sun just began its descent, a glowing orb behind a curtain of silver white clouds. Her mother would be so ecstatic to find out he had indeed arrived as promised. Emily smirked, thinking how unwanted a guest he was. Her step quickened, as she tried to get to the house before him.

Lieutenant Maynard kept his promise. However, he arrived in time for dinner. Her father would speak to him at length in the parlor, perhaps walk him around the grounds and take tea before they sat down to eat. Her father probably ate his lunch in his study at that moment and would not feel hungry again until dinner. Emily thought of how perfectly the soldier must have planned, too late for lunch and early enough to gain a dinner invitation. After the way he looked at her last night, she should have known he would seek a more intimate affair. This man's manner went more intimately than she ever experienced.

Voices floated into Emily's ears and she looked up to see Hettie and her mother. The women carried trays of food toward the men's barracks for their lunch. Closing her eyes, Emily paused at the bottom of the back porch stairs. She tried to focus her mind on her duties and not her worries. However, her duty would soon become her worry. She told herself that this moment was no time to turn into a fool. She would not dare behave poorly in front of the new help or the visitor. She must make up for her asinine staring and stammering from last night. She was determined to treat the visit like any other and took a deep breath to calm herself.

"He's only coming to dinner," Emily mumbled to herself. "It goes on every night—all over the world—no reason to act this way." Even if President Lincoln came to call, she was most sure she would not feel this nervous.

Jo-Hanna giggled, standing at her side while she danced in place. "My ma talks to herself too."

Emily's heart skipped at the child's words. She sighed heavily and gave her a sideway glance. A slight smile grew on her lips.

"Grown women have too many troubles to keep quiet over."

"What's that mean?" Jo-Hanna asked her.

"You'll see, all too soon," Emily said, climbing the steps ahead of the girl. "They call themselves men."

"Oh—" Jo-Hanna sounded not understanding, although her mother said similar things about her father.

Emily hurried Jo-Hanna inside, not wishing to allow a peek from the front door. She ducked in the kitchen to start hiding. Hopefully, one of the men would delay the Lieutenant by speaking to him outside about his horse or the things he did in the Army. She guessed a man like him would like to go on for hours over such topics. She hoped for anything to delay him, though no amount of time would be enough and then he would be with them until after dinner. There was still the closet under the stairs.

Trying to think of the tasks at hand, Emily gazed around the kitchen in a daze. Her eyes suddenly landed on the expectant girl. Jo-Hanna offered a delicate bow of her little lips as encouragement. Emily drew a breath, delaying now to think of things she could have her do.

"Man trouble?" Jo-Hanna asked suddenly.

Emily's eyes went wide, "What? Why would you say that? No-no." Emily tried to laugh off the astute observation of the girl. It would be wise to keep her very busy in the kitchens and away from guests. "Have you washed dishes before?"

The little girl nodded heartily.

While Emily desperately hoped one of the men delayed Lieutenant Maynard from his critically planned goal, he indeed met one of the hands upon entering the front lawn of the Conrad Farm. Joseph rode up the dirt path toward the towering house. His uniform was neat and pressed, thanks to Mrs. Howell. He looked as if the night before never happened. Beneath him, Manny trotted proud as a parade. He probably sensed Joseph's feelings over the visit. The animal could read him like he understood English.

Joseph's gaze locked on the farmhouse from the moment he emerged from the overhanging branches of the forest. The house proved a whole other sight in the light of day. The front gained no justice by the back, though every corner was impressive. The structure stood immensely proud under the guise of a Vermont farmhouse. Some of the features he discerned hinted at renovations it experienced from its original design. It claimed an age older than he first presumed, perhaps having housed generations of Conrads. The detailed windowpanes with the gingerbread, gabled roofs and cupola created a beautiful finish, which he found homey and unpretentious despite its size.

Joseph also saw it as a home belonging to a man wise in business and from a decent measure of wealth. Their money would easily replace the lost structure or cows. No amount of capital could have brought him back, if he failed in his efforts last night. Joseph's mouth flattened into a biter line. His selfless act should have received greater than the cold thanks the farm wife gave.

Joseph's thoughts of the ungrateful woman nearly turned his stomach and his course. His bravery did not impress due to her inexplicable snobbishness. He had not expected a thing for helping, until met with her mood. In the least, her daughter seemed appreciative. From what Evan told him that meant a great deal. His anger scattered with the reminder of the northern jewel he had discovered. For a chance to see her again, he would suffer the company of her dame or even another fire. The promise of the young woman bated him like a cold drink on a hot day.

Joseph remembered her soft expression when the calf nuzzled her hand before her mother stole it away. She loved the animal enough to name it. She would have been heartbroken if he perished. Joseph imagined the irritable mother shooing the bull off. She really wanted to shoo the man off. He knew nothing of the Conrads aside from what Evan begrudgingly revealed, but the little warning was helpful enough.

Back in the present, Joseph watched the old farmhand from last night hobble along on his bowlegs, smiling a toothless grin. His scruffy old face gleamed full of greeting and joy. Joseph grinned back, thinking this was the proper greeting Mrs. Conrad owed him.

"Afternoon to you, Lieutenant," the old man said, taking the reins from Joseph's hand and steadying the fine ebony cavalry horse, so he may climb safely down.

Jack looked up at the soldier with great respect. It took little prompting from Mr. Conrad to make him stand outside and wait for the boy. He understood his boss wanted the soldier to feel welcome and that his arrival went well. He would need his horse cared for by the best on the farm.

Jack looked over the stallion, gleaming like polished onyx in the sunlight. He whistled appreciatively, while Joseph slid from the saddle. The young soldier planted his feet on the icy ground and faced him, smiling genuinely.

Joseph knew just what the old man felt when looking at the charger. Manny was something to value by many standards, as one of the finest horses in all the United States. That was the given opinion of many who chanced a view. He would ride no less.

"Where ya get one a them?" Jack asked, while the stallion pawed the ground. It whickered and shook its great narrow head, the black main tousled like a ragged curtain in a storm.

"Kentucky—before the war, when I schooled at West Point," Joseph replied.

"West Point!" Jack said. He sounded pleasantly surprised. "Mr. Conrad's boy Michael goes there—just about to graduate too," he said with a devious smile.

Joseph heard the name and was reminded of someone Evan introduced him to years ago. His memory told of a friendly but shy man. Joseph wondered if he thought right. There could be no real question against it, for how many Conrads from Vermont would find their way into the Point and happen to live near the Howells? Joseph had spent no time with the underclassman while at school. Instead, Joseph preferred to busy himself with his training and a small group of friends from his own year, plus Evan. He wished he had felt differently.

"Is that so?" Joseph drawled, raising a brow. He eyed the older man and looked to the porch. The doorway called to him. Rather, the thought of seeing the young woman called to him. "Think you could keep an eye on him for me?"

"Oh indeed. It'd be an honor," Jack said graciously. He bobbed his head and the action made Joseph smile. "We'll see he's fixed up nice."

"Thank you kindly," Joseph said, touching the brim of his Stetson. "Nice to speak with you again—" Joseph trailed off, pointing out his ignorance of the other man's name. He forgot because of the alluring distraction a certain pair of blue eyes promised since the fire. He barely thought of anything else.

"Jack—Jack Benson, Lieutenant."

"I apologize—thank you, Mr. Benson. If you'll excuse me, I've an appointment with Mr. Conrad."

Jack nodded to him. He clamped his gums together and smiled closed mouth. When Joseph turned away and stepped toward the house, Jack continued to watch him. He thought only of what a good man he was and the honor of meeting him. Jack then turned the black horse toward the stables and walked carefully toward them, taking his time to watch his step. Jack remarked aloud how thoughtful the boy behaved. He apologized and thanked him when fitting. He respected him, as if his own father. He wondered how Mrs. Conrad could manage to think so ill of him.

"Right good man there," he muttered, eyeing the empty looking barn ahead of him. Manny whickered and nodded his head as if understanding. Jack smiled and continued, "Emmy would do good for herself with one like him." Manny shook his mane approvingly. Jack laughed heartily, sure the horse agreed.

Inside the farmhouse kitchen, Emily dashed about, continuing to direct the young Jo-Hanna in her duties. A pinched expression dressed her features, as if she felt unwell. Emily paused several times, distracted by the butterflies that twisted her stomach and batted her wits numb. She swallowed the dryness in her mouth and decidedly focused on the task at hand.

"All right, Jo-Hanna," Emily said, trying to gather strength for the coming struggle. "I want you to help Mrs. Conrad with the dishes right now. There'll be plenty everyday. When there isn't—and your sister doesn't need help, you can darn socks and mend clothes. There's a basket in the closet over there. You know how to sew, I hope?"

"Unhuh," Jo-Hanna nodded smiling, some of her baby teeth remained in her mouth.

Emily smoothed a hand over the buttons of her bodice and looked around the kitchen lost in thought. Jo-Hanna eyed the woman curiously, waiting for her next words.

"All right. Good," Emily said, returning to the moment.

Emily pressed a hand to the little girl's head like her father had done with her earlier that morning. A sudden knock came at the door and Emily nearly jumped out of her skin. Her eyes widen and she stared at the kitchen door expectantly. She listened as someone answered the door.

"Hang your coat over there and put your basket on the shelf. I'll be back to check on you in a little while."

"Are you nervous?" Jo-Hanna asked her, looking concerned.

"Nervous?" Emily repeated, frozen by the question. She watched the child nod and shook herself awake. Smiling, she said, "No—I'm—no, just busy."

"You look nervous," Jo-Hanna told her. "Is it a man?"

Emily's eyes widened, "Why would you ask that?"

"What you said earlier about men giving you trouble," she answered sweetly, climbing onto a stool to gather some dishes from the table. "Does my Daddy give you trouble?"

Emily watched her in awe. The child listened too well and proved all too intuitive in addition. Emily adjusted the collar of her dress, feeling it choke her. She wondered how she would survive the coming storm as uncomfortable in a regular dress as any other. Her heart beat rapidly, hearing the Lieutenant's voice through her panic.

"No—your father is no trouble here," Emily tried not to answer, but wanted to hear something other than the voice down the hall.

"Who then?" Jo-Hanna climbed down and dragged several large bowls to the sink.

"What—oh—no one dear," Emily smiled. "I think my lunch just disagreed with me."

"You should go lie down," Jo-Hanna said, continuing her duty.

"I wish that I could," Emily mumbled.

"Why can't you?"

"We have guests coming."

"A man?" Jo-Hanna rounded back the first question.

"Yes," Emily answered, feeling the floor disappear below her feet.

"So it is man trouble," Jo-Hanna smiled, busily washing a bowl.

"Fantastic," Emily whispered. Even a child had seen through her. "Just get to the dishes, Jo-Hanna, and don't think of another thing."

Emily could just hear the Lieutenant's voice through her words. The sound of it made her shiver with something not unlike fear. Turning toward the doorway, Emily abandoned her watch over Jo-Hanna and let the little girl complete her task on her own. Girding her fortitude as best as a coward could, Emily went to face the soldier. She took the first step toward the parlor where he would wait.

Unexpectedly, Blythe swung through the open pocket doorway into the kitchen with her blonde curls bouncing. She nearly plowed Emily down like a milkweed. Her sudden appearance startled the other girl and Emily placed a hand over her heart to keep it from leaping from her chest. Squeezing her eyes shut, she gasped.

Blythe swallowed hard looking at the woman fearfully and apologetically. She took a careful step back, balling her fist in front of her mouth. She watched Emily wide eyed and waited. This woman had a weak constitution to boot.

Emily opened her eyes, feeling her heart pound hard and threatening. She thought she would surely die of some sort of attack that day. Swallowing, she forced herself to compose and looked darkly at the new housekeeper. Already, Emily did not like her, but could not yet quite place the reason. It just hung on the edge of everything she did.

"Sorry Miss Emily, but a Lieutenant Maynard's come to visit your Pa. Mrs. Conrad told me to tell you right away, as soon as he came," Blythe declared, turning pink to her heart shaped hairline. She looked idiotic at best.

"Very good, Blythe. Go tell Mrs. Conrad now. She's in the lane bringing lunch to the hands. Thank you," Emily said. Her tone sounded clipped and breathless.

Blythe chewed her bottom lip, clearly sensing a tension between them. The woman's strange behavior stirred her curiosity and fears. Perhaps Emily Conrad was mad. Blythe knew she need heed more caution, or she would find her exit before sunset. Things would go rough at home, if that happened. She watched the Conrad daughter closely before carrying out her instructions. She thought about what the other girls said of her. No one liked Emily really, except the boys who were enchanted by her obvious charms. Blythe smiled to herself and exited the kitchen. Thoughts of her friend's words, upon finding out she would apply for work at the house, ran through her mind. They each suspected Emily would turn out to be a sneaky madwoman, or better, a randy whore who hid behind the guise of a pious farm girl. Blythe could hardly wait to find out which and make her report.

Emily pushed the girl out of her mind. She would rather sit in the kitchen with the warm fire and the little girl to keep her company. Pausing to shake off the pains of first meetings, Emily checked her dress. She coached herself to stay calm. Words Rose spoke some time ago popped back into her mind. She blushed at the crudeness. Without another moment wasted, Emily cut off her wandering mind and moved down the hall. She felt like a phantom floating in a surreal dream. Her legs must still stand beneath her body as she was upright, but they were numb.

Emily was sure she would faint before stepping through the opening. The image of his handsome face danced in memories. His penetrating eyes had reached into her and tried to uncover every secreted facet she fought to keep hidden. No matter how simple a matter, seeing him again would be difficult. Nonetheless, no one gave her the choice and she must go through with it.

Emily hesitated by a table that rested on the wall just outside the parlor, catching the quiet movements of the guest beyond. She swallowed hard and it hurt her throat. Suddenly the memory of his arm around her came into glorious review. She entertained the idea of going to the closet under the stairs again.

Biting her lip, Emily made herself do the opposite. She shook off the uncertainties and stepped into the parlor. Her father was hopefully in earshot, taking lunch in his office. This meeting would play out differently and it would finally change everything.

Inside the room, Emily found the Lieutenant with his back to her, hands clasped in the small of his back with his hat flipping up and down. He read the spines of her father's library intently. Emily immediately forgot everything she told herself and the strange sensations she experienced in the kitchen shocked her stomach once again. Then her breathing became strenuous added to by the tightness of her clothing. Taking another step into the room, she cleared her throat, more to moisten it than to make her presence known to him, although it served as both.

Joseph slowly turned and placed his powerful gaze on her once more. The stare appeared distant and cold at first, but warmed as he realized who had come. He watched her approach and offered a crooked smile. He almost looked a harmless little boy and just as nervous as her. Emily slightly relaxed and smiled back. Curiously, she liked him looking at her this time.

The moment presented more than Joseph hoped. When he turned, he felt his body disappear. Joseph clasped his hat under his arm to feel something other than his nerves. He held his breath, waiting for her to speak and kept his eyes on hers, not wanting a reprimand for ogling. She wore a simple dress and it made her all the lovelier. She was more beautiful than he recalled in the many dreams of the past night. Even an angel would be shamed at her side.

Joseph sensed her apprehension and saw she trembled slightly when joining him by the library. He adjusted his stance and felt foolish not speaking yet.

"Hello again, Miss Conrad," Joseph said.

"Good day, Lieutenant Maynard," Emily said. She eyed him a moment, hardly able to hold his gaze. Somehow she managed a bright smile, disguising her nervous shock. "Father will be along momentarily."

Emily offered her hand to him, holding herself amazingly steady despite the storm raging inside. The Lieutenant looked more handsome than she thought he would in the daylight. Although, she knew if he remained covered in soot from head to foot, he would still dazzle her. He took her hand and closed it between his. His touch felt gentle but strong. The other inclinations it brought assured her she would die before experiencing any. Emily cut off the voice in her head. She feared that it filled the silence of the room and not the silence in her head. Her heart raced in panic.

"Sweet Mary get me through this, and I'll never ask another thing of you again," Emily thought to herself, feeling as if she would wake on the floor without her senses, if this took too much longer. "Thank you for all you've done and thank you for keeping your word. Father's looking forward to meeting you," Emily added adeptly, once he released her from his firm grasp. "He was very sorry you left before he came back."

"You're welcome, Miss Conrad," he said in those enrapturing tones of his. He smiled suggestive of her thoughts. "I do apologize for having left so soon, but I feared the Howells would worry and they have enough to worry for—as you well know."

"Indeed," Emily let her hand drop to her side. It went cold, making her keenly aware of his very real presence. Emily swallowed hard and blinked at him while her mind stalled. She awoke before she embarrassed herself by staring at him. She felt the weakness in her legs and stepped back carefully, as not to land on her backside in an embarrassing tumble,. "Father is very understanding. He looks forward to thanking you for what you did," Emily said, watching him follow her, languidly like a cat that cornered its prey.

"I don't go back on my word, ma'am," Joseph said. "It was an honor to help," Joseph offered another smile to illustrate the hidden promise he made.

If honor held no stake in it, he would carry her to her room and have his way right then. Her pale blue eyes went to his mouth and he could see her blush slightly. She flicked her gaze back to his. She would like that, he thought, imagining her feelings. Trying to behave, he tucked his hands behind his back and waited to hear her speak again. His body buzzed though he displayed perfect calm. He locked himself into a stance a few paces away, before he made an all too forward advance.

"How is the calf?" He asked her. "Shakes is it? Named for the poet, I suspect."

Emily gave a questioning smile. A glimmer of something shone in his eye. She felt as weak as last night in his presence, but it would be more unbearable with no shadow to hide her blushes in. With great difficulty, Emily pushed off the fog he created around her senses and pointed to a chair to the right of the one she backed to. A small table would sit between them, giving just enough personal space without presenting the idea too clearly. She wanted to avoid shooing him aside in annoyance like her mother so desperately tried to do.

"Please sit down," Emily said softly, sitting in her chair. She felt safer tucked in the wings of the armchair and its cushions. She could not fall down. "Yes, Shakespeare. Thank you for asking. The calf is doing beautifully. I watched him go to pasture with his mother just this morning, as if nothing happened."

"Well, then I did my duty well," Joseph replied.

The setting of the parlor room was a fitting background for the dairy heiress. The blue area rug and wallpaper with the luxurious burgundy curtains made her beauty glow with an unearthly power, which quickly became more maddening by the moment. Joseph turned his gaze to the cherry framed window behind her and studied the expansive view of the porch and front lawn with the snow covered farm fields beyond. He smiled slightly warmed by her charm, hesitating to move to the chair she offered him. He wondered if he should dare throne himself beside such an entity. Joseph shook his head slightly, disbelieving such a simple place could prove the home of such splendor and he would stand privy to it. Accepting the seat, he set his hat on his knee and thought quietly to himself about what he would say next. He wanted to impress her and not frighten her away with his words. She seemed skittish but at least receptive to him.

Joseph's mind wandered. He studied the room soaking in each detail. The Conrads did just fine with finances from what he surmised of the less than modest but splendid décor of the home. His eyes turned over this and that, sighting the portraits on the walls, which told part of the family's story. The backgrounds of those paintings suggested generations lived there before them. He could not say for certain that Mr. Conrad gained the works through inheritance, instead of buying them with the home. Clues to lives before arrival in America laid about like treasures, from volumes he pulled from the shelves to antiques beside them. He could see it in the girl's manners. If he proved any judge, she had been raised with thought to refinement and society. However, she was not pretentious like most of the wealthy heiresses he knew. Instead, she sat beside him just herself, shy and sweet.

"Those are paintings of the first Conrads in America," Emily said, following his gaze to the walls. "They arrived during colonial rule, from England—that's father's grandfather," Emily added. She pointed to the centerpiece painting on the back wall. On the canvas, an unknown artist had rendered a portrait of a round and robust man, leaning against a post and beam fence with a small colonial farmhouse behind him. The tiny home must have been the original of the one they sat in now. "His name was Elias," Emily told him. "He nearly bankrupted the farm when he was my age and spent most of his life getting it back. Father turned the dairy into the business it is today."

"And I see that he's done well by himself," Joseph turned his gaze to her with a small amused smile.

"His mother taught him finances," she mumbled.

"The Conrad women are supremely educated," Joseph said.

"Father says there is no excuse for ignorance," Emily answered. "Gender does not matter because what makes a man a man and woman a woman is simply not needed to add two and two. What is needed both sexes have."

Joseph looked to her enraptured by the quoting. Emily lowered her gaze from him shyly. She wanted to eat her words the moment she said them. How could she make mention of such subjects with a stranger? Joseph shifted uneasily in his chair.

"Mr. Conrad is absolutely correct," Joseph responded, seeing her reluctance.

Joseph smiled, watching her for a moment, while her embarrassment afforded the chance. This young woman displayed intelligence equal to, if not rival to, many of the men he knew and was obviously Mr. Conrad's principal admirer. These were two things he had always hoped to find in a woman. Emily turned into an intimidating creature, but fear melted to curiosity and respect. Judging from his sense of Mr. Conrad given by outsiders, he should feel no other way. Joseph grew impatient to meet the man. Realizing his gaze lingered too long, he looked back to the paintings. The room was silent and for that he felt oddly uncomfortable in it.

The silence ebbed when Emily pushed back against the buttoned cushion of her chair, trying to relax if not hide behind the wings. Her hands gripped the arm rests and she twiddled her fingers on the leather. Realizing the man watched, Emily folded her hands neatly in her lap. She searched for something else to discuss that would not return to the matter of gender and sex. Often, Emily found little to say, especially when in the presence of a stranger. Her parents stood ever present guardians before her, but they remained absent that day. She knew her father had lunch in his office and her mother was most likely with him, but she should not have been left there to deal with their guest on her own. They knew she was a socially awkward nuisance and her mother saw how little she could be trusted the evening before.

Emily wished for Rose's experience. The house servant bloomed under the attention of men, whereas Emily withered like a sickly plant rooted in dry soil. Of course, Rose did things no decent young woman would dare, because she did not fear scandal. Instead, the maid relished it. Emily looked toward the archway and the hall beyond it. It must have been fun to carry on like the boys, running about doing as they pleased.

Joseph flipped his hat in a circle on his knee. Emily's eyes flashed to it. She looked startled but then relaxed. Sitting back against the cushion of the chair left her partially blocked by a vase of flowers. He smiled to himself, wondering how often Miss Emily entertained guests.

"Well—" Emily said suddenly. In the confines of her mind, she wished he stayed away and spared her this tension. His mere presence made her touchy. "Mother and father should come along soon," she said and looked toward the pocket door, but only saw the hall beyond with her hopeful gaze. "I do apologize for the wait," she tried to laugh.

"Not at all," Joseph said. He looked concerned at her clipped tone.

Joseph wondered why she kept so distant. Eyeing her, he thought she might own the same qualities as Mrs.

Conrad. Perhaps she only carried out an offensive duty for her beloved father. Joseph thought of the sweet blush in the light of the fire and again moments ago. He saw how she struggled, warring with hesitance. Perhaps he guessed right, that she rarely had guests. The hills of Vermont were sparsely populated and he did not recall many young men in his time there. Joseph looked to the floor with a troubled expression. Unable to help but stare at her, he thought maybe his forward gaze distressed her. But, had he correctly surmised what he thought he saw in her eyes last night? Her distraction might mean he strayed from his route. Attempting to regain the path, he would question her and perhaps fish out the truth of Evan. Besides, his curiosity was peaked. Was this her brother or her husband or was she promised to Evan Howell? He wondered why Evan had not divulged the truth.

"I can take the chance to speak with you now—since it's presented," Joseph said dryly, but mostly to encourage his speech.

Emily looked to him with owlish eyes, appearing like a cornered mouse. What could he possibly want to say to her alone? Her heart pounded.

Joseph hesitated, held solidly in her gaze. He took her off guard. He nearly laughed at the idea of succeeding in such a feat by pure accident. He was sure she could hold him off with little effort, if she had any of her mother in her. Joseph organized his thoughts before uttering another word. Overtly probing questions would certainly make her defensive. The moment was too important to waste in clipping banter.

"If I may ask, Miss Emily," Joseph finally said.

Emily opened her mouth to speak, but paused. She could hardly encourage a stranger to question her freely. She opened and closed her hand on the chair arm and waited for him to continue. She wondered what made him feel he had the right to ask her anything. Emily grimaced, thinking that sounded too much like her mother.

"You seem a mite distracted—you must miss your sweetheart," Joseph said, pulling her attention wholly to him. He watched her brows rise and then knit together in confusion. Depending on her reaction, he would continue fixedly from there out. "Is he away?"

"Sweetheart?" Emily cut him off, laughing. Through her smile, her tone smacked of outrage. Shockingly, Emily felt compelled to answer him. "Not exactly, Lieutenant, but I do miss someone," she said slowly and a blush crept onto her face again. He had all but said it.

Joseph's heart sank. He foolishly hoped to gain her side. He turned his gaze away and scolded himself for a foolhardy charge. He should have asked Evan who he was to her and not assumed from broken conversations. He should have asked about Michael. He should have asked Evan everything. How could he aim for her without being prepared? Not to mention, he had two short weeks before he would be back in Virginia with his company again. He had no time for subtlety.

Joseph's eyes instinctively went to her left hand, but the ring finger lie under the fingers of her right hand.

"I knew you looked far away," Joseph looked back to her, disguising his disappointment with a small laugh. Adopting a more respectful tone, he would amend his forwardness. He kept his eyes where they belonged and allowed another silence to ensnare them.

To look at another man's woman in such a manner was a terrible offense. Yet, he did it anyway. He hoped he had not disgraced her with his lack of control. His heart pained him, knowing he could never fix the damage of his rash actions. All he fancied himself to be was no more than a façade. His heart took to his throat with embarrassment. He deserved every ounce of what Mrs. Conrad threw at him, if he betrayed his dearest friend. He was no better than a surly drunk in a brothel. He could see his mother's shocked face and his father's deeply lined brow. He almost felt his father's hand on his shoulder. John Maynard never said much, but Joseph knew his feelings by his gestures.

"I'm just not used to him being gone—our lives have always been so—connected," Emily stopped the silence. She lifted her chin, tipping her head to the side. She looked to him with a smile on her lips. The tone of her words returned to playfulness. She saw the doubt in his features and wondered if he felt the same fears she did. "It hasn't been the same since he left."

Joseph's heart skipped a beat and his eyes lifted to hers with distress plain in their expression at Emily's words. She had fallen deeply in love. They had grown together, sealing their relationship early on. No chance to separate such hearts existed and he had no right to try to do such a terrible deed either. Joseph's thoughts worked for a reason not to continue. He broke his gaze from her to hide his shame. He was sure she would piece together his thoughts if he let her look at him anymore.

Joseph quickly realized he had gone too far to turn back. His need worked out reasons of their own, gaining added help from her pale blue eyes. They sparkled like jewels in the afternoon light of the window. He made his claim on her last night and he would not relinquish the reward to be gained even if it meant the end of a friendship. Joseph looked back to her, offering a wavering smile. He would cause the destruction of her family and his. He felt guilty, but it was a weak emotion, burning away in the fire driving him.

"Does he visit?" Joseph heard himself ask, unable to stop the question.

Joseph's heart pounded. It reminded him of cavalry charges against the Rebel lines, the days he would soon return to. Leaving should be enough incentive to let her go, but it only served to drive him with abandon. Joseph nearly yelled aloud to clear the devilish thoughts flooding his mind. He would not callously push Miss Conrad to indecent ends, merely to satisfy some random desire, and then take his leave, with no more than a thank you. His training and time away from his mother's drawing room had changed him more than he ever thought possible.

"No," Emily shook her head and looked at him with despondent eyes. "School won't let him come home. But, he'll graduate soon—I suppose we'll see him then," she revealed.

Emily blushed, sensing his intensity again. Strange feelings rose from her core and the need to escape from the parlor returned. She should have supervision and wondered how a soup lunch could keep her parents away this long. Emily adjusted in her seat, assuming her father meant for her to be alone with the Lieutenant. Her smile faded and she felt angry, grasping her parents had subtly turned their hopes to the stranger. Placing her gaze on the fireplace, Emily bitterly thought of how her mother made a point of punctuality that morning. This case was even more important to the woman since last night, even though she knew her mother despised him. However, if her father had it in mind he wanted his daughter to sit with Lieutenant Maynard alone, she would sit with him. If anyone heard a word of it, her reputation was at stake. Regardless, they meant to throw her at the feet of the hero, in place of Evan, and without even asking her how she felt.

Concerned for what would be said, Emily thought of the many acts that could have occurred by then. She felt her cheeks warm and a small smile curled the corners of her lips uncontrollably. Folding her hands over her stomach, she lounged back in her chair and drew a deep breath to focus back on hate, anything but the sofa.

"He goes to school then—where's he attend?" Joseph asked after a short pause in the conversation. He was confused by her response. Perhaps she had met someone else. He pieced together a story that told of visiting her brother at The Point and the lucky suitor there.

Emily's glorious eyes returned to him, stirring Joseph's insides into unrest and clouding his thoughts. Her intoxicating presence wiped his mind. Mere minutes ago he stood on the lawn discussing the Conrad son. Perhaps Emily was speaking of him, but what if she meant Evan or someone else? Looking at her pretty face, Joseph could not stop his pursuit even if he wanted to. From the moment he looked into her eyes, lit with the fire and the moonlight, he knew exactly what he wanted and no man would stand in his way. On the road to the Howell farm, he fell powerless against his feelings and it turned into sweet oblivion. Drinking from his emotions like a cup of strong wine, he felt drunk from their filling.

"West Point," Emily said. "Daddy wanted him to become more than a farmer," Emily said. She beamed proudly at the mention of the mystery man and it made her radiant. "So I begged Evan Howell to speak with him. He wouldn't hear of leaving the farm till after that. Now—now, I'm sorry I ever did."

Joseph felt elation wash over him. He squashed it down, needing to be sure.

They each smiled, but the emotions behind the expression were vastly different. While Joseph felt discomfort at being kept from his wants, Emily's emotions turned sad. Mentioning her brother brought back her guilt. She sat up and crossed her legs under her skirts. Resettling her skirts over her legs, she lowered her gaze to the floor. She hoped he would turn their conversation somewhere else, or her parents would finally arrive to rescue her. She thought about standing and excusing herself to seek them out.

"When did you come to the farm?" Joseph asked.

"I was born here," Emily answered, not wanting to speak anymore to him.

Joseph looked to her with another weak smile on his lips. Clearing his throat, he prepared to loft another of his inquiries at her. He heard the question bounce around his head. It was bold, but it would clear the path decidedly.

"How long have you been engaged?" Joseph asked, with a weighted and disinterested sounding sigh.

"Engaged?" Emily looked at him wide eyed.

This man believed her engaged to her own brother. If he thought on those lines and looked that worried, he most certainly sought her. What had Evan told him? She smiled and laughed, scoffing at the question and the idea she was being pursued. Then, she realized she held the power in their conversation. The Lieutenant indeed liked her. Emily forgot her guilt, replaced by delight.

"I'm not engaged, Lieutenant," Emily laughed.

Joseph smiled sheepishly at her, "He's your husband?"

"No," she giggled, "As I said—I don't miss a sweetheart, Lieutenant. You should listen to answers you ask for," Emily teased him with a playful tone, which she learned from Rose Benson. He smiled at her contented with the admission. "The young man of whom I speak is my brother Michael," Emily explained to him.

"How ignorant of me," Joseph said softly. He smiled handsomely and laughed, finding humor in the moment. "I apologize."

Excitement grew within him. The young woman stood unclaimed, waiting for someone like him to come along. Joseph could only smile and his heart expanded with hope to the point of pain. Now, the real game would begin a pleasant diversion from the war. He looked at her again in a lengthy stare that met her gaze moment for moment, until she felt forced to look away.

"No need to apologize, Lieutenant," Emily blushed.

By his choice of topics, the Lieutenant wanted more than just a visit with her father. Emily hoped she understood the signs exhibited to her. It would be embarrassing for her if she imagined interest where it did not exist. A man hardly acted with such attentiveness when displaying mere courtesy. His long stares had reached into her and that meant one thing.

"Conrad? A West Pointer, eh?" Joseph said, thinking aloud. His eyes rolled to stress his thinking and he squinted to show his doubt. Emily watched him smile and then laugh lightly. "Ah, yeah—that sounds right. Now I think of it." He paused again. "Matter of fact, I think Evan introduced us once at school," his eyes brightened fiercely. "You said Michael. Michael Conrad?" She nodded. Joseph rested his head against his hand. "Skinny boy—with—uh—sandy hair?" He smiled. "That boy's got too many brains and just as many plans."

"Oh, that's Michael!" Emily beamed proudly.

"Cadet Conrad's an excellent young man, as I recall. A real gentleman," Joseph told her, leaning forward in his chair to see her better around the flowers. "Wish I had the opportunity to know more of him. There's not much time with our studies and class obligations."

Emily felt easier in Joseph's presence when he spoke of her brother. If he truly thought so well of Michael, he might just be a good man. He looked too handsome to her with his honest eyes and decent manners. She told herself to ignore the superficial matters, because he could just be playing his cards as they were dealt. Only his actions during events such as the fire proved good character. Emily thought of Shakes, knowing he already showed promise. He had asked about the bull, after all.

"Michael takes after our father," Emily told him. "We're quite proud of him."

"Indeed," Joseph said. Her beauty distracted him and he forgot himself in it. While he studied her face, she cast her eyes away, flashing a small self conscious smile. "He's a good man and he'll make a good officer," he murmured and smiled assuredly.

Emily's face lifted and she looked to him with a darkening expression. The Lieutenant reminded her of her guilt. Her once bright smile faded to a deep frown. The entire world crashed on top of her. Her breath once again became labored and her heart beat hard against her chest. Michael would be a good officer and it was her fault.

Grasping the padded arms of her chair, Emily sat back against the cushion. Her head swam and she felt as if she would swoon. The tears burned her eyes, bringing with them the harsh feelings she harbored since Michael left for school. She wanted him home safe from the war. The unavoidable end to her meddling would only be death. She had murdered her own brother.

Emily prayed the war would stop before Michael graduated and he would come home safe. Emily licked her lips. Her mouth felt terribly dry. She ran her hands along the chair arms, thinking of a way to leave. She felt foolish to think escape from her torment possible. She dared to cause trouble in her life. Then, she would suffer the punishment that came with it. Emily closed her eyes and drew a breath. Her hands stilled on her stomach. Without opening her eyes, she knew the visitor watched her. She must look a mad woman to him.

Joseph could have thrown a snowball in Emily's face and received a better response. He watched her anxiety pulling down the corners of his mouth. He did not understand. She was so proud to talk of him, just a moment ago.

"Are you all right?" Joseph's voice reached her ears.

In Emily's withdrawal, she failed to hear Joseph's question. Lost in her misery, she saw her mother's accusing glance whenever someone asked after Michael. If she could not open her eyes and find this meeting a mere dream, Emily wanted the silence between them to last. Emily's eyes slyly trailed to the visitor's uniform. Michael would wear the same one when given his commission. Like a good girl, she should have left it to her father and not asked Evan to drag Michael into the army with him.

"I'm fine, thank you. My lunch seems to disagree with me," Emily sighed when his words settled on her. She opened her eyes to look at the parlor rug. The tone of her words sounded dead. Emily lowered her head into her hand, wanting to cry but embarrassed to do so before the guest.

"Can I get you anything?"

"No." Emily said curtly.

Joseph watched her openly curious. He meant for her to pull closer not away.

"What'd I say, Miss Conrad?" Joseph asked, letting her know he felt her withdrawal.

Emily lifted her eyes to him. His sheepish expression touched her heart without needing an apology to excuse his trespass. Before Emily could reply, her mother swept gracefully into the room. Her sudden appearance added tension to the room instead of relieving it. Emily looked to her with rounded eyes.

Margaret flicked her eyes from her daughter to the young man who leaned toward her too closely, bearing an expression of frigid assessment. Flicking her glance from Emily to their guest, she surmised in short order what she believed had happened. By the grave expression on her daughter's face and the guilt on the guest's, she could see he spoke out of turn. This obvious misstep was exactly what she expected of the heathen. Lifting her chin, she continued toward the Lieutenant with an air of irritation.

Emily watched her mother pass. She eyed the other woman's Sunday dress of dark maroon. Emily wished for half the composure her mother always displayed. Watching the older woman close in on Joseph, she thought over the last moments with him. If only Michael's situation did not bother her so. She could not help feeling so frightened. Soldiers fought wars and she made her brother one of them. Whether he was a good officer or not, he could die with the rest. How could she entertain the idea of happiness after causing so much trouble and heartache?

"Lieutenant Maynard," Margaret said, approaching Joseph's chair with her hand outstretched.

Joseph stood and grasped it reluctantly and quickly, as if the touch of her would poison him. The long fingers of her hand reminded him of an uninviting talon. That talon had swept away any chance at rectifying his error with the girl.

"My husband will come along in a moment. I hope you'll forgive our delay. You came during lunch. I don't see much of my husband during the day. So, we like to eat together in the music room, when we can," she added backing away from him with a stiff expression, wrenching her face into what she assumed a warm smile.

Emily's mother sat on the sofa, facing them with a disguised notion of his outright revulsion of her. She adjusted her skirt, crossing her legs and clasped her hands over her knee. She smiled broadly at the Lieutenant.

The tension in the room grew stronger. Emily looked to Joseph, noticing how stiff he had become. If he spoke his true feelings about her mother aloud, he could not be more obvious. She quickly adjusted her expression, masking her observation with disinterest and lowered her eyes to the floor at her mother's feet. Though her mother's present display exuded a huge change from the previous night, Emily suspected the meeting would go poorly between them, no matter what her father asked. Her parents would remain split over the subject. Eventually her mother would give over to her father, but by then it may be too late to rectify matters.

A weighted silence filled the room. Emily wondered at what drove her mother's actions. It may prove wise to hear what she had to say. Perhaps her mother's years gave her a power of perception higher than her daughter held. Emily planned to seek her mother's advice later when they could be alone. Only a mother could straighten the knots the Lieutenant put her thoughts into and protect her from any ill intent. After all, her mother held her best interest in mind.

Between last night and now, there existed no doubt that the man measured her willingness to accept his advances. Swallowing, Emily thought she carried the exchange too far to deny it now. She liked him the moment she saw him. The Lieutenant's questions insinuated his understanding of that sentiment. Emily looked to him. Her mother's voice filled the background. Emily closed her eyes and chewed her bottom lip. She felt her stomach drop.

Joseph eyed the elder Conrad woman with a wary look while she spoke to him. He saw the way her eyes regarded him in a cold and calculating manner. Joseph hardly thought this display sincere. Her words sounded friendlier than the night before, but it left him uneasy and keen on escape. She probably tried to mock him. He could only imagine what came next. He both mistrusted and feared the woman. He only wanted her to display fitting gratefulness. That would be enough for him to forget her transgression.

Before he could discreetly let Mrs. Conrad know how he felt and make a noble escape, Mr. Conrad joined them. The man smiled broadly from a cheery pink cheeked face. Joseph stood again, forgetting the wasp on the couch. The man offered his large strong hand to Joseph and he appreciatively accepted. He decided not to insult the family or leave so soon. He would first attempt to enjoy the new company. After all, he arrived for dinner and would not receive a dignified send off before then and it would give enough time to fix matters with Miss Emily.

"Good to finally meet you, Lieutenant Maynard," Stuart smiled, shaking hands. "I hope my daughter kept you well."

"The pleasure's all mine, sir," Joseph replied with a delighted smile. "Yes, she did. We had a very charming discussion. Thank you."

"Nonsense, young man. It's us who should be grateful for your presence," Stuart let him go, waving off his pretty words with a half laugh. He turned his face away with refusal, chuckling. The act reminded his guest of Santa Claus. "Would you like something to drink, Lieutenant?" Stuart offered him, returning a steady gaze to the young man's face.

"Thank you, Mister Conrad. I believe I would," Joseph smiled warmly in return.

Stuart reminded Joseph of a colonel from England he once met. He almost expected the man to tell him he served in the military, but retired some time ago. In that impression, he clearly saw the justification for Emily's regard of her father. Pandering to his ego, Joseph wondered how Mr. Conrad came by a match with such an ill tempered bride. Much must have happened between them since and he could see the result in the mood swings gone full around.

Stuart gave a warm chuckle from deep in his throat. He liked this young man already. Seeing him again only affirmed the judgment he made from last night's experience. Turning toward the open arch of the parlor, he called out to Blythe. When she entered, he looked back to the Lieutenant to request his preference.

"What would you prefer? We have fine well or some of our best milk?" At this he laughed, tucking his thumbs into his waistcoat pockets. "Best yet, why don't we have some tea? We've fine connections in England to get our leaves."

"That'd suit me fine, Mr. Conrad. Thank you," Joseph nodded.

Stuart backed away and turned to the young curly haired girl, who stood humbly in the arch, awaiting him. Ordering up their tea, he found his mind still thought on the boy behind him and the connection his daughter Emily could have with him. The Lieutenant seemed to be what he assumed women found attractive. The blush his daughter showed on her youthful cheeks the night before said so. However, Emily's now grayed demeanor warned he assumed too much. Then again, they may have breached a sensitive subject, like Michael. Stuart turned back to his family and guest, casting his eyes over his daughter. He watched her stare at the floor beside her chair. He then looked to the Lieutenant, not surprised to see he watched his daughter. Stuart detected a note of sympathy and regret in his features. Stuart felt sorry he arrived too late to help the pair avoid this falling out.

Joseph missed his host's eyes assessing him. He was too deep in a trance over the beguiling beauty of the girl. He went over their interview, turning his words over and over. He failed to discern why they damaged a perfect chat. Anyone would have appreciated the fine compliments he offered her brother.

"Please—sit down, Lieutenant," Stuart smiled, regaining Joseph's attention.

Joseph nodded and sat back in his chair, while his host placed himself next to his wife. Lifting his eyes, the Lieutenant saw an African woman descend the staircase outside the archway. She wore a fine gray cotton gown, fronted by a starched white apron, and a similar fabric cap on her head. Her gaze momentarily but warily turned to the parlor, as she stepped past the opening. Then, she went her way just as quickly as she appeared.

Joseph could not explain what he just saw and thought on exactly what sort of house he entered. The presence of an African servant in a northern home confused Joseph, thinking it far from the truth that slavery remained in practice here. He recalled hearing of a law passed to the contrary. He had not seen any Africans last night among the hands. She presented a most fascinating aspect of the Conrads.

Again, Evan had failed to prepare him for anything he stood to face in his visit. He merely stated the Conrads a pleasant family who he grew up near. He and Emily had been friends since childhood and all but promised to each other by their mothers. Joseph scratched his beard and his eyes returned to the girl. She still studied her hands, loosely clasped on her lap. Thankfully, the color improved in her face.

Stuart cleared his throat to regain his guest's attention from his daughter's obviously strong presence in the room. When Joseph turned his eyes toward him and his wife, he could see the embarrassment in the boy's face, realizing his attentions toward Emily discovered. Stuart glanced over at his wife and she appeared most troubled by the stares. Stuart half laughed despite her. Cocking his head in a gesture toward his daughter, Stuart thought to make light of the matter, but in a manner the boy would catch and the others possibly miss.

"Beautiful isn't it," Stuart said. He recalled his youth filled with coy flirtations and his heart lightened. "Vermont's a tremendously charming place," he added, covering his meaning with the view through the window behind Emily's head. Stuart imagined his wife serving his head on a platter for daring to present their daughter in such a manner. "It's most obvious to a soldier such as yourself, eh, Lieutenant?"

Joseph felt his heart pound in his chest, similar to the cadence it beat on the battlefield. His mouth went dry and his reply dried up with it. He could not make a sound. He swallowed his heart, gathering himself. After a slight pause, he found his words.

"Y-yes, sir. It is—quite," Joseph said. He forgot he no longer sat alone with the girl. He need be more careful.

At that moment, the African woman returned to the doorway. She carried a tea tray in her long fingered hands. The porcelain clattered, as the occupants of the room turned toward her with smiles. Joseph looked to each of them with surprise marking his features. The woman confidently approached the small table beside him and the young woman. There she set her load down and removed the vase of flowers to the windowsill behind. Joseph then watched her return to the tray, passing a momentary glance over him. Joseph quickly smiled to cover his curiosity. The woman's expression held a measure of defiance toward him. Joseph lowered his eyes from her penetrating gaze and awaited his tea. He would rather stare at the floor than allow her to dig out his soul like that again.

Hettie smiled softly and turned her attention to the porcelain vessels she brought to serve tea to the guest and family. That one glance told her a great deal. She prided herself on knowing a person with one look. This time her eyes told her she frightened him and was uncomfortable in the Conrad parlor. She wished she knew what the stranger sought so far from his home.

While she poured the tea into the first cup, her eyes pieced him together with what she had. His features held hints of gentleness. The corners of his mouth had small lines. He enjoyed laughing, perhaps a bit of a joker. Another line marked his right hand unnaturally between the fore and second finger. The wound had long since healed, probably attained in battle. His roving eye marked him curious. Such examples told of a character boyish and brave, but no threat.

Hettie offered Joseph the first cup, satisfied with her inspection, thus far. A great weight lifted from her shoulders.

"Thank you," the Lieutenant said. He took the delicate cup and saucer, watching her with amazement.

The Lieutenant's bearing and well kept appearance told Hettie he came from money. She noted the words he chose. He sounded intelligent, well above a normal education. He was interesting, at least.

"You're welcome," Hettie said.

Hettie gave a bright smile and then moved onto serving the family. She now knew the reason for Emily's girlish excitement. She could barely wait to tell Rose.

Joseph watched the woman work, as no ordinary servant or slave. She spoke freely with him, a right forbidden to slaves. His hometown of Frederick, Maryland made him no stranger to the institution. While she poured the next cup, Joseph watched her dark eyes glitter with amusement. He was embarrassed for staring, acting as though he never saw her like before. Joseph turned his gaze away, coloring a little in his cheeks and gave a small shamefaced smile at behaving so foolish.

"We could suffer the loss of a cow or that calf this season," Stuart said suddenly. Hettie offered him his tea and drew his jovial face to hers. "Uh—thank you, Hettie," he said, taking the cup from her with a smile of approval.

Joseph watched the housekeeper smile back and return to her tray, onto the next cup of tea. Stuart then sipped from his cup. Hettie continued to occupy Joseph's curiosity while she worked. He observed the surprisingly genuine warmth and thanks from Mrs. Conrad. It even came followed by a smile. That small moment illumined the cold matriarch in a new light. She harbored her ill feelings toward him over his origins or foreign purpose. Joseph almost laughed, thinking that his Maryland accent ruffled her feathers so. Joseph smiled, flicking his eyes over the woman. He watched her thin lips wrap around the edge of her white teacup. She looked like a camel stretching for water. At least they both had their prejudices now.

Joseph rubbed a hand on the back of his neck. He took a sip of tea. Joseph lowered the teacup from his lips and looked at the reddish brown liquid inside. He thought of what Mr. Conrad said to him.

"However, it'd been too much to suffer the loss of a Federal soldier," Stuart added, just a brief moment after his last word.

"Someone would have suffered without the milk," Joseph mumbled in response, his silky tones wakened Emily's attention back to him. "My life may be only one, but I'm willing to risk it for those in need," he added.

"On a farm? I don't think so, Lieutenant," Stuart said, smiling to see from the corner of his eye his daughter's renewed interest. "This area's been blessed with at least twenty births this spring."

"Honestly?" Joseph looked up with surprise. "That's grand, Mr. Conrad," Joseph's eyes flicked from Emily back to Stuart. He kept his gaze away from Margaret intentionally, wishing her to feel the way she made him feel.

At that moment, the Lieutenant saw the relationship between Emily and Hettie. The tall housekeeper passed a cup of tea to the smaller woman who sat before her. Emily eagerly pushed forward in her seat to accept her cup and whispered thank you. Emily sipped.

"May I have some lemon please," Emily whispered to her.

Hettie smiled and opened a small silver lidded bowl. With a serving fork, she drew out the bright yellow citrus and placed it on Emily's saucer. Emily looked up at her with a small smile. Hettie smiled back and touched her face. Then a questioning glance passed. Something other than the lemon went there. Emily then smirked with a shrug of her shoulders and turned her attention on her tea, squeezing the lemon wedge into it. She set the rind on the saucer rested on her lap. She took another sip. Hettie watched the girl a moment longer, but Emily sat back, ignoring her.

Hettie turned to Mr. Conrad and excused herself. She swept from the room, with one last glance to Emily, almost making the young woman giggle and spill her tea. Then the housekeeper disappeared. Emily's attention went to her cup.

"I do promise you that it would have proved a senseless waste," Stuart said. Joseph looked back to him. "If it meant your life. Nonetheless—I would like to thank you for your grand gesture, Lieutenant," Stuart's tone drew solemn and serious enough to belong to a preacher. "If there's anything we can do for you, or give, I'm much obligated."

Beside Mr. Conrad, his wife looked up from her cup of tea and gazed at Joseph. He moved his eyes to Emily, and saw the grave expression on the girl's face. She looked to her father with anxiety. Joseph slightly smiled and looked back to the husband and wife. Mrs. Conrad held fear in her eyes too. Did the women think their patriarch bartered his daughter as a thank you gift?

"Thank you," Joseph drawled. "But, all I ask is to enjoy your company for the evening." Nicely done, he thought.

Emily gaped between her father and him. No one missed the obvious meaning that swung through the room. Her heart pounded fiercely in cadent echo of her rising anger. She thought a father's job was to protect his daughter, not offer her attentions freely. Emily worried that if she did not take her leave right away, they would see to her packing off with him by nightfall. Emily lowered her gaze and drank more tea. The citrus accented liquid filled her mouth, but it failed to help do anything but keep her quiet. Swallowing hard, she felt her legs pulse, wanting to run the rest of her from the room. She quickly piped up to make a timely escape.

"Mother," Emily said in her soft tones. "Perhaps I should check on the new help—see how the meal's coming along," she explained.

"Go ahead, dear. I'm sure your father and Lieutenant Maynard won't mind. They've much to discuss." As Margaret spoke in her falsely pleasant tones, she turned her gaze from Emily to her husband and then to Joseph.

Joseph returned the gaze, noting something akin to triumph in Margaret's eyes. The woman wanted Emily gone as badly as the night before. However, he could not understand why she allowed her husband to dandle her in front of him and then send her off. Joseph felt a growl of anger brewing in his throat. He stifled it, wishing to continue his visit with the father under good airs.

Emily felt her limbs tremble as she stood from the chair that offered some support until that moment.

"Excuse me," Emily said. "It was a pleasure to meet with you again."

Joseph nodded, unable to say what he wanted.

Emily left the room with her head held high, determined to escape him despite her fear to move at all. With each step, she felt his eyes burn into her back. Once in the safety of the hall, Emily placed a hand over her heart and the other against the wall for support. She paused in the hallway to draw deep steadying breaths. Turning around, she put her back to the wall. Emily's frustration grew at her constant overreaction toward the Lieutenant, but this time she knew she had more to fear. She closed her eyes and focused on breathing. Unable to trust her parents, she hoped he would take his leave sooner than dinner. The thought of him ruined her lunch and now his presence would make the next meal entirely unappetizing.

Emily wondered at how she could possibly have wanted him to come back. After what her father had done, Emily plainly saw the reason behind her mother's warning. She released a weighted sigh and opened her eyes. Quietly sneaking down the hall, her hand unsteadily lifted and she covered her face to blot out the thoughts, coming in fast confusing torrents.

The sound of her parents and the stranger discussing some trivial matter reached her ears from the other room. Emily listened to them until she saw the door of the closet under the stairs. Calm returned to her body. Emily thought to hide like before. Instead, she reasoned out the fallibility of this meeting. Like Michael, he was a soldier and would not stay long. He faced a return to the army, stationed wherever they ordered. She need set her mind on more stable ground and not think anymore of someone who would be gone as fast as they arrived.

"What brings you up this far?" Emily heard her father ask, not missing a step in their conversation when she left them.

In the room, Joseph felt increasingly uncomfortable. He wished Emily had stayed. He wanted to spend more time with her, even if she remained silent. Joseph masked his disappointment with interest in Stuart's conversation.

"Mostly to get away from the rain and take a short rest while we got a lull in fighting. Second Lieutenant Howell said he wanted to see his family—he invited me—said I should see it," Joseph replied.

"Oh, the Howell boy . . ." Margaret's voice faded, as Emily walked away.

Emily listened from the hall. His voice made her heart beat hard. Emily felt the heat creep into her face and turned away, pushing off the wall to escape to the kitchen. Had Evan even planned against her? Emily shivered. The passage seemed miles longer. She thought no real escape existed from such a pursuer as Lieutenant Maynard, especially with her own family and friends helping him.

Joseph's voice carried down the hall and she could not hesitate in her escape any longer. Pausing, she eyed the kitchen door. Emily refused to accept the fate so many planned for her. She was not an object for sale to the highest bidder. She would see this man fail in his effort, before she added him to the list of her miseries.

Emily took the last steps to the kitchen. Once inside, she soaked in the sunflower yellow radiated happily from the walls. There, she found MaryJane kneading the dough for dinner with a small smile on her mouth. Beside the sink, little Jo-Hanna finished the stack of dishes from that morning and minded her own business, occasionally gazing out of the window to the yard. She looked so adorable that Emily smiled, forgetting the devil in the front room. She stepped over to her and stroked the reddish braid when she turned to look at her. Jo-Hanna smiled in return.

"Let me see how you've done," Emily spoke softly, and stepped back to the stack of clean dishes Jo-Hanna made. Emily looked over the pile, and they sparkled up at her, glistening wet and thoroughly cleaned. "Lovely, Jo-Hanna," she smiled then moved onto the other girl who seemed in a trance, pounding bread dough relentlessly. "MaryJane you're gonna deflate that bread permanently. Put it in a pan to rise," Emily told her firmly. MaryJane lifted her hands from the dough and peered at her with sullen brown eyes. "Don't be nervous. It's your first day we expect your mistakes," Emily said more softly and added a smile of reassurance.

"Oh, Miss Emily. I'm sorry," MaryJane said near tears. "I'm just so afraid your Ma will fire me if I don get it right, with the guest and all."

"Nonsense! We need your help," Emily soothed her fears. "Where's Blythe?"

"Upstairs with Rose," Jo-Hanna responded in her little voice. "They're cleaning while y'ave company."

Of course they worked up there, Emily thought. It was the furthest they could be from her. Emily's expression turned tragic with the realization she needed to step past the parlor door to climb the stairs. She needed to know what made Hettie risk herself. Her freedom was under constant threat. Without any doubt, if the wrong person saw Hettie, she would suffer execution for running away. She may have already condemned herself just serving tea. No one but Evan could certify the Lieutenant and he remained conveniently absent. If Joseph Maynard did not cause her untimely death directly, he could flap his ignorant jaws to any number of men who would. Hettie should have stayed out of sight. Emily blamed herself with the way she carried on about him. Hettie's curiosity had been peaked.

Emily wanted to join her friend upstairs, but there was no way safely around the parlor. Only her room could provide safety from the reach of the calf toting barn fire hero. Joseph Maynard hunted her like a lion would its kill, but with more cunning and deceit, bringing her father in to help him. He lured and coaxed, making her a wreck with unfocused emotions. Then, he reminded her of all the faults and wrong doings she had committed. Her response to him was abnormal at best, but he still pursued. Emily chided herself for being such a silly child. Emily shut her eyes and placed a hand on her forehead, trying to forget the thoughts the image gave her. Walking by the parlor would take the last ounce of her strength. The mere thought made Emily feel sure she would become hysterically sick. Sitting on a chair in the corner beside the brick oven and fireplace, Emily tried to regain her head before she fell to the floor.

Emily's effort to regain her composure made her look rather strange to the other occupants of the room, who now eyed her with concern. They had no idea what was wrong, but it certainly had them wondering. MaryJane exchanged questioning glances with her little sister and Jo-Hanna replied with a quick shrug of her shoulders. Emily was distraught over something or was just plain crazy.

"Are you all right, Miss Emily?" MaryJane finally asked.

"Oh—y-yes—I'm fine," Emily said. She looked at both girls and gave a hesitant smile. "I'm just a little dizzy all of a sudden—no need to worry about me," she added. With a heavy sad sigh, she rolled her eyes and said, "I'm just acting silly."

"It's the visitor. MaryJane felt dizzy after seein him too," Jo-Hanna glowed with the news.

MaryJane flushed and her mouth popped open in mortified outrage at the confession. She thought her sister trustworthy enough to speak in front of, but as usual she was wrong. Wiping her hands on her apron, she tried to keep calm, but then Jo-Hanna looked at her deviously. MaryJane was not surprised to see such a glint her sister's eyes. She never kept such knowledge to herself, spilling it at the first opportunity.

"MaryJane says he's a soldier a the union. She said he's—" Jo-Hanna persisted, before her angry sister cut her off.

"Shush yourself, child!" MaryJane hissed.

"Handsome," Jo-Hanna completed her sentence to spite her. "Is he?" She asked after she exchanged angry glances with MaryJane. She looked innocently to Emily.

"Why can't you keep quiet, Jo?" MaryJane almost sobbed, turning away.

"Please don't argue girls," Emily said lazily. She rose to her feet. "It'll do you no good here." After a pause, she added, "Besides, MaryJane, she's only curious, as all little girls are." When MaryJane remained silent, Emily looked to Jo-Hanna and answered her question, "Yes. He's a Union soldier, Jo-Hanna."

"Is he the same one my Pa told us saved the cows—he almost burnt up?" Jo-Hanna asked urgently, with wide brown eyes full of wonder and excitement.

"Yes," Emily said, half distracted by the little girl's pleasure at such an event. "He's the same one."

"Is he handsome—cuzz both Blythe and MaryJane said he is?"

"You're impossible!" MaryJane said angrily, tossing the bread pans onto the stovetop.

"Gently, MaryJane," Emily sternly spoke, turning to look at her with a reproving glance. "Not so cross—Mrs. Conrad doesn't like this behavior," Emily corrected her and received a mumbled apology.

Turning her attention back to the sweet freckled face of Jo-Hanna, she thought of her admission that Blythe stood there discussing the guest with them earlier. That at least answered why Hettie brought them tea instead. She knew that Mrs. Conrad would not stand for the girl flirting with their guest. Emily imagined the girl mooning over the solider. It mattered little now anyway, with the deed done. Emily continued to answer the barrage of questions from Jo-Hanna.

"As I wanted to say—yes, Lieutenant Maynard is very handsome," Emily smiled at her. "But, you need not concern yourself with the details of him. He'll go very soon and hopefully for good." Emily looked about the kitchen. She must reject the idea of him. "Put those clean dishes away and finish the rest. You're both doing a fine job," she spoke again touching MaryJane's shoulder reassuringly. "I'm going upstairs if anyone needs me," Emily sounded distracted and sad again.

In her mind, she already traversed the hall and made an escape upstairs. The girls returned to their labors and she moved to make the voyage for real.

The girls remained quiet until they heard Emily's footsteps fade. Then, MaryJane quickly turned on her little sister, fists clenched tightly at her side. A heated expression to rival any sinister creature twisted her expression. The little girl foolishly coaxed her ire and where their mother could not protect her. She would say her piece and see that no such incident happened again.

"You have to learn to keep your mouth shut, you little snot rag. It'll do you no good telling anything here," MaryJane pointed her sharp finger in the other girl's face and then sniffed about red faced and flustered.

"I's just asking," Jo-Hanna said indignantly. She pouted and crossed her arms, almost crying.

"You talk too much," MaryJane snapped roughly, stirring the soup in the pot where it hung over the fire, managing to spill a bit. "Damn!" She cursed.

V. A Choice

Mrs. Conrad had run out of topics to help her husband and their guest continue a conversation. Beside that, she felt quite unsure how to proceed, since she received so many curt answers. The Lieutenant openly displayed his displeasure for her. Folding her hands in her lap, she cursed her actions of the previous evening. She had failed to disguise her true feelings carefully, only effecting abhorred shame.

Stuart appeared most upset with the strife she brought to their home. He simply expected too much of her. The barn was on fire and then a pure devil came to seek her daughter. Stuart asked if she thought it such a great loss. What would the loss of most of their stock meant to her? If he failed to arrive in time to help them, their livelihood could have perished in the flames leaving them without income, and soon destitute. He was right, but at what cost? With or without her husband seeing what she saw, Margaret was determined to keep alert and one step ahead of Joseph. He would find a trial to gain her Emily, if she kept her wits and way.

"Well," Margaret breathed in a nervous sigh. She forced a genial smile. No response came and she looked to her husband.

"How would you like to view the acreage?" Stuart asked him before his wife could work more damage. His tone revealed a note of irritation. "Did you bring your horse or shall we walk it?" He managed a smile, although he thought of the discussion he would have with Margaret later.

"I rode my mount here," Joseph grinned, cocking his head to the side. It came clear to him the sire and dame of his jewel stood at odds. "But, I believe walking would be finer, sir—if that is all right with you. I ride too much as it is lately, Mr. Conrad."

"Of course—of course," Stuart chuckled and nodded understandingly. "Let me gather my things and we'll go."

When Stuart lifted himself from his seat and headed towards the door, Emily appeared in the archway. He nodded to his daughter with a warm expression and she stopped to smile at him before continuing. Stuart turned away first, to gain his coat and hat from the rack beside the door. He then waited for his guest to join them.

"I'll be upstairs with the maids, Daddy," Emily told him.

Stuart nodded and turned his gaze to the Parlor door. Joseph came along behind, standing from the chair to leave Margaret behind with no farewells. Joseph's intense gaze stuck to Emily and it displayed his lack of favor toward her mother. His eyes flicked to Stuart, awaiting him. He looked nervously between the daughter and her father.

Emily regarded Joseph with renewed disfavor. She saw his rebuff toward her mother. He acted unlike a proper gentleman, forgetting to excuse himself from the presence of a woman. Despite his perfect dance until that moment, Emily felt assured by this one misstep that she correctly decided against his advances. No one would disrespect her mother and think to win her affections, even if he did disturb her heart with the emotions it never felt. Before her heart could undo the careful work of her mind, Emily turned from him and climbed the stairs. She would not spare him another glance. However, his investigating eyes followed her until she disappeared from view.

"Come back soon. It's after three." Margaret's voice pulled the attention of the men back to her and away from her daughter. She stood in the archway behind Joseph. "Dinner shall be ready shortly, about five." Margaret smiled warmly at her husband, passing the guest to stand beside Stuart in the hall. She appeared to have taken little notice of the slight Joseph gave and the one Emily returned.

Joseph passed around them both to take his cavalry cloak and hat from the rack where the servant girl put it. After placing the items on his person, he pulled his gloves from where they hung looped over his belt and squeezed them onto his hands. His eyes trailed to the stairs several times. He could not help but wonder what he said that upset Emily so. He took each step carefully, from complimenting her family to playing the gracious gentleman. She still pulled away and now she loathed his presence. This girl took a great deal after her mother, but he warned himself against those terrible thoughts. He needed to talk with Evan before he decided. Something greater was going on that he was not aware of.

"Yes dear," Stuart smiled waveringly in return. He gave her cheek a soft loving pat, while Joseph got himself ready behind them. Shrugging his coat on his shoulders, he put his hat on his head and gave Margaret a searching glance. "You'll get to speak better at dinner. Make good then," he spoke low to prevent his guest from overhearing.

Margaret nodded with an unsure smile. They stood at odds with each other and she felt sure of her reason to do so. It was absurd that they need make friends, when this obvious threat loomed over them. She refused the night before, and she still refused now. She would behave merely civil and no more.

Stuart turned away from his wife and walked out of the great farmhouse, closely followed by Joseph. Both men cast squinting gazes over the rolling hills blanketed in a heavy melting snow. The clouds cleared away since before his visit and now a bright blue sky and cold white sun hung above the farm, filling them with fantasies of spring.

The buds on the trees would come along soon, leaving the barren gray stalks, now soaked with rain, studded with strange growths. The grass showed in patches where the snow laid trampled, yellow like hay. More snow would arrive before spring burst in full bloom, but the drought was a welcome respite. Despite its barrenness, the yard was a wonderful site, compared to the uncommonly cold parlor.

"I see the rain's cleared up," Stuart said, noting the obvious with a swing of his fashionable cane toward the blue sky.

Mr. Conrad's motion reminded Joseph of his own father. He felt a longing for home pang his heart. He had planned to see them on leave, but Evan pulled him further north. He could not define it if it meant his life, but he knew he had to go. It was now obvious to him fate played a game. The mere thought of the jewel enraged and delighted him. He had played with a few daisies in his time, but Miss Emily proved entirely different. He wanted more than just a moment, grasping at every bit he could.

"Mighty good for those head out there," Stuart continued, jutting his chin towards the grazing lands to the left of the house. "The grass will grow in plenty this spring," he added apathetically. Without the barn to keep them in, he would have the cows run out to pasture during the warm days and crowd them in the milking houses at night.

Stuart and Joseph spoke about the farm, as the first guided his visitor to the top of the hill and along the dirt path to the left of the house. At the crest they held a magnificent view of the pastures in the dales below, dotted by trees and shrubs, and marked out by stonewalls and fencing. In the far distance, the colored specks of another farm stuck out behind clusters of trees and still more fields.

They stood in the middle of nowhere, holding to themselves and thriving. Joseph admired Mr. Conrad's business abilities and sense. He wondered what the father truly thought of him. However, he rather intended to court Ms. Conrad and not her father, even if Emily obviously made other plans in her mind. He needed to figure out those plans and prevent them in order to place himself in her life.

When Joseph's thoughts came back to the present, Stuart still explained how he came to work the farm since the fire. He then turned their walk back toward the workhouses, which sat some distance behind the main house. From there he explained each landmark of the farm. Together, they passed in sight of the rose garden, and he told Joseph its story.

Generations ago a great matron of the family planted it in her traditional English style, of which she felt accustomed in her native land. Since then, it grew a bit larger and more eclectic. To Joseph's delight, he also informed him the garden served the women of his house as a refuge. The path by the garden led between the workhouses, up the hill on which it sat, then around it and finally off into a horse trail. The trail disappeared into the wooded acreage he owned for a mile back toward the Howell's fields. Mr. Conrad added that Emily would work in the garden soon, to clear away the debris of the winter and prepare it for spring. It was not the wisest thing to reveal, but he saw Joseph was a gentleman.

Mr. Conrad was most helpful. Joseph tucked his gloved hands into the small of his back, clasping them and smiled. He would find the garden from the back trail through the woods, and could see her there, alone.

"Is that so? Miss Emily gardens then?"

"Indeed," Stuart replied. "My girl won a blue ribbon for her roses last fair. She has the touch, some say," he smiled up at him. From there, they moved toward the dairy buildings. Stuart changed the subject to something a little more comfortable for the both of them. "We'll see the workhouses now, if you don't mind, Lieutenant."

"I would very much like to see them, sir," Joseph looked to the lonely palace of his jewel. It appeared sad, resting there in the wintry scene. "If I may say, you sure have a beautiful place here."

"You're right," Stuart drawled. "That's not all the folks find beautiful here," he hinted boldly.

Joseph smiled, "What do you insinuate?"

"The cows," Stuart stopped and looked at him earnestly. "My cows are the best around—good milk."

At that moment, the young bull Joseph had saved from the inferno trotted by Mr. Conrad and him. A rope dangled from its skinny spotted neck, dragging through the rutted lane, covering the fibers in sticky wet mud. Behind the calf, a young boy gave an exerted chase. His dungaree pants were covered in mud from the cuffs to his knees, smeared handprints stained the thighs. His small fingers were caked in mud, as well as his face where he rubbed it. Joseph could not help but smile at the filthy kid, thinking of his own escapades in days long gone.

"Come back ere you," the boy called out in a high pitched voice full of aggravation. On seeing the others in the yard, he came to an abrupt stop and tore off his muddied hat to them graciously. "Good afternoon, Mr. Conrad and Mr. Soldier." He nodded his head to each as he addressed them. The calf came to a loafing stop beside Stuart, as the play ended. The calf bent its head around to watch them.

"Good afternoon, Henry," Stuart smiled, offering a nod and touch to his hat in greeting. "I'd like you to meet my friend, Lieutenant Maynard."

"Nice t'meet you, Lieutenant," Henry reached out his muddy hand to shake Joseph's gloved one.

"Likewise, Henry," Joseph did not hesitate to shake hands, grinning at the boy with nostalgic memories.

Henry eyed Joseph suspiciously, like children do when faced by a stranger. He took back his hand, realizing it hung there covered in mud. He gave a small apology, which gained chuckles from Mr. Conrad, and another smile from Joseph who dismissed it as nothing. He tipped his blonde head to look at his uniform. His gold hair gleamed brightly in the sunlight, as he squinted up at the soldier, unsure of what to do or say next. He swished on his feet.

The men both smiled at him, awaiting his words, as they both knew he wanted to say something. The boy reminded Joseph of one about his age, assigned to his regiment since last summer. He pictured the red hair and freckled face. The little soldier beat out marches on his drum.

"Shakes's givin me a bit a trouble. But I'll set em ta right," Henry finally spoke, perhaps making up his mind about the soldier who stood with his father's boss. He heard the barn fire story earlier that day, but it turned a little scarier for him to see the hero for real before him. After a last glance at Joseph, he turned back to the little bull and ran after the animal before it wandered away up the hill.

"That's a good boy!" Stuart called after him with a light laugh.

Without further hesitation, Stuart led Joseph through an opening in the fence and hedges to the outbuildings behind. Joseph received the full tour complete with a lecture on the dairy business, the machinery used, and the animals he kept. In the milking barn, Stuart walked him over to the previously mentioned mother of the calf, May-Belle. Then, Stuart turned their conversation to a much more delicate subject. Joseph stood off guard by this time, feeling confident that Stuart intended no wrong, nor wanted to retread the path they nearly took earlier.

The matter of his daughter niggled at his curiosity. He saw her on the lawn last night, staring after Joseph like a pair of star crossed lovers forbidden to stand together by some angry harpy who wanted the boy for herself. However, only some of that rang true. The only threat to them was fear and reticence. Emily showed the signs of something he had not seen in his little girl. He wanted to see his daughter at last happy. Naturally, he wanted to know the young man's intentions before helping, not to mention sacrificing her parent's happiness. If such came to pass, Margaret would adjust. But again, he got ahead of himself. He could barely rein his wandering mind in, before it carried him away, but neither would he allow nature to take her meandering course.

"This here's May-Belle," Stuart leaned against the stall and looked over the haunches of the great black and white cow. "She's the calf's mother," he added with a pat to her rump. The animal turned her large head to look at them. "Mighty thankful to you she is," he said, looking to Joseph assessingly. Stuart paused, feeling out his words in his own mind. "Emily raised her. Her Ma broke her leg two seasons ago. Had to put her down," Stuart found himself explaining, floundering for how else to get back to the subject of his pride and joy.

"Well, I guess she owes two people now," Joseph said, looking back at Stuart already knowing his game. "Emily must have a big heart."

"Yes, she does," Stuart smiled and nodded, looking back to the cow. "She's a fine young woman," his voice sounded tinged with a distant thought unspoken. He continued, gesturing to May-Belle, "It's uncanny really—her ability with animals and such." Turning back to Joseph he took on an easy conversational tone, meant to set the boy at ease with his purpose. "She's saved some of the chicks in the coop. And once when she was little, she took care of a neighbor's dog that took sick, would have meant some of his business if the dog died. Sheep farmer you know. They need the dogs for work. It extends to people too. She's been helping the Howell's with Davie for years." Stuart held back on the finest of Emily's nursing efforts, unsure he should share any information on their housekeeper with him.

"Is that so," Joseph smiled, holding himself carefully aloof and guarding his expression. Inside he grew increasingly eager to learn more.

After a moment of silence that told Stuart more than Joseph knew, Henry clattered into the building bringing Shakes along behind him. The calf lowed, while the boy tugged him along to the stall where his mother stood. The men watched the boy unlatch the stall gate and wrestle Shakes inside. Once inside, the calf no longer fought the boy. Instead, he nudged his mother's underside until he found the meal he looked for. Henry backed out of the stall, wiping his dirty brow with a balled up handkerchief.

"I tol ya I'd set em right," Henry commented, mimicking the older men that worked on the farm. He regarded Joseph, rather carefully.

"Very good, Henry," Stuart nodded to him with a grand smile. He chuckled warmly. "Go see if your Pa needs some help. That's a good lad," he told him, not wishing the loose lipped child near while they spoke. He could stir up a good scandal on the farm. Once the boy went, Stuart returned his attention back to the matter. "Thankful to you for him. We haven't had a new bull on this farm in a long while. I'll need him to sire some new stock from the cows I bought last season," Stuart told him.

"Then I guess your fortunate I happened by," Joseph replied. "As I feel I am, for the opportunity it's given me."

"Yes," Stuart sighed in full agreement. "But understand that I could've afforded the loss a this calf more than the world could've suffered your loss. It was a brave thing you did, Lieutenant, but you must consider those who depend on you first—or will depend on you."

"I feel as though I should apologize," Joseph hung his head, wearing a remorseful smile.

"No—that's not what I meant. If you hadn't come when you did, you wouldn't stand here now," Stuart said, making Joseph a little confused. "Think on what that means," he added, perhaps seeing Joseph's thought process. He failed to mention Emily, but both knew she stood at the center of it.

The men fell silent for a moment, studying May-Belle and Shakes in avoidance of each other's gazes. The cow turned in her stall and faced them, chewing her cud and appearing to wonder why two humans would find interest in her. Her dark doe eyes watched them carefully. She sniffed the air around Joseph and stared at him. The feel of the large gentle eyes made Joseph nervous.

After his efforts last night, he now shared a connection with Emily. Fate bound Emily to him. He hoped to keep it that way. Joseph reached out and touched the wide glistening nose. May-Belle nudged his hand, gentle as a pet dog.

After a warm chuckle, Stuart led the Lieutenant from the line of stalls into the yard outside the milking barn. They walked along, noting the barracks set toward the back and paused to discuss them. Joseph heard the distinct sound of hammering and turned his attention to the eastern border. Several large draft horse carts sat loaded to their tops with hefty amounts of fresh lumber and mason stone. He watched men unload the burden and determined the sounds of construction came from just behind.

The Conrads were endlessly amazing, with their tenacity and adaptability. Mr. Conrad said they would capably rebuild soon, but to see it happen right away astonished him. He admitted knowing the means to deal with a great loss and it should not seem so foreign. He imagined his family would deal with such a disaster in much the same manner.

The men turned toward the construction, perhaps to walk down to where they planned the new barn a space from the old one. Joseph looked up to the southwestern sky. The scene looked dark and ominous, the clouds roiled with a storm. They then emerged onto the lane. The mud splattered with raindrops. Joseph watched little Henry run off toward the pastures.

The Lieutenant was ignorant of the careful observation of three sets of assessing eyes, weighing and measuring him with every move.

"That's him, Rose!" Henrietta Benson gasped acting like a giddy little girl at a dance. "No wonder Mrs. Conrad trussed Emily up so? It wouldn a been right otherwise," she added, as the other young woman joined her at the window. "Ain't he something ta see?" Hettie grinned at Rose. Her dark eyes gleamed with untold delight.

The women stood beside each other, gasping and smiling over what they saw in the lane below. They clucked their tongues and gabbled like chickens, ignoring the young woman that hid there to escape him. It was rare that such a chance came to their farm and they showed it.

Emily tried her hardest to ignore them, lounging in her cushioned chair that was tucked in a corner between her bed and the wall. Until that moment, she appeared adrift in one of her books, knees drawn up with her feet on the cushion. She stared at the page with her eyebrows pinched. She concentrated on the lines of the play, but they ran together making no sense. All that sunk in her head was what came from the housekeepers. Emily peered over the book at them and her mind worked hard on ways to rid of this new menace, which her parents tried to throw her at. She looked back at the page she had read four times already.

"I'll take kindly to being spoken to when I'm right here," Emily said suddenly, in a snappish tone.

"Come ere, Em," Henrietta ordered eagerly. She waved her hand and smiled. "You gotta see," she added when Emily offered a scathing look in response. Hettie's smile died instantaneously.

"I've seen, Hettie," Emily grumbled. She thought they knew that by now. Drawing herself out of her chair, she could still not resist another look, for some reason or another. "You brought us tea in the parlor—remember? It happened just a bit ago." Her tone even snapped at her own ears.

Emily made her way to the window and the fear returned to her body. She watched the housekeepers at her window. Hettie and Rose looked like two stuffed chickens, staring dumbly at the rain and clucking back and forth in giggly whispers. She could not imagine what he did that warranted such behavior, but she imagined that he only stood there. It appeared everyone but her fell madly in love with this man. How could she convince them she felt the opposite? They would think her mad. If she had gone crazy, it was the least of her worries, and least she chose to be.

Joining the maids, Emily scanned the lane. She half expected the same old scene and half expected to see him looking up at her with an arm full of flowers. Instead, she saw her father, walking with the soldier about the outbuildings. The pair stood there discussing something. Her father looked captivated.

"Ain't it somethin? A real soldier!" Hettie's brown eyes twinkled and she smiled at Emily, not knowing the pain and worry the girl felt.

Emily tried to smile in return, but fear boiled up inside her until it was impossible. Rose regarded her with a devilish look in her dark eyes, sensing Emily's feelings. Her black hair framed her pale face like a heart. Despite her sweet feature, Rose was no sweet hearted innocent woman. Rose said many things that made Emily's toes and fingers curl with shock. She imagined with dread the thoughts that ran through the jade's mind.

"Indeed it is," Rose began in her husky voice, wanting to play a game with Emily. Turning away, Rose stepped over to Emily's vanity and straightened it up. "I've not seen such a man before in all my days. Not many like him I'll warrant. What do you think, Em? Could I take um to the loft? Or do you wanna have this turn?"

Emily turned crimson, imagining herself astride the soldier in her hayloft, as they made love. Her eyes glared at Rose for forcing the thought into her mind. How could she begin to fight if they allowed her heart to wander about the idea freely? She pictured the Lieutenant kissing her in their torrid embrace and looked quickly down, hiding her face with a hand to her forehead. She rubbed the ache growing there.

Hettie looked at Emily with concern, furrowing her brow. She could just about see what went on with the younger woman now that she took a moment to look. Having such fun at Emily's stake could only lead to trouble. Emily hung the edge of exploding, but ready to react and in such a manner that no one could predict it. Drawing a deep breath, she could picture the innocent young woman doing just what Rose suggested, just because they expected something else of her.

"Rose—" Hettie hissed, putting a finger up in front of her mouth, trying to stop it before it began.

"What?" Rose straightened to look at them and folded her arms, grinning like she could not tell what her words did. She dropped her act of innocence when Hettie pursed her lips and looked doubtful. "As if she ain't thinking it. Look at her red with it over him," Rose gestured to Emily with roll of her eyes and point of her finger. She swayed her body with much animation, continuing and going back to cleaning the dressing table. "Not that I blame her. I'd let him make me think too—though I'd rather do."

Emily cast a shocked expression, listening to her devious giggling. Emily became outraged that her friend would dare to say such things about her and when she stood right there to hear it. Folding her arms, Emily pushed out her bottom lip in a childish pout and shifted on her feet. She could feel Hettie's eyes on her and she frowned. Emily did not enjoy this in the least. She fought to contain herself, believing the man would leave them soon.

"Don't you pay any attention ta her," Hettie said, annoyed by Rose. She put her arm around Emily's shoulders. "Where I come from we gotta name for the likes a her," she gave a reproving glare to the maid who smiled even deeper, proud as a fat partridge in its coop. "I'd tell you, but it ain't for a lady ta say," Hettie continued, looking back to Emily. The young woman looked at her with that sad owl eyed expression she made when someone trampled her feelings, as if she just lost everything.

Emily's heart swelled with longing, but the need was different now. She could not yet describe it, but it was forming. Emily wanted. She grimaced at the thought of the ideas popping into her mind, but caught herself and tearfully nodded to keep Hettie from examining her too closely. It was becoming apparent what passed. If Hettie saw, she would be mortified.

Looking back to the windows, her eyes burned furiously with unshed tears. While the housekeepers stood there, even if they were her dear friends, she could not cry. Emily stepped between Hettie and the window, keeping the woman's eyes from hers. She knew the whole story ran all over her face, but she would not admit to it. Even now she kept it secret from her heart.

Rose spoke true. Her mind worked on the visitor, if not how she suggested it. Her face was hot with embarrassment. It humiliated her to think that she lost so much control over the stranger, lusting after him like a brazen harlot. She felt his arm around her, an imprint from last night. Would he hold her too him like that again?

Unlatching the window panes, she opened them wide, and allowed the cold breeze to blow in over the casement and cool the hot anger burning her skin. Drawing a deep breath to settle the new emotions that rose inside her, she smelled rain in the air. Another breeze blew and it cooled her suffering. Her fears eased with the Lieutenant out of sight. No matter her inner struggle, she favored him.

Emily thought of her mother and father, attempting to aid the situation along. They had hoped her favor would turn toward another man in much this same manner not so long ago. Evan was her dearest friend, but Emily never loved him. Everyone believed and expected her to. She recalled how they openly planned with the Howell parents, as if it were all but said. No amount of refusal on her part convinced them. When Evan came home a few years ago, before he dashed their hopes by running away with the army, she told them it would never happen. She hated to think she let them plot her future again, after the pains of the previous episode.

Emily could almost see the nightmare before her again. They would tell her what a wonderful young man the Lieutenant was. Then they would say she should think of the future now. It was unwise to play like a girl who would have nothing to claim when the eve of life fell on her. True she was a grown woman, but that did not give them the right to make her choose a course, which merely pleased their designs and not her own. Emily made up her own mind about her future long ago, though she could not recite it, or chase after it if it came her way. What sense was in dreaming of a future she knew would not come? It proved as bad as doing nothing.

Heaving a resigned sigh, Emily saw what they failed to see. Dreaming of a future with this man pleased her a great deal. He pleased her to look at him and he promised fine support. A soldier held a commission and would find a job when he came home from the war. Not many would turn away a war hero. But, there in lie the problem, Lieutenant Maynard had to survive the war to claim her and survival was the most unlikely thing for a man in his position.

"Come on now! Shut them windows. Afore y'all catch your death," Hettie tried to pull her out of the draft and close the windows herself, but only succeeded in shutting off Emily's thoughts.

"Leave me be, Hettie," Emily growled. "It's too warm in here," Emily stubbornly held her ground, using her hip to push Hettie away. She took hold of the sashes.

"At least stand back. He migh see you!" Hettie begged, nervously backing away.

Rose straightened from her cleaning and watched Emily through the mirror of the vanity. She felt it best to stay out of these contests, though she started it and could not help but listen. She felt a little remorse for stirring the pot, but someone had to light a fire under the girl. Miss Emily was falling for the soldier. Giddy at the prospect, she could not wait to see how it would end. Smiling, she knew how it would end. Rose giggled again, cutting the quiet tension between the other women. Hettie gave her a quick glance and looked back to Emily who stood in the window.

"Things'r changing, Hettie Benson," Rose murmured.

"Don't be such a ninny. What's gonna happen if someone sees me?" Emily snapped after Rose spoke. What if she wanted him to see her? Emily wished she could make up her mind. Did she want him or did she hate him? She answered it easily. Both.

"You're watching like a vulture over a kill," Hettie replied outraged by Emily's uncharacteristic actions. "Come away! What will people say? You know they gonna find out. They always do," Hettie whispered her plea to sense, fearing the men would hear them.

"I suppose they'll hear us too!" Emily mocked her thoughts. She acted more like a dog with a cat up a tree. Hettie continued to back away, as if the devil stood before her. "You're ridiculous," Emily said, looking at her defiantly. She turned back to her beloved windows and watched the tree speckled hillside behind the farm buildings. "It's beautiful out there. Isn't it Hettie?" She smiled at the winter fields.

"It sure is, Emily," Hettie said to console her. "That's one good thing bout the North I appreciate. Now come away an let me shut them windows."

"You should appreciate more than that," Emily said. "You'd be dead for freeing the slaves and then running off. At least we in the North have some compassion." Emily turned and lowered onto her window seat feeling badly already about what she carelessly blurted out.

"Some a you do," Hettie said somberly. "But I've met too many that don't," she added sitting beside her. Hettie placed her arm around Emily's shoulders and hugged the young woman to her, sensing her remorse. She knew Emily's emotions lie tattered. She could not begin to control them.

"I'm sorry, Hettie," Emily said, looking to her about to cry again. "I shouldn't a—It'll get better someday."

"At least they ain't won yet!" Hettie kissed Emily's temple forgivingly. Smiling at the side of Emily's somber face, she brushed a stray lock of hair behind her ear. "They ain't ever gonna win."

Emily smiled ruefully, but knew the woman loved her no matter. She had not meant to bring up such horrible memories to threaten her with. In the time Hettie stayed with them, she had taken the role of an older sister or even an aunt to Emily, loving and caring for her no matter her race or bad temper. Hettie deserved Emily's respect. Emily felt disgusted with her behavior. She wished she was like the other girls she knew, so in control even when the situation was not.

In Hettie's eyes, she saw emotions ruled by innocence. Emily never meant to hurt, but lately Emily's tattered heart lashed out furiously. Hettie wished she could do more to ease the transition, but only time and patience would see it through.

The girl leaned onto Hettie's arm and they fell silent, listening to the construction of the new barn and the March wind. The breeze blew in through the open window, icy cold on their backs. Emily parted from her friend to face the open window again, as if called. Laying across the casement, she watched the outbuildings sadly. There was a choice to be made and she just could not decide.

The scent of the fresh air filled her senses, blowing away the hurt and replacing it with something like hope. She could not imagine a sweeter moment, but the thought of the Lieutenant weakened it. She smiled with her lips still pressed together and took a deep breath, feeling the sensations running through her at the thought of his eyes on her again. A heavy sigh escaped her. She could hear Hettie do the same beside her but for different reasons. She smiled deeper, thinking that no one knew what she thought. She could think about it for hours, more excited by the moment.

"Now that's the smell of freedom—sweet free air," Hettie closed her eyes smiling, as she turned beside Emily to look out at the sky. Opening her eyes, she followed the young woman's gaze to the buildings hidden behind the lane of trees. "They'll be comin out there soon. We should back up—or he'll think you like him," Hettie whispered, petting the girl's hair.

As if beckoned by Hettie's speech, the door of the storeroom opened and Stuart Conrad, followed by his guest, came into view in the lane behind the fence. Emily's heart froze at the sight of Joseph, carrying his hat under his arm and listening closely to every word her father spoke. She wanted to watch him without her moods to ruin the moment, just to know and decide.

"Your mother said dinner is ready," Blythe's voice entered the room from the hall. She stepped into the room with a dusting rag in one hand and a smile on her face. She looked at all their faces curiously.

Emily hardly believed she sat there hours, trying to read and listening to the women chat. She found her anger renewed at being bossed about, still not having her answer and no more time to contemplate it. She had not put a thought to the fact that if Evan did not marry her they would seek a replacement. Emily refused to blindly do what her parents expected. She wanted to make her choice. Her eyes followed the men, as they entered the lane to walk toward the construction. What could she do?

Rising and leaning out the window, Emily called down to her father, "You better come inside. It looks like the rain is coming! And, you know how it affects your leg."

Stuart laughed and shook his head. He nodded and raised his cane to her in acknowledgment. He walked towards the house with Joseph behind him. Joseph would have to wait until another time to see the rest of the farm. He looked up to her, flashing his grin and nodding. Emily forced a smile, staring sternly back. She reached for the window sashes and closed them sharply. The room behind was silent with no answer from the maids. She could feel their eyes on her. A brilliant blush flushed her cheeks. She flipped the latch and thought about her actions and her feelings. Why could she not decide if she hated him or if she fell in love with him?

"He'll go right by the kitchen and put the new girls into a fit," Hettie said worriedly, jumping up to hurry downstairs.

"He's already done that," Emily said.

Hettie touched her arm and brought Emily's gaze to hers. She smiled knowingly and tried to show her sympathy.

Shifting her gaze toward the door and back, Emily pursed her lips and said, "I better go. Rose needs to do her work." Emily would rather hide there, but couldn't. She was expected at dinner.

With the air of a prisoner facing execution, Emily returned to the first floor. She thought of how easily the man turned her upside down. She had not asked for this sort of change. It was something she had no resources to deal with or fight. As long as her parents worked to help him, she would reject his attempts. He could ogle her all he wanted, ply his charms, but none of it would change her mind. Her mind was made up.

When she reached the last step, Emily came face to face with the source of her torment. Her mood soured even deeper. She felt her throat constrict and her words, as he smiled. Instead of hatred, her body reacted with other urges. Biting her lip to halt the sneer on them, she rallied and thought of something a little cutting to say. Her mind was made up and her body was not going to switch things around.

"Good of you not to keep my father out in the damp," Emily said. The words alone had no blade, but her tone was sharp. Stepping to the floor, she thought to give him something more precise to take with him.

"I wouldn't readily allow such a thing, Miss Emily," Joseph smiled down at her, holding his frame purposely in her way.

"If you'll excuse me, I must check on the new help. It's their first day, and we wish to find the meal palatable. My parents will have to entertain you for now," Emily said mechanically, raw at how he kept her there. He would make her fight a difficult one.

"I'm sorry if I offended you," Joseph said. He detected the bitter tones from earlier still shadowing her voice.

"Not at all," Emily smirked up at him. She tried to route around him and leave him to his own invention. "Excuse me."

"Wait," Joseph stopped her, stepping to block her. While this private moment stood offered them, he knew he must seize it and fix the damage. "I'd appreciate seeing you again, Miss Emily. I most enjoyed your company. I haven't been able to see many ladies since the war. From what I remember—you surpass them all," he nervously tried to explain, offering a sheepish expression. "And I like to enjoy learning more of your brother," he smiled and slightly laughed at his foolishness.

"I apologize the young women don't entertain you often enough. Perhaps they are busy with the war themselves. About my companionship and my brother, ask my father. Now excuse me Lieutenant Maynard," With bitter tones unguarded, and even more bitter words replied, Emily turned away and walked to the kitchen, leaving behind a stunned Union Officer.

Emily did not turn back. She stepped down the hallway past her father, who eyed her wonderingly, pausing to watch her go. He heard her words to the visitor and felt shocked she rejected him so cleanly. Stuart smiled regretfully to his guest and continued to the parlor, holding his arm out for the young man to go with him. He half laughed, to reassure him. His dear Emily took on far too many of her mother's traits.

"Sorry, my dear boy," Stuart chuckled. "Emily is a busy young woman and takes after her mother. She can be very excitable."

"I rather think I angered her earlier when I spoke about your son," Joseph admitted.

"Ah—Michael," he stopped in the middle of the parlor and looked at him sadly. "We are all sensitive about him. As you can imagine, we won't know till the war's over, if we'll ever see him again."

Joseph nodded to him with understanding, "Do extend my apologies."

Stuart smiled and patted his arm.

Until dinner lay on the table, Emily hid herself from all of them. She worried her uneven temper would have another show. Worse, she might apologize for what she said.

The time came all too soon. Standing in the hall, Emily girded herself before entering the dining room. She changed her dress at her mother's appeal and rethought the current selection. Peering around the opening, she could see the table already set and the others waiting.

Entering, she tucked away her feelings and set her eyes on the far wall. Emily tried to think of topics she could participate in without being tweaked. The crystal chandelier sparkled less than modestly from where it hung above the center of the table. Her father bought it for her mother as an anniversary gift, after the gain of a small fortune. His business remained successful since.

Emily felt Joseph's eyes the moment they went to her. He watched her enter and approach the table. She heard his chair slide back and his effort to stand while she found her seat. She kept her gaze from him, instead watching her father seat her mother. Once her mother sat between her father and the guest, her father helped her. She was pleased to find the Lieutenant left her alone.

Joseph swallowed the dryness in his mouth, reseating himself. The family lowered their heads and listened to Stuart while he led the prayer. Joseph took the opportunity to make another study of the daughter. She had changed her gown from the lovely ivory to an exquisite gown of satin rose. He fought to keep his eyes from her, but she looked so stunning he could not help staring. His eyes grazed over the circlet of pearls around her fine thin neck and up over her mink locks, arranged much like he imagined the ancient roman women wore theirs. His eyes lowered to the features of her lovely face, and her blue eyes shone brightly, as she briefly caught his. Joseph quickly smiled at her with a nod, but she barely noticed him and he let his eyes wander to her low neckline. Ivory muslin served to disguise the tempting treasure hidden behind its foggy hues, but he could imagine she looked just as lovely there as the rest of what he saw. Joseph's gaze returned to her beautiful face and he could see she felt it, as they listened to Stuart giving their thanks.

The hue in Emily's cheek heightened, matching her gown. Emily felt exposed under Joseph's scrutiny and trapped like an animal in a cage. He stared at her much too long and too intimately, making her increasingly upset. She could only admit to herself in the secret spaces of her mind at how wonderful it felt to be appreciated, but it frightened her to sit in the midst of a battle for her freedom. She worried that her failure to prevent his trespasses continually invited more and spoke of feelings meant to be secret. Emily felt ashamed. She looked nervously to the fire behind her father's chair, touching her hair. Her ears just caught a minute chuckle from Joseph, and she knew he saw through her. Emily's chin lowered. He probably smiled again, too.

"Hello again, Miss Emily," Joseph tried to draw her eyes back to his, once Stuart completed the prayer.

Emily looked up with wide eyes, forcing herself to relax before she choked and look at him. She reminded herself of her choice.

"Hello Lieutenant," Emily replied to him surprisingly even. "I hope you enjoy your meal. It is our first with the new—cooks," she successfully finished, but would not yet congratulate herself. She would have to get through the entire meal without clawing his eyes out first. If she lunged at him, he probably would take her on the tabletop, not thinking twice.

"You've cooks, as well," Joseph said impressed. "I never would have guessed, Miss Emily."

"We do well with our cows," Emily responded, flicking her eyes to her father who received his meal from Rose. She could see the small smile on the woman's lips. Rose looked to her over her nose, raising an eyebrow. "Don't we, Daddy?"

"Indeed," Stuart said half listening.

"So I see," Joseph said.

Joseph tried to see the situation from a different perspective. Emily, by the propriety of her actions and her nervousness, stood an heiress to a rich and successful dairy on the verge of becoming a virtual empire. They offered her to him. He lowered his head and sat back. He saw their consideration of him in every word. Joseph nearly laughed at how she fought her parents. In fact, the idea turned laughable beyond his strength. He had survived several of the same experiences since coming of age before the war. None of the girls behaved quite like Miss Conrad over it.

At least this time, no one knew his family held claim to part of a very successful law firm out of Baltimore, or that he resided most of the time in a mansion in Frederick. His family came from old money, having left Europe in the generation of his grandfather's grandfather from Scotland.

When he spread his napkin on his lap, Joseph wondered what family would court a condemned man for their daughter's suitor. Yet he could not argue, as he already liked her too well. Emily offered both beauty and personality with defying intelligence. With those items, he was sure to be kept busy. He would have his way. However, time ran out to convince her.

Despite the suspicions of intended courtship hanging over their heads, they ate dinner with a congenial atmosphere. Emily slightly warmed to Joseph's company, aided by her father's dominance of conversation and resolute in her decision. She studied his uniform when he was not looking and listened though they continually spoke of the war.

Emily's eyes moved over her mother. She saw her mother look increasingly worried while they listened to the guest speak. Margaret lifted her eyes and offered Emily a small smile. Emily could see the fears of a mother clearly in her eyes and she no longer wondered at what drove her to try to chase him off. She smiled back amused at the idea that they worked in the same frame of mind. Looking to her father, she watched him smile and speak excitedly, enlivened by this visit. Still, Emily remained unsure of just how to deal with Joseph's flirtations and put down her father's campaign to win him to her side.

Evening soon surrounded them. The time came for Joseph to leave. Emily once again felt sure she would not deal with Joseph ever again. In that moment of farewells, Joseph somehow found a way to request another visit from her father. Carefully, he discovered when the Conrad's would go out and when they would stay at home. In his mind he made a devious plan, in which he could seize on opportunities to find her alone and hunt her without the difficulty of her parents' presence to stop him. Joseph stood inexperienced on such sneaky underhanded quests, but it must run something like military reconnaissance and in that he stood well practiced. Stuart easily accepted his request and invited him back with friendly speech that left her mother shivering with fear. Joseph smiled and shook Stuart's hand.

"Thank you for inviting me tonight, sir. It's been a pleasure to dine with you and your lovely family," Joseph spoke fluidly in silky southern tones. His eyes flicked to Emily and back to her father's face.

Stuart chuckled, "Of course, son, of course. Thank you for humoring an old man, and thank you again for all that you have done for us." Stuart let his hand go and drew himself up proudly. "Do come back if you feel so inclined. I enjoyed your company immensely."

Joseph nodded to him and to each of the ladies in turn. Before another moment, he walked out of the door and left their home. Stuart faced Emily and winked at her before continuing away to his study to read his newspaper, which he found no opportunity to look at that day, yet. Emily looked at the empty closed door thoughtfully and blushed. Her father knew all that went on between her and Joseph, even if she missed it.

Margaret faced her daughter and heaved a heavy sigh. Offering Emily a small smile, she went to her and put her arm around her.

"Come," she said to Emily. "Let's go to the kitchen and have some tea and put this at last behind us." Emily allowed Margaret to lead her away.

Suddenly, Emily stopped her and drew back. She wanted to lick her wounds in private. Going into the kitchen with her mother and the housekeepers would find all matters aired. Emily felt sure she could not endure the revelations she would receive.

"Actually," she began weakly, seeing her mother's surprised expression. "I'm very tired. I think I'll go to bed."

"All right dear. I'll have Hettie bring you a cup in bed then," she smiled, touching her daughter's face and frowning with rejection.

Emily gave her mother a small smile and turned away, unable to explain herself. Mounting the stairs, she escaped to the safety of her room to recover from the horribly stressful day.

Margaret watched her go until she walked out of sight. Sadly, she lowered her head, shaking it with motherly worry. Her daughter's reaction told her that she did not want this man pushed on her anymore than Margaret wanted to agree to allow him to pursue her. Turning away, she stepped to her kitchen.

Holding her hands together in front of her, she entered the bright yellow kitchen smelling the remains of the meal in the air as Rose and Hettie helped the other girls finish the after dinner chores. Smiling at the three new girls, Margaret warmly dismissed them with many thanks. The girls then hurried to gather their belongings and meet their fathers in the back lane to go home. Once they disappeared, she sat on a stool beside the worktable, and allowed her worry to show on her features.

"You all right, Mrs. Conrad?" Rose asked.

Hettie filled the teakettle with water and placed it on the fire, as she and Rose waited for the answer. Straightening from the fire, she looked to Margaret where she sat, crossing her arms and looking hurt.

"I don't know what Mr. Conrad's thinking with this boy," she finally blurted. "Throwing our Emily at his feet like some prize for saving the cows from the fire."

"I don't think that's his intention," Rose said, getting the cups down for the tea.

"No—Rose dear," Margaret sighed. "It is. He said as much himself."

"Mrs. Conrad," Hettie said, stepping back to the table.

"Yes, Hettie dear," Margaret lifted her gaze, smiling slightly at her.

"What does Emily want?"

Margaret scoffed at the idea of thinking Emily held any opinion about it, "She doesn't know what dress she wants to put on in the morning."

"That's not fair," Rose whined.

"No," Margaret said regretfully. "It isn't—but, Emily has been delicate since her brother left us. The poor thing has so few friends—and, she doesn't get out anymore. How can she begin to know what she wants?"

"I think she knows," Hettie said.

"Well—whatever she wants, she does not want Mister Lieutenant Maynard," Margaret said with a warning in her expression. It would prove the way of it, as far as she was concerned.

The women all fell silent no longer wishing to discuss the matter. The silence held with them not knowing what else to talk about. Soon the teakettle whistled and Hettie brought it to the table off the fire, pouring the water into the waiting porcelain brewer. As she prepared their tea, Margaret watched with pursed lips. Her expression tightened making her unapproachable still.

"Bring Emily a cup in her room if you would, Henrietta," Margaret suddenly said in clipped tones.

"Yes Mrs. Conrad," Hettie said softly.

Upstairs in the quiet of her dimly lit room, Emily pictured the Lieutenant disappear into the woods, as on the night they met. Hanging onto the moment for a few last minutes, she stared into the dark. He failed to bid her farewell like last night. Emily crossed her arms and sighed. Her attempts to throw him off worked and it left her dissatisfied.

Emily shook her head at herself and went about her room preparing for bed. She washed her face and hands and brushed her hair before braiding it. As she worked, she tried to keep her mind off Joseph, but each thought turned to him nonetheless, and as weary as she felt, she could not fight it. After undressing and putting on her nightgown, Hettie arrived with a cup of tea mixed with some lemon and honey to soothe her nerves.

Emily crawled into bed and put herself under her comforting blankets, as Hettie set the cup down for her on her nightstand and waited. Taking up the cup, Emily stared at the orangey liquid. The warm smell of the tea rose to her nose, and she found her mind recalling strangely enough, Joseph's scent. It felt just as warm and inviting as the tea.

Hettie watched Emily sit staring at her tea, wondering at what went on in the poor girl's head. Patiently, she waited for Emily to speak first, nearing the bed and then sitting. She folded her hands in her lap and studied her apron as Emily sipped the warm brew, remaining silent. So much happened in such a short time that she felt sure the poor girl felt overwhelmed. It reminded her of her reaction to her sudden match with Isaiah.

Waking Hettie from her quiet reflections, Emily set the cup on the nightstand beside her bed with a clink of porcelain and the spoon on the saucer. Sitting back against the headboard, she reached up and tugged on her long braid, twisting it this way and that, lost in her confused emotions again. With a heavy sigh, she let Hettie know there was a great weight on her heart, and she knew not how to unburden it. Emily suddenly smiled recalling the book she read. Her eyes went to it, resting to the other side of the cup on the stand. This situation proved much ado about nothing.

Rubbing her face, as if trying to rub away the things behind it, Emily assured herself the situation was resolved. No one knew for sure if he would come again. He showed himself a polite man and impulsive by his actions. However, he stood there on leave indefinitely and would leave when sent for by his commander. She should not expect him again, except perhaps when Evan came, which he would eventually, and most likely tomorrow. After that, there was impossibility.

Joseph revealed they just arrived yesterday. Perhaps then, Evan would release her from all of her fears and worries by saying that Lieutenant Maynard neglected to mention a fiancé or worse a wife. Smiling with pride at defeating herself, she looked up to Hettie to speak what lived in her mind, but it fell away when she saw the other woman's knowing gaze tear into her. Emily did not fool herself with these ideas. She hardly wanted him to be married. She wanted him to come and take her away. She wanted to escape to a place where war could no longer touch her life. She imagined a place where he would have become a friend to Evan by other means, and swept her into his arms to make her his wife. Her expression quickly changed to one of agony. Her heart could not sway from it and she realized her decision of the afternoon was made too late, because she regretted it.

"You need ta tell," Hettie finally gave up waiting for Emily to talk to her.

"Where do I begin?" Emily asked with a heavy sigh, exhausted by her fickle thoughts. "I'm not sure what happened since last night," she said before falling silent to look about her old dull room. It should hold more decoration than rested there, but she preferred to keep it stark for now, much like she felt her soul looked. "Should I ask mother about it?"

"Ask mother what?" Margaret said, entering the room suddenly. Her face showed a bizarre mix of warm comfort and cold warning.

"Mamma," Emily breathed and gave a smile of relief. "What am I to do?" She added when Margaret approached them.

Hettie got up from the bed, looking wary of Margaret as Emily's curious words passed between them all. She thought of earlier in the kitchen. Margaret told them her feelings regarding the stranger and it did not look promising for him. Hettie looked at Emily sadly, as she then guarded her expression. The young woman did not know on what trail she embarked and Hettie could not stay to explain.

"Good night, Miss Emily," Hettie said, excusing herself from the room. Her retreat showed just how uncomfortable she felt. "Good night, Mrs. Conrad."

"Good night, Hettie, and thank you," Margaret smiled before turning her attention back to Emily.

When Hettie left, Margaret sat on the bed beside her daughter. She regarded her for a moment before she pressed her to continue. Her little girl turned into a woman while she looked away. She smiled a small and loving smile at her.

"Now, what is this all about?"

"Mamma, why do I feel this way?"

"What way?"

"The Lieutenant's had my head spinning since last night," Emily explained.

Margaret's features darkened and her lips became a tight thin line. So, the evening turned out like she suspected. The devil tempted her daughter. Now he only needed to make his claim and she would leave with him.

Blast Stuart and blast the southern bastard to hell! Margaret thought to herself.

Margaret thought hard, but found no inkling of what to do other than convince her daughter she was a fool and to stop worrying so much about the soldier. He was just a stranger and they knew so little of him. If she wanted to be smart, she should let time prove what kind of man he really was, as time already proved Evan, but because little time existed for them to do so, it was foolish to worry.

"I would not bother thinking of him," Margaret said to her daughter.

The rest of her words followed through with her thoughts. When she finished, Emily felt more confused by her heart and annoyed her mother still hoped for Evan. Nothing Margaret said cleared away her daughter's anxiety over Joseph. Emily looked at her hands while they picked at the blanket over her legs. She thought on what her mother said, but she felt a warring within her at the same time.

"I just—"

"Trust your mother," Margaret said, patting Emily's leg. "Don't think anymore about him. He will return with Evan in a short while I'm sure, and you won't hear anymore of him." She paused to stand and turned the wick key of her lamp until the light nearly went out. Then, she blew it out.

Emily pulled herself down into bed and the blankets up to her chin. She felt frigid inside despite the warmth of her coverlets. She looked unsurely to her mother.

"There now—you go to sleep and it'll all look better tomorrow." Margaret kissed her daughter's forehead then left her to her advice.

Emily felt ice form inside her. She was helplessly pitched back into her mother's manipulations. The fear of what her mother spoke might have some truth, but all things pointed in another direction. Which was worse? Allowing them to force her into marriage with the lascivious Evan or with a man she might love.

Emily's thoughts stopped their dancing about the fears of what desires would bring. While she busily searched for help on a different issue, her other wish had been answered.

VI. Divine Intervention

Joseph left the Conrad farm for the Howell's a short time after nightfall. Evan would wait for news of his visit and dinner. Joseph smiled, riding through the peaceful dark on his black steed with a number three burned into its backside. Emily's eyes flitted about his memory and burrowed into his heart. He would tell Evan what happened with no assumptions before he could figure with his friend what ground he had gained. With all he learned of the Conrads, he also knew they planned on Emily and Evan marrying. He almost laughed, knowing that was not to be the future she enjoyed. Joseph was determined to bring her to Frederick, as his wife.

When Joseph arrived at the Howell farm, the house stood dark and silent. He quietly put his mount in the stall they set aside for his use. Then, he put his saddle and bridle away until tomorrow or the next time he would ride. Joseph patted Manny on his great rump, shutting the stall gate and left the barn. Outside, he found himself looking up to the starry sky. The fresh cool air surrounded him in its peace. He felt the joy of renewed emotions, those he had shut off since the war.

There came no sound for miles except the rush of the wind through the trees and the creek of the stirred fence. Behind him the barn door clattered. Though the silence offered a welcome respite he was glad to enjoy, Joseph's eyed the night warily. At home in Maryland, the distant gunfire could be heard. There in Vermont, he still expected a unit of Rebels to run out and take him prisoner. If there was anything a Union soldier feared more than wounding or death, it came in the shape of a southern war prison.

Joseph lowered his wary gaze from the glittery sky and crossed the frozen mud to the house. He quickly climbed the stairs to the back porch and found the back door unlocked. He entered, as if he lived there for years and took off his Stetson. With the Howell hospitality, he felt at home. If he never met Emily before this moment, he hoped for her to marry into just such a family. However, he was now there to see that changed. He turned to close the door behind him with a satisfied smile.

"Hello, Joseph," he heard a warm voice call to him from the dark.

Startled by the sound, he looked wide eyed, "Mrs. Howell?" His eyes adjusted to the firelight of the kitchen.

"How was dinner, Lieutenant?"

Joseph smiled with relief, taking in the welcoming but tired face of the tiny woman. She smiled at him with her eyes crinkling behind her small round spectacles. "Just fine. Not as good as last night though." She smiled at him, knowing he flattered her. "What are you doing up?" Joseph asked studying her as she rocked by the fire with a blanket over her legs.

"Davie," she sighed. "He's not feeling so well this evening."

Just as she spoke, Joseph heard the telltale cough from the front room. His gaze went to her with compassion, but she looked into the fire with a pained expression. He easily saw she choked off her tears, the same tears she fought daily over her sick son. Evan prepared him before their arrival, explaining that his little brother was a sickly child susceptible to all illness. Joseph lowered his gaze, not knowing how to excuse himself properly, but the kettle whistled low releasing him. He took a single step forward before she stopped him with her words again.

"Did you want any tea? Coffee?" Amanda said, moving for the kettle on the fire.

"No, ma'am," he replied somberly. "I had some before I left."

"Evan went to bed," she added. "He wanted to hear about your dinner with Emily. She's a lovely young woman, Lieutenant," Amanda smiled at him, pouring water into a copper pot.

"Indeed she is," Joseph smiled.

"They think she'll marry my boy someday," Amanda said. "May have been true at one time, but I think they have other aims, despite her mother," she added chuckling.

"That is what they said," Joseph said uncomfortable with this speech.

Amanda placed the kettle on a trivet. She paused, smiling at her little steaming teapot. She got caught in thoughts of long ago, perhaps when Davie was healthful.

"How did you like them?"

"I rather enjoyed their company," Joseph answered.

"Oh—I shouldn't keep you any longer," Amanda said, tipping out some tea into a mug. "You go on up to bed. It's late, and you need to rest so you're strong when you return to your unit."

Joseph smiled at her as she smiled at him with pain still obvious in her eyes. With a nod he continued his way to the stairs in the hall outside the kitchen. As quietly as he could, Joseph made his way upstairs to the room where he slept. Opening the door, he found a candle burning, most likely because of the thoughtful Mrs. Howell. She was a very kind and thoughtful host. Placing her as Evan's mother was difficult in light of what he knew of the man.

Joseph entered the small room, tossing his hat on the bed. He looked around at a loss for what to do next. His mind was distracted by a pair of blue eyes.

"Well?" Evan's voice cut through the quiet.

Joseph turned to see him enter the room, wearing an old dressing gown. His black hair looked a mess. Joseph smiled and continued to take off his coat. He wondered exactly how Evan felt about this Miss Emily Conrad. His friend entered the room with a shuffle and his hands stuffed inside the dressing gown pockets.

"What?" He looked up to him from the chair he set in to remove his boots. "Dinner was lovely. Their cook is good as your ma, but don't you go telling her I said that."

"Forget dinner," Evan smiled, sitting on the twin bed where his officer would sleep. "What happened?" He had been waiting for this moment for a long time and his eagerness was obvious.

"I ravished her in the garden before we sat down to eat," Joseph said, placing his boots on the floor beside his chair. "She's a lovely strumpet, Ev. You were right about the cow thing. Thanks for introducing us."

"Christ be serious," Evan said, never believing a word Joseph spoke.

"I had a good time meeting your friend," Joseph laughed.

"How is Em?"

"She's good—she's real good," Joseph said doubtfully.

"I'm gonna go over tomorrow and see her. I ain't seen her since her brother joined," Evan smiled. He looked dreamy, as he spoke of her.

"I wanted to speak to you about that," Joseph began, looking seriously at Evan. Evan regarded him just as seriously. "About Miss Conrad, Evan. I don't want to step on anyone's toes, but—"

"Oh—that again," Evan said annoyed. "Me an Em are just friends, Joe. Don't you worry. I know what her parents think, but she's like another sister to me. To tell you the truth, I don't think that much about her anymore. She's probably pissed as hell I don't write."

"How could you not?" Joseph said, standing. The image of the Vermont dairy heiress danced behind his eyes. He could see her cat like blue eyes, staring at him with that look of contempt that disguised something he felt sure of.

"Because I don't see her like you," Evan replied, watching his friend's back. He never saw her the way many of the boys looked at her. He grew with her and despite her obvious beauty and charm she became something else to him. "Her mother's gotta be pretty upset."

"Let's not talk about that," Joseph said, showing everything in his expression. Evan snickered. "Tell me something," Joseph turned to say.

"What?"

"What does it take to make someone like that smile at you?" Joseph asked.

"Awe, gees!" Evan exclaimed. "That's easy. She likes flowers like the rest of the women, but—if you really want to get to her. She loves to dance—and I bet she ain't been dancing since the war." After a pause, he added, "I heard you can dance real well. She'd like that."

"Dance?" Joseph rolled the thought over in his mind. He knew many thought him a fine dancer, from a long time ago at the Point. In Baltimore at the Partners' ball the law firm held yearly, he received many compliments to his ability. But where would one go to find a ball around here? "But where?" He said aloud surprising himself.

"Ole Bill Adams has a get together every weekend, as I remember," Evan smiled again, laughing. Raising a brow, he added, "My sisters are gonna be awful upset you won't be taking them."

Evan's three young sisters, ranging in age from fifteen to ten took a fancy to their elder brother's good friend from the moment they arrived. Lauralee the eldest mooned over him the worst. She flirted brazenly at every meal or any opportunity presented her. Evan and Joseph merely smiled, but Evan's father got upset with her antics. Thankfully, she slept soundly now and turned a deaf ear to their planning. Knowing Lauralee, she would burst into a terrible tantrum and run off crying to embarrass them all. Evan dealt with her enough that evening when she discovered that her intended took a fancy to Emily and went to dinner at the Conrad home. Emily was her rival and she hated her for it.

"Then I've all week to plan," Joseph smiled, ignoring the last statement and knowing nothing of the events of the evening in the Howell home.

"Nothing fancy, but I expect we better wear our uniforms, sir."

"It's the best suit I have with me," Joseph said, looking at his jacket speckled with rank bars, badges, and medals.

"It's the only suit you have with you," Evan smirked, and then laughed. "But I think it'll do just fine. Of course your welcome to borrow one a my old ones, or my dad's—that'd be real pretty," Evan added sarcastically.

"Thank you, I'll have enough trouble convincing her without," Joseph replied.

Evan eyed him, "She shove you off already?"

Joseph nodded.

"That's probably just her ma," Evan said. "Let me worry about it. I know what to do." The men looked at each other and slowly smiled. "You better really like this girl, or I'll shoot you myself."

Joseph laughed.

❧

The next day came and Emily found herself without much to do but fall victim to her endless thoughts. Putting her shoes on, she decided she would harvest some of the beautiful blooms from the greenhouse garden on the hill, whether it stood safe from Lieutenant Maynard or not. In a bright spring gown, Emily left the house. She swung a heavy wool cloak on her shoulders and her cap over her hair. The air felt warmer than that of yesterday, she thought, looking over the lane where the snow melted away. She grabbed a basket from the porch with the gloves and garden shears inside. Then, she walked down the stairs and behind the fence where the outbuildings sat lined up one after another. Stepping between the milking houses, she followed the worn dirt path towards the pasture.

The sun hung high above, spreading its warming rays over her. She held a sense of comfort with the light that shone down. This day promised peace, unlike the tumultuousness of the past few. Her mother was right. Matters turned out better after a good night's rest. Her worries had melted to nothing. When this lieutenant left, she would forget him and life would go on as before.

Cresting the hill the garden and greenhouse rested on, Emily stopped to peer over the pastures of the farm. The garden looked beautiful and peaceful despite the winter covering it. Listening to the quiet, she could hear the birds sing to each other. A breeze swept through the fields, bending the tall uncut winter grass. She took a deep breath and turned on her way. It was no good to stand there while work needed doing and she could occupy her mind. The temperature felt still too cool to stay out for long and her cloak already lost its warmth.

Emily soon rounded a tall holly hedge her ancestor groomed into a solid wall around the garden. In the center, a marble bench sat lonely beneath the great oak tree. She had climbed the tree with her brother as children, when her mother gardened below. Passing it by, she walked the narrow pathway, reaching the fogged windows of the glass building and opening the door. Emily entered the hothouse and placed the basket on the workbench. Bending all her attention to the task, she would try her best not to think anymore of yesterday.

The daffodils bloomed in the warmer environment earlier than they would in the outdoor garden. Their colorful blossoms posed a welcome sight to her eyes. However, she could not escape thoughts of Joseph. Though he went away last night, he haunted her just the same. Emily then reminded herself that if he returned. He came to see her father about the cows, not the farm girl he sired.

Taking the long shears in her hand, Emily started towards a cluster that promised some nice cuttings for the dining room. The yellow color would compliment the gold wood and olive velvet that decorated that room. Emily selected her blooms carefully. Her scissors cut carefully and she allowed the delicate blooms to fall to the bed. When a good amount lie cut, she picked them up and turned to put them in the deep wide basket she brought with her.

When she turned to select more, Emily found herself face to face with a dark clad figure, standing in the doorway. He closed the door and watched her intently. Emily shivered at the sudden fright it gave her. Recognition slowly set in and the scream in her throat died. She watched the chamois gloves raise to the brim of his hat until he touched it in acknowledgment of her. Emily swallowed and turned her gaze back to the basket she intended to set aside before he interrupted her efforts.

"Such a rare flower to find in a hothouse." He drawled, making her shiver again.

"What are you doing here?" Emily asked, looking sidelong. She was surprised at her sharpness, considering how her body felt.

Emily swallowed, thinking she spoke too harshly again, taking in his reproving slanted smile. Shaking off the feelings he filled her with, she neatly arranged the daffodil in the basket and turned away from him. If she allowed him to know he upset her, he would never go away. As she arranged the flowers to prevent them from getting bruised, she could see him moving closer and her body pulsed with fear.

"I wanted to see you," Joseph drawled.

"You should have asked at the house," Emily replied irritably. "There are things you just don't do. Like waltzing into a lady's flower garden and greenhouse while she's alone—and you're alone," Emily's continued, lifting her eyes to his face as she spoke. The sight of him made her choke on her words.

"I apologize," Joseph said, removing his hat. "I just wanted to ask if you'd go with me to Mr. Adams's event this weekend."

"Mr. Adam's," Emily said, swallowing. She knew the friendly politician nearly her whole life and attended many of his affairs. Since the war, that all changed.

There existed only a few able men to go around. "How did you know about Mr. Adams?" She asked suspiciously. *Damn you, Evan.*

"Second Lieutenant Howell, Miss," Joseph cleared his throat and looked down at his hands where he spun his hat nervously. He looked over his nose at her shyly, laughing and stilling himself.

"Well," Emily said, turning away to the flowers and brandishing the shears like a weapon. "You really shouldn't ask me. It'd be proper of you to ask my father."

"I want to know if you'd like to go, Miss Emily. I'll ask your pa when I'm sure you will," Joseph stepped around the potted plants and followed her to the row of white blooms she worked intent on.

"I like to dance," Emily heard herself say and looked up to his hopeful face. "I haven't danced in ages," she unnecessarily added, knowing it would only invite further advances on his part, but she could not stop.

Emily could remember all the young men that used to attend the dances in the town hall, or the church gatherings on Saturdays, but none could have begun to compare with the man standing before her now. Reminding herself not to react so hastily, she thought of how long it had been since she enjoyed any of those events, but tried not to allow her heart its way. With all the young men her age gone to war, there was no fun. The Lieutenant was simply available, and that explained the enticement. Of course, that stood apart from his stature, his fine cut uniform, broad shoulders, dark handsome eyes, southern accent, and his other well cut features too many to count. Lowering her eyes she blushed unable to stop her thoughts.

"I will go ask Mr. Conrad then," Joseph said, turning to go.

Joseph walked away without wishing her good bye. Emily followed him with her eyes, almost praying that he would not return and that he merely tried to see how easy it would be to have her. He acted so polite and proper before, but now he showed a much less cultured side. She wondered what happened since the night before and what she did to signal him to these means. Or perhaps, he simply no longer felt the need to act like a gentleman while they stood alone. It was more like Evan to do such a thing. She suddenly felt cold, seeing her friend's work all over the incident.

"Good bye, Lieutenant Maynard," she spoke, wearing a half angry smile and offering her icy tones unguarded.

"I'll see you when you return from your gardening, ma'am. Evan and his father are visiting for lunch and they brought me along," Joseph turned to say, wiping the smirk from her face. "I look forward to dining with you again," he added suggestively. "I hope that you do as well."

With that said, Joseph turned and continued to the door. He wore a triumphant grin on his face, but he knew he stood far from victory. Emily would act difficult just when she offered him an easier time of it. He placed his Stetson back on his head and strode out of the glass room with such a confident gate that he appeared arrogant. Talking with Evan had helped immensely.

Now all that lie in his way came in the guise of her wonderful father. Joseph would have to ask Stuart right away and before Evan or Mr. Howell mentioned the gathering. Mrs. Conrad would surely suggest Evan take Emily with him instead, if that happened. His friend would be unable to deny them. He almost feared to do otherwise.

Emily stood in the glass enclosure frozen. She still felt a little confused, but she thought she fared more favorably than the day before, not that her mother would see it that way. Her mother wanted her to forget about this man and refuse his advances at every turn. However, when he came around, she acted just the opposite. Despite her mother's attempts to the contrary, Emily continued to weigh and measure the options.

The fact that Evan brought the man home with him on leave, spoke of how well he thought of him. He was obviously a good friend, probably from school. If Evan thought so much of him, he would be worth knowing. Emily still doubted that reasoning, but her body was bending her mind to it already. She just hoped Evan knew what he was doing by helping him.

Emily found the ground pressing up from under her feet again, looking about as if she just woke from a late afternoon nap. She returned to the task that she set out for. When all was finished with her chore, she returned to the main house. She desperately hoped they would have gone by then. Unfortunately, her task had taken little time and it remained well before noon. She knew better than to assume the Howells came to only say hello and go away again. Unless something came up, they would sit in the parlor taking tea and waiting for lunch. No escape from Joseph Maynard would come that day. Echoing her fears, she heard their laughter muffled by the door and walls of her once safe home.

Emily glared at the closed door, setting the shears and gloves on the porch rail. She kicked her boots off just inside. Emily quickly ducked inside the kitchen with her treasures to place them in suitable vases. She meant to avoid the presence threatening her from the parlor. As she entered, she saw Jo-Hanna and Blythe busily cook the noon meal for the workers and the family with their guests. Emily patted little Jo on the head as she passed and went to the sink to arrange her fresh flowers.

"Get away from there," Hettie entered after likely delivering the tea. She shooed Emily away from her task. "Leave that t'me. You got guests."

"Father has guests, not me." Emily retreated to where Jo-Hanna rolled dough for biscuits. She took a white flower from her apron pocket and handed it to her. "I picked this one special for you."

Hettie offered Emily a cool expression. Emily looked back at her deviously. Jo-Hanna exclaimed with delight and offered Emily a big hug from her little arms. Emily patted her head and hugged her back. She took to the little girl so quickly and easily that she wondered how she managed to reject Joseph.

Despite the tenderness of the moment and the questions it raised, Hettie continued the task at hand. She told Emily she should go in the parlor with her mother and father. In return, Emily told her that she picked the yellow blooms for her room and if Hettie insisted on doing her work, she could also insist on finding the pale blue vase to put them in. Hettie listened to all of her words, shaking her head and speaking under her breath back to her. Hettie then pulled the flowers from the basket at the sink and prepared them for display. Whatever it took to put this lovesick bird under the foot of her lover, she would do.

"Flowers in your room? You haven't got one pretty thing in that cave up there and now you want flowers," Hettie mumbled. "Men'll make you do some strange things," she added, lifting an eye to her.

"Don't bring that up," Emily told her, crossing her arms. "You asked to do it, Henrietta."

"I was just thinkin you ain't had a bit a color in your room for a longtime," Hettie gave her an innocent look. "Bout time. You should be surrounded in pretty things at your age." She grinned. "Pretty—handsome tall things."

"Shush up—you're not that much older than me," Emily told her. "Why don't you have pretty things?"

"Doan talk to me with your age stuff and you know why, little miss," Hettie corrected her. "Go on with you, now. You got guests. Evan's here and you ain't seen him in a longtime. You should say hello."

"I would if you wouldn't keep bending my ear," Emily snapped at her.

Hettie raised a brow to her and stepped toward the pantry, which Emily also happened to stand in the path of. Looking as though Hettie came at her in anger, Emily turned tail and hurried from the room. She held other aims, but it did make the young woman do as she asked. Hettie smiled and reached out a hand to slap her backside as she went. The young woman took as much of her energy as her infant Ezekiel when she still cared for him.

"Get you gone," Hettie called after her. "Spoiled brat."

Emily slowed her step, giggling still at making Hettie upset with her. She traipsed down the hall, pulling the cap from her head and delaying. The smile on her face felt odd, an expression that she failed to wear too often lately. It felt good, but when she turned into the sitting room it faded away. There she greeted her guests with forced delight, distinctly avoiding Joseph, as much as possible. Then she sat in her seat behind the sofa, safely cloistered by the books and blocked from Joseph's view by her father. Her mother smiled approvingly at her, before turning back to the men. Emily realized she played the wrong cards once again. Fortunately for her, she received a chance to retrace her steps and start again only a moment after she sat.

"Say, Emily," her father drawled with a finger laid next to his mouth. He turned to see her better and opened the view for the Lieutenant. Stuart patted the wood embellishment on the back of the sofa, pushing himself to the edge. "Lieutenant Maynard's informed me that Mr. Adams will throw another of his parties. Why don't you go with the boys?" Emily saw the Lieutenant smile at her. It looked a devious expression after the greenhouse. "It'd be nice for you to get out of the house for a change wouldn't it?"

Emily swallowed. Her eyes flicked from her friend to Joseph. He wasted no time in making his plans known. Though he proved polite, he also acted rather pushy.

"I don't know," Emily said nervously. She looked to Evan who wore a broad smile. "It's been terribly long since I went out—with the lack of gentlemen to dance with the young ladies—I would have to stand out several turns to be fair."

"We won't dance with anyone, but you—" Evan said. He cut off his words when Hettie entered to bring Emily's flowers to the room. She sat the red vase full of the white blooms on the table by the window, picking up the other vase to take away with her. "But, if that beauty there would join us, you may have complaint."

"Never you mind bringin me inta things. I just came ta bring Em's flowers. Stay away from me, Evan Howell.

You're trouble sure as the devil, Evan Howell," Hettie snapped at him.

Evan laughed in return. He could not help but tease the woman. It was the only way he felt at ease in her presence. Every time he looked at her, she reminded him of the way they met. He had never seen anything like it until the war. Not to mention, he thought he knew what she saw when she looked at him.

Hettie's gaze turned from Evan's reproved expression to Emily. She made a small knowing smile, which the young woman quickly returned. Changing her tone and looking to the Conrad elders, Hettie asked if she could bring them anything. When they refused, she excused herself.

"Don't leave, Hettie. I'll be lost without you," Evan called after her. She paused in the archway to glance back at him with an arched eyebrow. Evan smiled at her beautiful face. "Can't you see when a man's in love?"

"Tell it to my husband boy," Hettie said and walked away.

"Don't tease her, Evan. She's busy," Emily said. Unfortunately, the attention returned to her, as soon as she spoke.

"Are you coming or do we have to find Lieutenant Maynard another girl to go with?" Evan asked. His eyes sparkled teasingly.

"Would that be so difficult," Emily said snottily.

"I'm sure one of my sisters wouldn't mind—how about Lauralee sir? She fancies you just fine."

Joseph smiled broadly at the jest, but his eyes showed the hurt at Emily's words.

"Evan," Mr. Howell said low. He shook his head.

Emily looked between the Howells and their boarder. Lauralee seemed a matter of conflict between them. The Howell daughter must like Joseph quite well for her father to disapprove of such a statement. Evan acted unwisely to make light of a family matter so easily before outsiders. Emily smiled at Evan and lifted a brow. How lovely to see the young man found trouble for his manner at last, but it little satisfied.

Evan lowered his chin with a grin. His father put a hand on his shoulder and squeezed, smiling at him.

"Emily?" Her father said.

Emily saw them wait for her response. She stammered, still thinking it over. She could not make the choice, although her mother may help. Emily took a breath, lowering her eyes to the back of the couch and then raised them to Joseph's and Evan's alternately. The Lieutenant pinned her right where she could not wriggle away. What would she do? If she accepted, then she meant to do exactly what her mother warned her to decide against. Ignoring her mother often proved unwise.

"I would be delighted," Emily heard her answer fly out of her mouth like a disembodied voice, before her mind finished calculating the outcomes. Emily wondered if she shared her body with a spirit determined to bring trouble to this house. "Thank you for asking," she added.

"Thank you for accepting our invitation, Miss Emily," Joseph finally spoke, appearing surprised that she accepted, but also pleased. "It honors me to escort you," he added at the sight of her mother's angry eyes.

"Rightly it should," Mr. Howell said. "Ain't a young man in this town that wouldn't kill you for the right you just won."

Emily rolled her eyes. She only accepted because she knew her father would be heartbroken otherwise. The room erupted in laughter at Mr. Howell's words, but Emily and her mother did not join in. Emily looked to the fire lost in her imagination. If she was a chess piece on a board, she had just stepped into the path of the queen. Lifting her eyes, she saw Joseph, watch her. He smiled quizzically in return, confused by her demeanor. Emily's mouth curled uncontrolled. She would have laughed, but Hettie appeared in the archway, stealing the moment and saving her. Her eyes lowered and she bit her lip to disguise their exchange from her friend. His attentiveness pleasantly surprised her.

"Lunch is ready, Mr. Conrad—when you are." Her voice took the silence.

Thanks to the grace of timing, Margaret held onto her reputation as a hospitable even tempered woman. Although, all present exchanged nervous glances, awaiting the opposite in that moment. She felt her husband's hand on her back. The gesture momentarily stayed her, but not for long. She would make her anger known to them before the day was out.

Despite the Conrad matriarch, lunch proved a more pleasant experience in comparison to dinner. Emily sat beside Evan and the Lieutenant at the end of the table in their son's seat. Emily spoke a great deal about her brother with Evan and what happened away at the war with them, ignoring Joseph. Lieutenant Maynard sat occupied by her husband and Mr. Howell, until Stuart joined the conversation with his daughter's.

Margaret ate her meal quietly watching, joining only when her husband or someone prompted. She kept her answers short or her mouth full. She watched the Lieutenant seek out another opportunity to chase her daughter and use Evan to help. When that occurred, Margaret's stomach turned over and her meal became unpalatable. She sipped her tea cautiously and took small bites of the displeasing food. She could only bide her time until the perfect moment came to put an end to it.

Margaret's eyes trailed to Joseph several times, while she calculated ways of ridding of him. Her efforts must heed caution and hide behind a mask of hospitality. She tore her gaze away, smiled and nodded yes without skipping a breath.

Upon one of Margaret's lingering and searching stares, Joseph felt her eyes. Everyone else was involved in their own topics and he sat back to relax from the banter and the filling meal. When his eyes locked on Margaret's, he clearly saw disfavor. Offering a meek smile, he received a quick sharp one in return.

Joseph was still confused by her hatred, having done nothing inexcusable. It seemed so out of place after he helped with the fire. Joseph's eyes flicked to Emily, while she laughed at something Evan said. Looking at her lovely smiling face, he wondered if perhaps Margaret fell under the impression that he posed an impolite threat to her daughter's future. The only questionable action he could think to have done happened only a few hours ago. Unless Emily told her and he doubted she had found chance to yet, there was no reason for her manner.

Throwing his napkin down onto the table, he drew a deep breath to steady the anger that rose within him. His intentions were not to make Emily's life difficult. However, he saw from the guarded exchanges and Emily's own hesitating behavior, his presence did. Looking toward Margaret, who pretended to sip her tea and listen as her husband discussed a matter with his longtime friend Mr. Howell, Joseph decided to play her game.

"I've heard from a very reliable source that you're an excellent quilt maker, Mrs. Conrad," Joseph began, attracting the attention of all at the table. So, they saw it too.

Margaret paused, caught off guard by his sudden attention to her. She sat with her teacup partially drawn to her lips. She quickly drew a sip and then placed the cup back down with a falsely pleased and astounded look. Wavering between nervousness and her true feelings for the boy, she set her hand on the table and felt the lacy cloth draped over it. She tried to smile at him, as best as she could manage. She only held his gaze for a moment, unable to bear it more. Stammering, she pressed her hands together in her lap and dreamed up a humble reply.

"I'm a fair hand at it," she finally said.

"Fair hand, Mamma? You won at the fair last year. It wasn't even your best work," Emily said with sarcasm.

"I merely meant to be gracious, Emily dear," she smiled at her daughter's question, but her eyes belied deeper anger. Emily exchanged wary glances with Evan. After a pause, Margaret added, "How came you to ask?"

"Mrs. Howell mentioned it in passing," Joseph replied. He looked about the table at all their faces. Evan flicked his eyes to him, shaking his head to make him stop.

"Oh—" Margaret said, feeling most curious to why they would speak about her. "Amanda is so sweet."

"My mother is a fair hand at it as well—we discussed my family last night and got on the subject," Joseph continued. "She made me the blanket I keep while I am with the Potomac," He added, touching the napkin he set on the table next to his empty plate. He wore a triumphant grin.

"You don' say?" Stuart drawled with a humph. "You haven't told us about your family. What—"

"Stuart dear," Margaret smiled at him. "Let's go back to the music room and let the housekeepers clear the table."

"Actually, ma'am," Evan said, rising to his feet. It was not yet time to reveal the story of Joseph to them. "We have to go. Ma needs help today. Davie weren't feeling so good this morning."

"Send our best to Mrs. Howell," Margaret said, rising from her seat with a true smile of triumph.

Emily looked worriedly at Evan, standing tall beside her. Lowering her eyes to the table with an expression of disappointment, she caught sight of Joseph and their eyes met. He offered her a wavering smile, but she did not respond in kind. Just looking at him made her stomach twist and the heat of her body rise. Flicking her eyes from him, she watched her mother successfully remove the guests from the house. She felt both embarrassed and angry. She wanted to spend more time with her friend Evan and not see him treated like some common pestilence because of the company he kept.

"I will see you soon," Evan turned to her. He took her hand and squeezed it. Then, he leaned down and kissed her cheek. "I'm glad you're coming with us. I miss the old days."

"Then you should write to me," Emily smiled up at him. "Thank you for asking me," she added.

Joseph smiled, "It is my pleasure, Miss Emily. Truly."

"I'm sure," Emily said a bit coldly.

"Thank you for coming," Stuart said to Mr. Howell, cutting off the conversation between the young people. He smiled, but his face soon lined with the worries of displeasure.

Emily lowered her eyes from Evan and Joseph. She felt her mother's angry gaze bore into her. Much would be discussed after the guests left. She saw her father and Mr. Howell shake hands and grin at each other in farewell. Evan touched her shoulder consolingly and turned away giving her a small comforting smile. She wondered where the hugs were that they so often shared.

The room soon emptied and Emily sat alone in the dining room, waiting for her mother to reprimand her behavior. However, Margaret merely leveled a cross glance at her and walked out, following her husband to the door with the guests. While Emily remained at the table gathering herself, Blythe entered to clear away the dishes.

Emily watched the doll girl enter. She went to work diligently. In Blythe, Emily saw what her mother wished her to be. Emily shut her eyes to keep them from filling with tears at the pain the thought gave her. She almost wished Evan stayed away and that her life remained a miserable existence, as before the fire. Shaking her head regretfully, she did not see Blythe eye her, going warily about her duties. Emily looked up and the girl glanced away from her quickly, piling the plates together, scraping the scraps onto one. Emily glared at her, but she would not take her frustrations out on the girl. Instead, she stood from her seat and escaped through the narrow door to the kitchen. Hettie would help, if anyone could.

"Mamma is angry with me," Emily said, stepping to the table where Hettie cleaned a chicken for dinner. "Is that the rooster?"

"Your Mamma done miss you already," Hettie said. She smiled at the second question, answering the first with wisdom beyond understanding.

"What does that mean?" Emily demanded

"The time comes when a young woman and a young man meet and want to come together," Hettie stopped and looked at her seriously, concentrating on her work. "It's obvious that time done come for you—so, your Mamma gonna miss you."

"You've married me to him already," Emily said, gaping with wide eyes. Her frustration turned to anger.

"No—not yet," Hettie smiled deviously. "You forget he's a soldier. Maybe after the war, but not now," Hettie continued then returned to her work.

"I'm only going to a dance," Emily whined.

"Mmmm—I don't know bout that," Hettie smiled nostalgically. "Bodies close—I saw that look in his eye."

"Don't!" Emily said, throwing herself down onto a stool. "Please—I can hardly keep my head about this."

"Well—sounds ta me like Miss Emily is in love," Hettie teased, laughing. "But don't worry darlin—those big hoop skirts a yurs'll keep him far enough away."

"Oh—Henrietta please," Emily said, after laying her head on the table.

"What?" Hettie looked at her seriously. "What's such a problem with this? If you like the boy—then like him."

"I don't even know him," Emily grumbled, sitting up.

"You know how he makes you feel," Hettie said, flicking sticky feathers off her fingers. "I seen the way you look at him when you don't think anyone'll notice."

"You're never around," Emily challenged.

"You seem to think so," Hettie replied. "It only takes a moment to see it in your little face."

"Shut your mouth," Emily said, gasping.

"I won't," Hettie said, placing the chicken carcass down on the table. "Emily, look. Honey, you ain't got the time to figure this out by playing games. Let him show his interest and let him get to know you. By the time he leaves, then you'll know."

Emily looked at her blankly, holding in all the emotions that stormed within her. She begged for change, but she meant something else. Perhaps she should have explained specifically in her prayers. Emily closed her eyes, but she saw only the Lieutenant. His eyes looked at her seeing all that she tried to hide from everyone. She asked for something to change her dull existence. It was anything but dull now. Hugging herself, she sat on her stool to think over Hettie's advice. Looking up at the older woman, Emily could see she already assessed the impact of her words.

"Well?" Hettie almost snapped.

"I'll wait until the dance," Emily said softly.

"You'll see him before that," Hettie grinned. "He likes you."

"He—where?"

"I don' know," Hettie hollered. "I ain't Lieutenant Maynard." She fell silent, picking harshly at the skin of the chicken. "But if I was—I'd figure out when you gonna be in the garden—alone."

"In the garden?" Emily said with fright. She looked at Hettie wide-eyed, imagining him coming into the garden like that morning, but with bad intentions on his mind. "Don't say such things. You didn't see how he looked at me." She pictured him claiming her in the greenhouse.

"Yes, I did," Hettie said distantly. "Oh—this is gonna be fun."

"Fun?" Emily said horrified, as images of him ravishing her and her allowing him to do it played out in her mind. "How can you call this fun? I feel sick," she said turning pale.

Hettie looked up at her owl like eyes and laughed. It already was too much fun.

The night of Mr. Adams' weekly dance came after one rapid but empty day. The time went without any side instances to affect matters more. Emily remained close to the house, helping her mother with her quilting and beginning one of her own. Between, she unpacked her old orchid hue ball gown and tried to fix it up for the dance. She barely found enough time to complete the dress and put the last touches on it in the afternoon of the same day she would go.

While evening fell, Emily stood in her undergarments eyeing her work on the gown with great disappointment.

No amount of Hettie's assurances could make her feel it good enough to wear out. Nonetheless, she only owned that dress. Hettie helped her to put it on over her petticoats before the men arrived. Once laced and buttoned up, Emily stood in front of the mirror gazing at herself. Emily was nervous her neckline plunged too revealingly. She tugged at it to draw it up and Hettie tsked, shaking her head in annoyance. She delayed for so long that in the end, she still stood upstairs when Evan and Joseph arrived to escort her to the dance.

"It's fine, little girl." Hettie grabbed up her hairpins and then grabbed her hand to draw her over to the vanity. "They're waitin on you."

"I'm sorry—I'm so nervous," Emily said, looking frightened.

"Your daddy's goin with you," Hettie said, looking at her in the mirror as she sat down. "You don't need to be afraid." She then braided and looped up Emily's hair. "Evan will be there," she added when Emily lowered her gaze and remained silent as Hettie worked. "He can't touch you with both them watching. For all the bad he is, Evan'd never let anything bad happen to you."

"I know," Emily said. "I'm afraid for other reasons."

"Sh—you look lovely," Hettie smiled.

Emily smiled back at her through the mirror. She did not have the heart to reveal her true fears. Instead she patiently waited for Hettie to complete her task and allow her to go downstairs to embark on an evening of distressing celebrations. Guarding her concerns, she did not want to speak of the matter any longer. It seemed that no one could understand what went on within her.

"That's why I'm afraid."

Hettie stared back at Emily through the mirror, understanding without another word.

Soon, the beautiful Miss Conrad finished her preparations and descended the stairs to join her father and other escorts in the parlor. When she came down, her father led the other men out to greet her. She smiled down at him, keeping her eyes from the others. Stuart smiled back at her with such pride that he made her blush. Without her brother to chaperone her with the young men, Stuart would take over the duty.

"You look absolutely lovely, my little girl," Stuart said. "I wish your mother felt better—she saw how hard you worked on your dress."

Joseph could not have said it better himself. He stood at the base of the stairs, feeling awkward as she descended like an angel from heaven to their lowly world. Emily humbled them all by her presence, leaving each man awed with her unearthly beauty. Joseph lowered his eyes rethinking his invitation. How could he expect to hold such a feral entity to him?

"Thank you, Daddy," Emily said sweetly, shaking Joseph from his thoughts.

If only Emily knew how similarly she made Joseph feel.

"Am I ever glad I came home," Evan said, drawing her eyes to him.

Emily smiled at him lowering her eyes self consciously. They remained silent for a moment looking at her and she continued down the steps to her father. Standing beside him, she felt safe and protected. With many thoughts rambling about her mind, she noticed that Joseph had yet to speak to her. Peering around her father's shoulder she coyly looked to him and found his eyes where they usually looked since their meeting.

"Well—shall we start out?" Stuart said, while Joseph smiled at Emily, and she shyly looked away from him. "Lieutenant," Stuart said. "Be so kind as to help Emily with her things."

Stuart smiled, drawing his daughter out from his side and passing her over to the Lieutenant. Joseph smiled down at her as she looked up at him, shyly complying with her father's request. Joseph gathered her cloak and other items, as Evan swept in to help. While Joseph fixed her cloak on her shoulders, Evan handed her one glove at a time, followed by a mink fur muff.

"You are a sight, Miss Emily," Evan said. "I'd nearly forgotten."

The four of them soon left the house together, making their way across the yard to the Howell carriage awaiting them there. Jackson waved to them from the driver's seat and climbed down to open the door for his passengers. He winked and smiled at Stuart who stepped to the side watching the young people climb into the leather interior. Both fathers could only watch with the pride such a position warranted. Though they long planned to see their children bonded by marriage, this event presented a wonderful result also. Emily had brought a great deal of joy to both families. If she planed to live her life with Joseph, they were behind her.

At that moment, Stuart looked over his shoulder back to the home he made for his family with the sweat of his own labors. In the second story window of his bedroom, he could see the shadowy form of his bride. She stood there, staring down at them. Raising a hand to bid farewell for the evening, he watched her back away. Stuart lowered his eyes back to the moment and thought about what went on between him and Margaret. He regretted having to oppose his wife in this, but he could not justify denying the joy of his life her own happiness. Margaret would adjust to Emily's maturity eventually, but she needed to allow her to make her own decisions now. Heaving a sigh, he knew Margaret would not be satisfied unless she had control over all parts of their life.

With the boys and Emily loaded into the carriage, Stuart and Jackson climbed onto the driver bench to leave them to their own cares. Inside the carriage, wrapped tightly in a warm cloak with a muff for her small hands to keep warm, Emily kept silent. She watched the light of the swinging lantern dance around the leather interior and felt the warm coals in the brazier beneath her feat. In her ears, the low murmur of Evan and Joseph's conversation buzzed. They spoke to each other about past dances Evan attended years ago. She heard little of what they said, trying to calm herself. Joseph's scent surrounded her, and the closeness of his body to her own made it difficult to focus on anything else but him.

Suddenly caught up in his presence and the effects it acted on her, Emily shivered. Thankfully, the weather remained icy cold in the evenings and they would think her shivering from the cold. Joseph quickly responded and adjusted her cloak around her. Unfortunately, while he tried to make her warm again, he also gave his undivided attention. Her eyes flicked to his face, widening and then over to Evan's questioningly. Evan's assuring smile little eased her fears, especially when Joseph took a blanket and spread it over their legs.

"Is that better?" Joseph asked, leaning close to her.

Emily pressed herself in the corner away from him, trying to replace the space between them. "Thank you," she meekly replied, not meaning it.

"Hey, Em," Evan started. "My sister Lauralee has a crush on Joe here. She wasn't happy when she heard you accepted his invitation to Adams' dance tonight."

Joseph released a weighty sigh and sat back with a smiling grimace on his face. Lauralee was but a child. Evan found teasing Joseph about his sisters an amusing game, whereas he never mentioned Miss Conrad in such a manner. His eyes returned to her when she did not reply, half smiling and half embarrassed by his subordinate's tale.

"You don't say," she murmured in response. "Maybe you should have brought her along."

"Yeah, dad would have spit nails," Evan ran his finger over the cushion by his head. He smiled at Emily. "So now that we're alone," Evan said after a pause, gaining a devious expression to his features. "What do you really think of my lieutenant?"

Emily looked down at the empty space next to Evan. She did not know how to answer that question without causing things she did not wish to happen. She could distinctly feel Joseph's leg pressed to hers through the layers of petticoats and skirts she wore. Her cheeks burned and she thanked the fates for the relative darkness in which they rode.

"I don' think she's enough experience of me to decide that yet, Second Lieutenant," Joseph replied before she could.

Emily half laughed, "I like you well enough so far, Lieutenant."

Emily reluctantly looked to Joseph, but could not hold his gaze. His smile devastated her even in the dull lantern light. Holding her breath, she waited for Evan to continue, but he did not. Instead, he sat back and looked at them with a scheming smirk. Emily turned her eyes away unable to stand it any longer and peered out the tiny window nearest her.

"Do you think Betty Anne will come tonight?" Evan suddenly asked.

Emily lifted her eyes from the window, "She moved to California last summer, Evan."

"California?" Evan said, scrunching up his face. "Why'd they do that?"

"Her father's business went bust," Emily explained. "They've nothing left."

"That's a shame," Evan said, recalling the promisingly lovely girl they grew up with. He teased her constantly in church every Sunday.

"Penelope Dunworth will come," Emily smiled.

"That knock kneed horse," Evan scoffed, recalling the one young woman that hounded him relentlessly and plain scared him with her terrible appearance. The girl looked the most ungainly creature he ever met with freckles and black hair like frizzy uncombed wire. She was as tall as a tree and just as knobby. He made a face of distaste and Emily giggled. "I don't think that's funny, Emmy."

"I do," Emily said. "Wait till you see her."

When they arrived, people walked the streets in their finest on their way to the Adams' gathering. Emily remained quiet but friendly toward Joseph throughout the rest of the ride. He spoke little as well, unsure of what to say to her. It was a strangely easy fight to gain her for the night, but then again he would see how the evening went. After all, her parents nearly handed her to him and not by her pronouncement. Though he wanted her, he did not want to gain success by such potentially terrible means.

The carriage drove into town, taking the road to the town hall, where they usually housed the dances. Mr. Adams was one of a few prominent townsmen, who held such gatherings, meant to keep morale high in such low times. He always did this, but with the war, Mr. Adams took the extra effort. Despite the lack of men for the women, he still held the dances and even posted the gatherings in town papers some distance away. They eventually became something to see, a parade of who is who in their part of Vermont.

"We're here," Evan said, feeling the carriage lurch to a stop. He pulled back the shade on his window to peer out.

Emily felt her heart beat hard in expectation.

Stuart climbed down behind Jackson and together they helped the young people out of the coach. Stuart still left Emily to the attention of her escort, who stood dashingly at her side, holding her arm in the crook of his. Though Emily stood apart from him, they came across as belonging together, and none who passed missed the chance to take notice of the lovely couple. Jackson wished them an excellent evening and remounted the carriage to return when the night ended, and bring them home.

"What a pretty picture," Evan commented of his friends. He turned to his companions and said, "Shall we then?"

After the carriage drove off, the four stood bleakly on the sidewalk. Slowly, they made their way to the hall, among stares and gasps of appreciation from the attendees already there. The sound of the music surrounded them. The sound awoke their wish for a good time, as they each climbed the stoop outside the building. People poured in by the dozens and some poured out, fanning themselves and wearing lively expressions, which the soldiers thought distant memories.

In the entrance, Emily clung to Joseph's arm, trying to remain with her companions. So many people stood present that it made the trek to the dance hall near impossible in her hoop skirt gown and standing so small of stature. Suddenly, she found the way cleared for them, because of Evan's boisterously greeting the people of his past. She watched their eyes draw to him and subsequently back to where she and Joseph stepped in behind him. They whispered to one another, casting wondering glances in her direction and eyed her dress. Emily felt more than uncomfortable.

"Your dress is lovely," She heard Joseph's voice call to her in a near whisper, as if he could read her thoughts. "I didn't get the opportunity to compliment you before."

"Thank you," Emily murmured still holding aloof.

"Your father said you made it yourself," he added.

"It's just one of my old gowns," Emily explained. "I worked on it a little since it was all I had."

"It's better than any I've seen this evening," he smiled down at her. She watched the crowd, ignoring him. "Perhaps you don't believe that—or perhaps I can only see the beauty wearing it."

Emily could not respond to him. Her eyes searched his with shock playing on her features. Emily never stood in the company of a man so forward with his designs. At least, she never saw it in that manner, or felt affected in such a way as this when it happened.

They crossed the threshold into the dance hall and Joseph lost focus on what he intended to say. He let it go while another distraction drew up to them. An older woman approached intent on Mr. Conrad. She smiled from her noble aged features, framed in steel gray curls drawn up into a pair of rolls on the back of her head, from which draped sparkling ornaments of stars and moons. By her dress and bearing, this woman came of prosperous means.

"Stuart Conrad," she grinned at him brightly. Looking around at all their faces and searchingly behind them, she looked surprised. "Where's Margaret?"

Stuart took hold of her hand and gently chuckled at the question, "Mrs. Murphy—oh, unfortunately Marge developed a headache."

"Oh—poor woman," Mrs. Murphy said not all that sorry. "Too bad she is missing this lovely get together. Mr. Adams asked me to decorate. Do you like it?"

"It's wonderful, Mrs. Murphy," Emily piped up excited.

"Emily," She smiled touching her face. "You are so lovely, my dear. And who is this?" She asked looking to Evan.

"Mr. Howell's son Evan," Stuart explained.

"My, my. I haven't seen you in years, my boy. Such a fine figure you cut in that uniform," she gasped, studying him. "And this young man," she said, spying out Joseph.

"My daughter's escort, Lieutenant Maynard."

"Lieutenant," Mrs. Murphy looked up at him awed. She offered him her hand.

Joseph gracefully accepted the fine digits of the older woman, "It's a pleasure to meet you, ma'am."

"Oh—a southern gentleman," she crooned.

"What say you to a spin around the floor while we talk?" Stuart said, drawing her attention back to him.

"I'd be delighted," Mrs. Murphy warmly accepted.

Stuart took Mrs. Murphy's arm in his and escorted her to the floor. The current song ended followed by applause. Then the bandleader announced the next tune they would play. Evan stepped to Emily's side and looked out over the crowd, adjusting his collar, as if it clamped too tight around his neck. Surrounded by the sounds and motions of the dance, the trio appeared out of place in their silence and stillness. The matter quickly corrected due to a handful of young women and their approach from nearer the band dais. Emily saw them first and quickly touched Evan's arm to send his attention in their direction.

"Penelope Dunworth," Emily whispered teasingly, with a jut of her chin to mark out the raven haired beauty, stalking toward them.

Emily smiled at Evan. He looked like a mouse caught by a cat.

"Evan? Evan Howell?" Penelope smiled from her pale ivory face. Her dark eyes sparkled deviously.

Evan swallowed hard, looking at her. His eyes shifted over her varying companions. He expected the woman to grow up as anything but how she was. Adopting his ease stance, practiced in his military training, he cleared his throat and tried to impress her with his accomplishments since they parted several years ago. Perhaps the young woman still fancied him.

"Second Lieutenant Howell, ma'am."

"I'd a never guessed," Penelope smiled at him, taking his arm in hers and pulling him away with her. "Come dance with me, I insist."

"Excuse me, sir," he saluted Joseph and winked at Emily.

"Behave yourself," Emily whispered.

Joseph saluted back with a smile. Evan always provided good amusement. While he lowered his hand back to his side, he noticed the other women that arrived with Penelope remained, hanging about him and Emily expectantly. Emily smiled and said hello to them, but Joseph kept his gaze away. If Penelope worked so boldly to drag Evan away, these young women would prove no different. He wanted to stay with Emily for every moment that evening. Satisfied with Emily's greetings, the women wandered away, leaving them alone.

"Would you like to dance now?" Joseph finally asked her.

"That's why we came," Emily coldly replied.

"Would you prefer Evan's company?" Joseph faced her with an angered expression.

"No," Emily cut him off with her response. Her expression wavered, almost regretful. "I doubt I could pry him free of his admirers," she added, ending hope that she may want to stay with him.

"No matter," Joseph smiled deviously. "I wouldn't' let you anyhow." If she wanted a game of cat and mouse, she would have her game.

With the game commenced, Joseph took hold of Emily's' hand and guided her to the floor. She took on a sullen expression, as if merely standing with him tortured her. Joseph spun her around to face him, and they took the first stance of the dance before beginning. He felt surprised when she boldly looked up at him. Her wide blue eyes reminded him of a sad puppy.

"I'm not sure I understand you," Emily said to him. The touch of his hand on her body felt like fire, and it ignited something in her that provoked her anger. She had made her choice and she needed to focus on that.

Joseph boldly looked back in her eyes, meeting her challenge, "What's so confusing, Miss Emily?"

"What do you want of me, Lieutenant?" Emily asked, while he led them around the dance floor. She showed surprise at finding him a veteran partner. "Does it amuse you to make me distressed?"

"Your friendship," Joseph replied to her question most seriously.

"Evan wants my friendship. Perhaps I'm mistaken," she said, sounding annoyed this time. "But, it seems you are pursuing more than that."

"Am I?" Joseph challenged her with an intense gaze. She blinked at him unable to respond. Smiling, he added, "Good of you to notice finally."

Emily stared at him, her jaw setting hard.

Stuart Conrad delighted in his time dancing with his partner unlike his daughter. While they swept about the floor, Mrs. Murphy smiled up at him admiringly and he regarded her much the same. They were friends most of their lives, from the time Mr. Paul Murphy brought her there from New York City. Since then, they enjoyed the greatest of respect for each other. Mrs. Murphy often found herself at the center of destructive scandal time and again and it strained many of her relationships. However, Abigail Murphy was no woman to cross and the only woman you wanted at your side in a pinch. She had a noble heart, gave honest advice to those in need and just the right amount of help to allow them to succeed. At that moment, she was what Stuart needed to ease his mind.

"Margaret is Margaret," Stuart said, pained by their discussion of his wife.

"And she doesn't approve of the pursuit of your Emily by this man?" Abigail said, uttering each word precisely and provokingly.

Stuart could not help but laugh. Shaking his head, he smiled at the question. Mrs. Murphy would not miss anything by her great intuitiveness. She saw the entire picture without needing her subject to reveal too much.

"Lieutenant Maynard saved my cows," he told her. "Risked his life for us—he's a fine man for that if you ask me."

Cocking her head to the side with a sigh of doubt, she said, "If you say so Stuart, but you know little else of him."

"I do say so," Stuart insisted, stirred by the way she made him see his wife's difficulty.

"Shouldn't your wife have some say in her own daughter's life?" Abigail asked him. "Perhaps she feels the way she does for a reason—but tell me, what does Emily think of him? She seems like a clever young woman."

"Margaret is acting unreasonable, Mrs. Murphy," Stuart began. "My little Emily," he said then stopped.

Then, his gaze traveled over the shoulders and heads of the other dancers, separating him from his daughter. He could just see her, a good space away in the arms of a virtual stranger that held unknown plans with her. Mrs. Murphy spoke true. They knew little of the Lieutenant, and he offered his daughter like a reward for a few cows. His expression turned tragic, but the glow of pride lit it up as he saw Emily smile up at her partner. Looking back at Mrs. Murphy, he could see her knowing and understanding. She smiled at him and it eased his mind a little. He still held the control and no pretenses existed to any marriage or acts of marriage.

"Emily doesn't know what to think."

Abigail could only laugh at this response. Patting his shoulder, she did not have to say anything. Her laughter only deepened when he guided her toward the younger pair who minded their own business, enjoying themselves oblivious to their intent. As they moved, the other dancers moved aside giddily laughing with them. Then the end of the song came and the dancers separated to applaud the musicians. Stuart stood beside Joseph and smiled up at him, looking down to his daughter who appeared lovelier than ever in her life. The breath of joy brought renewal to her.

Just as Joseph went to speak to Emily again, Stuart tapped his shoulder and begged a dance from his little girl. How could Joseph deny him? Stepping aside, he watched Emily smile at her father, her eyes sparkling with the love for him. Joseph would never deny them the opportunity to spin around the polished wood floor, or any floor they may stand on. To his surprise, as he bowed out, Joseph found himself quickly matched with the woman who spoke with Stuart at their arrival. It came just in time too. He could see the lonely young women, emerging from all corners with their hungry eyes on him, like wolves, closing on a fresh carcass.

Mrs. Murphy looked up at him with her deep brown eyes, as youthful as himself, and offered a small consoling smile. Despite her obvious wealth, she somehow reminded him of Evan's mother and he thought he sensed her good qualities yet undiscovered. Nodding his head, before too much time passed, or the wolves closed in, he greeted her politely. If she kept as close a friendship with Mr. Conrad, as he assumed, he held little to fear from her.

"Good evening, Lieutenant Maynard. I've heard a great deal about you," Mrs. Murphy's speech surprised him, still holding a note of the beauty it once held when she stood nearer Emily's age. "I know I'm little consolation to replace Miss Conrad, but may I keep your attentions on the dance floor for a time? I wouldn't want to see you wrongly distracted by the chattel draping these venerable walls."

"Contrary, ma'am," Joseph grinned. "It's a pleasure to make your acquaintance and have the opportunity to glide along this superb floor with you," Joseph bent at the waist and offered his gloved hand to her.

"Well mannered, Lieutenant," Mrs. Murphy said, showing her surprise openly as she took his hand. "I'm the widow Murphy, Mrs. Murphy, Abigail Murphy, or even just Abigail."

Joseph smiled, "Lieutenant Maynard, ma'am. Army of the Potomac."

As the music began, Joseph gently took her in his care and guided her around the room in the fitting steps. However, the old woman proved she could easily keep up with him, making him feel the fool. She felt as light as many of the women over half her age and held an energy they would die for. Joseph found himself having to adjust to keep up with her.

"I've already heard a great deal about you, as I am sure you will of me—if you spend any time in Vermont. Tongues still wag about me after all this time," Abigail told him, rising another grin, and without losing a single breath.

"Whatever for?" Joseph asked looking back to his dance partner, hardly believing scandal surrounded her.

"Nothing of any matter now," she explained. "Let the stories speak for themselves. Now, I wish to talk about you young man," she changed the subject, poking him in the chest. "Where do you come from? My guess is the South and I know I'm not mistaken. What is a southern boy doing in the Federal Army?"

Joseph laughed heartily, "Nothing will miss you, Mrs. Murphy. I'm from Maryland, and as you know we're split up the middle on who to side with. I picked my side. The union will stand and slavery be damned for it." Joseph colored when he realized he cursed before the matron. He just got so passionate about the war sometimes that he forgot himself. "Forgive me. I should be more careful. Being in the company of men all the time doesn't help my manners."

Mrs. Murphy brushed his apology aside, "You forget whom you are talking to." Joseph nodded to her. "I've three boys, all grown with their own families, and if you want to hear cursing, have a drink with them."

"Still ma'am, it's unbecoming an officer to use such language before ladies," Joseph insisted. "I was raised better than that."

"It's unbecoming a lady also, but I can tell you that I color my meanings, as often as my boys," Mrs. Murphy smiled softly. They remained quiet a moment, as she listened to the band play the music. "I fear we have gotten away from the subject. I wanted to speak to you about Emily."

"Yes, Mrs. Murphy," Joseph said, stiffening slightly. He wondered if he would politely receive orders to end his pursuit. "Please do."

"Oh—Lieutenant. There's no need to worry. I'm not Margaret Conrad," She smiled up at him noting the tension. "As I was about to say, she's the loveliest young woman I've seen in these parts for some time, aside from me of course," Mrs. Murphy began. "Don't you think so?"

"She's the most beautiful woman I've ever seen," Joseph said, looking to where she stood beside her father, while he spoke to one of his friends.

Emily looked enchanting in all her glittering jewels and the orchid dress that flanked her delicate form. Looking at her he found himself lost for words, but not lost for imaginings. He wanted to touch the soft velvety brown tresses, let them fall loose through his fingers and down her back over her shoulders. There never lived another woman in the entire world that could hold his attention for as long and made him feel so unable to control himself.

"Well, you are enraptured, sir," Mrs. Murphy smiled up at him. "She deserves such appreciation. And, well—you seem a proper young man—I wish you well in your pursuit," Mrs. Murphy spoke through his thoughts.

Mrs. Murphy read all she needed in the Lieutenant's eyes. The man proved no threat if she saw correctly. She prided herself on her ability to read people through their expressions. The only threat she found stood against Margaret's plans and rightly so. This young woman must walk her own path, not one her parents staked out for her.

The music and the dance ended. They parted with smiles.

"I'll put a good word in Mr. Conrad's ear—though I can tell you, he likes you already."

"Thank you, ma'am." Joseph bowed. "It has been delightful."

Hearing what he already suspected from the tongue of another only lit the fire he needed to burn his hesitation away. Fate had sent Mrs. Murphy, he wagered. She arrived just in time to make sure he would say all that needed saying at that moment. His strength returned to him and he remembered he was a soldier and a man, not a mooning boy with his first love. He would act gentle, knowing she preferred that, but he would act firm with his intents and never let up an inch until she fell into his arms to stay.

"Thank you for humoring an old woman, now get back to your friend," she said, indicating Emily with a nod of her head. "If I were you, I would not let her out of my sight or reach for long. Many a man would snatch her from you, if they could."

Joseph inclined his head to the venerable widow and she curtsied to him, wearing a warm motherly smile. After straightening, he turned and crossed the floor to where Emily stood. However, several of the young women placed themselves in his path, interrupting his chase, and he could only watch her walk away on her father's arms toward the refreshments. His ears soon filled with there nattering about his uniform and begging information about the war. Looking down to them, he saw how they grinned and fanned themselves. They told him that their brothers or even fathers went away to fight too. Their chatter continued endlessly, and he could only ungraciously grimace back at them. When that failed to prove enough, their rapid chatter followed the subject of dance partners and how a terrible shortage of them lately occurred.

To this point Joseph remained gracious, but he could bare no more from any of them. He would not waste the evening with these flippant females. He held no interest in them. His true desire hung on the arm of her father, just out of his reach. Their conversation bored him to no end, and it fast turned annoying, as they blocked his escape and path to Emily.

"That's unfortunate," Joseph replied to their complaints of no dance partners, lowering his eyes a moment to look at them.

Joseph lifted his gaze back to where Emily stood, but she vanished. His eyes searched the crowd for her, but she successfully eluded him. How could he have spent even one fleeting second with these grisly sows, when a proud treasure waited on the other side? He knew where he wanted to stand and he excused himself under no uncertain terms.

"If you'll please excuse me, I've someone t' return to," Joseph tried to push past, but they closed him in, driving him back. He grew restless to be elsewhere and wore it plain on his face, adjusting his coat instead of knocking them aside.

"You've come with someone?" A tiny and frighteningly porcelain woman said with wide black glass eyes. He looked at each of their faces, as if he saw a nightmare, and he plainly saw their disappointment.

"Do we know her?" Another pressed.

"Indeed," Joseph replied. "Most likely you would know her—Miss Emily Conrad," Joseph told them, keeping his eye out for the young woman he spoke of.

A knot of dancers cleared, and Emily stood behind them with her father. She looked over her shoulder to where her escort stood penned in by a circle of wide skirts. She smiled tauntingly at what she saw. She believed he justly received some of his own medicine back, recalling the way he cornered her in the garden and in the hall of her own home. Joseph nodded to her with a pleading expression, but Emily would not save him for the world. After he cornered her so, she thought it amusing. Turning her attention back to her father's conversation, she left Joseph to fend for himself.

"Oh—Emmy!" The women exclaimed with unfeigned delight in a high pitched squealing voice that cut through Joseph's brain. "She's such a sweet girl—how did you ever meet her?"

"Excuse me," Joseph stepped through them without looking back, holding his time as sacred. "I do have to get back to her now," he added.

"May I beg a moment with you," Evan said, suddenly pulling him aside when he stood within two paces of his goal.

"Not now Second Lieutenant Howell," Joseph said, as Emily walked away attached to her father's arm. She cast him a smile over her shoulder, triumphantly escaping.

"I need you to cover for me, I'm taking Penelope upstairs," Evan whispered. He saw Joseph roll his eyes and look toward Emily. "Em will be here all night," Evan said, looking to her and back to his officer. He missed the desperation Joseph had.

"And all her life," Joseph snapped, brushing past him. "But I may not," he turned back to say. "Do whatever suits you."

Evan opened his mouth to respond, but he remained silent, taking on an injured expression. He had not thought how far Joseph fell for Emily with only a few days between them. Watching him step away toward her, he started to smile. Shaking his head, he walked off in the other direction of the outer hall and Miss Dunworth, who waited for their tryst away from the party. Evan always searched out more entertainment at the expense of the unsuspecting females.

Joseph did not take too long in hunting down Emily. She watched him close in on her and her father. Her expression turned from one of mirth to one of fear. Joseph shyly grinned taking to her side, but switched his expression to benign indifference when her father caught sight of him.

"Ah—Joseph," Stuart smiled. "I've been taking good care of her while they occupied you."

"Thank you, Mr. Conrad."

"Em, why don't you go dance," Stuart took her hand and gave it to Joseph. She looked from her father to the Lieutenant gaping. "We'll be discussing business—very boring stuff," Stuart continued and Joseph drew her away. "Have a good time, dear."

Stuart waved her away and she found no choice but to go with Joseph. Taking her into his hold for another dance, he drew her reluctant gaze to him. Just looking in her eyes made him forget everything, including what he would say to her. Emily set her lips and sighed, slowly blinking her eyes.

"Where did Evan go?"

"To get some air," Joseph replied, covering as he was asked.

"He's going to be a father before he's even married," Emily blurted, already knowing what her friend got up to. "He'll bring shame to his family with his ways. I love him dearly, but—"

Joseph placed a finger over her mouth to silence her. She looked up at him with wide eyes.

"As I was trying to say," Joseph said, but his words soon failed him again when he removed his finger from her full lips and her gaze turned dreamy. Her sapphire eyes sparkled with the light of the chandeliers they danced beneath, like tiny diamonds glinting in the ocean. He laughed and smiled down at her.

Somehow that gaze lit his soul on fire. Joseph looked over the crowd in search of a more intimate place in which to hide and reveal his plans to her. Ducking beneath a staircase and catwalk, he danced her out of sight of her father and anyone who might find fault or care. Releasing her, he scanned the room quickly to feel sure that no one watched them too closely. Her father stood a good distance away, trying to peer above the heads of the revelers crowding the floor, but he did not identify their hiding place. Facing Emily, Joseph listened as the attendees burst into noisy applause. She stood there paying no attention to them, or even him. Instead, she straightened her petticoats and skirts. Smirking, Joseph stepped nearer and she popped her head up to see him. Her little heart shaped face looked solemn and endearing. Joseph sighed and took up her hands.

"Have you ever just known something, though you couldn't put words to it if you tried?" Joseph heard himself ask, as if he stood aside, watching a play of his life.

"Like Christmas presents?" She said still too innocent to understand where he headed with his line of questioning. "You can hardly wait to open your gifts, but you must. You know those gifts aren't what it's about, but it consumes your every thought," she ended her last words slowly.

"Every thought," he reiterated in low husky tones.

"Lieutenant Maynard," she said and then stopped.

"I think I've said all that need be said now," Joseph half smiled.

Emily blinked up at him feeling as though the meaning of this moment still passed her by. Fortunately for her, Joseph meant to define his meaning without question. He took her up into his arms and placed his mouth over hers in a gentle but passion filled embrace. On releasing her, Emily found her eyes drawn to his sensuous mouth, and she saw how he smiled at her reaction. Emily tried to draw a breath, but found it difficult. She licked her lips and turned her eyes up to his.

Now that Joseph found her so surprisingly receptive, he moved in for another embrace. The evening passed in much the same manner with many games of hide and seek from the adults that could end their game. Emily giggled and laughed, enjoying herself too much. She rarely left Joseph's side or the dance floor, even after Evan made his return.

Evan and her father busied themselves with Miss Dunworth and Mrs. Murphy once they found no humor in trying to cut in on Emily and Joseph's fun. The

Lieutenant's ability to duck supervision impressed her, but more impressive proved his dancing. He knew every waltz and reel that played. She wondered how she gained the blessing of this friend, out of all prospects. Emily prayed now that he would never have to leave her.

Stuart watched his daughter with a careful assessing gaze. He could see the smile on her lips and the look in her eyes when she gazed at Joseph. His heart swelled with pain, but a good pain. His youngest babe stood grown to womanhood. Now, it came her time to become the adoring wife of some worthy man. Stuart believed in his heart that she all ready found him. He stood with the other onlookers, watching her spin around the floor and out of his life.

When the revelry ended that night, Joseph parted from Emily regretfully. Until they met again, he would make due with dreams. Gaining pen and paper from an office nearby, he scrawled Emily a note, to meet him in the greenhouse if she would, sometime in the afternoon. Joseph doubted he would see her, but he need try. He knew calling every day would ask questions he could not answer, unless she wanted him to.

In the coach, Joseph offered Emily the folded piece of paper, where only Evan would see.

"Don't read it until you're alone," Joseph smiled.

Emily looked at him questioningly. She took the paper from his hand and looked at it. Her eyes went to Evan for encouragement. He smiled and shook his head.

"Uh-oh," Evan mumbled. He wriggled his brows at her.

"Hardly funny, Second Lieutenant," Joseph drawled. "Unlike you, my interests are purely that of a gentleman."

"Right—of course, sir." Evan replied sarcastically.

"Is there something I should know?" Emily asked, biting her bottom lip and looking at Joseph.

Joseph leveled Evan glare, "A life before now—perhaps I was not so thoughtful at times."

Emily laughed, "We have our faults."

Joseph smiled and kissed her forehead. She would forgive him his transgressions, like only an angel could. He watched her tuck the note away in her clothes.

"No one has more faults than Evan though," Emily suddenly said.

Evan looked at her shocked. His eyes went to his superior officer with anger. He thought he covered for him. Obviously he mistook his friendship. Evan shifted on the leather seat. If his parents discovered his foolishness, he was in for a bad run of it.

"No matter," Emily said. "We love you still, Evan Howell." Joseph and Emily laughed at Evan's expense. "Did you at least have a good time?"

"Very funny—witty," he folded his arms and leaned back to ignore them.

The coach lurched to a stop and the time to part came. Joseph stole one more kiss before she went from him. The coach bobbled, as the fathers climbed down. When the door opened, the three sat like good children inside, never betraying the conversation or kisses that happened moments before.

Stuart took his daughter's hand and goodnights given. Joseph touched his hat leaning out the door at beside Evan. Emily smiled at the boys and then turned away with her father. It ended too soon.

VII. Paying a Visit

The next afternoon, Joseph saddled up Manny under the pretense of exercising the animal. Evan joined him, making the cover all the more complete. They smiled and laughed, discussing what Evan did the previous evening. No matter how much Evan spoke, Joseph thought more of his experience at the dance. Emily danced before his eyes, wearing that purple and ivory dress. He remembered the feel of her in his hand. The whole night he wore his gloves, but he still felt her warmth on his skin.

The young men walked their horses out of the barn and swung up into the saddle. Evan's mother stood on the porch doing the wash with the girls. She looked up at them and waved. Joseph smiled and touched his hat to her.

"Hurry back! Dinner will be at six sharp," Amanda called to her boys.

Evan and Joseph nodded. They turned their mounts and whipped them into a race out of the yard, leaping the fence.

"They'll break their necks acting the fool," Amanda said worriedly.

Behind her, her daughter Lauralee watched with painful longing. They headed west along the road, probably to the Conrads. Lauralee drew a weighted breath and glared. If she knew her brother, they snuck out to see Emily.

Lauralee returned her attention to scrubbing one of her father's shirts. She ran it back and forth over the washboard with gusto. That woman stole her man without a thought. She hated Emily more than ever. She acted so perfect, living in her big house, finding no one good enough for her, least of all her brother.

"Lauralee," her mother called her name. "What are you doing?"

Lauralee blinked at her mother and realized she sloshed soapy water all over the porch and down her skirt. She stepped back and her mother took over, telling her to go change. If she could have, she would sneak out and see just what Emily did with her brother and the Lieutenant. It might be rather interesting.

Lauralee narrowed her black eyes to the distance. She knew a girl that worked in that house. Perhaps she knew something of Miss Emily. That would fix the bold girl, she thought, turning away and going in the house.

In the distance, Joseph and Evan raced along the road until they entered the tree line, disappearing from the sight of the house behind. Joseph pulled Manny up short and looked back. Evan charged up behind. They smiled at each other and then turned their mounts into the woods and picked along. Joseph looked to his subordinate, wondering what he thought of their sneaking about.

"Think she'll come?" Joseph asked.

"Sure as Lauralee's jealous," Evan smirked.

Joseph drew out his tobacco and papers, rolled a cigarette and laughed. "She's too young. I already told you."

"Tell her," Evan smirked. "Gimme one."

Joseph nodded. "Wouldn't' do any good."

Joseph passed Evan the cigarette he rolled and prepared another for himself. Removing a lighter from his pocket he gave it to Evan and took it back when his friend finished. Lighting his own cigarette he peered through the woods back towards the Howell home. He wondered about the little sister, just what she would do. It hardly mattered to him, since he planned to meet with Emily in a few moments. Putting the cigarette in his mouth, he puffed on it a few times and thought of the immediate future. The girl could become a problem.

A short time passed and the horses emerged on a trail, beaten through the woods by years of use. Evan turned them south and they continued until they emerged on the back of the garden. Joseph's eyes took in the greenhouse and the holly bush walls. His heart leaped up, thinking of what he faced. He hesitated, pulling Manny back. The horse pranced uneasily.

"What?" Evan said, also pausing. He half smiled at Joseph.

"She's there," he said.

Evan looked at Joseph quizzically. He stared at the steamed up glass of the greenhouse. Evan turned his eyes to it again and searched for what his friend saw. The hazy figures of two people showed through. So, she came after all. Evan smiled and shook his head. He never thought Emily the type to engage in such affairs. He felt almost proud of her, but then his smile dropped and he swallowed, realizing what he allowed. His friendship with Emily made her a sister and he helped his dear friend disgrace her. At least he accompanied him. He could protect her from anything Joseph may try, other than polite of course.

"Shall we go in?" Evan said.

"Ya-yeah," Joseph stammered, waking from his dreamy gaze.

"I expect you to be a gentleman," Evan said.

"Nothing less," Joseph patted his shoulder, smiling and putting his arm around him.

The men dismounted from their cavalry steeds and tied them off on nearby trees. Together they rounded the shrubbery and entered the garden. Joseph took the lead and approached the greenhouse first. They paused outside, knocking on the door. Both removed their hats and smoothed their hair, smiling and chuckling to each other. Then, the door opened and Hettie's face appeared. She looked them over with a serious expression, weighing and balancing.

"Afternoon, ma'am," Evan said to her. "May we enter unto your humble—glass home?"

"Evan," Hettie said, darkly stepping aside. "Lieutenant," she tried to smile at Joseph.

Hettie opened the door wide enough for both to enter the small building. The warm air clinging to the inside hit hard and they both shifted uncomfortably in the heat.

All stood quiet until the door clicked closed behind them, sealing them to their fate if they suffered discovery. Evan cleared his throat and motioned for Joseph to continue. He looked back over his shoulder, smiling slightly at Hettie. She remained by the door, watching everything they did. She gave him a flat stare he found difficult to read as other than dislike.

Surrounded by the heat and seeming unwelcome response, Joseph and Evan hesitated at the entrance. They both watched Emily work to pot flower bulbs from a pile at her elbow. Her back remained turned to them and she failed to show interest in their arrival. Evan looked to Joseph nervously and received a similar glance in return. The Lieutenant shrugged and they both looked back to her.

Joseph stood undaunted by Emily's reception. She may not welcome them, but he knew she stood there at his request. Joseph stepped away from Evan and Hettie to approach the young woman, but cautiously. Hettie looked to the man standing next to her. He smiled and she returned it warily.

"Been expecting you," Hettie said.

"We don't like to disappoint," Evan replied.

"Have a seat, Evan," Hettie pointed to a wooden bench behind them. "Tell me about your time away."

Evan nodded and passed a look toward the back where Joseph greeted his new girl. He smiled softly and sat on the bench, soon joined by Hettie. She waited patiently for him to begin his speech. Evan cleared his throat and thought of all he did since school and beyond. He checked on Emily again.

"She'll be all right," Hettie laughed.

At the end of the greenhouse, Emily clasped hands with Joseph. He smiled at her and she blushed, looking away. She pulled her hands back, recalling the soil covering her gardening gloves. She laughed lightly and he chuckled. Suddenly they needed no words to communicate.

"I missed you all night," Joseph said.

"You hardly know me, Lieutenant. How can you presume to miss me?"

"I do just the same," he replied.

"Go ahead," Emily said. "I've no power to prevent you."

"Don't you, Miss Emily?"

"I—" Emily stopped and looked up at him. She met his eyes and looked away. "What am I doing here? Meeting you in secret?"

Emily pulled the gloves from her hands. She threw them down and stepped toward the door, clutching her skirts. She looked suddenly angered and distraught. She could not answer why she met him like this. They need not hide what went on between them. Her father liked Joseph well enough. Why not allow him to court her openly? Emily then thought of her mother and the rousing fights she and her sire took part in since Joseph arrived.

"Here we go," Evan noticed the change and stood.

"Emily," Joseph called her back. He sounded desperate and looked much the same. Emily meant to leave him already.

"We're sneaking about Joseph—" She stopped again. "I hardly know you, but for what Evan has said. Why not call me at the house?" Emily faced him with a pained expression.

"Your mother would serve my head and your fathers for lunch," Evan interrupted.

"My mother is a problem," Emily said. "However, she would never forbid you at her door unless she discovered trysts as this occurring in her own backyard and against her better teachings," Emily explained, growing excited. She went to a worktable littered with plantings, "she thinks I am preparing the spring bulbs for planting."

"Then let her," Joseph said. "I would rather sneak than face her inexcusable glares."

Emily looked at him, swallowing hard. She felt the same, but she must live in her home whereas he would leave in a short time, leaving her to deal with all the results alone. Emily did not think that fair. Besides, her mother only worried what went on and held her good reasons.

"Lieutenant," Emily whined.

"Emily," Joseph said, stepping toward her, placing his hands behind his back. He stood above her smiling. "I will call at your home, with Evan." He paused, watching her lean back from him. "But—only if you honestly believe it the only way."

"I do, sir." Emily stepped back nervous.

Joseph's presence strained her emotions. She found her eyes flicking to his mouth and she felt the heat rise in her cheeks. Quickly she lifted her gaze to his eyes, but saw it done too late. He smiled at her knowingly. Emily looked away to the green plants that filled the room, then over to the vent where the warm air came in from the stove outside.

"Of course," Joseph crooned. "I would be unable to do this," he said, taking hold of her and pulling her body to his. Joseph cradled her in his arms, smiling at her shocked face. He kissed her mouth.

Shock waves raged through Emily's body. Held so close to him nearly cut off her thoughts and her air. Somehow, a voice leaked through the murkiness and Emily pulled away before he finished. She could not allow this to happen.

"Not now," Emily said, stepping away from him. The fog lifted slightly from her mind, but she could still feel him touching her.

"Only at night under the cover of darkness?" Joseph questioned, sounding rather sarcastic. Emily looked at him shocked. He offered his hand, smiling, "Perhaps a dance to warm you to me?"

"I was unlike myself last night," Emily snapped.

"She's just scared," Evan said.

"I'm not scared," Emily hissed. "And, you're not helping."

Turning away from the Lieutenant and Evan, Emily noticed Hettie at the door and feebly tried to ignore her. Evan cleared his throat, wearing an expression of worry, and stepped past her to rejoin Hettie. The pair sat on the bench, pretending not to notice her or Joseph.

"I think he's right," Joseph smiled.

"What do you think me?" Emily rounded on him, looking scandalized.

"Interested," Joseph replied. He stepped toward her, took her hand and guided her toward the back of the greenhouse. "And unable to express it for fear of her mother's retribution."

"Interested? My mother—" Emily snapped, cutting herself off when he smiled triumphantly. "You know nothing of me. Nothing at all," she said, narrowing her eyes.

"I know everything I need know," Joseph said, drawing her to him again. He danced her to the obscured corner out of sight. "You're afraid."

"Hardly," Emily said angered by how the feel of his body so close made her not only breathless, but forgetful as well. "You're enraging, Lieutenant. Let me be—go call at the house. I will play the piano—sing—but I will not meet you alone to kiss—or—or anything else."

"I never asked you to—I simply cannot help myself when I'm with you," Joseph replied, placing his mouth close for another kiss.

"You've the wrong impression of me," Emily said, her voice tremulous with his mouth so close to hers.

Joseph smiled, "Very well."

Joseph leaned back and drew a deep breath. His eyes rolled closed and reopened, looking at her with something like disfavor or perhaps annoyance. Opening his arms, he released Emily and she stepped back, looking at him almost regretfully. He smiled slightly and placed his hat back on his head. His eyes gained a different light, determination. Whatever she wanted him to do, to relinquish, he would manage.

"As you see fit, Miss Emily," he told her. "I will call at the house." He stepped forward and she stepped back. He smiled at her timidity. "But know I'll not walk away easily, ma'am. I've found something I want—you can ask Evan what that means. He'll know."

Emily's eyes widened. She once doubted his interests, but her suspicions now stood affirmed. However, she found difficulty in still deciding what she would do. Lowering her gaze to the stones of the floor, she saw him step toward her. Emily quickly stepped back to avoid another embrace. She felt her constitution only so strong when caught alone with him.

Joseph smirked knowing he worried her. Instead of closing her in another embrace, as he wanted, he stepped back. He would do what she wanted, exactly as she wanted. Joseph turned back, wanting another look at her. He placed two gloved fingers on the jaw line of her face. She looked at him and he offered a wavering smile, between joy and bitterness.

"I'll call at the house in a few moments," Joseph warned. "I suggest if you mean to see me again that you don't work too late."

"Joseph—"

Before Emily could explain to him that she wanted to see him, but she could not bring herself to meet with him alone, Joseph turned away. He stalked out of the greenhouse, holding his broad shoulders squarely. Emily frowned at his back. She meant to explain herself to him, but he acted uninterested in the reason she held him off.

Evan stood up from the bench watching his friend leave. The look on his face warned of trouble. Turning his dark eyes to Emily, he wondered what she just said to him. Evan dashed from the building behind his superior officer. The door closed behind them, but the words sounding in the garden could still partially reach their ears.

"Joe—what did she say?"

"Nothing—"

Hettie looked more worried than any of them. She lifted her dark eyes to Emily, not asking that which hung in the air all around them. The voices outside faded away and Hettie approached Emily. The young woman lowered her eyes and touched the workbench to her right, running her fingers along the rough dirty surface. She looked upset with the affect her words had on the Lieutenant. Hettie touched her arm and the young woman looked up at her. Hettie offered a small comforting smile, tipping her head to the side.

"I cannot go against my own mother," Emily said, fearing the idea of it.

"You cannot let her take what the Lieutenant brings you," Hettie said, touching her friend's face consolingly.

"He brings me scandal with his ways," Emily retorted, with a deep frown and tears building in her eyes.

Hettie said nothing. She saw both ends of this problem, but she knew one path would win the challenge. Folding her arms, she drew a deep breath and eyed Emily. She must make up her mind for herself. She stood at eighteen years old, a woman grown. The time came to act that role. She watched the Emily shift on her feet, altering between egos, child and woman.

"What would you have me do?"

"Make up your mind, Emily. He will only be here until the war calls him back," Hettie tried to reason.

Emily looked as if she would cry. She hugged her arms around herself and bounced back and forth on her feet. How could she decide to care for a man she hardly knew? No answers came to her.

"What do I do Hettie?" Emily whined. "I cannot defy my mother."

"You've the chance for something very few will ever enjoy," Hettie said. "Trust me if not him."

"What do you know that I can't see?"

"If I've ever known the grace of love—I know it shows its face here."

"Love?"

Hettie nodded. A slow smile bloomed on her lips. Emily regarded her unsure. What Hettie said always held weight with her. However, she found difficulty in taking in her present advice.

"Besides—you know you came here to see him—maybe kiss and cuddle," Hettie said. "You like him—that's fine."

Emily turned her eyes to the pale green glass of the hothouse. The fog on the windows reminded her of the fog destroying her senses. She could neither move forward nor back. She felt penned in and of her own doing. She looked over the leaves of the plants growing on the workbench. Flowers bloomed from some and buds lay unopened on others. Whether she was flower or bud, she had yet to tell.

"You gotta chance, Emily. You're free to do what you want," Hettie reasoned with her.

"You mistake my legal right with my social prison," Emily said. "I'm a woman and no better off than a slave, Hettie. My choices are made by my father and then by my husband once married."

"Then see what your father says," Hettie retorted. "All I hear are excuses. I may not have freedom legally, but I would not stop till I broke free of my prison."

Emily looked to her, seeing the point clearly.

"He's to call at the house," Emily murmured.

"Then we'll be there to meet him," Hettie said. "Don't let him walk away like this."

Emily and Hettie left the greenhouse to return to the main house. They laughed, walking arm and arm, never knowing they did so under calculating black eyes.

Prior to Joseph or Evan's arrival at the greenhouse, Lauralee went to her room, but soon decided to give chase to her brother. Stealing from the house, she ran through the woods and found the trail they left. Following it, she found the garden and the greenhouse with the pair of cavalry chargers abandoned outside. Lauralee hid just in time.

Evan and Joseph emerged, arguing over some matter. She heard little and understood less. She watched them from her cover, taking the horses back under their control and ride back up the trail. Once they disappeared, Lauralee ducked out of her cover and planned to follow. Partway, she heard the laughter of the two women. Emily and the black housekeeper came from the greenhouse and stepped through the garden. She could just make them out through the holly.

Lauralee turned back and ducked behind a great pine trunk. She pressed her body against the scratchy bark and watched. She glared and sneered with hatred at Emily's white capped head. She wanted to rip the dressing from her hair and choke her with the ties.

"I wonder how this will sound to the girls at church." Lauralee mumbled to herself.

Once Emily walked out of sight, Lauralee dashed off in pursuit of the soldiers. However, following the trail home proved wrong. Evan remained absent, as did Lieutenant Maynard. Lauralee climbed the stairs to her room, thinking they may sit upstairs talking, but found her father coming down in search of her. He looked at her darkly.

"Your mother's been worried sick," her father said to her.

"I went for a walk," Lauralee lied.

"Chasing your brother and Lieutenant Maynard no doubt," her father growled. "Leave them alone—they're too old for you to socialize with."

"I went for a walk alone," Lauralee insisted.

"Without telling anyone?" Her father grumbled. "You won't leave this house for a month—"

"Father—"

"Are you listening?"

"Yes father," Lauralee bent her head.

"A month," he said again. He paused, watching her. "And, after that you'll not go anywhere without a chaperone."

"Yes, father," Lauralee said.

Mr. Howell half smiled and patted her head. He understood she meant well. He continued downstairs and left Lauralee alone. He needed to see to splitting wood out back. The store was getting low.

Lauralee stood still on the steps until her father entered the kitchen. Turning on her heel, she continued to her room. A small devious smile played on her lips. No punishment would stop her. She had a duty to perform and it would end with Emily's punishment. Emily would suffer for crossing her and suffer long.

Lauralee hummed and then sang out loud, wearing a scowl that promised hell.

ര

During the following days, Joseph made his visits to the Conrad home and found himself welcomed in, despite the matriarch praying for his leave. Stuart and Evan remained always near, chaperoning as necessary. Still, Emily and Joseph enjoyed themselves and their friendship grew.

In this manner, Emily found the comfort she needed to continue. Though she knew of her mother's disapproval, it stayed merely a backdrop and she reveled in the attentions of her suitor. She no longer thought he would cease being a gentleman and show a more impolite side. Emily wondered if it all true, or if he was just cleverly working to earn something no one should have without a vow. How could she ever know, except to test him while they sat alone, or beg Evan to reveal some candid moment from the past. Would he reveal such an event and ruin his friend's hopes?

The chance presented itself on the following day when Joseph excused himself. Up to that moment, Emily sat alone with the young men in the music room, enjoying some piano music, which she played for them. Continuing to run her fingers dexterously across the strip of keys, Emily waited for Joseph to leave and waved Evan to the bench beside her. He closed in on the grand piano and leaned across the top, supporting his head in his hand. He looked at her suspiciously.

"You probably wondered when I would get round to asking you about him," Emily said.

"Actually," he smiled. "What do you want to know?"

"Tell me everything," Emily smiled. "Tell me of his character."

"Ah—well you see," Evan said, straightening. He sat beside her and clinked the low keys interrupting her play. "What ya see—is what ya see," Evan explained, tapping a key with each word. He smiled at Emily and she smiled back continuing her playing. "Joseph is the most sincere man I've met. Conscientious. Kind. Intelligent—"

"He intends to make me his," Emily said.

"Then you will be his," Evan replied.

"Is that fair? Shouldn't I have a choice?"

"What would you like?"

"To know if he means it—"

"He never stops talking about you," Evan disclosed, looking nervously toward the door and then back. "My mother says he's in love with you," he lowered his voice. Pausing, he looked at the keys distantly, seemingly sad. "I think he is too," Evan gave his honest opinion.

"Really?" She asked and giggled.

Evan nodded. "What about you?"

"From the moment I saw him," Emily said in low sad tones. "It scares the hell out of me," she admitted.

Evan sighed and put his arm around her shoulder, "It'll be okay."

Realizing what this meant, Emily stopped playing and looked down at her hands. They slipped into her lap and she remained quiet, thinking over her friend's words. If Joseph cared for her, it meant a great deal that he took the time and care to behave. He did all she wanted, just to sit at her side. She knew how she felt when the fire claimed the barn, when he carried her back to safety. She saw the appreciative look in his eyes on that night. It never changed.

Emily thought of every moment that passed between them since. Her mother made her fear him, doubt his designs and anything else, just to be rid of him. She let her too, and when she knew how she felt in her heart about this man.

Emily lifted her eyes to Evan, "I've been cruel."

"You've been Emily."

Evan smiled and Emily smiled back reluctantly. He touched her face and then quickly put his hands on the keys poorly playing a made up mishmash of notes.

"Stop! You'll put it out of tune," Emily laughed, smacking his hands away.

"Who taught you to play?" Joseph's voice rang through the room.

Joseph entered and sat on Emily's other side. Evan looked to him smiling and took his cue to step away to a window, giving them more privacy. Emily shied from him and turned her attention to playing a waltz. Joseph kept his eyes on her, studying every detail of her face and neck. Suddenly he found himself leaning close and placing a kiss under her ear.

Emily pushed him away with an elbow, smiling and giggling. One of her parents surely would walk through the door. It failed to make him stop, instead encouraging him to do more. It warmed her to feel him next to her with the confession from Evan. His touch burned her skin and she found herself wanting more.

"You do find ways to misbehave," Emily said, mockingly stern.

Emily tried to slide away from him. However, he cunningly sat himself on her skirt, trapping her squarely beside him. She looked at him warily. He smiled, pulling her into his arms. His hands ran up her sides. Somehow, she found her arms about him.

"You seem caught, ma'am."

Emily's heart beat in her chest like a great drum. She could not look away from him. She saw the intent in his eyes and after Evan spoke so well of him. She tried to pull back, but her skirt remained wedged under his leg and her body wedged in his arms.

"Quite caught, Lieutenant," she said. "Would you mind freeing me please?"

"Yes," he drawled.

"Lieutenant," Emily frowned at him, placing her hands on his chest, prepared to push him back if he dared what she thought.

"Meet me in the garden every afternoon at three and I will set you free," Joseph grinned.

"And risk my reputation?"

"I could do it here."

"Do what?" Emily challenged, pulling on her skirt.

Joseph chuckled and looked in her eyes. He did not say.

"Do you think I am no better than a woman who is paid to lie on her back to perform the services she gives?" Emily questioned him.

"I never said—" Joseph started, allowing his hold to loosen. He took his hands from her and leaned his elbow on the piano keys with a scream from the anvils and strings within.

"Emily," Evan said, seeing the anger in her face.

"You may leave sir," Emily yanked her skirt from under him. "Both of you."

With that said, she made to leave. However, Joseph jumped up and took hold of her swinging arm, pulling her back into the room. He looked down at her.

"If you don't like me—then just say," Joseph said. "Let me leave here tonight knowing I have no chance of winning you. Otherwise, ma'am stop toying with me."

Emily refused to look at his face. She took on a sullen expression, allowing the room to fill with the tension between them. She wanted to pull free of his grip and knew the accomplishment would be easy enough. He gently held her arm and she only stopped to hear what he said.

"You are toying with me sir—are you not?"

"No," Joseph breathed.

Emily recalled what Hettie told her in the greenhouse and now thought on what Evan said. Joseph at least cared for her and he never suggested they engage in improper activities. He merely meant to tease her, but she failed to see it that way.

Joseph released Emily's arm from his grasp and watched the thin limb fall back to her side. He would carry no further with her, if she failed to make up her mind about him. He hated chasing women that ran too far too fast. He liked a good game like the rest of the men, but this one obviously did not know where she went. Evan warned him that she might, but he thought his message clear.

Emily turned her body slightly and looked up at him. Her blue eyes appeared filled with tears. Joseph's expression softened and he uttered a barely audible apology. He touched her face and waited, knowing she would speak to him.

"I'm sorry, Joseph. This is difficult for me at best," Emily explained. "I cannot tell when you will leave—how can I give you anything more than I already have." She paused, studying the understanding falling on his face. "I've already let you do things most would condemn me for."

"Penelope Dunworth lets you do anything," Evan piped up. "Just so you know if anybody has something to say." Emily and Joseph looked at him shocked. "I wasn't the first either—as I gathered. Foolish me. I knew she liked me since we were kids."

"I would never expect Miss Dunworth's behavior from you," Joseph said, looking back to Emily. "I told you my intentions Emily. I meant them."

"He never goes back on his word," Evan said, lounging on one of the two sofas placed by the fire. He put his feet up on the leather upholstered back and pulled some fruit from the bowl on the table between his sofa and the next. "Swear to the Lord," he cried up to the ceiling. "As my witness, the bastards a mule."

Emily smiled and laughed at his familiar behavior. He planned to stay and Joseph would too. Emily looked back to Joseph shaking her head. She just could not decide.

"How long?"

Joseph drew a deep breath through his nose, clamping his mouth tight. He adjusted on his feet and looked in her eyes with a serious gaze. How could he answer the question?

"The rest of the week—maybe more," he said. "We're to be sent orders, as soon as they're given to our Captain."

"Then I shall see you every day at three in the garden," Emily said. "Feel free to come to the house also. I should like to see as much of you as possible." She looked at Evan eating the apple in his hand. "If Evan trusts you—then I will too."

"Honestly?" Joseph asked smiling.

"Don't you dare disgrace me," Emily said, warning him with a finger pointed at his chest.

"No—never," Joseph agreed astounded. "Never."

Between frequent visits to the Conrad home, Joseph also went to see the Widow Murphy in the township of Montpelier. She made him tea and spoke of the war and what they thought would happen. He knew there were other things he must do, but he could not bear to see Emily's eyes darkened again.

"It is no matter now, boy. I would wait to tell her until the last possible moment," Mrs. Murphy said, sipping from a dainty porcelain cup. "She understands your intention and that is enough."

Mrs. Murphy's sitting room spread around him much larger than many he had the pleasure of before. He felt lost on the couch next to her chair, as she carefully watched him over the rim of her cup. They finished a light lunch a little time before and relaxed to let it digest. He thought of other subjects than his visit. Mrs. Murphy smiled, lowering the porcelain vessel.

"Tell me what is on your mind, Lieutenant."

"Emily will be left behind," he said, rubbing his leg, as if it ached with unbearable pain.

"Not necessarily. There is always the post," Mrs. Murphy said dryly.

Joseph looked at her questioningly. What she suggested could well harm Emily's reputation and he knew what she thought of that. He could not do something so selfish and had promised. He remained always a gentleman after all.

"Cold comfort. Besides, it'd be indecent—" he tried to say.

"Only if you never marry her. People are a bundle of contradictions. If you are married before the close of the story, they will only remark on how romantic it was. No one will even think of the letters you exchanged or what they contained, let alone what you shared privately." She set her cup down with a clink and a smile. "Would you really want to spend months, possibly years, never hearing a word from her? I know Emily would not wish it."

"Now I can see why they say the things they do about you," Joseph grinned. "You're good, Mrs. Murphy. Very good," Joseph said, standing to take his leave. All this talk of Emily made him miss her.

Mrs. Murphy's eyes glinted at him and she laughed deep in her throat. She enjoyed such dealings. As a woman she stood unsurpassed at cunning and this talent proved the subject of what many people said behind her back. When she put her mind to something, she finished it. She did many things in her life that people spoke against, but she knew that if they found themselves pressed in such circumstances, they would do much the same as her.

"Do not let Emily's mother bother you. She can act very foolish sometimes, but she will come around. You are a charming man and she is sure to see it," she said escorting, him to the door, as he made ready to leave. "Besides, that which you have not told them will be of most use to you on that battle front."

"What do you mean?"

"Mrs. Conrad is a snob," Mrs. Murphy said bluntly. She sipped her tea. "From one those New York families I told you about."

Mrs. Murphy's eyes sparkled. She set her cup down and stood to walk him out. Joseph shook his head and laughed. At her front door, Mrs. Murphy helped Joseph with his coat. When he secured it, and stood buttoning up the front, she brushed the sleeves and shoulders like a doting mother. Joseph turned to her, offering a gracious smile. She returned the expression, touching his face. She acted kind to him despite his unfamiliarity in Vermont.

Nothing said Mrs. Murphy need take him into her home or behave more than civil, but she treated him as if he was one of her many sons. Mrs. Murphy claimed no children in her home at that age, but held onto her nurturing ways just the same. He could see that she enjoyed this chance to offer her aid. It provided opportunity to help her old friend Stuart and undo the ungratefulness his undeserving wife Margaret showed him.

"Thank you for the lovely lunch, Mrs. Murphy," Joseph smiled at her. "I'll think about your advice, and let you know what I plan to do," Joseph said. "I may need your help at a later point."

"Good luck to you, boy. I pray that God shine his grace on you in your pursuit."

Joseph returned to the small town where he found his treasure secretly tucked away. In the afternoon, when he found the Howell home, he met with a grave faced Evan. Joseph could only look at him with fear in his eyes. He already knew what the man would say.

Evan came nearer, wearing a sour sick expression, as if he held something rotten in his mouth. Joseph smiled at him, easing off the worry in himself. If possible, Evan's dark eyes turned blacker. Joseph could not deny the fear in himself any longer and his smile faded.

"Order's have come through," he drawled, reflecting the hopelessness he felt inside.

Joseph looked to the ground, closing his eyes. He rubbed them with the tips of his forefinger and thumb. The calendar said the seventh of April 1862 when he looked that morning. Reality crashed on him like distant cannon fire, shelling closer and closer. It only stood true to form that he would arrive at the Howells only to receive the call back. The Captain said, when they planned their move, he expected them to stand with him.

Joseph opened his eyes and looked to his friend. Evan kept his hands stuffed in his pockets. He stood like a boy. The wind ruffled his black hair. There was no more to say. As officers, they would do their duty and return. After all, it was their choice to attend West Point for this, regardless of the path it took them on.

"I'll need to tell Emily," Joseph said. His heart sunk at the thought. He already saw her face a mess with the news. The blue oceans of her eyes filled with tears and overflowed onto the banks of her cheeks. Her lips trembled, but there would be few words. "How long do we have?"

"Rest of the week here," Evan replied softly. "We need to be back in time for a maneuver they're planning."

"So they decided to stop hibernating."

"Come inside. Mom's been waiting for you," Evan said, dismissing any further thought on it. They acted foolishly, thinking it could go on forever. "Davie's feeling better."

Joseph dismounted and found Mr. Howell, waiting to take the horse for him. Mr. Howell nodded with a small smile. Joseph returned the same expression and turned to follow Evan into the house. He paused partway up the stairs, looking over his shoulder in the direction of Emily. He wondered if he dreamt a nightmare and would wake any moment. He hoped so, because he wanted to stay. Emily was more real to him than anything he knew.

Acres to the west, Emily sat in the sewing room with her mother and Hettie, as they each worked separate projects. Margaret's face showed more wear in the past few weeks. Emily knew why. She thought Joseph a wonderful breath of fresh air, which they needed to freshen their stale lives, but her mother only foresaw doom. At least, Hettie liked him as much as her father and Evan. As for their opinions, Emily thought the world spun around them, so it only made her love him more. In truth, if they all hated Joseph, she still would love him. No one was capable of stopping it. She smiled to herself and her heart beat faster at the thought of him. It only made her sad when she realized she must keep it a wonderfully delicious secret between friends.

Emily looked to her mother. The woman released a weighted sigh. She looked stressed by her labor.

"Mamma," Emily said. "Are you feeling all right?"

"I'm feeling fine, Emily." She replied without looking.

Margaret's tones were clipped and her face pinched. She rarely met her daughter's gaze when she spoke to her. In fact, she avoided Emily's company all together. They barely engaged in quilting lessons. When they did, she found fault with every stitch. Emily felt her rejection deeply, but continued to search for the place she held in her mother's heart before.

"Joseph will come for a dinner again, father said," Emily tried to make conversation.

"More work," her mother sighed with vexation.

"What do you mean, Mamma? You always liked company before."

"Nothing dear," she said, forcing a smile and her eyes to her daughter. She patted Emily's knee and continued her work. After a long pause she spoke again, sounding distant and unaffected. "He'll return to his unit soon or hasn't he said yet?"

Emily's heart stilled at her words, "I don't know."

Hettie's chin lifted. She studied the exchange between the women. The current question rang in her ears. She saw a dark storm on the horizon, trying to tear the family apart. She prayed the people good enough to take her in, give her a job and treat her like a human being would not be destroyed by the affects of her past.

Going to the closet door on the wall, separating the room from the parlor and line of closets between, she tried to mind her own business. Though Margaret spit out her words spitefully, Hettie loved her for her years of care.

Hettie gathered linens from the closet inside the passage. She tightened her lips. Mrs. Conrad did not need a housekeeper butting her head into family matters. She emerged from the closet space and eyed the girl in question. The ashen hue of her expression pulled the strings of Hettie's heart. Emily held back in defense of herself. She set her cross stitch on the table by her chair. Her gaze drifted out the window. The storm of emotions raged on the sea of her face.

"I better see if Rose started the girl's on the roast," Margaret dismissed herself, sounding strangely reenergized. "I wouldn't want him to feel unwelcome," her tone turned sarcastic.

Margaret's tone was unmistakable to either woman. Emily observed her mother's exit. She wished she would like Joseph, as much as the rest of the household. He had proven himself a wonderful man. If she gave him the least chance, he would easily win her over. Emily's eyes lowered from the vacant doorway. She felt Hettie place a hand on her shoulder. She looked to her friend.

"She'll come round. You let her be for now. It ain easy ta lose ya baby," Hettie said. She just did not want to see them fight, and perhaps a little time would mend whatever wrong Margaret felt from Joseph. "It's three o'clock."

Emily looked across the room to the old grandfather clock, ticking away the minutes. The brass pendulum swung back and forth, reminding her of a body swinging in the breeze. Emily drew a deep breath and shut out the horrible thoughts. She should feel happy. Joseph waited for her in the garden. Her mother's words would fade, replaced by his kisses. Rising to her feet, Emily led Hettie from the room to the kitchen.

Hettie dropped the linens on the worktable and gave MaryJane instructions for her and Blythe to set the table. Behind her Emily put her cloak on her shoulders and fitted her cap on her head. Hettie turned to find her own cloak, and they stood, looking at each other and slipping gloves on their hands. Emily smirked deviously at her and they darted out of the house.

Hettie never erred from accompanying her friend on these walks, even though she wandered the trail and outskirts of the garden aimlessly. She wanted to stand by, if Emily needed her. Besides, she could speak for her, if rumor took root.

In no time, they crossed the muddy lane and climbed the hill behind the workhouses. The roof of the greenhouse stood in view behind a line of cedar trees. They heard the rhythmic beat of horse hooves on the ground and knew they arrived just in time. Emily smiled at her friend. The crimson blush of her desire bloomed on her cheeks. She told her to hurry and ran up the hill impatient to see her lover. Hettie chased after, mumbling to herself and shaking her head.

When the women crested the hill, they found him still mounted on the back of his horse. He looked at Emily with dark eyes.

"What is it Joseph?" Emily asked him, knowing already.

"Nothing," Joseph replied, trying a smile. He eyed her, noting the wide gray striped skirt and how it cinched into her waist. His eyes trailed up the buttons of the bodice to her chin and then her eyes. He smiled deeper and she clasped her hands together before her waist, waiting. Joseph's eyes flicked to Hettie and her solemn face said he fooled no one. "How would you fancy a ride, Miss Emily?" He returned his gaze to his woman.

"Are you sure?" Emily beamed, missing his evasion of the matter in her excitement to ride the stallion.

Joseph held out his hand and Emily went to him. He pulled her up behind and felt her arms clamp about his middle while she wriggled into place. His smile turned genuine, but tears filled his eyes. He felt her press her head to his shoulder and it brought up notions of deserting the military for better prospects.

"Come back soon," Hettie said. "You're expected for dinner." Joseph nodded to her, touched his hat and turned Manny toward the forest trail, now clear of snow. "It might rain," Hettie added, seeing it failed to work.

"Hang on," Joseph said, warningly. He felt her clamp tighter and he laughed despite the feeling it raised in him.

Calling out to his mount, Joseph brought Manny to a run nearly instantaneously, but not nearly as fast as the charger ran in battle. Emily squealed as they darted up the trail until the farm was a shadow in the distance. Rounding corners and lifting fallen leaves, Manny brought his riders away from the safety of friends and family. They entered where the trail opened on a clear field, blanketed with tall grass and surrounded on all sides by the thick forest. Joseph slowed the speed to a trot and Emily giggled, squeezing Joseph.

"Where are you taking me, Lieutenant?"

"Where no one can hear you scream," he replied, reining Manny in beside a tall flat boulder.

"I scream very loud," Emily told him, touching his ear.

"I should like to hear sometime," Joseph replied, sitting atop his mount with her. He listened to her laugh against his arm.

Joseph's joy ended quickly. He must tell her the news. Sliding down from Manny, he steadied the mount by the rock and Emily lowered to the gray stone. With her feet firmly planted, she stood taller than him by half his height sitting in the saddle. He tossed the reins over the pommel and faced her. She smiled down at him, not knowing the secret he held.

Emily sat down on the stone and smiled up at him. She no longer feared the threat Joseph posed to her. She watched him, sitting still in her spot on the boulder, legs crossed beneath her skirts. When he leaned over and kissed her mouth, she put her hands on the back of his head, drawing him closer. Emily enjoyed every rush his touch caused, no longer thinking it improper or worrying over recourse.

The embrace broke and Joseph climbed up beside her on the rock. He stared into the woods, thinking of how he would tell her he must leave at the end of the week. He looked at the darkness surrounding the trunks and imagined the field covered in bluecoats, firing on the gray, darting in and out of sight. He saw the cannon lined up, heard the call to arms, the shouts to fire. The flag waved against the steely sky.

Emily put her arm around his waist and laid her head on his shoulder, drawing his attention back to her. She noticed he kept quieter than usual. Her face took on a somber expression, wondering if his attitude meant something bad for them. She drew a breath, feeling his arm wrap around her. She closed her eyes and soaked in the touch.

"What will you do after the war?" She asked him.

Joseph's gut clenched. It almost appeared she knew what he thought.

"Listen to you scream," he answered, saving the day.

Emily giggled, "Oh—Lieutenant. You're incorrigible."

"Entirely."

Emily tipped her head toward him in expectation of a kiss. Joseph smiled and granted her unspoken request. He placed a hand on the side of her face, holding her to him. The embrace lasted, lengthening in intensity.

Joseph broke the embrace, feeling his needs stir. He need take more care while they sat so far from supervision. He looked in her eyes, seeing she also felt the same. He watched her smile and bite her lip. He smiled back, but pain burned his eyes and tears threatened to spill over.

Emily listened to her heart, overflowing with echoes of words that reminded it would end soon. "I hope this never ends—forever," Emily sighed. She touched his face, looking at his mouth, a request. For a small time she forgot about crying and the ghosts stopped haunting her.

Joseph closed his eyes, thinking about the orders they received. He refused to think of what would come. The way matters currently played out, they each faced a long wait for the end of the war. Despite it, Joseph considered marriage. He refused to leave a widow or an infant behind. However, in his dreams war could not touch them and he thought about it a great deal.

"What's wrong?"

"Emily," Joseph breathed. He moved to face her, as they sat beneath the wide gray sky. The only way to tell her presented itself in the truth. "I received my orders to return to Virginia."

Emily kept silent for a time. She knew this would come. She heedlessly ignored the warning and went ahead to make a fool of herself. He would leave and all of it ended there with her disgrace. She swallowed and looked at the grasses, waving in a breeze across the field.

"I didn't want to hear that," Emily finally said. "I don't know what I thought when I—"

"We'll wait until this is over," Joseph sighed with a heavy heart. He clutched her gloved hands careful not to crush the delicate digits. "We still don't know how long it'll last."

"I don't want to wait," Emily cried, reaching an arm up around his neck. She never dared to act so brazenly. She pressed her lips to his.

Joseph's mouth closed over hers and she could feel the rush of emotion throughout her body. He trembled as she trembled, and she no longer felt sure he pretended to love her. She no longer stood assured of anything. The embrace broke and they sat with foreheads touched together, looking at their hands once again clasped.

"I will wait as long as it takes—I'll be here when you come home," Emily said with tears, streaming down her cheeks. They dripped onto the black suede of her glove and on the chamois of his. "Come to dinner, Lieutenant. Tell my father your news. He will want to know from you."

"Your mother will at least be pleased."

"Heartily," Emily half laughed. She wiped the tears from her eyes.

"Shall we go back now?" Joseph asked, as she moved to sit with her back to him. She wrapped their arms together and laid her head against his shoulder.

"No—I want to stay here a while," Emily said, clasping his hands in hers.

Joseph tried to smile, looking in her eyes to memorize them regardless of her tears. He wiped them away and stared.

Unseen in the distance behind the verdure of the woods, Lauralee watched the clandestine meeting of her rival and the object of her desire. Her gut roiled with jealousy and her mind worked on inconceivable cruelty. Her small ungloved hands dug into the mulch of the forest floor, imagining she dug out the eyes of her foe. A sneer of hatred marred her once promising features, and her eyes glinted with treachery.

Lauralee watched these meetings every day for the last week, reacting in much the same manner. She wondered why she tortured herself. In time, it would prove worth it. Emily would suffer for her indiscretions and Joseph would see what a trollop she was. Lauralee knew Emily was false, pretending not to think it unseemly. She sat there engaging in an affair away from any supervision.

"You'll pay, Miss Conrad," Lauralee growled to herself. "People will see what you're really like."

Lauralee stilled her hands on the ground, looking to them covered in black earth. Tears filled her eyes. She wanted Joseph to notice her from the moment he entered the yard. Yet, he failed to even look in her direction. He patted her head like a child, spoke to her like a child and complimented her like a child. Tears spilled down her face. She stood a grown woman, as much as Emily Conrad. She would show him.

Lifting her gaze, she saw the pair press their backs together, as they sat on the rock. She imagined herself in Emily's place. She knew he told her or would tell her he planned to leave soon. She cried the whole walk there, thinking it too late to make him see her as she wanted. Lauralee imagined him coming to her easing her fears, saying he cared for her, but must wait until she grew a little more, when her father would allow them to wed. Another year and she could marry anyone, perhaps follow him to Maryland and move into his big house to take her place in his bed.

Lauralee cried with longing. It seemed so unfair to her. She saw Emily fall into his arms again. They engaged in another embrace and Lauralee saw her passion denied.

She recalled the look in Joseph's eyes when he spoke of Emily. He loved her and she loved him back.

Jumping up, Lauralee ran off into the woods east. She could no longer look on the terrible spectacle. She sobbed and wailed, knowing she only earned a lengthened punishment for going out after him. Well then, they would both pay.

"Damn them both," she cursed, swatting the tears from her wet cheeks.

At the end of the week, Joseph bid good bye to a tearful Emily in their grove by the same boulder in the woods. Hettie stood a pace away, wiping tears from her eyes, while the pair discussed their plans to hold onto each other through the coming trial. She was reminded of her predicament. She missed her family and tears sprung to her eyes for them. She had remained for Emily so no one could say anything out of turn, but she found herself wanting to leave them for her rooms and the privacy they offered.

Evan and his father warned Joseph about Lauralee's frequent absences, believing her to follow him. Joseph confided to Mr. Howell, with Evan's help, all that went on between him and Emily. He understood the need for candor and understood the need Joseph held to see his beloved. He would deal with the matter.

Joseph and Emily stood in the field, holding tightly to each other, knowing it the last time until the war ended. Joseph looked down at her tear streaked face.

"I'll return. I swear to you—I'll come back," Joseph said, wiping her tears away. "I'll write as I'm able," he added, falling silent. "If you'll allow me."

Emily's feelings rushed in a torrent on her. Pulling him back into her arms, she said, "I would not ask you not to." She lowered her chin, quietly weeping. Her tears spilled on the ground at her feet. "Please do," she sobbed.

Joseph closed his arms around her and held on for too small a time. Emily wept against his chest, clinging to him in their last private moments. Looking up to the sky, he saw the sun rise from behind the trees. He must leave or suffer punishment for his disobedience to orders. Under this, Joseph made himself tear away. He picked up his Stetson from the boulder.

It felt as though his heart ripped apart, but he could not desert his post. Her hand slowly slipped from his and he watched her stand there alone, sobbing. He looked away, placing his hat on his head and mounted his horse. He must leave or suffer worse than this.

Turning Manny to make his way back to the road and meet with Evan before he arrived at the Conrad home, he looked back at her. She wiped her tears from her eyes. He smiled down to her and she looked up at him. No more time.

"I'll see you at the house?"

Emily nodded to him. Then he went from their field. Emily turned away and sat on the boulder unable to watch him go.

"Oh baby," Hettie rushed to her side. "Shh—we gotta get you back to the house," Hettie said. "Dry your eyes. You got plenty a time ta do that later. Come on now." Hettie encouraged her to get up and Emily reluctantly complied.

Only a short time later, Emily stood with her family and servants, dotting the front porch and lawn while they bid farewell to the grand hero and his friend Evan Howell. Both young men wore their Union Army uniforms, spit and polished, sitting on the back of their fine mounts. They stopped on the outside of the fence to speak with Stuart and Emily.

In the background, Margaret stood on the porch, leaning against the post and rail, watching her daughter carefully, lips tightly pinched. She adjusted her shawl, as a cool breeze whipped in from the west. Spring still needed time to warm up. She looked to the flowers, bobbing in the breeze, all well behaved pretty ladies doing what they should. Her gaze returned to the mounted soldiers and her husband and daughter. At least something did what it should.

Emily reached up to take Joseph's hand. It appeared she gave him a paper, but she could not be certain. Straightening, she peered at them more closely. Some of the farmhands came from around the house to watch the young men leave, joining Hettie and Jo-Hanna on the lawn. She looked at Blythe, who stood near. The girl looked blankly back at her. Margaret adjusted her collar and returned her eyes to the road.

The Lieutenant held her daughter's hand and kissed it. She felt disgusted by his action and could not wait for him to take his leave. He released Emily and gazed at her with longing. His hand cupped her face. She saw Evan, trying to peer round his shoulder to see what he did. Evan once would have punched a man clean out for taking liberties with her Emily, but now he stood a friend to the scourge who raped her.

"Joe," Evan said in low tones to him. "We've gotta go, sir."

Joseph held his gaze on Emily. She looked back to him with tears in her eyes. Her lips moved around silent words, I love you. He smiled and nodded, unable to return the sentiment there. She took hold of his hand again.

"Fare the well, Lieutenant Maynard—Evan," Stuart said. Joseph looked to him and he nodded to both boys. "Come back to us soon."

"Farewell, Mr. Conrad," Joseph said. "Thank you for all you have done." He looked to Emily regretfully, "Till I see you again, Miss Emily. Take good care of yourself." He flicked his eyes to Hettie. "You make sure she does, Mrs. Benson."

"I will, Lieutenant Maynard," Hettie replied, wiping the tears from beneath her eyes and trying to smile.

Joseph smiled once more at Emily and then pulled back to sit straight in his saddle. Emily's hand slipped from his and he did not look back. Together, he and Evan turned their mounts and started down the road that turned south from the Conrad farm.

Emily clasped her hands against her chest and stepped back. She felt her father's arm around her, a numb distant feeling. She wanted to feel Joseph's touch, but it now stood more a distant memory than her dreams.

Emily watched Evan turn back and wave. At her side, her father waved back to him. The cries and cheers of the farmhands and housekeepers followed. Emily sheltered her face in her hands and cried. She had only her memories to hold him to her now.

VIII. Duty and Honor

The Army of the Potomac has come a long way after so many disasters, Joseph thought, casting his eyes over the camp. He saw the billowing smoke rise from the various messes built between the units. He tried not to think of what memories that recalled and instead evoked the memory of the rabble, mixed volunteers and regulars, who filled the army in the beginning. Here they stood now hardy soldiers to the end. He grinned, thinking of the brave men who fought in this band of vagabonds, from battle after battle. He fought alongside them, an officer of the cavalry. It felt good to stand among them again, but more than half of him was elsewhere.

Riding to his tent with Evan close behind, he saw devastating loss still left its affects. He received and returned many salutes, but the fervor of yesterday proved absent from them. Each face they passed held a story, some wife or sweetheart left behind, the first baby born or the tenth in the family, starvations and hardships. Recalling what they fought for reminded him of a woman he tried to put in the back of his mind.

Joseph rubbed his eyes and made himself think of other times. Looking out over the tract between the tents, milling with men and faces, he saw the story of agony they unsuccessfully hid in their minds, principally the agony of terrible defeat at a place called Manassas. He came to them a green officer, but when it ended he held too much knowledge and tried to drown it out with mug after mug of stale beer. Like many others, poorly performed and lost battles damaged the precarious morale he kept, leading Joseph to cast his life to the alehouses.

However, fate sent them General George B. McClellan. The little man worked with the men in a way unmistakably well. He arrived in their midst, wearing an army issue cap and smooth long mustache. He peered at the rabble assigned him from dark angry eyes, thoroughly disgusted with the way his army ran itself. Joseph still heard the screaming, up and down the line, as they stood in the wraps of spirits. A voice never sounded so loud.

McClellan forced his troops to face reality. The new General commonly referred to by the men as "Little Mac," quickly proved a man Joseph felt glad to serve under. He returned his pride in wearing the Federal uniform, not to mention wearing his own skin with the return of his sobriety. The following months while they drilled, Little Mac put the Army of the Potomac back in battle fashion. It proved a bitter pill to swallow with beer sloshing about his brain, but he now stood grateful, for hindsight made it much clearer. Joseph smiled to himself, thinking of the days of saloons. Nothing made you forget better than whiskey and beer.

Far from the past, Joseph's hope stood renewed. The Army of the Potomac would soon rejoin the fight and the fight might end soon. He found Emily floating on his thoughts.

"Well here we are again," Evan's voice floated to his ears from behind.

Joseph looked over his shoulder with a smile and nodded. He found little to say. Six days passed since they left Vermont. They faced a hopeless many more before they would return to a life they began in a town hundreds of miles away. Joseph's features darkened and he entertained the idea of reporting to the saloon and forgetting his Captain. Emily would not leave his mind unless pushed out by a powerful force.

Looking at the tents and flags swaying in the breeze, the lines of soldiers milling around and hearing the sound of mock battle just out of sight, Joseph realized he could not drink her away. He recalled the day he and Evan found themselves rounded up from their favorite saloon. He sat across the table from Evan drunk with alcohol and misery. They both faced inquisitions for their poor actions, unbecoming officers.

Joseph stood before those men on the examining board with sweaty palms clutched behind his back, wondering if it meant the end of his service in the Army. He hung his head thinking of the damning blemish on his career and his family such an outcome could have left. However, Joseph found himself remaining in his commission while many others received their dismissal papers. This new order would now lead them on a campaign believed to secure the Union of the States undeniably.

Little Mac's drilling and preparing allowed Evan and Joseph to take the time they had to visit the Howells in Vermont. Their captain, Darcy Braxton, said that no earnest fighting would come their way until spring and he would send for them by the end of April when it came. Of course, his Captain also threatened both of them with legal action if they did not return on his request. Something told him Captain Braxton knew fate worked in untimely fashions, to bring much more change to a life than expected. The early spring came too quickly, but sweet despite the lingering cold. Joseph never felt the cold when under the gaze of his jewel.

Joseph found his Captain's tent within the set up about where it usually stood, twenty in and sixteen rows down from the western border of the camp. His should stand next to it with his belongings all set up by the unit corporal. Evan's would sit on the opposite side with a line of other second lieutenants. Reining in the horses, Joseph looked at the tent, slightly larger than theirs. He wondered if he faced the same man, in these times of change, a day could mean a whole new order.

"Shall we dance, Lieutenant Maynard," Evan joked.

Joseph looked to him smiling. He wrapped his reins around the pommel of his saddle and slid to the ground.

In mere seconds, the Corporal stood to take the mounts to the corral. Joseph yanked his saddle and bags from Manny's back, patted the animal's rump and bid him good bye for now. Turning to the Corporal, he ordered the man to see their belongings properly placed in their tents and call them to dinner, once it stood ready.

"Yes, sir," the man saluted and then smiled. Joseph smiled back. "You look well. Good to have you back, sir," He added.

"Good to be back," Joseph lied.

Joseph and Evan turned from the enlistee and faced the Captain's tent. They approached removing their hats and soon disappeared within the canvas confines. At the flap, a junior soldier announced them and opened the tent to them. They stood inside looking at the fair haired leader they left behind to visit the fairer idols of their lives. Joseph and Evan stood at attention, listening to him rustle some papers on a small table set next to his cot where he slept.

"Welcome back, Lieutenant Maynard—Second Howell," the man drawled.

"Good to be back, Captain Braxton," Joseph and Evan chimed together.

"You're just in time," he said. "We're planning to take the Peninsula—Yorktown."

"Yes, sir." Joseph said, looking up at the tent ceiling. From the corner of his eyes, he saw the Captain still looked over his papers and Evan turned his face to him.

"Something worry you, Second Howell?" Braxton asked.

Evan straightened his stance and shook his head, turning his eyes to the tent roof, "No, sir."

"You're dismissed," he said, lifting a paper up to his face to read.

Joseph and Evan saluted stiffly and received a paltry return. Pivoting on their heals, both men took leave of their superior officer.

One night passed followed by others. Soon the battle came and went a memory like a nightmare. Joseph and his unit rode into the tent city, beaming smiles on all faces. They beat the Confederates back. Each man knew that more of this turn around would bring the end of the terrible war. He felt convinced he would find his return to Emily before the end of the summer. They celebrated their success that night too soon.

Following the wonderful success of Yorktown, a bitter defeat at Williamsburg brought change to all of this. He sat on his cot, placed beneath his tent on the grass of a dry field, and thought of it. The battle proved one of the most trying times of his career so far and it beat back his hopes of marrying in the fall or winter to next summer and even never.

Joseph remembered it. Joseph had sat in the pouring rain, smoking a damp cigarette. He breathed the smoke deep, leaving the burning ember on his lip and pet Manny's soaked mane. The horse whickered and pranced to the side. Joseph crooned to him and he eased back down.

Joseph heard the slosh of heavy feet through the mud puddles, surrounding them at all sides. He lifted his head and the rain poured down his back off his brim, cold through the oil cloak that kept off the wet but not the chill. He saw Evan ride toward him on his brown mount, looking more miserable than Mrs. Conrad at another visit.

"Lieutenant," Evan's voice came to him through the rains.

Joseph raised his head to see who came to him. The rain dripped off the brim of his hat and down his neck from his uncut hair, soaking into his back. He looked as sullen as anyone there, but at least he sat on his horse, instead of standing in the mud with the other men who tried to make the road passable for the artillery. Joseph did not respond except to return Evan's salute. His eyes were like cold iron and his jaw set in a grimace of determination. As long as they stayed here, digging out of the mud, he and his men served no purpose but to act as pretty daisies to dress up the army's appearance. They could have marched miles from this spot if they did not have cannon to drive or the God awful supply carts to haul, laden down so heavily they sunk on stone.

"The major in command a the artillery wants us ta see about helpin getta cannon outta the mud," Evan said bitterly. He hated the idea of using his horse for a pack animal. It was trained to make charges not pull its back out on heavy carts.

"My horse doesn't pull cannon. He's a charger, Second," Joseph read his mind, but most of the men would have felt the same. They couldn't waste the horse's energy on these matters when they needed it for battle.

"I don' think he meant it as a question, sir." Evan regarded his friend for a moment, watching his expression change from slight irritation to absolute anger.

Evan turned his mount back around. It sloshed through the watery muck, back down the road where the men tried to push the carts through. Joseph watched him go and then studied his surroundings a moment longer, trying to work his ruff back down. Manny worked on the battlefield in charges like a gallant ballet dancer. He never worked to haul carts from mud holes. Most cavalry officers cared for their horses like a member of the family. The mount gave the means to work his job, the means of survival. To hurt that animal which eased your life was unthinkable. He could see his cavalry unit at the far end of the line scattered among the others, offering what help they could. He gave no orders for them to do such. Perhaps Captain Braxton gave it in his absence. More likely, the major of the artillery thought them idle, while they marched with the rest of the men who were not bogged down by ungainly carts. He probably took it upon himself to spread the orders. Joseph and his men were blameless for his misfortune. In this weather they could not expect to get far without trouble. However, he faced a direct order from a superior officer and his captain stood absent, unable to contest it. Joseph pushed his mount forth to comply with his orders, now he held control over his emotions again.

When he reached the canon, the Major sat atop his horse, governing from above by a fenced hill. He watched from a pair of cold black eyes, while enlistees and lower ranking officers dug with spades and lay planks to remove his cart from the mud. Joseph crossly wondered why the man had not hitched his own rotgut mount to the cart and pulled its knotty back out.

Nonetheless, he found Manny hitched to one of the carts beside Evan's horse. The two ponies that towed it before rested to the side, exhausted from the original efforts to release it. The soldiers laid planks and backed away to the rear of the cannon to push. If the fresh horses could not pull the cannon free on those planks, none would.

Joseph gave the word and the men pushed with all their strength, the strain reddened their faces. Snapping his reins, he and Evan put the horses in motion. The horses pulled, stepping unsure, hooves sinking up to the cannon of their leg. Their footing slipped and they stumbled. Both officers encouraged the animals with guttural commands, snapping the reins, and squeezing their knees into each horse's ribs. In a sudden burst, the cannon wheels rocked forward. The men pushed and the horses pulled. The cannon muzzle bobbed and rattled. The wheels creaked and groaned. Suddenly the artillery piece bounced loosely, carrying forward with sudden packed energy.

Joseph smiled at Evan, as the men cheered and waved their sodden hats for the success. The marching soldiers walking by lifted their frowning faces to look. Joseph shook his head and looked down to his charger. Manny snorted and chewed his bit, trying to spit it out and catch his breath. Joseph patted his neck, promising an extra treat that night.

"Damn! You still surprise me," Evan called out. He patted his horse's wet neck. "You rogue—" he kissed its mane. "I think I'll keep ya."

Joseph watched his friend carry on with his horse, smiling broadly until his eyes took crinkles in the corner. His smile faded, seeing the Major move his horse down from the tree line and fence, running along the top of a green hill on the other side of the road. It looked more like a high bank on a muddy river right then, instead of a highway.

Ignoring the Major's approach, Joseph and Evan kept the cart moving, unless it rutted in the mud again and they would have to misuse the horses another time. Joseph hated to risk his horse unnecessarily and he could not wait for the Major to thank him for complying with an order, as if he held the choice. Looking up again, he caught sight of the Major, watching them from close by. Joseph saluted him and received the return. The Major smiled small and nodded. Joseph supposed he thanked them for their efforts with that meager acknowledgement. If he allowed himself to think on, he would speak out loud and knew the words he wanted to say would serve himself a large reprimand.

"Bastard," Evan breathed boldly when the Major rode out of earshot. "He could do more than sit there and watch like a woman at tea."

"That would be unbecoming a West Point officer," Joseph added sarcastically. "It seems our upperclassman feels he's still in school and the dirty work belongs to those beneath him."

"Well I'll teach him a lesson he won't soon forget," Evan said, glaring ahead to where the man trotted his horse away. He saw the passage splash more mud onto the backs of those that made up his unit.

"Won't do any good," Joseph said. "Just get yourself in trouble."

"Right," Evan said. "I may not be allowed at the next battle—have to sit in my tent."

Joseph looked around at the scene. He knew it would be one of those times he would be thankful to leave behind. They faced another night, sleeping in hammocks slung between trees. No ground stood dry enough to lay a cot on. You would lie in the mud come morning.

All night, Joseph listened to sawing and singing. In the morning, weary from little rest and aching from the damp cold, he studied the muddy road paved with logs.

His unit ate breakfast quickly and Joseph saw them mounted and on their way. Captain Braxton showed his face momentarily and left Joseph to run the company with the other lieutenants. As usual, the man's mind was elsewhere.

When Joseph and the company reached the end of the corduroy, they watched the men half out of their clothes, working in rank mud. Axes and more trees were laid out. The rain fell lighter that day, but kept the road impassable. Joseph looked at the scene, knowing they faced more nights like the last. He wanted dry ground, like the rolling hills of Vermont dressed spring. He could lie in his tent and sleep comfortably, while a certain jewel smoothed his brow. Joseph looked at his uniform, soiled from days of marching. A bath would be nice too. He smelled as rank as a horse's ass three days dead in the sun.

Instead of having anything that resembled his daydream, Joseph sat in his tent, alone and dirty. He shook his head to clear his thoughts. He looked about the tent. McClellan's apathy had led them there. He could not stop thinking of the trust he and the rest of the men placed in him. The General still failed to seize the upper hand and receive the surrender. McClellan behaved like it was a ball, dancing about the enemy. Joseph wondered if the man was the leader they needed or just another charlatan. With only one small success and the Confederates counting dozens, it appeared they faced a long trial.

During the following days, with the guns quiet again, the Confederates made their escape. Joseph walked to Evan's tent. He wanted to forget the obligations of rank and tried to forget the images of the dead and dying. Before ducking in the tent, Joseph looked at his boots. The mud had gone from them, but he still felt filth clinging dryly to his skin. Despite the desolation, Joseph entered with a smile on his face. He could not say the same for his friend.

Evan sat on a mat by his cot, covered in grime as if he rolled in the mud. His mouth twisted in a snarl. The battle had ended some hours ago, but the affects continued their work on the men.

"You gonna take a bath, Howell?" Joseph kicked his foot.

"What?" Evan snapped back, feeling self conscious.

Evan pulled away when Joseph sat in the chair opposite him. He grimaced annoyed. How could Joseph smile in his face like that? Evan looked at him, as if mad. He was reading a letter from home. His eyes flicked nervously between the paper and the Lieutenant.

"You smell, boy," Joseph rasped.

"You're no rose," Evan said, trying to ignore him.

Evan lifted his hand to feel the beard that grew from his chin. His hand smoothed the coarse hair unsteadily and quietly scratched the dirt off. Joseph moved in the corner of his eye, not leaving. His hand shook as he returned it to the pages he held. It had been like that since the battle.

"What did ya want, Lieutenant?" Evan asked him irritably.

"Haven you heard?" Joseph laughed. "The reb's, my friend!"

"What about them?" Evan picked up his jacket and felt the long tear in the sleeve. "No, let me guess. They done surrendered to the fine and superior intelligence of the northern army's great leader," he added with sarcastic bitterness.

"No—unfortunately," Joseph smiled. "I just got news that they sunk a ship in the port and burned Richmond—sounds like we're finally gonna have em," Joseph said, amused by the events he retold. He thought Evan would appreciate to hear that not every point of the war on the Potomac counted a loss for them. His smile faded.

"Not after what happened out here," Evan said sullenly. "More like their heads swelled." He paused, looking at Joseph pleadingly. "Mac fowled this up. We had the victory—they sat in our hands, sir!"

Joseph quietly regarded him. A smile wavered on his lips.

"Ah!" Joseph sounded. He waved his hand, as if to brush away the negative thoughts of his friend. "We'll get them, and they know it."

Evan looked at him with a dark expression. "I hope you're right sir. This wasn't a thorn bush that done this," he showed Joseph the hole in his jacket sleeve, as it lie in his lap. "Some gray coat bastard stuck me with his bayonet—out of munitions or something. Lucky for me I've skinny arms."

"Did he get you?" Joseph said worried, seeing the bloodstain. He wondered how he had failed to notice before.

"Nah—just a scratch. No stitches or anything." He paused in a long silence. Tears welled in his eyes, making them shine. The orbs widened, staring into Joseph. "I killed him, Joseph," Evan said. His eyes lowered, taking on a hollow black cavernous appearance. "It's not the first time I saw a man die, but—" His eyes turned black. He did not want to look at Joseph, but made himself. "My parents raised me to hold life dear. What do you think God thinks of us now? Do we even care anymore?"

"Come on Evan. This is a war. He would have killed you surer than you killed him. Either way, you're right. This isn't the first time. Little Nate's faring better than this," Joseph mentioned the twelve year old boy that drummed for the army and ran errands for him. He stood a mere child, seeking to grow into a man and he found it a terrible cold station to inherit. Still, Little Nate held his chin up and smiled on what fortune gave him with the innocence of youth.

"I just—I'm not cut out to hold this commission," Evan said. "Nate's more of a man than me."

"You're a fine soldier, Second, and a good man," Joseph assured him. "One of the best, I'm privileged to know." Evan went back to his letter, shaking his head unconvinced. Joseph silently watched him before continuing, "Now I've to go and check on the rest of the men, make sure they're all right." He paused to glance back at his friend. Something dark hovered in the tent just beyond consciousness. Joseph feared they faced worse than defeat in battle. “Are you all right?”

Evan simply nodded, staring at the words. He held his coat in his lap like a child with a blanket. Joseph saw the shadow creep in on him. The shadow threatened to take him into a place where he would no longer have leave of his senses or cares. Remembering his duty to his other men, Joseph nodded back at him with a murmured farewell.

“You know where I am,” Joseph said.

Visiting home might have been the worst thing to happen to Second Lieutenant Evan Howell. Joseph exited the tent and told himself not to think so darkly. He peered up at the starry sky. Going to Vermont provided an opportunity to rest their minds from the monotony and terror of war. Besides, it was the only reason he knew about Emily.

Joseph thought to leave his friend alone for a bit. He would come back before he turned in for the night and see how he coped then. Joseph heaved a weighted breath and put his hands in his pockets. While he walked through the dusky camp glad to stand down, Joseph realized Evan’s words made him admit to his doubts. His negative thoughts laid in wait like the shadow over his friend’s mind. Some of the soldiers beat out a tune on old instruments to keep the despair at bay. Evan shook something loose that Joseph tied up and packed away a longtime ago. The revelry barely touched him.

Evan was full of youthful vibrancy when he came to the academy, and this attitude complimented Joseph’s. Teamed, they held enough energy to put a cannonball through a six foot stonewall backed with steel reinforcements. Many of the officers commissioned at the school believed they would make a strong force in the cavalry if placed together. It went easily to seek Second Lieutenant Howell with all the recommendations. Now they faced what they trained for and one half of the team stood crippled.

Joseph shook his head thinking it all over. The way they easily rallied the men to their sides now meant nothing in the grander scheme. They held no power to sway fate. Joseph wrapped a cigarette and lit it. He peered at the silver case of his lighter, engraved with good wishes from a man he hoped to work for someday. Congratulations, A. Wallace. May 1860.

Bitter feelings lifted to replace despair. Joseph tucked away the lighter in his jacket and walked on smoking his cigarette in search of anything that would make him smile, even for a small time. Williamsburg brought up only unhappy memories. He wanted to put it far behind.

Joseph's mind turned to thoughts of school. A certain cadet remained at school, missing this moment. Evan had faced such shock when he matriculated from the academy and joined them there a year ago. The green officer faired well, perhaps better than Joseph. However, time turned against him, infecting Evan with despondency. Joseph saw the real face of war. He lowered his chin, drawing from the cigarette. The evil of it had come to claim Evan as its next victim. Joseph was angry at the loss too, but he blocked it out. He saw the result of the mania men developed from battle. He could not let that happen to him. He had to keep it together in hope of an end.

Passing a campfire, Joseph's eyes dragged over the men who sat around it, drinking when they shouldn't. He never said anything to the superiors. He took a drink occasionally himself. Alcohol helped dull the pain but left it for later. The men sang a song and some noticed him while he passed. They swung their mugs to him, hollering a bawdy tune loudly. Joseph smiled and turned away down another path.

At the back of his and the officer tents of the company, the enlisted men pitched their homes. With this despair on their shoulders, they probably turned to drink and idleness, saving their hurts the only way they knew. Joseph decided to join them and drink away despair and longing. Spying his men and their roaring bonfire, Joseph recalled a moment of his past, when he told Evan his reason for staying, sitting and weeping into two mugs of beer like boys.

"It's too late to leave. I came here with some really big misconceptions—but I'll see it through or die trying by their rules," he had said to his friend. He remembered blinking blearily into his mug, perhaps rethinking the oath. "I hope it won't be to die in this god awful horse piss."

Evan's laugh echoed in his memory. Joseph saw his friend's face glow with the affects of drink. Evan was happier then. Nothing diminished his mood, a middle class farm boy headed for the ranks of higher society. He had no real need to drink away his cares. He had none. He drank to help his friend. He stood by Joseph, filling their empty days with vague masculine amusement. Standing there in the dark of night, looking at the fire in the distance, Joseph knew now was the time to repay him. Joseph wondered if he had found love only to lose his dearest friend.

To compound Joseph's fears, Cadet Conrad would join the military, a fresh officer from the Point. Joseph refused to think of what Emily's brother would turn into if he met the same ghost Joseph and Evan carried. A green officer required success to feather his nest and make a brilliant and strong career. Stellar recommendations brought Joseph to comply with a request to see the boy placed in his unit. At Joseph's side, he would learn how to defend his life and wage war in earnest.

In the wake of bending to Emily's will, Joseph wondered if he made a grave mistake. He kept his doubt and fears within, never mentioning it to his Captain. Joseph counted no success under his hat and gave up on seeing it sometime ago. The glory he once believed to exist in a soldier's duty faded. It would make him a poor teacher.

Evan had placed his own request, telling their superiors the man would make one of the finest officers the military would ever see and he came backed by the university. Taking back the request would raise other questions. It was trouble he did not want to bring to Evan.

Joseph knew Michael would definitely join the Army of the Potomac. He wanted to tell Evan, but realizing his own fears at the news, backed down at the last minute. Joseph looked annoyed with himself and threw the butt of the cigarette away to the ground with an angry flick. Perhaps he should have waited to manipulate matters and not agreed to please the woman he left behind. Trouble would come of it surely.

Shaking his head, Joseph let it go. He would soon see what his actions brought and not before it came to pass. He could hope for now the man would take a scrape to the leg and go home wounded, but alive. Imagining Emily's tear filled eyes and tear stained face, he hated the responsibility he brought onto himself. If Michael suffered anything serious, he felt sure Emily would blame him and that he could not stand.

"Lieutenant," an older soldier said.

The man waddled toward Joseph with the rocker and bars of his rank glowing on his arm in the firelight. The sound of his voice stole Joseph's thoughts away and he looked to see the man rush up to him with a cherry red face and bright smile. Joseph smiled recognizing his Sergeant, an enlistee he befriended when he first came to his commission.

The middle aged Irishman with orange hair, hailed fresh from the old world, trying to find a better life for his family in America. The moment he stepped from the boat, he had signed up. Men like him stood numerous among the ranks, fighting for steady pay, as they were denied elsewhere. To their disappointment, they found no reason to classify what they did receive in compensation as steady. However, they served their new country with the dedication and valor many natural born citizens lacked.

"Me and the boys wondered if you'd have a mite of a drink with us tonight, Lieutenant," he said to Joseph in a thick Irish brogue. His red brows raised and his high forehead crinkled. He smiled, already well into his drinking.

"Thank you, sergeant. That'd be fine," Joseph said, smiling at his companion horse soldier.

Joseph patted his shoulder, as the Sergeant turned and led him to the fire.

"We foun some fine beer, but ya mus'n tell," he said, waddling along beside Joseph. He paused to smile at him, trusting the Lieutenant's confidence. Joseph never breathed a word about the drinking in his unit, unless the men turned slovenly. Still, Joseph dealt with matters himself and fairly. The men appreciated him and his candor. "We're bout ta ave a sing along. Ya just sit there now," he pointed to a fallen log and Joseph sat down easily at his prompting. A man from Evan's unit played a tin whistle, a low tune that set the somber night background.

"Good evening, sir," the men chimed alternately, holding their mugs or some same vessel. A few held ramshackle instruments.

"Good evening," Joseph returned respectfully, looking at each of them.

The unit's respect for him showed in their eyes and expressions when they looked at him and it showed when they performed their duties. The men sought out his companionship like family and held little fear of reprimand for their occasionally disorderly behavior.

"Now we eard that ya foun a lovely lass up nort'," the Sergeant said, smiling down at him. He offered Joseph a mug of beer. Then, he winked to a dark haired man, standing across the fire from him who held a banjo in his arms. "Let us drink ta har," he raised his silver cup to the other men.

"To my dear, Miss Conrad," Joseph said, grinning. His eyes sparkled in the orange glow. "May we win this damn war, so I may go home to you soon and not find you spoke nuptials before."

"To Emily," one of the men echoed with a grin.

"Here, here." The Sergeant said reverently and drank down the contents of his mug. "By Jaysuz—if only we all ad a bit a nice fluff ta fight for. We'd win this war quick as lightnin."

"Your married—aren't you, Sergeant McGuire?" Joseph asked him, his brow furrowed in confusion.

"By the Virgin I am, Lieutenant Maynard," he said lyrically and smiled small into his empty mug, thinking of the woman he left at home with his babes. Lifting his glassy eyes with a spark of deviousness, he added, "But she ain a woman ta fight foor, but radder a women ta fight wid." McGuire said, falling to laughter with the men. It proved easier to laugh the absence away with a joke, rather than admit the truth of it. "Well now—what about a song?" He said to Joseph's knowing gaze.

"How's bout a little somethin I picked up in Kentucky?" Another man asked from his ruddy face, eyes gleaming with alcohol and a smile. He readied an old Irish drum in his capable looking hands.

"Where'd little Janey go to?" Sergeant McGuire asked, holding out his hand to pause the players. "Har fiddle'd make a shinning improvement ta yur song, me boy."

McGuire's watery eyes searched out the area around them until they settled on a young woman, owning a crown of curly blonde hair, tied up out of her face in a haphazard bun. She busily scrubbed some clothing in a tub beside the tent of an officer. Perhaps he brought her along for her housekeeping services and to keep up his status as a wealthy man, if not other reasons no one spoke about. Sergeant McGuire called to her and she tipped her face toward the fire. The Sergeant then bade her bring her violin to the fire to play a few songs and take a break from her work. The young woman smiled at him, glad to receive an invite to leave the wash for a time. She quickly complied with McGuire's wish, ducking in and out of the tent to find her instrument. She joined them at the fire, shyly passing a smile and hello to the men. McGuire smiled back at her with a warm smile, a wink and thank you.

Soon surrounded by the music, Joseph's mind drifted far away from where he sat. He forgot about the destruction and the death that lay around him. He no longer lingered on the ghostly shadows of Manassas. He let his voice rise with the others when they sang in a strong chorus guided by the instruments. The beer flowed down his throat freely.

The hour grew later and Joseph found himself listening to a sad tune played by the tin whistle and drum. His eyes wandered up the path between the tents, wondering if Evan felt better about his day yet. He meant to check on him. However, he saw the young man of his thoughts tread a confident gate in his direction, wearing a fresh uniform and his old smile. Joseph waved his hand to him and Evan increased his pace to join him at the fire.

"Ma said Em misses you," Evan said, teasing him with the contents of the letter he read earlier. "Stands out in her eyes whenever we're mentioned." Evan paused, searching his features with a painful smile. He missed Emily too. "Said the widow Murphy's paid a visit to the Conrads after we left."

"Why thank you, Second Lieutenant. You've told me something every man hopes to hear," Joseph smiled triumphantly. "But—uh—Miss Conrad wrote me since we left. She failed to mention missing me so completely in her version."

"Her pa let you?" Evan said with shock. He gaped at Joseph.

"No. I don't think they know," Joseph said. He turned his eyes away and put his palms together, elbows resting on his knees and shook his head.

"By God," Evan breathed. He accepted a mug of beer from McGuire. "You're gonna get in trouble with that woman's ma."

"I already am," Joseph grinned.

Evan returned the expression and laughed. Joseph told him of the woman's cold demeanor many times while they stayed at his parents' farm. Having faced it a few times as well, Evan believed him. He felt badly for Joseph, but the gains negated the risks. If he could have turned his heart to loving Emily, it would not have stopped him either.

Joseph thought about the letter he wrote to Emily that day. She would faithfully respond to him in a week or so. In his heart, she stood with him through every battle, begging him to be careful, so he would return. It broke his heart to see the tearstains that decorated the few pages he already received, smudging the scrawled words of her hand. He knew she knew everything he wrote her before she even received the letter. Unfortunately for them, the war was well covered by reporters. He recalled instances of them watching the battles, pen and paper in hand, jotting down notes while the battle raged. Joseph thought they should raise a gun and provide some support, better than their slandering tongues could do. She read the papers her father received and he knew Mr. Conrad would keep his little girl informed.

It enraged many of the soldiers who saw the reporters treat their life and death struggles like sport. They needed bloodshed and failure to make their wages. They did not see real men dying in the battlefields, instead behaving as though they watched actors on stage. Even worse, they saw coin. While men earned ghastly wounds that they would carry through life, they fattened their wallets. At one time, reporting was important, in that they alone could spread a needed word to the public. In the least, they turned the public's stomach against war.

Joseph drank from his mug, feeling as bitter as the aftertaste. He felt a folded piece of paper move in his jacket pocket. He kept one of Emily's letters with him, delivered into his hand from the Corporal earlier that day. Lowering the mug from his lips, he swallowed and tasted the terrible nectar once more. Joseph pulled out the letter, looking at the open envelope and his address written on the outside. Joseph slightly smiled at the paper and set his mug on the ground by his boot heel. He felt Evan watch him and offered it with two fingers.

Evan said nothing, taking the letter from him and unfolding the thirds. He looked at the paper with concern, slowly fading to a smile. She lifted his heart, too. She never failed them.

29th of April 1862
Dear Joseph,
I fear our exchange of letters will be discovered and deemed improper by father. I hide them well, and often Hettie helps, by getting the mail and sorting out your notes. Still, I am afraid. Would you consider it too much, if I ask you to disguise your letters somehow? Maybe, address it from a family member? I apologize, Joseph. I would let anyone know how we feel, except for the fear of being forbidden to hear from you again. Neither of us know how long the war shall last. Even one day is too long.

The days pass so slowly on the farm. With all the new help, there is nothing left to keep me occupied. I hate the South nearly as much as my mother for the pains they cause me. Don't they know all they cause? They must little care either, considering how they enslave human beings. How can they call themselves Christian, profaning God to justify themselves?

You would not believe all the things they did to Hettie. I've cried so many times with all the anger it builds inside of me. I wish you and your men the protection and skill of the angels and pray the rain stops soon. May grace guide you to victory and save our nation from the devil. . .

Far in the north, while she hastily wrote, Emily left smudges from her fingertips on the page. She paused, thinking to rewrite the letter, but the postman was due in moments. Looking at the pages, Emily softly smiled. She thought of how Joseph would only see how much she missed him.

Emily quickly folded her letter, stuffing it in an envelope, sealing the flap, and ending by hurriedly scrawling the address on the front. Rushing from the privacy of her room to the first floor and out of the front door, she waited on the lawn for the postman's arrival. Her eyes went to the bright sky. The sun still hung in the East. She should have checked the clock on the way out.

Emily's flight attracted the attention of her mother more. This new behavior had caught her eye more than a few times since the departure of the Lieutenant over a month ago. Margaret peered out of the parlor window, gently pushing the curtains aside. Concern pinched her dour face as she watched Emily pace by the fence tapping an envelope on her hand.

Margaret continued to watch from the window. She saw the unwarranted excitement that built when the postman rode up the south road. Her daughter gave him an envelope and waved before turning back to the house with a bundle of mail. Emily sifted through them fast, finding what she looked for and stuffed it into her apron pocket. Lifting her gaze, she looked around the yard suspiciously. Her face flushed.

Margaret shook her head and let the curtain close. Her daughter was up to something, she felt it and saw it. Placing a hand over her heart, she sat in the chair by the window. Her breath left her in her panic. She wondered if her little girl meant to run away from home and meet that terrible southerner somewhere. Margaret nearly fainted at the idea.

The front door opened and closed, waking Margaret from her imaginings. She stood quickly and went into the hall to meet her daughter. Emily gave her mother a small smile, passing her the packet of letters. She stepped aside to the stairs not knowing her mother watched everything from the parlor windows. Margaret's gaze followed her, thinking the worst actions her daughter could engage in. She remained hesitant, but spoke once her ideas got the better of her.

"Emily," Margaret called. "What is wrong?" She took on a benign loving tone and expression, which instead made her appear as though she ate sour grapes.

"Nothing, Mamma." Emily turned on the stairs to look down to her.

"Why are you so flushed dear?" Margaret asked, stepping up to her. "Are you feeling well?" She felt her daughter's forehead with a cold thin hand.

"No reason, Mamma. The postman just said I looked pretty today," Emily said.

Emily smiled through her lie and tried to bounce on her feet, like she saw the other young women do over compliments. She stilled seeing the shock on her mother's face. Emily clasped her hands in front of her and lowered her gaze to the stairs.

"The postman is an old man that should not be making eyes at young women," Margaret snapped out of shock. Her own daughter had turned into an unsavory liar and she knew just who to blame. "And you should not feel flattered by his compliments so deeply."

"Sorry Mamma. I won't do it again," Emily said, lifting her eyes to her mother's face. She took on an expression of a misbehaving little girl, chastened for a minor breach.

"No you shall not. Let someone else get the mail from now on," her mother said authoritatively. No question marred her direct order, and it should not turn out disobeyed. "I don't want him to get any ideas about you or our good family. The Lord knows what that'll bring us," her mother clutched at her throat with a shaking hand. That would put someone in the way of any more secret posts.

"As you wish, Mamma." Emily said nervously.

"What was it you sent with him?" Margaret asked.

"A letter to Michael," Emily lied. She held her breath while her mother assessed her.

"Go on then," Margaret waved her away and turned to the hall below. She mumbled to herself, as she sought the back parlor.

Emily hesitated, then quickly turned and climbed the rest of the stairway, glad to leave her mother behind. She raced to her room, where she could at last read the new letter alone. With bated breath, Emily awaited every secret missive from her absent lover. Now it finally came, allowing her the first deep breath drawn in more than a week.

Inside her room, Emily shut and locked her door. She tore open the envelope, letting it fall to the floor of her bedroom and read the black scrawls on the page. It made her feel cold to think the only part she held of him came in the form of lifeless scribbles. The pain burned her eyes and the tears built without the first word.

Joseph told her about the battles he fought and survived, despair on the tip of every line. She placed a hand over her heart worrying for him. She told herself he was fine. He lived. However, their letters took so long to pass into each other's hands, she could not be fully assured all remained just so. She dashed the thoughts from her mind, refusing to let them take root and grow more fear and despair.

May 15, 1862

Dear Emily,

If ever I needed a thing from you, it is now.

If this rain does not stop, I am afraid I will either float away or melt into the earth. It depresses me to no end, believing we will have to endure this weather until the end of the campaign. What I would not give to be under your roof right now. I would endure any number of cold glances and ill conversations with your mother, just to be dry.

It is nearing the time the Point will celebrate its next graduating class. I hope you keep your chin up and think of the accomplishment your brother makes. Do not concern yourself with his safety any longer. I will do all that I can to keep him from harm during his career. I am not promising more than I am able, capable of only a small influence.

In truth, I would rather shoot the boy in the leg and send him back to you where he belongs, safe and sound. I have heard promising news from Captain Braxton that Michael will indeed join us. No one knows what comes, until they open their orders. Wish him luck for me, since I am continuously detained by the Army's escapades in Virginia. You know I would shake hands with him myself if I could. Perhaps I yet will.

I am wondering, my dear, if you would care to hear how else I fair on this forsaken peninsula? I never thought you would ask, Emmy. Despite the rains and the hard march, I remain healthy and optimistic that our efforts will find reward in the end. Many of the men have taken ill from the weather. It has slowed us some, but I think that despite all, we shall prevail. I have faith in General McClellan, as he came to the Army and straightened us out the last time we faced such harsh odds. It is only fair to believe he will guide us true through this ordeal. When the smoke clears we shall find our United States, intact, as before, and you will find me at your door.

How do your days pass at home? I imagine you standing there in your bedroom, reading my letter, hiding from that mother of yours. Your forehead is pinched, just like when you work on your needlepoint, concentrating with all your strength. You may never know how beautiful you are to me, never knowing how often I just simply watched you. I will try to tell you for the rest of our lives, if God wills it. . .

Emily sat on her bed and turned to the second page. She could only imagine what Joseph wrote on all the sheets. Her heart beat feverishly for news of what her lover and Evan faced in the coming days. She wanted to read the war would end soon and Michael would not take part in battle.

A light patter on the door stole her attention. She looked up from the letter to the panel door. Neatly folding her letter, she put it back in its envelope and placed it in the safety of her dressing table drawer. Her mother probably found more to say about the matter with the postman, but Emily did not want her to find out the real reason she blushed. Smoothing her skirt, Emily went to her bedroom door.

Joseph had invaded her heart at the first moment she saw him. He was now the most important part of her life and no sensibilities could change that. She would risk everything for him, including her reputation.

Emily unlocked her door and turned the knob. She slowly pulled it open. In the dim light of the hallway outside, she faced a pair of large almond shaped dark eyes peering back at her. Emily's still heart beat again.

Realizing she faced Hettie, she stepped back to make room for the woman to join her. Hettie quietly entered the room with a smile, still holding the broom from her chores. Emily turned from her leaning into the hall to peek for any other occupants. The lonely hall stared back and she ducked back shutting and locking her door once more.

Emily turned back not sparring her friend a glance and dashed to her dressing table to recover her letter. Emily removed the pages from the envelope and unfolded them, placing the first aside to return to where she left off.

Hettie stood at Emily's side, looking between the paper and the girl's face. She enjoyed reading over Emily's shoulder and sharing in the girl's trials as an equal. It excited Hettie to know the wonderful secrets Emily kept and hear of what happened in the horrible South she ran from. She dreamed of one day reading, "I killed a man named Edward McAvery." Hettie knew it wrong to wish a man murdered, especially at the hands of a friend, but deep inside she knew only the death of that man would bring her peace.

"It's written in his hand," Emily told her, finishing the letter. She sighed with delight. "He's all right," she smiled, handing the pages to Hettie.

Hettie accepted the note. Reading the first line, thanks to Mr. Conrad's lessons, she scowled and said, "It's near two weeks old, Em."

"He can't post his letters easily, Henrietta," Emily said, trying not to grow concerned by the observation which echoed hers.

Joseph's letter went on with the drudgery of camp, amusing tales of his enlistees and some of the other officers including Evan. Emily clearly saw the difficulties he faced, describing the horrors of war and what he faced. Like her father, Joseph did not know what keeping her informed would do. He only understood that he needed to relieve his mind. Emily never complained of it to him in her responses. She would allow him to unburden his soul without guilt, no matter how much it hurt or frightened her to hear it. His health, body and soul, was more important than hers.

Emily feared the worst while she waited for her letters, but now she found reason to fear even more. Michael faced graduation and assignment to the Army of the Potomac under General McClellan, reporting to Captain Darcy Braxton, the same as Joseph and Evan. She supposed these officers needed much encouragement from their juniors to agree to such a move. Joseph did not tell her much more than his success in the matter. Emily hoped they would find her brother a good soldier or those that suggested his placement would certainly find trouble.

The letter from Joseph barely preceded Michael's graduation. In the morning they would go south to the train station and from there arrive in West Point, New York. Michael finally told his father that he planned to join the active Army, as his superiors requested him. They thought him a fine soldier already and competent to command a unit in their nation's struggle. Two days would pass before she saw him, but at least she would see him.

The trip to the southern end of verdant New York proved a somber one for the entire family. Hettie remained behind, afraid to alert anyone to her existence. They already endangered her once and felt that enough. This time they took Mr. Fordder's daughter MaryJane as servant. In Stuart's absence, the farmhands would watch over the home, keeping Hettie and the remaining housekeepers safe from harm. Emily found herself alone with only her father to protect her from her mother. However, Stuart did little to help. He paid no attention to the women of his family, sleeping the train ride away. He lay back with his mouth hanging open, drawing his air in drawn out snores.

Meanwhile, Emily embroidered some handkerchiefs for her mother's church group, sitting quietly and avoiding conversation. She used to enjoy going places, but this time was under a menacing shadow. She felt her mother's eyes on her, assessing what she thought she saw. Even MaryJane, normally chatty, avoided conversing with either of them. Emily wondered just how much her mother knew.

When they arrived, Emily could not wait to leave and hide at home in her room. Her mother's gaze held a note of disfavor, which Emily could barely stand any longer. She went to bed directly after dinner, complaining of a headache. Sitting on her bed in the room appointed for her in the rented townhouse, Emily unlaced the bodice of her dress, reaching behind herself.

A light knock sounded on her door. "Miss Emily," a small voice called from the other side of the portal.

"Come," Emily barely said aloud.

The door opened and MaryJane entered. She shut the door behind her, offering Emily a small smile. "I come to help ya get ready for bed, Miss."

"Oh—good," Emily smiled. "Just in time. These stays are giving me a difficult time."

"I'll get em," MaryJane said, going to the young woman when she stood with her back to her. "How are you feeling?"

"A little better," Emily admitted. "I think the embroidery hurt my eyes."

"Do you want me to bring you some tea?"

"No—I'm fine. Thank you, MaryJane," she sighed.

The room fell silent. MaryJane finished undoing the stays and then helped Emily out of her skirt and hoops, leaving her in her undergarments. Turning away, she found Emily's nightgown and brought it to her. She laid it on her bed with her robe and faced her. Emily removed her jewelry and then pulled the pins from her hair. MaryJane watched her. An expression of sadness came to the girl's features. Emily picked up a brush and ran it through her hair. She saw MaryJane in the mirror, hanging her head and looking expectant.

"Oh—MaryJane—what is it?" Emily barely found the strength to ask.

"Nothing, miss," MaryJane lied unconvincingly.

"MaryJane—"

"Your mother wanted Blythe to come with you," MaryJane began.

"You feel you don't belong here with us?" Emily turned to her.

MaryJane nodded, "But not just that."

"What else?" Emily asked sitting on her bed.

"Blythe couldn't come cause she'd been spreadin rumors bout you to the townspeople with Lauralee," MaryJane said. "I thought you should know."

Emily looked stunned, "So that's why she's angry with me." Emily paused and then looked to the young girl, admiring her jewelry and hairpins. "What else did she say?"

"Blythe said Lauralee Howell saw you in the woods with the Lieutenant. She said you made love out there—on the stone in the field."

"What?" Emily gasped. "I never," she cried.

"None of us believe it—Hettie told us he kissed you a few times," MaryJane said. "We don't believe anything Blythe says anyway. She always lies—and we know Lauralee does too. 'Sides, she's a crush on the Lieutenant."

"My poor father," Emily thought aloud.

"He doesn know," MaryJane admitted. "Your mother spoke to us in the kitchen one night—told us to watch what we said or our fathers and us could all look for jobs elsewhere."

"Oh—MaryJane," Emily cried. "I am sorry."

MaryJane nodded, "She's got Blythe watchin ya when she can." MaryJane paused. "Your father suspects Blythe of somethin—that's why she couldn come. Your pa is an awful smart man. I bet he'll piece it together and do somethin."

"I'm thankful it is you with us," Emily told her. Pausing, Emily let her tears dry on her cheeks. She could not let her mother win so early in the game. It came time to throw her punches. "You must do something for me," Emily said, holding her hand out to her. MaryJane sat on the bed with her, grasping her hand and smiling. "You must watch my mother and Blythe—tell me all they are up to."

"Like now," MaryJane whispered. "Oh—Miss. It scared me to tell you what I did say. Only Hettie put me up to it—when I could get the chance."

"MaryJane," Emily said seriously. "Hettie helps me now—but I need someone they won't expect. I need you."

"You are sneakin round with the Lieutenant," MaryJane gasped.

"Me and the Lieutenant trade letters," She admitted. "You may see it as sneaking if you wish, but—"

"You're in love," MaryJane giggled.

"Shh—" Emily quieted her. "You mustn't tell anyone."

"How romantic," MaryJane said dreamily. When she came back down, she added, "I'll help. Lieutenant Maynard was very nice to me."

Emily smiled and patted her hand. She would sleep easier that night, knowing someone watched over her.

The next morning, Emily rose easily when MaryJane came to wake her. She dressed and ate her breakfast in her room. A small while later, Emily joined her family in the rented parlor and they readied to leave for the academy.

Stuart and Margaret spoke little to each other and even less to their daughter. They left the house in silence and rode in silence. Emily wondered just how much they knew of her meetings and her letters. Her wondering only stopped when the ceremony began and drown out the thoughts with speeches from the blustering commanders.

After endless ramblings, Michael greeted them. He smiled broadly at his parents and sister, hiding the fear he felt inside. He had assumed the worry and now saw his mother's face wracked with it. He thought it wiser to hide his concerns, playing the stoic soldier.

Stuart took that moment to present his son with a small gift he meant to give him on this day for some time. With a smile, he reached into his jacket pocket and pulled out a small box with a plum ribbon around it. Michael looked at the presented box and turned a smile to his father accepting it.

"What's this?"

The family watched him, wearing smiles on each of their faces, proud expressions soon to suffer ruin with the information he would tell them. He waited, instead opening his present. Once the ribbon released the prize and the box lie open in his hand, he picked up a gold pocket watch and chain from the inside. Turning it over, he studied the craftsmanship. It looked nearly as fine of a piece as the one his father wore, if not better. Michael thumbed open the lid and looked at the clock face. The timepiece read correctly.

"There's an inscription there," Stuart told his son.

Michael turned it to the light, reading the words etched on the inside case. To our hero, we wish you a gallant career, 1862. The inscription burned his eyes. He took it from the box, passing the wrapping to his sister who took it without comment.

"Thanks, Pop," Michael said, trying to smile. He looked back down to the watch he held, letting a silence surround them. "I'm assigned to a cavalry unit in Virginia, the Army of the Potomac—must be Evan Howell's doing. Probably guilty for getting me into all this."

His father half laughed, "Something like that I'm sure." Michael watched his father put his arm around Emily. She smiled at him and he saw the worry strain her eyes. "You'll be needing that watch anyhow."

Michael smiled and looked at his family, detecting a story he felt sure he would hate to hear. Then again, if it upset his mother, as showed in her face, he might enjoy the tale.

"I won't come home at all," Michael told them, removing the attention from his sister. "I've to leave tomorrow to report on time."

"We know, son," Stuart said somberly. "It's all right."

"Tonight's the graduation ball," Michael said. "If it's okay—I'd like to take Emily."

Stuart nodded his ascent, rubbing Emily's arm. It assured him more than her. She could see the pinch in her mother's mouth.

That evening Michael took his sister to a ball in honor of the graduating class. He kept close to her side throughout the evening despite the men, tapping him out to have even a moment by her side, including his roommate Marcus. The man butted in more than most, stammering and stuttering, under her attention.

Under the respectful attentions of the soldiers, Emily positively glowed that evening. Those surrounding her radiated the glory back, like heavenly bodies, rising home. Many of the faces she saw that night would soon cease to exist as more than mere memories, passing in and out of time. Death faced them now, their training completed.

Emily smiled at her brother when he rejoined her, praying it would not be their last moments together. She never told him of the trouble at home. She found no power to speak it. She missed him, but could not pull him away from his duty to deal with family matters now. Besides, it was her responsibility to fix it.

"I want you to know, this was my choice," Michael told her. "No matter how mother makes you feel," Michael said. "I wanted this."

Emily looked into her brother's eyes. The tears welled in hers. She felt her heart tremble, releasing the blame to nowhere. She touched his arm and nodded.

"Evan will take care of you, if he can," Emily said. She just could not tell him the truth yet.

ℰ

After two days of rest back at home, the Conrads received an unannounced visit from an infamous acquaintance. A knock came to the door and Hettie answered it right away. Margaret joined her in the hall, not expecting anyone. To her shock, she found the notorious and rotund widow Murphy awaiting her. A fine city carriage sat outside, complete with finely dressed driver and decked out horses. The woman smiled warmly at her.

"Mrs. Conrad," the widow Murphy said, joyously. "I hope you do not mind. I came to call on your little Emily."

Margaret failed to understand the friendship the woman enjoyed with her husband and liked even less the reputation she brought with her. Margaret never condoned behavior such as Mrs. Murphy once engaged in and quite possibly continued. It only fanned her anger when the little round woman told her that she came not for Stuart, but rather to visit Emily. Her husband could endure what people may say, but a visit to Emily would only bring more curiosity to the developing events, which she learned of only weeks ago. What could this known jade want with her Emily? Was it her who coached the events and ruined the Conrads?

"Marge," Stuart's voice came from the study door behind her. "Call Emily. Good to see you, Abigail." His tone changed from commanding to charming.

"Oh—Stuart, it's such a fine night. I thought I would go out for a ride and then it dawned on me I have not seen your family in some weeks," Mrs. Murphy said, sounding all too familiar. She stepped to the husband and they shook hands, smiling at one another. "How are you Henrietta?" Mrs. Murphy asked when the maid came to take her cloak

"Fine, ma'am. Just fine. Thank you for asking," Hettie replied with a smile.

"Hello, Rose," Mrs. Murphy added, seeing the young woman pop in from the parlor with a duster in her hand. "How are you darling?"

"Mrs. Murphy," Rose said worried. She stared with wide eyes. "I-I'm good. And you?"

"Hettie," Stuart said. "Go fetch us Emily," he said when his wife appeared not to respond to his wishes.

"Yes, Mr. Conrad." Hettie turned and went to the stairs. She looked back over her shoulder to see a heated glance pass between husband and wife while Rose retreated to the kitchen.

Stuart then invited Mrs. Murphy to join him in the parlor to await his daughter. Margaret watched them walk away from her, clasping her hands before her breast. Her hands trembled with her anger. Her eyes flicked to Rose and away with something like disgust. Clasping her skirt, she reluctantly left earshot to be sure the maid went to put water on for tea. Nervously making her way down the hall, she looked back several times and saw Rose escape from the dining room back into the hall. The way her daughter befriended the housekeepers worried her, too. She feared Emily's judgment in friends led her down the wrong road. Without the support of her husband, what was she to do?

In the kitchen, Margaret found Blythe, washing the dishes from the supper preparations. Behind her, Jo-Hanna folded pastry dough around apples filled with raisins and cinnamon. She told the girl to make an extra one and expect a guest for dinner. From little Jo, Margaret turned to her sister, checking the food that cooked.

"MaryJane," Margaret said, gaining the girls attention from the ovens. The girl turned her brown eyes to her with an unspoken answer. "Please put some tea on dear, for Mrs. Murphy. She's come for a visit." MaryJane impressed her as a good girl, minding her business, seeking no trouble, and she worked hard.

"Yes, ma'am. Rose already stopped in," MaryJane replied to her mistress.

Margaret nervously nodded to her, remembering she must return to the parlor. She cast her eyes over the servants in the room, assuring herself that all went well. Turning her back on them, she crept out to the hall. Margaret heard her daughter's entrance along the stairs above. She joined her at the landing and dismissed Hettie from them, not wishing a house servant to hear what she would say.

"Mrs. Murphy is here to see you," she said once the housekeeper left them. "Would you have any idea what she wants?" Margaret asked her daughter, pursing her lips. She failed to disguise her displeasure at the woman's presence.

Emily looked at her mother confused, "I really have no idea, Mamma."

The pair regarded each other, the mother with disfavor and the daughter with defiance. Emily failed to see a reason for her mother's concern and passed by her with an expression near to anger. She heard what people said about the widow, but her father warned her to make her mind up on her own.

Of course, Emily doubted the widow's presence alone upset her mother. It must rank one of several items her mother noted, belonging to a list, which condemned her daughter. Since MaryJane told her of Blythe's loose tongue, she saw more and more of her mother's lack of trust. Her mother believed she planned something and would carry it out soon in full infamy. Emily felt the rift between them widen.

In Emily's eyes, her mother now appeared a woman who meddled too much and threw tantrums when her fantasies failed to come true. Her mother thought her a doll ever since she was a child. Back then, they planned for her wedding to Evan. Emily had her reasons for not loving the man as more than a brother, but none of them were good enough for her mother. Perhaps she should take Blythe's route and disclose his escapades, like the night of the dance and Miss Dunworth. However, Emily was not spiteful and cruel. She would not ruin a friend for her own ends.

Margaret carefully watched her daughter go to the parlor. She gave her a warning glance. Emily paid her no mind. She heard her husband speak to the guest in the other room and her stomach felt sick. Neither her daughter nor her husband complied with her wishes, when she only meant to guide them along the proper road. She had always known men and children strayed easily, but hoped that not to be true of hers.

Since their return from the academy, Blythe had discovered nothing to offer Margaret. She found herself watching once again and now wondering what Emily planned. Turning toward the parlor, she entered behind her daughter and masked her face in what she thought serenity. Emily played a dangerous game, going against her. She held the key to the girl's happiness.

Mrs. Murphy smiled up at Emily, "There's the lovely girl now."

Emily heard her father chuckle. Emily smiled shyly and alternated her gaze between them. Sitting in her usual place of late, her brother's chair, she folded her hands in her lap and waited. Silence filled the room and she felt her mother's angry expectant gaze on her. She looked toward her, where she sat beside her father on the couch. Her mother glared.

"What've you been up to dear?" Mrs. Murphy said, stealing Emily back to her. She smiled warmly across the small tea table separating them.

"Well, I shall excuse myself," Stuart said, both standing and interrupting the conversation about to begin between his daughter and the widow. "So you women can talk privately. Come Marge. I'm sure you've other matters to attend to before dinner," he smiled at his daughter and looked to his wife, waiting for her to stand. "I'm sure Abigail won't miss us," he stepped behind Margaret, guaranteeing she would also leave.

"I won't pretend that I don't know why you're here," Emily said once they sat alone. She kept her voice low, displaying the fear she lived with since coming home. She held her eyes on the lace edge of her top skirt.

The widow raised her brows at her, and laughingly said, "Indeed I would hope not."

"This is about Joseph," Emily continued.

"Very astute," the widow said, folding her hands in her lap.

"He wants you to keep an eye on me," Emily added. "He worries about my mother finding out—"

"No—actually I said I would watch over you while he kept himself away," at this she lowered her voice and pointed to the hall, where she well knew Margaret stood, listening.

"Margaret, whatever are you doing there?" Her father's voice came from his study. Emily looked to see him, pipe in his hand, glaring at the floor of the hall.

Rather suddenly, Emily's mother crawled out on her knees in front of the parlor archway. She smiled at them as if crazy and then looked back to the floor, searching for something. Emily already knew she looked for her conviction. She wondered how much her mother heard of her confession to the widow.

"I just dropped a needle I wanted to use for the mending," her mother explained. "I wouldn't want anyone to step on it." She produced a needle she kept in the folds of her hand and held it up. "Why here it is," she half laughed. Standing, she made a quick red faced retreat down the hall to her sewing room.

The widow smiled at Emily once her father went back to his office, "As I wanted to tell you, Joseph thinks he'll be gone for some time—I suggested that he write to you during his absence. Knowing your mother and her plans for you, I felt it might come to a problem. Stuart cannot manage her all by himself." She paused, leaning a little closer, "I'm merely visiting to assure myself you are well and you have been receiving his messages fine."

"All is well, Mrs. Murphy." Emily said, wanting to cry over what she just witnessed. "As you can see."

Mrs. Murphy smiled and nodded, "I shall make my visits regular. If you need me to post the letters or deliver them, I shall do that as well. You've a friend wherever you turn, Emily. Do not doubt that." She saw the doubt in Emily's eyes. "Your mother means well, but she often confuses the truth and ends up serving the devil in the end."

"Thank you, Mrs. Murphy," Emily smiled, seeing the trust she could hold in the woman and knowing, after the way her mother reacted to her visit, she must.

MaryJane entered the parlor carrying the tea tray. The cups and teapot rattled to announce her. She wore a small smile on her lips. The women fell silent while she served.

"If that will be all, Miss Emily?" MaryJane asked her.

Emily smiled and laughingly dismissed her. The young girl curtsied and hurried out. Emily watched the arch a moment after she went. She almost wished she held her place, the youth and lack of care. Emily quickly dashed those thoughts, knowing what praying for a change brought her the last time, and never wishing him away. She saw his eyes dance before hers as if he stood there now.

"Now, let us get on with our friendly visit," the widow said, setting aside her cup after a single sip. It clinked on the table and roused Emily from her memories. The widow smiled at her. "Oh—ho-ho—you do miss him—don't you?"

Emily could not fight the grin separating her lips. She swiftly discovered a true friend in Mrs. Murphy. Her conversation turned to guidance on the matter of handling correspondence with Joseph in a manner that would ensure success and go without detection. Emily listened to her intently, noting all she could. By dinner the widow and Emily found probable means in which to disguise their true designs.

Mrs. Murphy dined with them that night. Her presence reminded Emily of Joseph's by the way her mother avoided conversation and looked so sullen. Emily enjoyed her company thoroughly, as long as it enraged her mother. Soon she even dared to address her most informally, calling her Abigail.

~

Formal gatherings and celebration turned into distant memories all too quickly for Second Lieutenant Michael Conrad. He found himself on his way to Virginia, in a cramped train coach worrying if his mount would survive their journey or if he would need to buy another on the way to the camp. With his orders and commission, he felt full grown, but now he must fear more than the death of his horse.

Michael thought of home. He saw the blue walls of the hallway trimmed in dark wood. The polished wood floor glowed with glassy shine, stretching out before him to the back door. He wanted to walk that hall one more time. Forced to pay back the service the government afforded him, Michael hoped the price did not claim his dream of a return.

Michael thought of the day he graduated and the gift his father presented to him. He pulled the timepiece out of his pocket and looked at it. The train stopped with squealing wheels and puffs of steam billowing up to the sultry air. He put his watch away and listened to the conductor cry out the name of his stop. He stood up quickly and gathered his bag from the overhead.

A vast platform surrounded him, gaslights and weathered wood. People milled around by the hundreds, a great number of them wore a similar uniform to his. Waiting for the porter to find the rest of his belongings and his horse, he went to the claim area and studied his surroundings. He saw some dark skinned men, obviously belonging to a wealthy looking man that stood near the wall, also waiting for his belongings. He looked them over and his mind asked him why he stood there. What did he mean trying to seal his fate in blood? Michael lowered his eyes from them, seeing his uniform upset the man. Michael smiled to himself.

A man wearing the uniform of the rail line approached, leading a noble looking stallion toward him. The blonde buckskin cost him nearly his whole pay for the month. The seller insisted he present the finest horseflesh in all the states, even the parted ones. Michael haggled him down, but begrudgingly. A fine horse could save his life, so he had heard once or twice.

Tipping the porter nearly all his remaining money, in the form of minted coin, Michael packed up his baggage and led his mount from the area and onto the street. He counted seventy-two hours left to find his unit. He could spare no time to stay in a hotel for the night.

When his time was nearly up, Michael sat atop his mount, viewing the camp belonging to the Army of the Potomac. A sergeant busily cleared his orders, checking the lists of expected men and his identification. A moment later, Michael entered the camp with an escort in search of his captain. It stopped raining that day, but the sky looked threatening and moody. Riding his horse to where the men gathered, he asked where he should report. Having asked his way to his superior, he soon found himself pitching his tent with the help of a company corporal, who received orders to help place him. His pack and supplies lay in a heap on the ground with his cloak and cap draped on top.

"Well if it isn't the mother superior," a familiar voice called from behind, making him quit his labor.

Michael turned toward the familiar sound. His expression of distress faded to a smile. The raven haired neighbor he grew with since birth at last showed himself. He wondered since his arrival if he would see him.

"Evan," Michael sighed with a grin. They saluted. "Thank, God."

Michael stepped over some of his belongings strewn about the ground to join him and offer his hand for a shake. His eyes went to the man standing with him, noticing the first lieutenant bars all over his uniform. He could not place his name right then, but somehow he knew him. Was it first year at the academy? He saluted him appropriately.

"Second Lieutenant Howell," Evan corrected, taking his hand.

The two men shook hands. Evan's features brightened with a smile, seeing the familiar face from home. He thought such dealings lost to the past.

"Yes, of course." Michael nodded, lowering his hand back to his side.

The new officer's brave façade fell away and the misery of his fears showed in his eyes. He tried to keep his smile, but it did not touch the mirrors of his sister's own lovely features.

"This is your lieutenant," Evan explained the tawny haired stranger. "First Lieutenant Joseph Maynard. He went home with me on leave in March. Your pa might have told you about the fire and the gentleman that saved the cows."

"Oh—yeah, say!" He exclaimed, looking at the hero that saved his sisters pet bull from a terrible death. He then vaguely recalled meeting him first year. Such strange circles they moved in. "Let me thank you. What a hero," he smiled impressed by the legend of the man that stood before him. "That's great about Shakes. I'm sure my sister was really happy about that."

Michael offered his hand and they shook. The gesture spoke a great deal about the man. He met his strong gaze with his own and wondered if Marcus spoke true. If Joseph saved the cows, he met Emily. His sister must have swooned fiercely over this man. Yet, no one said a thing.

Joseph saw the sister glimmering just beyond reach in Second Lieutenant Conrad's features. The way he presented himself, it felt as if they knew each other nearly as long as he and Evan. His good nature lingered in his eyes, his smile, and his mannerisms. The Conrads once again impressed him.

"Your sister and the Lieutenant here, they've become good friends," Evan smiled deviously. He looked to Joseph, "I introduced you two a few years ago at school, but you wouldn't remember it now, Lieutenant."

Joseph nodded, "I remember something."

"Yeah," Michael agreed. "It happened a long time ago. But—well I can imagine after the fire, Em would take a shine to you. She loves that calf like her own baby," Michael told them. He regarded Joseph a moment to memorize his face better.

"Pleased to meet you finally, Second Lieutenant. Your friends and family think a great deal of you," Joseph said returning the gaze.

"Thank you, sir. The pleasure's all mine," Michael told them.

"If we can help you in any manner, have the Corporal call on us," Joseph told him.

"I certainly will," Michael said, placing his hands on his hips. He looked over his long absent friend for a moment. They stood in silence until he remembered himself. The Corporal still struggled with his tent while the other men stared at the mess. "Well I'd invite you in, but," he pointed to the sunken canvas.

"No matter," Evan said. "Join us at mess with the rest of the officers—when you get that damn thing up."

"I will. I will," Michael said. He bobbed his head and shifted on his feet nervously. He tried to disguise his eagerness, but it failed in the excitement of finding friends after so long alone.

Evan and Joseph sauntered away. They looked forward to their mess, both feeling too hungry to lend a hand to either the recruit or the Corporal. They disappeared in the crowd of men, meandering around the other canvas city.

Michael drew his eyes back to the wilted tent he would call home until the war ended. He looked at it, stark white compared with the grayed and dirtied tents surrounding him. Everyone in a mile would know he just came there. Michael hung his head, guilty to come so late to the dance.

The Corporal struggled with the tent stays some more. Michael woke himself and went to help. They soon worked the tent into standing position and Michael's belongings placed inside. Michael dismissed the enlistee and pulled out his gloves and hat. Putting both items on his person, he stepped out of his small airy accommodations and tried to find his way to the tent where the others expected him.

After asking the men he passed along the way, bungling through his commission, Michael finally found them. The front flap of the wide tent hung open and a long table stretched the center distance. In the chairs around it sat Evan, Joseph and another man Michael met earlier. While he stood there, two more officers stepped past him and entered to take their seats. More officers, Michael thought to himself.

Captain Braxton presented himself a secretive man when Michael reported for duty. He also came off cold and uninterested. However, his current actions betrayed that shell. He wore a glowing smile and his features looked warm in the lamplight. Michael watched all of them, hesitating still more. He checked his uniform and approached the entrance. Ducking under the flap, he heard the men fall quiet.

"Good evening, Captain Braxton," Michael addressed his commander, standing beside the table in stiff respect. "Lieutenant—Second Lieutenants," he saluted the others, half smiling at Evan.

"Welcome, Second Lieutenant Conrad," the Captain said with something like contempt, marking his features.

Michael regarded him cautiously biting his bottom lip, remembering the man sent him away callously, to fend for himself as he pleased. He knew nothing of what to expect of his superiors here. He grew used to those at the academy without thought that they would not always exist above him. Now, he stood hundreds of miles away from home and far from the sight of his university. He would start all over, as if the stress of a new post posed too little a hurdle by itself.

"You're welcome to a seat," Joseph said, pointing to the empty chair with the place setting.

"Lieutenant Maynard tells me that you and the Second Lieutenant are old friends," the Captain said, leaning with his elbows on the table and looking into him.

"Uh-yes, sir," Michael said after sitting. He looked at his empty plate self consciously. "We grew up together in Vermont," Michael added.

"Is that right? Well, that may explain why he requested you to join us in the Potomac," the Captain smiled, setting his attention on his own plate. He turned it carefully, as if studying its surface, but tried to keep from shaking his head and laughing.

"Requested?" Michael said perplexed.

"Yeah," Evan said, looking warily to Joseph. He did not want the boy to find out what went on to get him there and then figure out the reason. "Emily wrote to me requesting it. She thought maybe the man that got you into this mess could do his part to see you through it." Evan's eyes often traveled to Joseph's. His friend regarded him steadily, watching him struggle for an excuse. Evan could hear the Captain, snickering as he unfolded a napkin onto his lap. "I hope you ain't mad at her."

"No-no," Michael said, looking at Evan suspiciously. "She's not nearly as meddlesome as our mother—yet."

The table shared a laugh and then fell silent. A young Private started the supper service. The Captain received his meal first, then Joseph and the other lieutenants, followed by Evan and finally Michael. Michael hardly believed the meal set before him. However, he felt so starved he did not question it.

The prayer led by Captain Braxton echoed in his ears. A silence, broken by camp sounds followed and then the men set to eating. Conversation lifted the mood of the tent once more. Most of it concerned the subject of the new man. Once they satisfied themselves with mocking him, they begged for news of where he came from, the academy and everywhere else along the way. These men hungered for the news of home, draining him dry on every detail.

Near the end of the meal, Michael stared out the open flap of the tent. He saw the soldiers step by. A knot of officers paused outside, surrounding a shorter man with thick dark mustaches. His dark eyes peered into their mess and Michael found his heart and thoughts stilled.

The other men rose to their feet, wiping their faces, suddenly catching sight of the General. The knot of officers and McClellan turned toward them and salutes were given around. Every eye held a measure of nervousness among those inside the tent. Outside, the officers looked over the interior of their mess with cold assessing eyes. Michael felt the nervousness trembling through him.

McClellan stepped just inside the entrance. His dark gaze looked them over carefully. He held his hands behind his back in an ease stance that invoked images of his commander in chief. Michael looked toward him from the corner of his eye. The General presented nearly all the youth of Michael and his friends in a face hidden behind a dark mustache that hid his mouth. No gray marred the dark hair hidden beneath his cap. Michael flicked his eyes away. He did not want to gawk at the man and find a reprimand for it. He stood a graduate of

West Point, a refined soldier and officer. Gawking was the style of lesser men.

Awaiting the words of the General, Michael looked at the tent top and tried to work up some spit to wet his dry mouth. He knew the man commanded this army, but had not thought of ever meeting or seeing him. He heard so much of the war hero at the academy that he and the other boys raised him to the status of a celebrity.

"How do you and your men find themselves this evening, Captain Braxton?" McClellan's voice broke their silence.

"We are well, General—sir," Captain Braxton responded.

"I hear there is a new man who joined you today," McClellan stated without looking to any other man.

"Yes, sir. Second Lieutenant Conrad," the Captain suggested the fresh junior officer.

McClellan's eyes fell on him, as if Michael just entered the tent. Michael stiffly saluted and received one back. McClellan reached out a gloved hand and shook Michael's. The young officer gaped and his face flushed with embarrassment.

"I'm pleased to meet you, sir." Michael said, finding his words, laughing a little in excitement.

"My pleasure, Second Lieutenant. Welcome to the Potomac. I hope you'll find it well enough to stick by us for a time," the General smiled.

"I plan to enjoy a very long career, sir," Michael told him, grinning.

"Good," he smiled and then turned away. "Carry on," he called back to them. Darkness overtook his demeanor.

The men saluted and returned to their meals, paying no more attention to the visit. Evan smiled across the table at Joseph when Michael watched their leader walk away down the alley of tents. He still stood in aw, like a child meeting his hero.

Turning back to the company officers, Michael looked at them with stars still in his eyes. Lieutenant Maynard nodded to him and returned to his plate too hungry to care. Michael jumped back into his chair. He looked at his plate with half interest. Picking up his fork, he shook his head to clear the impression.

"Did you see that?" Michael said. He pushed a forkful of food into his mouth, chewed and spoke again, "The General himself."

"Finish your supper, lad. We might not eat for a while after morning comes," the Captain said with foresight.

The officers stopped smiling at Michael's youth, becoming sobered by the Captain's words. The meal continued until complete, held in a veil of silence, except for the metal utensils scraped against the bowls and plates. The lamplight flickered in a breeze, waking them each time to the understanding they feared. Tomorrow they marched. Maybe they would find a battle.

In the following days, through skirmishes met on their march to the south of the peninsula of Virginia, Michael displayed his great abilities and extensive enthusiasm. The first time they fired shots, Joseph felt unsure of the green officer, but Michael stood steadfast and brave. He faced the gray enemy with a stalwart determination. It reminded Joseph of the man's sister Emily. If he had the misfortune of her birth as a man, she would most likely turn out a finer soldier than any of them. Thankfully, she had come to them a very pretty woman.

At the end of the skirmish with the gray coats, Joseph searched out the other units of the company, taking a headcount for Braxton while the Captain prepared to report to their superiors. In the field among the bodies, Second Lieutenant Conrad stood beside Evan, helping one of their mortally wounded comrades until a doctor came. The young officer looked a little shaken, but no worse for his experience. Joseph approached Michael with a smile when the younger man stood to greet him. They nodded to each other after a flat silent salute.

"How do you feel about it now?" Joseph asked, looking around. His dark eyes blackened, reflecting the death that surrounded them. It reminded him of Emily at the barn fire.

"I'm all right, sir." Michael said, sounding tired.

"Good," Joseph looked to him. He half smiled at Michael's dirty face. He brushed a hand across Michael's shoulder to rid of a dust smear. The boy looked down and brushed off his dirty uniform, only succeeding in making it worse. Joseph laughed lightly. "Slow down—there's no glory for a dead man," Joseph advised Michael. "Pick your targets. Take them carefully. You'll get the feel soon enough, once this doesn't bother you so much any more." Joseph crossed his arms not sure he approached the subject as well as he thought he could.

"Does it ever get easier, Lieutenant?" Michael looked out across the field where dead men lie like sacks of discarded waste.

"No—," Joseph answered honestly. "Sometimes you think you got a thick skin, then you find yourself emptying your guts over the side of a fence at the sight of a leg blown off."

"Thank you, sir—for not coloring it," Michael said lowering his face, unable to hold Joseph's powerful gaze. He looked over the field again, sure that if he looked enough the affects would fade.

Joseph patted Michael's shoulder, knowing what the man felt. He watched the young officer, waver between insanity and loss of all feeling. He could not tell him any differently. He wished he knew how to lie, but a lie would just hurt them all in the end. Nor could he scare the man more than he already had. Nothing would keep the boy from becoming a soldier. Michael drew this lot of his own will. Now was the time to pay for that choice. It was time for them all to pay.

"Joe," Evan said, stealing the Lieutenant's attention from Michael. "He's gone," he said. Evan cradled one of his former soldier's head in his lap.

The man's face was pale with sickly death. Evan closed the eyes, passing his gloved hand over the lids. His mouth remained open, still drawing the last breath. The men could only look at him, laying there without peace in his final rest.

All wondered if this was their fate. The mask of agony would haunt their dreams, as the joyful features had once decorated their days. A ghastly reminder danced beyond the barrel of a rifle.

Evan stood, carefully placing the man's head on the ground. He backed away from the dead soldier, joining his friends. They kept silent, scanning the field and bodies. All three wished they could forget.

"I'll write the widow," Evan mumbled. He looked back to his enlistee. He would miss the man more than any of them, remembering the cheerful and fair heart. "Best to come from me."

"Good man," Joseph said. "Conrad—any casualties?"

"Three sir," Michael said.

"Write them up," Joseph ordered. "I need the report for Captain Braxton. Don't forget to send a letter to their next of kin."

Soon after the desolation of that skirmish, Braxton's Company faced more devastation. The pain of war reached to the home front, showing in the eyes of those left behind who awaited news of their loved ones. Joseph knew that when Emily read his letters, the events of the battles stood long since past and most of the details were already known to her from her father's papers. Waiting would have crushed him with the apprehension of what followed.

Joseph walked his path from battle to battle, destruction falling under pretty names of once pretty towns. The end to the beauty came with their arrival, rifles and bayonets bloodying the ground reveled in by farmers. All the while, Joseph thought of his honor and the promise he made so boldly to Emily. Beautiful memories soon became tainted with dark promise of a tortured death.

On horseback, he faced the overflowing and sluggish Chickahomony River beside Captain Braxton. The banks of the river swelled from the unflagging rain. At this level it threatened to destroy the Potomac's plans. Braxton told him they were headed for Richmond. The forces stood split along the banks and outlying posts awaiting orders. Joseph thought they may eventually meet with another army to finish off the Confederate's hold up. The only connections between the various units lie in unstable bridges, which they viewed at that moment. The flooding rocked them, threatening to drag them down the river.

"Captain," Joseph said, wrapping and lighting a cigarette. He became fast at the detail. "What if the bridge goes?"

Captain Braxton turned a gleaming smile to him, his blond hair glowing in the sunshine, "Boy, do you know how to swim?"

Joseph laughed though he found the jest less than amusing. He watched the river rage by, dragging driftwood and all else with it. Manny sauntered a bit under him. Joseph eased the horseback down. Obviously the animal liked the idea less than him.

"Captain!" A voice called from the distance. The company Corporal ran along the field between the waiting mounts.

Joseph pulled Manny out in front and met the Corporal. The young man gave him a ratty piece of paper, folded and wrinkled. Joseph looked at the paper, his expression looking more serious by the line. Lowering the page he went to his captain to pass the news.

"What've you there, Maynard?" Braxton took the paper from him. He read, taking on the same expression his subordinate wore. He looked to Joseph, handing back the page. Joseph regarded him warily. "Tell the men," Braxton said gravely. "They should know what they face. Thank you, Lieutenant."

After Joseph relayed the message that the Confederate forces expected them, they awaited further news and orders. All of them knew they faced great numbers and that Washington may not find it well to direct reinforcements in their direction. During the wait, the rains steadily worsened and, in the end, washed away the bridges, isolating the pockets of companies from each other and their enemies. They could not win this battle in such straights, but no one called the retreat. Joseph sensed the Confederates needed the win here to set their break to sovereignty permanently, but the Union meant to make it a hard fight.

The battle came despite the northern disadvantage. Lieutenant Maynard ordered his unit to march to battle. All the while, he foresaw his death and the utter defeat of the units closing in on the area with them. They entered the key town they needed to defeat on the way to Richmond. His unit closed in on the rail station, aiding the Union forces placed there, followed by still more. The rain poured down in sheets. Joseph was surprised to see the enemy driven back.

In the safety of his tent, Joseph lay under the blankets on his cot. He thought back to the charge his unit made on the gray coats. He pictured his saber hoisted high, seated on his horse, riding beside his captain. He felt the rush again, glorious guts, adrenaline and reeking death. Joseph never hesitated.

When he crossed the field toward the enemy, Joseph forgot about the man he pledged to watch over. Michael was left wherever he commanded his unit, somewhere behind him, hopefully near Evan. He left him laid bare for a bullet or bayonet of an onrushing Rebel. Second Howell would never leave him, even if cannon rained on their heads like terrible hail and flight became the only option.

Joseph wished Evan promised Miss Conrad her brother's protection. After all, Evan felt far more responsible for the younger man than anyone else. How easily Joseph forgot him, just proved that. Joseph rolled over to face the wall of his tent, guilt building within him, crushing his heart. He knew he feared the green officer's movements and wanted to protect him for a certain woman's sake. Though the kinship drew him close, he wanted to return to Emily and it made him fail her simple request.

Claming the rank of lieutenant, Joseph had a responsibility to his entire company and could not watch everyone individually. Every commander wished to keep their soldiers safe. Despite the promise he spoke to Emily, he owed them all. He gained his commission to serve his country, not hold hands and dance around campfires with the other soldiers.

Joseph closed his eyes to the shadows dancing on the canvas. The sound of rain lulled him to sleep. He imagined Conrad when the company pounded against the enemy flank. The young man's eagerness to fight showed in how he rode his yellow mount and shot his guns like a bandit. That horse danced beneath him, wheeling around and rearing, surrounded with a sea of angry gray coated men, fighting to preserve their lives and end the cavalry officer's. A rider never worked so fluidly with an animal.

Sleep claimed Joseph in its numb wraps until morning. The next morning at mess, he learned the Confederates lost their General. Braxton had word they replaced the loss with a well experienced man named Robert E. Lee. Joseph looked at him with widening eyes. Braxton only nodded and smiled. He dipped his biscuit in his runny egg and took a bite. No wonder they had failed to take Richmond.

"I know," Braxton said, still smiling broadly. He chewed his bite, took a swig of coffee. "By God—I never thought I'd see um again either."

"I went to school when they pulled his portrait from the hall," Joseph told him. "I knew it for real from that moment."

"Dark days," Braxton smiled. "Never mind Lee—how's that woman of yours doing alone up north?"

Joseph looked at his plate. He stared, taking in the news of his former superintendent. The Captain's last words settled in and he smiled. Then, he chuckled. He shook his head, filling his mouth with a forkful of potato hash. The salty grease tasted good, but not half as good as Emily's kisses. However, he would not share such information with the Captain, or any of the men for that matter, even if they kept it from Second Conrad.

"She's fine," Joseph said after swallowing. "Writes me back every letter."

"You get a picture a her yet?"

Joseph shook his head. Emily could not just commandeer one from the parlor. Her mother would rip her hide for sure. Anyway, her image remained unblemished in his mind, clearly remembered.

"Miss Conrad's nearly as famous as Lee," Braxton said. He wriggled his brows, sipping from his tin mug.

Michael ducked in and looked surprised to hear his name, "What's that bout Conrad, sir?"

Joseph cleared his throat and shoveled forkfuls of food into his mouth. He saw his Captain grin at him from the corner of his eye.

"We just said what a fine show you made," Braxton raised his cup to him.

"Thank you, sir."

"Excuse me, sir. I think I will finish in my tent. I've some letters to write," Joseph said, standing and taking up his plate and cup.

Braxton gave him a half salute with a grin of knowing. He paid no mind to his exit, returning to his meal. The other men filed in while he retreated from the possibility of taking a shot that morning while the southern rifles lie quiet. Walking away, Joseph's head throbbed with anger at the Rebels for holding them there and his own foolishness for not explaining to Michael. He hung his head with the shame. How could he think of keeping the matter quiet among these rogues?

Ducking in his tent, he set his plate and cup on his small table and found his writing paper and utensils. Pausing, he recalled Emily's smile and it eased his mind. At the outset of every letter he forgot just what he wanted to tell her. He wrote the date followed by her name. What should he hold back and what should he tell?

June 3, 1862

Dear Emily,

My God, it's a wonder I'm able to write you! Thank the Lord for this favor!

I must tell you, your brother is a remarkable soldier. I'd be proud to call him my brother some day, but let us speak of that later. I've much to take off my shoulders.

General Lee took over the Confederate troops and kept us from taking Richmond. What a scoundrel! I'd love the opportunity to strangle the pompous old windbag myself, even if he is a Point man. I wouldn't care if they hung me from a southern willow for the crime.

Then again, death would pain me miserably. How could I pass from this world with only regret at not seeing your beautiful face again? I would surely be in purgatory, lamenting how I destroyed all our hopes. I know you depend on my return, Emily. I warn you, I'm unreliable. I could die at any time. But please know, I'm not asking you to find another man to lay hopes on just yet. God knows, I would desert the Army to find you if you did and put a stop to such notions. Should I fear other men? No. I won't. I think Emily will stand at my side for all my life. How foolish am I acting now? I am sorry.

I want to thank you, Emmy. You've helped me remember why I'm here once again. I have remained unsure of my motives at times and my leader's motives even less. The past days awoke a fear inside me that I forgot since meeting you.

I'm sure you've heard of the move to Richmond. We lost ground fast. I don't know if we'll ever preserve this great Union. I once held hope. General McClellan has become an unsure figure in my mind, a figure sitting on his horse in the dusk of evening, silhouetted by the dark blue sky. I had placed my hope on those shoulders. At times, he reminds me of an apocalyptic horseman. I wonder if we follow a false prophet into each battle, condemning our souls to torment. I pray for forgiveness. I pray God will find understanding for all the soldiers.

Times like this, Emily, I need you to restore my faith in what we work so hard to hold onto. I often think of your friend Hettie and am reminded of the evil that brought us to this. State's rights cannot stand more important than the rights of men.

But, I don't want to talk to you about all this. I just keep jabbering about nothing, searching for something to write down and avoiding what is inside me. Forgive me? I face a long road to travel in this war. I fear an even longer road stretches between us. I wondered to myself if your last letter would end our time together. The scent of you on that lifeless paper covered in your words filled my head with so many ideas. I spare you the details my dear, if you may never know a life beside me and grieve easier for your lost Yankee soldier.

How are you getting on with your mother? Have you told her of us yet? I suspect your father already knows. He seemed so very shrewd. I think he knew the moment I looked at you. He all but said it. I want them to approve of me. I wouldn't blame them if they didn't. I haven't exactly been a gentleman.

I still have not told Michael. And, regarding your brother, this will interest you. Since that boy joined us, he has brought gray hair to my head! I wonder no more as to why your father went white. Michael's a fine soldier, but he charges out so fast. I've warned him, but he listens to no one. I fear what his quest for glory will accomplish. Despite pigheadedness, he's one of the most virtuous men I've yet to meet. He is definitely a Conrad, by all examples. You all boast great noble hearts, existing to do only good. We should all take example from your family. At the end of this, he will be a great hero.

I close my letter now and apologize if I've worried you unnecessarily. Don't worry after reading this letter. The words are only the outpouring of a scared fool. Know that I love you, and may Angels watch over you until—

Truly and Literally Yours,

1st LT., Joseph Maynard

In the time after Richmond, Michael did all he could to prove himself a fine soldier among their ranks. He revealed his lion's heart to those watching. Michael earned the favor of his superiors and his peers with ease. He spoke words seeping with trustworthiness, not telling a tale to anyone. All the aspects of his genuine personality made men think of a lieutenant whom they favored for similar reasons.

Michael fit like another piece of the puzzle, completing their company. Battles raged and days drew. They survived and others died. Michael's bravery hung like a brass ring above his head. He reached higher each time and so they all did.

Joseph hoped the over achieving would not keep on until it killed all of them. He saw the promise before and it ended buried within the corpse of a dead man just as often. He did not want such a fate for Second Lieutenant Conrad. He wanted to see Michael make his family proud and help his lieutenant keep a futile promise to a very dear someone.

Among the other officers, Evan and Joseph became his closest friends. Joseph was afraid of such since the boy came to the Potomac. It only meant more danger on the field. One misplaced notion of concern could see a man dead in seconds. Joseph wished Emily's request did not prove so threatening. Yet, he could not blame the girl for hoping her lover would keep a watchful glance over her beloved brother. He blamed himself for not wanting to carry it out, leaving it up to Evan or someone else while he ran from bullets and ducked cannon to preserve his own skin.

Inside his white canvas tent, Joseph reread his letter to Emily. The day came to a close outside, waning on the verge of dark. The rains had at last stopped.

Joseph laid down his letter and stared at the canvas wall, wondering what Miss Conrad would do while reading the note. He squeezed his eyes shut trying not to see her. She danced too clearly before his eyes, unreachable from where he sat. Emily's image faded reluctantly and he sat in the gloom, wondering when this torment would end, so he could go home again.

Though the weather turned fair, Joseph felt like winter lingered his heart. He heard Manny whicker and snort. He looked up at the horse's head, poking through the tent flap, and he wondered if the animal felt the same.

Manny lowered his velvety muzzle to nudge his human companion. He snuffled Joseph's hair, tousling it. Joseph laughed, a low somber sound, and smoothed back the tawny locks now hanging in his face.

"Joseph," he heard a voice call to him from outside his tent. His horse shook its head. "Joseph," the voice called him again. Joseph recognized the tones of Emily's brother.

"What?" Joseph cried irascibly. He looked at the horse and the black eyes regarded him questioningly. A rumble came from Manny's throat.

"Move your mount, Lieutenant. I cannot pass," Michael cried out to him.

"That's the idea." Joseph mumbled to himself, looking at the papers strewn across the trunk he used as a table right then. Joseph stood up on the mat he sat on, covering the trampled grass. He pushed Manny back outside. The horse only moved for him. "How'd you get untied?" He asked the big eyed animal, as if he did not know.

Second Lieutenant Conrad stood before him with a deadly expression, "That's a stubborn mule you got there." His expression reminded Joseph of the boy's mother.

"Yeah—he is," Joseph said, dumping feed into his horse's feedbag. "What did you want?" Joseph asked, strapping the bag on the horse. Silence followed and his eyes flicked to Michael's face. "Well, Second," he said.

"I was wondering if you heard from my sister, sir?" Michael spoke not so flatly, to keep his threat open. He leveled Joseph a glare, which said he came for other than a friendly discussion of the matter.

"Why would I hear from your sister, Mister Conrad?" Joseph said, adjusting the feedbag. He patted his horse on the flat plain of his head. The animal gladly crunched on his oats, watching them like an old gossip. Joseph avoided Michael's gaze, smiling a slanted grin.

Michael shifted uneasily, unsure he could follow his course of action with a superior officer, but honor laid in the midst. Decidedly, he would continue. He held out a sheet of paper, similar to the one that Joseph recently received. He said nothing, nor did Joseph. They looked at each other wrapped in a weighted silence, locking them together.

After another tense moment, Joseph took the letter from his subordinate, meeting his gaze strongly. His eyes burned like flames. He understood the threat of what this meant for him and Emily. His eyes slowly lowered to the paper and he read the words, written in the script that had become endearingly familiar to him. The page breathed her perfume, like the Main Street flower shop in Frederick. Reading more than the date, he wondered what Emily said.

Dear Michael,

It's with a strange unearthly urge I write you, dear brother. I remain unsure if I should tell you, confide in you something I haven't told mother or father. My heavy heart needs the therapy of exposing its turmoil to a kindred soul, older than the years of my age by little but much wiser. I need beg your promise that you'll say nothing to anyone. It would ruin all I've set out for.

Without another hesitation and the utmost of trust in you, I tell you my most wonderful secret news. I'm not sure of how close you are to your peers. You see, my tale concerns one of them. First Lieutenant Joseph Maynard has a vested interest in your safety because of me. When he happened into my life, we formed a friendship that time and distance could not destroy. Please smile dear brother. I assure you that this is only good news.

Joseph smiled to himself, reading the confession. He wondered how well these siblings cared for each other. She admitted little, but he stood there, defending her honor. It reminded him of his relationship with his fair haired sibling and how he split a few heads for her honor. He thought of his family much less now, since Emily consumed every thought. He told himself that after he finished his letter to Emily and this row with her brother, he would write his sister and let her know how he coped so far from them. He would ease her mind that he still held position as her brother and that she better behave herself while he stayed away.

Setting the thought of his sister aside, Joseph looked at Michael. The man appeared to chew his tongue.

"Read on," Michael said like a challenge.

Michael, I'd like your mind to rest easy about your little sister. I've done no wrong or anything improper. Many young women write letters to their soldiers in blue. I believe it helps keep the men alive. Perhaps the angels protect them with the power of our love. I do mean love.

I've written to your lieutenant from the time he left me in Vermont. I did so of my own will. I now know I cannot hide this secret forever from our parents.

With the greatest of strength and feeling I am bound to Joseph Maynard. I do not await your homecoming alone. I wait for Joseph with a heavy heart. To Joseph I send my undying love and prayers for his safe return.

If you hold such a matter as improper or wrong, I hope you will find the kindness to forgive me. In my eyes, it is not wrong. I pray for your understanding, confidence and assistance.

Love Always,

Your Sister, Emily

When Joseph finished reading the letter, he lowered it and looked up the lane of tents.

Michael crossed his arms and asked, "What is the meaning of this?"

"What does it say that concerns you so much, Second Lieutenant?"

"I'm asking you if I should feel concern over the matter, sir."

"If you are too thick headed, your sister need not fear— unless your tongue wags like a dog. Otherwise, don't concern yourself with it," Joseph said, passing the letter back.

"Don't concern myself?" Michael said heatedly. "How can you ask me to not concern myself where my family is involved?" Michael tore the letter back away from Joseph.

"You're right," Joseph admitted. He paused looking at him, placing his hands on his hips. "I don't think you should get riled. Emily told you something that no one can condemn. You understand me, Second? Your sister's a reputable woman. Don't worry more about it." Joseph then turned to duck back into his tent.

"I do worry sir," Michael said, following him. "She's right innocent," Michael cut off with anger. Joseph looked at him with an angry smirk. "So help me if you've taken advantage of her," Michael roared, pointing his finger in his superior's face.

"Now hold on," Joseph said, cutting off.

"With all due respect, sir. I'll kill you if you've been less than honorable," Michael told him. "And, I know your reputation."

Joseph regarded the graduate, his smirk dying on his face. Michael appeared a frightened boy, protecting his precious marbles from a bully. No matter, he meant what he said. Joseph looked at him unerring. His hands settled onto his hips and he thought about being Michael, his sister's honor on the line.

"You've much growing to do Mister Conrad. This war will make it go quickly. Whatever you learned of me at the Point—mark it up to schoolboy talk. I'm no less honorable than you. My designs with your sister are of the utmost." Joseph drew a ragged breath of disgust. "I would never dishonor Emily. I love her and that is all you need know, Second Lieutenant."

Joseph said no more, ducking back in his tent. A shrill whistle split the air. Manny lumbered forward and placed his head to his shoulders in the opening. The tent now stood blocked by the huge black body of a cavalry charger.

Michael stood outside for a long moment. His face worked through several contortions and his thoughts turned to revenge. Michael held the letter from home in front of him like a child would his blanket. Emotions raged within him to the point of confusion. He trusted his sister, but he failed to trust any man with his sister.

Men like Joseph proved persuasive and he feared what the man took from Emily.

Michael looked down at the pink blushed paper crumpled in his grasp, as if he just discovered it there. Joseph admitted to loving her. He never knew the man to lie and he gave up more than most saying it. He felt him as honest as Abraham Lincoln at one time. Turning away, he moved along the line of tents to return to his own. Could he trust him now?

While Michael stalked, Evan came along the dirt path trodden out by horses and wagons, as well as feet. He smiled a great grin. Michael wondered where he kept himself while his friend ruined his sister. He always knew Evan only cared for himself.

"Hey boy," Evan said playfully. When Michael looked up at him darkly, his expression became quickly serious. "What's wrong?"

"Em and the Lieutenant—" Michael said, nearly unable to speak. He handed him his letter. Michael watched the change in Evan's features. He knew the man already knew what went on. "Why didn't you tell me?"

"Your ma," Evan said, handing the letter back. "Em worried she wouldn't let them write to each other," he finished. He stuffed his hands in his pockets and shuffled his foot. "Nothing went on that you need worry about. You know I wouldn't stand for it."

"As if I can trust you," Michael said. "Everyone from here to home knows how you are."

"I wasn't the one visiting her," Evan smiled.

Michael regarded him for a moment hardly amused by those words. He took the paper and put it in his coat pocket. He would not risk anyone else knowing his family's shame.

"You should have seen them dance," Evan said, watching him glower. "Souls bound by heaven, Mike. One day you'll understand—right? They're meant to be."

Michael hung his head a moment without a word to say. Looking over his shoulder, he studied the graying tent where Joseph slept. How could he deny a dying man his last wish? He just hoped his sister held the strength to face what might come of her actions. He looked back to Evan and nodded. He found his gaze driven to the ground and Evan patted his arm reassuringly.

"I'll keep him in line, Michael," Evan said and smiled. "I have so far." He paused. "Besides, you didn't want her to marry me, right? Who else was there? It's the best match a girl like Em could dream of. He will do right by her."

Michael smiled doubtfully and the exchange ended. He turned and continued his way, stuffing his hands into his pockets. He thought battles gave him nightmares, but now his letters produced horror far greater. At least, here he could fight the enemy.

Evan watched him leave and then turned on his original rout, which led to places other than Joseph's tent. When he passed, he patted Manny's rump and the tail swished to flick him off like a bug. Evan laughed and patted the other side, then ran off before the horse kicked him.

Inside his musty old tent, Lieutenant Maynard tried to forget Michael's outburst. He finished his letter and dreamt of a future he hoped to share with his blue eyed jewel. Joseph hoped, in so doing, he could hold on until the war ended and he could return. He drifted to a day when he walked through the front door of a white farmhouse, hundreds of miles north.

Joseph took up his boots and polished them. Then, he mended a tear in his coat sleeve. All the while, he recalled the calvary charges. He thought of all the men who lost their lives for Mister Lincoln on General McClellan's request. He saw the Confederates intent on drawing blue blood. He heard the gunfire and felt his heart pound. His feet ached with the days of long marches, starting in the dark before dawn and ending in the dark of night. Cannon fire rang in his ears and he woke from the spell, staring at the blue sleeve of his uniform coat.

Lowering his hands, he let the coat droop to the ground, feeling the weakness in his arms. Drawing a deep ragged breath, he sensed Emily just beyond the northern horizon. She waited quietly in the garden or the field, where he saw her once a day for two weeks. Fourteen days told him enough to know he loved her. Michael could not tell him otherwise. Somehow, he would survive this, with the boy. Then he would drag Michael by the scruff of his neck to explain himself to his sister.

Later that evening, Joseph ate his dinner with the enlistees beside a bonfire. He distracted himself from his cares by engaging Evan in an examination of what he thought happened in the recent battles. The conversation grew lively, if not heated. Joseph enjoyed this mental swordplay and he felt sure that Evan appreciated the distraction it provided.

During these moments, Michael sat back and watched his comrades. This particular instance, he watched with a slack jaw, glancing from one to the other and back. He wagered a fistfight would break out at any moment. Each moment that passed without, left him more astonished.

"Fair Oaks was won only because Longstreet is an idiot," Evan argued heartily. "He bungles his orders every time."

"Doesn't that say the Rebs haven't a prayer?" Joseph said, adjusting how he sat on a fallen tree. He picked his plate up from his lap and rested his arm in its abandoned place on his leg. He grinned at Evan undaunted.

Evan refused to answer. He snickered and ate another bite of his rations instead. He could not imagine how anyone could remain so optimistic about a war. He wanted to strangle Joseph sometimes. Joseph's golden outlook made him crazy. He probably would act the same if he claimed a woman like Emily back home. His thoughts returned to the dance at Mr. Adams' and the raven curls of a girl he found there. He held her in his arms secreted away from everyone, in an upstairs office where he took his pleasure from her. She was a delight to dance with also, but something deeper was missing. That something, he saw between Emily and Joseph. He swore to God it started the barn fire. He wished a woman would strike him that hard and fall into his arms like fate.

"We made a fair win," Joseph reminded him when he remained quiet. The memory of the battles and the swollen river with the washed out bridge raged in his mind. It proved a hard win, not just fair. His mind reviewed the charge meant to reinforce the men held up in town. "We won—and we'll keep winning."

"Fine," Evan said, holding up his hand. "You're right. You're always right," he glared at him with fond disgust. "I'm just—" He stopped.

"What?" Joseph smiled.

"What if we don't win?" Evan's already dark features fell deeper into shadow, as if someone smothered the fire and the light it shone on them. "We've seen some bad things in our short careers," he gestured with his hands. He paused swallowing. "But—you weren't there when the Conrad's brought in Hettie. The woman was a mess—plain torn up." His eyes turned to Michael's and the young soldier turned his gaze to the fire to avoid the look. They both remembered the day when old Jack called Stuart out to the stables. "I can't live if I fail people like her.

"Just focus on preserving the Union. Worrying over the other will just stop you from thinking straight. You need a level head," Joseph said, catching the exchange between the neighbors.

"They brought in Lee for sure, Lieutenant. You told me yourself," Evan said after a quiet moment. "You know what kind of man he is."

They looked at each other knowingly. Michael's head rose at the sound of the name. He swallowed, thinking over what he learned of the man at the academy. He found it difficult to think that such a hero turned his back on his country. He remembered the story his classman told of removing the traitor's portrait from the wall of the lecture hall. The name only came out in uncivilized conversations and threats after that.

"Yeah," Joseph said, looking to the dark. "Captain says he's glad they got him. Compared with McClellan, the man is too cautious," Joseph smiled reassuringly at the men. "That'll be good for us."

"Nobody's more careful than Mac," Evan laughed.

Lieutenant Maynard knew what the junior officers thought. He went to the same school and saw and heard the same things. Lee was a hero, until he deserted for Virginian rights. Becoming a traitor was the worst offense you could commit. Although, Joseph still held a sense of respect for the man in his heart. Lee felt his convictions deeply with a strong sense of honor, which Joseph could entirely relate to. He lowered his head and put his empty plate on the ground by his boot heel. Joseph's parents groomed him a noble gentleman. He trained to learn the way of a military gentleman at school. Now his honor came from the Union, blue honor for the uniform he wore.

"I hope he's right," Evan said, looking somberly at his plate, empty but for a few crumbs.

"I don't like talking a this anymore," Michael said. "Let's discuss something else."

"Like your sister," Evan immediately picked up the opening.

Evan grinned deviously at his longtime friend, eyes sparkling like diamonds. He shook off the mantle of somber dark thoughts, preferring to provoke Michael. He sat full of mischief and rarely let a chance to use it pass by. Including, when Michael looked up. He wriggled his brows at the younger man and saw the motion fanned Michael's anger.

"Emily should not be concerned by either of you," Michael snapped, finishing a bite of his supper.

"I'm concerned," Joseph said, sarcastically. He looked between Evan and Michael. "Actually—I'm quite concerned."

"No you're not," Michael warned, slowly uttering each word. "Or have you forgotten our conversation, sir?" Michael glared powerfully at him.

"Yes. Indeed I have," Joseph said, smoothing the short shorn whiskers about his mouth with his ungloved hand. "It would prove wise for you to do the same, Second. Emily finds enough trouble with your mother. She doesn't need you making more for her," he told him, running the back of his fingers across his jaw line.

"No thanks to you, Lieutenant Maynard— sir," Michael said, adding his superior's title and name as a slashing afterthought. "My mother doesn't dislike anyone for no reason."

"I won't vouch for you on that," Evan laughed.

"I've done nothing to your mother. It's her that's done me wrong. I saved your livestock and she couldn't even thank me civil," Joseph said, standing on his shiny booted feet. He towered over the younger man. "She dislikes me because of the way I speak. I would have Mrs. Margaret Conrad know that many of her northern boys deserted to defend the South alongside their southern brides. Many wearing our blue coats are southern boys who fled north to preserve her precious United States of America, while she sits at home."

"Joe," Evan said, trying to prevent the words from turning to blows. Knowing the temperament of these two men, it looked like a powder keg washed in sparks.

"My mother does not often make sense, but—she cannot simply dislike you because you came from the South, Lieutenant," Michael said, disbelieving him.

"It's true," Evan answered for Joseph.

Michael's eyes flicked to his neighbor's son. Evan would not lie to him about something so serious as this. The young officer hung his head in shame. He misjudged Joseph, like many of the men told him. Joseph always proved a good man and all the officers and enlistees of the company swore to it. Michael wondered about the heroics Joseph performed on his family's behalf and compared it to his mother's idea the man meant to steal Emily. It seemed more likely to him the truth lay in his mother's inability to make Emily comply with her plans again. Joseph replaced any notions of marrying Evan and placed her far away once she married her new beau.

Michael felt like a foolish child, believing his mother acted justly. A stranger would not have known Emily lived there. He never knew a man to go out of his way, nearly killing himself to impress her. His father wrote to him about the matter at school. Joseph almost died for them. He almost died for the bull.

Dropping his fork into his tin, Michael put his dish aside. He looked at the fire, pressing the palms of his hands together. He wanted to apologize. However, affronting a man so deeply made it more difficult than just admitting he spoke wrong.

"Then I apologize, Lieutenant," Michael sighed, rolling his eyes up to him. He drew a deep breath and rubbed his hands together. "I hope you'll do well with Emily," Michael added, conceding defeat.

Joseph nodded with a bitter grin, and breathed, "Forget about it, second."

After a pause, Evan looked between them and said, "What did you want to say about that ungrateful swindler Lee."

"Never mind that blasted Rebel," Joseph drawled. "Let us drink to something worth our while," he said, picking up his cup and holding it out to the others. Michael took a bottle of something and poured them each a draft. When they held their mugs together, Joseph added. "To blue honor. We fight for blue till our lives are due."

"To blue honor," the others repeated.

IX. Endless Battles

Neither Joseph nor Evan were familiar with the kind of leadership General Lee would bring to the southern Rebel's. He planned to fight in the field and whittle them down. Each time, he tried to attack with the advantage of surprise. To thwart his efforts, Captain Braxton sent units out to scout the locations of the Rebel forces. McClellan would form a course of action against the enemy, route them out and crush them.

Of late, the woods of Virginia turned into a frightening nightmare, even in daylight. Riding their mounts on the dirt road, careful to watch in every direction, three units of Braxton's Cavalry tried to scout their surroundings. The gray coats of the Rebel Army blended into the foliage more easily than their navy blue. The only advantage came from horse sense. The chargers could smell danger and warned their riders of any unseen presence.

Joseph sat atop his mount with his jacket across its rump. Above his waist, he wore only the white shirt, without its collar, and the hat of his trade. His gloved hands wrapped the reins of his horse tighter around his wrist. The air clung sticky and hot.

Joseph reined Manny in, sensing a danger along the road without his horse's sense. The satiny broad black charger halted and thrashed its great head. Manny chomped his bit idly, making horse sounds. Joseph patted his mount's mane while the men behind halted.

A strange odor permeated the air. Joseph studied his surroundings, failing to place the source. His mind warned him to stay back, sensing the road ahead might prove deadly for his unit and those behind. Despite his senses, Joseph gave the men a glance over his shoulder. He gestured, wanting them to go slow and form a line to the left side of the road. They complied, understanding him easily. Joseph turned back to the road with their eyes on him. Moving ahead, he meant to draw out the hidden things ahead of them.

Joseph watched the road, flicking his eyes back and forth. Manny moved forward slowly and cautiously. He felt fate stir around his body. Something hid in those trees ahead, wanting to change the future they dreamt. Nothing could change what was happening. The horse's hooves clomped hollowly.

A twig snapped. Joseph pulled his mount up short. The horse pawed the ground and he looked back over his shoulder. His men stood back along the left side of the road, unmoving. Joseph whipped his head back around. Manny's head lifted and the ears twitch backward until they lay flat. The nostrils flared and the horse pawed its hooves wheeling backward. Joseph reacted to the horse in seconds and wheeled him around charging back to his men.

"Get to cover," Joseph screamed to them. He watched the men vanish into the forest followed by the crack of rifle fire. "Get to cover!" Joseph ducked the bullets, whistling past his head and drove his mount into the cover of the trees.

In moments, the three units hid in the brush among the tree trunks, surrounded by cracking rifle fire. The fog cleared around his head and he realized he lay on his stomach with a rifle in his hand. Shots burst from enemy barrels. Less than a breath later they bounced off trees, rocketed into the ground, and some hit flesh. Cries of agony beat his ears.

Joseph looked around, desperate to see where his men went. The men peered around the base of trees and shrubs, fallen trunks and limbs. Joseph checked his gun. He looked back to the men. Sergeant McGuire's face came into focus. Joseph nodded to him. The sergeant gave the word to return fire.

The horses screamed and hurried to the distance, their skins shivered with fear. Joseph saw the wild eyes and the flaring nostrils. The animals turned their muzzles into each other for protection from their unseen attackers.

The brush separated to Joseph's left and he saw the dirt smeared face of Second Lieutenant Conrad. Joseph fired his gun looking away from him. A man fell on the road, his uniform nearly matching the beach sand clay. Joseph watched ahead of him, waiting for the moment when he would use his gun again. To Joseph's right, Evan crawled to a large oak and leaned his back to it. His friend breathed heavy, clutching his rifle for dear life. Joseph turned his attention back to the range of forest across the dirt road they just traveled over and the man he shot. He listened to the volley of shots and the men reloading weapons.

Joseph closed his eyes and prayed, "Let this not be the last time we friends see each other in this life." The words resounded in his mind.

When Joseph opened his eyes, he signaled the men to stop firing. Everything turned still and chokingly silent. Joseph watched the road, feeling the sweat pour from his brow down his face. He heard his heart beat, like the ticking of a clock. His breath quickened and he licked his lips. With widened eyes, he saw gray ghosts emerge from the cover across the dirt tract. Joseph drew another dry unsteady breath and licked his lips to wet them again.

The Rebels acted cautious, bending slightly and looking back and forth while they crossed the open road. Joseph counted six. Jerking his arm to signal the men to fire, he lifted and aimed his rifle. He prayed for the men who trusted their blue coated enemy lay dead. The six dropped. Their blood poured out of wounds, soaking the gray brown road. More rifle shots from the other side of the road hit the trees above their head.

Flinging himself back against his tree, Joseph just caught sight of Evan jerking back violently. He drooped at the base of the oak tree and dropped his rifle from his outstretched still hand. Joseph's heart raced, fearing the worst. His friend's eyes were closed, as if he slept.

The shots paused and he crawled on his belly to where his friend lay, as still as death. The shots renewed just before he lay in the cover beside Evan. Sitting up, he propped his rifle against the tree. He looked to him panicked. He had prayed to late to protect him.

"God, Evan no," Joseph breathed afraid his friend was dead. Joseph shucked his gloves off his hands. "Evan," he called again, hoping it would wake him.

Joseph scanned Evan with his eyes, trying to find the wound point. There lie no sign of blood on Evan's uniform. Refusing to give in, Joseph tore open the man's coat. A snowy white shirt, just cleaned yesterday, lie beneath. He could find no obvious wound. Joseph could not think of what happened. Drawing a ragged breath he looked at the quiet face of his best friend. Then, he saw the blood. It dripped from his earlobe onto his shoulder, staining the white shirt red. Pain stung his eyes like hot ash.

Joseph sniffed, bit his lip and thought. He saw many wounds in his time. It took a nasty hit to do a man in completely. Gently placing his fingertips on Evan's head, he felt the skull. Before he gave up on the officer, he wanted to be sure the wound mortal. He saw minor cuts bleed like pipe leaks. Working his fingers gently and carefully, he found the place where sticky blood soaked the raven locks. Gritting his teeth, he pressed more firmly to detect a bullet hole. His fingers pressed, but found the skull intact.

Joseph shook his head and gave a bitter wry smile. Evan most likely struck his head on the tree, knocking himself cold.

Shots whistled through the air, pinging off the tree trunks and brush. With the relief that his friend was all right, Joseph concentrated on dressing the wound and getting back to the fight. He saw his pack out of reach.

Taking up his rifle, he fixed the bayonet on the end. Dexterously, he stuck it in the tie and dragged the pack back to him. Ignoring how easily he performed the task, he set his rifle back against the tree and looked for the small roll of bandages he carried.

"Keep firing," Joseph cried out to the men.

Joseph wrapped Evan's head and the blood made a rose blossom stain, quickly spreading to a smear. Evan needed a doctor to dress his wound properly and prevent infection, but this would hold him for now. Finishing his mediocre work, Joseph laid Evan back against the tree. He watched him for a moment, hoping he had not missed something else.

Evan's eyes finally fluttered open and he squinted blearily to the patches of sky that showed through the leaves. Drawing a deep breath, he looked at Joseph. He gave a small smile and Joseph looked at him concerned. A wavering return danced across his features.

"Oh—hey there, Joe. They got you too, huh?" Evan said dreamily. "Em's gonna be upset."

"You're not dead," Joseph growled. "Ass," Joseph cursed.

"That's good," Evan grinned. "I wondered how ya got in. Was sure I went to hell, soon as I saw you," Evan said. He laughed a little and then drew a sharp breath.

"I saved the cows," Joseph reminded him. Evan laughed and then winced in pain. "Easy, Second Lieutenant. You have a head wound—you're bleeding," Joseph said, preventing him from moving. "It's almost over. Can you wait until we get rid of them?"

"Yeah," Evan rasped, feeling the pain of his wound. His head spun and ached. "Get the bastards, sir," Evan breathed heavily.

"I'll be back," Joseph said, after nodding. "I've a plan."

In a scurrying rush, Joseph slid back to his own cover with his gun. Removing the bayonet to its useless place under the barrel, he readied his gun to fire on the enemy. The volley of fire remained regular. Joseph looked down his body to Sergeant McGuire, hiding several yards away behind a thick shrub. The Irishman winked at him. Joseph signaled him closer.

Watching the large red haired McGuire crawl from his safety to report to him, Joseph thought over his rapidly construed plan. No one had a count of the enemy soldiers they faced. McGuire reached him. The Irishman lay on his large middle, sweating like a well run horse. His eyes squinted at Joseph and he waited for him to speak.

"Send three men to see what we got out there," Joseph rasped.

"Right away, Lieutenant," McGuire grinned like a drunk madman.

Turning his head, McGuire ordered three men out. He and Joseph watched them crawl into the brush and disappear from their sight.

"Keep shooting at them boys," Joseph said, the sweat pouring down his brow heavier. He wiped his shirtsleeve across his brow.

"Lieutenant," a voice called to him. "You dropped this on the way down."

Joseph looked to see one of his men crouching and crawling his way over. He held a dusty blue jacket in his hands. Joseph spied the lieutenant bar and recognized a few other items on it as belonging to him. Joseph smiled at the man and took it.

"Thank you, Private," Joseph said.

"Wouldn't want ya to die without it," the young man smiled back.

"There'll be no dying t'day, laddie," McGuire patted his shoulder.

"What about them," the boy pointed to their handful of casualties laying across the ground.

McGuire raised his brows and looked to Joseph. Joseph glared at the bodies, half angry they died on him and half angry the enemy killed them.

"No more dyin then," McGuire corrected himself.

Joseph nodded to him and tried to smile. He raised his rifle and turned from the other men. He fired a shot into nothing, trying to kill them. The shot returned threefold and the volley renewed.

"How much ammo left?" Joseph called back over his shoulder.

"We're good for a while longer, sar," McGuire laughed, joining him at the tree.

A small eternity passed before Joseph saw the scouts return to them. Falling back, Joseph joined them to find out what they learned. Their grave faces made him think the worst and he imagined a force of Rebels on the other side of the road outnumbering them by hundreds. They counted near sixty men, as the Federal units converged. His eyes grazed the bodies, laying in the shade, respectfully pulled out of the path of bullets. They might prove an adequate force, if he played his cards right.

"There's bout ten of um, sir," the head of the scouting party explained. Joseph felt relieved. "They're pressed to the ground over there," he added. "It ain't doin us any good to shoot at um."

They could charge that number, but they would suffer more casualties. Joseph nodded to the subordinate and called a halt to the firing. No use to waste good bullets on trees. The men lowered their rifles. A few straggling shots followed from the enemy and then silence fell about the forest.

Joseph looked to Evan. The man's black eyes dug deep. He found himself in command of their two units and the maker of all decisions for this battle. Joseph looked from the shrubs to the dead enemies strewn in the road. More Rebels would camp up the road. It came time to claim the victory and leave while the numbers promised their success.

"My men will go—take them out." Joseph said.

"Glad ta, sar." McGuire grinned greedily.

Joseph crawled away from them, as Michael appeared in the brush. Now that the boy joined them, he would need brief him on what he learned and see that those who remained behind offered them a distraction. The units would be under his command on that side of the road for a time. He thought of Emily and wondered if he made the right move. He left Michael there to stay safe and now sent himself into the mouth of death. He almost felt the teeth biting his sides.

"Mike—Mike," Joseph rasped, sidling up beside him and the cover of the thick shrub around the tree. Michael pressed himself to the tree, peering across the way through the split in the trunk. "I'm taking some men around to route them out," Joseph said.

Michael's features looked pale and the sweat stood out on his face. He shook his head no, sliding down the trunk to his knee. His leg shook where he supported himself on it. Joseph watched him bravely hanging on in the face of death or capture.

"I'll go, sir."

"No—you stay here," Joseph smiled. "Watch Evan for me."

Michael looked over to the man laying at the base of the tree. He looked back to Joseph, "What do you need me to do?" It was an order not to be argued.

"Fire at the ground, just behind the bushes," Joseph said. "Wait until we've gone." Joseph paused swallowing. "You'll probably need to stand up. Take care you don't get your head blown off. I don't want to bring anymore dead men back with us."

"Yes, sir."

"All right, Second," Joseph crawled away. "Give us a moment to exit," Joseph whispered back. Passing into the brush, Joseph saw a young sergeant kneeling behind a bush. "Fergus," he called to him. Joseph jutted his head toward Michael. "Watch him for me."

"Aye, sir. That I will," Sergeant Fergus smiled and nodded.

"Michael," Joseph said. "You have the command, second."

Joseph watched the man join Michael at the double trunk tree. Joseph hesitated and then disappeared in the brush, following the rest of his men. Taking the lead, they made a wide circle back toward the way they came, knowing it clear of enemy soldiers. Finding the road a hundred yards from where they left the other two units,

Joseph halted them and looked over the road. The bodies on the road looked like stones. He looked the other way and then back to his sergeant. Nodding, he signaled the men to start across.

Disappearing in the brush along the other side, they continued quietly picking their way to where the scouts told him the enemy hid. Several tense moments later, the unit crawled in behind the ten Confederates. One lay dead at the base of a tree shot through the face, just under his eye.

Grim faced, they spied out each man and waited for their shot. Joseph looked at the enemy coldly and lifted his gun. Setting it against his body to absorb the kick back, he put a man in his sights, while McGuire assured each gray coat belonged to someone. Drawing ragged breaths he waited for McGuire to let him know they stood ready.

McGuire touched Joseph's shoulder. Joseph did not stir, except to wave his hand over his head. His soldiers lifted cocked their rifles. He saw the enemy look backward. The rifles cracked and the ten fell to the ground dead. They surprised them first, but a new surprise arose when three more emerged from cover. Joseph readied his pistol and he and his men came out of hiding aiming their weapons. He glared at the faces, holding shock like a bucket of tremulous water. He accepted their surrender.

"Pack them up," Joseph said in a deep rough voice.

Joseph lowered his rifle and he soon found himself riding back into camp. He stared ahead, bouncing with Manny. His coat hung open and his hat sat crooked on his head. Behind him, Evan rested on his brown horse, wearing a bandage around his head, looking like a Revolutionary hero. The soldiers outside the camp watched them come in, hauling the dead and wounded, including the enemy's. Three prisoners stumbled behind, hands bound and surrounded by men with ready rifles.

When the awe wore off, soldiers rushed to aid them. Evan slid from his horse with the aid of his attending sergeant. He would go to the medical tent with the rest of the wounded. Joseph accompanied him and waited for Captain Braxton while the doctor stitched up the scratch.

"You get better soon," Joseph said, smiling. It felt too quiet suddenly. "Mac's gonna need you soon." He looked like hell.

Evan regarded him with a wavering smile, as the thread suturing his scalp slid through his skin. He heard the clip of the sheers and nothing else. His eyes lowered to the ground under the tent. He studied the yellowing grass blades. The doctor shook some powder onto his cut and the unpleasant chemical made Evan cough. He evaded a response.

"Don't you go worrying my patient, Lieutenant," the doctor said, wrapping up Evan's head. "He's all the time he needs to get better," the man smiled at Joseph. "Now he's lost quite a bit of blood and needs some rest and plenty of food."

"I'll see you tonight," Joseph said, standing up to leave. "I'll bring dinner."

"You'd better," Evan tried a smile, but it pulled at the wound making it difficult. "I don't see any a them nurses ta keep me company. Where the hell are Barton's gals, doc?"

"Second Lieutenant," the doctor laughed. "I don't say as I know."

"You'll never change," Joseph laughed, turning away and placing his hat back on his head.

Not a step out of the surgery tent, Joseph heard a voice calling to him, "Lieutenant Maynard!" Joseph looked back to where Evan lay with stitches in his head.

"Uh-well, dinner may arrive a little late. Sounds like I'm in trouble," Joseph grinned and Evan smiled.

Joseph ducked out of the tent and met the company Corporal. The young man ran to him, stopping just before he bowled him down. Joseph eyed him with a grave expression. His head hurt already.

"Lieutenant Maynard," he said, saluting. Joseph returned the gesture. "General McClellan wants ta see ya, right away. Captain Braxton's orders, sir."

"I'm coming," Joseph rasped.

Joseph followed the man with a bearish gate and expression. The Corporal fell in behind and he looked over his shoulder to him questioningly. The boy smiled at him and Joseph looked away to where he walked. The men grew stranger by the day.

Sauntering to the command tent, flanked by guards and a table surrounded by officers, he waited for the Corporal to leave. Turning back, he looked at the men who worked on maps and papers, lifting in the breeze. They quietly discussed a maneuver, owing to his discovery of units to their east. The men paid him no attention and he cleared his throat. His eyes caught sight of Michael's report laying on top.

The officers looked to him. Their faces straightened and they assessed his appearance with alternating judgments. One flicked his finger up and an enlistee came to him. He whispered in the boy's ear and dismissed him to his duty. The officer smiled at Joseph and then they all returned to the work. The enlistee emerged from them and ducked into the tent.

Joseph lowered his gaze from the table of officers, feeling out of place among them. He adjusted his gloves on his hands and waited. Smoothing his dusty uniform coat, he tried to think what his captain and general would want with him. He hoped his appearance would not add to their displeasure of his handling the matter. That must prove the reason for the meeting. They meant to reprimand his poor execution of orders.

"Lieutenant Maynard," a voice boomed at him. Joseph lifted a sheepish expression to see Captain Braxton stand in the open tent flap. The golden haired man smiled at him. "Come inside, boy."

"Yes sir," Joseph entered the tent afraid of what he would face.

Joseph's superiors stood around the interior. Joseph respectfully gave a salute. Braxton smiled reassuringly and ordered him to ease. His captain abandoned him to stand among the others. Joseph let his hand fall back to his side and fell into an ease stance, tucking both hands behind his back. His eyes remained fixed ahead not seeing any of their faces straight on, as he learned at the academy. The officers took to their seats and silence filled the tent.

General McClellan sat ahead of Joseph, behind an extravagant table with a flag and decorations standing behind. Below his feet, he could feel the rug laid down for the General's comfort. Joseph ignored the decadence, as it was the whim of their leadership and privilege. He listened to his superior stand and felt his eyes measuring him. He looked displeased. However, he always looked displeased. Joseph swallowed. Perhaps they meant to dismiss him from his duty or reassign him. It may hurt, but it would give him the opportunity to go to Emily.

"Your captain has received a promotion that will remove him to another unit. He'll join the Federal Cavalry in Mississippi," McClellan's voice filled the silence. "His fortune is our misfortune, but he thinks we can augment the loss with one of his own men," McClellan said, rising and stepping to Joseph. He looked up at Joseph sternly. "Following recent events, Lieutenant, it's come to my attention that two of his officers should receive promotions." McClellan turned his back. "You see," he smiled bitterly. "If I promote one, a vacancy is left in another area." McClellan faced him. He tucked his hands behind his back and assessed Joseph. "Despite your poor appearance, Lieutenant Maynard, it gives me great pleasure to offer you the captaincy of your company."

"Sir?" Joseph lowered his chin and looked at McClellan. The man genuinely smiled at him. "Thank you, sir." Joseph said to the General. "I accept your appointment with great honor." He looked to Braxton and Braxton nodded with a smile.

"I believe it is us who should feel honored, to have such a man to serve with," Braxton said, stepping to him. The Captain passed a glance to the others in the room, patting Joseph's shoulder familiarly.

"Well said, Major Braxton," McClellan agreed.

Joseph felt the pride fill him already. Braxton must have spoken on his behalf. He thought after his self assessment of the spat in the woods. He recalled himself, holding the units solidly without a second thought. He proved quite able that day.

A few moments after he accepted the appointment and rank pins, his superiors dismissed Joseph. He stood outside the command tent elated. His feelings showed plain on his face. He could hardly wait to find a pen and paper to write home about his good fortune.

Major Braxton followed him out, placing his arm about his shoulder, "Shall we get a drink, Captain?" He smiled at Joseph, as proud as a father. "Oh, how's Evan?"

"He's much better," Joseph said. The words straightened his smile. "The doctor wants him to rest and eat. He lost a lot of blood."

"He'll rest even better when I tell him his good news," Braxton said. Joseph looked to him questioningly. "They want to promote Evan to stand as your first lieutenant. I wanted to keep you from being split up."

"We make a good team," Joseph said. "I don't know how I'd work without him."

"You'd move on," Braxton said knowingly. He saw the doubt in Joseph's eyes. "You'll loose many men, Joseph. Don't let it stop you from becoming a good leader."

The men regarded each other for a lengthy moment. Then, Joseph turned his gaze out over the field of tents. He held the rank of captain now. It felt good, but it meant responsibility of all the company units. He felt unsure that this appointment presented just what he needed. He could not refuse, as it brought honor to his family and the one he planned to join with.

"Let's celebrate this later," Braxton said. "I'm sure you have a few letters to write."

After Braxton left him, Joseph hurried to his tent to write a letter home and to Emily. His heart beat wildly with his excitement. Emily would glow with pride for his promotion. He only wished he could see the dazzle in her eyes. This good fortune would do much to heal the old wounds that plagued his mind and chase away the ghosts of aged battles. Captain.

Outside his tent, Joseph discovered the mail clerk who sorted packets of letters. He looked up and bobbled a salute, trying not to drop his burden. He handed a small bundle to him. Joseph took the packet from the soldier's hands, thanking him. The boy saluted again and Joseph returned it laughing. He sifted the letters.

"Captain looks good on you, sir," The clerk said before moving on.

Joseph nodded to him and returned to his letters. Joseph continued, flicking through the worn envelopes. The last, pale pink gleamed at him in the fire and moonlight. Emily Conrad had sent him another letter. He smiled, holding it to his nose and ducked into his tent. Inside he tore open the letter, dropping the rest onto his cot. He sat next to the small pile and read the words, like angel scrawls to his eyes.

8th of June 1862

Dear Joseph,

In comment to your previous letter—you dishearten me, darling. I no longer wish you to feel so. You must look better upon things. War is difficult on all of us and does not always go as we hope. It's true the good do not always prevail. However, I believe God stands behind the Union. He'll not let you fail in the end. Do not fret over it, my gallant soldier.

I hope you will find trust for General McClellan again. He is not one of the fabled four horsemen. He fights for the same thing you fight for. The Union. Know that you three do not fight in vain. Your injuries shall be medals, bold reminders of your success. I know you will bear them proudly.

Enough of this talk is right! I wish to write to tell you about the thoughts I've had lately. In particular, I dream of the day we shall sit on our rock in the field. Do you miss it? I can almost feel your arms about me and your mouth next to mine. I smell your scent. . .

Joseph leaned back on his bunk and thought over Emily's words. He could feel her along his body. Her small hand rested over his heart. He smelled her skin. Her soft hair brushed his cheek. The silk of her gown filled his hands and he nearly forgot where he stood. He rushed to write Emily back about his promotion, casting Evan and his dinner aside to do it. Sliding from his bunk, he scratched out a response. He would write his parents later and see to Evan's dinner in a few moments.

June 15, 1862

My Dear Emily,

I write to tell you once again that your family remains intact. Michael proves an outstanding soldier among all. It must run in the family. I heard from Michael that your family faced all dangers just as bravely, since the days of settlement in the colonies.

Now I will assure you, Emily, that I am also just fine. I passed the gauntlet unscathed once more. I find it hard to see straight looking back on it.

Our close friend, Evan received a wound in the skirmish this afternoon. A bullet scratched his scalp and bled quite a bit. The doctor assures me he'll heal fine, good as new.

I find it difficult to believe our luck after seeing so many men fall all around us. I will not bore you with those details. I'm sure that you will have read of them already when you receive my letter.

My fortune has brought still more glamour to my career. I've been promoted for my actions in battle. They say Evan will become my First Lieutenant. So now you shall write a Captain of the U.S. Army. I hope you're proud, Emmy. I wish I could see your beautiful face when you read this.

I still face a long walk back to you. General Lee continues wasting lives for his vanity's pride. Shove over and let go of your stale beliefs, I say. Maybe he will.

I must go now. I am to bring Evan his supper and do not wish to make the suffering wait on me.

Love Always,

Captain Joseph Maynard

Joseph read the sheet over. Satisfied with the quick note, he folded it into thirds and stuffed it into an envelope, addressing it from his sister. Leaving his tent behind, he went to gather his dinner and Evan's, post his letter and go to the surgery tent to sit with his friend.

Two days later, the surgeons judged Evan fit to return to his post. Major Braxton packed and took his leave for Mississippi. Joseph took over the full command of the company. On the following morning, they rode out on McClellan's orders. They filed in with the right flank, digging in north of the Chickahomony. The move soon showed how close death would come to claim them.

"I told you damn it! God damn Stuart!" Evan cursed, throwing his cap to the ground.

Evan kicked the cap and looked over the mess left them to clean up. He placed his hands on his hips and cursed under his breath. Bending down, he picked up the discarded cap. He dusted it off regretfully and placed it back on his head with a wince. Evan would have his stitches out in a few more days, near complete recovery. Sometimes he felt sluggish, but no more than before. They all felt tired. Stalking back to Joseph, he glared like an angered bear at everyone around. He turned back into his old self, but under the mantle of lieutenant.

"I should be shot for thinking we can win this goddamn war," Evan growled, looking around the clearing strewn with bodies again. The remains of their camp lay among them, including the carcasses of horses.

"No need to express yourself so, Lieutenant," Joseph said, understanding his friend's anger. However, such words would not help the wounded or clear the mess.

Joseph lowered his gaze to a packet of papers in his hand. He scrawled something down and passed it to the waiting Corporal. Looking up, he saw Evan bounce on his feet. He saw more comments on the tip of Evan's tongue.

"We can't win this," Evan lamented. "We never saw him coming," he added, looking to Joseph with tear filled eyes. "My sergeant's dead—half my men—but, I'm still standing here."

"I'm tired of hearing it from you." Joseph said. "You should be grateful," he whispered. "You'll get more men and carry out our orders."

Evan looked at him. His eyes ran up and down Joseph, as if he did not recognize him. Rank changed Captain Maynard or the pain bent him. Stuffing his hands into his pockets, he lowered his eyes from his commanding officer.

"We face a whole lot more, Ev. I can't let you fall apart now," Joseph said. "Count your men, give me your report. I need to oversee the graves."

Joseph walked away. He could not let emotions cloud his thoughts. He held a commission, which needed him to perform the duty of it thoroughly, letters for the families and burial of those remains not shipping home.

"Maynard!" Joseph heard a small voice call as he watched the men lower a horse into a long trench for burial. He turned to face a boy in a soldier's uniform, rushing towards him with a drum bouncing on his back. Little Nate was back from his mother's last kidnapping. "I've been trying to find you for hours, sir," he cried.

"When did you get back?" Joseph asked, not listening.

"Yesterday night," he smiled. "Come on—I's told ta come get ya. I couldn fine ya anywhere, sir. I done looked all over the camp."

"I've been right here," Joseph said.

"Yes, sir," Little Nate saluted Joseph, standing up tall. "Captain," he said, noticing the change of rank. "Cor! When did you get those bars?"

Joseph looked over the drummer boy, and then waved his words away, "Forget it, Nate." Rubbing his neck, he added, "What happened?"

"It's Second Lieutenant Conrad," Nate said. "He's been askin for ya."

"Where is he?"

"Over here," Nate pointed to a tree line they used as cover in the battle. "He jus keeps on sittin by a tree. He won help—won move. We think something's wrong. He looks sicker than a whore with the French disease—that's what Sergeant McGuire said."

Joseph's face turned pale. All he had hoped to keep away, swept in. His mind already worked on how he would tell Emily he had failed her. Joseph could not feel his feet beneath him as he ran to where Nate pointed. Shock fogged his mind. He felt his ears numb and his breath labored. His heart beat a deadly cadence in his chest. Shaking free of his reaction, Joseph gathered himself against the panic. Evan had just been wounded and he was fine. Michael would be fine too.

When he closed in on the knot of soldiers, surrounding the fallen part of a double trunk tree, Joseph lost his assurance of his summation. Michael rested against the part that still stood upright. His face looked pale as snow and he sweated a great deal, holding his coat on his leg. Joseph stood before him with searching eyes. The boy remained quiet, sitting on the stump of the broken tree.

"What the hell happened to you?" Joseph asked again.

"Nothing, sir," Michael opened his eyes, gazing blearily. A tremble ran through his body.

"My God," Joseph said, seeing the blood that stained the ground beneath him. He tore Michael's coat from his leg. "Why didn't you tell someone?" Joseph roared. The pant leg was purple with blood.

"They'll cut off my leg, Captain," Michael croaked in agony.

"No they won't," Joseph assured him. He tore open his pant leg with his belt knife. "Jesus!" He cried seeing the bullet wound. Looking at Nate, he ordered, "Get a doctor!"

Little Nate spun on his heel and ran off with his drum, bumping his back with the haste. Joseph looked back at the wound. His expression reflected his anguish and turned white with shock. They had only a small amount of time to fix this before the leg need amputation. The bullet wound looked painful, red and black. It sent a shock through Joseph that stung his heart. He failed to keep the promise he gave Emily but saw his hope realized at the same time. Her brother would return to her.

"What the hell were you doing, McGuire? Why didn't you call a doctor?"

"We only thought he were sick from what e saw, Captain."

"Shut up!" Joseph snapped. "Give me your whiskey Sergeant."

"Uh—sir," McGuire chuckled. "What whiskey?"

"You drunk bastard. I know you've got some," Joseph grabbed him by the shirtfront. "Give me the whiskey," Joseph demanded close to his face. "That's an order McGuire." He released his sergeant and looked back to Michael's pale face.

"A-aye sir," McGuire stammered. He searched his pockets for the desired tincture. He finally found the tin flask, buried within his jacket. He passed it to Joseph, "Here!"

"You're going home," Joseph said to Michael. He took the flat silver bottle, opened and poured the liquid on the wound. He wiped it clean with the cut off pant leg. More blood flowed.

Michael clinched his teeth and cried out in pain, "You—son of a—bitch!" Michael fought to regain his breath. "You cruel ass—stay away from my sister!"

Little Nate returned with the surgeon. The man's expression said all. Joseph looked at him with a deadly glare. He stood and walked the doctor away from Michael.

"This is very bad, Captain."

"He keeps his leg or I take yours," Joseph advised him.

The surgeon sighed and looked at Michael. Guarding his features, he said, "Ye-yes, Captain. I'll try." He routed around Joseph and went to Michael. He could not waste time arguing. Setting his pack on the ground, he pulled out an instrument. Looking to Nate, he said, "You—here boy, heat this on the fire."

The surgeon handed Nate the instrument and turned back to his work. Behind him, Joseph dismissed the soldiers to their duty. McGuire stayed with them. The surgery continued while they waited, among Michael's cries of agony. Joseph stood back, thinking of how he could tell Emily. Guilt played over his features.

“I need to bring this man to a surgery, Captain,” The surgeon invaded his thoughts. “I can’t do the procedure here. I’ll need to cauterize the wound and stitch it up, but we may need to amputate. The wound’s severe an-and it could get infected,” he continued. He looked at Joseph’s stony expression. “If it spreads, he’ll die.”

Joseph took hold of the surgeon’s coat and warned him, “You’ll treat him for it now. And, like I said a moment ago, Doctor, he keeps his leg. If anything happens to it, I will find you wherever you are.” Joseph took his knife from his belt and spun it threateningly. He glared at him, “That’s an order.” Joseph looked down at the man’s two legs and then in the surgeon’s eyes. He grit his teeth, “Do you like dancing?”

“Yes, sir,” the surgeon shakily accepted.

The doctor cautiously stepped back from Joseph. Turning back to the task of treating Michael’s leg, the surgeon knelt with his back to the man threatening him. Little Nate returned with his heated instrument and handed it to him. The boy smiled and the surgeon offered a weak smile in return. Sergeant McGuire stepped up to Michael, distracting the surgeon from his orders.

“Here. This’ll make ya feel better, sir,” McGuire said, offering a second flask of whiskey for Michael to drink.

Michael’s eyes flicked to him, hollow and distant. He took the flask without hesitation and pulled the stopper off. Placing the opening in his mouth, he tipped it up and poured some of the contents down his throat. The alcohol burned his mouth he winced at its strong flavor.

“Ready, Second Lieutenant Conrad?” The surgeon asked.

Michael lowered the flask and swallowed. He nodded his head. His distant gaze watched the heated instrument approach his leg. The surgeon pressed it in, cauterizing the wound. It presented the best solution to kill and keep out infection.

Michael screamed as the instrument burned him, attracting the attention of men passing by. Joseph folded his arms and lowered his head to his hand. He could not tell Emily. Lifting his eyes to the sky, he prayed he did enough to ensure the leg.

"He drank it all," McGuire said, taking the flask back from Michael.

Little Nate looked at the upturned flask with wide eyes, "That'll keep out an infection for sure—from what I hear."

McGuire and the boy looked at the bleary eyed Michael. A shiver ran through his body and then he suddenly stilled. They looked to his young face where a smile bowed his lips. Then, their gaze moved to the surgeon who shook antiseptic powder over the wound. He dug in his pack and found a needle and thread. The men turned their backs no longer wishing to see the procedure. After wrapping Michael's leg, the surgeon sat back on his heals, eyeing his work. He wiped his face and shook his head unsure.

"Well," Joseph's voice shook them.

The surgeon looked at Michael. He saw the boy shiver and nearly pass out. The doctor gasped for air and reached a hand to his forehead, running with sweat. He felt cool.

"He's going into shock," the man panicked. "I'll put it on your head, Captain, if he dies," he angrily said to Joseph, getting in his face.

"And reap all the glory if he lives," Joseph growled. After a pause, glaring at each other, Joseph added, "He's stronger than that. The man's just passed out drunk." Pushing the man away from him, he said, "Help us get him to one of the hospital carts."

The surgeon turned from him not offering another piece of advice. He already knew he would hang if the man died. The men standing by the Captain would swear to their leader's story. What else could he do than comply with the order? He hung his head, feeling a sense of respect for the man.

Sergeant McGuire and Joseph then looped their arms around the drunken Michael and dragged him from the trees. With all the strength left in their limbs after the exhausting battle, they brought Michael to a cart lined up to take the wounded to a Federal hospital and safety. Sitting him on the open back end, they propped him against the side, just in time to leave.

"Shit!" Evan exclaimed from behind them. "What happened?"

"You'll be all right now," the surgeon told Michael who seemed to wake from his faint.

"Yeah, doc. I feel just fine now!" Michael mumbled from where he lay, unable to hold himself up.

Evan tried to see his friend around Joseph and McGuire. He wanted to know what happened out there. He had lost sight of Michael during the raid. Evan lost his voice, as the reality of what he saw crashed on his shoulders. He swallowed his words and his throat felt dry.

Little Nate tugged his sleeve, "He got shot in the leg." His brows knitted and he looked at Evan's coat. "When'd you make lieutenant? Geez, I've been gone too long."

Evan looked to the red haired freckle face kid unable to respond.

Joseph stood with his back to Evan. He could not bring himself to look at his friend and explain. He watched the surgeon climb in the cart. Joseph cocked his head to the side looking away. He shook his head at a loss to concentrate.

"I'll go with him," the surgeon said. "I'll tell the doctors at the hospital that his leg stays on." He paused, taking in Joseph's smile of appreciation. He smiled back. "Direct orders from the General himself." He made to turn away, but hesitated and looked back to Joseph. "If I served in the field—I could only pray to serve under a man like you." He raised his hand to his brow and saluted with respect. "Captain."

Joseph saluted the surgeon. A broad grin split his lips. He watched the man prop Michael's leg up. Michael's head rolled toward them and he gave a small smile. Joseph smiled back and gave a respectful nod to the brother of his beloved. Michael lifted his hand to salute and then wave, but it came weak in his drunken and wounded condition. The cart lumbered away.

"Your dismissed, Second Lieutenant. Tell Em I love her!" Joseph cried after him. "Get back to us soon, Conrad! You're not done here."

"Don't worry—brother," Michael called back with a ridiculous grin.

Evan stepped up to his side, "He'll be all right. Right?"

"Write his family," Joseph said. "I can't—I can't tell, Emily. I failed her."

"It would be best coming from you," Evan insisted. "I'll write Mr. Conrad but you might want to send a telegram to Emily. You didn't fail her, Cap. You just saved his life."

Joseph glared into Evan's eyes. Evan tried to smile it off, understanding the emotions raging in him. Joseph blinked back at the cart disappearing in the distance. Joseph stalked off.

ঌ

Smiling brightly from a face framed by a handsome green bonnet, Emily approached the service window of her town's post office. She took the carriage with Hettie that morning to do some shopping for her mother and pick up the mail before the normal delivery. She looked back over her shoulder to the front window. She waited her turn, standing patiently behind a gentleman dressed in a striped suit. Emily smoothed her emerald skirts and checked her sac purse on her wrist. Fidgeting with her black suede gloves, she saw Hettie hung back by the posting board, behind her.

Hettie avoided trouble from the town folk, not wishing to bring trouble to her friends at the farm. She turned her back to Emily and peered at the posters and postings on the wall. Out of the corner of her eyes, she saw the postal clerk, curious over her every move. Turning, she kept her face averted from the gaze of the wary clerk.

Not everyone in the town accepted her like the Conrads, but they usually found no trouble.

The striped suit stepped aside and sat his bowler on a counter to do his dealings. Emily's turn finally came. She stepped up to the high window. She placed her hands on the small counter, a slab of wood peeking out from the bottom of the barred opening.

The postal clerk smiled down at her and nodded, "Morning, Miss Emily."

"Good morning, Mr. Young," Emily said. "Is there any post for the Conrads?"

"Let me see now," he smiled at her with a nod. He turned and looked over the shelves. "Oh, yes. Indeed. Quite a bundle. Graham will appreciate not carrying this in his bag today." He pulled the packet out and lifted a receipt and envelope from the top. His expression turned grave. "I've a telegram for you from a Captain Maynard. Is he the young man who saved your pa's livestock? Oh, and here's one from Evan Howell for your pa."

"Oh—yes," Emily said, startled by the telegram. "For me? Evan?"

"Sign here, Em," he nodded and pointed to the receipts. Emily took his pen in her hand and signed the receipt. "Thanks. You have yourself a nice day."

"Thank you," Emily smiled nervously at him and stepped back, gathering her mail.

Looking to Hettie, she showed her concern in her features. The man referred to Joseph as captain. She expected a letter from him soon. Perhaps he would explain the matter to her in his next installment. It appeared he had received a promotion during the time between. Emily turned from her friend, pondering the title and walked out of the building ahead of her. She realized that she knew little of Joseph still and the title could even be that of his father. He did not mention much of his family, sticking to her past instead. Then there was the mention of Evan's telegram to her father. Emily's heart pounded and she feared opening her message.

Hettie watched Emily leave, confusion pinching her brow as well. Looking to the service window, she saw the postal clerk turn away from her and pretend to busy himself with the shelves inside. She sighed heavily with and grasped the door, following Emily out into the light of day. The young woman walked up the brick sidewalk not speaking. Hettie remained quiet, waiting for her to speak first. A telegram often delivered bad news.

Emily saw Hettie's shadow trailing hers. Pausing, she looked at her friend's dark eyes and handed the letters to her without asking. Once Hettie accepted them, she tore open her telegram and read the lines, unable to wait another moment. She listened to the sound of horse hooves and carriage wheels, passing on the street and Hettie who walked behind, opening the parasol to cover them in shade from the summer sun.

Gasping, Emily stopped walking forward. Holding her telegram with two hands, she trembled all over her body. Tears sprung in her eyes and the pain constricted her throat. Her legs weakened beneath her and she began to fold at Hettie's side.

Hettie reacted quickly, wrapping her arm around the young woman's waist. Pulling her along the walk, she guided Emily to their carriage, waiting on the corner for them. She whispered words of encouragement, though she failed to know what happened. She saw the hot tears of anguish, blinding Emily's eyes. Hettie set her on the step of the carriage and clasped her hands about hers.

"What is it?" Hettie begged in a whisper.

"Michael's been wounded," Emily replied in a sniffling sob.

"Wounded?" Hettie gasped, both relieved and frightened.

"Shot in the leg," Emily elaborated, falling into her tears

"My God—" Hettie cut off. Tears filled her eyes and spilled down her face. "Come on. We gotta get us home."

Wrapping her arm about Emily's waist, Hettie helped the young woman to climb into the carriage. Once Emily sat securely on the leather cushion, Hettie took to the driver's seat. Her ears filled with the painful sobs of her friend's worry, but she felt nothing. Blinded by tears and denial, she snapped the reins and the horse pulled forward, wheeling them into the dirt roadway. The next moment she was aware of anything, their horse trotted down the road well outside town, mane and tail flying in the hot wind. She saw the stand of trees in the distance, which marked the forest before the Conrad farm. The Howell farm sat against the scene to her right, stark and wild.

When they reached the farmhouse, Hettie directed Emily to disguise her sorrow in a mask of serenity. They could not betray the news they already new and quickly find their source given up. Hettie expected that Mr. Conrad would appreciate Joseph's attempts, but she could not feel so sure about how he may react to his daughter, carrying on behind his back with the man. If they ran into the house awash in tears and told all they learned, the exchange of letters with Joseph would come to a quick end. Emily would face a long lonely wait until the end of the war.

Hettie drove the horse to the carriage house, handing the reins over to the man in charge. Smiling a thank you, she turned to help Emily down. The young woman sat on her seat, staring out of the carriage at the house. Hettie urged her down and the young woman woke herself, lowering her eyes slowly to the soft face beckoning her. Hettie reached out, knowing Emily lost her strength and will.

Hettie waved Emily to her and the young woman slowly responded, sliding down from her seat. Her face hardly disguised her worry, but Hettie already thought out another plan. Walking arm in arm, they made their way across the lawn to the farmhouse and Hettie told her to go to bed. She would tell the Conrad parents their daughter got a terrible headache from the sunshine on their outing and needed to lie down and take a rest.

"I'll come an get ya when they've read the telegram from Evan," Hettie said, as they climbed the stairs.

The women fell silent in the entranceway. Hettie took care of Emily's bonnet and jacket and shooed her away upstairs just as Margaret emerged from the kitchen. Hettie watched the young woman slowly climb the steps to her sanctuary. Practiced at faking her emotions on the plantation, Hettie turned to the coat tree and hung the young woman's coat up.

Margaret approached Hettie with a smile, "Well—you girls are back soon."

"Yes, Mrs. Conrad," Hettie said, walking past her, smiling back. "Emily's not feeling so good. Bit too much sun."

"Oh," Margaret said. "Is that so?"

Margaret remained silent. She kept her eye on the housekeeper until the woman disappeared in the kitchen. Looking to the staircase, Margaret grinned satisfied. She wondered when the news of the Lieutenant's death would come. Blythe found nothing to report for weeks. Margaret knew that meant the letters stopped.

"And that will be that," Margaret scrubbed her hands together, turning to enter the parlor.

Hours ticked by while Emily hid herself upstairs. Hettie remained in the open and continued her duties. She kept an ear pricked and one eye open, watching and waiting for Stuart to return from the field and read his telegram that would notify him about his son's injury. She hoped that true, but her eye went to the clock several times, seeing the time hardly change.

"Emily!" Hettie called from the bottom of the stairs in the late afternoon. Her face was wrought with agony.

Inside her room, behind a locked door, Emily sat at her dressing table with her telegram and a letter from Joseph that arrived at the same time in the bundle. Emily looked up from rereading the letter, eyeing the door. Hettie said she would call once her parents received the news.

Looking back at the letter in her hand, Emily found she could not move. She looked at Joseph's handwriting, assuring her suspicions about his captaincy. He failed to point out any future battles they faced, leaving her brother prone to an injury. She knew it would not.

Joseph owned no gift of foresight. Emily set the letter in her drawer and picked up a handkerchief. She wiped beneath her eyes and nose, worrying over what he did not say in the telegram.

A loud rap on the outside of her bedroom door startled Emily away from her worries for Captain Maynard. Turning a wide eyed expression to the dark panels, her pulse quickened and her breath shortened. Fearing her mother came to announce the telegram, Emily told herself that such news would have her mother swooning on the sofa. After nineteen years, her mother was at least predictable.

Emily hurriedly put her letter and telegram in the safety of her drawer, closing and locking it. She tucked the key in her corset between her breasts. Her parents would not dare look there. Drawing a steadying breath, she stood, facing the door. Another knock came. She called out to the person. Emily smoothed the bodice and skirt of her gown, crossing the room. Hesitating at the doorway, she wiped her face and guarded her features.

Emily placed her hand on the knob. The pain became real again. Michael took a bullet in the leg. She opened her door and lifted her face to look on the person who came to her. Hettie's eyes looked at her with regret. Hettie did not need to speak to let her know they had learned of Michael's fate.

A sob choked Emily and she backed into her room, covering her mouth with one hand and hugging herself with her other arm. She could not say a word. She crouched on the floor of her room in front of her bed. Hettie's hand touched her shoulder. Emily cried into her hands.

"They sent me upstairs ta get you," Hettie said in a harsh whisper. "Hurry, Em. They know. Mr. Conrad's read the telegram," Hettie said, urging the young woman to her feet.

"Why did this have to happen?" Emily murmured, stepping away from Hettie and leaving her room.

Emily rushed down the stairs, wishing to bring an end to her torment. Part way down, she looked to the parlor archway and saw her parents waiting for her inside. Her mother sat on the coach, sobbing into her handkerchief and her father stood with his back to the entrance, smoking his pipe. His expression was hard as he stared at the wall of books, holding Evan's telegram behind his back. Emily continued down the stairs, slowly closing the distance. Turning into the parlor, Emily folded her hands together at her waist. She looked at her mother and waited for acknowledgment. Her mother raised her chin and looked at Emily with a tremulous expression. Emily sat beside her, letting her mother fold into her arms. It felt good to feel her love again, but it wanted too terrible a price to earn it.

"Michael's been wounded," Emily heard her father say. The words sounded unbelievable to her ears, though she knew the truth already. "He's resting at a hospital, waiting for transport," he added, dropping into a chair.

Tears slipped from Emily's eyes, but she made no sound.

"Oh—Emily," her mother moaned, gripping her tightly. "Your brother's gonna come home. Don't worry. Your brother'll finally come home," she told her.

Emily remained silent unable to speak if she wanted. She knew longer than they about Michael's condition. Emily fought her emotions the entire time, even when they stood sure to cripple her, under the hope their finding out would release her guilt. It failed to happen that way.

Michael laid in a hospital somewhere and they knew no more. He received a wound in the leg but he would live. Emily felt numb to her toes. Lifting her eyes to her father, she saw a sad old figure. She kept a terrible secret from him. Lowering her face from him and burying it against her mother's trembling shoulder, she bit her tongue. She refused to tell her secret still.

The discussion on what they would do next began. Emily felt deeply sore with the decision her parents made. She would not go with her mother to the hospital in Washington and bring her brother home. Emily tried to protest, but her father would not hear of them all leaving. The dairy needed supervision and he would not see his young daughter in such a great city as their nation's capitol, guarded only by her frail mother and a young housekeeper. Emily demanded they should all go, citing that Mr. Benson knew how to run the dairy alone. She argued the close friendship with her brother and claimed she desperately wanted to go to him with her mother. She said her mother needed her at her side. Emily's arguing benefited nothing. Her mother agreed with her father and neither would hear anymore. There stood the end of debate.

Once the matter of what they would do was resolved, the Conrads ate a silent dinner. Much of the meal went uneaten. None of them had the stomach for it, with Michael miles away in agony. Emily left the table first to hide in her room for the evening.

Cloistered in the dark, Emily trembled and collapsed on her window seat, crying. She cried not for her brother, the fate of Michael was sealed. Rather, she feared what would come. Alone in the dusky light that filtered through her window, she clutched her small cross and prayed. Whispering against the cold metal, she shut her eyes and the tears lessened in her concentration. She prayed Michael's fate would not befall her lover. Without the ability to rest beside him, she would embrace her faith and wait to hear from her boy in blue. She was sure this meant the end to their good luck.

"May God be with you Joseph, that I cannot," Emily whispered, pressing her face to the glass and gazing up to the darkening sky.

The next morning came quickly. Just after dawn, Emily heard the sounds of people rushing along the halls of her home. Yawning, she rubbed her eyes and sat up in bed to listen more closely. Her eyes flicked to the gray sky in her window.

"Damn!" She cursed, flipping the covers back and jumping up.

Emily took up her robe from the foot of the bed and swung it on her shoulders, sticking her arms through the sleeves. Securing the belt, she looked for her slippers, eventually finding them beneath the foot of her bed. Emily knelt to dig them out and heard her mother's voice addressing her father. Time to go.

Emily quickly put her slippers on and dashed from her room. She hurried downstairs, working her unkempt hair into a single braid. At the bottom, she spotted her mother's luggage and smaller older bag belonging to Rose. Her mother's voice came into focus with a rush of hurried footsteps, for the morning.

Emily faced her mother, Rose, and a self satisfied looking Blythe. Emily wiped her eye and ignored the doll girl, setting her jaw sternly. Her mother touched her face and they bid farewell lovingly, belying the problems of late.

"Mrs. Murphy shall arrive within a few minutes to watch over the house with you, until your father returns," Emily listened to her mother say. She noticed the dark dress her mother wore, mourning the fate of her son. "Feel free to ask her to stay while I am gone. It would ease your father's mind."

Emily nodded her head, disguising her surprise at her mother's suggestion with weariness. She felt her mother pat her shoulder, as she stepped away to look over her baggage. Then, Rose stepped up to her and said her good byes. Emily managed a weak smile for her. The housekeeper would surely let Michael know their mother refused to let her come along.

"Hettie needs ta tell you something," Rose whispered, as she hugged Emily.

Emily pulled back and looked at her with an astonished expression. Rose grinned with a finger over her lips to keep her quiet. She nodded toward Blythe, who helped Emily's mother make sure the bags stood securely closed and ran through their checklist. Emily turned away from her to look at the young girl. She wondered what Blythe involved herself in now.

The front door of the farmhouse opened. Emily looked to the opening and saw Hettie enter. She stood dressed and ready for the day, making Emily tighten her robe around her middle. No one roused her. She would have dressed too. Hettie flicked her eyes to Emily, but said nothing and went straight to her mother instead.

"Mrs. Conrad," Hettie's voice filled the entranceway. "Mr. Conrad is ready."

"Thank you, Henrietta," Margaret smiled at her. "Help us bring the bags outside."

The servants gathered around the pile of bags. After a minor conflict, Rose claimed her own from Blythe, giving the upstart a warning glance. Hettie ushered them out, taking the next smallest bag and poignantly leaving the heaviest for the youngest. Emily smirked, pulling her braid around across her mouth. She watched them walk out the door. Blythe struggled to carry her mistress's trunk.

With her curiosity stirred at the way the other housekeepers treated young Blythe, Emily followed them out. Stepping onto the planks of the front porch, she shut the door and watched her father drive up in the carriage from the eastern backside of the house. The carriage lumbered to a stop several yards from the steps. Stopping there, her father climbed down and walked around the back to join them. He smiled up at the women gathered on the porch.

At that moment, Mr. Fordder appeared and took the bags from the housekeepers. Emily held onto her single long braid, watching them all work. Her father loaded her mother and Rose into the seat. Mr. Fordder strapped the bags down on the shelf in the back.

Emily looked to her father and he turned and waved to her. He called out that he would return soon. Emily waved to him. Her mother did not stir to look back.

"Blythe," Hettie said as the cart drove away. "Go inside and have MaryJane start Miss Conrad's breakfast. Make enough for two. Mrs. Murphy may arrive in time for the meal," Hettie ordered.

"Yes, Mrs. Benson," Blythe said sullenly.

Blythe entered the house, leaving the two women alone with Mr. Fordder standing on the lawn. Emily quietly watched her parents drive off. Emily clutched her braid, smoothing the plates. Movement on the porch behind her roused her from her thoughtful state.

"I'm sorry, Em," Hettie said. Emily looked at her blankly. "I didn't understand what's goin on until this mornin," Hettie stepped closer.

"What do you mean?" Emily half laughed away her friend's serious tones.

"Your mother—I overheard er talkin to Miss Holloway this morning," Hettie said, lowering her voice. "The girl's been watchin ya for your mother. She reports everything—snoops in your room when your not there. She foun some tidbits, but nothing important. Just the button he left. You're mother thinks he died in the battle that wounded Michael."

"What?" Emily gasped in shock.

"Imma talk to your father when he gets back," Hettie grinned. "I put one of your pretty necklace's in her coat pocket and some other things."

"You did what?" Emily looked at her with large round eyes, covering her mouth with one hand. "She'll get fired. What about her father?"

"She shoulda thought bout that b'fore she crossed us," Hettie said with harsh eyes. "She's splittin this family up for a scandal. She told your ma what her friend, Lauralee, oversaw in the woods. Thanks ta God, after Lieutenant Maynard left."

"Oh—oh, my God," Emily gasped. "Lauralee Howell?"

"There's no proof, cause I denied it," Hettie said. "We ave ta get rid a the pest, before she tears this house apart. I won see it done." Hettie paused and smiled deviously. "I sure can wait till your ma finds out Mr. Joe is alive."

Emily looked at the floor of the porch, tears standing in her eyes. The widow would come in a few minutes and watch over the house while her father remained away. It would give Emily the perfect opportunity to speak to her without her snooping mother about, but another set of ears posed a threat now. Emily lifted her eyes to her friend and nodded. Hettie touched her arm and smiled, then pulled her into a warm hug.

"I trust you, Hettie. You're the only one I trust other than Daddy."

"And Lieutenant Maynard," Hettie grinned, pulling back to smile at her.

"Oh," Emily said covering her mouth and grinning broadly. "I forgot to tell you. I've wonderful news. Joseph is a captain now." Emily paused to take in Hettie's shock. "He's got a promotion, backed by General McClellan himself."

"You don't say!" Hettie exclaimed. A smile bloomed on her face. "What a man ya found yourself. A Cap'n!" Hettie took Emily's hand into hers and dragged her back inside. "Since your pa's been teachin me ta read, I been lookin for books. I found this one inna spare room," she told her. She took the small volume out of her apron pocket. "It's one of your old books I think—a romance. Let me read it ta ya until Mrs. Murphy comes." She held the book up before Emily's eyes in the hall. "It reminds me of you two."

Emily read the title, Romeo and Juliet. She finished that before Joseph arrived and started her next Shakespearean play. Emily swallowed hard, remarking on the likenesses of her life to the misfortune within those pages. Love denied by prejudice and pride.

"I don't think I could stand it," Emily touched her stomach.

"Get you thinkin about Cap'n Joe," Hettie teased. "In his handsome uniform?"

"Henrietta!" Emily gasped. "Between you and Rose I will burn for the thoughts you make me have," Emily turned to climb the stairs. "Have you read much yet?" Emily asked turning back.

Hettie shook her head, and then said, "Can ya understand any a it?"

"Honestly?" Emily smiled, taking the first stair. "Some perhaps—but usually I am just confused." Hettie laughed at the jest and Emily giggled. "Come upstairs with me. I must get dressed before Mrs. Murphy arrives. I don't want her to see me like this—you know," Emily said turning up the stairs. "She reminds me of Nurse."

Hettie laughed again and joined her on the stairs, taking her arm and stepping with her.

⁂

The carriage driven by Stuart Conrad took the road south and soon turned west. The morning grew older and soon they arrived at the train station that would take them down to Saratoga Springs and from there to Albany and points south until they reached Washington D.C. at the end of the journey.

Stuart unpacked the baggage, allowing Rose to carry her carpetbag alone. He then took his wife's baggage and managed to escort both women regally to the ticket counter. Stuart settled their belongings with the clerk and paid for their passage to Saratoga Springs. Taking his wife's arm, he escorted the women to the train and they boarded with the rest of their meager packs.

Turning her back to the couple, Rose lifted Mrs. Conrad's handbag into the overhead with hers and sat in the seat by the window. The slat wood seats already felt uncomfortable. She hoped they would find more comfortable seats in the following trains they would have to ride. Her bustle pinched her delicate backside. However, Rose kept her mouth shut and listened to her employers give farewells.

"Keep an eye on Em, dear. That girl has me worried lately," Mrs. Conrad said in low tones to her husband.

Stuart kissed his wife's cheek, chuckling and smiling at her warmly. He saw no problem with his little girl. She acted responsibly despite what her mother thought and worried. He knew his wife always worried a little too much, but he could not begrudge her about her children.

"I will, Marge," he warmly assured her, touching her hand. He gazed into his wife's eyes until she blushed and looked away.

"I mean it, Stuart," Mrs. Conrad said, shyly smiling. "There's no telling what she'd get herself up to without us to guide her."

Stuart looked at his wife confused. He saw the housekeeper look at her with disbelief at the statement.

Perhaps he let his wife worry too freely for too long. Emily did not need guidance. She stood a grown woman. His wife seemed to need the guidance.

"We both know Em's a good girl. Don't worry yourself," Stuart said with a soft assuring smile. "Just bring Michael home and don't think of another thing. Mrs. Murphy and I will watch the house for you while your gone. We've all the other girls now—nothing could happen."

Stuart patted his wife's hand, but she offered him a doubtful look. He leaned in and kissed her cheek. Her expression remained unchanged. With a nod, he tipped his hat to his wife and took his leave. He would not argue with the woman in public and show himself a henpecked husband.

Rose watched Mr. Conrad turn and leave. She then watched Mrs. Conrad turn and sit opposite her on the narrow bench. Margaret clasped her hands and set them in her lap, wearing a pinch lipped expression. Her husband displeased her. Rose looked out the window, not wishing to gain a reprimand for staring. Stuart stood out on the platform, watching their windows. He waved his hands to them, holding his hat in one. Rose thought he deserved more respect than his wife gave him. She wondered how he kept his smile after so many years of marriage to such a harpy.

Rose's eyes flicked to Mrs. Conrad. She now smiled and waved to him through the window. The train whistle blew, but he remained with his eyes on them until they pulled out of the station and steamed southwest. Rose cleared her throat and then yawned, thinking of how long a trip it would be.

By the morning of the next day, the women found themselves stranded in the vast city of Baltimore. Margaret's mood soured further. She stood in the state that bore Lieutenant Maynard and his heathen family. She quickly turned irate when she approached the clerk at the ticket booth and discovered that no seats on the train to Washington that day stood open. In fact they looked clearly booked for the next week. Most of the steam engines stood diverted to military duty. He suggested they try to take a stage south. Most people reverted to the old form of transport since the difficulty of getting a train ticket began.

Margaret bitterly thanked the man, feeling as though she received poor treatment at the hands of yet another Southern Rebel.

Turning from the counter, she gathered her baggage to her and Rose. She told the woman of their predicament and together they left the station. Margaret pulled herself together and begged directions of a handsome looking older gentleman. He gladly directed her to the location of the coach and bid her a good day when they parted. Margaret kept her smile pasted to her face despite her roiling anger.

"Come along, Rose. We must hurry," Mrs. Conrad said. Rose regarded her with shock. She expected her to manage the bags alone. She looked at the trunk and back at her Mistress. "What's the matter, dear?"

"We can't carry these bags all over the city," Rose reasoned with her.

"I suppose you're right," Mrs. Conrad said, looking at the trunk and two other bags. Her eyes lifted to the woman who stood among them. "Indeed your right. I shall stay here. Fetch us a carriage."

Rose nodded and stepped away to do as Mrs. Conrad asked. She would feel more than thankful once they rested in their hotel that night in Washington, and they would, one way or another.

Nearly two hours later, Mrs. Conrad and her servant sat in the comfort of a stagecoach headed south to Washington D.C. and their soldier who awaited them there. The sway of the coach made Rose uneasy and she glared at the other occupants, wondering how she found herself in this position. Stagecoaches, she thought, were a memory since steam.

Rose's gaze shifted over the city, as it fell behind them. They emerged into the villages surrounding the metropolis and soon the country. Rose wished she insisted Blythe go. The little snit deserved to travel like this, in total discomfort. Rose's thoughts turned to home, wondering if anything torrid befell the girl yet. Rose smiled to herself. When Mr. Conrad came home, the girl would be accused of rifling through Emily's personal belongings. Then, she would be dismissed from her duties on inspection of her pockets, where some of Emily's jewelry hid. She had planned with Hettie thoroughly, to help keep Emily's secret safe from her calculating mother.

"Mrs. Conrad," Rose said, distracting the older woman. "Did the ticket man say when we should expect to arrive?"

"This afternoon," Mrs. Conrad's voice whispered. She smiled at the other people in the coach apologetically.

"Thank you," Rose said, sitting back.

Rose showed a sheepish expression to the people, who looked at her. Inside, she felt giddy. Margaret would receive her slap in the face the moment she returned home. She could hardly wait.

In the heat of the late summer afternoon, the stagecoach arrived in Washington. Mrs. Conrad and Rose stepped onto the street and looked in awe. The city was enormous. Turning on the baggage handler, they squeezed directions from him of a decent hotel around the Federal Army Hospital Michael rested in. For a congenial tip, the man spilled his honest answer and gained them a carriage, putting their bags on board, also.

Rose sat in her seat behind the driver, thinking Mrs. Conrad quite useful at times. Neither of them lifted a bag since Baltimore. She smiled and placed herself on the soft seat. Her limbs were worn from the ordeal.

"Once we have our rooms situated, we shall inquire at the hospital for Michael," Margaret planned aloud. "If they will allow me, I should like to take him to the hotel tonight. We had better pay for two rooms."

The carriage pulled away. Rose watched the streets in awe of all the uniformed and well dressed young men, going about their business. She smiled too broadly for Margaret's taste and won a reproving glare. Lowering her gaze to her skirts, she hoped the hotel lie close, or mother and son would share a hospital room.

The carriage pulled up in front of a grand looking hotel and stopped before the entrance. The women stared at the façade with their eyes drawn along the high floors above their heads. The like of such finery was rumor until that moment. Margaret quit gawking first and accepted the aid of the driver to climb down, followed by Rose. Margaret had seen such things as a girl in New York.

When they stood on the carpeted walk, a porter met them to take their bags. The porter welcomed Mrs. Conrad and Rose to the hotel, bearing a ruddy face and broad smile framed by a grand mustache. He welcomed them in and they stepped ahead of him through the broad French doors. On the other side they faced a wide and deep grand lobby fitted with glimmering chandeliers and an airy feel from the numerous surrounding windows. People walked past them looking like dukes and duchesses in their expensive gowns.

Mrs. Conrad moved quickly and approached the front desk, wearing a smile for the clerk. After placing her handbag on the counter and responding to the desk clerk's welcome, she looked over her shoulder. Rose looked around the lobby, gaping like an idiot. The woman's eyes drew in every detail and she turned several times to stand sure of what she saw. Margaret saw the porter smile at Rose. He touched his hat to the servant, chuckling at her naivety.

"Miss Benson," Margaret said. "Do come over here, would you," she called her over before the woman successfully embarrassed her again.

Rose dropped her eyes to her mistress and crossed the distance between them. She watched Margaret turn back to the desk clerk. In moments, she secured two comfortable rooms and the porter left them to arrange their belongings. Mrs. Conrad faced Rose and smiled. Rose felt uneasy despite the show of warmth.

"Should we take tea before we go to Michael, or head straight out?" Mrs. Conrad asked her housekeeper. They both traveled under terrible circumstances and felt weary, she could tell.

"I would not ask you to wait, ma'am. I think we've a little more in us ta get to the hospital now," Rose said what she thought Mrs. Conrad wanted to hear, though she was ready to collapse.

Mrs. Conrad touched Rose's arm and turned away to the clerk. For a moment, Mrs. Conrad showed her old warmth and Rose forgot about the anger she harbored at her. In the lobby, she waited patiently to the side while the clerk arranged transport to the hospital. Events at last went smoothly on their voyage, but Rose felt uncertain she wanted to see Michael in his reported state. However, Rose would face Michael wounded. The women settled into the carriage and just as quickly alighted the steps that lead to the main door of the hospital.

Stepping just inside the door, Mrs. Conrad and her servant discovered an old rickety side table pulled up next to the entrance with a soldier sitting at it. He looked over some papers and then lifted his chin to consider the women. Mrs. Conrad smiled at him despite his cold manner. She took the telegram from her pocket and gave it to him. She waited while he checked his ledger.

"Private Fenwick," the man called over his shoulder. A tall man replied with black mustaches, dangling to his chin. He came to stand next to the other soldier. "Take Mrs. Conrad to Second Lieutenant Michael Conrad. He's in the west wing twenty-fifth bed right."

"Yes, sir," the man said, taking the telegram from him. "Come with me, ma'am," the soldier motioned Mrs. Conrad and her companion forward.

The Private led them along the tall corridors to a long whitewashed room with a vast glass window at the opposite end. The interior intimidated to say the least, lined with scores of men bandaged and wounded. They looked a fright, as their hungry eyes turned towards them. She drew a steadying breath, deciding not to leave her son here to succumb to the effects of some disease. She cared little what the soldiers of the hospital would say. There was nothing they could do here that she could not do at home. She grasped her purse tighter to her side and glared into the Private's back.

Margaret felt all too exposed, making her way down the center of the room between the two rows of beds. The Private stepped quickly ahead of her and she noticed each of the beds had a number at the foot with an 'R' after. Her boy lie reduced to a simple number. Margaret's face pinched and she felt the tears stand in her eyes. She covered her mouth with a handkerchief and followed onward, glancing back to see if Rose came along.

The young woman's expression grew dim at the sight of what war had done to the men. It was like she walked through hell. Rose swallowed hard, trying to calm herself. Rose's dark eyes went to Margaret's face, but Margaret turned away from her.

The sad sunken features of the sick men followed them, appearing like ghosts appearing with a warning for the living. The glint of fever showed in many an eye and the bandages numbered too many to count that seeped with gore. Nurses worked among them, looking lost in their efforts. Some of their eyes went to the visitors, coldly assessing and offering frowns.

Suddenly the Private halted and Margaret nearly ran into his arm. She stopped short, placing her hand over her mouth. She excused herself and he smiled down at her and nodded. Margaret watched him step from her and maneuver between the beds. Margaret looked at the white metal rungs of the footboard. At the top a plate read twenty-five R. Margaret's eyes flicked up to the man whose face was turned from her, as he lay sleeping. She failed to believe the pale boy her son.

"Second Lieutenant," the Private said, trying to wake him gently.

The soldier slept in a bed dressed with stark white linens, paying the visitors no mind. His leg lay propped on some pillows, wrapped in white cloth bandages from the knee up. The rest of his leg stuck out on the mattress naked. Margaret's eyes traveled over the foot, it held its ivory color and not a streak of black to forecast disease or death. The boy rolled over and Margaret at last recognized her son.

"Leave him to us," Margaret said. "I wish to get him ready to go home. Do whatever paperwork it is you need." She paused, looking at the man's doubtful expression. "I'll not leave him here a day longer."

"Yes, ma'am," The soldier said. He nodded to her and Rose. Then, he turned away, taking his leave of the woman. It appeared all too easy to just say they planned to take a commissioned officer home.

"Mom?" Michael breathed confused.

Margaret watched the Private walk away and her gaze shifted to Rose. The maid had an unspoken question in her eyes. Margaret raised her brows to keep her quiet and Rose looked away. Margaret returned her attention to her son. She smiled softly at his sleepy features. He looked well for a wounded soldier and she felt relieved to see his leg still attached.

Rose stepped toward the bed, grasping the foot with a shaking hand. Michael looked better than she had first believed. Her eyes trailed over his neighbors and back to him. He faired better than any she saw there. Rose smiled proudly. Michael was quite the man now.

Rose lowered her eyes, recalling how he teased her when children. She suddenly felt sad. Tears burned in her eyes for him.

"Help me get him up," Margaret said, going to the head of her son's bed. She would waste no more time. She wanted to move him home as soon as possible and that started with leaving this place for the hotel. "We have to get his clothes on him. I won't walk him out of here without his uniform on."

"Mother, when did you get here?" Michael asked.

"Yes, ma'am," Rose whispered.

Margaret touched her son's brow gently and smiled. Her boy was barely awake.

"Yes, it's me boy, now get up. We're taking you home," Margaret said, forcing him to sit up. "Come on now get your clothes on."

"But, I can't," he breathed looking at her. His eyes went to his leg and then the foot of his bed. He squinted at the blurry vision. "Rose?"

The girl stared at him helpless. It eased his heart to see her face, more than he would let his mother know.

Looking away, Michael complied with his mother, unable to do otherwise. Rose helped him put his shirt on while his mother gathered the rest of his belongings. He looked to Rose and a grin split his face.

"Thought you'd miss me dying?" He asked, thinking himself funny.

"I'd a killed um sure if they dared to kill you before I got my chance," Rose snapped. She rapped him on the head with the back of her hand.

"Oww," he called out. "Hey, I'm already injured here. I don't need a head wound, too," he added, rubbing his sore head.

Margaret wheeled her son out of the hospital, taking him to rest in the clean hotel for the evening. The next morning, they would arrange the return trip and her son would have a peaceful rest. Margaret did not show any signs of fatigue after the lengthy restless trip. Her mind bent on getting her boy home, rest for her could wait.

The next morning, Margaret stopped at the front desk to see if her plans were realized. The clerk met her with smiles and good mornings, following up with an assurance that her whole return trip lie solidly planned for her. Margaret looked at the man with an approving smile and a measure of surprise. She never discovered such service in all her dealings in Vermont. It made her miss the city life all over again.

"Thank you very much, Mister Colson. Do you have a telegraph service, as well?" Margaret inquired of him.

He smiled and nodded, "Yes, Mrs. Conrad. Of course." He stepped to the edge of the counter that went behind a door marked office, holding his hand out for Margaret to follow him. She shifted reluctantly to the side and stood before the door patiently waiting. The clerk opened it and guided her inside to the office. "If you'll wait here a moment, ma'am."

Margaret sat down in a chair beside a cluttered desk affixed with what she assumed to be a telegraph instrument. Wires and gadgets decorated the surface and a pull switch on top with what looked like a finger pad. She smiled at the piece of technology, imagining her husband's delight to know just when she would arrive home. This trip proved remarkable and she now wished Emily accompanied her to see the wonders. It stood too late for such meanderings now and she told herself Emily remained safe at home, healing from her loss and preparing for her brother's return. She took a deep breath relieved things would finally be as they should.

The telegraph clerk joined Margaret at the side of the desk. She relayed her message for Mr. Conrad, about her expected arrival time in Vermont. At the end, she gave an added message to the postal clerk that he see the message delivered within an hour of receiving it. Satisfied with her job, Margaret tipped the clerks for the dutiful work on her behalf.

Margaret smilingly inquired about breakfast in the dining room. She stepped from their offices, telling the clerk to arrange for her and her son to eat in the dining room. Then she told him to send a healthy breakfast to her second room for her servant, collect their bags and prepare their bill. Margaret turned away and climbed the stairs to her room on the second floor. She could barely contain herself at the prospect of her success.

Margaret collected her son and they enjoyed a leisurely breakfast in a vast sunroom fitted with tall potted plants and statuary, including a fine cherub fountain. Michael insisted on paying for the meal with his wages from the service and did not step aside when it came time to pay the bill. Margaret blushed and covered her face, as he gave the banknotes to the waiter. Michael smiled at her, assuring his mother he made enough to pay for the meal.

In the lobby, mother and son met with Rose to await a carriage to the coach station. Meanwhile, Margaret tried to convince her son to leave the wheelchair behind, he would find no use of it in the house with all the stairs and traveling would go roughly for them. Michael agreed and when it came time to leave the hotel, he gave the piece to the hotel for patron use. The clerk found the gift acceptable and took the worth of the chair from the Conrad bill. Margaret insisted it a donation, but the clerk demanded he must relieve her of its worth. When the matter lie settled between all parties, the carriage to take them to the coach station waited outside.

In little time, the three travelers found themselves cramped inside a hot rickety old stagecoach, wheeling north. Michael stared out of the window, thinking of how lucky he was, keeping his leg and surviving a bullet. The hot dusty day passed him, stirring up memories of battles. Turning his eyes back into the coach, he watched his mother study the same scene, with a somber expression. He wondered what she saw.

Michael sat back and laid his head against the leather cushion of his seat. He saw battlefields stretched out over every point of the scene outside. He imagined lines of soldiers entrenched against the enemy. He saw cavalry ready to charge. His leg bobbled, as they crossed a rut in the road. He winced from the pain and the images stopped.

By midday, the trying ride ended. The coach stopped and they left the rocking conveyance. Margaret and Rose took an arm each and helped Michael to a stationary bench inside the coach station. Rose left them to gather the baggage and arrange for transport to the train station. An hour later, Margaret rested beside her son in the Baltimore train station. She sat upright, watching everything that went on around her without the least sign of weariness. Lowering her eyes to her son, she placed a hand on his shoulder and squeezed. She gave him a small smile.

Michael offered her a weak smile in return. His leg hurt since the coach ride, a nagging ache that distracted him from everything. His gaze shifted down his leg, stretched out over the top of his suitcase and his mother's. He drew a deep breath, holding the long silence they fell under since sitting there. His eyes moved to the plain wooden cane, resting in his right hand. He received the piece before he left the hospital, army issue.

Sighing, Michael wished he lay in his bed, half sleeping while his sister read to him from one of her many books. Her presence set his mind at ease. She acted more the loving mother than the mother they shared. Although, he knew his mother tried to nurture them both. Her ideals got in the way and she controlled their decisions to see them to what she thought best.

Michael's gaze shifted around the stuffy train station. He saw the people like him, waiting to go home. He wondered if his career as an officer ended. The thought of the military brought up other matters he needed to speak to his mother of. The matter nagged his mind since Joseph became his superior officer, since he showed himself a noble gentleman and held the reputation of such with all the men and probably the women who knew him. Since, Joseph saved his leg.

"I met that man Evan brought home," Michael said. He watched his mother adjust uncomfortably at the mention of Captain Maynard. "He's my captain—one a the finest men I've met."

"Indeed he seemed that way," Margaret said through tight lips. "He saved our cows. It's such a pity."

"I heard he almost died for Em's calf," Michael said, looking to her. After a long pause, "Did you know some of the men on our side come from the South?" He watched his mother's face contort with horror. "A few of the Johnny Rebs come from the North."

"Where did you hear such a horrid thing?" Margaret said. Her lips trembled.

"I done seen it, Mamma," Michael answered. "I wouldn't have believed it if I hadn't." He paused, thinking of what she said. "What do you mean pity?"

"Well, the gentleman died, did he not? In the battle you were wounded in?"

Michael scoffed. He could see the hopefulness in her eyes. "No," he said. "He saved my leg." He laughed looking to Rose with a question. "He's just fine far as I know."

Rose smirked triumphantly. There was a story here.

Margaret thought over the feelings she held for the southern man who came to her home. Their conversation went silent. She had thought Lieutenant or Captain

Maynard, whichever he called himself, dead. He tried to disguise himself with his gallant well to do birthright and not what he was. She felt herself sicken at the idea the man was alive and that he was her son's commanding officer. He probably shot Michael, or at least he stood responsible. Blasted southern wolf in sheep's clothing!

"Then, we are thankful to him on two counts now," Margaret said not meaning it.

The blast of a train whistle blew through the station, startling the group from the tense moment that seized hold of them. The tracks were empty, but the telltale rumble of a steel steam car announced the arrival clearly. The large black engine pulled into the tunnel, dragging several carriage cars behind it. Steam billowed from beneath the wheels, hissing from the train's inner workings. Michael stood, using his cane to support himself and offered his hand to his mother.

Margaret waved her son away and stood on her own. She clutched at her small handbag and motioned a passing baggage handler to their side. The valet joined them, placing their baggage on a cart already laden with more belonging of other passengers. Together the three went to join those who boarded the train to New York City. It may be an exhausting trip, but they would take it to return home quickly.

After Michael's removal from the front, Captain Maynard and his company moved with the migrating Army of the Potomac. At the center of it, Joseph could not see how the battles would end. His memory was soaked in images of picket lines and trenches. He still saw the barrels of endless rifles, aimed at the enemy in warning of the might they held. The enemy never fell back, certain of their righteousness. Instead, their maneuvers allowed Joseph and his men to have their revenge. The Federals met the onslaught with a strong arm, wanting more than anything to beat the Rebels solidly. Eventually, a full victory was granted the Federal forces. They managed to come out nearly unscathed and the Confederate men at last took the heavy loss.

Joseph thought of the gray coat fall. He went over the memories and it seemed they finally gained a long awaited advantage. He mused he might see Vermont before the first snow of the season.

On a hot day at the end of June, Joseph and his company fell back to the James River. His orders from the top read confusingly, but mentioned something about the rails and to prevent their loss to the enemy. He should find General Porter along the way and join with him to make his move against the enemy. Joseph thought it strange that he should join with the other general and it felt like an omen when he read the words in the orders.

Joseph felt the niggling of a warning in the back of his mind. He could only regard the orders as a glorified retreat. Indeed the trains may supply them their needs, but he thought it cowardice to run back there, after gaining so much ground. They should have called in other units to do the job and let them continue their advance. He pictured his former superintendent, drinking to them in scorn, laughing at the Yankees as they ran like confused chickens in his yard.

With Porter, Joseph found his company assigned as cannon fodder. During the maneuvering, his men fought bravely, holding against the enemy forces for some time. Mounted horseback, Joseph watched the sunset. Something bothered him about the vision of the bright orange sun falling behind the dark tree line, as it cast fiery rays over the landscape. Fire.

Night came and the fighting turned severe. Joseph kept his units back at the orders of his commander, Porter. A useless charge in the dark would only lose more of his men. Joseph preferred not wasting his men for sport. He looked them over, listening to the crack of gunfire in the dark. He also hated to see other men wasting their lives for foolishness in his stead.

"Captain Maynard," a familiar voice called from behind.

Joseph looked to see the Corporal, who stood behind the line of horses. He held a paper up. Joseph motioned the man over and his companions parted to allow him to pass. Joseph waited for the Corporal to stand at his knee.

"I've orders from, General Porter, sir," the Corporal said.

Joseph eyed him harshly. He took the offered paper and read the lines scrawled inside. He handed it back to the Corporal and nodded. The Corporal turned toward the company and loudly called the retreat. Joseph shut his eyes for a fleeting moment. He felt weary of running away. If only they would face the threat in a united front and push back the enemy for good.

Opening his eyes, Joseph turned Manny and led the line of his company units away from the fighting. They found themselves surrounded by thousands of navy coats. A sea of Federal soldiers planned to make a retreat in one rush. The guns blasted behind them and Joseph looked over his shoulder. The Rebels planned to follow the rush and overtake them.

"Company!" Joseph screamed to his men. He could see some of their faces. "Keep together! Head for the river," Joseph ordered them.

In the sea of bodies that made the retreat, his horsemen picked along, trying to keep in their saddles and keep their horses on their legs. Manny faltered in his step and protested, fearing to step on a human that found his way under foot. Joseph leaned him down and kept him moving ahead. His heart raced in his chest with fear like he only knew in a charge. The relentless Rebels chased them.

Joseph wondered how far his company would reach, before the hand of death closed on them. He feared capture more than death, but neither stood as a sensible solution. Looking back over his shoulder, he saw the desperate faces of his men, including Evan. Turning his attention ahead, he spotted the bridge they need cross. Men already converged on it and more crossed in the river itself in a desperate attempt to get away. It looked like a herd of animals running from a predator.

Joseph refused to look back, until they were safe. His men would follow him and with Manny to carry him, he need not worry how they would escape. He held his eye on the bridge and the sea of men he rode among. Their efforts turned to a blur.

Evan sat behind Joseph on his brown stallion. He kept his eyes on his captain, checking over his shoulder to assure himself that his new sergeant rode close behind with his eyes on the rest of the men. He looked back. The sound of a bullet whizzed past his head and roused him to look back. An explosion burst behind them. He shook and his horse reared.

Evan eased his mount back onto all fours and continued retreating. His eyes searched ahead for Joseph. He saw Manny's glistening black rump. His eyes widened to see Joseph slumped over the neck of his beast. Without care for a man between him and his friend, Evan snapped his mount into motion and rushed him to Joseph's left side. Reaching an unsteady arm, for the way his mount tried to hold next to Manny, he grabbed Joseph's arm. It felt sticky wet.

Without hesitation and knowing he felt blood, Evan pulled Joseph straight into his saddle. His expression looked strained with pain. One of the Rebel rifles sent a bullet nearly true.

"Don't let go yet, Captain. We've almost got there," Evan said to him. He watched the bleary green brown eyes turn to him. Joseph drew his breath hard. "Think of Em."

Joseph nodded, feeling weak. He put a hand over his upper arm where Evan released him. Grasping his reins tighter, he managed to sit up and complete the retreat to the bridge. Another explosion of cannon fire fell not far behind and propelled Captain Maynard and his company to safety. He thought the night could not end soon enough and the eyes of sapphire danced about his memory. He felt her hand in his and the silk of a purple gown, she said she just fixed up out of an old dancing dress. His eyes turned black.

Sitting in a rickety chair balanced on its back legs, Joseph stared up at the ceiling of the surgery tent. He winced and sucked in a breath of air through his teeth. Every stitch the doctor worked into his arm stung like a bee. He counted five times the surgeon told him he almost finished. The man was a worse liar than McClellan. However, he thought better of pulling his arm back and putting his shirt back on before he finished.

"Cap," Evan's voice came from behind the blood smocked surgeon.

Both Joseph and the doctor looked to see him. He stood their, smiling at them with his cap in his hands. His chamois gloves held the stain of Joseph's blood on the right palm and a smear on the top of the left. Joseph tried to smile back. With both of them there like that, war proved a gory ghost and not the applicable answer they had sought. At least both sides agreed.

"We lost five enlistees in the crossing," Evan said. Joseph looked away from him. Evan lowered his gaze and stepped closer. He thought about the other words he needed to say to him. "General Porter wants to give you a medal. Some of our superiors viewed the collected manner in which you worked our retreat. Our company suffered some of the fewest losses. They think its cause a you."

"Its not me," Joseph said, setting his chair back on all legs. The surgeon washed his wound in preparation of wrapping it. "I've only been lucky enough to get the finest rabble of the whole lot."

Evan grinned and sat in an empty chair, facing him out of the way of the doctor. He hoped Joseph would keep them, by his own design or that of fate. Evan drew a deep breath and set his cap back on his head. Resting his elbows on his legs, he leaned forward and looked at the Captain. He drew a soft rose hued envelope from inside his jacket.

Joseph eyed the letter in his subordinate's hand. His name was written across the front in a calligraphic handwriting. The black ink looked like heaven. It filled him with electric excitement and at last he found a reason to smile.

Evan laughed and smiled, "Thought you might appreciate seeing that."

Joseph took the letter from Evan. He looked at it another moment. Joseph never felt so thankful he stood alive to accept such a gift. His wounded arm settled back to his side and he looked up to see the doctor, smiling down at him. Lowering his gaze, he saw the bandage around his arm.

"You hungry, Cap?" Evan woke him. "Mess should be ready."

"If you can stand to sit with me while I read this," Joseph said, holding up the letter.

Joseph stood, putting his shirt on, and grabbed his coat from the back of the chair. He picked up his hat from the table the doctor's instruments rested on. Putting the Stetson on his head, he felt the stitches pull and he grimaced.

"As long as you don't cry none," Evan said. "Ain't nothing worse than some blubbering old man." He stood to join him.

Joseph looked at him with a warning sneer, "I'll make you cry."

"I look forward to that," Evan replied stoically. A slow smile slipped.

Together the officers left the surgery to return to the company. They joined the other low ranking officers at the company mess, which sat in sight of the enlistees gathered around their own tables. Dinner tasted better than any he ate in his life, even in the prosperous dining rooms north of that tent. The cigarette he smoked made a fine finish. In fact, the dinner proved so enjoyable, he forgot the letter he laid down beside his plate, intending to read while he filled his belly.

"Joe," Evan murmured. "You going to read that letter from Miss Conrad? Or, you thinking of holding it like the woman herself?"

The men around the table chuckled low and kept their eyes away from the Captain, not wishing him to turn them into the butt of a joke. Joseph smiled looking over them. He drew the envelope into his hand and blew out a breath of smoke. Setting the cigarette on his lip, he tore open the envelope with his thumb and pulled out the neatly folded letter inside. The smell of her perfume surrounded him, driving away the smell of unwashed men and horse waste. He read.

23rd of June 1862,

Dear Joseph,

It was frightful to hear of Evan's misfortune. I hope he feels better and this does not hinder you and your men from the goal you set yourselves. He can be quite a baby when sick. How does Michael fair? Is he busy with his duties? I do not know a soldier's life, but you remember to write to me as often as is possible, and without fail. My brother is not so diligent or so honest as his commander.

I'll not worry about him, since he rests in your capable protection. I'm sure he is fine. He writes Mamma and Daddy, but not me since he left school. I guess I got used to hearing from him myself. You're going to say I'm spoiled. Well, it's his fault if I am.

I nearly forgot. Hettie wants to say hello to you. She wonders if you've received the luck of meeting a man named Mr. Edward McAvery. She told me he owned the plantation she ran from. She asked that if you do see him, please give him a bullet straight through his stone heart for her. That is all I will say about that matter. I cannot think of those things right now. They darken my already shadowed life.

Tell me how your plans go. Where are you now? Is McClellan a better leader? I've heard little from the papers over the last few weeks. I now try to wait for word from your letters. It's agony, hearing my father read the news, not knowing if you're one of the numbers listed.

Joseph, please come home to me. I could not bear losing you. Every day I grow sicker from the thought and I wonder how long I can bear it. Now you see my heart opened to you in full. Call me a fool. Call me brazen. Call me whatever you like, but I won't leave words unsaid between us.

I love you.

I miss you dearly and more so everyday you stay away. I pray for your return, so we may spend the rest of our lives together. I pray you've the same thoughts, but lifeless words do little convincing.

Joseph, come home to me soon. I enclosed a picture, so you may remember me as we met. If the war goes on any longer, I fear I shall become an old maid. I hope you would retire before then and come claim your brazen headstrong Vermont girl. . .

The rest of Emily's letter turned personal and Joseph folded it up to save for later. Placing it back in the envelope, he found the photograph she spoke of still tucked inside. He held it up in front of his eyes.

Still surrounded by the scent of Emily's perfume, he stared at the gray hues, an injustice to his woman's true beauty. For a few moments, it transported him to another place safe from war, wounds and death. He dreamed of a life with his beautiful Vermont dairy girl. He saw their children, running all around his house in Baltimore. He pictured his family in the expansive backyard where Emily would make a new garden. He heard the joyful prattle of children, climbing over him and competing for his attention, after he arrived home from a long day at the office.

Deep in his thoughts, safe from the war, raging just outside his little tent, he assured himself that he would write a reply soon. First, he need secure himself away from his comrades. He looked up and saw their eyes flicking from him to each other. He looked to Evan, sitting beside him with his eyes on the small photo. The man wore a grin like a devil.

"What's that, Cap? A picture of your Miss Emily?" Evan asked him. "I think the boys would find interest in that," he added, taking the photo. He looked at it first. "I do miss my old friend. I'm sorry I ever introduced you two."

"You would have made her a dishonest woman, Lieutenant Howell," Joseph played back.

"No," Evan said. "But, I would have hurt her dearly."

Evan passed the photo onto the other officers, smiling. They passed it around with only a little interest. With respect to the Captain, they would not gawk at his intended bride, like a barmaid with a loose neckline and virtue. The photo returned and he tucked it in his jacket.

"Lovely woman," one of the officers complimented.

"Indeed, Lieutenant," Joseph smiled. "If you gentleman will excuse me. I shall write back to Miss Conrad before Mac takes the opportunity."

The men chuckled at the jest, recalling the many runs they made in the past days.

Joseph left them behind for his tent. He quickly tucked Emily's letter in a place of safekeeping and drew out his supplies to write his return letter to her. The next would contain her response about her brother. He hoped she received his telegram, knowing the state of communications was a mess.

Joseph scratched his steel tipped pen across the surface of his letter paper.

July 2, 1862

Emily My Love,

Your words restore my morale, not to mention the success of your photograph. I will keep it tucked in my breast pocket, close to my heart and always at the ready. Now when I find the need, I can once again look upon you in more than memory. Seeing it now, I miss you more than you or anyone will ever know. I wish I could take you in my arms and—I better not say. It will protect you if someone discovers your letters from me.

I want to say that I write to you to assure you I am well. I took a minor wound in my left arm. The doc gave me stitches, some stinking sulfur and a fine white bandage with his sendoff. I guess I have some luck that way.

I would like to apologize about Michael. The last letter I received from you must have posted just before my telegram. You made no mention of his status in it. I want to explain that, too. The battle he received his wound in couldn't have turned worse. They surprised us and the units suffered for it. I hope you're not angry with me. I did my best, Em. It was near impossible to keep an eye on him for long. Even Evan tried. You'd understand if you were here.

I hope you'll send news about Michael's recovery. I heard they discharged him, but I'd wager he'd get his commission back with no fight. He is needed here. Say hello to him for all of us and he is still welcome. He'll know what I mean. The men miss him. Michael brought life to his unit and his absence darkens our lives. It's a shame we no longer have him to look forward to at the end of a long day.

When I mentioned you visiting, I remembered a funny story I learned from my Sergeant, Mr. Seamus McGuire. A rumor is running through the camp that one of the enlistees, claiming to be the brother of another turned out to be his girl. Both were dutifully dismissed, but now all the men look at one another strangely. I hope I've not given you any ideas. . .

Joseph did well to write his letter when given the opportunity. He even found time to post it. However, the word shot through the camp in the early hours of the morning to fall back. The gray coats chased them. In a notable rush, the Federal army evaded the enemy again without fight.

Until nightfall, his company retreated from the ghost of battle. Finally his superiors judged the distance they crossed plenty to keep them safe. They stopped and made camp. Seeing to the day to day of his commission, Joseph only joined his men at their campfire when they had a meager dinner ready for all units.

When Captain Maynard sat down, he noticed Sergeant McGuire's wary glance in his direction. Joseph offered him a questioning glance in return. The man shakily saluted him and placed his attention on his meal without a word. Joseph returned the salute and glanced over the others of his unit. Their wary eyes avoided him.

"What is it now?" Joseph asked, lowering his plate.

"Ave yourself some more chicken, Captain," Sergeant McGuire said, pointing his fork at the poultry, cooking on the fire.

"Thank you, McGuire," Joseph said politely. "Now answer my question," he demanded in a distinctly angered tone.

McGuire lifted his eyes to Joseph and regarded him carefully. He drew a fork full of rations to his mouth, stuffing it full. The nervousness showed plain on his face while he chewed, but Joseph would not look away. McGuire shifted his eyes to the other men. They pretended to not notice anything. He hoped to hold his suspicions to himself, but alas his idiotic staring gained attention. In the least, he could see his question answered.

Joseph straightened from putting some meat on his plate. He sat back on the log they laid on the ground. His eyes searched each of their faces carefully. He smiled and shook his head. He thought he knew these men and they him. He failed to understand what this mistrust came from. He smiled and turned his face to his plate, cowering.

"McGuire?"

"Aye, sar." McGuire's face rose from his plate, looking like he failed to hear Joseph the first time.

"I asked what's wrong with you?"

"Awe, sar. T'ain't nothin ta worry bout," he tried to assure Joseph, but he could see by the Captain's eyes that he would not reroute. "We wondered if Second Lieutenant—Mister Conrad—if e wur—"

"He's gone home to his family with both legs, my best guess," Joseph answered. He ate more of his dinner.

"That's good, sar," McGuire said, just as quickly returning to his own food.

Joseph lifted his chin to drink from his mug. He saw the exchange of glances between the men around him. He lowered his cup and sighed with a roll of his eyes. Something else bothered the men and he failed to imagine what. Joseph cut the chicken on his plate staring at it. He put the piece in his mouth, chewed and then swallowed the bite. He eyed the men, as suspiciously as they regarded him.

"What about Mister Conrad?"

"Nothing, sar—nothing." McGuire insisted a little too nervously.

"If this is anything to do with his sister—"

"Ahk-no, sar. We just wondered how he's doin, but ya answered tat for us."

"This is about the woman. Isn't it," Joseph said, looking them over. Their gazes would not meet his, but he could see the guilt. "For Christ sakes," he cursed. "I can't believe you'd think Second Lieutenant Conrad a woman," Joseph looked at them with scorn. He pulled the photo he obtained a few days before from his pocket. "Here, she just sent me this," Joseph said, passing the small photo to McGuire first. "Do you honestly think he'd have gotten through Point with no one knowing the difference?"

"It's jus ya asked for um ta join our unit—an ya ad this ere thing with the Miss Conrad, his sister," McGuire laughed. "I'm sorry, Captain," he said, placing his tin on the ground by his feet. The Irishman wiped his hands clean on his trousers and accepted the photo. He held it carefully and an honest grin of appreciation bloomed on his face. A long low whistle came from his teeth and he tipped it towards the firelight for a better look. "Look at har," he said. "Ain no way that ugly mug Mike's this here beauty," he smiled and winked at Joseph. "Ya done nice for yourself, sar."

McGuire passed the picture on and the sentiment reiterated around the fire. Eventually, the object returned to its owner. Joseph tucked it away in his pocket and returned to his meal. The men turned back into their normal selves, assured Michael a man.

"I'm sorry, sar. Things just've been a mite strange round here," McGuire apologized again. "Will e come back soon?"

Joseph smiled at him and said, "I don't know yet." He looked at his plate and the mess filling it. "He's got a limp that'll keep him off the back of a horse for some time. I hope for his sake that we've seen the end of his military career."

The men agreed with the Captain's words.

They all agreed on that, but they knew they would miss him if true.

☙

Just as the guns of war blew over Joseph's head, a smaller war brewed in Vermont, on the Conrad Dairy farm. It began when Mr. Conrad confronted one of his latest employees in his study at the request of Hettie. The house servant claimed that Rose and she saw young Blythe Holloway, sneaking around the rooms upstairs for days. She skulked suspiciously about the house all the time. Hettie told him his daughter was missing a necklace and some other items from her jewelry chest. When Emily backed up the story, Stuart called the young woman in his office, given no other choice.

In the interior of the study, Stuart asked the child to defend herself against the allegations. Through a fit of tears, she claimed the women of the house merely tried to get rid of her, because Mrs. Conrad made her spy on Emily. She relayed the tale she told Mrs. Conrad, which she learned from Lauralee Howell. With every passing moment, Stuart grew angrier. He stopped her in the middle of her wails and asked for her to turn out all her pockets, including those in her coat and bag, which he brought in the study for such an examination.

Blythe tearfully complied. When she emptied her apron pockets and purse, they found nothing. However, her coat pockets showed a slight bulge. Stuart took the garment from her hands and pulled the contents from it himself. He discovered a necklace and some other items he gave his daughter as presents last Christmas.

Stuart sighed heavily and looked at the young woman reprovingly. She bit her lip and stood silent. He told her she brought shame to her family and she should no longer report to work at his home. She would not gain references from him to any other household and the matter stood dropped once her parents searched her rooms at home and replied to him with what they found.

Blythe gathered her belongings and dismissed herself from Stuart's study. With her head hung, she paused in the hall. Sniffling, she held herself in a manner as if to lick her wounds. Her chin lifted and she saw Hettie first, with her arms crossed and a sneer on her face.

"You oughta think twice before ya try ta ruin a woman's reputation," Hettie said to her.

"I didn't mean any harm," Blythe said softly.

"I suppose Lauralee didn't either," MaryJane spat.

"Don't you go gettin involved," Hettie told the little girl, putting an arm about her. Hettie looked back to Blythe. "You best get on outta here, before Mr. Conrad finds you hangin about."

Blythe turned away, tearing open the door. On the other side she found Mrs. Murphy and Emily waiting. She hesitated a moment, but pulled the door closed behind her. Stepping onto the porch, she boldly faced her fate.

"Miss Holloway," Mrs. Murphy said. "I'll see that every fine house in this state and that of New York will know of your treachery. You won't find a comfortable position for some time."

"Yes, Mrs. Murphy," Blythe said. She stepped toward the stairs, but Emily blocked her path.

"I would like to say my peace," Emily said, surprisingly upset. "You tell Lauralee she should watch what she says about other young women, when trying to better her station. She just might find the plan turned on her head."

"You're mother knows what you done," Blythe growled. "The truth of it'll come out one way or another. You wait an see," she warned.

"Your threats don't frighten me. You say one ill word about this family to anyone, and you'll see charges of theft brought against you."

"I didn't take your jewelry, Miss Conrad. Someone put them in my pockets," she ended with a glare at Hettie.

"I don't know a judge in the state that would believe that tale," Mrs. Murphy chuckled.

"And you know a few, don't you?" Blythe hissed.

Emily slapped her, "Don't you dare show her disrespect."

Blythe cradled her cheek and looked sourly at Emily, "I wanted to leave," Blythe said. "But, you kept me here. I wouldn't have said a thing, if you didn't make me." Blythe stepped back. "I hope you're punished for your ways," she growled at her.

"It's time to grow up and accept responsibility for that which you do," Emily replied. "Good luck with your father tonight."

The girl dashed from the porch and into the dark. She would have a long walk home to think over the punishment her parents would give. The town would see to her after.

Emily watched the girl run along the road in the moonlight until she made only a tiny shadow. She crossed her arms and leaned against the porch pillar. Drawing a deep breath, she took in the vast night and felt her heart ease. With the snake out of the hole and the venom taken out of its fangs, a bite could do no real harm.

Mrs. Murphy stepped closer, "Are you all right, darling?"

Emily looked to the woman and nodded with a small smile. She allowed the older woman to guide her back inside.

That night the present Conrads took part in a lavish dinner of quail and cranberry sauce with the most luscious seasoned mashed potatoes Hettie ever made them. Among the fare numbered fresh vegetables, such as carrots, beans and peas, from the garden the workers kept up. Then, loaves of bread arrived from the capable hands of Little Miss Jo-Hanna Fordder, by use of her mother's recipe and permission. To drink, they enjoyed some of Emily's fresh fruit punch, squeezed and worked from recently bought citrus and other summer fruits, by the daughter of the house alone. Lastly, a chocolate cake prepared by MaryJane and coffee and tea service from the gallant Mrs. Murphy was served.

The spirits of the house rose despite earlier and Stuart allowed the servants to eat with his daughter, his guest and him in the dining room. Laughter, such as what rolled out of that room that night, never existed in the farmhouse since the children turned to adults. However, they soon would see another light cast on the farmhouse, another dark shadow.

In the days after, the Conrads received word from young Miss Holloway's family. They apologized for her behavior and explained she was the victim of the suggestions of her closest friend, Lauralee Howell. Mr. Conrad put the matter behind all of them and dismissed any hard feelings between himself and the Holloways, but let Mr. Howell know of the allegation toward his daughter. He thought it best his friend know what Blythe said of his daughter, but soon found the allegation true. It saddened him to think Lauralee stood at the center of all the trouble.

Jackson Howell dealt with his daughter swiftly. He turned her life most uncomfortable, by letting everyone in the parish understand her crimes. The girl never bothered a soul again, but gave the town gossips much to discuss.

Mrs. Conrad had returned to her quiet home with her son and a bittersweet homecoming. He greeted his father and sister with the servants in the hallway. Then he accepted proud greetings from the farmhands and shook hands with the smiling Mrs. Murphy. She wished him well and blessed him under his mother's cold gaze. Not wanting to leave their warmth, he regretfully excused himself because of his sore leg. Leaning against his mother, he made his way upstairs.

Emily watched her brother go, wearing a worried expression. She felt her father's eyes on her and looked over her shoulder to where he stood. He smiled at her and she offered him a weak one in return. Her father patted her shoulder to console her.

"Well," Mrs. Murphy sighed. "I better go. I'm sure I've outstayed my welcome."

"Not at all, Mrs. Murphy," Emily said, sorry for her mother's cold behavior.

"Oh—my sweet Emily," she said touching her face. "This is family time."

"If you must," Emily hung her head sadly.

"Remember," She said, tipping Emily's chin back up. She smiled at her lovingly. "I am going to Europe in a few days. I will stop by before I go, but you shant see me for a time after that."

"I will remember," Emily told her in a small voice. "Write to me. I will miss you."

"I plan to, darling," she said warmly. "Let your father take care of you and have a wonderful evening."

With that said, Mrs. Murphy turned and accepted her belongings from Hettie and Rose. Emily watched her father bid the widow a good voyage and a safe trip home. He kissed her cheek familiarly and she him. They clutched hands and said farewell. Emily walked behind them and stepped up the first stair. She turned when the door popped open and watched Mrs. Murphy leave, waving a last farewell.

Upstairs, Michael sat on his bed. His eyes looked distant though he watched Hettie and his mother unpack his belongings. He roused when his sister stepped in the room. She smiled at him warmly and entered to sit on his bed beside him. She picked up his cane from the nightstand, spinning it around in her hand.

"Doc says I won't need it much longer," Michael told her. "Should be walking fine in a few months or so and go back."

"That's wonderful," Emily smiled.

Behind them, Margaret straightened from her work and hurried over. She hardly enjoyed the conversation between her children. Pulling the cane roughly from Emily's hands, she shooed her daughter from the room. Her boy needed rest and not to think of going back to the service.

"Nonsense, Michael," Margaret said to her son. She felt all their eyes on her. "You'll rest and not think about that. You've had a long trip and a harrowing experience."

"She's just looking at it, Mamma," Michael said, stunned by his mother's rudeness to his sister. "Em's done no harm. I feel fine."

"You need rest," she insisted. "Go on, Emily. Leave your brother alone."

"I feel fine and I'll return to my unit when I'm ready," Michael defied her. He tore the cane back from her hand with surprising strength. "I'll make due on my own. Going to have to sooner or later. Especially now I'm not a child."

They all knew by the determined look on the man's face. He would get well soon. He wanted to return to his commission before the war ended. He told Hettie to leave his uniform on the chair, ready for wear, washed and pressed. She complied despite his mother's wishes.

Once Michael lay settled, Margaret left her son's room, shutting the door. Emily awaited her in the hall. She told her mother of their discovery regarding Blythe and the young woman's resulting dismissal. Margaret seemed unmoved by the development, but once her daughter stepped away from her she took on another bearing. She covered her mouth with a shaking hand and stepped into her bedroom shaking her head, muttering under her breath. What would she do now to keep an eye on Emily? With Joseph still alive, her daughter still risk being his victim.

Just after the dust settled, Emily lay with Michael on his bed, listening to tales of her chivalrous hero, as the afternoon lengthened. She imagined him on his black steed, charging down the enemy. No bullet touched him. They fainted at his glory. Michael told Emily everything he knew about Joseph and she drank it in thirstily. However, Emily could not read the fear in her brother's eyes or understand the reason he held back.

"All the men love him," Michael said.

"I knew it," Emily smiled. "He just has that way."

"Yes, he does," Michael said with a bitter smile. He hated to see his sister mooning over his commander. "Say, Emily—"

"Pssst," the sound came from the doorway. Both Emily and Michael looked to see Hettie, standing in the doorway. "Em," she waved the young woman to her.

"Your welcome inside," Michael told the housekeeper.

"A letter came," Hettie whispered, stepping into the room. She showed the envelope and stuffed it back in her pocket, smiling to see how Emily jumped up for it.

"A letter," Michael said not guarding his voice.

Emily and Hettie stood together at the door and turned to hush him harshly. They looked to each other with a smile. Hettie led Emily into the hall, walking arm in arm. They whispered quietly to each other, watched by Mrs. Conrad.

Margaret had heard Michael's call a moment ago and thought he meant for her. When she went to the hall it was then she saw the housekeeper give an envelope to her daughter. Clutching her hand to her heart, Margaret knew she witnessed the one event she waited months to see. Ducking into her son's room, she tried to get closer to Emily's room without the girls knowing she saw them.

"Did you need me, darling?" Margaret asked her boy.

"No. I didn't call," Michael said confused.

"I thought I heard you call," Margaret told him.

"I was talking to Emily and Hettie," Michael said. He looked at his mother wonderingly. She appeared nervous over something. "What is it?"

Margaret's gaze shifted about the room. "What dear? Oh—nothing," she tried to smile at him. "I'm still worn from out trip."

Michael nodded unconvinced. He warily watched her leave his room.

Through his door, he saw Hettie pass to the stairs. His expression turned to a scowl. His mother suspected the letters between the Captain and his sister, assuming the worst.

Michael grabbed his cane from where it leaned by his bed. He needed to throw himself between the women before one harmed the other. Flipping his blankets off his legs, he climbed out of bed, leaning against the wooden cane. His wounded leg pained him and trembled. He would collapse in the hall, if he made it that far. Sitting back on his bed, he put his cane away. Michael lowered his head into his hands and listened, helpless to do anything.

Margaret carefully stepped to her daughter's room at the end of the hall. Peering through the half open doorway, she saw Emily with her back toward her. The young woman looked yet unaware her mother spied her covert behavior. Her head bent slightly forward and her arms tucked to her sides to the elbows, where they angled back up to her hands full of guilt.

Margaret frowned. With her suspicions confirmed, she felt deeply cut. Her flesh and blood had gone against her. Margaret stepped back and leaned against the wall outside her daughter's room. She pulled a handkerchief from her skirt pocket and wiped her eyes. Clandestine communications between her daughter and the lieutenant would ruin her family's reputation, all the way to New York.

Trying to find some excuse for her daughter's unseemly behavior, Margaret thought perhaps a letter from her brother arrived late, after his arrival home. Wiping her eyes, she knew Emily would not hide away any of Michael's messages, not when she shared them at the dinner table whenever she received one. Often Margaret saw letters come for her daughter and none came to dinner or any other meal. Drawing a deep breath, she dried her eyes and stepped from the wall. This matter needed her attention. Sniffing, she tucked her handkerchief away and sternly set her expression. She would not allow one of her foolish misled children to destroy all she worked for. She would embarrass Emily into right. Her daughter must soon see she wronged herself and her family by courting the devil.

Margaret looked through the door, remembering the way Emily and the Captain mooned over each other when he visited. She clutched the high neck of her dress, thinking of the rumors circulating. Her daughter went unescorted outside her house, entering secluded places with the stranger. The townspeople whispered the secret back and forth and eyed her suspiciously. Margaret wondered how her young Emily found herself so easily lured to the garden and the fields beyond, so far from her mother's protection. She never denied his visits. She felt sick at the thought of a southern man touching her precious daughter, promising her things he never intended until she gave into his lusts. What had they been so secretive for, if not trysts?

Stepping into the room, Margaret shut the door nearly closed behind her.

"What are you about, Emily?" Margaret asked dryly, startling her daughter.

Emily turned to her mother with fear clear on her face, eyes as wide as saucers. Her mouth popped to answer, but she stood wordless. Emily's mind raced with a torrent of horrifying thoughts. She backed away, tucking her letter behind her. By the expression on her mother's face, she already knew. Emily knew her mother did not like Joseph. Now, she gave her the reason to shut him out of her life forever. Emily could not allow that, no matter the cost. She loved him desperately and she needed to hear from him, if not be with him.

"I asked you, what you're about?" Margaret said more forcibly. Her tone did not display her rage. She clutched her hands at her waist and revealed the storm she felt in her heart only through her eyes.

"I'm reading a letter," Emily answered nervously.

"I can see that. From whom, may I ask?" Her voice sounded falsely soft.

"My friend, Mary," Emily said, crumpling the letter in her fist. "The sister of the gentleman who saved our cows," she felt herself having to explain. "After he left, she started writing me, and—we've become—friends."

"Your friend, Mary!" Her mother questioned, knowing better.

Margaret dove toward her and tore the letter from Joseph out of her daughter's hands. She held it up, shaking it like a terrible weapon. Now her daughter thought to boldly lie to her. She looked at the crumpled notepaper, reading the print at the top and turned her eyes to the handwriting below.

"Does your friend Mary write this," she dared her daughter. "My dearest love Emily—" She read before her daughter cut her off.

"Mamma!" Emily cried out. "Stop! Stop it!" She pleaded, but her mother found no forgiveness that day.

"Your words've succeeded in restoring my morale!" She exaggerated. "What need ail this poor woman, Emily?" She feigned shock. Emily wept in her hands, falling to her knees at her mother's feet. "She goes onto say," her mother acted proud of her actions. "Not to mention the photograph you sent—" At this, her face turned red with rage. "Where did you get the picture from? Is it the missing one from the parlor? Never mind," Margaret growled. "Good Lord, I miss you more than you know. I wish I could take you in my arms and—" At this she gasped exaggerating the feelings meant to show there. "He best not say."

"Stop," Emily sobbed, looking up at her with a tear streaked face, full of agony. "You never liked him," she accused her mother. "You're doing this just to spite him! Stop it—stop it!" She stood and tore the paper from her mother's hands. "These are my letters and I forbid you to touch them." Emily folded the sheets. "I'm a grown woman, Mamma."

"Forbid! Forbid!" Margaret gaped at her daughter in shock. "You—forbid!"

Emily kept her eyes on the crumpled sheets. She held them gently, as the tears slipped from her chin to soak them. Margaret felt her ire rise at the way her daughter thought her sin more worthy of her protection than her good name. Her heart beat hard in her chest and words formed in her mind.

"How dare you defy me," Margaret hissed.

Emily glared at her defiantly from a reddened face streaked by tears. She would not allow her mother to ruin everything she planned, just from assuming her daughter's behavior. Her mother's ridiculous hatred of Joseph came from her foolish assumptions. It must stop. She would take the matter to her father and he would help. If not, Michael would speak for the Captain. Of any of them, her brother knew what kind of a man Joseph was. He lived with him in the army and Joseph saved his life.

"You're my daughter," Margaret reminded her warningly. "You'll not forbid me to do anything in my home." She paused eyeing her. "Your behavior's unseemly child. I'll not allow you to ruin your reputation and your family's over a dead man. I—forbid—you to ever see him again, and don't think to dare write anymore."

"Make me—father won't," Emily snapped back.

"You brazen little—hussy!" Margaret gasped. "You're no daughter of mine!" She yelled, slapping Emily across the face and knocking her to the floor.

After a long pause, kneeling on her hands and knees, clutching her cheek tenderly, Emily sadly said, "You can't possibly be my mother. No mother would stand in the way of her daughter's happiness." Emily trembled, looking at her letter. She held it out like a weapon. "Joseph's the only reason Michael's alive. Without him, his leg would lie in a pile somewhere in Virginia. He could lay dead in a pile in Virginia," Emily said, rising to her feet. "Admit it! Admit it! He's the only reason we have our cows left to us! He's the only reason we remain whole!"

"Michael wouldn't have faced any of it, if you hadn't meddled," Margaret spat.

Margaret heard her son's words echo in her mind from the train station. She could hear the way Michael spoke to his father about him last night at dinner. Captain Maynard was sure to become a hero if he survived, already claiming several medals. It made Margaret sick in her stomach and her head rang like a hammer and anvil. She saw a devil, fogging their eyes with his fakery. He used tricks to woo them to his side. She saw through him, despite it. He planned to ruin her family, starting with her Emily, then Michael and finally her husband. No one helped her to thwart him, not even the housekeepers, long since lost when Emily fell.

"Margaret," a deep voice filled the room. The women's eyes went to the bedroom door to see the father of the house who stood there tall and stony faced. "I want to speak to you—alone." His white brows hung darkly over his deep blue eyes and his face reddened in that manner when something angered him a great deal. His tone remained remarkably calm. "Now."

Margaret took one last look at her daughter, letting her hands fall to her sides. Emily's eyes held fiery anger. Margaret looked away from her and stepped from the room, disappearing with her husband in the hall. Here came the end of her fight.

Emily watched her retreating mother, wondering what changed the woman. Her eyes flicked to her father and he smiled reassuringly to her. Emily felt her heart ease at the expression. However, unless her father believed in her, trusting her implicitly, it may just prove the end of her letters.

"Dry your eyes, Emmy," he said and stepped away. "And, see to your brother. I hear him calling."

Emily nodded and lowered her eyes to the partially torn and crumpled letter in her hand. She failed to finish the letter before her mother burst in on her. Her heartbeat hard against her chest with the passion she felt for her boy in blue. If her mother succeeded—she could not think of it. Emily threw herself onto her small bed and sobbed like a child.

In the hallway, Margaret preceded her husband down the stairs. Hettie watched them go from the door of their bedroom where she had been cleaning when the ruckus broke out. Their steps stopped and the study door closed downstairs. Hettie quietly stepped to Emily's room. She hesitated, worry dancing across her features. She could hear the helpless little girl inside and she feared the family was falling apart.

Hettie entered Emily's bedroom, holding a dust rag in one hand and clutching her skirt with the other. Emily's pain reminded her of her own. It became increasingly difficult to see the girl through such tender days. Swallowing her pain, she blinked back tears and sat on the edge of Emily's bed to lean over her. She ran a hand over Emily's back consolingly. Her sympathy was all she had to give.

"It's all right, Em. I'll listen at the door and tell ya what they say. Ya go see Michael. I'm sure he's wonderin what all the yellin's bout," Hettie said, urging her to sit up. "Come on now, before he gets outta bed."

Hettie helped her to her feet and held her to her side, walking down the hall. She left Emily in the doorway of Michael's room. Peering in, she saw him sitting on the edge of his bed with his cane in his hand. An expression of anguish marked his Apollo features with deep lines. A tear slipped from his eye. Hettie smiled slightly at him and pressed a hand on Emily's back to urge her to him one last time.

Michael put his arm around his sister when she sat beside him. He waited for her to talk. He heard most of the argument from where he helplessly sat. Not too long ago, his mother's controlling temper existed as a mere joke. Now, he saw his mother fought to control his sister's life with some strange imagination that her suitor presented a threat to the family.

"It'll go all right," Michael said. "I told him what the Captain did for me. Pop likes Joe. He said he liked him, soon as they met."

Hettie turned away and descended the steps to the last stair, pressing her body to the wall. Going against all she had learned, she listened for Emily's sake. The voices were clear and clearly raised in opposition. Hettie stared out the oval glass of the front door, soaking up every word. Her heart raced with fear. This laid the only real obstacle in Emily's way aside from the war. All they kept of each other lie in a dressing table drawer and a trunk down south. It kept the lovers moving toward the day of reunion. Hettie lowered her chin, thinking how precariously that dream tottered on disaster. She prayed Mr. Conrad's heart would see to his daughter's happiness.

". . .people say—" Margaret's voice sounded in Hettie's ear, but was cut off at Stuart's growl.

"I don't give a damn about what people say!" Stuart hollered, sitting in his high back chair behind his desk. He faced his wife who sat in his meeting chairs opposite him. "You won't listen to them. That boy's a hero and a good man."

"He's taken your daughter and turned her into—"

"Come now, Margaret. Your daughter was not brought up that way. You don't trust her?"

"She met him in the garden and our fields unescorted."

"I don't care if she met him in the Howell's hayloft. I saw how they looked at each other. I know," he looked away from his wife disappointed. "I looked at you that way once. Did you think it a sin then, too? I won't hear any more of it." He paused, drawing a deep breath. He touched his pipe smoldering in the tray on his desk. "I want you to apologize and stop this nonsense. You're plain mad with the need to control your children's lives. You cannot do that Marge. You'll destroy our family."

"Stuart dear," She said softly, touching her heart. "Don't you trust my judgment? I know what's best for Emily and Michael."

"You wanted him to stay on this farm and rot," Stuart grumbled. "You wanted your daughter to marry one of the most disreputable men in the county."

"Evan's not so bad and what's wrong with the dairy? It's good enough for us," Margaret argued.

"Miss Penelope Dunworth is visiting family in New York because of Evan's indiscretion," Stuart told her. "She's due near our Lord's birthday. You want that blemish on this family, but not that of our daughter who only kissed a boy? Why is it all right for him to carry on in such a manner and not Emily?"

"Evan isn't the father of that baby," Margaret demanded. "I won't let you believe it and I won't let my little girl marry a southerner. Don't you remember what happened to Hettie?"

"Don't throw Henrietta into this. Just because Captain Maynard comes from the South doesn't mean he's a bad man. Emily will continue the letters, as long as favor allows. It may be all they ever enjoy of each other." Stuart weighed her in his gaze. "Go. I'm through discussing the matter. Now, you'll do as I asked."

Hettie turned from the study door and crept up the stairs before her employers caught her listening. She grinned from ear to ear, bursting at the seams to tell Emily the good news. Her step fell light and energetic as she scurried into the room to find Emily weeping on her brother's shoulder. He smoothed her disheveled hair and tried his best to quiet her. Hettie smiled at him still clutching her dust rag. He looked up at her and relief came to his features. .

"Mr. Conrad told your mother you're ta keep writin," Hettie said. "I heard him say it. He wan's Mrs. Conrad to apologize to you, Em. I bet you won hear none of it from er, though."

"I don't care," Emily sobbed. "Just don let them take Joseph away," she wiped her face with her brother's handkerchief.

"Come on now," Hettie said, taking her hand and pulling her to her feet. "You been stronger than this till now. How much longer you got till e comes ta get ya? You won need hide them letters no more, and I think it's only the beginning. This is good."

Emily sniffled, standing there limply. She remained unresponsive.

"Em," Michael said. "Let me see to Mamma. You just give it time. She'll come round in her own way soon enough."

Emily lifted her head and looking into her brother's mirroring eyes. He smiled up at her confidently. She smoothed the unkempt hairs from her reddened features. Would her life ever be normal again? She wondered if

Joseph could last through the war, if she could wait that long for him to come home. Emily turned to the door, feeling the dark shadow of doubt and despair, closing around her again.

"Thank you, Michael." She said solemnly. She stepped out, pausing in the doorway. "Thank you Hettie," she said, lifting her eyes to the woman, but unable to hold her gaze.

"I owe him for letting me keep my leg. He's done so much for the men," Michael called to his sister, when she walked away. He raised his voice and added, "I'd be honored to call him my brother."

Emily hesitated in the hall. She looked to the window at the end, shining white light on the wall. Her tears slowed and the terror of losing him faded for a moment. It would not end as her mother's fault if she lost him now. Shuffling along the hall, she tucked herself in her room. Hettie entered behind her and closed the door.

"I'm here if you need me," Hettie said.

Emily sat in the small wooden chair before her bureau. Taking her letter from her pocket, she smoothed it on the writing surface. The pages, now crinkled and torn by the fight, stood a testament to a once close bond that conceit and foolishness ruined. Her mother once loved her, but it fell to the past when she grew to womanhood.

Setting aside her hurts, Emily finished reading. In a few moments, she drew fresh sheets of paper from her top drawer. She put her pen to ink and then to paper, scrawling her thoughts in plain exposing text.

Behind her, Hettie stroked her long hair with a brush. She tamed the snags put there in anger and rearranged the calmed locks as before. Hettie was more of a mother to her. Hettie walked her through the dangers with gentle guidance, never telling her she must or must not. When Emily finished the letter, she read over the words.

11th of July 1862

Dear Joseph,

I'm glad to find you in greater spirits. You are quite welcome to the photograph and I'm glad you enjoy it. I feel sure my mother will not miss it.

Thank you for worrying over Michael. We received your telegram and Evan's on the same day. Evan forgot to tell my parents of the severity of his wound. I could not tell them for the sake of our letters, but mother went to Washington right away. He's resting at home now.

I think it encouraging that Michael is so well liked by the men. He is glad to be home, but I think he would rather be with you and the soldiers. His sense of duty is honorable. However, I fear he won't return to you anytime soon, if ever. He can barely walk yet, but at least he holds hope, still having his leg. It is because of you and so many prayers that he's intact.

Don't think of apologizing any more. I understand what it must feel like for you. I placed too much pressure on you, I'm sure. If anyone, I should apologize. It is my burden to bear the guilt of sending him off in the first place.

Enough with sadness and mourning, I rather liked the idea of dressing as a soldier and accompanying your sweetheart to war. Hettie and I find it astounding a woman did it. She told me not to get any ideas in my head. She doesn't like the idea of returning to the South.

I must share something far more astonishing. My mother has found our letters. . .

Emily wrote of the near fatal run in with her mother. It came from her with difficulty, revealing her innermost pain. Teardrops marred some of the words, but clarified her meanings. Folding the pages, she told herself that it hurt a great deal to know what her mother thought of her. Emily once wanted to turn into the woman that bore her. Then the woman, who bore her into the world, ground her underfoot and made her fight for her own place. She saw the real person behind the mask of propriety, and it was a frail beast steeped in fear.

Later in the evening, Mrs. Murphy arrived for dinner. Emily met her in the parlor, bearing a sore expression. Her blue eyes were larger than usual, widened in despair. She sat in her chair and waited for MaryJane to bring them tea.

"What is it dear?" Mrs. Murphy asked with a bright smile.

"Mother might be down for dinner," Emily said weakly. "She's suffering a terrible headache and is resting it off."

The widow saw the young woman's lie. Her smile faded slightly. Without asking further, Mrs. Murphy already knew something happened. The woman always claimed a headache when something went other than her way.

"How's your brother?"

"He's well," Emily smiled now. "He'll come down shortly."

"Oh good," Mrs. Murphy beamed, pleased to see the matter proved other than the boy. "I want to speak to him about all his time away, before I leave."

"It's very interesting, Mrs. Murphy," Emily said.

"But not as interesting as why you've been crying," the widow said.

Emily's face turned to her with a glance of shock in it. She stammered a few times, but the widow raised a brow dismissing her paltry explanations. Emily sighed and then told the entire tail, not stopping when MaryJane entered with tea.

Mrs. Murphy finished tea with Emily, but when Stuart showed she left his daughter to speak to him in his study alone. She claimed her fault in the matter. She told him of how she advised the young man to write to Emily in his absence. She thought no harm would come of it. Mrs. Murphy admitted that she should have known better considering Margaret.

Stuart surprisingly laughed the whole matter away. He told the widow that matter stood dealt with and no more need saying. He offered her a drink of his fine cognac and quickly changed the subject. He smiled at Mrs. Murphy offering her a glass.

The bell in his office rang. He looked at it shaking by the ceiling over his door. It wobbled on a thin curl of metal. He set his glass down and stepped to the widow's chair.

"Dinner," he said simply. "Shall we?"

"Yes, Mr. Conrad. I'm famished."

Stuart nodded and walked to the door, opening it for her to pass ahead of him. The widow exited, but paused in the doorway looking up at the stairs. Stuart stepped out to see what interested her. His wife stood on the steps. Her eyes peered down at them coldly. He looked at her with a warning in his eyes.

"Good evening, Abigail," Margaret said. "I'm glad you could come."

"Go on ahead to the table, Mrs. Murphy. We'll be along," Stuart said.

Mrs. Murphy complied without further prompting. She smiled to Margaret and then walked to where Hettie stood in the hallway. Her ears pricked to listen, but the Conrads kept their voices low and her eyes filled with the image of young Michael who traversed the steps just to see her. He smiled broadly as she entered and she smiled back, leaving his parents to themselves outside.

The evening soon wasted away with the family entertaining their guest in the music room with tea and cakes and Emily's piano. It was a lovely moment that allowed them to feel far away from the threats of war, except for Emily whose heart always looked to Virginia.

❧

Many days became history while Emily's letter wandered its lengthy path to Joseph's waiting hands. When he received the message, he stood eager of news from home, but did not find the usual words that glowed like sunshine. He felt responsible for the pain and anger these women experienced. If he never showed his face in their barnyard, they would still be a loving family.

Joseph hid from his unit, especially Evan who became keen on reading over his shoulder and ribbing him over every word. Joseph was in no mood for taunting. After seeing Emily's tearstained words, he felt raw. His thumb rubbed over the blur of a scribble. He already fought one hopeless battle and did not need another. Many became curious about the girl called Emily, since they saw her picture and knew her brother so well. She hung above their heads like the famous actress Louisa Drew, but she new nothing of her fans.

In response to Emily's letter, Joseph responded by declaring his feelings. He apologized for his part in causing the pain and told Emily to be strong. Her father would not allow her mother to separate them. She need fear no more from her mother's fears, for they had done nothing wrong. Joseph asked Emily to think on the idea that her mother forgot her own youthful indiscretions, excited to worries at finding her daughter grown. He wondered if Mrs. Conrad had behaved in the same manner, but she vowed not to let Emily take part in such dealings. Somehow, age often turned events about in a mother's mind.

With the matter aired, he voiced his other fears in the following passages.

Sitting back from the cloud of uncertainties, Joseph thought of the other news he received. General McClellan officially ended his campaign on Richmond. Washington planned a new tactic. Joseph already stewed in his bad mood and needed no encouragement. He felt like a child, torn around by rootless parents, having no aim or goal. As long as Washington held the authority to tell their soldiers what to do, he would be their pawn in a needless game of chess. Washington never listened to the real men who worked the field and faced the enemy. They only saw them as the cause of failure. They expected to win by their obtuse means and none other.

Joseph shut his eyes and rubbed his face. No wonder little Mac succeeded in so little with his army. Joseph felt badly for his leader. His mistakes compounded with Washington's ignorance and arrogance, and he took everyone's blame alone.

X. Change

Summer aged, growing hotter. Each day ran into the next, marked by battle after battle. The time left Joseph more restless than ever. He wanted to be anywhere but Virginia. Foremost, he desired the company of a certain young woman hundreds of miles from where he was. There he could forget his duty and guide her through the difficulties she suffered at home. However, he was a newly raised captain and refused to ask for leave. The fighting came too frequent and something larger threatened at a distance. Besides, his request would never find approval. He already took too much time earlier that year. In its stead, Joseph made due with letters and time went slowly.

After escaping skirmishes and battles little scathed, Joseph faced another old ghost. He sat atop his horse and faced a frighteningly familiar scene. Manassas, laid out there, the killer of many hopes and dreams. Having fought there once and lost, he knew that well. Now, Joseph's company again stood on its grounds, sent by Washington as reinforcements meant to aid in preventing another southern victory. They arrived late and provided little aid to the men already embroiled in battle. Driving the blade of despair deeper, the man who they suffered their last defeat with at that very place was in command. Joseph conducted his company of cavalry to the best of his abilities, hoping he may ease some loss somewhere for his temporary new general, Mr. John Pope or his assistant Porter. Joseph tried to believe his efforts meant more, and the battle would be the turning point of the war. He hoped they would finally put the Rebels on the run and halt the secessionist army. He wanted to go home and see the rest of his men sent home too.

Captain Maynard received word the rest of McClellan's forces dallied in their march to join with them. Joseph quickly surmised his commander's hatred of Pope from his disguised refusal. This act of immaturity on Mac's part made Joseph wonder if he ever meant to take victory or if he meant to win only on his terms.

The southern army stood to defeat them, regardless of efforts and the plans of the men behind the Federal Army. In the evening, smoking fires lit the dark city like a scene from *Inferno.* Joseph foresaw the coming loss. They received word the railroads were destroyed again. He hung his head. They broke their backs to fix them a mere year ago to no avail. He and his men were forced back with that reality weighing on their minds.

Joseph had wanted success for his men, to finally kill the ghosts haunting them. He should have known the moment he rode out that was impossible. Then, he faced a small respite with the retreat to think well on the misfortune. He and his men were useless into the second day.

Standing between the warnings of the former defeat and the current worsening battle that occurred two miles away, Joseph still wanted to be in the thick of it. He sat nervously on the ground beside his horse. The animal was content in the cool grass of the shade despite the blast of artillery so close. Manny nuzzled Joseph's arm, desiring his rider's attention.

Somewhere to his left, Joseph's current commander ignored orders to join the fight. McGuire claimed it was out of spite. Joseph and McGuire decided they hated the foul bastard, no better than the rest, as they let other men die over their personal quarrels. They took care not to dirty their boots in the mess it made. They had political nests to feather and blood drew flies.

While Sergeant McGuire discussed the matter of their commander with Joseph, Lieutenant Howell swaggered up full of his usual disdain. The men looked at him with a wary eye. Howell calculated something and it showed in his eyes.

"He's gonna be in trouble with daddy if he don't move," Evan said, sitting beside Joseph. His wounds were long since healed and he wore his cap without the bandages to skew it.

"Shh." Joseph smiled, placing a finger over his lips. "Got word Longstreet moved in ta join Jackson. If we attack—" He shook his head warningly.

"Right. I may surrender my commission as a man—and find myself shot like I signed up for," Evan said, looking up to the sky and squinting.

By evening, defeat was but a small reach away. Joseph imagined the news that reached the homes of the United States civilians. His heart ached at the thought of Emily worrying, not knowing until the letter he planned to write later reached her so long from now.

The battle stretched into the night. The Rebel forces snatched victory out of the Federal mouth before it could taste it. Bombarded by artillery, the Federal army fell back again and again. With the rain pouring on their heads, coupled with flashes of lightning and bursts of thunder, the bedraggled Federal Army entered Washington. Joseph rode atop Manny, a dark figure cast in iron anger, leading his units to their camp.

Captain Maynard was right. Miss Conrad received many messages from people about the battle. They named it after the first, calling it the Second Battle of Bull Run. Her father read her and Michael the details from the newspaper. Two long days of hard fighting won the Federal Army a slew of casualties and another loss. Two days the enemy, embodied under the personality of General Lee, threatened her future. She listened to the articles her father and brother collected with fear, knowing Joseph might be among the men still unlisted. She held her breath, not waiting for Joseph's next letter, but the one following that. Until it came, dated later than the end of August, she would not know if Joseph lived or died.

Miles away from the Vermont parlor of the Conrads, Joseph and his good friend tried to make sense of the mess. Twice defeated in the same spot wounded all their egos. They both wondered how they earned a diploma from West Point, never supporting such weak kneed tactics. Embarrassment was too weak a sentiment to explain the way they felt.

"He thought he'd get another feather for his cap," Joseph said, referring to the general that commanded for the duration of the last battle. "And God struck him down," Joseph added. His features looked shadowed and his eyes distant and hollow. He saw more than his share of terror that day

"I wish God struck his ass before we got involved, not those men out there," Evan replied, as they sat with the men outside the tents. "Bull Run—bullshit run," Evan spat.

Joseph kept an eye on his forces, having long since removed the lines between officers and enlistees at mess. He wanted to see the affects of war on them and act before they were lost. He needed to feel assured their health and morale was good, to keep them running like a well oiled machine. Their trust and appreciation for his pains won their deeper favor.

Joseph carefully studied them throughout the meal. He could see the marks of battle, showing in their eyes while they ate and spoke quietly. Each tasted his food, as if he never would again and looked at one another, as if it would be the last.

"Sir," the Corporal said, approaching around the other men. "Your tent's up—and the other officers."

"Thank you, Corporal."

The man saluted and stepped away. Joseph watched him go, eyeing the tear in his jacket. He set his tin down and stood from his seat beneath the mess tent. Looking down at Evan, he offered a small smile and patted his shoulder.

"See he gets that jacket fixed—or a new one," Joseph murmured. "I'll write the letter to Mrs. Fergus." Evan nodded and he stepped away and came back. "Don't forget to run your turn at the camp perimeter when you're done there."

"Sure, Cap," Evan nodded, but his tone was darker than usual.

Joseph stepped away from him and the rest of the men. He took his rain cloak and Stetson from a Private who stood near the entrance. They saluted and Joseph ducked out, racing through the rain. In the near dark of the tent camp, he found his canvas hovel and flipped open the flap ducking inside. Joseph's eyes scanned the weather beaten cloth, keeping the rain off his belongings and him. He removed his soaked rain cloak and hat, hanging them on the pole in the center. He looked around again with dark eyes.

Drawing a deep breath, Joseph lit a lantern and then unbuttoned his uniform coat, removing it and hanging it on the back of his rickety folding chair. Scrubbing his hands in his dirty hair, he sat down hard on his cot, worn and tired. His russet gaze stared forward at the ground, flecks of green shining in the lamplight. The colorful hand woven rug made his mood ease, as there was no stain of blood or torn flesh to find on it. Sliding from his cot to the ground, he buried his face in his hands and remembered Michael's sergeant.

Joseph lost Sergeant Fergus that day. He had taken the man into his fold after Michael's injury. The rest of Michael's unit was spread among the others by order. They would not spare them another Second Lieutenant. They had none to give.

Fergus was one of the quieter soldiers who stayed to himself rather than join in revelry with the other men. On rare occasions, he joined them for a much needed drink. He was a fine soldier and Joseph was truly glad to have the opportunity to meet him in his career. He thought the man would wind his way through the ranks with ease, eventually winning a commission from his career instead of purchasing one. Joseph had even pictured the Scot as a general one day. Michael would be most upset by the loss.

Joseph sat down at his little table with his writing tools. He pulled out a sheet of his letterhead. He planned to write a letter to the man's bride. If anyone held right to the duty of telling her, Joseph owned it. He fought to form the words that would say *your husband will not return to play father to his new son or his three year old daughter.* Joseph froze at those thoughts. It struck too close to his heart.

Joseph pictured Fergus, riding on his white horse, rifle hoisted to shoot. It hit him quickly, sending him to the ground from the saddle. Joseph wheeled back to him, but too late. The ball gored through his throat. In his hands, he still clutched the rifle given him on signing his name to the tour. He could not erase the stare of the wide eyes still expressing shock.

Joseph pulled the picture of Emily from his shirt pocket. It felt a little damp from the rain and cold, unlike how he remembered her. He smiled slightly, knowing she surely could help him feel better anyway. The gray hues of her photo made him forget anything but her. Despite the trials it followed him through, the pictures was in its best condition as if she just gave it. He thought he should buy a wallet to keep the photo in, so the rain would not ruin it by the end of the night, as it poured ever heavier. He could not imagine the loss of such a totem. Joseph stared at the face.

The Captain shut his eyes and placed his head in his hands, praying Emily would never receive a letter like he would write that night. He already asked Evan to send it, if such came to pass. He also bore the same request to his parents, if they did not receive notice from a Lieutenant Howell. Asking such a favor stung at his heart. He did not want them to have to think about it.

Placing his pen to paper, Joseph scrawled the achingly painful letter, unable to put it off.

September 1, 1862
Dear Mrs. Martin Fergus,
I regret to inform you that your husband, Sgt. Martin Fergus died in battle today, August 30, 1862. He has journeyed gallantly from our world, defending his nation and his family against the Confederate States of America. I will send his belongings in the following days with his last month's pay. Please accept a gift from the men of our company to make the going easier, ma'am. If ever you have need of someone's help, call on Captain Joseph Maynard, Frederick, Maryland.
My Greatest Condolences,
Captain Joseph Maynard

Joseph folded and stuffed the letter into an envelope, sealed it and turned it over to write the address on the outside, copying it from his ledger. While he finished, his tent flap flipped open and Evan entered with a soaking head and broad grin. Joseph flicked his eyes over him, as if the man mad. He continued writing the address.

"Saw Miss Clara Barton headed out where we come from," Evan said, shattering the moment. "God bless that woman," Evan added, shaking the rain off his cloak.

Joseph sat silently, gazing at the address. He pushed it away and picked up his photo of Emily. Her blue eyes lie lost in the fading gray hues, but he could remember them. He would never forget.

When Joseph did not respond Evan stared worriedly, then said, "Are you all right, sir?"

"Fine, Lieutenant Howell. Just fine," Joseph replied lazily.

"I just came back from out there—from scouting," Evan said.

Joseph pulled his watch from his coat pocket and flipped it open. It took him near an hour to think and write. He put the watch on his table and leaned back, rubbing his eyes and stretching. He felt the fatigue in his limbs, pulling from places he never felt. Joseph yawned and looked to his bed. He got up and went to it under Evan's gaze.

"Supposed to report to you, sir, when I finished," Evan took to the chair Joseph abandoned. He saw the watch and the letter. He smiled bitterly. "The perimeter seems fit and fine as a new corset. It'd be nicer to sit in the city," Evan told him. "Casualties are real bad all over. There isn't much help to bring them from out there either. The trains run them in by the hundreds, with no one to take care of any," Evan explained. He gave a big smile. "Clara and her women are helping where they can," Evan said, looking to Joseph who sat sullenly on his cot. "Poor bastards," he muttered when Joseph made no response. "We lost ten in the company. General McClellan is sending us their replacements in three days. He wants them trained up in time for our next dance."

Still there came silence. Evan looked to the letter and the address. Sergeant Fergus now numbered one of ten killed in action that last two days. No more than a number now.

"Did you get his remains sent home?" Evan asked. So many lay in unmarked graves, scattered all over the damn blasted Virginian fields.

Joseph finally placed his gaze on his friend, as if to say something, but Evan spoke before he could. "Those damn Rebs are walkin all over us, Captain," Evan whined. His voice held all the anger and hurt of the years he spent there. It came into his eyes, threatening to spill over. "Curse them fur this, Maynard! You just can't sit here. That pompous windbag shouldn't be general. Neither a them! They're alone in this—them and their handmaiden—McDowell. Damn I shoulda known when they involved him. He's poison," Evan said bitterly. He wiped his jacket sleeve across his face already wet with rain, now wet with hot tears of frustration. He saw the faces of those who used to be his friend's and he saw their gray and bloodied corpses. They turned his dreams to nightmares. He had not slept well in weeks from it.

"There isn't much more to say but that, Evan," Joseph drawled in somber tones. They sat in silence for a long moment. Joseph took out the picture of Emily again. She chased away his nightmares.

"Is that Em?" Evan asked, ending the silence. The question successfully changed the subject and saved him the embarrassment of bawling like a child.

"Yeah," Joseph smiled with a halfhearted laugh, more like a forced breath from his nose. He passed the picture to her best friend and his.

"Good Lord! What a beautiful sight she is," Evan slowly smiled. "How can you keep yourself away?"

"I've never seen in my life, a lovelier woman than Miss Conrad," Joseph agreed also smiling. "I never will again."

"Joe? Is there something you want to tell me?"

"I think she's the one," Joseph said. "If I can ever get out of here before some slob takes her from me."

They looked at each other and they smiled. Evan lowered his chin and shook his head.

"No, don't worry none about that," Evan said. "I'll shoot him," he said straight. A smile slowly came to his mouth.

☙

Word passed from the venerable halls of Washington to Joseph's ears in a few days. He would see Little Mac given the nod to keep command over his forces and take that of John Porter's. As for Pope and the feared leadership of the cavalry, Joseph saw that matter dealt with and the commander who had lost both Bull Runs removed from his seat. Joseph stood shocked at the development, but remained stony faced when he heard it. Washington claimed its scapegoats for the loss of the battles so far, branding the dismissed officers daft and destroying their careers.

McClellan's restoration soon saw the men's hopes fully restored. They wanted revenge for the affronts the Rebels served them and their General groomed them for it. McClellan sat on his mount, viewing the men while they ran drills, practicing the new manner in which they would face the enemy. He looked older and careworn. His features turned stern and his manner gruff. People avoided him, not wishing to come closer than they must. Joseph included.

On one of the quieter days of their recuperation period, Joseph and his men ran through exercises with their horses, carefully watched by the corps commanders. Joseph sat to the side, dolling out orders and watching the General. He discovered he wanted to know less of the man. It turned that the more he found on Little Mac, the less Joseph liked the man. Joseph lowered his gaze from the thick dark mustaches and Union Army issue cap.

"It's over. We ain't done a thing in days," Evan said. "I think they're givin up."

"It isn't over yet," Joseph replied. His gaze shifted over his men. He watched them bobble a maneuver. "Come on you dandies—you know how to do it," he called out to them. "Now do it right," he ordered. His commander, Colonel Donnelly smiled and nodded to him. "I can feel something coming," Joseph continued with Evan. "Something real bad. Something I don't want to face."

Captain Maynard drilled his men, displaying their talents to his superiors. Their expressions revealed their appreciation of his efforts and the greater efforts of the men who ran back and forth in front of them. Joseph's eyes flicked past his superior officers, easing his watch on his company.

An enlisted man ran through the crowd of soldiers gathered a distance away, down the hill from where he sat on his horse. The man rushed through the camp, jostling men aside and shaking a fistful of papers before him. Joseph squinted to see more clearly when the man drew further away. He felt with his gut that something closed on them.

The soldier disappeared into a broad tent surrounded by several guards, mainly placed for show. Joseph returned his attention to his company. His eye caught the wary gaze of Lieutenant Howell and he smiled uncomfortably. He crossed his arm over his saddle pommel and leaned with the brim of his hat disguising his face.

"What is it Joe?" Evan asked.

"The command tent," he whispered to Evan. "Messengers."

Joseph watched Evan's dark eyes go to the tent. They then watched the man duck inside. He turned his head and looked, careful not to alert their commanders to their lack of attention to drills. Joseph flicked his eyes over them, called the next order to his men. They lined up for display and carried it out against the dummies hung for them to feint on.

A moment later, Evan elbowed Joseph and jutted his chin to the tent. A man with more gold than blue on his uniform rushed from the inside to where General McClellan oversaw the war games. Both the Lieutenant and the Captain watched him pass a paper to the officer on McClellan's left. The man took it, read and passed it to the General, wearing an enormous grin. Mac did not display such joy for what he saw. He looked over the field, mouth moving to form orders. The man on his left saluted the one on the ground and he turned to some runners gathering behind. His voice appeared raised, by the way he held his head back, his face reddened and his mouth opened wide.

Joseph swallowed as his throat dried. His eyes flicked to Evan and he saw the fear in him too. Joseph straightened in his saddle, gritting his teeth. He put his gaze on his men. They would find out.

"What's happening?" Evan asked him, knowing the Captain knew no more than him.

"Something bad for us. I'm sure," Joseph said bitterly. "We'll know soon enough."

It came by the runners. He watched them spread out over the field towards the corps commanders, including his. Joseph braced himself for what would come and every muscle in his body tensed. He hoped this was the end and he hoped they faced a chance for revenge. Emily floated in the back of his mind. Revenge for his fallen friends and bruised nation or Emily? He was yet undecided as to which would satisfy better.

The runners relayed their message with a beginning and ending salute. They backed away and disappeared in the crowd of soldiers. Just out of sight, the dark shadow again loomed on what nearly felt like the horizon. Joseph found his hope for the end of the war dashed.

Colonel Donnelly rode around to join Joseph. Both he and Evan stiffened in their saddles. He sat silent beside Joseph. His eyes looked over the field. Tension wracked his shoulders.

"Dismiss your men," he ordered Joseph. "Drilling's done for the day, Captain," He said looking to Joseph. "Report to me in one hour."

"Company halt!" Joseph cried out powerfully. The men stopped in their horse tracks, waiting for him. "Dismissed! Fall out!"

The soldiers gladly scattered while the officers remained behind with grave expressions.

"You may fall out, Captain—Lieutenants," Donnelly said dryly.

The sound of dozens of arms lifted, snapping the proper greeting between superior and subordinate.

Joseph rode from the field with Evan, "I'll of course tell you what they say, Lieutenant."

"As always, Captain," Evan said. "Shall we take tea while you apprise me of the orders, sir?" He jested, smoking his cigarette like a dandy.

Joseph smiled at him. He turned away, shaking his head and chuckling.

"Make sure the Corporal has it waiting for my arrival."

Captain Maynard soon found himself in the dim light of the command tent, listening to what news came to them by the messenger. The world crashed on his shoulders, destroying his hopes. Lee would make an attempt at Maryland, Joseph's home. The narrow state provided the Federals a buffer between the North and the Rebel forces who fought against them. The campaign on Richmond fell to the back of their minds, awaiting the invasion. Tiny Maryland must remain in the Union. If Maryland fell, so would Washington.

Once dismissed from the meeting, Joseph returned to his tent and sent a man to bring him Lieutenant Howell. When Evan arrived, Joseph stood beside his cot and table, pouring a short shot of scotch from his secret stash for himself and one for his guest. A cigarette hung from his lips and he squinted through the smoke of it. Joseph looked to him and smiled. He sat at his table and pushed the shot toward Evan.

"They make for Maryland," Joseph said once his friend sat and took hold of his drink.

Evan looked at the burnished liquid, swallowing hard. His eyes flicked everywhere but to Joseph's face. He thought of the family who came as close as his own, from the stories his commanding officer shared. Evan lifted the shot and slammed it back. With a trembling hand he set the glass on the table by Joseph and watched the man he called friend. They might as well invade Vermont, for the way he felt.

Captain Maynard smiled and filled Evan's empty glass halfway again. He had not taken his first drink yet. Joseph set the bottle down and then turned his glass in his fingers. He remained silent watching Evan. The man's gaze lowered to the scotch. Joseph's cigarette smoked on his lip and turned red at the tip when he drew from it. He took it from his mouth and blew out the smoke, flicking the ashes on the ground at his feet.

"What are you gonna do?"

"What they tell me," Joseph drawled more easily than he thought. He paused to watch Evan eye the scotch. He seemed afraid to take the drink. "You know—" he smiled, rocking back in his chair, stretching out the weariness in his limbs. He yawned and took on a relaxed look despite the future they faced. "I could probably name the men who'll leave Frederick as rebels. It's their right to fight for what they believe in, right or wrong to me."

"Are you going to write your parents?" Evan said. "You can get them outta there before this shit comes down on their heads."

Joseph saw what this invasion meant for his family. He picked up the drink finally. He put the glass to his lips, his eye on Evan and drank. He thought of his sister, his mother and the servants who worked in the house.

Then he thought of his father and finally the old family house, which he grew to love. His heart tightened and he winced the scotch down.

"I'll send Nate," Joseph rasped. He looked down at the little table his father gave him. It served Mr. Maynard before his birth, during Indian moves. He ran his hand over the rutted surface.

"You better send him soon," Evan said, picking up his glass. "I hear his mother's looking for him again."

Joseph sent a message with his personal service provided by young Master Nate, to a large old house found among the other grand homes of Frederick, Maryland. He sacrificed nothing to time and mistakes, giving the drummer boy enough cash to carry him by civilian means, fast and safe. He outfitted the boy in the clothes he wore on the last escape from his mother. He knew the boy would do the job better than any, wily enough to escape a doting mother at every turn. Besides, his leaving broke no rules of the military, not ranking an official soldier, but rather earning his pay by the errands he ran between battles.

Standing outside his tent with the red haired boy who reached a height just above his elbow, Joseph directed Nate to the job he would complete for him, witnessed by Lieutenant Howell. He counted five single dollar currency notes while the boy's eyes widened. Joseph folded them in his fingers and stuck the bills out to him. The boy reached and he pulled back, tucking his wallet in his jacket.

"You'll get more when you return with their reply," Joseph said. "You remember what I told you?"

Nate nodded and held his hand out. Joseph smiled down at him and surrendered the bills. He took his letters from Evan and gave those to Nate as well. The boy finished, tucking his money away and then accepted the envelopes.

"Don't tell anyone, but Mr. Maynard. Okay?" Joseph continued. The boy agreed. "Now—the letter to Mr. Stuart Conrad—have Mr. Maynard post, as soon as you give him his."

"Yes, sir," Nate said.

"You sure you're ready?" Joseph asked smiling.

"Sir, yes, sir," Nate replied, stiffening and saluting.

"Go on with you now," Joseph held an arm out to point the way. The boy took off at a run. "Safe journey, boy!" He called after Nate. He turned and waved back at them.

Joseph watched him disappear among the tents. He wondered how long it would take the boy to complete his orders. He smiled for Nate's bravery. The boy went without question, trusting him implicitly.

While he waited, Joseph dreamed fiendish Rebels murdered his family. He feared the worst with every passing moment. The soldiers practiced their maneuvers, but it did little in the way of distraction. Time ticked away, wasting itself on waiting. Joseph thought often of the warning he sent his parents and the plea to Mr. Conrad. He wrote them hastily and opted for unembellished details. It made him ache inside.

The other letter he scratched to Stuart. It left him more fearful, knowing the man just discovered the damaging letters to his daughter. Joseph hoped he did not presume too much, asking the Conrads to house his family. He hoped that despite Mrs. Conrad's hatred of him, she would bless his request. It was the only means by which he could calm his mind and assured his loved ones safe. He could not ask the favor of the Howell's when Davie was still sick. Amanda Howell had enough work, without him adding to it again. What would he do if the Conrads refused them?

September 3, 1862

Dear Mother and Father,

I've received the gravest of news from my superiors. The Rebels plan to invade Maryland, possibly Frederick. Know that the Union won't let you go without a fight. I ask you to be brave in sight of Lee's impending invasion.

While you are under threat, it is my suggestion that you retreat to a safer vantage. In the least, send Mary and Mother north for a while, if you will not send yourself. I beg that you all go without delay and send word on your decision, that I may rest my mind when I come to fight. If you leave soon after you receive this letter, you will make it there unhindered I am sure.

I'll send letters of introduction to the Conrad family of Vermont. They're dairy farmers in a village north of Montpelier. I met them on leave with Lieutenant Howell this past winter. I assure you they are respectable people, well thought of in the town.

Again, I beg you to go and leave the house under the care of someone you trust. I cannot bear the worry over any of you.

I love you.

Love always your son,

Captain Joseph Maynard

Within a week, Little Nate returned worn and tired, carrying a message for the Captain from his family. Joseph paid the boy and sent him with Sergeant McGuire to get some food and rest. Ducking into his tent, Joseph found his parents gave him an emphatic refusal. They thanked him for the warning, but would not think of leaving the family home. His father said his mother would not leave without him or their house servants, hoping for mercy from the Confederates.

Joseph set the letter aside and breathed a weighted sigh. They would not cower or hide. What did he expect of a grizzled old warrior and his bride? However, with the abolitionist tendencies of the Maynards known by everyone in the village, they assured their son they would send Mary where he suggested with their housekeeper Phoebe.

Joseph felt angry at first, but he understood. His mother would never leave her husband's side, especially at such a time as this. The thought warmed his heart a little, but a chill crept into his bones. He wondered about his girl and if she would stand at his side the same. If the war took much longer, he was sure his jewel would shatter.

Evan burst into his tent, shaking him awake, "What did they say?"

"Won't leave—they sent Mary, though," Joseph replied.

"They'll make it just fine," Evan assured him. "They're civvies, Cap,"

Joseph looked at him annoyed. Plenty of civilians died at soldier's hands in this war. They both knew that.

⁂

Shortly following the departure of the red haired boy, the Maynard house buzzed with the preparations to send their daughter to safety. Mr. Maynard posted the letter, as requested and sent his own letter of introduction with his daughter. If his son thought so well of these people, he knew to trust him, but he also knew he had little choice. The Maynards brought Mary to the train station with her mouse haired escort and bid them farewell.

John kissed his daughter's fare cheek and patted her golden head, as she stood above him boarding her train, an innocent angel of God. She smiled back at him reassuringly. He took her hand, squeezed and then let her go, stepping back for his wife to bid farewell next.

"See you soon, father," Mary said to him, her dark eye holding a tear. "Me and Joey."

Mrs. Maynard reached up. She put her arms around her daughter, crushing her to her body. The embrace nearly pulled her back down from the train. Mrs. Maynard begrudgingly released her daughter and listened to the tinkling laughter. She touched her nose with a gloved finger and handed her purse to her. She nearly forgot it back on the bench where they waited for the train.

Mrs. Maynard looked up at her daughter, standing a head taller than her on the black iron step. She touched her daughter's cheek and kissed the other. Stepping back, she smiled and let Mary board, to run to her safety up north. Mary did not understand the danger she ran from. She never wanted her to understand.

"Be on your best behavior—and write us, darling," Mrs. Maynard demanded warmly. "Everyday if you want." She smiled.

"I will, Mother."

"Take good care of our girl, Phoebe," Mrs. Maynard said to the maid.

"I will, ma'am," Phoebe softly spoke. Her pale face was bleached with fear.

Mary waved to them and went inside the train car, leading her maid. She reappeared further down, in the window of her cabin. She waved to them with a smile. She sat on her cabin seat and smiled through the dirty glass at them. Her parents waited with smiles also, until the steam engine pulled away. They waved good bye.

In the evening, the matter seemed a distant thought with only a longtime to pass before either light of their lives returned to them. The gray coats came and they were thankful to have sent their youngest to the safety of the far North. The days following the Rebel arrival came with confiscation of homes to fill the need of command posts and barracks for the officers. The families went from them forcibly at the hands of their oppressors, without a care to what they would do.

Somehow, the Maynard mansion evaded the eye of rebel commanders. A day or more passed and the explanation came to their door.

The Maynards were spared the rape of their town, by a Confederate soldier who once lived among them and called himself friend. He did not like slavery, but he felt the southern states were right in their claim of state's rights above Federal rights. He came into town wearing his dandy butternut uniform, riding high like a French Cavalier, and he headed straight for the Maynard mansion.

Sitting atop his gray dapple stallion, outside the wrought iron fence, Colonel Francis Wesley McFadden faced the sprawling mansion. He drew a fat cigar out of his mouth and grinned up at the home from a heavily bearded face. Colonel McFadden then dismounted and secured his noble mount to the fence. Not waiting for an invitation, he stepped inside the front yard. He took his broad brimmed hat from his head and smoothed his black hair back with a gloved hand.

Somehow, the Rebel officer looked nervous. It seemed unlike him, for his great height and broad shoulders. He carried a pistol on his belt and a gold hilted rapier. He looked altogether well kept and presented an impressively handsome figure on first inspection. He smiled touching the doorknocker and breathed Mary's name.

Knocking on the dark panel door, Colonel McFadden awaited admittance to the home he dreamed of while away. Dancing back and forth on his booted feet, he grew impatient, but soon heard the sound of footsteps within the home. The door opened to him and he saw the face of a woman he did not recognize. He expected to see little Miss Phoebe.

"Good afternoon, sir," her small voice spoke to him.

"Good afternoon. My name is Colonel Francis McFadden," he introduced himself noisily, with a broad grin. "I've come to see Mr. Maynard, ma'am. Is he at home?"

"He's in the study," she answered him unsure. "Come in. I will see if he has a moment," she added, opening the door wider to him.

McFadden stepped inside, twirling his hat in his hands. He looked around the wood panel entryway and the carved staircase, leading up to his beloved's boudoir. He paused looking at the stairs, spiraling up the wall, with carved panels on the underside and carved banister to run its length. He grinned deeply. He wondered if Mary rested the afternoon away, sleeping in her underclothes in her room, like he knew the young women did in the heat of the day.

"Colonel McFadden," the housekeeper's voice called him. "Mr. Maynard will see you."

McFadden nodded to her and entered the room she held the door open to. She closed it when he passed and retreated to the back of the house. Mr. Maynard asked her to warn Mrs. Maynard of the visitor, although she already meant to. The people in the Maynard house held their own ideas about this man.

John spoke with the visitor for a short time in his study. The meeting stood closed to all, but his wife waited in the hall with the servant, just back from the stair landing. Silence wrapped the house for an eternity. The door of the study then opened.

Colonel McFadden emerged from the closed meeting. He saw Mrs. Maynard, waiting for them. She wore a frightened expression, but he tipped his hat to her with a grand smile. He excused himself with his condolences that he must return to his men. The housekeeper rushed to the door ahead of him and opened it. He paused with a thank you and made his exit.

The attention turned from the doorway of the house to the doorway by the stairs. Mr. Maynard stood in it with a solemn expression on his face. His wife stepped to him with worry plain on her face this time. She flicked her eyes to the housekeeper and the woman retreated from the hallway, hurriedly.

"What did he want?" Mrs. Maynard asked her husband.

"It's very good we agreed to send Mary when we did," he said. "Let's sit in the parlor, Lucretia. I need to discuss something with you."

John took his wife into the parlor and spoke quietly to her for a long while. They both knew Francis favored their daughter and hoped to gain her favor in return. He assured John he would see their home left unscathed and them unharmed, but it held a price. He asked for permission to court Mary. John proudly told him that she visited friends up north, not saying where. He said she would not return for sometime, if a battle broke out there. He wanted his little girl safe from harm.

Thankfully, McFadden understood and let the matter pass this time, instead asking that John encourage his daughter in his direction. He held means and standing now. By the end of the war, he would be a wealthy man with great position in the new Confederate Government.

John said he would mention it to Mary and those words satisfied him. He added that he felt sure the young woman would see it her own way in the end. He knew

McFadden understood, the way of women and all. It was then that McFadden took his leave.

Lucretia kept the matter between her and her husband. She found no need to worry her son, miles away and unable to help. He would drive himself mad about the issue. She saw the way he handled Mary's unwanted suitors before. At least for now, this one seemed dealt with by them.

Sitting behind his desk, Stuart Conrad sifted through the letters that arrived for him that day. He affixed his glasses to his face and read the front of each. Correspondence from other businesses he used to run his, bills and other items were the bulk. Somewhere in the middle, a thin envelope made of fine grade paper caught his attention. It came with his name on the front, but he saw the like in the house before.

Flipping the envelope over, he discovered the fine preprinted name of Captain Joseph Maynard, with his home address. He smiled and chuckled at the surprise. He thought for sure the Captain misaddressed his letter.

Picking up his letter opener, he slit the fold of the flap and pulled the note from within. Unfolding the letter, he smiled at the more than respectable letterhead. He read the letter and found it correctly directed to him.

September 6, 1862

Dear Mister Conrad,

It's with a heavy heart and worrisome soul that I write to you. Please feel assured that at no other time would I ever be so bold to ask you a favor. I heavily and humbly realize we hardly know one anther. My predicament, however, leaves me no choice.

It seems, sir, that General Lee invades Maryland. My home, in the aforesaid state of this blessed Union, is in his path. I fear rightly for my family's safety. I requested that my mother and young sister visit with you until the threat has passed. If my mother refuses, you will only be put upon to care for my beloved sister, Mary Maynard and her accompanying servant Miss Phoebe Lansing. I can readily assure you they will prove no problem for anyone, but only an asset. She's adept with the needle and unafraid to help. She understands the graveness of the venture and that she stays with you only from my concern for her safety and your grace.

Mary will respect your wishes to the utmost and do any work you will need of her in your home. I've enclosed my recent pay to cover her meals and my father will send a monthly allowance to care for her needs. Miss Lansing will provide my sister with any service she requires.

Please expect her arrival within a week of this letter, carrying references to your wife's tastes. Thank you for your hospitality. I would not impose without genuine concern.

Sincerely,

Captain Joseph Maynard

"My God," Stuart said, jumping to his feet, tearing his glasses from his face and stormed from the room. His voice rang out loud, "Marge!"

~

The evening sky drew long, with purple tufts of cream mixed with orange, fading into strawberry punch. Lucretia kept her eyes just above the black shadowy trees, standing on her back porch wrapped in a banded shawl. In the distance she heard the sound of thunder, but not one cloud spoke of a storm, not a storm like they knew. She watched on, feeling her heart thump against her rib cage. She drew a deep breath and a tear slid from her eye, down her face.

The door to the porch opened behind her. She did not look away to see who joined her. The door shut. She listened to the steps, holding her chin high. She felt an arm go about her shoulders and then she looked. Her husband stood beside her. He offered a small smile and she tried to return it.

Lucretia laid her head on her husband's shoulder and watched the sunset. She prayed for her boy and her family.

"It'll turn out all right, Lucy" John assured his wife. However, his expression said otherwise. "We'll see the kids soon."

Miles from there, Joseph faced the countryside he grew to maturity on, now torn up by the blast of artillery. The sun set on the first day of the fight. He wondered how many more days would follow until the end. He felt tired and unsure he could last.

The sound of hoof beats rose above the gun blasts, meaning someone rode close. Joseph looked over to his left, along a line of men mounted horseback. They watched the battle, bearing the marks of war. A lone rider pounded down the space behind them. Evan.

Lieutenant Howell aimed his mount for the space beside Joseph, slowing his steed to a walk fluidly. He clucked the brown stallion into position. Joseph eyed him, seeing his face lined with concern. He has sent Evan to Colonel Donnelly for orders. He saw that whatever the commander told his lieutenant greatly bothered him. Perhaps he asked for another charge.

Joseph looked out over the field. The Rebels appeared lost right then. It made sense Donnelly would call them in again. He rubbed his face waiting for Evan to speak.

"Donnelly said to loop in from behind—off the right," Evan said. "Over there."

Joseph nodded. The order went up the company lines. He led them from the holding point, marching horseback behind the other waiting troops and lines of firing rifles. Joseph guided Manny to their head, turned and faced them. He trotted Manny backward to their left side. He watched them fix guns.

"Boys!" Joseph cried. He lifted his rifle, "We're going in—let us come back out." He cast his eye over them. "This is my home men. I expect to keep it that way."

Joseph maneuvered his steed to the center of the line. He looked left and then right. The men sat at the ready. Looking ahead, he drew his lips tight back across his teeth and called the charge. Everything turned to a blur, echoing with the cry of a heart's need to survive.

Much further away, in the great hilly and vast North called Vermont, Emily Conrad stood in the cupola, gazing southward in the sunset. With her arms wrapped tightly around her own shoulders, she wistfully watched the graying autumn sky. It rolled into the fire of the orange East. A tear dripped from her eye. All the beautiful colors of the season were a wash of fire and it reminded her of the fire that changed her life. Like a phoenix, it burned the old and left the unsure promise of newness. She survived the resurrection, but feared she would fall from the sky to burn again.

Wiping the tears of her fear and longing from her eyes, she tried not to think the worst. Drawing a deep breath, she heard the floor creak with the weight of someone behind her. She stiffened with the fear that her mother discovered her hiding place there in the cupola. Her heart burned with resentment. Her mother stopped behaving irrationally only at the order of her father. She hated and mistrusted her for defying her wishes regarding Joseph. Emily wondered what could ever make a mother's love end this way.

"Emily?" A familiar voice said. "What you doin way up here all alone?"

"Oh—Hettie," Emily sighed with relief. She turned, smiling at her. The tears streamed down her face. Hettie stepped to her and touched the tears away. "I'm just looking over those hills and that old gray sky," she looked back to the windows, gesturing to the scenery. Emily drew a deep breath to steady herself, but it did little. Hettie smoothed her hair and put her arm about her. After a long pause, girded with Hettie's strength, Emily added in a tremulous voice, "I wonder if Joseph's looking at it right now." A chill of despair ran through her body, sensing something.

Hettie moved closer to stand at her friend's side. The housekeeper's dark eyes watched the scene beyond the window. Her arm slipped to Emily's waist, still trying to offer her support. Their heads leaned together, and for a moment they appeared as sisters. They looked as if they always stood that way together, hewn from the same stone. While her large brown eyes drank in the expansive landscape that whispered promises of freedom, she sensed that Emily's blue gaze saw the trap of death, closing its fingers about her. Hettie understood more than anyone else.

Among the pangs of memories and new moments, Hettie still felt wonder grow in her heart. She soaked in the essence of the only place that offered her a chance at what any human truly desires. Her eyes scanned the south road, stretching down until it disappeared in the trees. She ran so far from her prison, nearly died of it, but she stood there now. She often asked why. Now she understood why.

Placing a consoling hand on Emily's head, she kissed the girl's forehead and worked the art she knew best. Emily needed someone to guide her through this time. She whispered strength into the girl and fortified her thoughts against what would come. She could tell by the trouble the path already revealed thus far, Emily would need all the support she could get.

"I come up here at night and wonder if my family's out there," Hettie said. "I think about if they're okay or if somethin's happened to um. I wonder if they even miss me," Hettie told her after a short pause. "I wonder if Isaiah's waitin ta come home ta me. How can he be all right? My baby—God Em, I hope they're all right."

All the while Hettie spoke, Emily recalled the tales Hettie told her of people that seemed more like characters in a novel on her father's shelf than real life. They lived out in the distance, fading in and out of shadows like fantasies. Now that she faced her own loss, Emily really understood the heartache her friend felt. She knew nothing of them since she left six years ago. Her son would be so grown, if they still lived.

The tears formed in Emily's eyes again, large and round. She listened to her friend's words and they slipped in large droplets down her cheeks. Hettie was the only person on the farm to wholly understand her situation. No one knew suffering like Henrietta Benson. Hettie sat Emily down on the cushioned bench beneath the windows. She turned and cried on her friend's shoulder.

"Shh—now," Hettie hushed Emily and quieted her own fears. "I know what y'all thinkin. Don't you worry. They'll come back to us. They're gonna come home," Hettie said through clenched teeth, trying with much difficulty to stifle her own fears.

To have her family back was Hettie's single wish, but she wondered if it even possible. The plantation owner acted kindly to the house slaves, but only because he thought them a usable lot in other matters. The men and women he owned and kept in the house would spy on the rest.

Master McAvery treated the females especially well, though the women saw it another way. When his wife went away, he needed a few to keep him warm on the sultry southern nights. Hettie grew sick at the thought of the girls forced to lay with him. Even when his wife stayed home, he sought the attentions of the women in the slave quarters. He came late at night and picked one to take right there, dismissing the rest like a useless herd of nothing. If ever sin existed, laying with that man was the highest and they were forced to commit it for survival.

Hettie refused Master McAvery when approached. He gave her a choice the first time he asked, though he ordered the others to it. Then, he aimed for her like hunted quarry. At that point, Hettie realized she must find a way to leave or give in to him and despise herself forever. Instead, she chose the more dangerous route.

Hettie and her sister conspired with the white folks who secreted slaves from the plantations, making it look like a runaway. However, the matter cleared when a house slave revealed the true intent. Hettie's sister hung for the crime and the master whipped her back, still wanting a taste of her flesh. The wounds proved so deep and so numerous, Hettie became ill. Her husband requested the help of their outside friends. It was the last she saw of him and their boy.

Hettie told the story to the Conrads when she felt better, explaining herself uneasily. She found no reason to feel ashamed for her sufferings, but feared the strangers from experience. Imagining her sister's face, as it once looked when she lived, Hettie watched Emily pull a letter from her skirt pocket. She offered it to Hettie. Hettie eyed Emily warily and then took the envelope. She read the address with less difficulty than when she arrived on the farm. Her lessons were more useful than Mr. Conrad said.

Looking up to Emily's sad eyes, Hettie wondered what kept the young woman from opening it. The devil himself could not have stood in the way of Emily when she got a letter from the Captain. She passed it back and touched Emily's hand. Joseph wrote regularly, except lately. However, the papers explained the Potomac lost themselves in maneuvers. Hettie thought perhaps Emily would need assurance that he survived, but she had not read her letter.

"What ya waitin for, Em?" Hettie asked, rubbing the girl's shoulder. "He didn send it for you ta hold."

"I'm afraid," Emily's voice trembled. "After the last I learned."

"From Joseph or about that girl ya knew?"

Emily looked up at her fighting back her fears, "About Penelope. I never thought such a thing could happen. I feel so badly for Evan. He doesn't even know." Emily looked at the letter in her hand. "Such bad news only brings more."

"He'd not send a letter to you if he's dead, girl."

Emily reluctantly opened the letter, pulling the folded sheets from within. She read the words silently, drinking in every line thirstily. Suddenly, she smiled and spots of color came onto her cheeks. She covered her face with a hand.

"I'll leave ya be," Hettie smiled broadly and rubbed a hand across the young woman's back. She stood and went to the staircase. At the top, she hesitated and turned back. She regarded Emily a moment and laughed. "Come see me when ya done, Em. Silly thing."

Once Emily finished reading her letter, she rushed down the stairs to the third floor hallway. She came through the door leading to the cupola with the papers ragged in her hand. Her cheeks still burned a hot crimson from the words her lover sent. Surrounded by the energy, she would not waste a moment to respond.

Ducking in her room, she secured the lock and went to her dressing table. Unlocking the drawer, she placed Joseph's letter inside and secured the drawer again. She went to her bureau and gathered some paper. Settling in her chair, she readied her pen. Emily swallowed hard looking at the blank sheet of pink paper. She drew the key from between her breasts, pulling the chain with her fingertips. If she lived, the letters remained safe from discovery, but only as long as she lived. Emily drew a deep breath. Her mother would not succeed. Emily knew the right of her actions by her heart. Putting pen to paper, she wrote her reply to Joseph.

5th of September 1862

Dearest Joseph,

I beg you to please place a warning at the head of your letters if you ever send such content as the last. I swear my face will burn for days now!

I heard from father that your men do not fare as well as hoped. I fear you might be feeling low again and have avoided telling me. I send you all my love and I enclose half of my locket as proof. When you return to me, I will have it repaired. Until then, hold it as a symbol of our undying love only parted by distance.

Oh—if you are given leave, I wish you to know I want you to see your family before me. You missed them the last time when you went with Evan. I can only imagine how they worry over you from my own worries.

Michael sends his greetings, Captain. (Salute) He believes he'll return at the end of the year or early next. It's grand. His leg heals wonderfully, but he still limps slightly. I don't believe it permanent. What can we do to stop him? I am afraid for him. I think the wound is a warning. He should stay out of the war. Still, there I am, helping him to get better.

Tell me how you are. Truly. . .

✎

With the southern threat removed from Frederick and the camp so close to home, Joseph requested leave for the evening. He took his close friends Lieutenant Howell and Sergeant McGuire, rewarding them with a home cooked meal for their pains on his behalf throughout their time in service together. They stood outside the Maynard front door in their finest uniforms, wearing handsome grins that belied their trials. It felt like homecoming.

Drawing his hat from his head and his gloves from his hands, Joseph knocked on the door. The men straightened themselves one last time while they waited. Joseph looked them over, dashing a hand over Evan's shoulders to sweep off the dust from the road. He nodded at him and Evan looked worriedly over his jacket. A laugh escaped Joseph and he faced the door just as it opened.

The golden light of the foyer spilled out onto the porch. A uniformed housekeeper, older and dustier of feature than Miss Phoebe, stood in the opening. She looked at them blankly a moment. Then her mouth popped open and her eyes widened with surprise. She covered her mouth and cried out.

"Joseph," she said.

"Is my mother at home?" Joseph smiled at her.

"I's sure you wouldn come back," she gasped. She pointed to the floor inside the broad hall, "Wait here. I'll get them."

Stepping inside, Joseph motioned for the men to follow. He turned back and saw the housekeeper climb the steps to the upper floor. He smiled to himself, satisfied to stand once more in the home of his grandsires. He looked at it, drawing in every aspect.

Joseph faced his companions. They too soaked in the scene, gawking like children at a summer fair. He smiled at them. They had been aware of his family's standing, but he did not speak of it.

With a whistle, McGuire winked at him and gave a nod, "So this be how the owther alf lives, eh."

"I guess so," Joseph replied. It was just home to him.

Evan smiled at him, hanging up his hat and gloves. Joseph stepped over to do the same. They whispered to each other about the house while McGuire stepped deeper into the hall, getting a good look.

"Joseph—my boy," a softly aged and familiar voice said. It called to him from the base of the stairs and Joseph turned to see his mother. "You look well for a man at war," she smiled at him.

"It's good to hear your voice, Mother," he said, smiling at her.

"Did you forget your manners? Who are these lovely young men?" She asked, meaning the soldiers who stood in the hall.

"Sorry," Joseph said sheepishly. "This here is Lieutenant Evan Howell," Joseph said, shoving him forward to meet his mother.

"Ma'am," Evan nodded with a grin. He took her hand and slightly bowed. He straightened and clasped his hands at his waist.

"Pleasure, Lieutenant Howell."

"And this is Sergeant Seamus McGuire," he said, indicating the gawking Irishman just joining them.

Lucretia turned to see the Sergeant and smiled, "I'm pleased to make your acquaintance."

"My name is Lucretia Maynard, Joseph's mother."

"I sees our ugly captain dun take none after his beautiful mother, Ma'am," McGuire said, taking her hand and lifting it to smile over her knuckles at her.

"Oh—how flattering you are, sir." Lucretia laughed. "Come sit in the parlor," she said stepping ahead of them to the carved wood archway and the vast sitting room beyond. "How long do you have?"

"Dinner," Joseph answered, casting his eyes to the floor as he entered.

"That'll do," his mother smiled at him after sitting on her couch. "I'd rather see you at dinner once in a while than not at all." She paused and added, "Your father will come right down."

"Boys at the point had you pegged when they said you're rich," Evan smiled, sitting beside McGuire on the opposite facing sofa.

Joseph smiled shyly at him, taking to the chair set between and at the end of an old low standing table. He did not want to discuss it.

"Did you school with my son, Lieutenant Howell?" Lucretia asked, guiding them into a friendly conversation.

"Yes, ma'am. A year his junior."

"Where are you from?" Lucretia asked

"Vermont, Ma'am," he replied. "I'm sure you've heard tell of it. Joseph said he sent Mary there when the Rebels came," he continued.

"Oh, you're the boy Joseph went with on leave," she smiled at him. "I must hear more about this place, and the Conrad's is it?"

Joseph half laughed, "After dinner, Mother. I promise."

"Joseph," a voice resounded from the archway.

Everyone turned to see Mr. Maynard enter the room with a smoking cigar in his hand. He did not smile or betray any joy in his expression. Joseph jumped up from his chair and faced him. The sight of his sire filled him with awe. John smiled and chuckled unable to hold the grave expression long.

"Father," Joseph said. "How are things?"

"As well as they can be," his father replied, putting the cigar back in his mouth. It turned red at the tip and smoked.

Joseph saw that something bothered him, "What is it, sir?"

Joseph waited for him to answer. His father lowered his eyes to the rug and put his hands in his trouser pockets. His mother and father exchanged knowing and worrisome glances. Joseph turned toward his companions and saw they noted the same.

"Francis McFadden," his father drawled, stepping to the sofa where his wife sat. He took her hand and sat on the cushion beside her. "He paid us a friendly visit to ask for Mary's hand—he suggested our home would become a command post or barracks otherwise and that we would be put out."

"What?" Joseph rasped unable to believe such a cowardly threat. "I'll never let him—I'll find that bastard and tell him the deal," Joseph growled.

"The matter's settled," John lifted his hand to settle his son down. "He was wounded in the battle, yesterday. He lost his foot, from just above the ankle," he continued as his son sat back down in the chair. "He'll not bully Mary or us again."

"None's more deserving than him," Joseph said. He stared at the table, chewing his thumbnail. Anger wrenched his features. "I wish it had been me who got him."

"That's the way God watches is flock, mate," McGuire smiled and patted Joseph's knee.

Joseph's eyes flicked up to his as the servant entered, clearing her throat, "Dinner's ready in the main dining room, ma'am."

Evan looked at the Captain and mouthed the words, "Main dining room." He pursed his lips impressed.

"You've excellent timing," Lucretia smiled at her son and the guests. "Shall we?"

They enjoyed a quiet dinner similar to before the war. However, Joseph worried over the matter of his sister. He knew the man well and recalled the name easily. Francis Wesley McFadden was a few years older than Joseph and came from a long line of military tradition, going back to the old world of Europe. He graduated from the point while Joseph was only a freshman. Joseph remembered the man indifferent toward him, until McFadden's attentions fell on Mary. Mary was only a girl then, barely sixteen and two years younger than Joseph. She had been very pretty her whole life and grew lovelier everyday. Now practically a woman, she awakened ideas in Francis that slept while she wore pigtails and short skirts. Unfortunately for his sister, he could not return from school to protect her, as he once had. He knew the man mistook her fear to turn him away as unquestionable interest. During the rest of the year at West Point, McFadden courted danger, all but saying he intended to make Mary his.

Evening drew into night and dinner came to a close. With the end of the banquet, the time for the soldiers to return to their post arrived. The reality grieved both father and mother. They hoped for end to seeing Joseph go, but they must do as expected. Joseph's father served in the military before him, until he found it dissatisfying to remove people from their homes because the government marked them treacherous and inhuman. They drew the ability to comply from that experience.

In the wood panel hall of the Maynard home, Lucretia followed the men to the front door. She hung back a little while they gathered their things. A small smile trembled on her lips. She vacillated between pride and pain, watching her son.

"Thank you all for coming. Don't be afraid to visit us again when you're given the time," Lucretia said.

The men nodded to her. Joseph approached and gave a deep hug. His mother kissed his face and looked up at him with a tear in her eye. She touched his cheek and smiled.

"I'll come again, soon as I can," he told her.

Joseph let his mother go and turned to the door the housekeeper held open for them. His father followed the men onto the porch. They all shook hands and the companions of his son bid farewell and stepped down the stairs to their waiting horses. Joseph faced him alone.

"Keep your head," John said gruffly. He smiled. "I expect to retire when you return, boy."

"The only thing you need to worry about is what to do with your time," Joseph told him.

Joseph nodded and then took his father in his arms and gave him a long strong hug. They patted each other's backs and laughed away the tears. When the embrace ended, they regarded each other. Joseph placed his hat back on his head and smiled. He turned away and walked down the steps. He crossed the yard and reached the iron gate. Joseph turned back and waved. His mother joined his father on the porch and the pair waved back.

The next day, Joseph and his company moved west. Word came in while he dined at home that General Lee thought to try again. Joseph recognized the area and surveyed it with curious pride and censoring worry. He would draw Rebel blood there, reprisal for their trespass.

Joseph once fished the creek meandering nearby. His father took him there on an outing, between cases. He eyed the land, familiar and yet unfamiliar. He spent many summers basking in the glory of the sun and boyhood. His childhood was lost in the past, but he hoped the split of the Union would not take his home from him, too. The fear of loss left him full of hate and lusting for revenge. He turned away from the scene and lost himself in the Federal camp. They would wait for the enemy to come.

While he waited for the battle, Joseph took the small hours of the morning to write to his beloved Emily. He could not sleep for fear of dying the next day. Sleep would take his last moments. He was among many who felt the same.

Joseph wrote his letter, hanging on the edge of despair. He held back information, thinking to spare Emily. He would not mention what he thought the future held. Instead, he forced himself to concentrate on the future he wanted. His heart threatened to break. If Lee succeeded, his jewel may never become his wife.

September 7, 1862

My Dearest Love Emily,

I write to you in the small hours of the morning, while I still find chance to. It's three o'clock. I cannot sleep. So many thoughts harass my conscience. Has my sister Mary arrived yet? I hope she has. Thank you for accepting her into your home, as I'm sure you have.

Emily, tell my sister I miss her and love her. I went home yesterday and the matter of Mister McFadden is finished. When Maryland is safe, she can return home without worry over his undesired attentions.

Does Hettie keep you company? Tell her hello for me. She probably reads over your shoulder anyway, so I'll say it. Hello Hettie. No McAvery yet, but I keep my eye out.

Now for you, Emmy. I miss you more than you may ever know. I miss the meetings in the garden and greenhouse. I miss our rock and field. I hope you try to smile when you think of or time together and do not grieve. My heart is full of so much to say. I hope that I am able to unburden it of its long tale.

I stand on the cusp of a great battle. I feel it in my bones. I cannot be certain I'll survive, but know that I love you, as foolish as it sounds. Of you alone, I am sure. . .

Joseph told the tale of his heart and the pages lengthened. He rested the papers on his writing table, in order to dry the ink while he carefully addressed the envelope. It felt strange to use his name. He sighed studying the job done. Would these be the last words between them?

Before he folded the pages of the letter and placed them in the envelope, he noticed a teardrop in the middle of the last page. Leafing through, he found more on other pages. His hands shook with anxiety at the idea of her seeing him so vulnerable. How could he not have noticed while he wrote? He wiped his face with the back of his hand. He would copy it over and take extra care. He shook his head and breathed deep. Joseph reached for more letterhead.

"Last call for mail!" Lieutenant Howell said, popping his head into Joseph's tent.

"I'm almost done," Joseph said, stuffing the original letter into the envelope with no time to copy it.

Joseph stood and Evan entered. It came too late to repair the tears, and he would think no more of it. He sniffed and wiped his fist under his nose. Evan said nothing and took the papers from him. Joseph sat on his cot, turning his face away.

"I'll take it for you," Evan said, turning to go.

With his letter and his friend gone, Joseph lounged back in his cot. His thoughts closed in on him. He was alone with his quilt and his ghosts. He stared up at the tent roof, recalling the life he once knew. He saw the shadow of his boyhood, walking along the path to the creek. He held a fishing pole in one hand and his father's strong hand in the other. He brought him there to escape the women at his grandfather's home, the mansion he ate dinner in yesterday. His sister annoyed him with her crying. She was just a baby. He squeezed his eyes shut and tried to think of Emily and the future that he must live for, the babies they meant to have together. His eyes closed and he made himself sleep.

When the Army of the Potomac drew up to face their rival, Joseph was unsure he would see the hills of Vermont again. His throat felt dry and constricted and his heart raced. Even though he heard the buzz of life all around him, Joseph's beloved Maryland reeked of death. His eyes searched the beautiful countryside, then the sky. His hand mechanically went to his breast pocket where the stiff picture lay near his heart. He reminded himself to buy a wallet when he found the chance.

Somewhere in the great North, Emily sat or maybe worked on some task. Perhaps she hemmed a skirt or embroidered. But, whatever she did, he hoped that she prayed for him. He needed much help. He was tired of the fighting and unable to find the energy to go on, let alone pray. Images of his fallen comrade flashed in his mind. He reached a gloved hand out and patted Manny's mane.

"So many times I've been at this starting gate, and it never gets any easier," Joseph said. His dark eyes coldly assessed the view before him.

"At least you got something to look forward to," Evan said with a wry grin.

Joseph looked to his friend and chuckled, "What is that supposed to mean?"

"Nothing," Evan answered, looking at him darkly. He swallowed hard and looked away, wiping Joseph's smile away with the turn.

On rolling farmland near his favorite fishing creek, the battle took place. Joseph recalled the event as a blur of bullets, blue and gray, mixed with artillery. He only heard the snap of distant firing rifles and the hollow boom of cannons. When his unit received the call forward, he became deafened by the gunfire. He eyed the gray sky of the morning.

Peering over the field, Joseph was amazed the Federal soldiers held a chance at success. As the battle progressed, it drew into the hardest fight the bluecoats faced yet. If they failed, it meant annihilation for the Union. Men rushed and guns blasted like hell's trumpets. To either side, haunted scenes of marching men, cavalry and guns at the ready played out. The pounding cadence of beating drums, blasting cannons and cracking rifles echoed. He saw them fall on both sides. The bold behavior of the southern army unnerved him and the clumsy command of his comrades stilled his heart.

Joseph knew he was no one to question the experience of the generals. He only recently rose to captain and left his thoughts unspoken. He would fight as they ordered him, if they ordered him to. Colonel Donnelly's messenger arrived and ordered Joseph to draw his company back to their holding position.

Returned to the cool shade of a field north of the battle, Joseph watched the sloping hillside, lined a hundred yards or more away with trenches. He fought his personal battles inside while his fellow unionists fought less than a mile away. Joseph drew a heavy breath, feeling like a coward. His eyes swept to the field beyond the entrenched soldiers.

Joseph felt sure the clash would end with only a mutual slaughter of thousands. He knew in his heart there must be some other way, but humankind had yet to discover it or accept it. His eyes drew up to the sky and he thought of something Evan once said to him. What does God think of us now? Joseph lowered his eyes knowing.

Joseph sat up from laying against Manny's back. The horse lay in the grass behind him with his lanky legs drawn up under his body. Joseph patted the animal's neck. Manny made sounds in his throat and shivered. His tail flicked the ground, swatting flies away.

"I bet that's Hooker," Evan pointed to a line of trees where smoke rose. Joseph looked from his horse to where he suggested. "Things might be looking up."

Joseph's gaze turned severe. He saw a unit of cavalry and infantry headed toward the trees, but not them. Joseph tore a piece of tall grass from the ground and tore it apart. Throwing it away, he refused to speak. He knew he would spout off unwanted scores of curses and comments he kept inside.

While Joseph played spectator, he thought of the man that resembled his beloved's father. He swallowed his fears as much as he could, but it made him sick. He wondered if their forces could afford a loss here. He feared a loss because he knew the reputation of the General. Burnside had ill served the army in times of need before. He was slow to act and this day affirmed it.

Joseph wished the commander would insist his troops be brought in to assist, but he probably rather keep silent and wait. Burnside had no stomach for fighting. He mused on volunteering himself. It would ease their conscience that someone wanted to die, instead of cowering and nest building. He could not imagine experienced commanders shrinking like girls.

Captain Maynard looked over his right shoulder to the sea of bluecoats that sat between him and the commanders. He felt sick, making them watch like weak kneed women. While they rested and lounged in the field, men were dying.

"To hell with their politics and scheming," Joseph muttered under his breath. "They play with our families and friends—like it's a game."

"What Joe?" Evan asked not hearing him.

"Bernie won't call us in," Joseph said, looking at him in an angry sidelong glance.

"Ask me—I'm glad for it," Evan said. "You should feel the same," his dark eyes looked like black pits of horror. Something ate at his soul.

Joseph looked back over his shoulder to the shinning brass. They milled around the ground, unheard chatting and joking, as if they were at a party. He watched a paper pass from one of the uppers to a runner. Joseph licked his lips. He hoped. He turned back to watching the field.

"Cap," Evan started to say before the runner approached them.

"You're company's to report to Pleasanton," the man said, giving Joseph the orders handwritten on the paper. He looked down at them overflowing with self importance.

"What for?" Joseph asked with sharp sarcasm. He knew the answer, but wanted the annoyance his question would give the upstart.

"I don't have answers to your questions, Captain. Sir, I just deliver orders and tell you to go," the man said, not pleased to recall he ranked below them.

"Thank you, Private," Joseph took the paper, refusing to look at the enlistee.

This was the second time the commanders moved with little regard for Joseph's men. Standing, He growled a heavy angry sigh. His horse got to its feet with him. He refitted and checked the bags and other things on Manny. All around him, the other men did the same. He heard Evan shouting for them to stand ready. Joseph looked over his weapons, lingering on the pistol he pulled. He shoved it back in the holster and raked the battlefield with his eyes.

Swinging into the saddle, he turned Manny east to report to his position. Evan followed suit close by and the rest of the officers and other soldiers fell in behind. Joseph's eye went to the commanders. Some looked his way, but quickly avoided his gaze. An argument brewed among them. He knew what this meant as likely as the paper that passed his way a few moments ago.

Joseph heeled his mount forward trying to beat them to it. He could have led this army far more efficiently given half the chance to do so. For now, he planned for one simple future. He did not harbor any ideas of greatness or political schemes. He simply wanted Emily's affection. Desiring the same ends as the men who would die around him already made him a better leader.

Passing behind the knot of high ranking officers, the Private stepped in front of Manny and called them to a halt. Joseph could barely hold back the great distaste he felt for him. When the time came to stand and fight, his commanders halted him. Perhaps they needed a lesson in why they fought the war. It just might inspire them to action.

"Captain," he said gravely. "Disregard the orders. We need you here, sir," He spoke in slow low tones. "Tell your men," the Private saluted him.

Joseph saluted the little weasel back only for protocol. An angry glint in his eye revealed his feelings clearly without words. The skulking runner stepped back and Joseph gave the order to Evan who gave the order to the other lieutenants. The company turned back in perfect formation under the watchful eye of the commanders.

Joseph turned Manny last. While his men went to relax, Joseph sought his own place to smooth down his rough. They would not move in and they would do nothing. He found a stand of trees and dismounted from Manny, fixing his reins around a branch to stay him. Joseph then took out his frustrations on the verdure, tearing branches and shrubs with his gloved hands.

Several yards away, Evan stood with McGuire, watching the tree stand tremble under Joseph's efforts. McGuire looked to the Lieutenant, holding his thick hands on his broad hips. Neither man said a thing. Evan half smiled and folded his arms, adjusting his stance.

When Joseph emerged from the trees, his features were unreadable. He walked ahead of his ebony charger, picking leaves from his uniform. His gaze lifted and he saw Evan and McGuire smiling at him.

"God save, Emily," Evan said under his breath. A smiled brightened the darkness in him. Joseph joined them and he said, "Take a deep breath, Joe." Evan patted his shoulder.

Joseph glared over the field, "Bastards! Every one of um." He looked to his companions' faces. "They have no idea what they're doing," Joseph dared to say. "This is my home and I can't even fight for it."

"We will," Evan assured him. "Just remember the less death you face, the safer you are for Emily. You can return to your woman still."

Several wagons entered their field from where Joseph tore up the trees. All three watched it rumble by, carrying some kind of supply for the troops. The guns boomed louder behind. Suddenly the air filled with the sound of a shell sailing through the air. It crashed in the ground ahead of the trenches, sending up a geyser of black earth. He noticed they barely moved so use to the event.

Evan removed his canteen from his mount, unscrewed the top and took a long drink of water. He looked at it with a sour expression as if disappointed by its content. He probably wished for whiskey, but more likely the warm fluid tasted awful, steeping in the metal all day.

"What I wouldn't give to pay back old Jeb now," Evan put his canteen away.

"Forget about it, Evan," Joseph looked at him darkly. "We won't see a fight."

"As I said before, you should be thankful, Captain," Evan replied seriously. He pointed his gloved hand to the men killed from the blast. "Those boys—none of them ever gonna see home and their Emily's again."

Joseph felt anger rear up in torrents inside him. His cold eyes seared through Evan with a fire hotter than the end of a freshly fired cannon. He ground his teeth and clenched his fists. He hated the whole war and thought to resign right there. Evan silently returned that gaze, knowing he hit a cord. The man knew him too well to fear the expression. His point was merely well made. Evan should pat himself on the back for reminding his friend of the ever present danger of not going home. Joseph spat then cursed, looking away from him.

"Captain!" A voice called from somewhere behind Evan.

"Mail," Joseph whispered, focusing his eyes on the Corporal who walked speedily toward them. He used one of his saddlebags to hold the company mail, slung over his shoulder.

"Mail," he added holding a packet of envelopes.

Joseph approached him and gained a small packet of envelopes.

"Thank you, Corporal." Joseph turned away after an exchange of stiff salutes.

"You too, Lieutenant Howell, sir," the young Corporal said.

Joseph stepped back to where Manny grazed on the fall grasses. He sat in front of him, sorting his mail for the pink envelope he always expected. Pulling it free of the others, he noticed Evan joining him. They rolled cigarettes and smoked, blotting out the sounds of the heavy fighting. Joseph rolled back to rest his head on Manny's ribs.

Evan laughed, "Imagine getting' mail at a time like this." He sifted through the pile, shaking his head and looking gloomy. He took the cigarette from his mouth and blew out the smoke.

"That boy did real well delivering those letters!" Joseph declared in a tone different from the one he just used. "Must've rode all night," he muttered.

Joseph showed Evan the letter from the man's sponsor and neighbor.

13th of September 1862

Dear Captain Joseph Maynard,

It would be our greatest pleasure to have your sister, or any of your family, stay with us. Do not worry. We do not and cannot feel imposed upon by your request, owing you so much. Anything we can do for you would be small in comparison to your sacrifice.

We eagerly look forward to Mary's arrival. It will be enjoyable to have another young woman in our home, for Emily mostly. As an afterthought, you neglected to mention our expected guest's age. We half expect a child, but fear she is a grown woman.

We regret that your mother will not be accompanying her. If she changes her mind, our home is welcome to her. The invitation stands open.

Again Lieutenant, do not worry on this any longer. Mary will be as one of our family. Rest assured she will be cared for and kept safe. We send our greatest of hopes for you with this letter.

Sincerely,

Mr. and Mrs. Stuart Conrad

"That's Margaret's writing," Evan sneered. "He probably dictated it," Evan laughed.

"Was still kind of them to accept," Joseph smiled back. He smiled at the papers in his hand. "They let Em sneak a note inside," he said, holding up the small pink square.

"Lil Nate's back, sar," McGuire's voice woke Joseph from his letters. "He's standin o'r thur," he pointed past Evan's shoulder.

"Thank you, Sergeant," Joseph nodded and stood. He made his way to where Nate stood by one of the units, sharing some snacks they had. Young Nate saw more of hell than any boy should expect, and he bore the effects better than most of the men around him. Joseph watched him smile. "Nate—Hello," Joseph greeted him. He came to stand in front of where the young boy sat.

"Hello, sir." He quickly stood and saluted stiffly. He stood just above Joseph's waist.

"You've done well, soldier." Joseph told him, with a smile like a proud father.

"Thank you, sir."

Joseph smiled at the boy's protocol. After a pause, he added, "Here's the pay I promised." Joseph reached into the small black buttoned pouch on his belt. He paid the boy five dollars, something he would only see after several weeks of hard work. It was a small matter to

Joseph, considering his commission and funds from his parents. He would not suffer.

"Thank you, sir," the boy said, displaying open excitement.

"Don't lose it. I can't replace that easily," Joseph pointed at him.

"Never, Captain. You can count on me." The boy stared at the money in his hands.

Joseph never saw eyes so bright, except those of a certain young woman he held the privilege of knowing. Joseph tousled the boy's hair. He turned back to his friends and rejoined them by his horse, now laying on the grass.

The battle played out, cracking gunfire off to the right. Evan paid no mind to the racket. He looked up when Joseph sat, but turned his eyes back to his letter held tightly in his hands. Joseph picked up his discarded mail and the note from his jewel.

"Ma wrote," Evan said morosely, flicking the last of his cigarette past his feet. He lowered the letter in his lap. "Davie's sick again." Evan's dark features desperately shadowed. "Doc says he won't make it this time." He looked out over the field, while a long pause tightened on them. When he looked back to Joseph, his eyes stood full of tears. He added, "Emily's been going over to see after him. Did they say anything about Mike?"

Joseph saw the fog of despair collapse around his friend, even at the mention of Emily. Evan's little brother meant a great deal to him. He remembered the boy was ill when they visited. The family explained it as his nature to be sick, but it did not make the matter easier. Joseph wished he could do more than pretend nothing happened and play with the boy, as if he were healthy like the rest of his family.

Joseph remembered the cough at breakfast one morning. It brought Mrs. Howell to her knees on the floor in front of him. He could still see her, holding Davie to her chest and patting his back to make it pass.

He nearly lost his breath forever that time. He saw his face so red with the desperate need of air.

"No," Joseph replied gloomily. He moved on to his own letter and felt glad for it. He unsuccessfully kept himself from the words, which spread across the page in flourishes, bringing emotions he dare not express there. Emily guaranteed him a smile, even at the mention of her name. "What's—"

"You said Em wrote?" Evan asked, cutting him off with the need to hear something that may lighten his heart, before he fell to tears in front of his men like a woman.

Joseph held up the pink paper from Mr. Conrad's message and the bonus of a blushing page that smelled sweetly of a woman's perfume. He smiled slightly and a sparkle glinted in his dark eyes, softening them. Evan gave Joseph's arm a quick and hard knowing pat. He laughed and the worries over his sibling scattered. Joseph watched him lay back on the grass with his knees up and put his cap over his eyes to blot out the sun.

"At least there was some worth to the time sitting here idle," Joseph said, going back to his reading.

"Not for me," Evan said, meaning more.

"Evan?"

Evan looked to him. Joseph's eyes pulled into his soul, seeing through him. He looked away unable to hold his friend's gaze. He knew Joseph saw his secret.

"What?"

"You've been moody for weeks," Joseph scoffed. "What's going on?"

"Oh—I don't know," Evan said, yanking up some grass. "A war maybe," he said sarcastically.

"It's more than Davie," Joseph said. He puffed his cigarette and squinted at the smoke.

Evan looked at him crossways, replacing the cap on his head and putting his arm to prop himself up. He wondered how Joseph saw him so clearly. Pitching the grass past his feet, he folded his arms over his knees and drew them up to his chest. He clamped his mouth shut and studied the field, thinking over his answer, if he would answer.

"A few weeks ago, my father wrote me a letter," Evan said. His expression turned tragic. "You remember Miss Dunworth?" He looked to Joseph only long enough to see his nod. "She's carrying my child." He looked back to see Joseph draw from his cigarette. He blew out the smoke slowly.

"What?" Joseph rasped hardly believing what he heard. "Evan—what are you gonna do?" Joseph choked.

Evan shrugged, "Not much I can do." He looked to the Captain and smirked, "Penelope used to chase me round when we were still kids. Guess she still had it for me." Evan's expression turned tragic. "I wish I never saw her again," he admitted.

"You don't mean that," Joseph said sternly. His friend thought to toy with a woman and then walk away without responsibility. "You ought to do right by her."

"I would," Evan said. "But, they won't tell me where she is and Donnelly won't even give me a few days leave to marry her."

"Sounds like the son of a bitch," Joseph growled, finishing his smoke. "He's no conscience."

"Pa said he'd continue to try the Dunworths—see if they'll tell him," Evan half smiled. "Nothing better than being a father."

"Yeah," Joseph smiled at him receiving a glare. "How about a husband first." Joseph shook his head at Evan's reproachful glare. "You know better than to carry on as you do. You had to know sooner or later this'd happen."

"Maybe," Evan said bitterly. "Why do you think I wouldn't marry Emily or even involve myself with her?" Evan paused looking at Joseph's searching expression. "I respect that girl too much to ruin her like this. You understand."

"And you didn't respect Miss Dunworth?" Joseph questioned him.

Evan shook his head no. He lowered his eyes to the ground feeling sorry for himself. Adjusting his arms on his knees, he thought over the results of his actions.

Somehow a smile bloomed on his lips. He shook his head and whispered to himself.

"I'll talk with Donnelly," Joseph said. "If we can survive this and get you some time—I'll see that my father writes the Dunworths about the matter—"

"No!" Evan blurted. "It's up to Penelope to tell me where she went to. I don't want anyone else involved in my mistake," he added, looking desperate. "I'm prepared to fix it."

"All right," Joseph said. "Then, I'll just ask Donnelly for a week for you." Joseph looked to the field worried the matter may come to a close for Evan sooner than they both thought. "You try to find where she is."

"I want her father's permission," Evan said, looking through the rest of his unopened letters.

Joseph laughed, "You can't have everything, Lieutenant."

Evan said, "Maybe I can." He held up a strange envelope with no return address.

Joseph eyed the letter, obviously written in an expressive hand. His eyes flicked back to Evan's. Despite the stress of the matter, the man looked bright. He wore a broad grin and perhaps hoped it came from the woman they discussed. Joseph smiled back, thinking Evan a better man than his friend thought himself.

"No time like now to open it," Evan said, slipping his thumb beneath the folded end. He tore it open and pulled the handwritten pages from inside. Sorting to the last page, he read the signature and smiled. "It's from Penelope."

"Well? Read it," Joseph urged him forward.

Evan held up his hand and returned to the first page, still wearing a bright smile.

September 11, 1862

Dear Lieutenant Howell,

I have recently received your request to know where I am keeping myself. Before I disclose the location, my father told me I am under no obligation to do so.

However, I believe that I am. Still, I do not hold you responsible. It was my actions that brought us to this predicament as well. Hesitantly, I shall continue.

Upon the discovery of my pregnancy, my parents told your mother and father of the situation and my claim that you are the father. You know the truth of that. They heartily believed I lay with no other man and went with the wish of my parents to keep the matter a secret. My father is quite angry with both of us, but if you make good, he will come around.

Once my stomach began to grow, they sent me to New York City to visit with family and attend finishing school. At least, that is what they tell people. Honestly, I am with my Aunt Gertrude. She is helping to take care of our unborn child and me. She said it would be wise to tell you where I am and let you take responsibility if you will. When anyone asks, she's taken to answering that my husband is away in the war. Everyone seems contented with that response and I do not suffer from my condition.

Understand that I will hold you to nothing, but I wager that your curiosity about my location is more than curiosity. I pray with a still heart that you will come to me and make me honest once more. Again, you must not feel that you are obligated to take me as your wife. My Aunt prepares to see the baby adopted to a nice family and one is ready to stake their claim.

I only wish this tragedy had not become ours and that you would have asked me to be your wife for feelings in your heart. I am a foolish child, already knowing you never felt more than a passing fascination. I changed a great deal in your time away, but I don't think you have.

I will never be angry with you no matter your choice, for I am in love with you and always will be. Keep well.

Love Always,

Miss Penelope Dunworth

P.S. I hope to see you soon.

Evan wiped a finger beneath his eye and drew a deep breath that filled his lungs, relaxing him despite the mood. His gaze studied the papers in his hand and read the address, far north in New York City. He let his hand fall to his lap and looked to Joseph. He treated Penelope horribly, claiming untrue facts about her. He felt like a cad. His heart clenched.

"She wants me to marry her," Evan said, blushing.

Joseph laughed, "And rightly you should."

"I thought she'd want me dead," Evan laughed. He paused, looking at the letter. She told him something that pulled at his heart. That never happened before. "She said—she loves me, never was with another man."

"You need no more reason than that," Joseph told him.

"Donnelly won't let me go," Evan said. "I can't make her wait—"

"Leave him to me," Joseph said.

Evan nodded and looked over his friend's expression. He failed to judge him, despite his dishonorable act. Evan drew another cleansing breath and felt release.

"Let me see your letter," Evan said, nodding to the pink paper in Joseph's hand.

Joseph smiled and passed the page to him. He waited for Emily's letters with just as much need.

13th of September 1862

Dear Joseph,

I'm sorry but this will only be a quick letter, my love. I wrote hastily to add to my parents' message. I miss you, and it gets worse everyday. I love you.

I'm so excited at the prospect of meeting your sister soon. The house is buzzing with more excitement than when the barn burned down. I simply cannot wait until she arrives. I just know we'll become good friends.

I also continue to find myself waiting with more enthusiasm for the arrival of your next letter, even in the light of the battles I read. They assure me you survive and so with you our plans. I hope all is well when you receive this message. I feel you in my heart. Be brave and I will try also. I think it is a matter of days before the end comes to this war. I hear of the draft riots and hope

Washington will call an end because of them. Fare you well, my love.

Love Always,

Your Emily

P.S. Michael is almost fully recuperated! You should see him walk!

The moment Joseph finished the smaller letter, he heard the approach of heavy footsteps on the ground. Joseph forgot his other mail, tucking them in a bag. He looked over his shoulder to see Evan's new sergeant run toward them. His face shined red and oily in the sun. Whatever agony he felt was disguised in a broad smile beneath his long thick mustaches. Joseph smiled back at him.

"I just heard the funniest damn story, Captain," Sergeant Harley Daniels laughed, collapsing at their feet. Evan sat up from his lounging position on the ground beside Joseph. "I heard women and children hid in a farm up yonder," he motioned with his thumb and wheezed with laughter. "When the fightin started—" he wheezed again. "When the fightin started, they came a runnin out." The man laughed harder. No doubt, he pictured the whole odd occasion. Joseph stared at him blankly, failing to find the humor in frightened women and children. "They went runnin cross the field tord the Rebs! Flyin like geese—" he stood up and mimicked what he believed their flight. He threw himself into a crouch in front of Joseph and Evan. Then, he continued, "They fallin all over the ground, thinking they gettin shot at, but ain n'one gonna shoot at um er round um. So's both the armies just sit there watchin and laughin—and the women kept a runnin n'every time one of um falls they scream n'run faster thinkin she's shot dead! Awe, sir. It musta been a sight. I tell you. Even the Rebs laughed."

"Is that so?" Joseph asked with a smile at the man who lay on his ample belly, shaking with mirth while his eyes filled with tears.

Evan laughed, resting on his elbow. He liked the Sergeant the moment he met him. Evan lay back down and lowered his hat over his eyes. Daniels hit the bottom of his boot and he looked to him. The man lay on his side smiling at him.

"What's at ya, Lieutenant?" He asked, widening his eyes.

Joseph saw Evan scramble for an answer, looking desperate to his friend for help.

"Captain!" Joseph heard someone yell.

The Captain turned where he sat to see the source of the sound run toward them.

"We're moving over the bridge!" The Corporal hollered, rousing the other men to service.

"Move um out!" Joseph yelled to the units under his charge.

Joseph quickly gathered himself with a racing heart and mounted. It came all too soon that he and his company crossed the bridge the Corporal spoke of. On the other side, they faced a wall of rebels, ready to kill every last one of them. They held their positions across the creek inside the village on a street where people once lived in peace. That place should have welcomed them, but now it intimidated them with the dead strewn over it in heavy numbers.

Just beyond and within sight lie General Lee's headquarters. If they pushed hard and chased, they would have him at last. Joseph formed his lines. His men drew up with him. Lee must be taken that day, for Maryland and an end to the war.

"This better be it," Joseph said to himself.

Guns fired and the Union Army pushed forward, forcing the Confederate lines in front of Joseph's Cavalry to run back to the safety of where they came from. The sound of war clashed around them. They were off from their retreat. Joseph's men charged into the middle of it. They made a wide sweep away from the street full of bodies and blood, moving behind the divisions of butternut fighters, as the others kept around the front. Somehow the southern men moved back without much loss despite them, Joseph cursed his own name at the missed opportunity to beat the men that bested them every time. When the maneuver ended, the commander of the troops he was sent to aid thanked him for his trouble.

"You're a good lad, as I've heard." The Major General looked pleasantly at him, his eyes sparkling. "You deserve your bars, far as I can tell. Don't be so harsh on yourself," he told Joseph when he tried to explain his failure. "Now, Captain Maynard. Take your men and wait in the rear of the left flank. I'll send orders soon."

"Thank you, sir." Joseph said not feeling any better.

When he turned his mount, the considerate gesture from the higher ranking officer continued. He reached out a gloved hand and patted his back. Then, he half smiled, seeing much in Joseph that he liked. His performance proved more than admirable and he knew how to ride better than many horsemen he knew. He rallied his men around him easily. They followed him like a wolf pack. Of any company of cavalry, he would stand most proud to command such as them.

"I should keep my eye on that one," The Major General told the man next to him. "A fine soldier, as I ever saw."

"Yes, sir." The other man smiled. "I'll write him down for you."

The Federals rallied together and made to run again. Night soon fell, but their respite went undiscovered. Rest did not come in war, when guns raged angrily, hungry for the taste of blood and death. By midday the next, it looked sure they would lead a final Federal victory. Still, Joseph did no receive orders to call his men on further attacks. Instead of stewing over the matter, Joseph took the quiet time to write his mother. He worried much over the safety of his family and usually avoided communications in fear of learning the worst.

September 19, 1862

Dear Mother,

I feel assured at last. Maryland is safe from the threat of rebel marauders. However, I wish you to act with caution and not call Mary back home yet. In fact, she should stay with the Conrad's for some time longer. I don't believe this singular defeat will prevent Lee from yet another try. I think Maryland is important in his plans. Then again, he may only use us as a distraction to gain ground elsewhere unobserved.

How has the house fared? I'll come see for myself, as soon as I am able. I don't trust my dear mother to keep from coloring the details of the occupation. I've yet to learn of all the damage caused by the Rebel scourge from my one brief visit, although I've word it is bad.

I received a letter from the Conrads. They can barely wait to meet our girl Mary. They are glad for the companionship for their daughter Emily. I'll have to tell you more about the Conrads at another time. Very nice folks. You'd find their little girl, Emily, most interesting.

Right now, I must cut this letter short, to see it sent to you. I will write again soon, Mother.

Love Always Your Son,

Captain Joseph Maynard

"Ya know Miss Barton's here," Evan said, approaching Joseph where he sat against a tree. Manny stood over him, gazing at nothing.

Joseph smiled devilishly at him, "You gonna get wounded so you can woo that woman?"

Evan laughed, "I already have a woman."

"Then why are you talking about the other one?" Joseph wondered.

The color rose in Evan's cheeks.

"Be quiet. She's a regular hero," he said. He took his cap off and spun it in his hands. "I was just telling you," he added in a whine, sitting down. His happy expression faded to shadow again. "Besides, if we get hurt—there's someone out here to do more than the hackers we got."

Joseph looked at him sullenly. Earlier, he asked Donnelly for Evan's leave time and received a stern refusal no matter the reason Joseph gave him. He kept it secret, hoping a quiet time might develop and change Donnelly's mind. Besides, Evan surely would suffer if he knew. They all suffered too much already. Thinking of his secret, Joseph looked away to the fields and trees disguising his features in a study of the defenses set up around their perimeter.

"I keep thinking," Evan said, sitting next to Joseph.

"About," Joseph said, whipping a hand under his nose to relieve an itch. He kept his eyes away from Evan.

"I'm glad I told you," Evan admitted. "I feel like the weight's lifted."

"Good," Joseph said, offering him a quick halfhearted smile.

"I mean it," Evan said, sensing Joseph's lack of enthusiasm. "Things don't seem as bad." Evan paused and snickered, "I'm real excited now."

"Good," Joseph said, again offering a mere smirk. "I just hope we can get you to New York soon. With this fighting so thick—"

Evan looked at him with the smile dying on his features, "Donnelly said no again."

Joseph hesitated, "No—he." Joseph tried not to respond.

"I figured he would."

"I don't think it's anything other than the battle," Joseph told him. "You've got to understand that." Joseph looked to him, seeing if his words made him feel better. "I know he'll approve your leave when it's over."

"I understand," Evan rasped. "But, Penelope might not and I know the baby won't wait. I have to get there before the end of November."

"She will and I'm sure you'll see her soon," Joseph assured him. "Get some rest. You'll need your strength come morning."

Evan looked at the Captain darkly. Joseph could see him, gritting his teeth in anger. Perhaps he thought of more to say, though the conversation turned away.

Until the next morning, Joseph's units remained in position, sleeping on the ground under the stars. Joseph listened to the night. A rifle shot sounded in the dark, shaking him full awake. He looked down his body to the trenches yards away. He saw the men skulking about. A long saber like instrument glinted in the moonlight, held tight in each of their hands. His eyes flicked up and he spied the large outline of McGuire, sleeping on his back with his mouth open in a snore. Joseph smiled slightly and kicked him in the shin. McGuire rolled away from him snorting and licking his mouth.

Joseph sat up unable to fall back asleep. They faced a horrible scene and his mind recalled the bodies in town. Above the snores, he made out a cadence of unearthly cries and groans. He peered into the night, knowing he listened to wounded men suffering without help. Joseph hung his head and begged for an answer as to why this was necessary.

Looking to the navy blue horizon, Joseph thought of the lack of ambition in trying to win the war for Washington. The stars twinkled down at him. Suddenly the world became a cold unfeeling place, more than he ever knew. If they all died tomorrow, the fight that raged today would be even more meaningless. Watching the white sparkles bedecking the blackened sky, he thought of how little any of it mattered. Tomorrow would come and go with or without them.

The dawn eventually rose, but gray and stark. The groans died away, replaced by cartwheels and marching. Gunfire filled the remaining space. The scene played out before both sides like the fabled second coming, following the reign of the four horsemen.

Joseph took his coffee and continued to smoke. His distant gaze watched the fit soldiers gather the dead and wounded. A cease fire stood agreed on by both sides, to allow the civil collection to pass quickly. Joseph counted his men and found that all stood accounted for from the last count last night. A nick here and a nick there, but they survived. Such blind luck could not last.

Despite finding all of his men present, Joseph saw the faces from other days gone by. He remembered the smiles and laughter, now hidden in masks of mocking death. A wagon full of corpses passed behind where he tried to pass the morning, waiting for his orders. The creaking wheels gained his attention and Joseph looked over his shoulder toward it. He saw the features of a muddied and bloodied officer. The familiar features bit at his mind, stilling his heart like snake venom. He had seen him at school, a year or so ahead of his class. Major leaves confirmed the suspicion.

Joseph looked into his coffee mug. Cadet Carlton Sanders supplied him and his roommates with the finest liquor he could scrape up from the means of a student. Joseph made friends with him and discovered his story similar to Evan. His family saved every penny to make him a better life. This is what that money bought them.

Joseph rubbed his eye. He felt the anguish stab his heart. He squinted into the sunny arch of trees where another wagon came along, the same stand of shrubs he attacked a day ago. Joseph hoped they would send the body home and not dig a mass grave to place him in. Carlton was a man who deserved better than that. Every dead man on those carts deserved better than that, no matter what side of the flag.

"Nate!" Joseph hollered for the drummer boy.

Nate jumped up from the grass where he snoozed beside his drum. He hurried to the Captain's side. The officer pointed to the cart and gave orders. The boy nodded and ran off to follow them.

Joseph swallowed and it tasted bitter. His brows pinched as if he would cry, but he could not do such a thing there with all the men watching. Carlton was a stranger now, even though they schooled together for two years, and it did not warrant him losing his composure. He turned his back from the retreating cart and the boy who went to find out what would happen with the body. Joseph went to help where he could be of use.

Though Joseph turned his back to the scene, he could not get rid of the image of his friend in the cart. From there it became his own fate and he saw Emily crushed by his loss. He had seen her face awash in mournful tears, the day he left. What would she do if he died, never to come home and fulfill their unspoken promises? He fell in love with her the moment he saw her in the firelight. His heart would not let her go. But, he wondered what if it stopped beating? Could hers let him go?

A small while later, a runner dismissed the company under the command of Captain Maynard to clean themselves up and eat a decent meal back in the tent city. Joseph and his men mounted their horses and rode through the reeking mess to their canvas homes. Joseph said nothing to any of them, ducking in his tent to be alone.

With his letterhead spread out before him, his mind filled with many ideas, but he forgot what to say. He thought too much and failed to place one idea above another, except one. Placing his pen to paper, Joseph scrawled a small message that would answer all of Emily's questions at once.

September 20, 1862

Emily,

I am alive. I love you.

Joseph

Though Antietam ended, the memories remained. Joseph wondered how kindly Washington looked on the General of the Potomac and the performances of his underlings. He thought ill of it himself, so he doubted Washington would feel much better. Despite his growing dislike of the man, he prayed God to bless McClellan for seeing him through alive this far. Then, he wished God to remove Mac from command and bless them with a better leader.

XI. Thoughts of Home

Stuart Conrad bent over his desk, fixing a small addition problem in his ledgers, thankfully in his favor. With his glasses balanced on his nose, he erased the entries incorrectly written and replaced them with the correct numbers. The door to his study opened and he looked up to see his wife enter, wearing her bonnet and cloak from an outing. She went to gather the young Maynard woman from the train station with Jack.

Stuart looked out the window to see the carriage drive by toward the carriage house, listening to his wife speak, "Miss Maynard is here. She's waiting in the parlor."

Stuart smiled up at his wife and set the ledger down on his desk. She made great strides since their last fight over the matter of Emily. She softened toward him and saw the ill of her ways. It felt good to have her back, but at times he saw the darkness falling back on her.

"Thank you, dear," his voice carried softly in the rooms. He set his pen down and stood. Joining his wife on the other side of his desk, he took her stole and guided her out of the study to the hall. She smiled and leaned her head on his shoulder. Stuart hung her stole up and they joined their guest in the parlor. "Welcome, Miss Maynard," Stuart bellowed happily.

Mary rose to her feet with a broad beautiful smile for him. She offered her hand and he took it giving her gloved digits a small squeeze, "Mr. Conrad?"

"Indeed," he smiled at her tired eyes, nearly a copy of her brother's. However, she looked far fairer than he.

"Thank you for taking me in," Mary said to Stuart and Margaret. "My brother worries about me a great deal."

"With reason," Stuart suggested the sofa to her. He took to his chair and his wife sat beside the young woman. "We are most glad to have you as our guest. Your family is always welcome to our hospitality," Mrs. Conrad said.

"Thank you, Mrs. Conrad," she turned on the sofa to point to a young woman who stood by the fireplace. "This is my servant Miss Phoebe Lansing. My father sent as an escort and aid to me," Mary explained the uniformed girl.

Phoebe nodded her white capped head to them with a small smile. She kept her hands neatly folded before her, resting against a crisp white apron over a fine but simple black gown. By the clothes of both servant and guest, it became increasingly obvious what lifestyle the Maynard's enjoyed.

"Very pleased to make your acquaintance, Miss Phoebe."

"Thank you, sir."

Stuart turned his attention back to the other young woman and said, "We'll enjoy our lunch soon. While you wait you are welcome to refresh yourself and settle into your rooms upstairs." He stuck his hand out toward the archway where a pair of young girls gathered. "MaryJane and Jo-Hanna will show you the way."

"Thank you kindly, Mr. and Mrs. Conrad," Mary said standing. She turned to her servant while her hosts rose to their feet, "Phoebe will you join me?"

"Yes, Miss," she replied shyly.

MaryJane and Jo-Hanna grabbed one end each of the large trunk, while Phoebe took a pair of suitcases, leaving her own baggage in the hall. Mrs. Conrad acted quickly and called Rose to their aid. Soon all their guest's belongings and those of her servant moved up the stairs.

The affect the Maynard family had on others soon became obvious. When the golden headed Mary passed Michael's open door, he sat bolt upright on his bed and stared disbelieving. He looked at his healing leg, thinking he passed into the kingdom of heaven or an angel came for him at last. He quickly gathered an ebony cane from the side table and stood, grasping the gold hand piece in his fist. He pressed the gold tip to the floor and lifted himself with some effort from the bed. Intent on seeing who came to the house, he hobbled to his door, but he only saw the mousey haired housekeeper on the stairs to the third floor. Down the hall, the guest bedroom door shut.

Michael looked around disappointed and turned back into his room. He shut his door behind him and sat on his bed. Suddenly he remembered what his father said. Captain Maynard's sister would arrive today. His face took on an expression of shock and fear. She saw him in a terrible state of undress, not to mention unshaven. He touched his jaw line feeling the prickly hairs on the skin. Michael cursed and quickly hobbled about his room to snap his appearance back into shape.

Michael soon stood before his mirror, washed and dressed, shaven and preened. He buttoned his shirt up to his neck and attached a collar. His door opened and his mother stood before him with a small smile. She eyed him a moment, no doubt thinking him handsome. He buttoned his collar, looking back to his reflection.

"Miss Maynard's arrived. She'll join us for lunch," Margaret smiled. She shut the door behind her and entered. "I see you want to come," She helped him fix his collar. "The meal is about ready. I'll help you downstairs now."

Michael nodded with appreciation to his mother. He hated people seeing him limp about. His leg still felt soar and the fall from his horse he told no one about had put him back some weeks. He used the limb as little as possible because of the pain. However, the less he used it, the stiffer it became and he saw the problem with that. He walked the lane since last week, but time would only see his leg back in regular use.

The family gathered round the dining table. Emily arrived for lunch with a bright smile for her brother. She went out to check on her bull before Mary arrived and watch him frisk in the corral grown to adulthood too quickly for her liking. She sat next to Michael and told him all about it while they waited for the guest to descend to them.

Their father entered next to take his seat at the head. He nodded to his children, safely gathered to him once more. Then, their mother arrived with their guest. Mary moved to sit beside Michael and Emily. Both men rose from their chairs, Michael with some difficulty. He saw her eye the cane rested against the table at his seat. Still, she smiled at him and genuinely, not a bit of pity.

"You're just in time for some fresh apple cider. Would you like some? Our orchards have done quite well this year," Stuart asked, watching his son labor to push the visitor's chair in. He hobbled back to his seat and Stuart nodded to him approvingly.

"Yes, that'd be fine. Thank you," Mary replied, watching the young man limp to his chair. She knew without asking, the wound came from the war. His mother mentioned it on the carriage ride there.

Michael placed himself again, disguising the pain well. His eyes flicked to his sister and he saw the smile playing on her lips, as she spread her napkin on her lap. He smiled at her leaning back in his chair with a hand on his chin. His eyes went back to the guest and he studied her fair hair and fine facial lines. She did not notice his assessment, engrossed in a response to his father, made of soft sultry tones.

Michael smiled to himself, thinking of the Captain trapped all the way down in Maryland. The man barely showed in any fine turn of her features. He lowered his gaze and drew a deep breath to steady himself, as he felt more than he should for his commanding officer's sister.

Rose and MaryJane emerged from the kitchen entrance, carrying trays of steaming food. Behind, Hettie approached with two silver pitchers, sweating in the heat. Mary's eyes went to her with the same curiosity Joseph showed the first time. The family acted unconcerned, already knowing the Maynard's stance on the issue.

"How did you come by owning slaves in the North?" Mary asked, coloring in her cheeks with anger. She watched Hettie pour her a glass of cider and set it on the table again.

"We don't own Mrs. Benson," Margaret explained. "She works for us."

Hettie looked at the new girl with a furrowed brow.

"My apologies, Mrs. Conrad, Mrs. Benson. It's unfortunately so common in Frederick and Baltimore that it seemed the only explanation," Mary said, lowering her eyes and voice with embarrassment. "It's good to hear you've found work for pay," she added after a moment.

"Your family is abolitionist," Margaret stated with a smile. The girl nodded, affirming what they already knew. "It's an honorable duty to fight for those who have had their rights stolen from under them."

"Indeed it is, ma'am," Mary said, still feeling awful.

"Young Michael here is a Second Lieutenant in your brother's company, Miss Maynard," Stuart gently guided their attention to other conversations.

"Is he?" Mary asked eyeing him with a blushing smile. "My father didn't mention that. You know Joey well then?"

"He saved my leg, Miss."

"I was wondering how he came to know you all the way up here," Mary looked around the table and back to Michael. "That must be why he sent me to you," she smiled nervously, soaking in every feature of his face. She looked away to her plate shyly.

MaryJane served the guest first. Mary watched the delicate bowl of thick soup. It smelled delicious and she realized how starved she was. She welcomed the distraction from the young man at her side.

"Actually," Michael said receiving his meal next. "He came here cause our neighbor Evan Howell. He serves as his lieutenant now. I was still at school then," he explained.

This Michael was handsomer than any of the boys yet met. His eyes and all of him was exactly what she once tried to explain to her friends. They so often pressed her to tell them what she found attractive, as she rejected nearly every suitor. Well, there the man sat, justifying her and showing her daydreams not a waste of time.

"Captain Maynard saved our cows from a barn fire," Stuart added.

Mary looked at them shocked to hear such news. Her parents hid a great deal from her, probably not wishing her to worry.

"Joey's a right hero then, huh. I just hope he's left a good impression on all of you."

"Indeed he has," Stuart smiled, looking to his daughter, as she received her lunch.

"I'm glad of it," Mary said, quietly watching the other young woman.

Stuart's and his wife's plates were filled last. Then, Mr. Conrad led the family in a short prayer and they put all attention on filling their bellies. The conversation that followed concerned the visitor and her family, but the Conrads never pried too far. Mary warmed to them quickly.

"We are glad to have you join us, Mary. Perhaps when this dreadful war is over, Captain Maynard and you will return to visit?" Margaret offered, knowing it would go politely accepted and stopped any more nonsense on her own part.

"Thank you," Mary smiled, surprised. "We will take you up on that I'm sure."

During the meal, Mary watched Miss Emily Conrad closely. She knew Joseph kept his eye on Vermont for some reason. She wondered if Joey's intent lay in not keeping her safe from stray bullets, but to tell mother the girl was a good match. Mary lowered her chin and ate from the plated second course. She would see about this young woman in time. However, she acted too meek so far, remaining silent throughout the lunch. Still, she was a delightful contrast to the gabbling gooses that usually followed her brother about town.

Mary lifted her chin and savoring the meal. It tasted better than anything in the past few days and equal to her memory of home. Her eyes went to Emily again. The young woman looked like such a harmless and pretty thing. She conducted herself in perfect manners. Mary's eyes studied the dress she wore to the combs in her hair. She was so quiet, but Mary already liked her.

That evening, Emily sat at her bureau set to write a letter to Joseph, assuring him his sister arrived in fine and good spirits. She dipped her pen in the small pot of ink, careful not to soak the tip too deeply. Someone knocked on her door and she set the pen to paper and flourished the date. She kept her eyes there, next fashioning the greeting.

"Come in," Emily called to the visitor without looking up.

Michael popped his head in and smiled at her. Emily looked up at him to see who came and went back to her task. Her brother shut the door and hobbled over. She thought of her first words.

"Writing Joe?" Michael asked her. Emily nodded, wearing a somber expression. "Don't tell um, but I think I'm in love."

"Michael!" Emily gasped, spraying drops of ink on the sheet. She dropped her pen and turned in her seat, looking at him as if he went mad that day.

"She's an angel, Em," he claimed.

"But you know nothing about her," Emily reasoned with him.

Her brother looked to her with a raised brow, "And I suppose you know all there was to know about Joe the second he stepped out of the fire."

"I know a great deal more of him than any of us know of Mary," Emily said, turning in her seat. She put the ruined sheet aside and cleaned her pen on a rag. She started again. "But, I won't tell him."

"Thank you, dear," Michael said, standing back up. He touched her shoulder and left the room shutting the door. "Though, this would even the score."

"Score?" Emily questioned unimpressed.

Emily set her pen down and looked at the lamp, filling her room with a golden glow. Perhaps, she should wait a day or so to write. Then she would find more to tell him of his sister. She looked at the sheet, blank except for the date and greeting. She felt afraid to send him another letter.

"I'm afraid this will make me miss him more than ever," Emily murmured.

Michael reached and closed her in his arms, "I'm sorry, Em."

The next day passed pleasantly with introductions in the past. Emily acquainted with Mary alone and introduced her to life on their enterprising dairy farm. Michael remained always close. He hobbled on his leg less and made a concerted effort to keep up with their steady. The muscle pained him to walk for too long, but he gave his all not to be left behind. Despite his protests only good would come of using the limb, the women brought him inside and they took tea in the music room.

Mary spoke to him, distracting him from fears of not returning to the army. He could not ride with a bad leg. He could not face that fact. She sipped her tea and told him her stories, making him laugh and smile. He forgot the pain of his injury.

After another walk about the grounds in the sunny afternoon, Emily returned the guest to the house where she could refresh herself before dinner. She stood with her mother and brother, watching Mary continue down the hall ahead of her servant. When Mary went from sight, Emily's attention went to her family. She saw her mother smile at Michael and she patted his cheek knowingly. Michael's eyes studied her askance a moment. He said nothing, but his face soon flushed red. Emily covered her mouth to keep from laughing aloud. He glared at her and she walked away to follow where Phoebe and Mary went.

"What is it with these Maynards?" Margaret laughed.

Stuart entered the hall from the parlor where he read his paper. He rushed with the newspaper held in his hand, waving it back and forth. His voice cried out in raucous joy. Joining his wife and son in the hall beside the kitchen, he pointed to the front page and a bold type header. He handed it to his wife, wearing a big grin and red face to match his sons. He hunched down and slapped his knee. He laughed and wheezed unable to speak for all the joy filling him.

"What is it, Pop?" Michael asked, looking at the paper over his mother's shoulder.

"Right there boy," he pointed to the article. "Emancipation—the president passed the bill!"

Stuart danced around the hall. Hettie entered on the scene from outside, carrying a basket of apples from their stores. She eyed them worriedly and tried to smile. Stuart danced to her after she set her burden on the table. She watched him warily, as if he had gone made. Stuart laughed and drew her into his arms. He danced her about the hall singing, "Glory, glory, hallelujah. . ."

Hettie laughed, begging them to tell her, "What's happened?"

"You're free, my girl. Absolutely free!" Mr. Conrad called out.

Hettie's face turned flat with shock. She looked at their faces and her body trembled, as her eyes filled with tears. They said she stood a free woman. She drew a breath feeling faint. Perhaps they kidded her.

"Free?" She asked.

"What's going on?" Emily asked, returning from the stairs. She gave an unsure smile.

"Henrietta Benson is a free woman," Stuart told his daughter.

"Hettie," Emily said excitedly.

Rose entered from the closets. She looked at them agape, holding a pile of linens. She joined the Conrads in the hall, discovering what the noise celebrated. Her little bow mouth turned to a smile.

"Come sit down, dear," Margaret led Hettie down the hall to the parlor and set her on the sofa. The rest of the family ushered in with her and Rose. Margaret looked at the housekeeper and said, "Have the girls bring her something to drink." She nodded and moved to dash off.

"There now," Margaret cooed. "You sit there until you feel better."

"I've something better in mind," Stuart halted Rose. He held his arm out to stop her from leaving. "You sit with your friend Miss Benson."

"Thank you," Rose spoke softly, turning to rejoin Hettie.

"I'm free," Hettie looked at her hands, long since shackled by the sin of slavery. She saw no manacles there now. "I'm free," She breathed again, feeling Rose put her hands on her shoulders to comfort her.

Stuart danced back from his study with his prized bourbon in a crystal decanter and a glass with a draft already poured. He offered the strong drink to Hettie. She reluctantly took it and looked at the liquid inside.

"That'll settle your nerves," Stuart grinned.

"Oh, Daddy. That's only because she won't feel a thing," Emily cautioned him.

"Go on. Drink it," Margaret said surprisingly. "Lord knows I needed it once or twice."

"What about my husband and my boy?"

"They're all free," Stuart said.

Hettie drank a sip of the whiskey. It burned her throat and she grimaced. She handed the glass back to Mr. Conrad. He refused and she took it back to her lap.

"Can I get word to them?" Hettie asked.

"We'll try," Margaret said. "If you remember the name of those who helped you, I'd start there."

Hettie nodded and sipped more bourbon, "Yeah. I doan trust anyone ta tell ya the truth." She looked at the Conrads. "I mean except you, of course."

"We'll inquire," Stuart said. "I've an idea that may just work."

Hettie looked up at him and then drank down the rest of the whiskey in her glass. She winced at the liquid's bite.

The following days went similarly, with excitement brewing all over the farm.

Michael still insisted on attending the ladies, shortening their walks. In compensation, Margaret took the young people into town to shop and carry out other forms of distraction and entertainment beyond the farm. Once Michael leaned less on his cane, they traveled farther.

September faded into October. The evenings often passed beyond the farm house, trying to keep the women entertained. Under this new vitality, the whole family felt refreshed. The drudgeries of farm life and work no longer dug them so deeply. Most impressed, Stuart enjoyed the company of Mary Maynard and delighted in how well she got on with his children. Somehow the young woman even won over his wife and Joseph turned to a discussable subject.

Mary could barely wait to speak of Joseph. She learned from her servant Phoebe, who learned the tale from little Jo-Hanna only the second day, Joey and the Conrad girl had fallen in love during his visit in March, just as she suspected. It lightened her heart to find they passed letters back and forth and it explained his callous inattentiveness towards his family. She would have to speak with Joey about that. Just because you fall in love, you should not throw over your family.

Later that day, Mr. Fordder came to see Mr. Conrad over hiring his son Christian on at the farm. Jack's second looked much relieved to have his boy back among them. Together, they joined Mr. Conrad in his office. Emily watched the young man limp like her brother. He too had been wounded in the leg, but unlike Michael, a bayonet stabbed Mr. Fordder's son.

Emily stepped past the open door to return Joseph's letters, worrying she saw the face of things to come. She since learned of Joseph's survival through terrible battles the papers called Bull Run and Antietam. She read about the fight for his home state of Maryland. Despite all that occurred in September, the war continued and she knew he would face new trials and she would wait to hear how he fared through them. His simple note pressed against her side, where she tucked it in her pocket always at the ready to see her through.

Climbing the steps to her room, she thought of how Michael grew stronger. The day of his return to the army hung just out of reach. She sat in his room that morning while he wrote a letter to reinstate his commission. He seemed so excited, as if what he did were harmlessly apply to an office. He smiled and planned, just like she dared to plan about Joseph.

It worried Emily. She could only imagine the days he would face. If Joseph died, she thought weeks would pass before she received news and that may only come from Mary. Who would tell them of Evan? If her brother died—she refused to think anymore of that. It was more than enough that he nearly had.

Alone in her room, Emily cried overwhelmed by her fear of an unavoidable end. She thought of the weeks she may spend, begging for a safe return, only to learn it impossible days ago. Her hopes and dreams may lie shattered on the battlefield. Could she find someone else to love and bury the part of her heart that had become Joseph? In his absence, her love never faltered and the fact remained she loved no other man. The thought crippled her. There would never live another man that she would love. With little hope left in her heart, Emily prayed that fate would not see fit to take Joseph from this world just yet.

Emily put off her letter for days.

1st of October 1862

Dear Joseph,

You should not think of me at three o'clock in the morning. You should rest! You make me worry more than necessary, because you will not care for yourself. I swear I'll have white hair like father by the time you return!

There is a surprise on the farm. A new hand, Christian Fordder, started work with us this week. He returned from the war wounded in battle like Michael. He informed us that he had been stuck by a Rebel out of munitions. He limps, but father believes he will work as hard as the other men and his father assures us the same. Besides that, Old Jack seems to really love him and so does his daughter Rose. They are to go to the dance this month together. I can hardly believe how well she behaves, in an effort to impress the man. I wish you were here to join in the fun. It is pure madness and does my heart good.

Mrs. Murphy is away in Europe. She writes me about her travels and is having a wonderful time. It seems she too has gained a new companion. He's a widower and seems quite smitten with his new American friend. I wonder if he will travel home with her. I half imagine a wedding. I hope to go to Europe one day. It excites me to think of those old places. Mrs. Murphy had invited me years ago, but my mother refuses. I think it would have been amazing.

Despite the madness you and my friends give me, your sister soothes my mind. Mary came at the end of last month, September 22. She's a lovely young woman and we get along beautifully with her. Even mother enjoys her company. I am so glad she came.

Mary tells me a great deal about Joey! But don't worry. I'm more in love with you than before. You're a wonderful man only made more charming by the tales of your past.

To answer your questions: Of course, I still miss you. How can the days possibly stretch out so long as they do? I help about the house all day, but it does not help much. I grow more and more afraid and it grows worse by night. Then I find nothing to do but lay in bed and stare at the ceiling. I would talk to your sister, but it would not be fair of me to keep her up all each night until I fall asleep. How do you pass the nights where you are? Evan must be exhausted.

I always think of our time in the garden and the field. I wander out there sometimes and sit. I dream of our meetings when I finally find the pleasant gift of sleep.

You've no idea how your letters help me through. They are the only way I feel sure you are all right. I wait for each one with excitement building and nearly burst when they get here. The last I received frightened me, but it came after the battle.

I wish I could be with you my love. Soon. I miss you so.

Hettie said to return your hello emphatically. Her lessons are going exceedingly well and she looks to the future brightly a free woman. Did you hear the news where you are? Hettie is finally free! She tells us it is a wondrous feeling, but she fears all it means. I know I cannot understand, but I feel better, knowing no one will take her from us. She's my dearest friend. I can only hope she will stay at my side.

With this event, we expect to see her family soon. Daddy sent letters to some friends, hoping to lead Isaiah and Ezekiel to our farm. I know we must wait until after the first of the year, but after all this time, it is not far away at all, but Hettie can barely contain herself.

There is another matter I wish to discuss with you, Captain. When you come to Vermont again, I expect you to. . .'

Emily

October lengthened and the fears of the war dulled by the relief the Maryland visitor offered them. Joseph still wrote faithfully to Emily, but letters appeared for his sister, as well. Mary shared them freely with her and Michael in case any news arrived in them that he held back in the others to Emily. In this way they forged a friendship that would last throughout their lives. For Michael it turned into something far deeper.

Later that month, a response to Michael's reenlistment request arrived. His commission stood accepted and they expected him to report to Captain Maynard, Army of the Potomac at the end of the month. They requested a certification from his doctor on his arrival with some other items. If he proved unfit for service, the doctor may send the correspondence to his commander and the matter would stand resolved.

Michael told his father right away, presenting the letter to him in his study where they always found him. Michael kept a serious expression and his father eyed him darkly. He took the letter and read it for himself. Michael turned away, leaving his father alone. He knew how he felt about the matter and he did not want an argument.

Inside his study, Stuart lowered his head to his hand. The words brought him a headache and he rubbed his temples to rid of it. Lowering the paper to his desk, he drew a deep breath. He hoped to keep Michael at home. He looked out the window and remembered the little boy that used to run about the lawn carrying on like a wildcat with his sister and the neighbor boy. Their long lost laughter echoed in his ears.

Outside the study, Michael stepped down the hall and found his sister and Mary, preparing to take a walk without him. He hurried down the hall to join the women, nearly stepping perfect on his leg. Michael smiled at Mary and took up his coat from just inside the kitchen door. After he put it on, they left the house through the back door and disappeared along the lane headed for the garden and secrecy.

"Not without me," Hettie called to them, arriving from the workhouses with milk jugs. She hurried to bring the milk inside and dashed back to join her charges on their walk. "You know your mother won't approve of you all going off together."

Emily and Hettie left the other pair alone in the garden. Emily's hollow darkened eyes spoke of sadness neither of her other companions understood. She sought the shelter of her field and the stone she sat on with Joseph, planning their future. Hettie proved the only one to know the real pain filling her heart. Neither knew when their suffering would end.

Left behind in the quiet of late fall, Michael sat on the bench beside Mary in his family's garden. She smiled and drew a deep breath of the crisp air. Her dark eyes looked up to the yellow leaves still clinging to the tree sheltering them. Michael smiled at the side of her soft face. She lowered her chin and smiled back at him.

Michael knew what he wanted to say, and while Emily walked with Hettie, he meant to make it known to Mary. He kept his hands to his sides, having kept his feelings the same. Mary might have suspected his emotions, but he never made them known. He hid in fear of her, making no real advances at all. He simply conversed and enjoyed her company as a friend.

"I'll return soon," he said. "I hoped to have more time."

"I thought you wanted to go back," Mary laughed, touching his hand with her gloved one.

"I did," Michael said, looking at the small digits. He took them into his hand. "Until, I met you."

Mary studied Michael's features. The smile she wore faded. Mary pulled back her shoulder closest to him. She let her hand remain in his. She could not speak, hearing what she only guessed for weeks. Michael looked in her eyes and she blushed, giving him another smile.

"Forgive me," he said. "I don't know how to say this. I'm sure you've heard it a million times before. I don't know how to say it right, but I'm gonna give it a try."

"Trying can't harm," she smiled, still letting him hold her hand. It was a good sign that his efforts succeeded.

"I've fallen in love with you," he blurted, knowing no other way to say it.

Mary smiled, turning her face down to their hands, clasped together. She blushed, a deep crimson to rival the autumn leaves. Men boldly told her of their feelings before, but never so honestly. Too many tried. However, they failed where he now succeeded, saying nothing pretty, making no promises and not disguising torridness. Michael meant what he said and she knew it.

"That's the best I've heard it said so far," Mary finally spoke. After a pause, she turned her chocolate eyes to his and smiled. She wanted to tell him how she felt, too. The excitement ran through her like lightning. "I'm—"

Before she could speak, Michael pulled her to him and laid his mouth on hers. He kissed her without fear of results and received an equally eager response. From behind them a gasp shuddered through the, raging silence. Michael ended the embrace, still holding Mary to him. He gazed over her shoulder, grinning. Mary looked with a blush on her cheeks.

Emily stood in the arch with her hand over her mouth. "Michael Conrad," she gasped. "Were you brought up in a barn? Do you not know how to behave with a lady? I leave you alone for a minute and—"

"Emily Conrad—you've no room to speak," he pointed his finger at her.

Emily put her hands on her hips in response to his sarcastic remark. She could not feel angry with him, but she looked unhappy that he took advantage of Mary while she turned away. While she scrutinized him like their mother, he distanced himself from Mary and smiled sheepishly. He forgot about the chance of getting caught.

"Sorry, Mary," Michael said. "It won't happen again."

"I didn't mind," Mary said, sliding her hand to his on the bench.

Michael lifted his chin and smiled at her.

Near the end of October, Emily received a long awaited response to her letter from earlier that month. It took much longer to find her than usual. That fact worried her when she saw the post date stamped on the outside. Perhaps his feelings changed and he now found their correspondence a part of his duty and not a distraction. The small note she received, one line in all, back in September warned her of the changes coming over her beloved. Emily cloistered herself in her room, wishing away her doubt.

October 22, 1862

Dear Emily,

. . .Tell Hettie congratulations. She's worked hard for this. And, do not worry. I wager you will see your family soon. You are a hero, Miss Benson, and someday you'll be celebrated.

I am happy for Rose and Mrs. Murphy. I cannot wait to hear Mrs. Murphy's stories. Europe is a grand place. You would enjoy London most, I think. We shall see eventually. I will take you, if you still want to go.

Your last letter leads me to think more happens at your home than you tell me, Miss Emily. Perhaps I'm only a suspicious old goat, but I know my sister and I know your Michael. I fear he thinks to even the score with me.

If not, he may see something in my sister many men see. I suspect he has already fallen in love with Mary. I understand, from former experience. My sister is a charming young woman. We're all proud of her, just as you are of Michael.

If I suspect correctly, it allows for an odd situation. Don't you think? Our families would end up bound by double bonds. I mean that, my jewel. I do think of marrying you and you should know of my designs. Shall I spell them out for you and leave you crimson until I return?

"Emily," Michael's voice interrupted the message from Joseph.

"Oh—hello, Michael. When did you get back?"

"I just got home," he answered. "Mamma wants you to come downstairs."

"What is it?" Emily asked, lowering her letter to her desktop. She stood, watching her brother with concern.

"Hurry up," Michael said, not answering. He disappeared from her doorway, but his footsteps echoed down the hall.

Emily followed her brother out of her room and down the hall to the stairs. She stopped at the top, looking down. Her mother stood at the bottom waiting for her. She saw the grave expression of her mother and her heart stilled. She thought everything had been set to right about her letters. However, this showed her mother retracted her earlier decision. Swallowing her fears, Emily stepped slowly down the steps and discovered guests in the parlor.

Mr. and Mrs. Howell looked frightful. The lines in their faces deepened and their color looked ashen. When they turned their eyes to Emily, they reminded her of dark caves found only in nightmares. Emily found her breath taken from her and her heart beat rapidly. Only two events would bring the Howells to such ends. *Oh, God, not Evan.* She panicked thinking her prayers neglected her friend.

"Emily," Mr. Howell nodded to her respectfully. His voice sounded raspier than before.

"Good afternoon, Mr. and Mrs. Howell," Emily tried to smile. She saw her mother hold her arm out to her and invite her to sit on the couch beside her. Casting her eyes about the room, she saw her father by the fireplace and her brother by the bookshelves in the back corner of the parlor. He hung his head in his hands, rubbing his forehead as if it ached. "What's going on?"

Mrs. Howell looked to her husband, avoiding Emily's searching gaze. She clung to her purse tightly and Emily noticed the tracks of tears laying pale on her cheeks, highlighted by the gray light coming from the window behind her. Mrs. Howell cried for some reason and it still alluded to the two reasons Emily tried to forget.

"We've bad news, Emily," Mr. Howell drawled. Emily looked to him, girding herself against what she feared to hear. Her stomach twisted and her knees buckled. "I am sure your father told you of our son's indiscretion earlier this year."

"Yes," Emily admitted, looking to her father momentarily.

"Mr. Dunworth stopped by our farm this morning," he continued. "It seems that Penelope took sick at her aunt's in New York. She won't be coming home till spring."

"What do you mean?" Emily heard herself ask from miles away.

"Evan cannot get leave from his commanders," Mr. Howell went on. "However, when he can, he's promised to marry Miss Dunworth. We just received his letter on the matter."

"Oh—is that all?" Emily smiled deeply. "You think I'd be upset?"

The Howell's looked at her worriedly. They did not respond.

"I know you must feel that Evan brought shame on your family," Emily said. "But, I know he will do right by Penelope. He is a good man and never meant for this."

"We just thought you should know, Em," Mrs. Howell said with a wavering smile.

"Thank you," Emily said. "I am glad to know you feel concerned for me."

Mr. Howell nodded to Emily with a smile, "You're a good girl, Emily."

"I try to be," Emily said, looking to her mother for approval. "Will Penelope ever return?" Emily asked.

"Not until she marries Evan," Mrs. Howell admitted.

"I can hardly wait to see her again," Emily said truthfully. "Imagine, Evan becoming a father under any circumstances and married too!"

All but Michael found amusement in Emily's words. They shared a hearty chuckle. It soothed Emily's mind to hear her friend's, kept so far from her, were all right. She thought of her letter, waiting for her to finish it upstairs. Now she would wait until bedtime, knowing the Howell's would stay for dinner. Despite her good feelings, nervous angst shook inside her heart, realizing that her family and Evan's still planned a future for them together until Penelope Dunworth disrupted the outcome. It proved a better affair than any of them knew and she felt thankful for it.

~

Evening fell over the torn up countryside of Maryland. Joseph undressed with only the light of a pale oil lamp on his table to guide him. He neatly folded his clothes, hung up his jacket and sat down in his undergarments to polish his boots. He lifted the shoes into his hands, studying the surface marred by dirt and scratches. They lasted longer than the last pair, but only because of his commanders who decided to hold his units back while they sent others to their deaths.

Joseph smirked at his thoughts. His frazzled mind coiled with anger. Evan told him to be thankful he had the grace of staying back. He would return home and marry his girl.

Joseph picked up his shoe brush and polish. Setting to work, he thought about the woman he left behind. He was thankful he never took his claim of her. If he had, he would most likely be in Evan's predicament. He shook his head, feeling awful that Evan and the young woman need suffer so over one moment. Joseph scuffed the brush across the toe of his boot and tried to forget, but knew only one solution could ease his mind.

Though his heart suffered afterwards, writing letters home to Emily still soothed his restlessness. He wanted to court her like a proper gentleman should and prayed the war would end every moment of the day. He lived merely from the drive to see her, to feel once again livened by her true lovely tones, instead of the photograph's deadpan gray. He sought the sound of her voice, tickling his ears from the confines of his memory. He realized he nearly forgot the sweet melody. Instead, he heard the cadence of artillery.

The war ruined many lives, Joseph's included. He saw it firsthand among his units and among the others stationed there. In the eye of ever soldier, he saw the families torn apart, waiting in suspension for a fated end. The pain in his heart left him to wonder if the United States was honestly worth the effort. He loved his country, but loved his family more.

Joseph reminded himself of the reason they stood on the battlefield. This war was more than the right of a state to decide what laws and rules its citizens adhered to. Washington usually allowed such before the war. The true matter contended on that ground came in the form of those men not created equal in the eyes of others, but argued equal under the precepts of the Constitution. When the Federal Government tried to end the institution of slavery, their conglomerate of states balked. They vehemently declared it was the right of their people to decide and they meant to defend it. Joseph heard the ring of the forefathers in those words, but would not back it up. He would not use a document guaranteeing rights to all men as a means to keep some bonds, merely to serve him cheaply.

While Joseph sat alone in his tent, preparing to lay down for the night, he paused listening to the distant sound of boot steps. The tent flap opened behind him and he saw the ebony head of his comrade. Joseph knew it was Evan. No one else dare walk in on him. He would serve trespassers a fist in the mouth or worse.

Joseph faced Lieutenant Howell with a sullen expression. Evan tried to do his best to keep the Captain from losing heart. He offered Joseph a smile and sat in the spare folding chair. He set a bottle of whiskey down on the table, an arms length from the side of the tent he occupied. Joseph watched him and smiled for the gift. The last time he saw Kentucky bourbon was nearly a year ago, in Mr. Conrad's study.

"Thought you might like that," Evan said. "Thanks to McGuire. He smuggled it for me."

"I did not hear that," Captain Maynard said, sitting on his cot. "Nor do I see it."

Joseph pushed the blushing paper on the table aside and found a pair of glasses for them to drink from. He opened the bottle and poured.

Evan watched him carefully. He saw the letter when he entered and recalled the tear filled gaze, peering back at him from a rough mirror pinned to the back post of Joseph's tent. The tears still stood in Joseph's eyes when he faced him. Evan ignored the signs and accepted his glass of whiskey with a grand smile and thanks. Joseph raised his glass to him and drank the first glass in one large gulp. Evan eyed him, finally understanding how bad he was. He held his glass, watching Joseph take up the letter and fold it back into its envelope. He lifted the lid of his trunk, set between them like a coffee table and simply put it where he kept the others. Closing the lid, Joseph poured more whiskey, leaned back and put his feet up on the old blackened trunk. He looked more than tired, but tired was the only thing he could feel then, if Evan knew him well.

"How's Em?" Evan finally built up the courage to ask, sitting back in his chair. He drank some whiskey, but not so fast as the Captain. His eyes went to the top of the tent, a dirty dingy gray now. Every time he spied it, the tent looked older and dirtier than the last, as if dragged through the muck on their way to the next camp. "Any news?"

"She's fine," Joseph said. "Mary gets on well and she says the bull is nearly full grown now. The farm prospers and her brother will return within the month. This letter will barely precede him."

"You don't say! I can't wait to see the old boy," Evan smiled.

"Fine," Joseph said bitterly, not listening. "Everything's fine."

Evan eyed him. The fight had gone out of the last man who had that look. Evan drank the rest of the whiskey in his glass. He tasted it and poured another. He would bring whatever remained of Joseph home to Emily in the end. Now, he once more had something to live for.

"Is this about Mac?" Evan asked, feeling warmed and strong from the drink already.

"At this point—I don't care who the damn general is, as long as this ends soon," Joseph rasped. "And I don't see anyone doing it but him."

"Losing him makes me nervous," Evan admitted.

"Everything makes ya nervous," Joseph smiled.

"I was just getting used to him," Evan drank his whiskey. "That's all."

❧

Cold settled around the North and Emily felt familiar longing in her heart, reflecting the desolation of November. She suffered the same emotion a long time ago, but Joseph chased it off with his arrival come March. Emily climbed the stairs to the cupola, carrying her letter from her hero. She sat beside the window and read. Come February and March, who would chase the clouds away?

Time turned to the gloaming of evening. Rain streaked the windows, pinging against the glass. Emily stared over the hillsides, dreaming of her far off love. The cupola became her refuge, distanced from the excitement, which rushed through the house. No one bothered her there. Tonight, they were busy with other things. Between the first two floors, preparations for Michael's return went on. He needed to pack soon and leave on a train early the next morning. He returned to the war. Nothing, not even Mary, could have stopped him. He was a brave or foolish man. Emily could not decide which.

Outside in the rain, Emily saw Mary walk beside her brother. Michael carried an umbrella above their heads. Emily touched the glass, wiping away the fog to see more clearly. She noticed her brother stepped strongly without the use of his cane. She watched them disappear behind the workhouses, up the dirt road that lead to the gardens, with Phoebe not far behind. She knew exactly what would be said.

Picking up her letter, she wandered down the stairs and went back to her bedroom. She must write Joseph before tomorrow and send the message with her brother. Sitting at her bureau, she took out her writing tools and paper, but paused. Picking up the envelope, which contained Joseph's last message, she breathed in the smell of the paper, wondering if he lingered among the scents. An ink fingerprint lay on the seam. She ran a tremulous hand over it. She could not remember how he smelled.

Emily set the letter on the top of her bureau, smoothing it. She sniffed and tears spilled from her eyes. She cried not just for Joseph, but the young woman in her garden, bidding farewell to Michael. She wondered how much suffering would be enough to see the war ended.

Wiping the tears from her eyes, Emily attended the need for her letter. She set her inkwell on the bureau and took up her pen. With one last swipe to her cheeks, she set to her most enjoyed duty of the day. When she wrote, it often felt that she sat talking with him.

Emily wondered if Joseph would ever receive the letter or if something would happen before Michael reached wherever they were. Forcing the tired old fears from her head, she told herself nothing would happen. He would come home, marry her and take her back to Frederick to start their family. With a heavy sigh, she dipped her pen and then scrawled her thoughts. She had to believe that.

14th of November 1862
My Joseph,
It took your letter longer to reach me this time. Is anything wrong? You probably have been moving around too much to write me. . .

We're quite busy tonight on the farm. I'm only glad for the work. It helps fill the empty days. We prepare for both winter and Michael's leaving.

I can't say if my brother loves your sister or not, he swore my secrecy. Being a trustworthy young woman, I gave my promise and intend to keep it. I see that they're only friends as we've all become here. My mother included.

Mother took an extra special shine to your sister. Perhaps it helps her amend the way she treated you. I feel sure now that she'll mend her error when you return. We get along much better. She apologized, but things are still strained underneath. I think she now understands our relationship and knows she cannot stop what will happen. It is God's will. . .

Hettie sends her prayers to you and mine also come with this letter.

Love Forever, Your Emily

By late November, the coming winter failed to bring an end to the war. It seethed with apathy and the army and life moved slower. It appeared for then time was weary and sought to rest, only forced to move unyieldingly forward.

Wrapped in a gray mantle of leafless trees and yellowed grasses, Virginia looked different to Michael. He gazed about the trail from the back of his borrowed horse, thinking over the train ride south and the excitement he felt at returning. Now he felt apprehension. However, the doctor saw him fit to serve and he must comply with the orders of his superiors. He had driven hard to reinstate his commission and return he must.

Guided by a lanky stone faced sergeant, Michael eventually discovered the hiding place of the Army he left behind. The man led him along the packed dirt road and out into a wide field, once farmland by the look of it. Michael paused in awe. His eyes scanned the tent city.

"There you are, sir," the man spoke the first words since hello. He saluted Michael.

"Thank you, Sergeant," Michael responded. "Fine job."

Saluting the enlisted man, Michael heeled his mount back into motion and rode toward the line of graying white tents. Men and animals came into focus among the smoking scene. He drew a deep breath, thinking again that he could return home and make the doctor claim him unfit for service. Shaking off hesitation, Michael entered the lane cut in the ground between the tents, a worn path of beaten down grass.

Michael's eyes took in the scene with both dread and longing, competing within him. He would face battle soon enough and he hoped he remembered how to shoot a rifle or even the pistol at his side. He smiled at the faces turning up to him as he passed. He felt foolish and out of place among the men there. No one recognized him.

Drawing further into the camp, Michael sought the tent he remembered from vague memory. Just like the first time, he stopped and begged directions of the more knowing soldiers that stayed in his absence. They directed him with a point down the lane. Michael thanked them properly and returned their salutes. Guiding his mount the rest of the way, he traversed the maze of tents and messes to find Joseph's tent set beside Evan's as always, within a stone's throw of the mess tent. It was like his first days all over again.

Michael smiled and dismounted. He walked the rest of the way, holding the sight of his friends milling around, oblivious to his presence. The fears ebbed and he only found the longing to stand back among them, not worrying about a single rifle.

"Michael Conrad—as I live an breathe," a voice called to him.

Michael turned to see Sergeant McGuire, waddling his way. His face beamed rosy and he smiled broadly. Michael stopped and greeted him a friend, forgoing the usual propriety due an officer. The man took his hand in his thick fists and they shook. McGuire patted his arm and looked him over. Michael looked around his shoulder for Sergeant Fergus.

"How've you been?" Michael asked. "Where's Fergus?"

"Oh—jus fine, lad. Ya needn't a come back, but wur glad ta ave ya now ya come. Did ya appen ta bring that er beautiful sister a yers?" he said, falling to wheezing laughter.

"You haven't changed a bit, Sergeant," Michael smiled at him. "Where's the Captain?"

"Feedin' his harse," McGuire said, pointing to the rope and stake corral where they kept them. "Ya might wan ta ask him about your unit."

Michael looked around and saw the company horses corralled together. His blonde still stood among them. He thought the Army would take it for another man. Joseph's legs moved among them near the satin black stallion. He smiled slightly and then looked back to McGuire. He decided not to press the man about Fergus, guessing what had happened. He would miss him.

"Come. Let's go see um. I warn ya, he's been in a dark mood a late," McGuire urged him forth. "P'raps seein ya will fix that."

"Might—since I brought a message from my sister," Michael said. He pulled out the envelope to show him.

"Ahh—good. Good," McGuire laughed. "He needs some a that."

Michael approached the corral and found Captain Maynard in a dark mood, just as McGuire described. However, Joseph managed a smile and welcome for his friend. Michael wasted no time in handing the letter from Emily to him. He bore it like a gift, knowing the healing it offered.

Joseph was glad to see Michael's friendly face, though he preferred he would have stayed at home with his family, before he got himself killed and made Joseph responsible for it. He never told him of the promise he made his sister. He thought Michael might erupt with anger if he heard Emily held no faith in him. He warily eyed the note.

"She wrote it the night before I left," Michael told him. Joseph ran his thumb down his name. Michael patted his arm. "Good to see you again, Joseph," Michael said when he looked up. The man barely uttered two words. It reminded him of his guide. "I'll tell you about my trip later," he smiled. "I want to get unpacked and settled in. Unless we're moving?" Joseph shook his head no. "Good," Michael said and went to turn away. "You can brief me on my unit later. Uh, Cap—one other thing," at this he took on a devious expression. "I want you to consider us even."

"Even for what?" Joseph said in confusion. He squinted at him, smiling back.

"I'm sure you'll find out sooner or later, my friend," Michael's smile turned roguish. After all Joseph put him through, he would enjoy this.

Joseph regarded him with confusion for a moment more, and then shook his head, looking away. He placed his hands on his hips and adjusted his feet where they stood. When his gaze returned he received a salute and Michael dismissed himself, still smiling broadly. Joseph watched him go, giving a halfhearted return to the gesture. He thought hard about what his friend said. He remained, standing with his hands on his hips, thinking it over. Joseph's eyes lowered to the envelope in his hands. He smiled. Then, he laughed. The author of that letter was the contested matter. However, he found no answer to why Michael thought the matter settled, unless Emily said something. Perhaps Michael simply meant his leg.

Joseph's face quickly straightened. He lifted his scruffy chin and peered after the Second with hard cold eyes. He watched Michael's telltale saunter and recalled his arrogant smile. He acted that way after meeting Emily. Putting his letter in his pocket, Joseph gave pursuit. His sister stayed in that house for over a month by then.

"Michael!" Joseph roared at his back. "So help me!" He followed him through the camp of white tents. "I'll tear your damn legs off."

Michael laughed and turned back to face the Captain. Joseph's angry gaze made him wonder if he looked that way when he had discovered the relationship between the Captain and his sister. Something about Joseph's state of mind and stature made it more worrisome.

Joseph's dark eyes flashed green fire. He opened his mouth to speak, but the words he wanted to say fell powerless on his tongue. He seethed inside, unable to balance friendship and family. He took less than kindly to any man using his baby sister to even a score with him, over whatever imagined wrongs they held, but what if Michael truly cared about Mary?

"Nothing like that, Captain." Michael held up his hands, trying to soothe him.

"Nothing like what?" Joseph reiterated, not so sure the boy meant well. "Clarify for me a little, Second Lieutenant," Joseph demanded, wavering between smiles and sneers in a manner that defined his dilemma.

"I think the world of Mary," Michael answered. "You've no idea."

"I can imagine," Joseph said, stepping closer for a fight. "Many men have been beaten black and blue for looking at that girl the wrong way. If you've so much as—"

"I've been no less honorable than you," Michael assured him, quoting the words that he received after he asked the same question. He stepped back, intimidated.

"It'd not bother me to shoot you for her honor," Joseph said flatly with a maniacal grin.

"Nor would it me, for Emily," Michael said, holding his ground now.

"Keep a decent distance from my sister, Second Lieutenant Conrad. She's no plaything for you to discard when you grow weary of her charms," Joseph told him, putting a hard finger to the junior officer's chest. "I gave you fair warning. I will not hold myself accountable for the actions I take if you don't."

"We are even," Michael reiterated slowly. "As I said before," Michael looked boldly into his superior's smoldering eyes. "I gave you fair warning about Emily. I didn't expect the same to hold less true with your own sister."

Joseph offered him a raw glare. He turned on his booted heals and stalked off. He would not let this episode with his sister get the best of him. More than likely, Michael wanted revenge for his own sister. He probably blew smoke in the eyes and nothing more. He would write to her to find out for himself. Until then, he planned to continue grooming his horse to smooth his nerves back down, before he pummeled Michael to death and found himself with a court martial.

Within the course of days, the affront Joseph felt faded to dull annoyance and his mind turned to other more important matters. While Michael familiarized himself back to the life of an officer of the United Sates Federal Army, Joseph tried to grow used to the new leader he served in that same army. General Burnside was a familiar character that Joseph fought under the command of on other occasions. The General led their company amid several ruined battles, which Washington blamed McClellan for. Joseph dreaded this change, knowing who was truly responsible. He knew Burnside would drag his feet, even without Mac to support his apathy. This meant a longer road to the conclusion of the war and the beginning of his life. It would make a hard road for all the men of the Potomac.

The matter worsened when Burnside again displayed his incapability to lead. In December, the Union Army faced a difficult period of watching and waiting. Unable to maneuver around obstacles, Burnside predictably delayed. In the meantime, engineers constructed bridges for a supply path over ravines and rivers. Joseph could not understand the master plan behind the construction in the dead of winter. He wondered what tactical advantage Burnside believed he would gain from this insanity. No failure McClellan accomplished was as appalling as this. If only Washington would realize the same.

"Joe—Captain," a sullen voice called to him where he sat alone, finishing his coffee in the mess tent by a warm stove.

Joseph looked up to see Michael enter warily. His face hung in shadow, but not from the roof of the tent or the overcast day. Joseph set his tin cup on the rickety table. He waited for Michael to continue.

"Yes, Second Lieutenant," Joseph said when Michael held his tongue, stressing rank.

Michael reluctantly stepped closer, pulling his hat from his head. He lifted his sunken blue eyes back to Joseph's face. He stammered a few times and paused again. Joseph laughed and shook his head. He took another sip from his cup.

"You should know that I don't plan to kill you yet," Joseph told him. "I still need you and as long as you're here, I know my sister is safe."

"That's not it," Michael said. He eyed Joseph and Joseph eyed him back. "I received a message from my father today."

"Usually those things offer good news," Joseph said sarcastically.

"Not this one," Michael told him.

"Is it Emily?" Joseph asked suddenly concerned.

"No—thanks for that at least," Michael advanced to where Joseph sat and gave him the letter from home. "I can't speak," Michael explained, half laughing.

"What could be that bad, Second?"

"Read the second paragraph," Michael directed him.

Joseph read the second paragraph as his subordinate directed. His eyes swept over the words casually, quickly turning troubled with what they saw. He lowered the page, drawing a deep breath through his nose. He looked to Michael and found the younger man unable to look at him in return. Joseph's head ached.

"How do we tell Evan?" Michael groaned. He dropped hard on the bench with his back to Joseph. "I can't tell him."

"I'll tell him," Joseph said. He stood, taking up his hat from the back of the chair.

"He meant to make good on his mistake." Michael shook his head and watched Joseph step past him, "You're going to tell him now?"

"I don't believe waiting would be suitable," Joseph said gruffly. "I don't want to explain why we said nothing when he gets a letter from his father."

Michael looked at the dirty canvas of the mess tent. His eyes looked distant and angry. Joseph's shadow cast over him and he looked to see the Captain exit. Michael jumped to his feet, casting all conflict behind him. The moment called for their utter solidarity. When Evan was settled, they could return to the matter of their sisters.

The walk to the Lieutenant's tent took longer than any time Michael or Joseph remembered. They stepped with determination, their eye on the gray shelter. Neither considered he may possibly be absent. Instead, they ran words repeatedly through their minds, preparing for the moment they would speak them.

"Lieutenant Howell," Joseph called out, stopping in front of the closed entrance.

"Enter," Evan called back. His voice sounded strangely normal, as if it should have shook with the knowledge they had.

Joseph cast a glance back to Michael, hesitating to enter as Evan bid. He waved a hand to Michael, urging him forward with him. He flipped the tent canvas back and ducked into the narrow space beyond. Evan stood in the center, fixing his uniform. His dark eyes lifted to Joseph and he smiled welcoming him.

"Good morning, Captain."

"Good morning, Lieutenant," Joseph returned, taking a quick study of the interior. A letter lay open on his table. "Would you sit down, please?" Joseph asked, holding his hand out to the cot.

"Sure," Evan responded, casting his eyes to Michael who entered behind Joseph. "What is it?" Evan asked, looking up at them from his seat on his bed. "Did Donnelly finally approve my leave? It'd be better than never."

Both Michael and Joseph sat down on the spare chairs. They looked to Evan with sympathetic gazes. When he stopped speaking, Evan showed a measure of understanding. His eyes flicked between Joseph and Michael, waiting for what he guessed they would say.

"Mr. Conrad sent a letter to Michael," Joseph said. "It's about Miss Dunworth, Evan."

"Did she have the baby?"

"No," Joseph said, looking to Michael for help.

"Penny got sick back in October," Michael explained. He watched Evan's chin drop. "Father said she never recovered," He continued. "She wasn't strong enough."

"Penelope and your baby," Joseph finished. "They passed away during the birth."

Evan drew a hard breath, "What was it? What did we have?"

"A boy," Joseph rasped. "You had a boy," he repeated.

Evan lowered his head into his hands, weeping like a child. Joseph watched him, feeling his heart beat slowly for several tense moments. His eyes lowered to the ground beneath his friend's cot. He discovered himself lost to understand the pain Evan felt and the fear of it rose. Joseph found it hard to breath.

"Captain," Michael said. "I think we should leave."

"No," Joseph said. "If it were me, I'd thank my friends to stand by." Joseph reached out and touched Evan's knee with the tip of a finger. "Whatever you need," he said. "Just ask."

"I didn't have a chance to make it right," Evan sobbed. "She died with the stain on her soul that I put there—my son wasn't even born innocent."

"None of us are," Joseph told him. Joseph slid to the edge of his chair and patted Evan's shoulder. "Let's drink this off," he suggested.

"I want them buried with my name," Evan growled.

"I'll send a telegram," Michael whispered.

Evan looked at Joseph with red eyes. His tears slid down his cheeks unhindered. He swallowed hard, feeling the world spin round him. He pictured Penelope's face, smiling at him when they met again at the dance. He saw her passion filled eyes in the dim room upstairs away from the party. He could almost feel her ebony curls between his fingers and her body pressed to his. His heart trembled and he lowered his chin to his hands, shielding mouth with his hands. He shook with the agony of his misfortune.

The arrival of the holidays brought a longing for the old ways before the war. Despite these feelings, the Federals would not see home until the South was defeated and that likelihood reduced with each loss they took. The men held an air of depression, appearing as a bunch of miserable vagabonds haphazardly tied together to fight.

The only manner in which to feel a whole human came from lifeless sheets of paper, holding the flourishes of meandering thoughts. Each soldier exchanged letters by some unseen bureaucracy to their absent loved ones in the hope of remembering why they served their country. After so long a time, indeed they needed a reminder. Their hopes fell to dust each day they failed to achieve their goal. Joseph's thoughts since visiting Vermont had remained among its fields and farms, but he owed a duty to his blood kin too. Joseph constructed his letters, granting holiday well wishes to the only important addresses in his whole list. His parents headed the line, after being cast aside for so long.

December 3, 1862

Dear Maynards,

I send all my wishes for a Happy Holiday season. It saddens me that we cannot all be together during these special days, but know I think of you always. . .

Mother, I find it especially difficult to write home, wondering how beautiful our home will look dressed for the season. Will you make the pudding I like so much?

What I wouldn't give to have some. When I return home you'll just need to keep some waiting for me. . .

When Joseph finished his letter home, he wrote a short holiday note to the Conrads. He thanked them once again for taking Mary into their home and into their hearts. Without them, his younger sister would have suffered the southern invasion and the attentions of a soldier who unworthily sought her hand and would seek any means to gain it. Joseph called them guardian angels, alighted on earth to ease men of their difficulties.

With the last duty of respect completed, Joseph took out fresh sheets of letterhead and pushed the envelopes, containing his previous letters, aside. He hunkered down in his tent, feeling the fragile heat of his small stove as it battled the chill of winter. He tried to sketch a bright note to his jewel despite the bleak setting. Not long after he started the letter, his heart ached with the pain of what kept him so far from Emily at Christmas. More than anything, he wished to lay down his gun, take up the reins of his horse and ride north. He often dared to hope it might come to pass, but as he sat there he knew it impossible. He would not abandon his duty and leave would not be granted.

All the paper in the world could not hold all the sentiments Joseph wished to share. Since the army strictly rationed the paper supply and his own grew limited as well, he conserved his ideas to a few pages.

December 3, 1862

Dear Emmy,

I won't bore you with details of my military woes. I feel assured from your previous letters that you hear enough. I want my letters to fill your heart with happiness in my absence. And, though I am absent, I wish you a bright and happy Christmas. You should know I'll sit at your side in spirit since I am unable to come in person. If only I could see your face when you receive the package I sent you. I hope you like it. I discovered the mystery item in one of the charming towns we marched through. Remember. Don't open the box until Christmas. It is a gift for the holiday. Promise? I know you'll be excited the moment you receive it. . .

Michael serves us better than before he left. I wonder at times just what about Vermont makes you heal so well. What did your family do to him up there? Maybe we should send all of our wounded to you. Your mother would certainly not care for me then!

How are things on the farm? With winter you must have little to do again. Our fields will lay covered in snow. The garden, too. Do you still take walks out there? I had a dream last night. It was late with only the moonlight to show the way. I found you in the garden. You turned to me with this smile. I felt more alive than in months. I couldn't help but. . .

It will be so good to see your face again. I send you all of my love, Emmy. I wish I could be there. Someday soon. . .

After Joseph folded the last letter into an envelope and set it on his table with the others, he woke from the fog it left him in. He drew a deep breath. The realities of war loomed in every direction, from the tent walls to the coal stove. The wind blew and he felt the chill of the winter cool his skin. He shivered.

Joseph took up his quilt from where it lay folded on top of his trunk. He wrapped it around his shoulders and stared at the ground. Watching his breath, he tried to convince himself that someday soon all these trials would fall to the past. It little helped to warm his freezing body then. Joseph closed his eyes and tried to rest them from the worn sight of the military camp. He listened to guns in the distance, always firing. The cadence of death left him to wonder if he could find sleep without it.

"Captain—" Evan's voice roused him from his troubled rest.

"Come in," Joseph said morosely, standing from his chair. He dropped his blanket from his shoulders onto the cot and replaced it with his uniform coat.

Lieutenant Howell entered, flipping open the loose canvas flap that closed Joseph inside. He smiled, but his features looked no brighter than the Captain's. Scrubbing a hand through his raven locks, he took to the spare chair.

Evan looked up at the Captain. He stood, buttoning his coat over a grayed white shirt. His eyes lowered, noticing the wear in his pants and the dull dusty appearance of his boots. Evan stuck his polished boot out. The Joseph of the old days usually replaced his tattered belongings with new finer garments and always kept his boots polished. Evan lounged in his chair, crossing his arms. He lifted his eyes to Joseph's unshaved face. Even the beard looked a bit let go. His heart skipped with worry.

"The men made dinner. If you want any," Evan told him.

"Yeah," Joseph said, forcing a smile to his lips. He smoothed his jacket. "I'll be right there," he added, sweeping his eyes toward the opening of the tent. He saw Michael's legs dance back in forth in the gloom beyond. "Second Lieutenant," Joseph drawled apathetically. "You may come in, unless you prefer eavesdropping."

"Michael told me about Mary," Evan grinned before Michael entered.

Michael stepped inside the tent and glared at him. Evan chuckled and looked to Joseph. He figured mentioning loved ones would lighten his friend's heart some. However, he saw it made no difference. Evan brushed his hand across his leg, ridding of imaginary dust. He felt uncomfortable with the Captain in such a sour mood.

"He probably told you more than me, Lieutenant." Joseph said, looking at the Second Lieutenant sternly.

"Want me to help you kill him?" Evan smiled.

"Not that again," Michael whined.

Joseph smiled, picking up his hat from the hook with his wool cloak. An edge of anger accented his features with a glint of warning in his eye. A sister's honor gave many a man reason to fight on. Perhaps Joseph needed that other reason to live. Evan and Michael both watched him place the hat on his head and the cloak on his back. He finished and looked to them expectantly.

"Just tease him about Em," Evan said playfully. "That'll straighten em out," he added while, rising to his feet. He slapped the back of his hand on Michael's chest, humoring only himself. "Like that time in the garden."

"What're we having, Lieutenant?" Joseph said with a reproachful expression.

Evan saw his joke fall flat between his comrades. He straightened his jacket and his face, "Daniels made his stew, I think." He followed Joseph into the cold evening, "Whatever it is—it smells good."

Joseph said nothing. He felt hungry enough to eat a dead horse. Besides, the comment Evan made left him more skinned than his letter writing. Since Michael's return, the matter of brotherhood turned to conflict between them. It made him sick to think that he lost a friend to differences neither of them could move past, even though they faced death every day.

Joseph lowered his head to his hand, thinking of how terrible he behaved. He was not interested in destroying their friendship. He knew Michael and knew the kind of man he was. He rubbed his temples as his head throbbed. For so long, Joseph fought off suitors for his sister's hand. Now, he would need to let Mary decide for herself.

"Michael," Joseph said. He stopped walking and looked at the younger man, putting his hand on his shoulder. "I need to say—"

"No need," Michael said, grinning. "Me too. I know how you feel. Em and all."

Joseph nodded with an inaudible response. He smiled slightly and patted Michael's shoulder. Following a brief pause, Michael held his hand out to him and they shook. The hostility died that moment. After all, they had no time to carry on like boys. Both men smiled.

"Destined to become brothers—damn touching," Evan said. He walked into them, putting his arm around both and pushed them forward to the officer's mess tent. "But—I'm hungry, so let's eat, ya damn daisies!"

The matter between Joseph and Michael was resolved. However, the matter of North and South raged as heated as ever. Joseph reflected on the early December battles, several days after one of the worst defeats of his career. In his memory, the Potomac faced the Confederacy in an uneasy clash. Again, the same faces looked at them over the lines, wearing dour expressions. Except for the color of their uniform, the enemy appeared no different from Joseph's comrades. Did the Federals have the right to win this war justified by self-righteousness?

By the end of the battle, the Confederate Army reclaimed their honor, serving them as many casualties as they took months prior on Maryland soil. Joseph knew this meant the dismissal of their newest commander. He was unmoved when the order indeed came through, until he learned who would replace General Burnside. Both shock and anger competed for position in his heart. He still pined for Little Mac and the comfort the commander once loaned when seated above him. However, Burnside granted still more misery before he took his leave.

Joseph observed the infantry march on foot through the freezing rain, through the mud of the riverbank, retreating over the water and giving into failure. The Rappahannock flowed by gray green with chunks of ice mixed in it. Beside his men who rode on weary mounts, artillery and wagons stood with their wheels stuck deep in the mud. He looked with anger to the men who tried to force their cannon out, but his hatred was meant for another.

Laying under the blankets of his cot and wrapped in the pathetic heat of his tent, Joseph fought to dismiss the memories of the cold rain. Joseph wondered if he woke to the reality of springtime and the winter had gone no more than a hopeless nightmare. Not even the whiskey he took favor to drink touched the iciness. It stood hard in his stomach and churned it like a wild ocean. Joseph rolled over and shut his eyes, but they opened again. He wanted to blot out the vision of the damned tent he lived in for nearly three years. He hated it and everyone associated. He squeezed his eyes shut tight, daring Lieutenant Howell to step inside and mention Emily right then. He hated even her, for staying in her comfortable home and sending him words of encouragement to see him through. A tear of regret seeped from the corner of his eye.

Joseph's hand reached to his neck and pulled out a fragile silver chain. On the end dangled one half of a delicate oval locket, engraved with pale letters. He read them. I love you. His eyes stared at the words, reading them several times, reminding him exactly how he felt and why he despaired Christmas day. A feeling of utter discouragement pervaded throughout the troops, magnified in light of the holiday season. Christmas turned into a dismal event, gray and stark with its joyless arrival. It haunted Joseph's mind with unwanted thoughts of those who would now never enjoy time with their families. He counted himself among those not to return, believing he was a dead man with a meager excess of allotted time.

With Emily's words repeating in his mind to defeat his despair, Joseph fell asleep at last. In the dark of his dreams he saw Rebels jeer him and his fellow soldiers, as they embarrassed themselves all their efforts. His mind at last went blank and then he woke to the dawn and another new order.

In days, the new year would ring the freedom of the men he stood there fighting to guarantee rights for. Dressing and preparing for breakfast, Joseph wondered what the new commander of the Potomac would do first to finish the fight between the states. He hardly thought Joseph Hooker belonged among them. He heard of his reputation and thought such a man would fail at leading them, just like the rest. Of course, those of better repute performed no more than extended marches in wide circles and the slow torturous murder of the army. Time would prove the General's plans.

Joseph swallowed his pride, realizing he held no power and could not be blamed for what took place. He left his tent to join his subordinates. From that moment forth, he vowed to work his commission like any other job and hoped to just survive it.

"Lincoln's paying a visit to check on the boys of the Potomac," Evan said somewhat derisively, as approached Joseph from the lane between their tents. He was dressed and wide awake, already carrying out duties by that time.

Joseph turned to look at him, "The President?" Evan set his lips in a thin line. "We're not ready for this."

"I know," Evan said. "Thought I'd get to you before Donnelly. He's out for blood this morning already." He paused, eyeing Joseph carefully. "I'll see to the units. Eat your breakfast, sir." Evan paused eyeing him. "You might want to trim that thing up a bit," he indicated the beard that was becoming untamed. Joseph glared at him. "Just a suggestion."

Joseph grit his teeth and thought of all the tasks he had to perform before Lincoln's visit. Least of his worries was grooming his beard. Joseph watched Evan salute him and stand there, waiting for a return. He caught himself and shifted his hand to his brow sharply. Evan lowered his hand to his side slyly grinning. He watched his friend pivot on his booted heel and leave back towards the enlisted tents. Evan held the company together while he fell apart, throwing himself into his commission with both feet since his tragedy. Joseph lowered his eyes to the ground, adding guilt to the list of sore feelings. He couldn't even manage to look decent.

Joseph ate his breakfast with the other straggling officers that morning and returned to his tent to find Michael, waiting with a report on Evan's progress. The news brightened his mood, easing his concerns. The men would be ready for the visit, hours before it would take place. With murmured thanks, he dismissed the Second Lieutenant to his duties and ducked in his tent to prepare himself.

After redressing in his finest uniform and snapping himself back into the shape of earlier days, Joseph reported to Colonel Donnelly and gave their progress. The man seemed distracted with other matters. He listened for three sentences, stuck his hand out for the written report, which Michael had scratched down quickly, and dismissed him to his preparations. Joseph swallowed hard and eyed him. He wanted to speak, but thought the better of it. He stiffly saluted and left to find his officers and their units.

Around noon, Joseph led his spit and polished company to the field around the camp. They drew up in tight formation. Joseph held himself in line with his other officers. Evan and Michael sat mounted to his right, shaking in their boots while the President ran his examination. They stared out across the dead grass fields to the tree line, avoiding direct eye contact with anyone. Their mouths lay in straight hard lines, unmoving for fear of reprimand. An icy breeze blew down the line and the sound of carriage wheels came to his ears. Joseph's eyes darted up the line of horses.

An open hansom pulled by fine black Morgans, drew the President and his men by the lines of soldiers. Joseph held his breath when the carriage slowly neared. Joseph saw the tall hat of the commander in chief, sticking above the others. Lincoln towered over everyone in height and rank. It was odd to see him as a simple man out for a ride. He was the leader of their country and held all these soldiers' lives in his hands.

When Lincoln passed under Joseph's gaze, he stared the President into memory. He looked thin like a rifle, tall like a tree and dark like the night. He had an intimidating appearance, thin wrinkled skin stretched over his thin bones. His broad hands resembled paddles. In his eyes, he held the same shadow as the soldiers he inspected. Joseph looked back to the field before him.

"That weren't so bad," Evan whispered, not moving.

"Quiet," Joseph hissed, not looking. "It isn't over till we're dismissed," Joseph warned.

"Yes, sir."

Horse hooves sounded on the ground and Donnelly came to Joseph, facing him with a dark expression. Joseph saluted him and Donnelly returned the gesture with a narrowing gaze. The other men followed the example. The Colonel eyed them and looked back to Joseph.

"Company," he said darkly. "Dismissed."

"Fall out!" Joseph cried, turning his mount first.

Evan rode next to him back to the camp and Michael trotted up to his other side. Joseph tried to ignore them, drawing a deep calming breath. He felt raw.

"It's going to be a long winter," Joseph spat.

"Already has been," Evan agreed.

"If it ever ends," Michael added starkly.

Following the inspection, Joseph led his men to where Lincoln planned an address for the Union forces. He hoped to raise morale. By all accounts, they needed it. Reaching the lines of men who waited for the President's speech, Joseph and his officers dismounted. The Corporal and a knot of privates took the mounts, meaning to tend them in their owners' absence.

Once the officers lined the inner circle and the enlisted men filled in behind, Mr. Lincoln stepped to a raised podium. Placing a pair of wire rimmed glasses on his more than adequate nose, he read his speech. Joseph remembered little of what he said, struck with awe by the frail figure. He knew he stood witness to an important moment, but his thoughts wandered over the man's appearance again. Like many of those around him, he revered Lincoln as a god and he was confused by the figure he saw.

The grave voice of the President fell to silence among the applause and cheers of his soldiers. The commanders of the army presented themselves, blown up and preened for the occasion. They dismissed the gathering back to their daily duties in loud clipped voices. Joseph turned from them with Evan and Michael ever at his side. The three wandered back to where their tents waited, thankful for the conclusion.

Returned to the camp, Joseph parted from his companions and collected his mail from the Corporal who found them no matter where they were. With a small smile, Joseph freed the pink envelope from the rest. Emily always came through when he needed her.

Ducking under the canvas flap, he hid inside his tent to read.

Joseph sat on his cot, placing the other less important letters aside and looked at the pink envelope. It looked to have gone through its own battle, wrinkled and stained, the letters disfigured by some spill. He thought it reflected his image and sense of the war. He thanked God the letter reached him, knowing the same tattered old war that wreaked havoc on them threatened the postal system, as well. He did not want to know what it would be like without mail.

12th of December 1862

Dearest Joseph,

I just received the letter you wrote me on the third of December. The post takes longer lately. With the snow and ice up here, there is no wonder. Consider yourself lucky the temperature is all that freezes where you are. We lost the chickens in the bitterness. Father plans to buy new in the spring. At least they gave us something to eat and I finally got my wish to have the horrid rooster for supper. He won't give anyone his spurs again. I have to say, me and little Jo-Hanna are glad of it.

How does your family fair with you away at the holidays? I wish you stayed with us now. I can hardly imagine how your mother feels while my heart aches so. She must be strong, like you. Mary shows similar strength in the face of her despair. Your father decided to leave her here with us until after Christmas or even later. He fears a return of the southern forces. We civilians cannot guess Lee's next move. She hates the idea, but we persevere to make a good holiday for her.

Oh—and please don't worry over the matter of details you send. Nothing you tell me is boring, Joseph. I want you to always share your troubles. Don't be afraid to reveal a thing. I hope you've never spared me a single detail. I think it will help later, to understand what you've gone through, so your adjustment will not be so difficult. Besides, the newspaper leaves no imagining worse than you say.

How is my brother? He has not written yet. He sent a message to mother and father, but those letters hold none of what he wants to say. I know you said he is performing well, but how is he feeling? Perhaps I should ask Mary, since she's received mysterious letters at our home since his absence. I hope you are not fighting over the matter. After all, imagine how he felt when he discovered our secret. It's so romantic really.

The package you sent arrived with your letter. Mother put it in the music room with the tree and guards it from me with Hettie's help. I can hardly wait to open it, but it's only a few days now. I'm sure I'll love whatever you gave me. I thank you now, with a kiss.

My Christmas glows less bright for the absence in my heart. However, my family and friends pull together and I manage to smile for their sake. Knowing Mary suffers the same, I feel easier with a compatriot. I hope wherever you remain stationed, your Christmas is wonderful. Perhaps you will go home despite what they think. . .

Leave failed to come despite hopes and wishes. Like his men, Joseph remained miles away from home. The cheerless new year arrived soon after, more stark and cold. The artillery soldiers shot off rounds and they fired some pistols, passing drinks around to celebrate, but the underlying mood held on. They stood prisoner to duty while the slaves walked into long awaited freedom.

For New Year's Day, the farm seemed somber to Henrietta Benson. In the past, the celebration began from the moment she rose in the morning and ended only after midnight when they returned from the town hall dance. Rolling a pin over a batch of dough to make cinnamon rolls for breakfast, Hettie thought of what Mr. Conrad may have planned for them. Lifting the pin, she picked off the bits of dough sticking to it and put them back on the slab flattened on the floured table. Hettie drew a deep breath, studying her dusty fingers. Today marked the first day of her freedom, but no one noticed and nothing was different. She thought for sure something would have happened to mark the occasion.

Hettie lowered the pin and smoothed the dough again. The door in the back of the kitchen opened, admitting MaryJane. Hettie lifted her chin to see the girl better and MaryJane smiled at her. She went to the silver drawer in the hutch to gather the utensils for breakfast. Hettie watched the young girl work, wanting her to say something, but she remained silent at her task. Hettie sighed again.

"Did you get the linens?" Hettie asked MaryJane.

"Yes, Mrs. Benson," MaryJane replied with a little smile. "I used the gold set."

Hettie looked at her with her mouth half open to speak, but she forgot what she wanted to say. She knew the gold set as Mrs. Conrad's best. Hettie's lips bowed in a soft smile, feeling a measure of reassurance. Perhaps they meant to meet at breakfast with her. Setting the pin down, she picked up a knife and cut the strips for the rolls. Out of the corner of her eye, she saw MaryJane leave the room.

"Mrs. Benson," a small voice called from the hall doorway behind her.

Hettie looked to see little Jo-Hanna. She stepped in the kitchen carrying eggs, now delivered from outside the farm daily. Hettie stepped to her without hesitation and helped her out of her winter coat and hat. Jo-Hanna set the eggs on the table, just in time for the rest of the baking. Hettie used the last of their supply on the rolls.

"What are you making?" Jo-Hanna asked her, watching Hettie hang her coat and hat on a hook by the door. "I'm starving."

"Cinnamon buns," Hettie told her, coming back to the table. "You wanna make me the icing?"

"I can try," Jo-Hanna smiled. The little girl made Hettie remember her boy, probably the same age but hundreds of miles away, most likely not to shine his face in her life again. "I've never made it b'fore."

"It's simple," Hettie told her. "Come on over and sit."

Hettie gathered the items the girl needed. Jo-Hanna's big brown eyes watched her carefully and she listened to all that Hettie said with a reverent silence. Hettie returned to the table and smoothed a hand over her head, smiling warmly. She set a heavy but small stone bowl on the worktable and added a spoon that clattered on its inside. Jo-Hanna's eyes went to it.

"Now," Hettie said. "Y'all need some fresh cream, a bit of butter, and vanilla," Hettie added, settling those items on the table as well. "I'll get the sugar."

Hettie stepped to the pantry, lining the wall even with the hallway. She opened the heavy wooden door and stepped inside. Her booted feet made hollow sounds on the root cellar door beneath her. Looking over the shelves, she whispered the word sugar to herself repeatedly. Somehow the powdered sugar can hid from her eyes. Setting her expression with concern, worrying they owned none, Hettie touched her finger to her lips and scanned one last time.

In the door of the kitchen, between the worktable and the hallway, Jo-Hanna saw Mr. Conrad and his chief, Mr. Benson. Mr. Conrad held a green bottle with a fancy label and his companion clutched a fistful of flowers. Jo-Hanna smiled and giggled. They both entered quietly and the first placed a finger over his lips to quiet her. They smiled warmly and asked without words where Hettie kept herself. Jo-Hanna pointed to the pantry. She knew today was important from the buzz in the house.

"Ah—Henrietta," Mr. Conrad said, looking to the shadowy closet. He went to Hettie when she stepped out toward him, holding a round tin. "Mr. Benson brought you a present."

"Mr. Benson," Hettie said, warily eyeing her employer. She then saw the tiny old man step out from behind him. "Jack?"

"Here y'are, Missus Henrietta," Jack said with a gummy smile. "Congratcheations ta ya pon yur mancipation."

Jack held out a lovely bouquet of yellow flowers and ferns. Hettie's eyes went wide with surprise. She hesitated before accepting the gift. Her eyes filled with tears and she quickly set the tin on the table with a clink. Covering her mouth with her hand, she took the flowers from the old man and cried. She never received such a gift in all her life.

"They're beautiful," Hettie said, touching the blooms carefully. "Thank you, Jack," she added with a full heart. "They're mine," she whispered.

"At last you are free," Stuart smiled. "I brought you some champagne—you can save it for when your husband arrives, or drink it tonight at dinner."

"Mr. Conrad," Hettie said, taking the bottle he offered her. "I can't take this."

"Of course you can," Stuart said, tucking his hands behind his back. "I won't hear of you refusing our gift. Mrs. Conrad would be most upset."

"I bet she'd be mo upset losin a bottle a yur stock ta me," Hettie said, shoving the bottle toward him.

"She suggested it," Mr. Conrad said. He smiled at her.

Hettie turned the bottle to look at the label. She recognized it. Mr. Conrad kept it since she arrived there. He said he would use it on a special occasion soon enough, but not to open until he asked. He said the matter important. She always watched over that bottle, never realizing he meant to give it to her.

"Have ya heard anything back yet?" Hettie dared to ask, meaning her family.

"Not yet," Stuart admitted. "Soon I should think. I only just sent the letters. They must find their way to them." Stuart watched Hettie's expression fade to despair. "Oh-now, no tears for that. Have more faith. God will see them back to you unharmed. Just a little bit longer."

Hettie shook her head. She failed to find the right words to say to him and kept silent. Stuart stepped closer and gave her a fatherly hug, patting her back. She never knew her father and she almost despaired for that as well. It warmed her heart, knowing he meant to lend her some of his strength. Hettie smiled and blinked back her tears.

"I better get these in some water," Hettie said, parting from him.

Stuart chuckled letting her go. Before another moment passed, several footsteps clattered down the hall with a determined stride driving them. The occupants of the kitchen looked to the door to see who arrived. Emily swung in the room, still removing her hat from her outing with her mother and Mary.

"Good morning," Emily said to them. Her eyes went to Hettie and her treasures. "What's all this?" She asked already knowing.

"Mr. Benson brung me flowers," Hettie smiled almost blushing.

"They're lovely Jack," Emily told the old man. His old face turned crimson and he nodded. Emily approached her friend and put her arms around her. "I brought you something, too," She said, stepping back. She pulled a box from her skirt pocket. The ribbon and paper glistened like a Christmas bauble.

"For me?" Hettie asked. "We jus had Christmas, Emily," she added.

"Yes it is," Emily said. "It's never too early or late for presents." She paused. "Well—I hope you like it. I picked it out by myself."

Hettie reluctantly took the gift, "Thank you." Hettie reached out and drew the silver cameo onto her fingertips from Emily's neck. Joseph's Christmas gift went morning, noon and night with her. "If it's half as nice as this—I'll surely love it."

"Go ahead," Emily urged her on. "Open it. I can hardly wait."

Hettie pulled the silky bow and clawed the paper from the box. Carefully placing the wrapping aside, she took the top of the little box off and looked at the item within. A locket pin lay on a layer of blue satin, gold glinting around an enameled American flag. Delicately touching it, she gasped with tears springing to her eyes. She picked it up and held it, wanting to feel assured of its reality.

"Oh—Em!" Hettie gasped. "It's lovely."

"Turn it over," Emily said.

Hettie flipped the oval with her friend's help. On the back, a golden embossing of the President's head lie in profile and below was an engraving, which read Freedom 1863. Hettie rubbed a thumb over the engraving. She felt frozen, thinking of its meaning to her.

"I thought you should have something to mark this day," Emily smiled up at her with glinting sapphire eyes. "Something you could pass down to your grandchildren—or maybe a daughter."

Hettie reached out and crushed the young woman to her, "You always know what to do."

"Cause you taught me," Emily said warmly, holding her arms around Hettie's middle. "You're my best friend."

Hettie laughed, "Someone's got to be." She touched Emily's face and added teasingly, "Who else's gonna put up with you. Joseph?"

"I've still got my daddy," Emily played back.

They heard the men's laughter.

Hettie stepped back from the young woman and looked at her new pin with a smile. Tears ran down her cheeks and words again failed her. Her friends remembered, despite her doubt. Looking up, she wanted to thank them, but Mrs. Conrad entered the kitchen next, eyeing them with her usual pinched expression. Hettie hesitated and lost the chance.

"Happy New Year, Henrietta," Mrs. Conrad said.

"Happy New Year, Mrs. Conrad," Hettie said back.

"Congratulations, Hettie," Mary's voice lyrically filled the room. She dashed from the hall to Hettie's side at the sink. Her cheeks were bright pink from the cold January air. She smiled at the former slave and gave her a warm hug. "Here," she said offering her a gift as well.

"Miss Maynard," Hettie said. "You didn have ta go an do this." Hettie opened the gift and found a lovely pair of enameled earrings. "Thank you," she breathed, feeling a little speechless. She then offered more thanks to the others, filling the room. "This is all too much, really."

"I've news of my own," Mary said, placing her arm about Hettie's shoulders and facing her hosts. She decided to take the pressure off the woman at her side with her own news. She smiled at the gathered faces warmly. A letter arrived from home and the words it contained cheered her with hope. She fought for her words, lost in her excitement. "My father sent a letter," Mary finally said, grinning. "I'm to go home in February. Joey's assured us Maryland will be quite safe by then."

Mary received her own round of congratulations and happy smiles. Everyone knew that she wanted to go home after the first few weeks, but not for any lack of hospitality. She missed her home and her parents a great deal, never being far from them in her young life. Looking to Hettie, she smiled when the woman touched her face. It meant a great deal to feel the love of the people in that home. After all, she knew when her brother returned from the war, they would become part of the family. Not to mention, her second set of parents if Michael saw fit to marry her, but then she would not be afraid to live so far from Frederick. Not with Michael at her side.

Despite her excitement at returning home, she saw Emily kept her face turned down and said nothing. Mary's happy expression faded to concern. She released Hettie and stepped closer to her friend, standing an arms length from her. She put her hand on her shoulder, but Emily refused to look at her. Her heart wrenched.

"Are y'all right, Em?" Mary asked, fearing she hurt Emily's feelings.

Emily nodded her head and swallowed the pain, knotting up in her throat. Mary became a dear friend to her in her brother's absence. They shared a common bond and similar difficulty. Without Mary, she would not stave off the sadness and fears, hunting her each day. Hettie alone was not enough anymore. Only Mary chased away the darkness, because she understood exactly.

"I'm glad you are going home, but I will miss you," Emily finally spoke.

Mary laughed her cares away, "Is that all?" She stepped to her, taking Emily's hands into hers. "You can always come and stay with me." She grinned, "It won't be long before Joey comes home and maybe you'll come live with us."

"Emily," Margaret snapped their attention away from the last statement quickly, but not out of spite. "Michael sent word he'll visit soon," she offered an open letter to her daughter as proof. "You won't feel lonely long," her mother smiled, trying to warm Emily's cold feelings. She stepped closer to join the young women at the sink side. "Who knows—we could arrange a visit in the springtime." Emily lifted her chin. "Mary's right, darling," she continued. "The war will end soon and make trips easier than ever before."

Emily looked to her mother with little confidence in what she said. Her mother changed her mind all too quickly. Perhaps her fears held less weight with Mary, but she did rank Joseph's sister and a key to the end of her hopes for her daughter to marry Evan Howell. She doubted her mother gave up so easily on anything. However, she supported Mary's statement and a light of warmth and love stood out in her expression. Her mother now sympathized or tried to.

"You mean it?" Emily blurted. She could see the honesty in her mother's eyes.

Margaret smiled and touched her daughter's arm. Her attentions to Emily died the moment she defied her with Joseph. No hug, kiss, or touch came from her to her daughter since. Placing a hand on the side of Emily's head, she ended the shunning. She pressed her lips to Emily's forehead and sealed the promise.

"I do," her mother smiled.

"See," Mary said. "All's well."

The hours between the first of the year and the following month passed quickly. On a cold February day, Hettie found herself awaiting the arrival of the postman at the end of the path leading to the Conrads' front door, praying for just a single word on those she left behind. Tightening the shawl around her neck and shoulders, she watched the horse and cart draw up with the familiar man at the reins. He touched his hat, bidding her good day and offered her a warm smile.

"Fine day, Mrs. Benson," the Postman said to her. "Got quite a bundle of letters here for you. How are the Conrads?"

"Good, Graham," Hettie answered him. "How's your family?"

"Very Good. Here you go," he said, handing the packet over to her. He nodded with a smile and turned away. Snapping his reins, he said, "Have a good day, Mrs. Benson." He waved and drove off for the next delivery.

Hettie watched the postman leave. The wheels of his cart bounced and jarred over the frozen ground. Last night brought a terrible ice storm and she thought the post would come late. She supposed they meant to deliver no matter what, for the comfort of those they served.

Turning her gaze east, Hettie studied the arch of trees in the distance. The other side of the stand opened on the Howell holding. She wondered if Evan would return with Joseph and surprise Emily. So far, no word came. Even the Howells said nothing of the like. Perhaps no one expected a visit from the boys. After all, the war turned hotter day by day, despite the cold temperatures of Vermont. She wondered how Michael found the grace to cart himself home.

Lost in thought, Hettie found herself unable to look away from the arched limbs of the tree branches. They glowed silver in the bright morning sunlight. She felt warm in the rays, but her feet were cold in the snow surrounding her boots. She shivered. A bundle of contradictions formed all around her. She felt joy at her freedom, yet despair at the loss of her family. She felt warm from the sun, but frozen by the earth. Drawing a deep breath, she realized the awe of the opposing items drawn from within her broken heart.

Hettie wished against all odds that her husband and son would find her. She mused then, looking at the road stretched up a hill, disappearing among the trees. She could almost see them walk along the dark trunks, bold stride matched by their strength. They held purpose and meant to come get her. She eyed the trees angrily, knowing it only a powerless wish.

Suddenly, a figure moved just above the horizon of the road. She stepped around the fence to see better, guessing Michael arrived early. Then, Hettie thought it a squirrel looking for food. However, the form grew larger, as if springing from the ground. Hettie watched with curiosity.

On the distant eastern road, a man walked toward their farm. She spied the smooth skin of the dark head, no hair to speak of. Beside it, another figure emerged. This one paled in comparison, long and skinny. It bent at the middle a little and carried a large bag at its side. The head looked funny to her, perhaps dressed in a broad flat hat. Hettie looked closer and saw a third person appear. Her heart raced and her breath left her. A child walked with two men toward their farm.

Hettie covered her mouth and continued to study the strangers, unable to make out their features at the far distance. Counting, she tried to reason their presence without giving herself false hope. The letters in her hand fell to the ground. She could not mistake the broad shouldered tall man in the middle. He moved with confidence she saw in only one other man. He should have walked in a field among others like them, a king and his vassals.

Hettie gasped, "Isaiah." The sound of the name brought tears to her eyes instantly and they slipped down her cheeks uncontrollably.

Taking up her skirts, she bent her body into a run. The distance little mattered now. She knew who came to the farm. Mr. Conrad told her to keep faith and she prayed to God every night since her arrival. Finally, her prayers were answered.

Unhindered by slippery ice or binding skirts, Hettie closed the distance between her and the men. The tears blinded her eyes, but she knew her path. She cried out her husband's name and dropped her skirts from her hands to hold her arms out to him. So long she prayed for this moment and she already felt him holding her.

Leaping from the icy ground, Hettie threw her body at the largest figure in her blurred vision. Instantly, he caught her and she felt his strong arms close about her. His voice sounded in her ears and she feared the dream would end, as it always had, in the late empty night. Lifting her head, she swiped the tears from her eyes and looked at the strong handsome face of her husband, smiling up at her with the glow of love in his black eyes. His face wrenched with emotions and a single tear slipped from the outer corner of each of his eyes.

"Henrietta," he stammered through his own tears. "My girl—ya alive."

"Isaiah," Hettie breathed. "You're really here." She bent her head and touched her lips to his forehead. Then, she found her emotions released. Breathing in the sent of him, she spread kisses all over his face until he laughed and kissed her mouth.

"Isaiah," Hettie said. She placed her head on his shoulder and wrapped her arms about him. She closed her eyes, trusting for the first time he would remain when she opened them again.

Isaiah set her on the snowy road and kissed her forehead. He smiled down at her, drinking in every detail of her face and dress. Isaiah kept his hand on her arm, not wishing to let her go for anything. He watched Hettie take notice of the others with him. A bold wide grin bloomed on his lips.

"Uncle Dodd," She said, reaching out for the arm of the old man.

Uncle Dodd proved no real relation to her, but everyone called him uncle where they came from. Isaiah stepped aside and Uncle Dodd nodded to the last member of their party. A young boy stood by her side, reaching a height past her elbow. Ezekiel. Hettie breathed his name, collapsing on him with tears, hugs and kisses. The boy took hold of her skirt and whispered Mamma.

"Oh—my God," Hettie cried. "My baby," Hettie said, picking him up despite his size. She crushed him to her chest and wept. "My little boy—so grown now."

"Wur together now, Mamma."

Back at the farmhouse, the Conrad family, their young servants and their guest rushed from the front door and onto the porch. Hettie's cry had penetrated the walls, lifting a frightful alarm among the occupants. Their searching gazes met with a vision of their friend, running along the road to a trio travelers emerging from the forest. Their hearts froze and their expressions turned troubled.

Suspecting the identity of the strangers, Stuart stepped to the stairs and peered with sharp eyes at the distant scene. He saw the mail laying in the snow and gathered them up. He drew a deep cleansing breath of the chilled February air while a slow smile spread on his lips. He triumphantly laughed and clapped his hands together. He looked to his wife, shaking a delighted fist at the sky. Margaret clutched her shawl tighter and joined him on the lawn, wearing a worried expression. Stuart chuckled and put his arm around her, giving a reassuring squeeze.

Margaret turned her face to her husband's, recalling all the reasons she loved him. Suddenly, the moment filled her to the brim with tears and she cried. Margaret wrapped her arm about Stuart's middle and tugged him closer to her side. She looked at the scene, taking a handkerchief from her dress pocket and wiped her eyes. His letters had worked, she thought with much pride.

"See that," Stuart said. He watched Emily dash past them, after jumping down the stairs with Mary close behind. "That's what a letter and a little faith gets you," he cried out as they stopped on the snow covered lawn.

"I can't believe it," Emily breathed.

Emily watched Hettie take her son's hand and turn back toward the farm. She never saw the woman wear such a large grin. She smiled to herself, feeling the power of it. Emily's eyes then slipped over the men who walked beside her friend. She took his hand into her free one and then they put their arm about each other. Emily recalled the stories of him. Her imagination failed to compare.

In moments, Hettie's boots crunched along the snowy path back to the farmhouse, with her family. Her heart skipped and soared. It amazingly mended in just a few moments, thriving with relief. However, she felt her husband and son both hesitate, still suffering the lessons of the past. She looked up to see the concern in Isaiah's features. She looked back at Emily and Mary and then the Conrads and the maids on the porch. Hettie touched her husband's cheek, drawing his attention back to her. She understood his apprehension.

"These are the Conrads," Hettie told them.

"The man who sent the letter?"

Hettie shook her head yes.

"They white folks," Ezekiel said a little loud.

"Shh," Hettie quieted him. "It doan matter what they are. They gave me a home an a job. They made me better an they brought y'all back to me. We owe them some respect."

Isaiah started forward again and Emily rushed to him with her hand out. She smiled up at him unafraid and confident, "Pleased to meet you." She paused and waited for him to shake her hand. He took it, wearing a stern expression and shook. "My name is Emily Conrad. Welcome to my father's farm." She looked at the little boy pressed halfway through Hettie's skirt, wearing an expression like his father. "You must be Ezekiel."

"Emily," Uncle Dodd gummed the name. "My Mamma's name was Emily."

"Was it?" Emily asked, looking at him. "I'm honored."

"This is Uncle Dodd, Em," Hettie said. "Uncle to all of us back on the plantation."

"Pleased to meet you, sir," Emily shook hands with him. He nodded and smiled. "Come with me and I'll introduce you to my mother and father."

Isaiah reluctantly followed Hettie along the snowy lawn. His eyes swept over the other woman with Emily and up to the porch where more young girls stood with two older folks. He wondered if the farm was a home for girls. His eyes took in everything, including the three floors of the house. It reminded him of the plantation he left behind in Mississippi.

"Are you sure bout them?" Isaiah asked his wife.

"I trust them," Hettie said. "Ya no reason ta be afraid."

"So's ya say," Isaiah raised a brow.

Hettie laughed and put her arm back around him, "Ya love this place. I promise."

"Come inside," Margaret called to them. "You must be starved and it's freezing out here." She smiled from her perch at her husband's side on the porch. "Come along. We've been waiting for you," she held her arm out to them invitingly. "Welcome to our home."

Isaiah led his boy and wife to the steps of the huge farmhouse. He looked up at the people warily, as they called him closer. He wanted to believe it safe and should have, seeing how good Henrietta looked. However, he learned a hard lesson where he came from and it left him fearful. He drew a deep breath and let his wife go. He reached a strong hand out to the fine suited man who waited for him.

"I'm Isaiah," he said in a deep strong voice. "Pleased to meet you, Mr. Conrad."

"As am I," Mr. Conrad smiled. He stepped down the stairs to stand even with him. "Come inside. Let us get you something to eat. Are you thirsty?" Stuart chuckled and patted Isaiah's back. "You don't need to fear us son. I swear on the Bible."

Isaiah looked at him, trying to smile. He hesitated and then stepped up the first stairs, finding each after easier to move up. Soon, he stood in the hall and then he sat in a large room with a polished wood floor. On the wall beside his seat sat a fire, roaring with life renewing warmth. Uncle Dodd sat next to him and his wife took to his other side. His son sat alone on the opposite sofa, appearing anxious. Behind him, the young women stood in front of a large brown piano. The plantation owner kept a white one in his sitting room.

"Would you like tea or coffee?" Mrs. Conrad approached to ask.

"Whatever you feel fit to give, ma'am?" Isaiah answered.

"He likes coffee, Mrs. Conrad," Hettie replied for him. "As I remember." Isaiah looked at her anxiously and she smiled. "It's all right—you'll see."

"Uncle Dodd?"

"I've been wantin ta try some a that fine thing they all call tea," Uncle Dodd replied, finding no hindrance in accepting the Conrad hospitality. "If it won be any trouble for you, ma'am."

"None at all," Mrs. Conrad grinned. "It'll come in just a moment."

"And what would you like, young man?" Mrs. Conrad asked the boy.

"I don' like either," Ezekiel said with large round eyes.

"Y'ain had either," Isaiah said.

"I know," Ezekiel said. "Cause I doan like it."

"How about some milk, Ezekiel? It's fresh and just what a growing man needs."

The boy nodded and smiled with approval at her referring to him as a man. Mrs. Conrad patted his shoulder and smiled.

"I'll bring you some lunch," Mrs. Conrad laughed before she slipped from the room to see to their order.

Emily dashed from her companion's side and sat on the sofa beside Ezekiel. The boy slid away from her to the other side and watched her warily. Emily smiled at him despite his obvious fear and turned to eye the couple she faced. She looked to their clasped hands and smiled, hoping for her own reunion soon.

"Hettie told me all about you," Emily started. "I want to hear more."

Isaiah swallowed hard. He saw a hard transition before him. Behind him, Uncle Dodd laughed and slapped his back. Indeed, he faced a long transition.

৺

"Miss Emily," Ezekiel cried out, running into the kitchen with a battered letter in his hand. He stepped to her side grinning. "This jus came for ya."

"Thank you, Zeke," Emily murmured, taking the letter. She smiled at his bright eyes.

With his delivery given, Ezekiel spied Jo-Hanna who busily washed dishes at the sink with her sister. He felt the laugh leap in his heart at the idea of annoying her again. Carefully stepping behind Emily, he crept up on the other girls. His expression turned devious. Hesitating, as not to let them know he stood behind, he carefully took hold of Jo-Hanna's apron string and pulled. The string gave way easily and the apron fell to the floor around the stool she stood on.

Jo-Hanna cried out and grabbed at her fallen garment. She looked with anger to who dare bother her while she worked and saw Ezekiel, laughing with his hand over his mouth and pointing at her. Since his arrival, he found it amusing to annoy her at every chance. She thought it the opposite.

"Zeke!" Jo-Hanna cried.

Ezekiel ducked and grabbed her apron off the floor before she could recover it. Turning from the kitchen, he ran to the door with it. He shook it tauntingly and stuck his tongue out. Now came the best part.

"Zeke!" Hettie called him from the worktable, shaking a long wooden spoon at him. "You give that back right now young man." She set her hands on her hips. "I'll thrash ya little bottom. Are ya hearin me?"

"Give me back my apron," Jo-Hanna demanded, stepping after him.

Ezekiel laughed and dashed out of the kitchen.

Jo-Hanna gave chase, but Ezekiel dropped her apron on the hall floor and ran outside, slamming the back door shut before anyone could catch him. He always took the same route, to find safety from them in the workhouses. Exasperated, Jo-Hanna picked up her apron and checked it over for soils. Once dusted off, she returned to the kitchen and secured it back around her waist. Her gentle face was sunk in a deep glower. She mumbled under her breath and rejoined her smiling sister at the sink to continue their chore.

"How's it feel?" MaryJane asked her.

"Be quiet, MaryJane," Jo-Hanna whined. "I was never so mean to you."

"I see it differently," MaryJane grinned at her sister's sad little face.

Hettie shook her head and mumbled under her breath about her boy. He carried on like a hellion since he got his legs under him again. She supposed the lack of a real mother to watch over him brought out the worst of his behavior. She shook her head, hoping her reemergence in his life would help. She turned from the kitchen door back to the table and Emily.

"The letters from Michael," Emily interrupted the renewed silence. "He wants me to meet him in the garden at sunset tomorrow evening. He's brought me something from Joseph that Mamma and Daddy can't see."

"Michael?" Mary's voice entered the room. They looked up at her surprised. "I heard the commotion upstairs," she told them. "Is that Zeke bothering you again Jo-Hanna?"

"He never stops," Jo-Hanna whined.

"It's typical of a man," Mary patted her arm. "Don't think they'll change." Mary turned from her to her sister, "Phoebe needs the iron, MaryJane. Would you bring it to her?"

"Yes, Miss," MaryJane said, looking up.

"Now," Mary said, stepping toward the worktable. "What's this about Michael?"

"He's brought me something from Joseph," Emily said.

"Hmmm," Mary said, trying not to laugh. "Sounds devilishly good. I wonder what my sneaky brother's gotten himself up to now."

"We'll have to wait for tomorrow," Jo-Hanna said.

The women looked to her surprised. She heard everything said in the house. The women's eyes returned to each other, warily assessing each expression. They burst forth, laughing at Jo-Hanna's words.

The next day arrived like all the others before it. It passed slowly, taunting those who knew of the letter to near madness with anxiety. When sunset came, masked behind a mantle of gray clouds, all three women turned positively uncontrollable. Under her mother's wondering and assessing gaze, Emily excused herself and Mary to take a walk in the garden to spend the energy they suddenly found themselves bound with. They rushed from the parlor before permission came to them and quickly tied on their hats and shoes, followed by coats and gloves.

The women giggled like little girls and hurried down the hall to the back door, passing Hettie along the way. Mary reached out and took hold of her arm, urging her to come with them. Hettie's expression turned bright and she followed with no further prompting. They waited for her to gather her belongings from the peg inside the kitchen and then they dashed from the warmth of the house to the freezing temperatures outside.

Stepping down the stairs, Mary and Emily whispered and giggled to each other. A cold blustery wind whipped along the lane, threatening to pull their hats and coats from their bodies. The giggling stopped, replaced by fear. Mary and Emily pulled closer to each other.

"That's a foul wind," Hettie breathed, worriedly.

"Do you think he'll be all right?" Mary asked nervously after a stretched silence. She expected to see a wounded bedraggled ghost.

"I think he'll be just fine," Emily breathlessly replied.

The women stepped behind the fence blockading the work buildings from the main house, the sunset remained a mystery, but the darkening evening told the time. They looked up the path to the garden, apprehensive to continue through the dimness and see ghosts. They tried not to think how Michael would appear, holding to his image from the day he left.

"He'll look well," Emily said, noticing Mary's reluctance. She took hold of the girl's arm and patted it. "He's never looked badly in all his life. I swear to you."

"I hope so," Mary said unconvinced. "But—oh—I shouldn't worry," she said and then smiled. "He's here to see us and alive is well enough for anyone."

Emily smiled back and they laughed lightly. The excitement returned and she turned attention to what they faced. They climbed the hill path, concentrating on each step, as not to fall down in the snow. Emily swung her arm out and took hold of Hettie's hand to balance between her two companions and help them.

The three women reached the top of the hill and stood within sight of the holly wall garden and the greenhouse beyond. The tall oak at the center hung starkly above. It appeared a forbidding place. They paused to look at it and another wind dusted sharp snow around them.

"He's there," Hettie whispered. She pointed a finger to the rump of a horse, standing to the side of the garden.

"Shall we go see my brother?" Emily asked.

Emily held her companions arms and stepped forward first, dragging them reluctantly with her. She remarked on how similar that horse was to the one she saw a year ago after the fire. Holding the smile on her face, Emily infected the others with her enthusiasm. Studying the dark holly leaves, Emily thought on the contents of the letter and forgot the anxiety of her friends. Her brother remained vague on the matter of what he brought from Joseph for her, probably prompted by his superior. Suddenly, Emily felt her necklace shift. It dangled her Christmas gift just above her breasts and reminded her of Joseph. She preferred to see him than receive any gift he could send.

Hettie distracted Emily from her new bauble. She stopped walking, falling behind both her and Mary. Emily looked back to her friend and saw the surprise in her enlarged eyes. Hettie still watched the horse tied off on a tree by the garden. Her wary gaze flicked over it and the garden wall, while her mouth worked around soundless words. She touched her lips and appeared concerned by some matter Emily failed to understand. Emily smiled and breathed a short small laugh, reaching to pull Hettie with her.

"Come on. He's waiting," Emily said grasping her arm tight to her side.

"Uh—Emily," Hettie started to say. "That can be Michael's horse—it's black—"

Hettie's words cut off when they emerged into the garden to find two men, now awaiting their arrival. Mary gasped her brother's name, putting her hands to either side of her face. Emily stood watching him, not seeing Michael who stood a pace behind him. Joseph looked to them and smiled, sitting on the bench with his elbow on his knee and his Stetson held in his other hand that rested on the marble. He looked surprisingly well, as if he never left.

"Joey!" Mary gasped again. "Michael!"

Emily released her companion's arm and remained where she stood. Swallowing her fears and emotions, her eyes filled with tears. She watched Joseph rise to his feet and step toward her, leaving his hat behind. He wore an expression, like the day he left. Her heart pounded hard against her rib cage, perhaps trying to reach him. She thought she would faint and the awkward emotions from their first days rose up again.

Mary dashed to Michael's waiting arms with no such hesitation. Emily heard their laughter distantly, beaten away by the song of her heart. She stood alone under Joseph's gaze, knowing Hettie backed out of the garden, by the distance of her footsteps. His piercing gaze pinned Emily where she stood and her breath left her not to return. Her body trembled, anticipating his touch.

"Emmy," Joseph breathed.

The sound of his voice brought the tears from Emily's eyes to her cheeks. She sobbed his name and lifted her small hands up to him. She found herself unable to move, waiting for him to come to her. His smile ripped into her heart and she felt her knees weaken.

Joseph smiled. "Where have you been Miss Emily?" He asked.

"Waiting for you, Captain Maynard," Emily replied, trying to smile through her sobs. "I never thought I'd see you again," Emily cried.

"No hell or high general can keep me from you, Miss Conrad," Joseph said softly.

Joseph closed the shrunken distance between them in one step and pulled Emily into his arms, lifting her from the ground and nearly crushing her against him. His eyes closed and he drew a deep breath. The smell of her filled him with bittersweet agony. He felt her pull closer to him and his need for her stirred until he found her mouth with his. Closing his lips on hers, his emotions burst his heart. He filled his hands with the fabric of her dress and leaned into her deeper. His tongue parted her lips and he tasted her. Emily's hands pulled at his coat, bringing him still closer and she met his enthusiasm equally.

"Captain," Michael's voice destroyed the moment.

Joseph released his jewel from their kiss. He looked at her eyes, studying his mouth with that hazy gaze of her passion.

"Need I remind you that's my sister you're taking liberties with, sir?" Michael continued.

Joseph smiled and let Emily slip down his body to stand on the ground close beside him. He turned toward Michael, "And you need reminding that is my sister you have your mitts on." Joseph pointed at Mary, tucked tightly on Michael's side. "But—I believe I've the finer of the two."

"Not so. Not so, sir," Michael smiled. "God outdid Emily when they made my Mary."

"Enough from the both of you," Hettie snapped, entering the garden. "They both beautiful girls. Doan make em jel'us a one another. They jealous enough with the likes of you runnin all over Virginia alone."

"Awe, Hettie," Michael said, stepping from Mary. "I forgot how pretty you are," he came towards her, holding out his arms. "Now God outdone all women when he made this fine—"

Hettie smiled knowing his game and cut him short, "You may wanna be more careful a what ya say, boy.

My husband's just yonder, itchin ta release some a his anger."

"Your Husband," Michael said, stopping with shock clear on his face.

"You deaf from the guns, Michael?" Hettie asked sarcastically. "Yeah, I said my husband." She folded her arms and looked at him crossly.

"He found you? How?"

"Yur gentleman of a father sent word ta the one's got me out," Hettie snapped.

"Well where is he? I wanna meet him," Michael said, holding his arms out and looking around.

"He's working, which is more than I can say for either of you'," Hettie scowled between the young men. "And doan get him in trouble, draggin him round with ya. We've had enough."

"I'll see um after dinner then," Michael said, smiling a little.

"And doan ya give my boy any ideas. He's nuff trouble for us as it is," Hettie added.

"They found Ezekiel?" Michael said, gaping with surprise. He reached and held his hand out for Mary. He clasped her hand and drew her back to his side. "How did they find him?" He asked, turning back to Hettie.

"The master sold em down the road after I left," Hettie said, pursing her lips and raising a brow. "I knew he'd do somethin like that ta get at me, but I never thought he'd do such a stupid thing as ta send um two doors down the road."

"That's wonderful," Michael cried. "I mean that you found him," Michael corrected. "Where is he?"

"In the house, helpin the girls," Hettie said.

"Or harassing them," Mary said dryly.

"You be patient, Michael. Ya can't hug and hold in the house. Mrs. Conrad would have an attack sure as bees fly. Ya stay here."

"Yeah," Michael breathed. He looked to Mary's smiling face. "Your family isn't going anywhere now."

Under Hettie's advice, they remained beside the oak, talking and holding each other for a while longer. The cold felt miles away even when the breeze stirred their clothes, chapping their lips and face. Time got away with them until the dark drove them to return to the farmhouse. They parted with whispered good byes, sadly wandering in different directions.

"Come along, ladies," Hettie urged them with her.

This time, Hettie walked in the middle, holding the arms of the younger women to assure they followed her. Both Emily and Mary looked back over their shoulders, watching their lovers mount their battle chargers and swing them round to come to the house by the eastern road. Their absence would only last a few hours, but it would feel like a lifetime.

Just before nightfall, Michael and Joseph mounted the stairs to the front door of the farmhouse. Both men wore broad grins and laughed, speaking to each other. Joseph patted Michael's back and let him step to the door. He watched the Second Lieutenant knock on the wood and took a deep breath. Although he saw her moments ago, he felt nervous to visit with her parents, considering the last time.

Promptly following Michael's knock, Hettie opened the door, sternly looking at the two of them. Joseph spied the small boy at her side and knew him for Ezekiel.

"Wah! Soldiers!" Ezekiel cried out.

The door opened wider and Michael smiled at her stepping in. He turned back and waved Joseph to follow him. Joseph hesitated removed his hat, and then nodded, taking a step forward. He paused when Hettie cried out to announce Michael's arrival.

"He brought Captain Maynard with him," Hettie continued to call into the parlor.

Joseph stepped inside the house behind Michael. He saw Mr. Conrad and his wife approach from the parlor and nodded respectfully to them. Hettie took hold of his hat, drawing his eyes to her smiling expression. She lifted it from his hands and he smiled back at her. When she stepped away, the sound resounded louder until they filled the hall to the ceiling. Joseph's ears filled with the sound of the Conrads, welcoming their son home. His eyes drifted to staircase and he realized the loud footsteps approached from above.

Emily and Mary hurried down the stairs to join them. Emily hesitated to go to Joseph's side immediately, allowing his sister to hug him. When he let Mary go, he turned to Emily and gently held her hand and lifted it to his lips, kissing the knuckles. He released her and smiled at her blush.

"Good to see you again, Captain Maynard," Emily said, as if no one knew of their relationship.

Joseph laughed, "Miss Conrad, thank you."

"Why don't we settle in the back room," Mr. Conrad said. "Hettie," he looked to her with a smile. "Go tell Mary Jane to bring us tea. Leave Ezekiel with us and get your husband. I'm sure the boys would like to meet Isaiah."

"All right, Mr. Conrad."

Emily led Joseph down the hall, stepping backward and holding his hands in hers. He watched her father and mother walk ahead of them. Neither acted as if their daughter's behavior strange. In the back room, they parents smiled at him from their seats and indicated the opposite one of the chairs. Emily parted from him with a small frown and joined Mary at the piano. He and Michael looked at each other and Michael smiled, assuring him he could sit.

"Do sit down, Captain Maynard," Stuart said, sliding over for Ezekiel to sit between him and his wife.

Michael held his hand out, pointing to the farthest seat and took to the other side of the cushion. Joseph stepped carefully, recalling the moments that were snatched in that room so long ago. Lowering himself to the cushion, he tried to smile at his hosts, but felt uneasy in their presence. After Emily told him her father secured their correspondence, he never thought of about what seeing them again would be like. He half expected Mrs. Conrad to plainly share her views of him.

Joseph's fears left him when a dark shadow appeared in the archway. Both he and Michael looked with astonishment to the man who loomed there, nearly as tall as the opening. At his side, Hettie appeared and touched his arm, prompting him to enter. When he moved into the light, he revealed a somber and strong face reflected in the youthful one between the Conrads. Michael and Joseph rose to their feet speechless. He dwarfed the entire room, including them and Joseph was considered tall among men.

Hettie led her husband to Michael first, "Michael Conrad, this is my husband Isaiah."

Isaiah took hold of Michael's offered hand with both of his and shook strongly, "Pleased ta meet ya, sir."

"No—just Michael, please," Michael laughed, smiling up at him with awe filled eyes.

Isaiah then drew him into his hold, "Thank ya for bein so kind ta my Hettie. I owe y'all a lot for what ya done."

"You've got the biggest damn arms I ever saw on a man," Michael rasped, peering over Isaiah's large bicep.

"Ya suppose ta say ya welcome," Hettie said sternly to Michael.

"You're welcome," Michael breathed.

Isaiah released Michael with a deep throaty laugh and patted his shoulder. His dark eyes went to Joseph and Hettie introduced him. Isaiah shook Joseph's hand, studying his face to memorize it. By his stature and uniform, he guessed his relationship to the family.

"Emily did all the work," Michael told him. "But, I suppose Hettie already told you," Michael continued. Isaiah looked back at him. "Em's got the touch. Any one sick, she makes it right in a snap. Plant, animals, people." Michael swallowed hard, standing under Isaiah's assessing gaze. "Sorry we couldn't do more for you."

"Y'are now," Isaiah touched a finger to one of Michael's buttons.

Michael let out a weighted bitter sigh, "Not very well." He looked over the brass buttons. "Our commanders seem more interested in personal matters than keeping the states together, or freeing slaves."

"I bet they are," Isaiah grinned, understanding fully.

"Come sit down Isaiah," Stuart smiled up at him. Vacant chairs sat at either end of the table between the sofas. Isaiah nodded with a smile to him and stepped from his new acquaintances to his seat. "You too, Hettie."

Hettie clutched her hands together and followed to the other chair, offering a respectful nod to her employer. Since the first of the month, Mr. Conrad treated them more like equals than staff members. Of course, he had that way about him. Looking warily toward the farm owner, her eyes shifted to Emily's hero, watching him walk to where his sister and intended bride rested.

"So tell me," Michael began the conversation with a brilliant smile to Isaiah. "Exactly how did you find Henrietta all the way up here?"

Isaiah rubbed a knuckle on the side of his nose and cleared his throat. He then offered Michael a smile. His deep voice rumbled hesitantly before he told the tale. His eyes held the younger Conrad's with both respect and confidence. Hettie told him much about the Conrad family and he saw the truth daily, especially in the way they treated his son.

MaryJane entered after the family sat in deep discussion, bringing the tea service with her. She scooted about the room, offering steaming cups, lemon, honey, or perhaps just sugar with a tad of cream. She smiled up at Joseph, offering him a cup touched with just a squeeze of lemon, as she remembered from long ago. He took it graciously smiling back at her. She felt her stomach twist and her hands shook nervously. Stepping away, she meekly nodded to his thanks and continued her duty with painful self-awareness.

Later in the evening, with their bellies full from a grand feast, Hettie settled Michael and his companion into their rooms. Michael commanded her attention first, seeing him fitted with a pitcher of warm water, soap and some towels. She moved around his room, helping him prepare for bed. All the while she ignored his teasing. Once his nightshirt rested on the foot of his bed and his slippers by his nightstand, Hettie left him. Entering the hall, she grumbled under her breath and joined Joseph who patiently waited for her.

"You want me to take care of him for you?" Joseph asked, grinning.

Michael's voice called out, begging Hettie to return to him or send for Rose.

"He's an incurable ass," Hettie said with stern eyes. She gestured Joseph to follow her.

"I'd wager that's true," Joseph said, going to the door she opened beside Michael's.

Joseph stepped into the room and looked around the darkness while Hettie lit an oil lamp. He set his suitcase on the floor beside the only chest of drawers. Hettie crossed the room to a high piece of furniture, set on a pillar between the two windows. It held a porcelain basin and displayed a pair of cabinet doors. Hettie opened the cabinet to reveal towels and a pitcher. She drew the shining white vessel from its shelf and set it in the basin.

"Mrs. Benson," a small voice called from the hall. Joseph turned to see young Jo-Hanna enter with a teakettle and bucket of water. "I brought Captain Maynard's wash water. MaryJane's not feeling well."

"Thank you, Jo," Hettie smiled.

Hettie took the items from the little girl and Jo-Hanna turned to leave the room. Hettie looked up to see her stop with a smile in front of Joseph. It brought a smile to her lips to see him shift under the child's gaze. He offered her a nod and greeting.

"MaryJane said you make her sick," Jo-Hanna spat out.

"Tell MaryJane, I'm sorry," Joseph replied.

"I will," she smiled up at him. She dashed from the room.

Joseph stepped toward the bed, setting his hat on the top of the chest of drawers by the lamp. He saw the lights of the carriage house through his windows, otherwise black. He wondered if the garden hung just beyond in the darkness.

"I'm glad to see your family safely home with you," Joseph said to Hettie.

"Thank you, Captain," Hettie said. She poured the hot water into the pitcher and followed it with the cold.

Turning to face him, Hettie explained to Joseph when to expect breakfast and how they ran the rest of the day in the house. He gave her his full attention, nodding when fitting. Hettie looked at him almost reproachfully. She then turned to go, leaving him to rest.

Joseph picked up his suitcase and placed it on the bed. While he opened the lid, he heard Hettie enter behind him again. She crossed the distance between them and put her long arms about his chest. Squeezing him tight, she patted his back and then kissed his forehead, drawing him down to her lips. Releasing him, she smiled into his clear dark eyes.

"What was that for?" Joseph asked bewildered.

"Thank ya for makin her happy" Hettie answered. A blush crept up on her cheeks. "Lord knows men've tried, but Em's been waitin for you."

Long after dark when Stuart sat alone in his study, reading over his paperwork, Michael and Joseph crept downstairs. Michael entered the door at the bottom alone, to ask his father if they may speak with him. Mr. Conrad nodded, viewing his son through a pair of rectangular wire frame spectacles. Michael then waved Joseph in from the hallway.

Stuart watched the boys enter, half out of their uniforms. They looked to him healthy as the last time he saw them, but a tad thinner. Stuart silently thanked God for the grace and continued to smoke his pipe and watch them. With a welcoming smile, Stuart pointed to the two chairs on the other side of his desk with a thrust of the papers he held in his hands. He stood from his cushioned leather chair and went to his filing drawers to put the papers away. He listened to the young men sit and then clear their throats.

"What's this about, boys?" Stuart asked around the pipe stem, as if he didn't know.

Michael shifted in his seat. The sweet comforting scent of his father's pipe permeated the room not helping Michael's fear to ease. His eyes nervously went to

Joseph and set his superior off guard. The matter of his sister's courtship would not pass easily with his father. He loved Emily dearly and hoarded her away from unworthy suitors, meaning all men who competed for her hand. The only man to enter their father's mind as a prospect ruined the chances by committing an unforgivable sin that caused the death of an innocent young woman.

"Father," Michael said and then stopped. "Father I've come to help ask your permission for Joseph to court Emily."

"What for? He can't do it himself?" Stuart cut in. He looked up from the final item he had been searching the perfect spot for. Looking back to the files, he spread them open with his fingers and slipped the paper inside.

"He—he's, uh," Michael stammered, crossing and uncrossing his legs.

Stuart looked to his son, assessing him and disguising his inner emotions. He clutched his pipe with one hand. He puffed, sending rings of smoke into the air. Turning, Stuart returned to his comfortable leather chair. He spun it to the side and leaned back, placing his feet up on the unseen ottoman by his desk drawers.

"I aim to make your Emily my wife someday, Mr. Conrad. If you will allow it," Joseph smoothly interrupted, spurred on by his anxiety and Michael's floundering. He would not allow a little nervousness stand between him and the woman he loved.

Stuart's study went to the Captain. He looked seriously at him for a long moment. He either half smiled or grimaced, Joseph could not tell the difference. Then, there came a lull, which made him increasingly uncomfortable and doubtful of continuing further. Though Joseph rethought his move, it already stood too late to retract the question. Joseph swallowed hard and looked at Emily's father. His mouth felt dry and he found it difficult to breathe or even speak.

"Ya do—huh?" Mr. Conrad drawled dryly.

Stuart's eyes switched between the young men. He enjoyed this game and wondered if his wife played it for the same reason. He turned his gaze to the windows between the shelves of books to his right. He only wanted to know Joseph truly cared for his daughter.

"Yes sir," Joseph replied, as if to a superior officer. Sitting there, he thought of the General who formerly commanded the Potomac.

"What's the use of courting her when you're away all the time?"

"I love her," Joseph said.

Gazing into the windows overlooking his farm, Stuart thought over the idea thoroughly. To Joseph, he knew he appeared more distracted with what happened in the reflection on the glass window than in the room they shared. He heard his guest chairs creak and his eyes slipped to the potted plant set in the corner between two windows.

When Joseph shifted in his chair, making the leather creak, he gained more than Stuart's attention to his uneasiness. Michael touched his arm and looked warningly. His subordinate's simple glance told him they stood on the edge of failure.

Stuart turned his gaze back to the young Captain. He appraised him with his eyes, wondering a great many thoughts about the young man. His daughter claimed to love him and he declared the same of her. However, Stuart still felt confused why he made the request now, so long after he went about it anyway.

"Emmy's a beautiful girl, Captain. She's just like her mother at that age." He paused smiling thoughtfully. "I should have known this would come soon. I think Margaret knew. Right scared her, it did." He cast a glance at Michael, and then returned his attention to Joseph. "You don't need my permission to do what you've been at," he chuckled, leaning with his elbows on his desk. "Perhaps you wanted me to tell you I approved of it?"

"I apologize," Joseph said stricken. He looked to Michael quickly and saw his companion also taken back by the older man's words.

Stuart nodded and chuckled. He put the mouthpiece of his pipe in his mouth. His eyes sparkled deviously.

"It's not like Emmy to try to hide anything from us," Stuart explained. "I understand why she did. She feared her mother would try to keep you apart." He paused, eyeing Joseph. "My little girl was lost the moment she laid on eyes on you," Stuart leaned back and continued. "But—I still see the good in you. I only ask you to take care—we live in a dangerous time. I think when you come back, it would be just fine."

"I will, sir." Joseph said, trying to ease Mr. Conrad's mind.

Joseph wanted to say something else, but it cleaved his tongue to the roof of his mouth to even think it.

"You'll do your best," Stuart corrected him.

"I'll do my best," Joseph smiled at him. "Thank you, Mr. Conrad," Joseph stood and offered his hand for a shake. Joseph felt his mind urge him to speak more.

"Good night," Stuart said, returning to his work cluttering his desk surface.

Joseph's looked back over his shoulder and thought his opportunity passed. Stuart puffed on his pipe and acted like their conversation never happened. He felt something hit his shoulder and shifted his gaze to where Michael stood by him in the doorway. He offered Joseph a weak smile. With a nod, he followed him upstairs.

The next morning after breakfast, Michael and Joseph took their sisters for a sleigh ride over the hills and fields of the farm. During the ride, Joseph sat in the back with Emily quietly holding her to his side. The need to hide their feelings from outsiders was gone.

"I spoke with your father last night. He thinks courting you would be just fine, when I return from the war." Joseph said, taking her hand in his.

Emily lifted her chin from his shoulder and looked into his eyes with a wide smile, "You asked him?"

Joseph nodded touching her cheek. She looked radiant that morning, all the better for his missing her.

"Was he angry?"

“Not in the least, Miss Conrad,” Joseph said with sarcasm.

“Well I guess that is my fault,” Emily said, lowering her eyes from his and slightly turning away. “I didn’t exactly behave appropriately.”

“You didn’t do anything wrong,” Joseph assured her. “I doubt anyone who sees us would think so, secreted letters or not.”

Emily smiled and looked back to him. Until that point, she had treated the affair like a secret, failing to realize how obvious it was to everyone. She saw Joseph smile back, peering deep into her eyes. She hoped her action would not prove an eventual mistake. Thoughts of lustful escapades filled her mind, like they filled her dreams. She felt her cheeks grow warm. Joseph’s eyes crinkled and laughed slightly, telling her she blushed brightly.

“Now, sir. I should say you owe me,” Michael said in mock sincerity. He coolly studied his superior, holding his sister, as they rested on the backseat beneath a blanket. “But—keep your hands where I can see them,” he added, wishing Joseph to worry. His sister claimed her price and he would see it paid.

Mary smiled over his shoulder at them, placing her arm about Michael’s waist.

“Mother’s going to be so happy,” Mary said to her brother.

Joseph and Emily spent a greater part of the week immersed in complete contentment. Traversing all the places they haunted a year ago together, they felt hope renew their strengths for the coming separation and ignored the fate that hung over their heads. Neither imagined a future without the other in it. They dared to plan, even if small.

“I’m sure you’ll return soon,” Emily said, walking down the isle of the greenhouse where plants grew like in summer. Some bore flowers, trying to shame her beauty. Her hand brushed over the blooms.

“Daddy said General Hooker replaced Mr. Burnside,” she said with tears in her eyes.

"Yes. He has," Joseph said. "I'll go in a few more days as planned."

"If the war does not end before then," Emily smirked, knowing it a hopeless dream.

"I'd rather retire and come home," Joseph said.

"It would dishonor your family, Joseph." Emily faced him and said, "It is not in your heart to leave something you believe in."

"I'm not so sure I believe anymore," Joseph admitted. He stepped close to her at the back of the room, feeling like they stood surrounded by a jungle. He placed his hand on the side of her face and leaned in for a kiss.

"Daddy says Mr. Hooker's units are followed by prostitutes," Emily dodged him.

Joseph snickered looking at her, "They are."

"Do the men often use their services?" Emily dared to ask.

"Some," Joseph breathed. He closed in on her again.

"Do you?" Emily stopped him, studying his lips.

"If I were interested in that," Joseph said in low tones with a smile. "I'd have the woman I love." He paused, looking in her eyes. "I do not wish the shame Evan suffers for either of our families."

Emily's head rose from her chest and she turned from him to a tall green plant, bearing some yellowed leaves. She picked them off and said, "I am no kind of woman to do that anyway."

Joseph smiled, approaching her, "I love you, Emily." He placed his hand on the back of her head to feel her soft mink tresses. He watched her still and shut her eyes, uneasily drawing a breath. He pulled her back into his arms and kissed her neck, "I could bare no other touch than yours, least of all a whore." Joseph turned her in his arms and tipped her chin up to look in her eyes. "Trust me?" Joseph mumbled. Emily licked her lips, and nodded. "Good." He smiled, picking her up. He twirled her around, extracting a squeal. He chuckled and sat on the bench, putting her on his lap. "Now, where was I?"

The blush in Emily's cheeks deepened. She looked radiant and he felt his insides stir to see her so. Joseph caressed her cheek and watched her in silence, soaking in every moment he had left. He leaned in and kissed her mouth, placing a hand on the nape of her neck. When he released her from the embrace, she looked at him eagerly. She chewed her lip and pulled at her gloves. He smiled comfortingly, but the tears spilled down her cheeks despite it.

"We'll never see each other again," Emily whimpered.

"I will see you again," Joseph said.

"Joseph, please," Emily demanded. "How many bullets can you dodge? How many battles can you survive? What if they capture you?" She paused with a sob. "I don't know what I would do, never seeing you again." She looked to the glass of the building that sheltered them, thinking wild thoughts unlike her. "I know I said I'm no woman to do it, but what if we never have our time together?"

"Don't say it," Joseph said, placing his fingertips over her lips to quiet her. "I can't stop myself, Emily. Don't ask me to do it." After a pause he added, "I will come back to you. I swear to it."

"Joseph," she breathed, looking into his eyes. "If you love me, why will you not make your claim on me?" She paused, searching his eyes. He tore his gaze from her. Emily touched his face, making him look back to her. "I love you," she said tremulously.

"I'll miss you more than you know," Joseph said. "Don't make it worse."

"I'll die here without you," Emily said. "Give me something to hold onto."

"My promise is not enough?" Joseph questioned her.

"Not for my heart," Emily said.

Joseph studied her expression. She looked like a wild reflection of the young woman he knew. She took off her gloves, casting them aside. He kept his eyes on her face, appearing serious. He felt her hands unbutton his jacket, making his stomach tighten. Her eyes lowered to where she worked until it hung open. Then she smiled at him and he knew she was sure.

"Emily," he breathed. "What if—" he tried to ask, but she closed her mouth over his.

The end of winter wrapped them in freezing temperatures, but they could not feel it inside the greenhouse and lost in their passion. Joseph set Emily beside him on the bench and shook off his jacket, letting it fall to the brick floor. Wrapping his arms around her, he pulled her close and kissed away the tears. Her hands pressed to his neck and shoulder burned like a brand and the length of her jolted him like lightning. Joseph released her mouth and pulled her legs around his waist. He kissed her again.

When the embrace ended, they stared into each other's eyes frozen in time. Moving almost too suddenly, he reached his hand around to touch her soft pale cheek. She licked her lips to cool them, waiting for the next kiss. The feel of her in his arms, held in such a torrid position, broke the dam carefully sealing away his desires. Joseph forgot his honor and propriety, including his grand designs or fears of becoming a man like Evan Howell.

Using the weight of his body, Joseph pushed Emily onto the bench. His lips kissed hers and she met him eagerly, wrapping her legs about his waist. Joseph made his claim on her and now he must return or suffer the consequences by God's hand. When it ended, they thought no more of his departure, just the next meeting.

XII. Darkness

The events of February turned to pale memories and Joseph soon found himself back among familiar masculine faces. The men connected with him and the old navy blue uniform they wore, welcomed him back like a homecoming. March passed quickly and the weather turned brighter with the springtime. Joseph counted the days since his leave from Vermont. The last he saw his Yankee girl was nearly two months ago.

While Nature changed her dress, she showed no feeling toward violent men. The fight Joseph returned to had lasted far too long. The sentiment carried over on other soldiers. With little success and minimal leave, they all pined for other places and different times. He noticed the units grow keen and tire quickly when it came time to perform duty. He felt the same reaction in himself when he tried to keep them in line. Taking leave in February to see Emily proved a strangely unwise decision at best. He left his concentration in the north, bringing back a listless shell. It warned of danger, but he could only ignore it and falter in his guilt over one stolen afternoon in the greenhouse.

Outside the company mess tent, the soldiers of the Union Army went about preparations for their daily maneuvers. Evan and Michael sat to either side of Joseph, quietly eating their breakfast and drinking muddy coffee. The spring air occasionally blew in over them, already making the meal cold. They did not comment, long used to such hardships.

"Do you think this'll do any good?" Michael suddenly asked. He aimed the question at Joseph, but it went unnoticed. From the corner of his eye, he saw Evan look up and listen. "I mean what they're planning?" He continued.

"What?" Joseph asked.

The sound of Michael's voice went around him never settling in. He looked at the younger man with disinterest and his tone spoke of the same emotion. His lack of enthusiasm turned into a permanent fixture of his personality since his return in the beginning of March.

"Cutting off Lee's supplies." Michael said, as if obvious.

"If he doesn't find someone else to give him what he needs," Joseph drawled neutrally. He only cared if it meant the end of the war.

Captain Maynard knew better than to think the end came by this point. He shoved another fork full of mushy food into his mouth and stared ahead at the passersby. Sore to the touch about his problems, Joseph tightly closed his mouth in effort to no longer speak that morning. While he found himself unable to carry out his true wishes, his conversation would remain short.

No one in the camp knew Joseph better than his lieutenant, Evan Howell. Evan leaned back and looked to Michael around Joseph's shoulder. His expression told the boy to button his lip. Any more small talk would see to a sour answer or a fight Joseph would finish. Second Lieutenant Conrad would be wise to let it drop until a later date. Evan turned back to his food.

Michael easily read the meaning silently held in Evan's expression. He sat straight and looked into his plate with wide dejected eyes. He stuck some rations in his mouth and swallowed hard. He only meant to brighten the morning with a chat and possibly find hope for their efforts, seeing it nowhere else. Everyone knew they stood in the middle of nowhere to fight a war that no one cared about.

Michael shoved a fork full of what he assumed eggs into his mouth. That would keep him from saying another word, especially ones he may regret. He eyed his plate of meager rations. He told himself he numbered among the lucky. Word spread about famine among the Rebels with images of their searching the woods and fields for enough to stave off sickness.

Setting his plate down, Michael looked to the sullen expression of the Captain. He sat there the entire time, pretending to study the other soldiers passing the mess. Michael wondered what he thought, suspecting something like his sister. He hardly blamed the man, understanding through his attachment to Mary. It was the only thing that kept them going.

"We go to Richmond," Joseph said. "You better get your things packed. The army's moving out soon," he added, rising to his feet. He walked out of the tent without hesitation.

Michael watched him go, seeing Evan held little interest. He finished his breakfast and looked to him askance. Michael shook his head and grinned. They tried to keep information from him a great many times, but always they ended telling him something.

"What is it now?" Michael said.

"He didn't say anything to me," Evan said. He lifted his mug to his lips and took a drink. Wiping his hands, he swung his legs from under the table. Throwing down the cloth, he stood and said, "Best do what he says. I'd wager he's no patience today."

Michael nodded and complied. Together, they left the tent to the care of the enlistees running the mess. Stopping outside, they looked up and down the tent lane and saw the camp collapsing around them. A din of demolition filled their ears.

"We're late," Evan said. He turned and trotted off to find their units.

Michael hurried after him, wondering why he came back at all.

Days passed with little incidence until the beginning of May. The rains returned like last spring. It appeared to those who fought the battles, they merely repeated last year again. However, this time hope waned more and the weariness in the soldier's eyes showed darker. The sentiment of the civilian population reached their numbers, pulling out the last vestiges of any reason to continue.

While still carrying out their orders, Joseph's company camped among the other Federal Army troops in a field safe from the reach of Richmond's protectors. The camp lay silent beneath the starry sky. The last wisps of smoke lifted from the dying embers of mess fires. Shadows loitered along the ground and others moved around the perimeter. A horse whickered uneasily and shook its mane at some unseen menace.

The sound of horse hooves, as they struck the packed dirt road, beat like a heart, growing louder with every round, until the animal and its rider appeared from the surrounding forest. The soldiers on watch readied their rifles or pistols, awaiting the signal. Their eyes remained fixed on the figure headed toward them. It slowed to a walk, failing to brush aside or take heed of their raised guns. The trill of city pigeon cooed in their ears. This meant a messenger of their side.

The guards kept their guns ready, but allowed the rider to close in on the entrance to the camp. When he sat above them on his war steed, they clearly saw his Union uniform and lowered the muzzles from his chest and head. For his sake, he better prove what he appeared.

"I've a message for the company commanders," the soldier said.

A lieutenant stepped up and took the paper from his hands, "What message, Corporal?"

The Corporal released the papers to him and watched the man read, "I have to get the men up and moving now, sir."

The Lieutenant read the message while his expression turned increasingly grave, "They lost Chancellorsville to the south." He turned to the soldiers by him and spread orders, "Get the commanders up. Make sure every soldier in this camp wakes now!"

The men with the guns turned and fell into their orders. The Lieutenant faced the Corporal again and passed the note back to him. He gave a meek smile and nod. His eyes remained bleak.

"Get you to your duty, Corporal."

The soldier saluted the officer. He folded his letter with one hand, tucking it into his blue jacket. Pulling the reins of his mount, the Corporal turned him and trotted into the tent city. His orders clearly explained his responsibility to see the message brought to the officer in charge, no matter his underlings trying to carry it out over his head.

Only moments later, Captain Maynard's Corporal entered his dark tent. The look in his eye spoke of terror, as did his hesitance to wake his superior. The Corporal stepped to Joseph's bed and eyed him while he slept. Of late, Captain Maynard had a quick temper. He could only hope tonight would not bring him a terrible reprimand for his actions.

"Captain Maynard," The Corporal whispered harshly. He turned and lit Joseph's lamp. The Captain failed to wake. "Captain Maynard you must get up. Orders have come to retreat."

Joseph rolled on his cot and made a noise like a refusal. In the next instance he sat up and looked to his subordinate. He yawned and stretched, wiping a hand over his bearded face. The Corporal shook his head and Joseph looked at him both groggy and disapproving.

"Sir, General Hooker sent orders—he's called a retreat to Frederick, Maryland. We need to leave now, sir."

"Oh, goody," Joseph drawled. "Get the lieutenants up," he said and stood, throwing his covers back. "Have them assemble the rest of the men."

"Yes, sir." The Corporal seized Joseph's jacket and pants from his chair and handed them to him. He saluted stiffly and made a dash for the exit.

With his clothes in his hand, Joseph hurriedly dressed. He sat on the edge of his cot and squeezed his feet into his boots. In the next moment, he rounded up all his belongings and crammed them into his three trunks. Just as he shut the lid on the last one, a pair of soldiers entered and helped break down his tent and take away his bed and other items. Joseph watched the cot, as the men prepared it for packing. A strange despair glinted in his eyes.

The urgency of the retreat echoed in the actions and expressions of the men who broke camp. In the background, clouds rolled in to blot out the starry sky and the rumble of thunder sounded closer. The warning of the coming storm reminded Joseph of what was surely to come. Like times before, Hooker would pull back and quit. Then, Washington would send a replacement. He eyed the carts loaded with ammunition and other items.

After a few minutes, Joseph stood in a field to wait for his horse. He recalled his pleasant imaginings during sleep, wishing to return to them. He listened to his voice call out hollow sounding orders. His dream had turned to a nightmare.

Sergeant McGuire approached, leading Manny by his reins. Joseph nodded to him and received the same greeting in return, with a half forgotten salute. Joseph flapped his hand to his brow smirking. He grabbed the reins and climbed into the saddle. They faced a long march, yet again, and it looked like that would take place in a lovely rainstorm.

Nudging Manny into motion, Joseph led his units out of the encampment and into the line of marching Federal soldiers. Joseph looked back and saw fire still burning among the remains of the site. As he watched the orange flames flicker, the wind howled through the trees. Then, the rain came. It fell lightly at first, but quickly intensified, turning the road to mud and soaking them to their bones.

"Awe shit," Joseph heard Evan curse. It made him smile.

Several weeks later, they found refuge in Frederick. Colonel Donnelly called Joseph to his tent and debriefed him on the matter of their retreat. Joseph found the news Donnelly shared difficult to accept, though he already guessed most of it. When he left the commander's tent, he called his own staff meeting.

"General Hooker has resigned," Joseph said, refusing to cut corners. He looked over his men, including Michael and Evan. "We've yet to have the name of his replacement, but Colonel Donnelly assures me we'll know very soon." His eyes swept over the small group. "He also told me that fresh troops are to arrive soon to augment our losses. I want you to share this information with your sergeants. The new men are to be trained more than suitably. Report their progress to me at the end of their exercises. Lastly, you need to know we'll move from here in a couple of days. The commanders have reason to believe Lee will try for another position in the north. We march to cut him off before he pisses all over the countryside." Grown weary from the drudgery, Joseph drew a deep breath and looked at his subordinate officers. "Any questions?" He asked, hoping they felt secure with the little information he gave them. "Dismissed. Mess will be at six."

The Lieutenants rose to their feet and saluted the Captain. Joseph stiffened and returned the gesture. With dark eyes, he watched them exit the tent. In the least, Hooker moved them to familiar ground and he foresaw a delightful evening ahead. Unfortunately, the rest of the soldiers would enjoy no such event. They would spend their night at campfires and share army rations.

Joseph was thankful for the blessing of being near his home. He used the time to visit with his family again. However, all matters eventually found an end. The visit passed no differently. Time would not wait for Joseph. When Captain Maynard returned to the camp, he found Evan waiting for him outside his tent. The dark haired man smiled up at him. Joseph smiled back, wondering what he thought. Since the death of Mary and the infant, Evan hung back more than usual and treated events more darkly than before. Joseph missed his old friend and hoped the smile meant more than a glimpse at him.

"We're getting General Meade," Evan said. "Donnelly came by earlier to tell the officers," his dark eyes glinted deviously. "I told him you went to check the perimeter.

Can't believe that worked." Evan laughed. "How are the folks?"

"Good," Joseph answered, ignoring the first information. "They send you their good wishes and to Mike—and to Sergeant McGuire," Joseph explained, feigning annoyance. "They sent this," he added holding up a covered basket. The delicious scent of fresh bread and other contraband reached Evan's nose and he grabbed for it. "Share it with Mike and McGuire."

Evan took the basket and his features turned depressed, "Do ya think we'll make it now, Joe?"

Joseph's smile faded to a frown. His eyes searched Evan's face, lit by the orange glow of the fires nearby. Evan hardly met anyone's gaze lately, beaten by guilt. Joseph drew a deep breath and formed a reply. He could not ignore what Evan asked.

"I can only pray," Joseph said.

"I think I'll go to bed now," Evan said after they fell silent for a time. His dark gaze penetrated the scenery laid around them. He then looked to Joseph offering a small smile. He placed a trembling hand on his neck and rubbed. "See you in the morning, Cap." Evan stepped away, but paused suddenly recalling the item held in his hand. He lifted the basket slightly, swinging it toward Joseph. "Tell mom thanks from her boys."

"I will," Joseph said, forcing a smile. He waved Evan farewell.

Evan turned and disappeared into his tent. Joseph watched the flap settle back down. It seemed a breeze disturbed it. He wondered if he imagined the moment, but realized the basket he brought from his mother no longer rested on his hand. Joseph lowered his gaze with a mournful expression.

The next morning, plans carried out the same as days before, but with the added excitement of preparing for a march north to avoid the Rebel forces. In the later hours before lunch, General Meade made a quick inspection of his army, showing himself those yet unfamiliar with him. For Joseph, Evan and Michael, it proved merely a reintroduction. They learned much of the man from their days at the academy, considering Meade attended the institution.

When the young men first saw him in other than a portrait, they noticed a great deal about him. He appeared nothing like the other Generals Joseph served under and proved by rumor to act unlike them as well. At full attention, Joseph and his comrades studied his features from where they stood on the ground in front of their trusty chargers. They noted everything from his dark and crumpled eye sockets to his balding crown and pointed beard. He studied them, too. However, they each felt sure he looked at them differently, weighing and measuring what his escort said of them and deciding to keep them among his numbers or serve them a dismissal.

General Meade passed along their lines continuing with no further hint of his thoughts. Joseph watched him go from the corner of his eye, daring to turn his head ever so slightly. The sound of boots on the ground brought his attention round again and he looked to the tree line eight hundred or so feet away. He knew Donnelly stepped out to dismiss them, but made himself wait for the order.

"Dismissed," Colonel Donnelly called to them. "Captain Maynard," he added, taking Joseph's attention away from leaving.

Joseph joined his superior, casting a glance toward the retreating forms of both Evan and Michael. The man probably had something unpleasant to say as usual. Joseph barely contained himself with the excitement to hear it. He stepped up to him, straightening his face and masking any anger in his eyes.

Joseph soon returned to his comrades. They walked away slowly, as not to listen or loiter. Joseph held trouble in his gaze and it wrestled with his mouth. Evan and Michael faced him and stopped.

"We're moving north tomorrow," Joseph told them. "Colonel wants the men ready."

"Where we going, Cap?" Evan asked unmoved by the warning.

"Pennsylvania," Joseph answered.

"Where's Pennsylvania?" Michael asked, pretending he did not know.

Joseph looked to him with a smile and almost laughed. He clapped his hand on Michael's shoulder, walking back toward their camp to rally the men. Evan followed with a smile. Michael shrugged away his joke. If he did not know, he could not go.

"Just another goddamn town in the goddamn way," Joseph clarified for him.

Despite discouraging experiences and little other choice, the Army of the Potomac moved bravely onward. With the defeat of Chancellorsville tucked behind them, they faced another day of war and would until the day Washington sent them home. The ghosts of fate whispered in each man's ear, just beyond their reach, as they raced north in pursuit of beating the Rebels to it. Their morale rose and hope for victory turned to need. Each man behaved more determined than ever that they rid the countryside of rebel scourge.

&

Placing each step carefully, Ezekiel crept down the hall from the kitchen to the parlor. He heard Mr. Conrad's warm tones, which beckoned him from his chores. Every night he sat outside the parlor door, listening to the man read from the newspaper. Ezekiel leaned forward as he walked, not making a sound. When he reached the archway of the parlor, he placed his back against the wall and slid down until his knees touched his chest. A small smile brightened his youthful features and he wrapped his arms about his legs.

Since the soldiers left, he wanted to know more about what they did far away from the farm and why the girls were so interested in them. His mother and father said they fought to keep America one country and to free the slaves. Ezekiel doubted their word, but curiosity got the better of him. While he listened to the news, rolling off Mr. Conrad's tongue, he saw the truth of what his parents had said.

"The Union Army of the Potomac will cross the Maryland-Pennsylvania border, to protect the North from the southern threat posed by General Lee's Confederate forces. It is projected the Potomac will clash with the Rebel Army in a massive battle that may decide the war. As you read this minute article, our soldiers march to their deaths or possibly for our countries greater glory—"

"Stuart Dear," Margaret said.

Ezekiel peeped around the opening to see the couple who faced each other. Mr. Conrad sat in his chair by the window and his wife on the sofa. Closest to the opening, he spied Emily with her head lowered to a thick book in her lap. She wiped her eye and drew a steadying breath.

"Is there anything in there about Mrs. Murphy's grand welcome home soiree this weekend? I'm sure Em would much prefer to hear about that. She had so been hoping to visit Mary. It breaks her heart to know these things that prevent her."

Ezekiel heard Emily's mother speak and watched the young woman look up from her reading. He saw the hollow look in her eyes like his father used to keep when they lived on the farm down south. He touched the door casement and felt his features sink into sadness. Emily always stepped about with such joy. She never spoke a foul word to him and treated him with the respect fitting his age. She was at his side for every bump and bruise, like a big sister.

"Yes," Emily breathed. "I would, actually."

Ezekiel saw tears glisten unshed in her eyes. She set her book on the chair she sat in and rose to her feet to walk out of the room. Without noticing him, she went to the stairs and climbed. Ezekiel leaned back against the wall and watched her go. He felt his heart crush in his chest.

"Zeke," his mother's voice called softly. He looked to see her, watching him from the kitchen. "What are you doing down there?"

Ezekiel jumped to his feet with a smile for his mother. He closed the distance between them and said, "Emily's crying." His mother touched his forehead with her brow furrowing and a frown forming on her lips. "Mr. Conrad said the Potomac is going to face General Lee's army in Pencil something. Is that where Mr. Joe and Mr. Michael are?"

"Pennsylvania," Hettie said for him.

"Pennsylvania," Ezekiel repeated, still looking concerned for Emily.

"And, yes," Hettie nearly forgot to answer his question. Her face pinched and she distractedly added, "I should go to her," Hettie said to him. "You need to finish sweeping out the kitchen."

"Yes, ma'am."

Hettie touched her son's head and brushed past him into the hall. Ezekiel stepped into the kitchen, looking at the sink sadly. He felt his anger grow inside him. If the masters of the South never existed, Emily's soldier would be safe with her. He shook his little head and picked up the broom he abandoned. They still managed to beat them down.

ᘓ

"I don't think it's just another goddamn town, sir. People'll be talking about this for years," Evan called out, laying on his back behind a tree.

"I don't think this is the time, Lieutenant," Joseph said, firing his pistol across a field littered with the bodies of the wounded and dead.

The cavalry horses shied behind a stand of trees at the back of a small colonial farmhouse. They whickered and nervously pranced while shot zinged through the air around them. In a knot they backed off, ears twitching. Both Evan and Joseph crouched with their arms over their heads. The whine of an artillery shell sliced through the air. In a loud explosion, the ground burst several yards ahead of them, spraying soil and body parts. Joseph looked to Evan and received a dark glare in return.

Straightening along the trunk of an oak, Joseph judged the field. Picking his target, he aimed his pistol and fired. Quickly ducking back down, he picked up his rifle and began the load process, placing the pistol back in his holster on his hip. His eyes caught sight of a round figure in blue, dashing from cover to cover. Lifting his chin, he set his rifle on the ground at his side and took out his pistol, reloading that as well. He looked calm, considering.

Sidling up to Joseph, a sweat covered McGuire said, “Donnelly’s sent word ta pull bahc ta the cematree.” McGuire fought to catch his breath.

“Sergeant,” Joseph nodded and looked to Evan. Flicking his eyes back to the ruddy Irishman, he added, “spread the word.”

McGuire nodded, showing no fear but that which rested in his eyes. They obviously were pinned under enemy fire, but Donnelly had given orders. Joseph rose on one knee, taking his rifle with him. He then stood and fired at any gray coat he saw. He looked down to Evan and saw the man hesitate to move.

“Pull back!” Joseph cried out.

Evan carefully leaned his way up the tree that offered him protection, until he stood on his feet. He looked to Joseph, terror wrenching his dirty face. He nodded and swallowed hard. They either ran or stayed and became prisoners or worse.

“Move out,” Joseph hollered, waving his chamois gloved hand toward the stand of trees. He watched the men retreat, taking their mounts with them at a run. “Fall back!” He urged them.

Joseph looked to Evan and nodded. The time to make their run came. Turning their backs on their retreating units, both officers hoisted their weapons and propelled themselves backward. To their left, Joseph saw Michael help a wounded man back onto his feet and pull him to the safety of the trees beyond their small clearing. McGuire appeared by the stand of trees, holding the reins of each mount. He proved a brave or foolish man that day. Ducking only occasionally, as bullets sounded close, he smiled and handed their chargers over.

“Good day ta ya, sars,” he said. “If there’s nuthin else, I’ll take my leave of ya.”

Somehow, they mounted and followed the rest of their men. Gathered with the rest at the cemetery where

Donnelly sent them, Joseph took his head count. With a small black book in his hands, he marked down their losses. Scratching his brow, he drew a deep breath and thought over each name. They fell back further south away from the city with every contest and lost a handful each time. By then, they held a line at the cemetery without much loss of ground or life.

"The rest have minor wounds," Evan said, finishing his report.

"See they get medical attention," Joseph muttered. He looked up from his little book and studied Evan. "Where's Michael?" He asked alarmed.

"Reporting to Donnelly," Evan replied smoothly.

"All right," Joseph drawled with a nod. He squinted at Gettysburg and tucked his book into his jacket pocket. "Let's hope this is done then."

At sunset, Joseph watched the battle below as it continued. His eyes swept over his company spread before him, awaiting the unavoidable. Through the rifle cracks and artillery shelling, he heard the commanders discuss maneuvers. However, Joseph heard mere snippets of their murmured conversation over the battle noise. Shutting off their words, he returned his gaze to the field.

Above them the sky glowed purple and orange. The light grew dim and night would soon surround them. Joseph wondered if there would be peace this night. The night before witnessed continued attacks from both sides. Joseph wiped his face with a chamois glove, trying to erase the exhaustion. The graves of strangers observed the events of the day, marked by gleaming white stones etched with dead letters. He hoped their presence was no warning of what came for all of them in these days.

"Been awhile since we had a decent dinner," Evan said, thinking the sky looked like a blueberry tart with whip cream clouds ready to eat.

"It'll be a while longer," Joseph drawled in that manner that marked him since his return from Vermont.

Instead the sky looked like Emily's eyes in the night with a fire lighting them.

"Captain," Evan's voice stole his attention. Joseph looked to where he sat in the saddle next to him, leaning on the pommel, as if relaxed and not worn out. "You never said what happened on leave."

Joseph eyed him, "Not much to say."

"You haven't been the same since," Evan smiled. "Did Em tell you to go?" He straightened his features when Joseph looked down at Manny's mane. He sensed the turmoil in his friend. "Joe?" He asked worried. He knew Emily could be brash when pressed.

Joseph lifted his scruffy chin and looked over the field, brushing his hat back to scratch his forehead. He felt his heart pound with fear other than death. Releasing a weighted breath, he drew the reins of his mount tight in his fist. With practiced is, he sauntered him right, to stand a hair's breadth away from Evan's.

"You can't tell any of this to Mike," Joseph said, taking hold of his arm and lowering his voice to a hoarse whisper. He looked desperately into Evan's dark eyes. "He'd turn his rifle on me as sure as Lee himself."

Evan looked at him, leaning back, "Sure—I won't tell."

Joseph released his best friend since academy, appearing dismayed by both his actions and thoughts, "Me and Emily—I—we met in the garden." Lowering his eyes from Evan's, he continued with a frown, "She told me things she shouldn't have." He sighed, looking up to the sky, "She cried and I—"

"It can't be that bad," Evan scoffed when Joseph stopped.

"It can," Joseph murmured. "But—" he cut himself off again with shame.

"What is it Joe?"

Joseph lifted his eyes and Evan saw the tears stand in them. Joseph never showed such emotions before his men. Evan guessed the war finally broke him. He waited for Joseph to speak, knowing not to push him.

"I've ruined, Emily," Joseph said bitterly. He shut his eyes and shook his head.

"What?" Evan asked choked with shock. He never thought Joseph the type to play his games, Emily especially. "What if? Damn it, Joe!" Evan cursed out loud. He saw several heads turn in their direction. Joseph looked to him wide eyed. Lowering his voice, he added, "You're gonna do right by her aren't you?" He paused, feeling the pain of his loss again. "Don't end up like me."

"I'll do right by Emily, even if it never happened," Joseph swore, meaning it.

Evan smiled suddenly and laughed. He tried to imagine little Emily as a seducer. His mind would not wrap around it. Patting Joseph's arm, he looked away and shook his head with a big grin on his face.

"I told you the cow thing would work," Evan jested to put his friend at ease. "Women love that shit."

"That isn't funny," Joseph said most seriously.

"Yeah, it is," Evan laughed. "But—I swear I'll still keep it from Mike." He drew his expression more seriously with his tone. "But, you owe me for it, Captain."

"Captain Maynard," Donnelly drew out his last name as he approached on horseback, looking at ease with the scenery.

While Donnelly closed in, their conversation precisely ended. He passed him a written set of orders, explaining they came direct from the top. Joseph took the paper and opened the folds to read them. His eyes raked the lines, quickly taking in the meaning expressed. Joseph lifted his face to Donnelly and saluted. Donnelly offered him a nod and his dark eyes flashed with an unspoken apology. He flicked his gaze to Evan and then took his leave of them.

"What now?" Evan asked once Donnelly left earshot.

"We hold here," Joseph said. "They're breaking through."

"I mean with Emily," Evan said seriously. Joseph looked to him and he slowly smiled.

By sundown, the battle of Gettysburg ended with only random shots fired from rifles in the dark. The hard fighting had ended. Thousands of dead soldiers lay on the ground, needing attention from their comrades for suitable burials. The groans of the wounded called for mercy. Joseph gathered his men about him again to take the count. His little black book rested in his gloved hand with a leaky pen to jot down his thoughts. Against the morbid backdrop, he saw them fed and refitted with ammunition.

Joseph sought out his officers, sharing their meager rations together. He sat with them at their fire and filled his belly just enough to take the edge off his hunger. His eyes searched each of their faces. They spoke quietly to one another, thankful for each man's presence. When Joseph looked to Michael, the younger soldier smiled and sat up.

"That was one hell of a fight, sir," Michael's voice cracked the calm.

"One I don't wish to repeat," Joseph smiled. He looked to Evan who picked something from his food and flicked it away with annoyance. Joseph elbowed him. "Don't you agree Lieutenant?"

"Yeah," Evan said distracted. "Whatever you say, Captain."

Joseph laughed, knowing he heard nothing. He turned his eyes back to his men. None of them held joy in their features. He held onto his smile despite the desolation.

"We're drawing back to Frederick in the morning," Joseph said to lighten their spirits. "Would either of you two be interested in seeing some of the folks who live there?" Joseph asked, clearly meaning Evan and Michael.

Joseph watched their faces as they exchanged knowing glances. Delightful smirks lit up their darkened features. At least they laughed now.

"If I may, Captain," Michael piped up immediately, wearing a hopeful expression. "I would."

Evan laughed out loud at his friend's expense. He gathered himself and said, "I don't think the entire army could hold him back. I cannot wait to meet your sister."

Joseph smiled and took a long sip from his tin cup. He lowered it and swallowed. Releasing a sigh, he gave Michael a sparkling glance. Now came the time for merriment.

"Then get the completed casualty report for our new units to me before noon tomorrow and the letters for the widows," Joseph ordered. "If you'll excuse me," he added, setting his dishes down by the fire and rising to his feet.

Michael's chin drooped at the Captain's words. He studied the food on his plate and felt his stomach tumble with anxiety. After nearly dying, seeing Mary was the only thing he wanted to do. He lifted his eyes slightly at the thought and Joseph's shadow passed before the fire. He felt the Captain's hand pat his shoulder. Then, Joseph disappeared. Michael released an exasperated breath.

"Always a price to pay," Michael whined.

"Well," Evan smiled. "You are courting his sister."

When the dawn rose on the next day, Joseph rode at the head of his units in the march back to Frederick. Casting his eyes over the heads of the infantry who walked ahead of him and over the tree lined roadway, Joseph allowed his mind to wander. He dared to daydream while the hope from the success at Gettysburg fueled him on.

Suddenly, the world felt uneven. Joseph woke to realize that Manny took a misstep. He watched his head hang low, seemingly exhausted. Joseph's heart pounded against his ribs. Quickly dismounting, he guided the horse to the side of the road and out of the way of the moving army. Joseph whispered and patted Manny all the while he examined his legs and hooves. Stumped for an answer, Joseph returned to his great narrow head and looked at him with hands on hips. He shook his own head confused by the symptoms.

Joseph lifted his chin and watched the cavalry units ride past. He saw the sorrow for him in their eyes.

Gritting his teeth to set his jaw, he looked back to his trusted mount. Joseph placed a loving hand on his muzzle and rubbed. Using soft words, he urged him to take a step forward.

Holding his breath, Joseph saw the horse stumble weakly to him. He whickered and lowered his nose to the ground. Joseph's heart clenched at seeing Manny stricken. He spent years training his horse, teaching him to expect his every move. Manny knew how to move without command. More than skill alone bound the horse to his rider. Manny became one of the few companions he looked forward to seeing everyday. He could not lose him now.

"You're just tired, boy," Joseph patted Manny's forehead between his eyes on the white stripe of his fetlock. "So am I," he rasped. He looked at his companion mournfully, but Manny only blinked and turned his head to look behind him. Joseph's greatest friend since the Point became a casualty of the war. Losing a horse may prove a fact of war to a horse soldier who enjoyed longevity, but he hated it just the same. He hoped Manny not in either category, especially that of abuse. Manny served him soundly too often for that.

"Captain," Joseph heard someone call. Donnelly approached on horseback. "What is wrong?"

"My horse can't go another step, sir. He's finished," Joseph told Donnelly.

"That's too bad," the commander said, more because this event stood to slow them down than to give comfort. "You best start marching then, Captain Maynard."

Donnelly saluted arrogantly, sporting a malicious grin. Once the man's back turned to him and he rode away with the rest, Joseph glared daggers into him, muttering curses under his breath. He gave this man his all and Donnelly cared very little.

Joseph dismantled his belongings from Manny's back. He pulled his saddle belt loose until the saddle fell to the ground. He then followed up with freeing him of the weight of the packs and saddle pad. He left Manny's bridle on, planning to lead him by it. In his moment of despair, when he believed he might need to free Manny to chance, Little Nate trudged past at the head of an infantry unit.

Nate trudged along, his drum bouncing on his back. He looked worn and tired, just like the horse Joseph thought to save. Joseph whistled the red haired boy over. Nate looked up, still marching boldly on. A bright smile bloomed on his freckled face. He rushed to Joseph who waited for him with hands on his hips.

"Hello, Nate," Joseph smiled.

"Hello, Captain, sir." He smiled up at Joseph with a small hand raised in salute.

"Good to see you well, soldier," Joseph said in earnest, saluting back.

"Thank you, sir."

"What say you to escorting Manny for me? Would you take him up north?" Joseph asked, putting his hands on the charger's muzzle to show him. "I'll give you ten dollars, if you take this horse to Vermont," Joseph bribed him. "I want him brought to the Conrad Dairy Farm dead or alive. Preferably the later," Joseph directed.

"I can find it, sir." The boy's eyes glowed with delight.

"Here's five dollars to get you there," Joseph said, digging in his belt pouch for the note. At some point, the boy would surely think Joseph carried the U.S. Mint right in his pockets, if he did not do so already. "You brave enough?"

"It'll keep my mother off my tail," Nate said, cocking his head to the side to look up at Joseph. "I'm more fraid a her than a Rebel rifle."

Joseph smiled and handed over the greenback, "You'll get five when you come back."

Joseph told him the directions and wrote the address down on a slip of paper from his small notebook. Tearing it from his book, he gave the boy the paper and watched him read it. Backing up, he waved Nate with him. Joseph bent down and picked up a bag. He handed it to Nate, telling him he should only receive a treat once or twice a day, although the horse liked more often. Then he grasped a bulging sac from beside his scattered belongings. He handed that to Nate, too.

"That feed won't last long," Joseph said. "Make sure you catch a train north as soon as you can," he further directed. The boy simply nodded, never telling if he truly understood.

Joseph rose to his feet and looked at Manny's dark eyes, carefully watching them. Joseph patted his fetlock again. The sound of horses approached from behind and made him turn. Evan and Michael sat atop their mounts. Their faces expressed clear concern.

"What's happening, Captain?"

Joseph turned away from his friends. He gathered the reins of his horse in his hand and gave them to the small boy. Joseph took his drum from him and set it on the ground beside his belongings. He swore to keep watch over it while the boy stayed away. He then helped him to mount.

Joseph rattled out instructions to not ride the horse hard. Manny was too tired for playing and needed a rest. He then asked him to stay in the train car with him once he paid his passage. Joseph thought the world of the charger, but could only hope Nate saw that clearly

"All right," Joseph said, looking straight up into Nate's eyes. "This horse means a lot to me. If he dies because you treated him bad, I'll find out," Joseph warned, pointing a finger. He paused and then whispered good bye to his friend, insisting he would turn out all right. Emily would take care of him. He turned back to the boy. "Give me your hat and coat," Joseph held out his hand. "I want you to disguise yourself until your at least safe on northern soil," he pushed Nate's coat into his pack. He straightened and pulled a letter from his jacket pocket. "Give this to Emily Conrad only—and thank her to work her magic on the poor beast." He gave Nate a solid pat on the back to send him off. "And here's enough money for feed and the train."

"You can count on me, Captain Maynard. I'll be good to old Manny. Don't doubt that," he assured Joseph.

"Good," Joseph smiled. He saw Michael dismount and step to his belongings. The Second Lieutenant picked them up and gave a share to Evan. Then, he turned and secured the rest of the load to his animal. "Try to walk him and ride only when you must."

"Yes, sir," The boy nodded his understanding.

"Those are orders, boy," Joseph said.

"Sir. Yes, sir."

"Go find a place to rest him for a few hours—then get started."

Under the scrutiny of his subordinates, Joseph turned his back to his animal friend. Displaying a hard grimace, he joined the rest of the men who made the long march to Frederick. Evan and Michael looked to each other worriedly, but would not give in to his dark mood. They clucked their tongues, calling their mounts into motion.

"We'll take turns on my horse, Cap," Evan suggested.

Joseph shook his head and hand at Evan in refusal. He continued silently forward, feeling sick in his stomach. Riding another horse smacked of treachery in his heart. Forgoing the agony, he thought to walk, as he saw most of the soldiers do since he joined the Potomac three years prior. Somehow they slogged through it all, so he followed suit, but with his subordinate officers, riding behind him.

"I suppose this isn't the time," Michael said warily. He eyed the back of Joseph's head. Turning his gaze crossways, he looked to Evan for any warning to leave off. "Donnelly sent us back. He wants you to confiscate another mount, soon as you come across one suitable for duty. He said to say, he can't afford a dismounted cavalry officer," Michael relayed the message, as told him by his superior.

Joseph bared his teeth in a bitter expression of anguish. "Pompous ass," he said under his breath.

"Easy, Cap. There's ears," Evan drawled.

Joseph spent the night pondering his misfortune, which left him with little sleep. In its place, he stared at his picture of Emily. The faded tones of gray made him wonder what she thought of the events that would be splashed all over the papers. He prayed the newsmen treated the matter of Gettysburg gently for her sake.

The next morning the march renewed. This time, Joseph walked at the head of his units, as proudly as if he still sat atop his great war stallion. Thankfully, their route allowed him a view of many farms before noon and Donnelly found no reason to complain at his delay to select a new mount. Perhaps he understood the delicacy of his situation.

When the road took the bend toward Emmitsburg, Maryland, Joseph spotted a fine looking fence, which enclosed an expansive farm lined along the left side of the road. Peering through the trees, he saw well groomed fields and neatly kept buildings. The scene called him to take a closer look and he heeded it with wisdom. Joseph stepped from the line of marching soldiers to stand at the fence and, as always, his friends followed him.

"Is that a horse farm?" Evan said, disbelieving the luck.

Joseph studied the broad cleared fields bordered by an old forest of pines. In the distance several horses wasted the day, lazily grazing or standing with not much else to do. Joseph stepped forward along the road bordering the fence. His eyes never left the fields. His pace quickened. He swiftly stepped the distance toward the house. Then he saw her. Joseph slowed a hundred or more yards from the main house. He was frozen for several moments, watching her frisk in her corral. He looked back to Evan and Michael who dismounted to see what he stared at. He gave them a broad bright grin. Their expressions gave away their awe. Joseph looked back to the mare and found she reminded him of a wild spirit who traveled far north to rest. Her red coat gleamed in the bright sunlight and he fell in love all over again.

The three men approached the noble farmhouse, studying the fence and hedges that lined the path to the front door. More neatly clipped verdure edged the base of the porch. Without hesitation, Joseph walked up the wooden steps to the green door. He had left his companions on horseback to wait in the yard. He cast a hopeful glance to them over his shoulder and then faced the doòr, giving it a solid knocking. Joseph adjusted his uniform jacket. He hoped he looked presentable. After an already lengthy march that morning, he could imagine he might frighten those at home.

Sitting in his saddle, Evan turned his head to see the particular mare in question approach the fence and hang her head over to watch them. She shook her mane and whickered before turning her bright black eyes to the man at her farmer's door. Evan laughed lightly, slapping Michael's arm to gain his attention. He pointed to the horse surprised at her reaction to them.

"Hey, Captain," Evan called out, looking toward Joseph on the porch. "She's waiting for you."

Joseph turned his eyes to the fence and saw the red mare closely watch him. She weighed and measured his worth, as much as he did with her moments ago. Shaking his head with a wavering smile, he turned back to the farmhouse door and knocked a second time. The scurry of slippered feet met his ears from behind the blockade, followed by the muffled tones of a woman's voice. The green door swung open and a small woman of middle years appeared. She peered at him from behind wire glasses. He smiled and removed his hat, bidding her good day. She smiled at him, disguising her concern at the sight of his uniform with little success.

"Pardon me, ma'am," he laughed away her worry. "My name is Captain Joseph Maynard, Army of the Potomac," the sound of his voice noticeably put her at ease. "I wondered if I might ask to look at one of your horses? You see, mine's been lamed and my commander asked me to buy another as soon as possible," Joseph continued, explaining his presence quite charmingly.

"Maynard?" She questioned. "You wouldn't be one of the Baltimore Maynards would you?"

"Indeed I am," Joseph replied astounded to know his name came that far.

"We've heard a great deal about your family in the society pages, Captain."

"I hope all good," Joseph laughed.

"Indeed, sir," She smiled breathlessly. She touched her hair self consciously and offered him another smile. "Our horses are the finest these parts have to offer," she stammered unsure. "Let me find my husband. It'd be best for you to deal with him."

"Of course, ma'am." Joseph bent his head. Then, he retreated two steps back along the porch to the stairs where he stopped to wait.

The woman shut the door to her home. "Bernice!" The woman's voice rang out through the walls. "Bernice, where is your father?" She questioned.

"Out in the barn feeding the horses," a young woman's voice replied, as the door reopened.

"I'll fetch him," she said to the woman. "You bring some water to those men out there," she commanded. She looked at Joseph and said, "It'll only be a moment. I apologize at keeping you."

"No matter, ma'am. Take your time," Joseph smiled.

The door shut on him for the second time.

He shook his head confused and turned to face his companions patiently awaiting him. Joseph smiled, thinking of the time he met Emily.

"You're famous too?" Michael stared. "Don't that just beat all?"

Joseph shrugged, not unused to his name being known to strangers.

Rather suddenly the door popped open behind him and a young woman in a dull blue dress stepped onto the porch. She carried a stoneware pitcher and three cups on a tray. She smiled at him from pink hued face, spattered with freckles on the cheeks and nose. Her red curls bounced on her neck when she stepped toward him. Joseph nodded respectfully to her and removed his hat.

"Mother asked me to bring you water," Bernice explained. "For your men, too."

"Lieutenants," Joseph called to them. The soldiers dismounted and came up onto the porch. "Miss—"

"Bernice Wallace," she filled in her name for him.

"Miss Wallace wishes you to have something to drink," Joseph said.

"Thank you, ma'am," they said together, seizing the cups from the tray.

Bernice smiled at them, almost giggling at their antics. In turn, they bowed and shuffled before her, removing their hats. Joseph excused himself intent on another red head that day. Before he went his hand clamped on the scruff of Michael's neck, and he pulled him away beside him. His call for an angel stood answered a long while ago.

"I want you to tell me what you think of her," Joseph said to Michael's questioning glance.

"I think she's nice," Michael foolishly said.

Joseph glared at him, helping him down the stairs a bit roughly, "The horse, Second Lieutenant." Stepping to the ground, they crossed the emerald grass to where the horse waited. "Do I need to remind you that you court my sister, Conrad?"

"No, sir," Michael hung his head shamefaced. He spun his hat in his hands.

Joseph grabbed the hat and smashed it on his subordinate's head with playful irritation, "Then look at the horse."

A short time passed before the head of the house joined him. They haggled while Evan laughed and conversed with the women freely. A decent price was eventually met, but not in the conventional manner. He paid the owners what he could afford then for her, even though the man stood a staunch unionist with a big heart and wanted to give her for nothing to her admirer. They proved more than happy to oblige the soldier, but Joseph would not take advantage of them. He thought they showed fear and not loyalty

With the horse brought around from her enclosure, Joseph saddled her up and accepted the bridle she wore until he could get a military one to replace it. This evening she would receive a branded U.S. and be his until she left the world.

Joseph swung into the saddle and found the mare responded well to him. He called to Lieutenant Howell who entertained the women on the porch. Waving a hand, he signaled the time to leave. The last of the Potomac units just passed the farm and they fell behind. Evan smiled to him with a nod of understanding. He excused himself with noble bows and flourishes, all to impress the young Bernice. Joseph allowed him the moment, noting that Evan smiled and stared the most he dared since last November.

Once all three mounted their steeds, they turned from the yard expressing more thanks. Then, they reached the road and trotted behind the rest of the army to catch up with their units some time that day. Joseph felt invigorated at sitting in the saddle again and the soldiers at his side were livened, as well. Joseph looked to his longtime companion wonderingly. However, Evan said nothing until they rode among their units again.

"God made an angel," Evan suddenly breathed, unable to contain himself before their friends. "After this here war is over, it'll be my duty to find Miss Bernice Wallace and marry her," Evan crowed. He paused, feeling the eyes of the men assessing him. "Mrs. Wallace asked me to dinner if I've the chance before or after the war," he smiled, leaning toward Joseph.

"All that from a smile?" Joseph asked him sarcastically. "Or was it the cup of water?"

"What about the water?" Evan sat up straight, looking chastised. "As I recall, a cup of water set you up rightly."

"Ah—that water's a menace," McGuire clipped in with his thick accent. "Worse'n whiskey when a woman ands it to you." He winked at the boys.

With his new mount, Joseph rode on to their next campaign. She brought him good luck like Manny. She quickly earned her name, given her by McGuire's suggestion. Joseph thought nothing better than an Irish name would suit her. He called her Aoife. It fit, considering the manner of both namesake and the mare.

Having survived Gettysburg and a few clashes with the enemy after that, a rest period came to the Potomac. Joseph decided no better time presented itself for a short leave to Frederick and the home of his parents. As promised, he brought his usual companions along for the jaunt. They followed the road to Frederick and then bore off the fork toward the road lined with large houses. The bright happy colors, gables and fancy gingerbread lifted their spirits. Joseph knew the way home from anywhere in the world.

When they rode through the village, the citizens stopped and called Joseph's name, waving and smiling at him familiarly. Joseph seemed like a celebrity among them. At the end of the lane he turned sharp left and followed the cobblestones in front of brick sidewalks and mansions that loomed larger than the next.

Joseph smiled up at his home, settled in the end of the street. A candle burned in the parlor window since the war began and was still there, but now accompanied by another. Joseph set his jaw sternly. He did not fully accept the love his sister felt for Michael, convinced the young man only meant to play with her, as his only means to take a swing at him over Emily.

Joseph missed the exchange behind him. Lost in his thoughts, he heard nothing of Evan and Michael's conversation. Evan struck Michael's arm, making him look to the house. He pointed to the window with the two candles. He and Michael grinned at each other like children.

Within the fine walls of the Maynard family home, young Mary stood in the parlor making her last adjustments to her fine clothes and hair. She gazed into a silver hand mirror. Looking past the reflective oval, she saw Phoebe press her face to the glass of the window. The house sat in perfect view of the lane outside. The men could not sneak up on them.

Mary's heart leaped up at the thought of her beloved Michael coming for dinner. This was the first time he would meet her parents. Filled with nervousness, she joined her servant at the window. She gently touched her back. When Phoebe turned, she handed her the mirror and dismissed her to other duties. Phoebe smiled knowingly and touched her shoulder to ease her mind.

Phoebe turned away, leaving her young mistress to her vigil. In no time, the young man they met in Vermont would grace the house with his good presence. She smiled to herself, trying not to laugh at her mistress's anticipation.

"Mother!" Mary called. Her face flushed, as she stepped back from the window. "It's him. It's him."

The three men rode in a triangle formation along the center of the road, with Joseph at the head. It resembled a small cavalry charge.

"Who dear? Who?" Her mother asked, rushing in. Her tones sounded startled.

Mary went to her mother's side, dancing on her feet like a little girl begging. She fiddled with her perfectly placed hair, looking desperately at her mother.

"Michael, Mother—and Joey!" She paused with her eyes wide. "Do I look all right?"

"You look lovely, darling," Lucretia told her daughter, suspecting the feelings that excited her for sometime. Mary never stopped the tales of the Conrad man who served with Joseph. Mary smiled and then dashed toward the door. Lucretia quickly cut her daughter off. "It's unseemly to be too eager, dear."

Mary's expression turned quickly sad, but she backed away from the door at her mother's advice. Her mother put her arm about her waist and squeezed reassuringly.

"Plenty of time later for rushing to him," Lucretia said.

Outside, the three soldiers reached the front gate and a pair of grooms took the horses when they dismounted. Joseph smiled and greeted them with handshakes. They had worked for his father for years before he left for the academy. When the three finished with the servants, they walked to the front of the home, talking and laughing, swathed in good moods. Joseph climbed the steps first, one then three sets of boots scrapping on the stone. Joseph took hold of the doorknocker and struck it three solid claps. The men patiently waited, adjusting coats and removing hats.

Behind the door, Lucretia waited for the knock. When it came, she bowed her head to Phoebe and stepped back, pulling Mary with her. The door swung open before her eyes and she felt her heart still for a moment, until her son stood within her view. She covered her mouth with a shaking hand and gasped.

"It's good to see you again, Joey," Mary smiled, lunging at him with her arms outstretched. She crushed her big brother in her arms, shutting her eyes and resting her golden head on his arm. He squeezed her back, letting her know that he missed her, too. Mary released him, taking hold of his gloved hand to guide him in the house. "You're all just in time for dinner. Hello Second Lieutenant Conrad. Lieutenant Howell."

"Ma'am," the other men said at the same time.

Michael looked at Evan reproachfully, catching him eyeing Mary. Evan shrugged and gave a sheepish grin in return.

"Hello, my boy," Mrs. Maynard said in a delicate and aged voice. Joseph's mother stood in the foyer to greet them with warm smiles. Tears were in her eyes. She held out her arms and Joseph rushed to her like a little boy.

"Mother," he said, crushing her to him. "How've you been? Lord, I've missed you?"

"Worried as any mother should be—and I've missed you," she laughed, squeezing him back with a relieved sigh.

"What're we having for dinner? Are you making me that pudding?"

Joseph's mother leaned back from him, smiling up in his face. She patted his chest covered in the brass buttons and her eyes took on a cheerless glow. Joseph turned into the man she always hoped he would, but she feared it meant the end for him. Tears strained as she looked up at him, gathering her thoughts. She only held the faith of her prayers, pleading for his safe return from the war.

"You haven't changed, my boy, after all that schooling," she tsked at him. "Not how is my father? No, is the practice doing well? Have we any money left? Did the Confederates beat you down? No—my son asks what's for dinner," she mocked him to keep herself from crying. "No matter," she dismissed her questions before Joseph responded. "Will you introduce your new friend, or shall I do it myself?" Lucretia stepped out from behind her son and smiled at the golden haired boy behind him. In an instant she knew the man by her daughters prattling. "I've heard a great deal about your visit to the Conrad's, Joseph. This must be Michael," she looked at him, holding her hand out. Michael took it, bending slightly at the waist. He smiled and gave her fingers a gentle squeeze. "Good evening to you, Second Lieutenant Conrad. Mary made good friends with—Emily, I think it is. Your sister."

Joseph slowly stepped up beside his mother. She reached across his chest and patted the pocket where he kept the photograph of the young woman she mentioned. It seemed she knew right where to find it. Joseph clasped his hands behind his back and bounced on his booted feet. His gaze accused Mary of betraying him. She simply smiled back at him and winked. Joseph shook his head, laughing to himself. He felt sure he would have to explain why he failed to mention the young woman any sooner. How could he explain something he found no words for? Only seeing would lend justice to it. He smiled and mouthed a thank you to his sister, clamping his lips shut to typify his sarcasm.

"Yes, Emily is my sister," Michael said, releasing Joseph's mother.

"I've heard a great deal about both of you," Lucretia smiled at her daughter. "It is satisfying to place the man with his name at last. I hope we may gain the chance of the same with your sister." She turned her gaze to her son with a glint of playfulness.

"Come sit in the parlor," Lucretia suggested to her guests. "It is nice to see you again, Lieutenant Howell."

"Thank you, ma'am," Evan replied, as Phoebe approached them, accepting their hats and gloves. She nodded with a smile to each.

Lucretia and Mary headed them into the parlor. The women sat together on one sofa, pointing to the other and the chairs at the ends, "Come sit." She smiled up at them. "It'll be a short time before dinner," Lucretia said, watching them take to their seats.

Lucretia spoke with her guests for a short while. Then another loud set of clacks on the brass doorknocker tore through the hallway. She saw Phoebe step quickly to the door. Lucretia continued to speak, picking her fingernails together. She crossed her legs and waited. Warning tingled her spine.

Phoebe quickly opened the door without opening the peep window to see who came to the house. Her gaze settled on a tall angry looking man. Francis McFadden could not pick a worse time to show his face in the Maynard home. He stepped in, making Phoebe step back. She put a hand up in front of her mouth to keep from calling out.

"I demand ta be let in—I want to see Mr. Maynard this instant," Francis bellowed, smelling distinctly of whiskey.

Phoebe froze where she stood, blocking his path into the parlor. Francis glowered down at her. Hobbling forward with his cane, he swung his great arm out and roughly pushed her aside. Phoebe called out in a terrified shriek. She quickly shut her eyes and covered her head, to protect herself from unwarranted blows. She fell to the floor.

Phoebe looked into the parlor from where she lay on the floor trembling. All three soldiers rose to their feet with looks of concern on their face for her. She looked away from them and gradually rose to her knees, to push herself to the furthest wall for safety.

"Phoebe, darling," Lucretia dashed to her side, crouching down to help her stand. "Are you all right?"

"Yes, ma'am," Phoebe said still unsure.

"You've no business here," Joseph's voice filled the rooms with anger. He stepped to Francis sneering.

The Confederate entered the room, leaning on a cane. His foot failed to exist beneath the cuff of his pants. However, he made an impressive figure in the room, glaring around at the gathered Union soldiers. Something passed that he did not appreciate. Then his eyes raked Michael, carefully holding Mary behind him. He saw the way she peered at him over the other man's shoulder, frightened. He felt sick to see her hands grasp the boy so familiarly, as if the whelp could protect her like he could.

"I won't leave until I speak with your father, Yankee," Francis said embittered.

"No," Evan piped up brazenly. He saw Mr. Maynard rush down the stairs with a worried expression on his aged features. He knew they needed to get the crazed ape out of the house before he hurt anyone else. "You'll leave now."

McFadden laughed at him, "Make me, boy."

"If you insist," Evan grinned with a shrug of his shoulders.

Together and against the pleas of the women, Joseph and Evan wrestled Francis from the Maynard house. Michael joined them, finally prying Mary's desperate fingers from his arm. He saw his comrades push Francis down the stairs to the yard. Michael tore his cane from his hands before he used it like a hammer on their heads. He sauntered behind, watching them tear open the wrought iron fence gate and push the barbarian into the street. Michael threw the cane hard. It clattered on the cobblestones, bouncing and rolling away.

"Don't let me hear of you showing your face round here again, boy!" Joseph hollered.

Francis rose onto his remaining foot, seething with defiling anger. He glared over his nose with red eyes. Catching his breath, he wiped the back of his hand on his mouth. He could rip them to shreds right there, but another idea popped into his cold and calculating mind.

He wanted something more permanent to take care of them.

"I'll get ya, Maynard!" Francis warned. "No doubt—I'll get ya."

Lights flicked on in the other houses. People drew from indoors to their porches to see the commotion on the street. They whispered to themselves, *The Maynard boy is at it again.*

"Leave off, reb," Michael joined them at the fence. "You already lost this fight."

Reluctantly, Francis turned from them. He glowered and muttered under his breath, still warning them out of earshot. Using the stub of his ankle, he limped to where his cane lay and picked it up roughly. He grinned to himself madly. The plan continued to form in his drunken mind.

Francis thought he made his intent clear to Mary. She would become his wife when he could make it possible. Since the war came, she suddenly acted ignorant of that agreement, as if she was too good for him. Well, he would show her and her puppy what kind of man they played with.

Picking his way through the streets, Francis went to a broken down building pressed against another building and about to fall over. He hobbled up to it and lifted his cane to knock on the chipped and peeling door. He muttered at the occupant to hurry and banged the head of his cane on the door again. The rickety portal shook open and a man squinted out at him over a lamp.

"I've a job for you," Francis grinned, bleary eyed.

When it came time for them to leave at the end of the mostly enjoyable night, the mood of the joyous house turned somber. The dimness overshadowed the home's grandeur. Joseph's mother offered a package of food and other comforts to send them on their way, with her extended hospitality and love. Good byes never came easily anywhere.

Lastly, Mary bid farewell to her hero in blue. They stood on the porch, holding hands. Mary blinked back the tears in her eyes. Michael touched her face and looked at her with longing. He wanted to kiss her trembling lips, but her parents watched from the door. Heaving a resigned sigh, he took up her hand and kissed that instead. Mary sobbed and one tear from each glassy eye slid down her cheeks until they dripped from her chin. Michael wiped his thumb across her cheek and smiled.

"I will see you again soon," he said in soft tones.

Evan clapped his hand around Michael's shoulder, giving him the out he needed to step away. She could blame him for Michael's leave. Evan smiled at Joseph's sister. He thanked her for her company and explained they must leave. She sniffed back her sobs and consented.

Mary remained on the porch with her eyes on the blurred figure of Michael. She sensed her parents, standing just behind her in the doorway. Until they disappeared, she kept her vigil. When Michael no longer rode on the street before her, she lowered her face to her hands and cried. It was too much to miss both of them.

During their night of travel, the three men whispered about the visit at Joseph's home. Evan goaded him about his sister and Michael. Joseph smiled and smoked his cigarette, trying his best to ignore him. Once again, he felt sure Second Lieutenant Conrad simply wanted revenge. Not even Evan dared to look at her the way Michael did. He could see something stronger than need drove Michael, but it was not love.

"Pardon me, my brilliant companions," Michael said with his head full of elation. "I must find a forgiving tree to empty myself on."

Their horses lumbered to a stop along the road. Michael dismounted, throwing the reins of his mount back across the pommel of his saddle. He stepped into the thick brush, leaving only a tremble in the delicate branches to mark his passing. Then, his horse followed, reluctantly pushing through the scrub.

Joseph crossed his forearms. He smiled and looked to Evan who laughed at the scene. The laughter quickly ended and both their faces straightened. The distinct sound of horse hooves, rushing along the road filled their ears. They looked to each other with wide eyes, half frozen to the spot they held. Joseph flicked his cigarette to the ground and snapped his horse reins, panicked to find a hiding place.

Suddenly, the road lit up with bright lantern light. Joseph reined Aoife in, making her paw the ground for footing. When his horse stopped, he scanned the scene surrounding them. He counted six gray coated soldiers with their rifles pointed at both Evan and his chest.

Joseph guessed the smell and glow of their cigarettes gave them away, or maybe, the constant chatter he allowed them to engage in. Whatever the cause, there came no use in fighting. He lifted his arms, giving himself over. He thought of the inglorious end imprisonment would bring to him. His heart raced, knowing he would never see Emily again.

"Well, lookee what we got here," one drawled.

"Dandy little Yankee off'cers," another laughed. "Ain they just purdy."

"Purdy as a rich gal at a ball," a third added.

"I thought Colonel McFadden said there's three."

"Made enough noise fur twenee," a plump greasy young man laughed.

They laughed and eyed each other with angry smirks, turning their glares on their prisoners. They stepped closer, pressing their rifles into Joseph and Evan's sides. Joseph flicked his eyes to Evan and he did the same.

Flashes of Emily filled Joseph's mind. Each moment assured him his jewel fell out of reach forever. Anger flared in his eyes, but Evan's black gaze kept him still.

"We aught ta kill um," the fat one said.

"We can jus shoot um," the first one insisted fearfully. "Colonel said that one's the brother."

Joseph and Evan exchanged glances. They knew exactly what happened. Gritting his teeth, Joseph silently promised himself that he would serve Francis both his fists, when he had the chance. The rifle in his side moved, reminding him of the Confederate presence. He looked down at him and saw the man's sneer.

"Buhsides, they're officers," the first continued. "We're s'posed ta bring um ta the Captain. We'll be heroes," he laughed. "Chris one of um could be Meade himself for all the Colonel told us!"

"Meade's an old man, ya fool," the man with his gun pressed to Joseph said. He reached over and knocked his comrade on the head. "Colonel said they's a captain and a pair of lieutenants." He paused, looking about nervously searching for something. "Well we ain't got time ta fine the other one."

The smell of old whiskey and beer reeked every time they spoke. Joseph's nose curled at the horrid odor. They were less than the romantic image that supporters of the South promoted. He found himself reminded of a sour old acquaintance of his father from Baltimore.

"Pull um down and tie um up, boys," the only one of any rank said, stepping into the lantern lit circle. "Colonel McFadden's gonna be keyed." He grinned, around a smoking cigar, reaching up to spin it. He held his rifle in the crook of his arm like a hunter. "Make sure they behave."

The Confederate marauders laughed at them like demented demons. The Rebels reached up and took hold of Evan and Joseph's jackets, propelling them off their saddles to the ground. Both Joseph and Evan struggled, as it proved their nature to always try and fight, but more of the need to land on their feet. However, their actions interpreted the first way. Landing in the dirt, Joseph suffered a rifle butt to the side. He curled on the ground, fighting for breath. Joseph nursed his side, gritting his teeth until the Rebels yanked him to his feet.

"There's plenty more where that one came from, Yank!" The soldier growled near his face, baring teeth.

Evan fared little better. Joseph looked to him. He saw the pain clear in his friend's face. They both leaned, favoring a side. He looked to the gray coat standing by him, holding his rifle suspiciously. Once tied, Joseph saw Evan limp forward where their captors led them. He took more than a hit in his side.

Behind, an unoccupied pair removed the belongings from Joseph and Evan's horses. They threw the saddlebags at their backs, laughing and taunting. Neither Evan nor Joseph said a word. It would not have mattered, except to give pleasure where it stood unwarranted.

"Come on," the leader cried out. "We ain't got time fur this. Get their bags," he continued. "I ain't feeding them our rations."

From the safety of the thick shrubs, hugging the base of the trees on the roadside, Michael watched Joseph and Evan herded away. His heart beat in his throat, sticking his tongue to the roof of his mouth. In his panic, he froze in the darkness and hid. Even if he called out for help, no one would come, because no one lay in reach.

Michael hung his head and closed his eyes while helplessness filled him. If only they rested in Frederick for the night, they might have suffered a different fate. The excitement of seeing the Maynards had clouded their judgment. Lifting his chin, he watched the last enemy leave the road, taking the light with him.

Michael waited until he stood alone on the dark road. They left the horses bare of all but saddle and tack. Michael's heart pumped, warning him to leave quickly. He suspected how the Confederates found them there and further suspected they meant to imprison him instead.

Michael quickly gathered what belongings were left, strewn over the road. He threw it all in one discarded bag and slung it over his shoulder. Taking hold of his horse's bridle, he swung into the saddle. Michael turned around and gathered the other horses to him. Looking down the road to where the Rebels took his friends, he drew a deep breath and wished them luck. Then, he dashed back toward Frederick to see if he could find help.

~

Trudging along the road with sore feet beneath him, Little Nate prayed this farm he approached the last. He searched all over for the Conner Dad Dairy and failed to find it. The last place, Howell, sounded promising, but they insisted he try the next house down the road. He thought sure the people there related to Lieutenant Howell. However, since he lost the paper with the address on it in the rain, he was reluctant to think anything sure. Still, he followed the instructions he remembered.

Raising his head, he spied the tall white farmhouse set below in the flat field. He stepped out of the woods the road ran through before it turned south. Placing his hand over his eyes to shield them, he took further study of the farm. It looked massive to say the least, sprawling over its acres. In the distance, he saw black and white cows grazing in a field. He grinned, thinking he found the right place.

Little Nate's pace quickened and he covered the distance between the forest and the dairy farm in moments, hauling a lumbering black stallion behind him. When he entered, carrying his pack and bedroll on his back and leading Manny by his reins, he met with an old man stepping out of a carriage house to the left of the main building.

Nate squinted up at the stranger, "Is this the Conner Dad Farm?"

"No—it's the Conrad farm," Jack told him with a smile.

"No—that's it. I just forgot," Little Nate said relieved and excited.

"What do you need, boy?"

"I was sent by Captain Maynard to deliver this horse and this letter to Emily," Nate explained, holding up the letter. He pulled it back when Jack tried to take it. "It's for Emily only. Captain's orders." He eyed the old man suspiciously until he stepped back. "Captain Maynard said to ask Mr. Conrad's permission for his daughter to nurse old Manny back ta proper health. I don't get paid otherwise."

"I thought I recognized um," Jack said with a proud smile. "Let's get um settled in the barn," he said holding his hand out for the reins. "Then, we'll take you inside and feed you before you talk with Mr. Conrad."

Nate gladly surrendered the reins. He followed the old man toward the building he came out of.

Soon, Little Nate sat in the farmhouse kitchen, eating a heaping plateful of fresh food. He looked up at the dark skinned woman who served him and smiled. He thanked her with surprising good manners before filling his stomach. She touched his head, welcoming him with a smile.

Beside him sat Mrs. Murphy, who had returned in late March from a lengthy exploration of Europe. Emily remarked how refreshed she looked. She thought Mrs. Murphy would prove tired from such an extended trip and lengthy ship ride home.

"I'm past it by now—though I don't approve," her mother said, gaining her attention. Emily looked to her, noting how sternly she looked at her. She stepped back from the doorway to join her in the hall. Margaret folded her arms and sighed. "All I hope is this man will do right by you."

Emily looked at her anxiously, "He will, Mamma."

Margaret let a silence take them. She pressed her thumb to her lip and thought. Lifting her eyes back to Emily, she released a resigned breath. What more could she do? With little other choice, she turned Emily toward the front door and walked her dawn the hall.

"Then, take care of that horse, child," Margaret said unquestioningly.

"Yes, Mamma," Emily said, grinning. Emily trotted toward the door happy that she held her mother's faith once more.

Emily entered the stable and went to the first stall, reaching over the door to unlatch from the inside. Stepping in, she gathered a blanket and a lantern. Exiting that stall, she traversed the passage between the others until she found where Manny rested. He lay on the floor of the stall fast asleep. Emily cocked her head to the side watching him. Other than his lethargy, he appeared well to her. Emily shrugged her shoulders, not knowing what made him sick. She set the lantern and blanket on the floor outside the stall.

Unlatching the stall gate, Emily stepped inside with him. He stirred a little, but quickly settled back to sleep when he recognized her smell. Emily set her jaw with frustration and her brow crinkled with concern. Worse cases plagued animals before Manny, but this time it mattered more to her. Joseph could not lose his horse for her failure.

"Well," Emily whispered. "I'll give you a rub, check you over and see how you feel after that." Manny whickered and shook his mane when she neared him. He shook his tail and shivered. "All right, let's give it a go, Manny." Emily began the process.

The next morning, as Emily washed him down, she saw her father drive off in the carriage with Little Nate beside him. He meant to bring the boy by the train station and see him safely off. She smiled softly watching Nate's proud little head beside her father's arm. He proved a wonder, finding them up there all on his own. Manny whickered at her side, regaining her attention. Then, he nipped at the back of her dress. Emily pushed his head away and continued the bath.

"You've the manners of Joseph for certain," she told him.

The horse wriggled his lips and shook his head up and down, as if laughing silently at her jest. Emily could only smile. When that task ended, she led him out into the bright stable yard. He still moved with effort and it worried her. She watched him wander aimlessly about the yard before abandoning him for other tasks over a few hours.

When she returned at noon, he stood at the door to come in. Emily laughed at him lightly and guided him back to his stall. She placed a feedbag on his long muzzle. Then, she gave him a good rub, which he received gratefully. He ate well and it eased her mind.

"You have ta get better, Manny. I promised Joseph you would." The horse chomped on his oats noisily. "I know you don't want to disappoint him. So, let's see about getting some rest and good food back in you for a time."

She checked his leg once more, simply puzzled.

❧

In August, Joseph and Evan found themselves placed within the lines of the Army of the Potomac's most wanted prize, Richmond. They both thought they would see it someday, one way or another. However, tucked in the back of a rickety prison cart fell last on the list of how they thought to achieve that goal.

Rattling over cobblestone and dirt streets, the cart eventually rolled up to a well guarded gate built in front of an old warehouse. Joseph looked between the bars at the forbidding structure. He saw a uniformed Confederate step from the guardhouse to the cart and take a handful of papers from the driver. The man bitterly smiled, folding them up. He signaled the driver to carry on and the cart lurched forward.

"Welcome to Libby, Yanks. Final destination," the guard mocked.

Before they were admitted, both young men suffered searches and were relieved of any possessions that posed a danger or could be of use to someone else. Joseph passively stood by and allowed them to seize his belongings. Most of what he called his came to him under army issue and he cared little for any of it. However, when they grabbed the wallet with the picture of the beautiful woman, wearing a satiny gray dress, his patience died.

"Lookee here," one of the men announced, holding it up to show. He let out a long whistle and wriggled his brows. Another man stepped up and took a look, expressing the same appreciation. "What'ya doin here with that there purddy lil thing at home all lonely?" His eyes glinted deviously, meaning his game. "I could go on up n visit for ya. Perhaps she needs some consolin—now that your in prison and all," he lewdly suggested his meaning.

Joseph remained silent. His steel bladed eyes bored through the man. He betrayed no outer emotion except for the ticking muscle in his cheek. It spoke volumes for the rest of him. The Confederate smiled, studying the photograph again. Taunting men like him must be a barrel of great laughs, to keep on so distastefully, day after day. Joseph was sure the man never missed a chance, even when he knew he stood out of his league, like right then.

"Wha'd a gal like that think a her hero now? Providin that she—uh—still thinks a him?"

Joseph returned the grin with one of his cool ones, "Thank God he isn't an uneducated lowly born southern Rebel."

A long pause took hold of the room. The jeers and snickers of the guards came to an abrupt end. The two men watched each other closely. The tenseness of the room thickened, pressing against something that hissed to fill the silence. The other men in the room shifted their gazes between them, waiting for the next move.

"Your a southerner too, boy," he paused eyeing him darkly. "You jus been fightin on the wrong side." He stepped around to where Joseph stood and tapped him on the chest with the wallet of the photograph. "For that—you've lost ya rights ta send letters—t'anyone." He added a 'sir' with great distaste to the end. "I'm gonna make sure you don't find it easy here. I'm gonna be at you every minute—till you die."

The guards in the room shoved their things into their shackled arms and took hold of both Evan and Joseph. They roughly ushered them through a door into a dim passage. Evan looked at Joseph and shook his head. He wished Joseph kept quiet a little more often. He had to admit to himself he was about to do the same for his friend's honor and would have fared far worse.

Ahead of them, the guards opened the door on a dark room. They stepped back to give the new prisoners a preview before casting them inside. Wearing smirks, they watched Evan and Joseph take in the scene with growing horror. Sunken faces like zombies appeared in the dingy shadows and a rank suffocating air swept over them. The guards stepped forward and forced the prisoners through the door, slamming it closed and bolting it behind them.

Inside, the current populace surrounded the newcomers, begging for news of outside and introducing themselves. Joseph pushed a path through them, refusing to answer. Evan followed, apologizing for both of them. He hardly wanted to visit, feeling painfully repentant. Together, they found an empty spot to claim and put their meager belongings down.

"Joe," Evan whispered. "Look at me," he urged when Joseph sat in a corner, lowering his chin on his arm. "Don't let them beat you down. That'll kill you as sure as your going to starve." Evan fell silent, but Joseph said nothing in return. "I want you to send messages to Emily through me. If she doesn't hear from you, I can't imagine what'll happen." He crouched down and sat on the wall butted against his. "Anything you need to send, do it through me." Joseph still said nothing.

On the following day, Joseph gazed out of the window at a gray green canal, thinking about escape or suicide. Urged by a handful of six other officers, both Evan and he ate less than palatable provisions, provided by the already arranged messes among the prisoners. The food they served came in care packages from home, already stale or half bad. Only a fraction came from the confederacy. It lent little or no hope to the despairing hearts of the men.

Following the worst breakfast of their lives, the door opened to the cell room and the Confederate guards entered, brandishing weapons. They spread mops and buckets of whitewash to everyone. Those with weapons eyed the prisoners, sneering mock grins. The head guard looked around at them and ordered a wash of the entire room.

Joseph watched officers with bent backs, turn their hollow eyes to the task ordered them by subordinate ranking whelps. He gritted his teeth about to refuse. Evan turned to him with a wary gaze and shook his head. Joseph watched him take hold of a bucket and drag it to a corner to start scrubbing. Joseph looked down at his hand, clutching the mop handle given him and the bucket sitting at his feet. Growing discouraged with their lot, he bent down and flipped the bucket handle into his hand. He picked it up and slowly stepped to the wall behind him. He dipped the mop three times, twisted it out. Then, he dragged the dirty coils of mop rope along the dim flooring.

In the depths of his despair and his first full day closed, Joseph sat for sometime mooning over his photograph of Miss Emily Conrad. He was unknowingly being observed by one of his fellow prisoners. When Joseph turned and looked at him, the man self consciously returned to scribbling in a worn old book. Joseph stood and approached the long rickety table where the other man sat, under hanging meats intended for use at some point.

"What are you writing?" Joseph asked, forgoing the usual respect due an outranking officer. He saw the badges and pins of a Lieutenant Colonel on his jacket. Since his imprisonment, Joseph refused to speak until that moment without need.

Joseph's voice gained Evan's attention and he sat up from where he lay on his bedroll in their corner. He looked down the length of his body and watched.

"Memoirs," the man responded, looking up at him. A bright glint showed in his eyes and he managed a smile despite their surroundings. "Captain," he added noting the bars on Joseph's shoulders.

The man pointed to an upturned crate across the table from him. Joseph sat down with his darkened eyes intently studying the man. He introduced himself as Lieutenant Colonel Cavada and set his book down between them on the table. Gently smiling, he asked Joseph about the picture, and about the young woman. They quickly fell into a conversation about her and the other man's various experiences.

Evan let his head fall back on his balled up jacket and saddlebag. He hoped this meant the end of Joseph's silence. He could not take much more. Prison would surely drive him mad like that.

However, it affected Joseph little. For several months he spent his time in apathetic depression. Evan stayed at his side wearing a gaze that read of unspoken I told you so. While they enjoyed their days in seclusion, a meager and bitter hope rebuilt. They no longer faced death by threat of cannon or gun. No bayonet could reach them. Prison, though harsh, provided some protection.

⁂

Until August, Emily received letters regularly from Joseph and then they stopped. She waited weeks after the usual time, thinking that Joseph engaged in battles or movements that kept him from his regular output of letters. Her mother watched her from the house when she went out to collect the mail. She saw her somber gaze, but her mother never said anything. Emily wished within her that she would.

One gloomy day in mid August the Howells arrived in their horse drawn carriage. Stuart felt sure it was only a friendly visit, until he saw the grave features of Jackson Howell stonier than ever he had seen them. He swallowed the ill feeling and answered the door himself. Inviting them into the parlor, he gathered his family with him and sent young MaryJane to heat water for tea and bring them the nice cakes she made.

Stuart stepped into his parlor and the smile on his face faded. The sunny day outside darkened with a sure mood of terrible luck, falling on him.

“Stuart,” Jackson began in a dry grave drawl. “We’ve brought your family some bad news.” His eyes swept over the women.

Emily’s gaze grew anxious. She sensed his next words. They both died, or Evan or just Joseph. She felt frantic inside and clutched at her mothers frail hands, clutching back at hers. Emily’s eyes drifted to her mother’s and she felt surprise at seeing her expression of empathy. She gave Emily’s hand a gentle squeeze and placed her arm about her consolingly. She must have seen the fear in her eyes.

Jackson handed her father a sheaf of papers. He took them and read. When he finished, he motioned his wife forward. She stood and Emily felt suddenly alone. Everyone's eyes went to her. They stared with dark mournful gazes, as if they said sorry. What could they feel sorry for? If Evan died, she felt the one who should feel sorry. If Joseph—she refused to think of that.

Margaret finished the letter, turned and handed it to Emily. She looked up at her mother with large round eyes. Reluctantly, she took the papers and read them. While her eyes traveled over line after line of horrific detail, her heart pounded hard against her ribs, aching with anguish. Emily quickly tossed the pages aside and rushed from the room in a storm of tears. Blindly, she hurried up the stairs wailing.

In the kitchen doorway, Hettie listened for what news the Howell's brought. Her dark eyes reflected a moonlit glow of agony. She felt pain like she left back at the plantation miles away. She knew the Howell's never paid a visit unannounced without a worrisome reason. Her worst fears stood confirmed when Emily left the room, sobbing like a child whipped good.

Hettie clenched her fists at her sides and walked up the hall to the stairs. She prayed everything was all right. The worst of events played out in her mind, repeating and driving her mad. No good would come of tears like Emily's or visits like the Howell's. She swallowed hard, accepting she could not change the past. No matter what happened, she needed to help Emily face it.

A distant slamming door told Hettie right where Emily hid. She hesitated outside the parlor and looked inside to see the Conrads consoling the Howells. Then, the Conrads accepted condolences from the suffering Howells. Hettie needed no more to piece the matter together. Strengthening her constitution with her mind, she placed a hand on the banister and made the first step up. She never thought this day would come. She had herself convinced they would return. Her heart ceased to beat or she ceased to feel a thing. She remembered the boys in their small times together and a tear slipped from her eye.

After a tense silence, Hettie reached the landing and traversed the hall to Emily's room. She wiped her eyes and passed the doorway of the bedroom where Joseph slept for a week. She felt her heart clench. If anything happened to him, Emily would never recover. She eyed the door that shut the young woman in her room. Approaching it, she saw it partially open and peeked inside.

Emily lay across her bed, crying with such vehemence that Hettie no longer doubted her guess. It somehow assured her the matter was less than feared. If Joseph passed away in battle, she knew Emily would have destroyed the house and ended with a leap from the cupola before anyone could stop her.

Hettie pushed open the door. The hinges creaked and she hesitated, looking to Emily with large unsure eyes. Her expression softened. She waited for the girl to look up, holding her breath expecting an outburst. Nothing happened. She lay there trembling with the force of her agony.

Sitting on the bed, Hettie stroked Emily's tousled hair. "Tell me," she said softly.

"Joseph's in prison," Emily sobbed. "Hettie, I'm never gonna see em again. I'm never gonna see him again!" She said, sitting up. She turned and threw her arms about Hettie's neck and sobbed against her arm.

After the shock settled in, Hettie silently cried. Hettie could no longer rein in her tears and they slipped down her cheeks. Her dark eyes searched the white walls of Emily's room. Memories of her enslavement danced in her head like demons around a fire. Slavery felt like prison and Joseph was a prisoner of the South. Hettie knew just what it felt like to be under the control of wretched and unforgiving southern men. She shuddered, remembering it all too clearly. God save Captain Maynard, he must come home.

"He's gonna come home, Emily," Hettie found her words, spilling out on her tongue. She held her friend close and they both cried. "He's got to come home."

"He promised me," Emily wailed. "He promised."

Hettie shut her eyes and cradled her friend's head in her hand. Her own family had returned to her, by some other worldly grace. She never thought to see them again before the Conrad's. She held no hope of such a reunion. Somehow, these people carried the devil's own luck. Hettie prayed it hold true just a little longer.

"I blame myself," Emily said, lifting her head to look at Hettie.

Emily studied her friend's black eyes, full of pain too. She stood and went to her window, wiping the tears away. She gazed into the lane and at the buildings, like the day he emerged from one with her father. She half expected to see him again. She leaned against the pains, holding her hand to the cool glass. She sniffed and shut her eyes to the scene.

"It's my fault."

"No, Emily. Don't do that," Hettie muttered under her breath.

"I asked him," she turned and stepped to her mirror. Hettie drew a deep breath of relief. Emily gazed at herself and added, "I said what if you get captured? I cursed him by my fear."

"Nonsense! Curses aren't real! You're just looking ta blame someone for it. They're in a war down there. Men get killed and men get captured," Hettie argued.

Emily turned to her friend. Her face reddened with grief made her look wild. "Can he keep his promise now, Henrietta?" She demanded

"Could he ever?" Hettie pressed her. "You've gotta be strong. This isn't gonna be easy. Lord knows I know." She paused, taking on a softer expression. "Now, Joseph made his promise to you, and he means ta keep it. Trust in the Lord and he'll allow him ta follow through." She pulled Emily up into her arms. "I tell you what I did when my men were lost to me. Come sit."

Surrounded by darkness and disease, Joseph and Evan discussed their future. With so much time to loiter aimlessly, it seemed the only distraction. In their meanderings, they dreamed of days yet to come. Dreams

they would not give up on yet. They believed in their hearts that all would right itself, whatever happened. Though they would not say it out loud, they determined to hold out hope. Dreams were the only property they still owned, which the guards could not steal.

"I knew as soon as you saw Emily that you'd fall in love. I thought you'd be round for the rest a my life. I just didn't think this'd be it," Evan said. His features sunk in with hunger and despair. The only time he brightened was when the sound of music drew from the depths of the prison and met his ears. To him it was life and freedom, reminding him of the past campfires with his men.

"This isn't the end, Evan. I promised Em I'd come home and I keep my promises. We'll go home. I just don't know when."

Evan looked at him with despair drawing his mouth down. He nodded, refusing to think what his mind rambled over. He rested his thoughts on hope. As long as they drew air, they might go home again. He focused on home and breathing.

Sadly, the months passed them by, while they were indefinitely separated from friends and family. By some means, a package reached Joseph from the Conrads just before the one from his family ran low. He found food, some money, tucked in by Stuart no less, a letter and a blanket from Hettie and Emily. He could smell her on it. By the packages appearance, it suffered an ample search. Even his letters had been torn open.

Nevertheless, he sat thankful to receive what remained. He opened the first letter and read the date. By what lie scrawled in the top corner, the guards held his package for sometime, stealing from it. Thanks to the Conrads wisdom, they sent him canned goods and nothing fresh. He smiled bitterly at the box and pushed it away to read his letter. Someday he would have his revenge on these men and they would rue the day they ever met him. His thoughts quickly turned to the cause of his problem. Joseph imagined the day he met with McFadden once again.

Unfolding his letter, he forgot about the prison guards and his sister's crazed suitor. After all, more important matters pulled at his heart and he needed to care for them.

29th of August 1863

Dear Joseph,

I never should have uttered those words that day in the garden. I am truly sorry. Hettie tells me not to blame myself, but I cannot help feeling responsible. I often think of our last day together, and our last words. I'm afraid I brought this on from my fears.

I just ask you to keep your promise and not to be angry with me. I love you. I want you to come home. How funny that sounds. Home is with you—with me. Come Home Joseph! Come Home!

I do not care what bonds they place on you. Your place is with me. We sanctified that. I pray to God you will be set free soon and in good health. It's all I can do not to come down and make them release you. If I had the power I'd wish you safely away. Please Joseph come home soon . . .

Tearstains and the tilted letters of the last word on the page explained why she did not write more. Emily could not. Joseph understood. He could not have written more himself. His heart ached, imagining what she went through. His head lowered to his arm and he cried, unable to do anything else.

Joseph wanted to go to her. He would hold her and tell her she was a fool. She was the last person to blame for his capture. He pointed the finger correctly at McFadden and at himself for his asinine mistake. Not many soldiers rode through the dangerous woods of Maryland, smoking and laughing freely. He promised her and he failed to even try to uphold the promise, callously believing himself immune to misfortune, as if his entire career had not proven otherwise.

From that moment forward, Joseph lived for each letter that arrived for him from Emily. They came regularly, still full of the cheer and hope she held for his return. Emily cleverly addressed them to Evan, assuring his unspoiled receipt. Evan handed over the message with a grin. Josèph recognized the envelope without the need to read the handwriting on the outside. He took it from Evan's outstretched fingers and stepped to their corner for the little privacy he could gain in the open room, full of more men like him. He slid down the wall to sit on the floor and his blankets. He slipped his thumb under the slit and opened it. The smell of her perfume hung strongly on the paper.

11th of October 1863

Dear Joseph, my love,

How are you coping? I know you cannot write to me, but try to send word somehow. It makes me mad, waiting so long without any word. I miss you and your letters. Perhaps I should come to Virginia. It would only be a matter of days. It felt easier knowing you lived free and had a chance to find safety when threatened. Do the guards abuse you, my love? I wish I knew what happens to you there. I wish I could see for myself that you are all right. I've heard many horrible stories in the newspapers about those prisons.

Michael sent word to let you know he keeps Aoife with the unit to train her. Sergeant McGuire picked a beautiful name for her. I hope to see you and your new gallant charger soon. Manny arrived months ago. I wasn't able to tell you. Little Nate, as he called himself, delivered him safely. I hope he doesn't catch the devil doing this for you. He's such a brave little boy. I wish I had half his heart right now.

But, you're probably eager to hear about your stallion. He was so exhausted when he arrived, but Daddy and I have fixed him up right. When you come home, he'll be here waiting for you.

I have good news. I hope you recall when I mentioned the new worker on the farm and how Rose felt about him. They are engaged now! I can hardly believe it. You should see them. They are so in love. I cannot wait for the service and celebration. Rose is so deserving. Christian is a wonderful man. Unfortunately for us, she will no longer work, needing to take care of their home.

I won't see much of her after that. Still, it is a wonderful event.

Mrs. Murphy sends her love. She wants you to know you are in her prayers. She tells me to beg you never to give up. You need to come home to your Emily.

Mrs. Murphy has helped me through much of this time. I hope you and Evan support each other and find strength there.

I pray to God every night to keep you safe. I can barely contain myself, dreaming of the next time you will visit us again. Mother and father are both equally afraid, but none so much as Hettie and I. We pray more than the old Church ladies. In the morning we pray together twice, at lunch and at least five more times before bed.

I often dream of the day we'll come together for the rest of our lives. I still feel your touch on my skin. I hope it'll always be like that. . .

Emily's hopeful and loving words broke him to tears again. He no longer held back the frustrated agony, burning at his eyes and in throat. His heart beat wildly with his panic. Lowering his face into his arms, he hid his despair from the prying eyes of other prisoners who sat nearby.

Evan reached out to take the letter from Joseph's hand. His concern furrowed his brow. Searching for the cause, he read the pages himself. He thirsted for a piece of home, as much as the next man, but somehow he never managed to cry with frustration. He understood Joseph had more heartache than him. Evan could only imagine the pain his friend felt. He was glad of not having someone to return to.

Joseph wiped his face and drew a steadying breath. He looked up to the dirty window, set high in the wall above them. Evan saw his features grow darker and more sullen. Each day that passed, Joseph continued to withdraw into himself. He still barely spoke, using the gift only when necessary. Evan's chin dropped and he folded the papers in his hand. He looked at them, seeing the words through the paper. He set it on the dingy floor at Joseph's feet.

When the Christmas and New Year holidays arrived, Joseph kept to his corner. He sat against the wall when awake and laid with his face to it when sleeping. The light in his eyes dimmed and he turned to ignoring Evan with the other soldiers. When more active, he stood at the wall, staring out the small window, barely able to see the world beyond where his thoughts went. The prison walls slowly rotted his caged spirit.

Joseph's eyes searched the wintry landscape of the Christmas Eve city, recalling the promise he made Emily. He promised. The rowdy play and music of the other soldiers became a numbing background. His eyes moved to watch a lone guard cross the courtyard below with his rifle across his chest. He saw the red glow of his cigarette and his thoughts turned to the last escape attempt by one of the prisoners.

One man disguised himself as a Confederate and tried to escape, during the guard change. It made some feel guilty they did not try the same, but when the man was caught and he never returned, they thought themselves the wiser. Yet others found it inspiring.

Joseph and Evan had stood in the courtyard, taking part in their compulsory exercise, which the guards used to search the prison quarters. They walked together, keeping their eyes on the other prisoners. While they walked to stretch their legs, one of their ranks bolted from their lines. He ran with all his meager strength toward the gate. In moments, he fell to the ground under a handful of Confederate guards. They all watched helplessly as their captors beat him into bloody submission. Then, they dragged him away. He also never returned.

There was no hope of escape with every attempt put down time and again. The men trapped in the warehouse fed on lacking provisions, leaving them not only on edge, but weak as well. His uniform already sagged on his thinning frame, but Joseph never considered escape. He convinced himself from the first day that he would die in this wretched place and never see his beloved Emily again, no matter what he said aloud of hope. He promised to come home.

Lowering to his haunches on the floor in the corner, he crossed his arms over his knees and looked to the men. His frighteningly sunken eyes bored into them. He wondered how dead men celebrated this day so happily. With a bitter grimace, he lay on his bedroll and put his back to them. He set himself to sleeping, as often as he could in avoidance of time.

"Why don't you join us, Joe?" Evan's voice roused him. He looked over his shoulder and Evan continued, "It'd do you some good."

Joseph gave him a dark glare, "Christmas is for men with hope."

February of 1864 rolled around after long nightmarish days and brought with it an epidemic of Smallpox. Joseph survived the disease as a young man, losing a little brother to it. Unfortunately for his newer companion, Evan held no such experience to strengthen him. Joseph saw him soon show the symptoms.

Following the first of the month, Evan remained on his bedroll uneasily drawing his breath. His face glistened with a high fever and he listlessly moved to find a comfortable place to lay. By the afternoon, he showed the disease in full, wearing a soar rash on his face, hands and feet.

"You will get through this," Joseph said to him, mopping his brow with a rag.

"God's punishing me," Evan rasped. "I'm going to hell, Joe," he whined. "I can feel the fire."

"You're already there," Joseph smiled, but it did little for his sickly features.

The next morning, Joseph rose first and gathered their morning meal, bringing it back to feed Evan. He remained under his blanket, shivering. Joseph folded his legs under him and sat. Odd pustule marks surfaced on Evan's face. Joseph eyed him with concern, and then woke him. Evan's deep brown eyes looked glassy and unreal, as if he existed out of his body. Joseph smiled at him and showed him the watery oatmeal.

"Ready to eat?"

"I'm not hungry," Evan replied with some effort.

"I don't care," Joseph said firmly. "You will eat if I have to squeeze it down your throat," he warned.

Evan looked at him blankly and said nothing.

During the days of Evan's sickness, Joseph fed his ailing friend extra rations, taken from his own plate. He wanted to assure himself that Evan would survive the illness and what better way than more food. Growing weaker from the lack in his diet and his friend's encouragement, a dark cloud descended on Joseph. He filled with self blame and anguish, wishing to change the events of the evening McFadden set his jackals on them.

Joseph soon looked a skeleton and became unresponsive to anyone but Evan. He watched the events of the prison with madness illuminating a strangely in his eyes. The other men avoided him altogether, leaving his corner empty except for him and his one friend. He wished they had given the courtesy sooner.

With the dawn light filtering through his little window in a surreal gray glow, Joseph crouched by Evan as he slept. He watched him a moment, judging how he felt. He touched his forehead. Evan's skin felt cooler to the touch. He gave a bitter smile and pulled his hand back.

Evan's eyes rolled open and he looked up at Joseph, "Captain?" His head throbbed less and he felt hungry for the first time since falling ill. "I think I'm feeling better."

"Get some more sleep," Joseph directed. "Breakfast'll be a minute."

Evan moved his head to nod. He watched Joseph stand, seeing how his clothing hung off him like a scarecrow. Evan felt his heart leap into his throat, as the reality of their position closed in on him again. Then, Joseph collapsed to the floor. Evan sat upright, but the other soldiers already gathered about him. Evan's head swam weakly.

"Lay back, Lieutenant," A man urged him. "We'll see to the Captain."

Evan said nothing, feeling his tongue stuck to the roof of his mouth. His eyes surveyed the men who picked Joseph up and moved him back to his bedroll. He saw the bruise on Joseph's face, blooming along his cheekbone where it struck the floor. Evan turned his head, unable to watch more. He stared at the ceiling of the room, fighting to hold onto his hope.

The other soldiers took over the duty of caring for both of them, showing respectful concern for another's life. When they brought Evan his lunch and tried to force food down Joseph's reluctant throat, the door to their cell opened. A small group of guards entered, escorting a pair of Southern Army doctors. The moment Evan saw them, he knew they came to select those among them who needed medical treatment and see them transferred into the city military hospitals.

Several of the men, who still suffered amid the pox epidemic or at the end like Evan, received the mark to transport north for medical treatment. The doctor stepped closer and Evan prayed they pick him and Joseph. He looked to his friend, sleeping soundly beside him. His exhaustion and starvation left him weak and sleepy. If they did not pick him, Evan knew he would die. The doctor stepped to him.

"What's your name and rank, officer," the doctor said, peering at Evan gravely.

"Lieutenant Evan Howell, sir," Evan replied in a rough voice. "Third Potomac."

The man nodded and scribbled something in the book he held, "At the end or beginning of your illness?"

Evan looked at him concerned, "My fever just went this morning." The man nodded. "I can barely lift my head." He nodded again.

"What's wrong with him?" He asked, jutting his chin at Joseph.

"Starving," Evan said. "He cut his rations in half to feed me."

The doctor paused concerned, but only nodded again. Evan saw the guard from their first day stand nearby. He stepped closer to look at them. He sneered with a sickly triumphant grin. Evan looked away and nausea turned his stomach. The man planned trouble and it meant one of their deaths, if not both.

"He ain goin nowhere," the guard sneered to the doctor, meaning Joseph.

"I don't think you understand," the doctor laughed in the younger man's face. "That man is dying and we're running out of graves here."

"He doan deserve any grave, Major."

"No matter what you think of him, Sergeant," The doctor reminded him of his rank. "I say he goes. I believe that is an order."

The guard eyed his superior like an arrogant adolescent beaten at his own game, "Yes, sir."

The doctor nodded to Evan with a smile, "His name and rank, Lieutenant Howell."

"Captain Joseph Maynard," Evan answered, watching the guard step away disgusted. "Third Potomac."

The man looked to him and smiled, understanding the connection.

In the evening, the hospital carts rolled in and lined the courtyard outside. Their acquaintances, sharing their torment, packed up their small amount of belongings and placed them close by. The minutes ticked by in long tense moments until the soldiers came to collect Joseph and Evan for transport. Only Evan knew what happened. Joseph remained asleep and barely aware of the world around him when awake. Evan gave his thanks and bid farewell to the unfortunate prisoners left behind.

In the cold temperatures of late February, Evan and Joseph exited the prison, hopefully never to return. Evan viewed every moment in the dusky light. Then, the back of the wagon closed the view to him. He lay back on his litter and shut his eyes. The wagon lurched forward. Evan released a breath of relief.

When they arrived at the hospital, Evan made sure they were boarded together. While his status improved,

Joseph remained essentially unchanged. Concerned that his friend willed himself to die, convinced he would never escape Libby, Evan begged a young nurse to help him write a quick note to Joseph's intended wife, asking her presence at the hospital. Emily proved the only person who could save Joseph now. With a pretty smile and an Irish brogue, the nurse assured him she would send the telegram when her shift ended. Evan gave her what little money he still had and asked her to keep the rest as a fee for her trouble. The nurse smiled at him again, but with her thanks, she refused to take the money of a sick man. She planned to return tomorrow with the difference and a receipt.

True to her promise, the nurse performed her duty and returned the next day with Evan's money and a receipt for the message. He thanked her with a flirtatious smile. Her red hair reminded him of a young woman back in Maryland. However, her bright smile and freckles were far more attractive than the one she resembled. Evan watched her work, bending his mind to make friends with her. A hospital would be much easier to escape than the prison, especially nestled in the middle of the city. They could walk out with her help and disappear, like they were never there.

"If ya be needin anything else," she told him. "Ask fur Nurse Healy," she said.

"Thank you, ma'am. I will."

Later in the day, the nurse brought him a return to his message sent last night. He took it with trembling hands and looked at it, surprised by his emotions. He hoped Mrs. Conrad took pity on them and that his parents no longer felt ashamed of their son. His eyes went back to the pretty girl who watched him. He gave her a small smile to ease her mind.

"Do you want me ta read it ta ya?" She asked, clasping her hands at her waist.

"No—thank you," he said. Evan opened it and found one line. "Tell him I leave today." He lowered the page and smiled up at Miss Healy. "You've saved this man's life."

"If he loves his fiancée that much," the woman smiled. "He deserves to live."

"Loves her like no other," Evan agreed, looking to the bed beside his. Joseph slept again. "Say," he flicked his eyes back to her. "Ya haven't told me about yourself."

"There isna much ta say, Lieutenant," Miss Healy began. An attractive blush lit her face. "I come from Cork in Ireland, but I'm sure ya guessed that a'ready. I work here, cause n'one else'd hire me."

"I'm glad for it," Evan whispered.

"I'm sure y'are," Miss Healy lifted a brow to him. "That's nuff chatter fur now, Lieutenant. I'll bring yur suppers an talk ta ya while I try ta get the Captain ta eat. If yu'll excuse me, b'fore the head nurse takes ta shriekin at me like a banshee."

"Of course, Miss Healy. I look forward to dinner."

Miss Healy shook her head and took her leave. Evan pushed himself up against his pillows and sat the telegram on the table between his bed and Joseph. He looked to his friend who lay listlessly under stiff hospital blankets. Joseph's color improved with the aid of daylight pouring in from the large windows at the end of the room. Evan drew a deep breath, hoping Emily's arrival would be in enough time.

"Hey, Cap," Evan said in a low voice. Joseph refused to open his eyes. "Emily's coming. You just hold on. She'll get here soon."

~

Having booked passage for themselves and two servants, the Conrads prepared for their journey south. The time could not come quickly enough for Emily. By the time she stood on the platform awaiting the train, she was filled with more fear than if Joseph had died. Ever at her side, Hettie stood with her arm about Emily's shoulders, offering what strength she could.

Mrs. Murphy whispered to Emily, softly smiling while the Howells and Jack Benson spoke with the elder Conrads. The Howells could not leave their ailing son and make the journey with them to see to Evan. Stuart assured them he would send word upon their arrival. If anything could be done for either boy, both would be equally cared for. Mrs. Howell took little consolation from Stuart's words. She tearfully listened to Margaret echo them in her own manner.

Emily's eyes flicked to the station clock. The train to New York City was due to arrive soon. From there they were set to take a steamship down the coast to Virginia and the Confederate held city of Richmond. Evan's telegram gave them little other information, but they needed none to come to his call. Once the Conrads took their leave, Mrs. Murphy and Jack were in charge of the farm. Hettie and Isaiah gave the last instructions regarding their son. Emily watched on, as if she dreamt the entire moment.

"He gives you or that little girl any trouble," Isaiah told Mrs. Murphy. "He deals with me when we get back."

"I am sure to see to it, Mr. Benson," Mrs. Murphy laughed. "Don't you worry about him. Ezekiel's a good boy. He'll behave for us."

Though she little believed her words, Mrs. Murphy wanted to see the Conrads quickly off with little thought to their farm. She understood their need to worry about the soldiers and not their home right then. She could see the crushing look in Emily's eyes.

The steam engine pulled along the tracks and the platform surged with energy. Before too much longer, the train sat ready for loading. Jack shook hands with the Mr. Conrad and waved to the women, as they boarded.

Stuart led his family and servants to their compartment. He helped Isaiah put the women's bags on the shelves before they sat. Hettie's quiet words consoled his daughter. It was the only sound until the conductor checked their tickets. Stuart settled between his wife and child, noticing his daughter's pained expression. His heart clenched to think of how much she hurt, having her dearest friend and the man she loved at the mercy of they knew not what. He touched her face and smiled at her when she looked at him. She offered him a weak return and went back to the window.

During the passage south, Emily remained nearly mute. She stared at the passing countryside with large eyes. Her unshed tears stood in them, sparkling brilliantly. The beauty of those orbs tried to take in the scene if only to distract the mind behind them from its terror.

The Conrad party changed trains after arrival in Albany, New York and once again in Westchester. From there they entered the city and booked an evening in a hotel until they transferred to the steamship early in the morning of the next day. The trip to Richmond was the longest road Emily ever traveled. By evening, they stood within the city limits.

Emily would not wait for the following day to see Joseph. Her mother and Hettie escorted her to the hospital named in the telegram, while her father and Isaiah settled them in their hotel. Emily walked halfway down the street before they missed her. She held her telegram in her small gloved hand and wore a stern expression of determination on her face. Emily's companions raced to keep pace until they found the hospital.

The building loomed tall with scores of windows peering down on them. Confederate soldiers guarded the exterior; making it known the services performed inside came to military men, possibly prisoners. Far from frightened by the nearness of the enemy, Emily approached a man by the entrance. When she presented herself to him, she loosed her tongue for the first time since leaving Vermont and asked for admittance. The man surprisingly replied to her politely and they were admitted beyond the gate.

The stark interior of the hospital put Emily's heart into a panic. She took quick short breaths and shook nervously. Hettie grasped her hand and squeezed. She could feel her friend's shaking, despite her attempt at fortifying her. Both of them felt as though they entered a wasp nest. Looking sharply around, she found the closest person and asked for help.

The soldier eyed Emily and Hettie with unreserved disgust, seeing how they stood so close. Emily set her jaw and sternly glared down at the man, grasping tighter to her friend's hand. They hàd no time to discuss politics and she was sure the man had no means by which to do battle with her.

"I am here to see Captain Joseph Maynard of the Union Army of the Potomac," Emily snapped, stepping in front of his eyes. "I suggest you take your eyes off Miss Benson and show me where you heathens are keeping him, before I see you hauled out of here and thrown on your ear in the street for treating a lady less than respectfully."

His dark eyes shifted back to Emily. He gave her an amused expression, "Young woman, your Mamma need teach you manners." He paused, seeing the elder woman step closer with a less than amused expression at his words. He cleared his throat and said, "I'll see to finding out where your Yankee officer is kept. Wait here."

Emily followed him with her angry eyes. Her sharp tongue served her just as well on the farm. She drew a deep breath and looked up the dark hall, studying the ecru and black diamond tiles of the floor, anxious to be on her way. He was only rooms away and she could not reach him. Tears threatened her eyes again. Emily thought on her next steps, if the Confederates refused her beyond that point. Her breath caught in her throat at the idea.

"Miss," a soft voice said. Emily lifted her eyes to look in the face of a nurse. The woman's soft green gaze and freckled face set her at ease. "Did ya ask bout Captain Maynard?" She asked with an Irish accent.

"Yes," Emily said breathlessly. "I did. I've come to tend him? Where is he being kept?"

"Are ya Emily?" She asked hopeful. Emily nodded somewhat confused and the woman beamed. "Come with me," she said, reaching between Emily and Hettie to take her arm.

Without an ounce of hesitation, Emily followed the nurse up the dim hallway into the den of lions. Beside her, the nurse walked with determination and bravely held her head high. Emily felt the other's woman's confidence fill her. Either Evan blabbered on about her or Joseph was well enough to speak. Emily prayed with every step deeper into the hospital that she did not face a nightmare, but a wakening from the one she was already in.

"Lieutenant Howell says very nice things bout ya," the nurse explained. She faced Emily on the stairs, offering her hand and smiling, "Fur'give me manners. M'name's Claire Healy." They shook. "Yur friend, Lieutenant Howell's been the politest man I've met in this hospital. Yur fiancée's lucky ta ave him. They seem like brothers, thur so close."

"Fiancée?" Margaret breathed questioningly.

"Oh," Claire stammered. "Evan'd made it seem ya were engaged."

"Merely friends, Miss Healy," Margaret said with a smile. She looked to her daughter with a warning in her eyes.

Emily kept her mouth shut and looked to Claire with a smile.

"Let us continue," Claire urged with a bright smile. "I doan wish ta keep ya any longer. I'm sure the trips been horrible nuff." Claire saw more there than she let on. It was a shame the girl's mother disapproved. She had thought Captain Maynard a grand choice from the way Lieutenant Howell cared for him. "I shud prepare ya for what yu'll see. The prisons ave little food since mos Confederate soldiers starve daily. Much a what yur imprisoned soldiers receive comes ta them from families." She paused to draw a breath. "A recent epidemic a smallpox took quite a few of the men. Lieutenant Howell was lucky ta survive and he credits Captain Maynard for his life. He said e fed him most of half of his rations on top his own." She shook her head and looked to Emily consolingly. "He looks very thin, Miss, but he's in the clear, far's I can tell. The doctors think he's mad, brought on by bein at Libby." She saw

Emily's panic stricken expression. "I think he misses you," she softly smiled.

Claire stopped outside a long room lit with lamps and candles. She put her hands behind her back and waited for Emily to absorb the scene. Emily stared into the interior. By the expression on her face, she could not wait another instant.

"Are ya sure ya ready, Miss?"

"Take me to him," Emily said without trepidation.

Claire nodded and led the way into the hospital room.

Emily lifted her chin high and floated into their drab white walled room with her mother and Hettie close behind. Her passing drew the eyes of the wounded soldiers in the beds and they leered hauntingly. Her eyes searched them, growing increasingly eager the deeper they traveled. She heard the whistles of appreciation and her nerves stretched taught.

"Watch your manners, you slobs!" Evan shouted from his bed. "These women deserve your respect. That's the Captain's girl!"

"Yes, Lieutenant," some of them murmured sullenly.

"Sorry, Lieutenant," others added.

Evan looked to Emily with an apology. He was embarrassed to sit among the unrefined brutes and thought better of calling them there, especially Mrs. Conrad. Seeing the women's well kept appearances, he imagined how he looked. His black hair was terrible mess, laying on it day and night. He scrubbed a hand through his hair, trying to straighten it.

"Where is he Evan?" Emily said desperately, dashing around Claire to reach his bed.

"Right here," Evan answered. He indicated the bed beside his. "I wouldn allow em to put Joe anywhere else. Not after what he did for me."

Emily rushed into the narrow space between the beds. Her silken glove gently touched his bearded cheek. She wanted to cry, seeing how awful he looked. He never looked so weak, so consumed. He made no motion to acknowledge her and she believed the skeletal form long since expired. Tears sprung to her eyes, knowing the last bits of the proud man she fell in love with were laid out before her.

Emily could not take her eyes from him. She saw Joseph behind the dark circles and lines marking his handsome features with the stress of his trials. She brushed her finger down his jaw, forgetting her mother stood just paces away watching. Joseph jolted at her touch and awoke. His hollow eyes peered through her. They were darkly distant, frightened and mad. Though he seemed far away, Emily knew he still lived in there somewhere. She could not mistake the shades of green that sparkled with their hope. She smiled at him, crying.

"Emmy?"

"Joseph," she breathed, smoothing his hair back.

"Emmy," Joseph breathed, weakly smiling with what little strength remained in him. His hand gripped her skirt tightly.

"I'm here, Joseph. I'm here now," she said, taking his other hand. "You're going to get better. I swear it." They stared at each other not able to drink in enough all at once.

"We'll write your family tonight," Margaret added. "They should arrive within days."

"Where's Hettie?" Joseph asked, not seeing Emily's friend in her usual spot attached to her side. He no longer felt assured he did not dream. "You're never without her."

"I'm here, Captain," Hettie answered, approaching his other side. "Don't worry about where I'm at. Miss Emily came a long way to see you."

"Now, you see her, too," Emily said.

"I don't want to see anyone but you."

"Then you don't have to."

Claire approached the distant side of Evan's bed, and watched the reunion. She smiled and a tear streamed down her cheek. Evan's eyes went to hers and she wiped away the tear embarrassed to cry in front of him.

"You've done a fantastic job, Nurse Healy."

"Thank ya, Lieutenant," She smiled shyly at him. "It was a pleasure ta perform."

"How do we get them out of here?" Margaret turned to Claire with a stern expression.

Claire stammered, "Well—well, thur still prisoners a the Confedrahcee, ma'am. They canna leave."

"So they think," Margaret said. She patted Evan's hand and smiled at him. "Devise a plan, Lieutenant Howell. You are the military man."

Evan stammered. He had been thinking of a plan for weeks, but nothing would work.

"No—I think I know a way," Claire said, lowering her voice. "But, I'm out of a job if they fine out I helped," she looked about nervously.

"That is a chance you're going to have to take, Miss Healy," Margaret said.

"After I've been kind ta ya? How can ya threaten me?" Claire asked, pinching her brows with anger. She clenched her fists at her sides. She felt something touch her hand and looked to Evan who grasped for her. His eyes halted her anger and she frowned.

"We'll need help nursing them," Margaret said. "You may stay with us for wages and board. My husband can help see you placed in a nice home."

"Nice homes doan take Irish."

"Then they're not nice homes," Evan said, distracting Claire from Mrs. Conrad. "I'd hate to see anything happen to you over me."

"I'll do it," Claire said, looking at him. For some reason, the Lieutenant inspired her to do things she would normally be terrified to do. "I doan know why, but I will." She drew a deep breath and looked back to Mrs. Conrad. "Meet me in the west alley at three in the morning. N'one'll be round an the guard's passed out drunk by then. I'll move them ta the recovered ward and sneak them out on my watch. Bring a carriage and doan think ta stay another night in Richmond." Evan smiled at her. "Oh—I'm sure ta ang fur this."

Margaret looked at her with a serious expression, taking it in. It seemed the only sensible plan, if they could pull it off. It was risky, especially with Joseph so weak. Her eyes trailed to her daughter. She leaned over his bed, with her head on his arm. Their hands were twined and she knew she could not part them again. Margaret's eyes went to Evan. She and her husband owed him a great deal. They had seen to him getting into West Point and ending up in this situation essentially. She heaved a weighted sigh, tired and worn from their travels. What else could they do but try?

Margaret looked to Hettie. Her servant would suffer the worst of them all if they were caught taking part in such business. Hettie nodded without hesitation. Margaret let her gaze slip over the room. She could not leave them there, only to be returned to prison for however long the blasted war would carry on.

"Very good, Miss Healy," Margaret said. "My husband will see to your being compensated amply for your trouble."

"Y'are the bravest people," she said, eyeing each of them, forgetting her part in the plan.

"Only for our loved ones and those who help them," Margaret smiled.

"Miss Healy," Evan grinned. "I've never been so impressed by a lady in all my life."

Claire gazed at him wide eyed. She blushed and lowered her chin smiling at the compliment. She quickly took back her hand and tucked them both behind her.

Emily stayed with Joseph and Evan until night fell and Claire at last secured permission to move them to the other ward. The doctors examined Joseph's improvement and looked over Evan, also. The men determined the patients out of danger. They would not require constant monitoring. At Miss Healy's recommendation, they placed the men in the wing by the kitchens. She said the smell of food would whip up their appetites and the look of them said they needed it.

The doctors turned to the Conrads and the head surgeon explained they planned to move them right away. If the women pleased, they may return in the morning and find the men in their new quarters. The doctor passed his card to Margaret and she took it with an impassive expression. She gave a false smile and tucked it in her purse with a thank you.

Emily kissed Joseph on the cheek, “I will come back tomorrow. Rest easily, Captain.”

“I won’t sleep a wink,” Joseph said.

“I’ll watch em while your gone, Em” Evan’s deep voice cracked through the silence. “You go get some sleep.”

“Thank you, Evan.” She whispered back, as her hand slowly slipped from Joseph’s.

Emily reluctantly left him to the care of the doctors and nurses in the hospital. She looked back over her shoulder several times before she left the room. She turned away, swallowing her fears. He was alive and that would be enough. Emily walked down the hall with her head held high followed by Hettie and her mother.

Margaret put her arm about Emily’s shoulders. She sensed her young daughter’s fears. Margaret pulled Emily close to her side and kissed her temple. She smiled warmly.

“It will be all right,” Margaret assured her. “Your father and I will see to that.”

“Do you trust her?” Emily asked.

“You’ve no choice and Evan seems to,” her mother replied.

“Then, that is enough for me,” Emily said unconvinced.

XIII. The Dawn

The dark alley between the western wall of the hotel turned hospital and the next building, of undefined nature, looked imposing in the dark of night. The pocket watch Stuart carried with him read two minutes to three in the morning. He blinked at it, weary from his travels, but afraid to fall asleep. He watched the door set several yards away, guarded by one man who slumped in his chair. The nurse his wife spoke of would exit there with Evan and Joseph. He hoped this young lady had the fortitude to perform her task as discussed.

"Y'all right, Mr. Conrad?" Isaiah whispered.

"Worried," Stuart answered. He smiled at him in the dark. He wondered how the nurse handled the issue of other guards, eyeing the one passed out at the door. There had to be more. His gaze lowered to where his daughter solemnly watched from inside the carriage.

A light suddenly flickered from the door. Stuart touched Isaiah's arm and he looked up the alley toward it. Their carriage carried forward slowly. Stuart held his breath until he saw a woman helping a man support the listless body of another between them.

"My God," Stuart rasped. "They look dreadful."

"I've seen worse," Isaiah grinned, though the worry lingered in his dark eyes.

Stuart quickly climbed down and opened the carriage door. He smiled at the brave young woman, taking the bag she carried. His eyes settled on Evan. The young man patted his back assuredly, while Isaiah helped

Joseph into the interior. Once Joseph rested in Emily's arms, the nurse faced Stuart and gave a quick curtsy. She turned to run back inside.

"Where are you going?" Stuart questioned.

"I'm goin back," she said as if obvious. "I'll be missed." She paused, looking up the alley. "The guards'll return soon. Ya need ta go."

"When you leave tonight," Stuart said. "Leave for Washington. I don't know what kind of trouble will come of this for you or us, but I don't plan to stay here and figure it out."

"Washington?" She asked, looking starry eyed. "I haven the fare fur that."

"Take the first means out of Richmond," Stuart said. He took out his wallet and gave her money. "You helped us this far, Miss Healy. I cannot leave you hear to suffer alone for this. We will meet you at the train station in Washington."

Claire eyed the money warily. She took it in her hand, folding it over her small fingers. She looked past the white haired older man into the dark of the coach. She saw his wife and the black woman from earlier. Her eyes flicked back to Stuarts. She tucked the money in her uniform.

"At the station—Washington," she repeated it, agreeing to the sense of his instructions. She dashed back to the building to cover up what she could of the escape until her shift ended.

Escape from Richmond came all too easily. They left the Confederate stronghold well before dawn. Emily held Joseph throughout the ride. The pair slept soundly, under the watchful gaze of her family and Evan.

In the later hours of morning, the Conrads converged on Washington and the train station. Arriving in Washington felt like a holiday for the war heroes. They were at last free and the threat of prison was far behind. Abandoning their carriage, they waited for the rest of their clandestine party. Claire soon appeared with one lone piece of luggage. Hanging on her arm was a young man she introduced as Liam. He was her son, bearing the same red complexion. She hung her head self conscious under their stares.

Evan looked most astounded, but kept his mouth closed, welcoming her openly. In truth, it mattered little to him, considering his own past. He smiled at the boy and received a grin in return.

"I should've mentioned my son," Claire said apologetically.

"Nonsense," Stuart said. "I'm sure you forgot in the fray."

"No," Claire said. "I ad time ta tell Lieutenant Howell, but—"

"You weren't married when you had him?" Margaret asked.

"I was, ma'am. But, e left me on the trip o'er," Claire explained, annoyed by the woman's question. "He was sick, b'fore we boarded—wouldn hear a delayin ar trip. Stubborn man—they buried im at sea," she grew somber at the tale.

Emily looked to the young woman with sad eyes. She had long feared such things to happen to her. When it came so close, it left her terrified. Her gaze shifted to Joseph. He looked back at her with hollow, but seeing eyes. He smiled.

"Well," Stuart said, offering her his seat on the bench by his wife. "Sit down. The train won't come for a bit longer."

Evan stood up and offered his place on the bench. She thanked him and sat, drawing her boy into her lap. Evan put a hand on her shoulder and squeezed. She looked up at him and he smiled.

Stuart's gaze shifted over the group in his charge. He smiled weakly and turned his back. From the archway toward the west entrance, a couple approached with a steward in close tow. By their manner and dress, Stuart already guessed who they were. With a grand smile, Stuart approached them. He introduced himself.

"John and Lucretia Maynard," the distinguished man said for both of them. The woman on his arm looked ashen. "Where is he?"

"Over here," Stuart smiled. He held his arm out to indicate the way.

Their eyes took in the scene at the bench. A young woman rested her head on Joseph's thin shoulder. They held hands fast. They only cared that he was all right. The Maynards hurried to Joseph.

With a grand smile, Stuart left them to greetings. He wanted to settle their arrangements and see to comfortable transport to the house Mr. Maynard gave him the address for.

The arrival of the Maynards proved a wonderful surprise for their son. Upon seeing them, he drew himself up with the little strength he had left. With tear filled eyes, Lucretia Maynard threw her arms about her son's neck. He stammered and stared at them. Then his tears flowed. During the days of his imprisonment, he convinced himself the people who surrounded him now would never do so again. Isaiah offered his help when he leaned on the verge of collapse.

"You've no idea what it means to see you all again," he said, as all the pain he tucked inside him poured out.

"You've no idea what it means to see you safe again," his mother said, smiling softly at him.

"Mr. Conrad," John addressed Stuart who stood beside the girl his son had been holding hands with.

"Oh—Father," Joseph said. "I'm sorry," he held out his frail hand. "This is Mr. Stuart Conrad and his wife Margaret, Mrs. Henrietta Benson and her husband Isaiah," he pointed to the man, holding him up. "You know Lieutenant Howell. The young woman beside him is Miss Claire Healy and her boy Liam. She helped us to escape. And, finally, Miss Emily Conrad," he said breathlessly, looking at her beautiful face, as she smiled at his parents.

Lucretia stepped closer to Emily and took hold of her hands. She told the woman of how long she waited to meet her, having heard so much from her children. Emily looked sidelong to Joseph, unsure of how to respond.

"This is a treat," Lucretia said.

"Mary insisted on coming, but we sent her with Phoebe to prepare the townhouse," John told him.

"You opened it?"

"Yes—where else did you think we'd stay?" His father smiled at him.

"Porter!" John called. A uniformed man approached. "We need tickets to Baltimore." He said wandering off.

"Is there anything else you want to tell me about your life, Cap?" Evan smiled at him. "I keep getting these fantastic surprises."

"No, Lieutenant, nothing else," Joseph said guardedly

"Ya sure? Cause I think Em would be real interested."

"Evan," Emily chided. "This is no time to tease him."

It seemed forever before the cabs delivered the Conrads and Maynards to a large townhouse in Baltimore. The guests settled into their rooms and spent a full day, resting while Lucretia and her daughter tended Joseph. After supper, Emily joined them and together they fed Joseph his meal. The four discussed the events of how Joseph met Miss Conrad in Vermont and soon Lucretia pieced the entire ordeal together. His supper eaten, Lucretia left Joseph to the care of his beloved Emily and urged her daughter to do the same.

Late in the evening, Margaret searched the house for her daughter and found Emily asleep in her chair by Joseph's bed. She lay on his hand, held tightly in both of hers. Margaret's eyes studied the pair, sleeping close to each other. His hand held just as tightly to hers. A smile wavered on her lips and tears sparkled in her eyes, as she thought of what her husband said in the study nearly a year ago.

The love she saw between them was all she wanted for her little girl. She thought of how she tried so hard to stop it. Biting her knuckle, she forced back the tears, forming in her eyes. She never felt so sorry.

Margaret slowly stepped into the room and stood beside Emily. Trying not to startle her, she gently placed her hand on her daughter's shoulder. Emily's head rose, and her eyes quickly went to Joseph. Margaret smiled and turned her head chuckling.

Joseph slept. Emily touched his brow and studied him with a sad solemn face. He drew a deep breath and opened his eyes. Emily smiled at him and he smiled back, touching her face gently.

"We must go to bed," Margaret whispered. "He'll be here in the morning."

"Your mother's right," Joseph said, sounding strangely weak. "I can't run away yet."

Emily looked to her mother with doubt. Emily looked back to Joseph and stroked his hand with her thumb. She knew there stood no use in arguing with either of them.

"I'll bring your breakfast," Emily promised.

"Will you bring me breakfast," Evan asked, laying forgotten across a chair in the dark corner of a bookcase.

"I can't wait," Joseph told her.

Emily reluctantly released his hand and rose to her feet. She turned to the door, holding her gaze on the dark hall outside. If she looked back, she might not leave. Placing her trembling hands on her waist, she stilled them to keep her mother from noticing her fear. She lifted her chin and noticed Mr. Maynard coming through the door.

"Goodnight, Miss Conrad—Mrs. Conrad," he smiled at them. "I just came to say good night to my son."

"Goodnight," Emily said, continuing out with her mother.

"Goodnight, Mr. Maynard," she heard her mother say.

"Oh, Lieutenant Howell," Mr. Maynard said, closing the door. "Good you're here."

The moment the sun rose, just peeking over the buildings to the east, Emily rose from bed. She peered out the window and quickly turned to getting dressed. When she finished, Emily dashed from the room and downstairs. She gathered Joseph's breakfast from the cook, thanking her for her trouble.

Emily spun out of the kitchen, carefully carrying the tray of food in her hands. She traversed the stairs and entered Joseph's bedroom. She placed the tray on the nightstand and pulled the chair from the wall to sit beside him. He slept peacefully and she paused to watch him. Sitting on the cushion of the chair, she pulled the tray closer. She took up his hand and gently woke him with the call of her voice.

Emily's help would see Joseph regain some strength, but not enough to stave off further illness. Two days after their safe arrival in Washington, Emily entered his room to bring him breakfast. She found Joseph, standing before one of four tall windows that overlooked the corner of the street below. He had opened it and now stood in the cold March air. Emily quickly set the tray on a chest of drawers and went to his side.

Joseph stood nearly dressed, just short of stockings and jacket. She looked up at him and her great joy turned to dismay. Joseph's hair lie pasted to his face by sweat and his mouth worked into a tight grimace. Emily touched his shoulder and she could feel the flames of fever beneath the shirt. His hands looked white around the knuckles where he clung to the draperies to keep from falling over. He avoided looking at her.

"Joseph," Emily said in a surprisingly calm tone. "You should lie down, now. I've brought you breakfast. I'm sure your starving."

"I'm not hungry," he rasped.

Emily put her arm around his middle and helped him back to bed. He felt wet with perspiration and his body burned her wherever she touched. Once he sat on the edge of the bed, she took off the shirt he wore. She let him lie back on his pillows and removed his pants. Then, she pulled the blankets over him. His eyes rolled glassy in his head. He tried to gaze out of the window from the bed. Emily's fears renewed.

"How are you feeling this morning?" Emily asked, fetching the tray of food from the table by the door.

"I'm not feeling so good, Miss Emily," his voice cracked dry.

"I know, Joseph." She propped him up on his pillows.

"It's hot in here," he said. "I wanted to open the window."

"You have a fever," Emily said, picking up the cup of juice on his tray.

"I told you I wasn't feeling well," he said, half laughing.

Emily sat on the edge of the bed and helped him to drink the glass of juice. He grimaced at the first sip and tried to refuse. Emily ignored him. Looking at his tray, she selected the toasted bread and decided the rest too much for his body right then. She picked up the first piece and found him cooperative by that point.

The door to Joseph's room opened. Hettie arrived. Emily calmly requested she have someone call for a doctor. Meanwhile, she wanted Claire to help her tend Joseph. Emily knew her abilities to heal limited, but at the least her presence might ease his mind. The rest would come from the doctor's pills or potions, which would work their affects to heal him faster. Wearing a worried frown on her face, Hettie complied and turned out of the room.

"What's going on?" Evan appeared in the door. He stepped in, buttoning his shirt. He saw Joseph's state and stared. "I'll get Claire," he said and quickly went to carry out his words.

The doctor arrived by midmorning. After Hettie admitted him to the house, he trudged up the stairs, an old figure bent with tiresome age. He used a shiny ebony cane with a silver tip to keep from toppling over, as well as Hettie's arm. He looked to the dark skinned woman with surprise at first, but his face changed to a warm smile. He nodded to her with a thank you and adjusted his wire frame glasses on his thin nose, allowing her to help him.

The doctor stepped in Joseph's room and offered a kind smile to those who stood around and made his patient more comfortable. Setting his bag on the nightstand he turned to them and asked if they would mind leaving while he examined Captain Maynard. He patiently waited for them to take their leave. When they shut the door on the room, he began his task.

"You are not feeling so well, Captain Maynard," he said in his aged voice. "Let us see if we can fix that," he smiled at Joseph.

Outside his bedroom door, Emily stood with Mary and Evan to each side. She clung to the other young woman, both on the brink of tears. Evan frowned, stroking Emily's hair. She came all the way from Vermont to see Joseph well again. Her family risked their lives to help him escape from his enemy's hands. They brought him so far. Loosing him at that point turned it into a mockery. She felt Mary lay her golden head against hers. Her friend gave her a strengthening hug, but nothing helped.

"When I get my hands on Francis McFadden he'll pay fur what he's done," Mary swore between clenched teeth. "He did this to Joey. I'll see um pay."

"Me and Mike'll see that debt paid, Miss Maynard," Evan testified darkly.

Emily looked into Evan's face. She saw the deadly and powerful rage echoed there. She recalled such determination expressed in his father's features on occasion. Before she could ask what had happened with this McFadden, the door to Joseph's bedroom opened. She faced it and watched the doctor step out, shutting the door behind him. He turned to her smiling and approached with certainty. His small eyes studied her closely from behind his small round glasses.

"Are you the Captain's wife?" He asked her. Emily blushed despite her concerns and shook her head. "Well then, I've rarely made a mistake and I am sorry for my presumption."

"Doctor," Margaret said, stepping up and placing a gentle arm about his shoulders to guide him to the right people. "This is Mr. and Mrs. John Maynard. Joseph is their son."

"Ahh—yes," he breathed heavily through his nose. He strode oddly toward them. "He has caught a bacterium of some sort, but nothing to worry over if taken care of. These things happen in the hospitals all the time. He was in a hospital before? That's what he said. Anyway, disease spreads quickly there. I'll see to some proper medication." He paused to look at them. "He'll of course need much rest, no excitement." At his advice, all eyes turned to Joseph's father. He ignored the accusation by adjusting his lapels. "I shall write a prescription and send you my bill."

While her family waited with Joseph's and the doctor, Emily returned to Joseph's side. She mopped his burning forehead and spoke softly with him, as he lay there as helpless as a baby. His eyes never moved from her once they met her soft frame. His hand rested on her knee, as if to assure him that she remained there. She told him of the doctor's prognosis.

"You need to stop thinking about returning to your company," Emily advised him. "One thing at a time, Captain." She hated to tell him those words, but he needed to hear them. He spread his energies too thin. "They will do just fine for a time without you. You need to worry about getting better now."

Hettie entered the room with a porcelain basin of water and her arm draped with cloths. Emily thanked her and set the items on his stand. She wet the first rag in the cold water and placed it under his neck, following with one on his forehead. Placing her trembling hand against his warm cheek, she begged him to rest. He only looked at her sullenly. Emily kissed his hand. His eyes still watched her, but he said nothing. The rise and fall of his chest was the only sign that he lived.

"Now you are angry with me?" Emily smiled. "Would it make you feel better if I read to you, Captain?"

"If I were better, Miss Conrad," he said. "You would be in danger right now."

"But you are not," she smiled at him deviously. "I will read to you."

"If you must," he said sarcastically. "Read me the paper," he said.

"No," Emily said, standing and rounding the chair. "The doctor said no excitement." She went to the shelves of his books and read the spines.

"Then you should leave," he jested. "Seeing you brings up all sorts of exciting memories."

"What one do you like?" Emily asked, ignoring him.

"The pink skirt," he answered watching the back of her dress. She looked at him and he smiled. "Bleak House," he finally answered.

"Good," she said pulling the book from the shelf. "I have not read this yet."

"You'll enjoy it, I'm sure." He looked to the open doorway. "Where is Lieutenant Howell?"

Emily wandered back to the chair at his bedside.

"Out with Miss Healy," Emily said, opening the book and leafing to the first page. She felt Joseph's eyes on her, but she quickly immersed herself in reading the pages aloud to him. The uncomfortable feeling faded.

The prescription, which the doctor promised, arrived in the evening by means of a courier. Joseph received his dosage and Emily sat with him while he ate his supper. He ate only a little during meals, but drank more, which Emily saw as good. Though she wished to remain at his side, she made herself leave when he looked like he needed to sleep. The fever subsided in another day, but he was still obviously weak.

Following the setback, Joseph strength and health grew rapidly. Emily quickly had her hands full, trying to keep him at rest. Eventually, she gave into his whims, allowing him to sit by the window or read by himself. In the least, he fed himself and finished what was on his plate.

One particular day, Emily stood exasperated at his bedside while he repeatedly insisted on joining their families for breakfast in the dining room. Emily pushed him back down on his bed, but found herself toppled into the bed with him. He wrapped his arms about her and rolled until she lay tucked tightly beneath him. He smiled down at her and kissed her mouth.

"Do you yield, Miss Emily?" Joseph smiled full of as much vigor as ever. His eyes sparkled devilishly.

"Are you insane, Captain?" Emily asked, pushing her hands against his chest to move him off her. Her heart raced with fear of their discovery. "Let me up, Joseph. What if they come to check on you?"

"No one's up yet. They don't wake for a few more hours at my best guess—and I've had a great deal of time to learn their schedules," he told her. He took her protesting hand into his and pushed it back against the bed. "I've missed you more than you'll ever know," he said memorizing every facet of her face. His voice revealed the seductive mood he played and he longingly gazed into her eyes.

"Joseph," Emily trembled, knowing she could not win this battle. "I don't want them to see us like this."

"Hettie's outside the door," he looked to see the woman he spoke of, turning her attention quickly elsewhere. She muttered something under her breath. "If anyone comes, I'm sure she'll signal us."

"What is it that you intend with me, sir?" Emily asked, becoming outraged and strangely interested.

Joseph smiled, sliding to her side. He pulled her skirts up to her knees and said, "I merely thank you for the care you gave me."

"Joseph," she chided, feeling his hands slip down her side. Her words stopped with a kiss and his hands reached beneath the many layers of her skirt.

"You shouldn't have started this," he said, releasing her mouth. He worked her legs apart with his knee and smiled at her.

"Me," Emily gasped. "I've done nothing. You're being a scoundrel."

Joseph's eyes looked through hers deep into her soul, "Can you tell me you don't think about what we did?"

"Everyday," Emily said then suddenly turned crimson, realizing how she answered.

Joseph's mouth curled into a sultry small smile. He looked at her face, that of an angel. He could not help himself for all the need he felt for her inside. His features slowly straightened and he let his hand slip up her leg to her hip, feeling the soft fabric of her undergarments. The silken bare skin of her body was just out of reach. Emily licked her lips nervously, watching him with her face slightly turned away. He lowered his mouth to her neck, he kissed her there, nuzzling and nipping. He kept her arms pinned above her head until he felt sure she would not fight him.

"Damn," Emily breathed letting her arms close around him when he released her. "Why do I let you get to me like this? I wasn't raised in a brothel. I should for decency sake refuse these attentions, but I c—"

"Shh—Emmy. Enjoy it," he said cutting her words short. He released her and sat astride her waist, looking at her pinned beneath him. "How shall I do this?"

"Not at all," Emily said, wriggling from beneath him. "You're still too weak."

Joseph moved quickly and caught her, pulling her back into his lap. He brushed her loose hair aside and kissed her shoulder. Emily froze in his hold and then shivered, breathing his name. Wrapping his arm tight around her waist, he worked the laces of her gown slack. He would not let her deny him the pleasure of making love to her, even if his parents and hers slept only a few feet away.

"Let me love you as my dying wish," Joseph said, pulling her skirt up to where he could snake his hand beneath again. He kissed her shoulder and slipped his other hand into the neckline of her dress.

"Don't say such things, Joseph. I don't want to hear—" Emily turned her head to look at him, but he used the moment to kiss her quiet.

Joseph released her, looking into her eyes. "What would you like to hear?" He grinned, laying her back on his bed and winding his leg about hers. "Soft moans of pleasure?"

"Joseph—" Emily rasped, as he pulled the neckline of her dress down. She saw the disappointment when her corset blocked his view of her entire breast.

"Why do you women wear so many clothes? It's going to take me forever to get you dressed again."

"So whatever it is you intend will be stopped by exhaustion," Emily said smartly.

Joseph smiled at her. His hand slipped up to her belly under the skirt and yanked the corset down, revealing her breasts to him.

"It'll take more than that to stop me, Miss," he leaned down and kissed her mouth.

"Oh bother," Emily breathed against his face when he let her go, feeling his hand claim her. "What if Evan finds us?"

"He's not welcome to help," Joseph replied.

Spending so many days with Evan only affirmed her feelings and left Claire sorry to see him return to the military. While her son played at her feet, she watched Evan unpack his uniform in the light of the April morning. He laid it out on his bed and turned to her. His smile faded, finally seeing her there. She swallowed hard and fought back the tears in her eyes. He looked so handsome, well fed and clean.

"I loved my husband," she said to him. "But, it didn keep him alive." She crossed her arms and thought better of telling him how she felt. "Without someone's help, I'mna sure how my son'll eat."

Evan rested his hands on his hips and looked at her with a wry grin, "The Conrads said they would help find you a place."

"As a housekeeper?" She looked at him hurt. "I'm a nurse," she said.

"And a proud one," Evan said, crossing his arms. He stepped to the window seat she rested on, picking Liam up and setting him on his lap. "Your mother's proud. Isn't she, Liam?"

"Proud as a partridge," he said, reiterating something he heard somewhere.

"I've an idea," Evan said, looking at her. "I wanted to ask you for awhile now, but I couldn't." He paused and Liam squirmed out of his hands, climbing down to the floor. "Why don't you go with the Conrads back to Vermont? You can help my mother care for my little brother. He'd appreciate Liam's company and Mom needs another hand. My sisters are too busy scheming to do as they should."

"You told me they don't have much," Claire said. "I canna ask a wage a them."

"I'll pay you," Evan said. "I'll send part of my commission each month."

Evan held his breath, waiting for her answer. Claire showed him a grand smile. She looked to her son, inspecting the uniform he left on the bed. The tears poured from her eyes. Evan stroked her arm and patted her shoulder, chuckling with surprise at her reaction.

"How can I thank you?" Claire cried because she had to let him go.

"I'll let you know, when I think you're up to it," Evan smiled.

Claire's tears stopped and her expression changed to one of warning, "I ardly think so, Lieutenant. Yu'llna get that from me unless ya put a ring on me finger."

"Wait for me in Vermont and I might," Evan laughed. Claire smiled at him and her beauty made him forget everything but the moment. He blinked and drew a breath, trying to clear the fog she put in his mind. "After everything," Evan whispered. "How could I be worthy of you?"

Claire looked at him askance, "Evan?"

Evan placed his hand on her cheek and pressed his lips to hers. "Nothing. I better get ready. I still haven't seen Joe. He's getting stronger and Emily's going to need my help. Make sure you give her a hand when I've gone. God knows what he's done to her already."

Evan jumped up from her side and went to his uniform, now draping the floor and Liam. Claire watched him deftly rescue his jacket and pants, before exiting to put them on. Claire stood from the window seat and went to her son playing with other items of Evan's occupation. She picked him up, carrying him out with Evan's cap on his head.

⁂

In early May, Joseph felt nearly ready to return to the cavalry. Surrounded by family and friends, he told them he still felt unsure of returning. However, the choice belonged to his superiors and he owed them and himself the respect of complying with orders. The Army would not release a healthy captain of the cavalry this late in the game, after so many had deserted. Besides, his honor nagged him to go back and the souls of his friends called to him. Separate from the families, he begged Emily for understanding and she tried to give it.

Despite the eventuality of leaving, Joseph determined to enjoy what little time he owned with his beloved. Early each morning, she went to his room. There they laid together in the gray glow before dawn. It took little coaxing on Joseph's part. Emily only wanted to stay with him in his arms.

The families ate breakfast together the third day before Joseph planned to leave for the Army. Emily sat beside his sister, carefully eating her cheese omelet. He watched her with concern, where he sat between his father at one end of the table and his mother at his left. Across from him, Mary smiled knowingly and winked.

"Uh-Joseph," his father said, wiping his mouth on a cloth napkin. "We've been asked to attend an event the night before you leave. I expect you to attend. It's for the firm and it'll give you a foothold with the partners."

"That'd be lovely," Lucretia gasped. "You could take Emily and show her off."

Joseph smiled and lifted his gaze to Emily. He saw the nervousness in her expression.

"I'd love to join you," Joseph replied.

"Oh—Emily," Margaret said excitedly. "We'll have to get you a new dress, dear."

"Lovely, may I come along?" Mary said, touching Emily's hand.

"I hope that you will," Emily said with a furrowed brow. "I'm afraid I wouldn't know what to wear."

Mrs. Conrad left the house later that morning, with Emily and Mary to see her daughter fitted with a new dress. Mary helped them find the perfect shop, one she used on occasion. Stepping behind the door, they quickly found themselves surrounded by clerks more than willing to help. The women took Emily to a backroom and brought several gowns for her to try. She eventually selected a pale blue dress of shimmering satin.

Next, they selected the perfect pair of shoes to adorn Emily's feet. The clerks brought her a set that matched the material of her gown and accented on the toe with seed pearls. Once Emily was redressed in the gown she came in, they selected a fur stole for her shoulders, white with silvery blue ties. Then they offered a pair of silvery satin gloves. Mary suggested she take them and they did. When they left, the shop promised to have the gown to her by tomorrow evening, delivered at the Maynard flat.

Mrs. Conrad paid them their fee and they left with the accessories, to await the altered evening gown. From there, they went in search of other items Emily needed for that night. When they returned, supper stood ready for them in the Maynard dining room. Hettie and Phoebe helped them with their packages and coats.

"Dinner is just about ready, Miss," Phoebe said to Mary. "Your mother and father are waiting for you in the dining room. They have a present for Miss Conrad."

"Thank you, Phoebe," Mary smiled. She shucked off her jacket and handed it to her. "Emily," she smiled, taking her friend's arm.

Mary and Emily entered the dining room ahead of Mrs. Conrad. Inside, the rest of the Maynard clan gathered with Mr. Conrad and young Miss Healy and her son. The food rested on the sideboards, waiting for them to eat.

"Come in. Come in," Mr. Maynard urged them. They took to their usual seats and the men, except for Mr. Maynard sat. "How was your shopping?"

"We enjoyed ourselves thoroughly," Mrs. Conrad beamed.

"Good. Good," Mr. Maynard smiled. "My wife and I thought you might need something else, Miss Conrad." He indicated a long box near her place setting, wrapped in festive ribbons.

Emily picked up the box and looked at it. She felt awkward accepting a gift from Joseph's parents. She did nothing to deserve it. She looked up to them with a questioning glance.

"Open it," Lucretia said. "I can barely wait to see your face."

Emily hesitated. She stared at the bright box. It reminded her of the gown she selected. At her side, Liam squirmed and picked up his fork. Emily looked to him and he smiled up at her.

"Is it your birthday?"

"No, Liam," Emily answered.

"Why'd you get a present?"

"Because we love her," Mary answered for her. "Don't we, Joey?"

"Very much," he said, giving Emily a devious look. "You are going to open it aren't you?"

"Y-yes," Emily stammered. She set the package on the table and pulled the ribbon from the box. Then she picked the paper apart. The silver box turned to a long black lacquered box. She tipped open the lid and found a necklace and earrings inside. Three strands of pearls forced her mouth into a gape. She nearly swooned when the aquamarine drop glinted in the lamplight, surrounded in diamonds that glistened like moonlit snow.

"It matches your eyes," Liam said in his small voice.

"Our point exactly," Mr. Maynard smiled, placing his hand on his son's shoulder. "We hope you will accept this gift as gratitude for out son's health. Without you, we might have lost him." He paused to watch her pick up the jewelry and study it in her hands. "Do you like it?"

"It's loveliest jewelry I've ever seen," Emily breathed.

"For the loveliest woman in the Union," Joseph said, bringing her eyes to his.

"How did you know the color of the dress?" Emily asked.

"We have our ways," Mr. Maynard told her.

The evening of the ball, Emily stood bathed and dressed in her new gown, standing before a full length mirror. Hettie fastened the stays, tightening the bodice around her ribs. It fit better than any dress she wore. Emily smoothed her hands over the laced bodice. The silver crisscross ties glinted. The pearl tone lace felt silky beneath her hands.

Margaret appeared at her dressing table, carrying the box with the gift from the Maynards and the hairpins they bought days ago. She set them down and looked at her daughter. She smiled warmly, as pride filled her. All too quickly, the shame of her actions took over. Margaret lowered her chin and spread the items on the dressing table surface to distract herself.

"Awful nice of the Maynards to get this for you," Margaret said, opening the box and picking up the pearls. "Just lovely," she added when the aquamarine drop glinted in her eye. She could barely imagine the cost.

Hettie completed the stays and stepped back to let Mrs. Conrad place the choker on Emily's neck. She draped it in front of Emily's eyes, bringing it down to her throat. There she fastened it and looked at the piece against her daughter's skin. A tear glinted in her eye at how lovely her little girl looked.

Hettie offered Emily the matching earrings and her gloves. She stepped back and watched her attach the jewelry to her delicate lobes. She smiled softly, recalling the first dance Emily attended with Joseph. She felt sure the next grand ball would be their wedding.

Emily slipped her hands into each of her gloves, pulling them up past her elbows. She buttoned them at the wrist and faced Hettie with a smile. Behind Emily, her mother stepped back to look at her. She offered them both a shy smile, hoping she looked half as lovely as she thought. When her mother pressed her hands together in front of her lips, she felt most assured.

"Hettie will you do my hair? You always do it so well," Emily begged her. Hettie nodded her head and cleared the dressing table. Emily faced her mother and saw the tears stand in her eyes. "Oh— Mamma," Emily said, crushing her mother into her arms. "Thank you so much."

"If it weren't for me, I'm sure you'd be much happier."

Her mother turned away, hanging her head with guilt and sat on the edge of Emily's bed. Emily stepped toward her, but Hettie touched her arm stopping her. She lifted her eyes to the housekeeper and Hettie shook her head. She pointed to the chair at the dressing table, waiting for her. Emily felt unsure of which direction to go in. She had only a short time before she must stand ready beside Joseph downstairs.

When her mother sadly spread the fur stole on the end of the bed, Emily made up her mind of which ranked more important. She stepped from Hettie toward her mother. Reluctantly, she sat with her at the foot of the bed. She need clear matters with her mother, before she saw her hair played with.

"I know you were only frightened for me," Emily said, reaching out a hand to touch her mother's back. "In your place I'd have done the same. Joseph's forgiven you and so have I. You must forgive yourself now. No one bears you a grudge, Mamma."

"Oh—Em," Margaret turned and hugged her with a tear filled grin. "How I've longed to hear those words from you." She pulled back, holding Emily at arms length to look at her. "You're a princess, my girl—an absolute princess."

"I'll say," Hettie piped up. "Spoiled rotten and wise mouthed too," Hettie said crossly. "Now, I think it's high time her highness sat in this chair and let me place her coif like she asked," Hettie added sarcastically, shaking her brush at her. In her other hand, she wielded the heating tongs fresh from the fireplace.

Emily pursed her lips and stood to join Hettie at the vanity. She sat in the chair, looking at her half finished appearance in the mirror. Hettie started with brushing her long mink locks. Then, she endured the long process of curling and pinning. With every passing moment, Emily grew increasingly eager, until she felt sickly restless.

Suddenly the clock struck seven o'clock, Hettie placed the last curl and pinned it. Emily finished the last bit of cosmetics while Hettie placed the jeweled comb at the top of a cascade of curls falling over her right shoulder.

Seven marked the time to leave. Twirling up and out of her chair, Emily turned to get her stole from the bed. Mary pushed through the door wearing an emerald hue dress with the stones themselves about her throat and ears. Her hair bore small sparkling stones on a weblike net that covered the golden braids at the back. She carried a black satin bag in her gloved hands and smiled at her new friend.

"I can't wait to show you off," Mary said. "My sister'll be the most beautiful young woman in all of DC."

"And what about yourself?" Emily asked, placing her stole on her shoulders with the help of Hettie and her mother. They adjusted the ties and Emily soon started out of the door. She looked to Mary and thought she looked more like the princess. "I'm sure I barely compare with you."

"I can't convince you otherwise?" She laughed. "I'm sure we shall make a pair won't we?" Mary said, taking her arm. "Joey's waiting," Mary whispered when they took the first step down. "I can't wait to see what he thinks."

Emily's eyes scanned past the polished wood and carpeted steps. At the base of the winding stairs, Mr. Maynard waited beside his son and Mr. Conrad. Joseph wore his full dress uniform, accented by gold embroidery and brass buttons, thankfully shipped to him with other items by Michael. It became the officer without appearing regally gaudy. Emily glided down the stairs on the arm of his sister, holding her eyes on him. She softly smiled and felt the heat rise in her cheeks.

Joseph watched her descend to him like an apparition. No woman he ever knew looked so fair in all his life. He believed God sent an angel to him, as thanks for rescuing the lives of some unfortunate cows, bound to die in a terrible fire. He adjusted his jacket, self consciously.

"I could have warned you, but I hardly knew," Mr. Conrad chuckled proudly.

"What a vision," Mr. Maynard smiled up at the women. His eyes flicked to his wife, just descending behind them. She smiled down at him, taking hold of the banister in one hand and her skirt in the other. "I'll be the proudest man there, with the loveliest three women in all the US," he said, beaming at his lovely wife.

A short while later, the Maynard carriage had traversed the streets of the capitol to pull up at the front of the home of Mr. Albert Wallace. Outside, several finely dressed women and their escorts entered the mansion through a set of enormous doors. The carriage door popped open and the Maynard driver stood to the side, allowing Joseph to dismount first. Joseph turned back and helped the women down.

Emerging last ahead of Mr. Maynard, Emily climbed down, viewing the scene with awe at the finery she saw. She felt used to splendid things with the success of her father's farm, but nothing she knew compared. The Town Hall ball she attended ages ago with Joseph seemed so diminutive now.

When they all stood on the sidewalk, the coach driver shut the door and drove away, to wait for the end of the evening in the Wallace carriage house. Joseph offered his arm to Emily with a smile and she took it, turning her awe to a happy smile. She turned her eyes to follow their chaperones. Mr. Maynard and his wife walked proudly along the sidewalk and up the cobblestone walk to the front steps. Several of the people tipped their hats and bid them a good evening, allowing the Maynard party to pass them. Emily placed her gaze on Mary, hoping the young woman could lead her in the proper manner of action from there.

At the front doors of the grand Wallace home, servants greeted their party to accept their hats and cloaks and to escort them inside among the other revelers. Joseph surrendered his hat and helped Emily remove her stole. He placed her back on his arm and watched her stare wide eyed at the foyer of the partner's vast home. He explained to her wonder why a Baltimore lawyer lived in Washington. He saw her only half listen, while she tried to soak in the sights of paintings adorning the high red walls and the glimmering fixtures above their heads. She looked down to the marble floor stretched out beneath their feet.

"I've never seen a home like this," Emily admitted to him. She looked up at Joseph and smiled. "I'm sorry, Joseph. You tried to tell me?"

"That's all right," he patted her hand. "I'm glad you are enjoying it. I was only saying that Mr. Wallace is trying to retire from the firm. His son has been with them for ten years and served his term of apprenticeship, so to speak. Mr. Wallace is now interested in government," Joseph continued, as they turned into a vast ballroom with a deep granite floor. "Father will fully retire once I've served my ten years as well."

"You're joining the law firm in Baltimore," Emily stated gravely. "When will I see you?" She looked up at him with sad eyes.

Joseph smiled down at her, placing a hand on her jaw. While it closed around her jaw like it did when he meant to tempt her into sin again, his eyes glinted with deviltry. He leaned in close to her his lips, wavering in a wry smile. Emily's mouth opened, as if she would speak.

"Every night I come home," he said, holding her with his gaze. His hand slipped down to her arm and he patted it where it rested in the crook of his. They stepped forward again. "That way," he continued the other line. "The firm will remain Wallace, Maynard, and Reese. Not just Wallace and Reese."

"Your father's a partner?" Emily asked, shocked to hear the news after so long. In all the time they spent writing, Joseph never mentioned this much of his family.

"Yes, he is," Joseph answered, as they came into a room filled with men and women of Washington society. "And these are his friends, if you can call some of them that."

Emily smiled at him understanding the joke. She quickly forgot what he said, dazzled by the jewels and gowns that shone bright before her eyes. She caught many appreciative glances herself and several bold jealous glances from a handful of young women gathered by the punch bowl. They fanned themselves and watched her wander by on Joseph's arm.

Despite their obvious disapproval, they approached with forced smiles and begged to know whom Joseph escorted. Joseph proudly presented Emily to the entire collection of debutantes. They spoke familiarly with him, trying to ignore his companion and make her feel especially excluded, now they knew. When Emily failed to prove an unknown cousin, she quickly became a rival. Though they each presented that much to one another, Emily stood the worst sort among them, an outsider who threatened their society.

"If you'll excuse us, ladies," Joseph said. "I've a host to find and thank for his hospitality," Joseph smiled at them. He nodded respectfully. When they protested, he insisted and pushed his way through, holding Emily to his side. "I haven't seen Mr. Wallace in years now. I am eager to meet with him again. Excuse us."

Freed from the crowd, Joseph brought Emily through the throng, searching for his father and mother. He guessed they would be wherever the host stood, most likely awaiting his late arrival. He felt sure they would understand how they became separated, knowing the behavior of the young women. At least some things never changed.

Above the heads of the crowd, Joseph spied the venerable heads of his sire and that of Mr. Wallace. Heading a course straight through the crowd, he found himself quickly at their sides. Emily stood beside him, distanced by the hoop skirt she wore. He preferred the fashion to shrink and allow her to stand closer, like when they lie in bed early in the morning.

"Good evening, Mister Wallace," Joseph said when presented, with a strong handshake.

"Boy," Albert exclaimed his white brows rose on his red face. "I haven't seen you since you went to school. By God the army made a fine man of you."

"He was turning into a fine man before the war," Lucretia corrected the partner.

Albert inclined his head to her, "Merely a compliment, ma'am." His attention turned to Emily standing at his side. "And who is this striking creature? Is this your wife, Captain Maynard? I've not heard tell a such thing, but—"

Emily ducked her head and gave a small curtsy, as proved suitable. She offered her hand to the older man with a smile. "This is Miss Emily Conrad of Vermont, sir," Joseph introduced her.

"A fine state, Miss Conrad," Albert took her hand and inclined his head over it. "I prefer to visit the area of Burlington when I am up that way," he added. Turning his attention to the others he asked, "Did you know they plan to build a horseracing track in Saratoga, New York? They say that they race on the streets up there. As if the one track weren't enough." He looked back to Emily, smiling, "I hardly believe your trade is in horses, young lady. What is it the Conrads keep themselves busy with in Vermont?"

"My father is a dairy man," Emily replied in her soft sweet tones. "Finest in all the North."

"Without a doubt," Albert smiled, taking a drink from a tray to offer to her escort.

Joseph took the glass with a murmured thank you. Mr. Wallace offered Emily a drink as well, but she politely refused. Then Mary and her mother refused the refreshment. However, Mr. Maynard accepted with a gracious smile. Emily lowered her chin, drawing a deep breath. She hoped her refusal stood blameless of the precedents. Mary squeezed her hand reassuringly, letting her know all would turn out right. She lifted her chin to look at her friend and saw her infectious smile. Emily smiled back.

"What brings you to Washington Miss Conrad?" Albert said, returning to her with his dark assessing eyes.

"It's a terribly long story," Emily said.

"Nonsense," Mr. Wallace said, appearing interested. "Do tell me."

"My friend from home, Lieutenant Howell serves with Captain Maynard. He wrote to me from the hospital. My parents of course set out to rescue both of them."

"I won't assume your mutual friend introduced you. How is it that you came to know Joseph all the way down here?"

"Circumstances, which unless you are going to try a case—you don't need to know the detail of," Mary interrupted with a calculated smile on her face. She adjusted Emily's arm into hers, locking them together at the elbow.

Albert raised his drink to her in submission. "I believe dinner shall occur soon. Shall we go to the dining room to find our seats?"

Everyone consented with soft voices. They followed their host from the ballroom into the adjoining dining room. Serving men guided the various guest to their tables. Emily felt surprised that she would sit at the main table with Mr. Wallace and his wife. An empty seat sat waiting for his son who would come a little late because of a case he worked on in town. Soon the rest of the guests poured in from two entrances to find their tables.

"This is Mr. Reese and his wife Violet," Mr. Wallace introduced them. "Miss Emily Conrad."

"Pleasure to meet you, Miss Conrad," Mr. Reese said. He looked much younger than the other partners, but older than the sons soon to take over.

"Thank you," Emily said sweetly.

"She's lovely, Joseph," Violet said.

"Thank you," Joseph said, looking to Emily with a smile. "I thought so myself."

"Still with the sense of humor," Mr. Reese grinned. "It's good to see you so well. I suppose we have Miss Conrad to thank."

"Indeed," Lucretia said. "She kept him from the brink when he escaped prison."

"Mother," Joseph said, trying to stop her.

"You escaped prison?" Violet gasped.

"War prison," Mr. Maynard cleared up the question. "With the help of Miss Conrad's father and Joseph's lieutenant."

"My word! How exciting," Violet grinned.

Emily watched in awe. Since entering the magnificent room, her eyes never stopped roving. She took in the high vaulted ceilings and the chandeliers that hung on long sparkling chains from them. The walls were decorated with paintings in heavily ornamented frames. The wallpaper served enough, but excess ranked the fashion of the day. Behind Mr. Wallace and his wife, a portly older woman with gray shot through her brown hair, sat an enormous fireplace complete with roaring flames.

When the guests sat, Albert Wallace stood up and attracted their attention to him. The room turned silent and he gave a well thought out speech to welcome them to his home. Emily watched him, soaking in each word. She never heard such eloquent language used by anyone. The mayor sometimes spoke in that fashion, but in Vermont where it remained largely unsettled, pretty words held no real weight with the people.

The speech ended and Albert seated himself once again. Taking a sip of his drink, he watched as the servants performed the duties according to his design. Their table received service last, as all the guests were considered more important than the host that evening. At their table, the servants served the women first. When Mrs. Wallace sat with her plate filled, they turned to the men. With everyone served, Albert gave word to dine at their leisure.

The food tasted unlike anything Emily enjoyed before. Rich and full, she wanted more than she could possibly eat. Somehow, she kept control of her appetite, reminding herself that she should appear a gracious guest and a lady. When dessert came, she managed to feel full to bursting despite her care.

Following dinner, the men relaxed with a drink and cigar in the rooms the various sitting rooms filled before. Emily and the females of the Maynard clan separated to other parts. They lounged in chairs and fainting couches in a line of backrooms that appeared like a Grecian palace, added to by numerous windows and curtains. Emily stared out the windows to the lawns and gardens beyond.

More servants entered with more refreshments as they wished, or waited beside windows and doorways for them to call. Emily felt out of place from the moment they entered the space and nervously sat on a couch to relax away dinner. She wanted to stay on Joseph's arm, where she felt safe. The eyes of the women around her were cold and assessing at best. They did not want her there.

The snobbish women excluded her from all their discussions, although Mary alluded to her so many times, it became impossible. It proved Mary's only means to tell them Emily Conrad was there to stay, with or without their approval. Mr. Wallace and his wife accepted her and so they better follow suit. Those among them from Baltimore society would not dare to treat her so terrible once she married Joseph.

"I've heard that President Lincoln will come tonight," One of the older women speculated.

Emily ignored them and watched the fiery sunset out the windows. She only cared that Joseph would wait for her when they left the room. She wondered if this was a sample of what her life would be like after the war. She felt small and frightened again, like when she first met Joseph. Her eyes turned to the big windows. The sunset streaked the sky with red, purple, and orange. It felt silly to speculate when the South's submission was so far off. No matter how they suffered, they kept fighting. How long could Joseph survive?

"Where are you from Miss Conrad?" A soft voice asked her, before she could drive herself mad with thoughts of his death.

Emily turned her attention back to the group of women. An older matriarch sat at the edge of a couch, looking at her expectantly with a small smile on her lips. The other women in the room stared at her expectant.

They looked uninterested in truth, considering they already knew all they needed to know of her. Emily was Joseph's intended and that meant the rest stood out in the cold.

"A small town near Montpelier," Emily replied.

"It's mostly farms out there, isn't it?" The woman asked.

"Yes, ma'am." Emily answered.

"A lovely place I'm sure. What is it that your parents do in Vermont?" The woman asked.

Emily looked surprised that all the information about her had yet to circulate about the party already. She looked over the faces of the eager group. The younger women about her own age seemed annoyed that someone spoke to her. They rolled their eyes or made faces when they knew she saw, whispering to each other behind their fluttering fans.

"My father is a dairy man," Emily said, swallowing her fears. She held no secret to feel ashamed of. Joseph and his family never inquired this of her, and they accepted her. That was all that mattered. Besides, she felt quite proud of her father. He was an excellent man. "We have the largest dairy farm in our area."

"Is that so dear," the woman smiled, but it somehow did not touch her eyes.

"Vermont is not a big state," one of the young women said, intending to upset her.

"No, it is not," Emily agreed. "However, there is no county in your larger states to compare with it. And if there were, it would be doubtful that anyone but my father could dominate the dairy market or any market for that matter, as large."

"My father controls the senate," one bragged. "The largest market in the country. He sent my brother to West Point and he graduated in Captain Maynard's class. We've known each other since we were children. How is old Joe?"

Old Joe? Emily's thoughts questioned this little name. She felt the reassuring hand of Mary on her back. These women tried to make her run screaming back home.

However, nothing they could do would make her leave her beloved captain now. They could bring death itself to her door and she would face him down without a single thought.

"Emily's brother is a graduate of the point as well, and so is her neighbor," Mary piped up proudly. "Her father helped put both of them through the school." She paused, smiling at their annoyance. "I'm going to marry her brother, if I have it my way," she added with a wanton air.

"Mary," Mrs. Maynard said reprovingly. A smile blossomed on her lips.

The girls twittered with this news, nearly scandalous. Everyone believed she would marry within the firm, either Reese's other son or Wallace's unmarried, who happened to miss dinner that night. Now there stood a new threat on the horizon. New money wanted to be added to their small close society. It would ruin everything.

A servant entered the doorway and announced that their host requested they move into the ballroom for the continuing festivities. Mary took hold of Emily's arm and guided her at the head of the group. She whispered words of reassurance into her ear, trying to erase the memories of that horrible inquest she just suffered.

"They're jealous, my heart," Mary said to her sad little face. "Joseph would never marry the likes of them and you proved it. I'm so glad, too. I don't know what I'd do if Joey had never met you." She squeezed Emily's arm. "I couldn't stand to have one of them for my sister."

"Thank you, Mary," Emily said, lifting her chin.

Emily put her arm about Mary's waist and together they walked to the ballroom, holding to each other for support. There they met the Maynard men. Joseph smiled at Emily and shook his head. His mere presence erased all the sadness from her features and mind. He took her arm in his and led her to a quiet corner to listen to what happened in the other room.

"How has the evening been?" He asked, suggesting his knowing. He gently touched her face with the back of his hand.

"Wretched," Emily replied, near to tears. "They despise me because of you."

"Good," Joseph said, grinning. "I don't wish their friendship on anyone except the Confederates," Joseph told her.

"All very funny, until you have to deal with them," Emily said, refusing to look at him.

"You won't have to deal with them anymore," he said, kissing the knuckles of her gloved hand. "I promise you that. Mr. Wallace adores you and they would not dare upset him. I'll speak with him and see what he suggests."

"I expect you to keep your promises, Captain. All of them," Emily blushed at the feel of his warm lips so near her skin. "Or I will take it out on your hide personally," she added playfully. Her eyes took in some of the young women who harassed her moments ago, stepping through the tall open doorway.

"I hope you will," Joseph said, turning her away from the jealous gazes. He guided her away as the band struck up a waltz. "Tomorrow morning before I leave perhaps," he suggested.

"You'll have me with your child before I wear your ring," Emily said, following his lead about the dance floor.

"Am I not careful, Miss Emily?" He asked.

Emily looked up in his eyes, smiling, "I cannot say. I'm no woman to know the ways of how accidents occur. Perhaps you should consult Evan."

Joseph grinned and continued the dance, ending their conversation. They soon forgot everything but each other and the music. Their eyes locked together, and their hearts beat in time. Neither wished to stand anywhere but right there. All around them the dresses of other revelers spun in time with the grand music, following through each waltz.

By the sixth song, the music ended. The dancers and onlookers clapped their hands approvingly. Mr. Wallace stood on the raised dais where the musicians played and waved his hand at them, begging for silence. The crowd became reluctantly quiet, and Albert started his speech. At his side stood a young man his arm in a sling under his coat. He looked well kept, but something in his face said not all stood in complete order.

"That's Mr. Wallace's son, Lieutenant Daniel Wallace," Joseph explained. At that moment Albert introduced his son. The guest clapped a welcome to him, and waved his hand and nodding graciously. "He was wounded at Manassas by a Federal charge. He hasn't been able to use his arm since." Emily looked to him wonderingly. "The doctor's find no reason for it. The bullet barely tore his flesh."

If this man standing before them received his wound from a battle with the Union soldiers, it only meant one thing. She knew that Maryland hung between two loyalties until the Unionists gained control of the senate seats. She gazed at the man with the lame arm, her lips partially opened. She saw few Confederate soldiers in her young life and all when she came to Washington.

"Daniel was a Confederate soldier until that point," Joseph continued. "After his wounding he turned to denouncing the practice of war. At least he didn't lose a leg like most."

"That could have been my brother," Emily thought to herself, starring at the shaggy haired man. Emily sighed, upset by her thoughts. She cared little for what Albert said, and could not bring herself to care. It only served to remind of what she wanted to forget.

The Wallaces stepped back when several suited men joined them. They looked far too serious for the mood of the ball. Emily watched them take to opposite ends of the stage. This regained her attention quickly.

"What's going on?" She asked, trying to get a better look around all the shoulders and heads.

A notably tall man walked to the center of the stage, wearing a finely tailored suit. His grave features spoke of the heavy toil on his mind. He stepped to the center with his long thin arms behind his back. A black beard lined his jaw and chin leaving the upper lip bare of whiskers. A resounding round of applause rang out to his honor.

Emily recognized the tall figure of her nation's leader easily. She saw his picture many times, but it never did justice to the real features of the man. He looked more creased and dark in the face, a contradiction to the heart held within. When his voice echoed through the room it sounded like the distant low rumble of cannon fire. Emily stood awestruck even more than when she entered this palace. His speech turned from wrangling support for the war to the revelry of the evening.

"It is my honor to share this evening with each of you and it is my hope, despite the dangers that are all around us, we will take this time for our enjoyment. In my experience there is no greater healer than laughter and music. Our mutual friend, Mr. Wallace has been gracious enough to provide us with both tonight. I will not keep you any longer, for my wife waits to enjoy a spin around the floor as much as all of you. I wish you an excellent evening."

The president spoke in a deep rich full voice, gripping the lapels of his jacket. His dark eyes swept over the faces turned up to him. He nodded to their applause. He was not the best speaker, but he spoke what he meant. He stepped back from the edge of the stage, and followed the suited men to the dance floor where Mary Todd waited in a regal gown of amber silk.

"By God," a man near them exclaimed in a whisper, echoing everyone's thoughts.

Emily turned to Joseph with dazzled eyes. She never thought Joseph's presence to bring such good fortune. In return, he smiled down at her and the music once again played. He offered his arm seemingly unaffected by the President's presence.

"Joseph," Emily said, taking his arm and allowing him to guide her back to the ball floor for another dance.

"Why did you never tell me you held such company? I find that I know very little about you."

"I swear I hardly knew myself," Joseph admitted. "Although, I've had the honor of seeing the President on two occasions while he inspected our units."

"Life holds so many surprises," Emily said, twining her fingers round his hand and feeling his other hand slide to her back, as they started another waltz.

"And so many more to come," Joseph said.

The evening came to a close and the Maynards returned with their guests to their townhouse. Emily and Joseph bid each other good night unable to say the words they needed to, with so many eyes on them. Emily climbed the stairs to her bedroom flanked by the other women, including Hettie. Behind the closed door of her room, Hettie helped her out of her many garments and removed the pins from her hair. She sat at her mirror, cleaning the cosmetics from her face. Hettie smiled softly at her through the mirror.

"How was it?" Hettie asked.

"If he were not returning tomorrow," Emily said tremulously. "It would've been grand."

"It's almost over," Hettie said. "I can feel it."

"I wish I could feel it," Emily looked up at her with round sad eyes.

"Because you listen with your fear," Hettie told her, brushing her hair straight. "Listen with your soul." She set the brush down and braided Emily's long locks.

Emily slipped into her nightgown and climbed into bed. Hettie tucked her in and kissed her brow. Her friend stepped away and prepared herself for bed. When the light went out, Emily tried to sleep, but fear besieged her mind.

The house fell silent, pressing in all around her. Outside the sound of horses and wheels on the streets below continued. She watched the sheers of her balcony doors billow in a breeze. Hettie left the window open.

Unable to sleep, Emily rose and went to the open door. She peered out across the midnight scene of Washington. The sounds pressed in on her from all over.

It grew louder, from the street to the hall. The ticking of the hall clock drove her mad, reminding her of how the minutes rolled away. She looked back to the bed and saw Hettie sound asleep. Emily shut the doors and turned to try again for sleep.

Moonlight filtered inside, creating odd patterns on the walls and floor where the firelight could not reach. No one stood watch outside Joseph's door that night. He no longer needed supervision since he got better. If she went to him, no one would know. Her heart ached and she wondered what she should do. Her hands grasped at her nightgown, feeling the soft cotton. It could be the last night on earth so close together. She looked at her bedroom door, questioning just what she was about to do.

The clock struck three and she felt her heart wrench. She had laid there for a long time without a wink of sleep. That realization quickly decided for her. Unless she sacrificed everything for one more night, she would never sleep again. They had hours before his preparations to leave began.

Emily crept through the dark room to the door. She opened it quietly. It pressed in on her with a strange pressure that scared her. She stepped backward from a broad shouldered white shirt as it entered. It turned and her heart skipped. Joseph had come to her.

"Em," Hettie's low voice called. She sat up in bed and blinked at the forms by the door. Her eyes popped open with shock.

"Shh—" Emily put a finger up in front of her lips.

"I couldn't wait," Joseph whispered.

Emily looked at him not answering.

"I'ma leave," Hettie said, crawling out of bed. She took up her robe from the foot of the bed and swung it on. "I've been meaning ta spend the night with my husband anyhow."

"Thank you, Hettie," Joseph breathed.

"Don't," Hettie said, taking hold of his face with her long fingers. "I'm not gonna be blamed," she snapped with her disapproval.

Hettie glared at him. She then turned away, tore open the door and left them alone.

Joseph looked down to Emily, standing before him. Her sad face looked to the door her friend exited. Hettie spoke true, but they did not fear an unwanted pregnancy less than his return to his commission. Joseph drew her into his arms.

Following an early full breakfast, Joseph stood out on the front stoop with Emily behind him. He watched Sergeant McGuire step along the sidewalk, away from the pair of horses he tied off on the black posts outside. He smiled up at them from his round face and laughed happily at seeing Joseph. Joseph smiled back and held out his hand welcoming him.

"McGuire," he said.

"Good ta see ya, Captain," McGuire replied. "Good morning, ladies." He pointed to Emily with a smile and question in his eyes. "Thar she is. By God, if I were only a younger man."

"Come in. I'm not quite ready yet," Joseph grinned.

McGuire entered the flat at his commander's invitation. His eyes noticed the stack of luggage at the base of the stairs. He looked up following the winding staircase and took in the chandelier over his head. Cursing in Irish, he shook his head. Joseph touched his arm and indicated the parlor to their right. He nodded and went along.

Emily sat in a chair before the window, placing her back mostly to them. An older woman stood behind her, clasping the chair back in her hands. Opposite her, Mary sat on a sofa by Mrs. Maynard, holding a handkerchief in her fists. Her expression showed her dismay. Joseph introduced him to the well dressed man, opposite Mr. Maynard at the fireplace and smoking their choice of pipe and cigar.

"Why don't you tell them about Evan and Michael," Joseph said. He turned to see Miss Healy enter the room with a tray of tea. "Miss Healy would prove most interested in Evan," he gestured to the red haired woman.

"Oh—I've heard bout you, Miss Healy," McGuire said, bringing a smile to the woman's face. "Where's tha boy—Liam, I think the Lieutenant said."

"Aye, Liam. Evan spoke a me?"

"At lenth," McGuire said, taking hold of her hand. He patted it gently.

"Don't forget Michael," Joseph interrupted. "The Conrads would appreciate a word about him."

McGuire turned from the young woman whose hand he held, "Lieutenant Howell and Mike are doin jus fine," he smiled at them all. "We're glad to ave um back." He saw their somber expressions remain unchanged. "Oh—I almost forgot. Mike sends his best ta Miss Maynard." His eyes searched out the golden haired woman.

She looked up at him with tear filled eyes. She pulled an envelope from her skirt pocket, "Would you take him this, for me?"

"Most sar'tan, Miss," McGuire stepped over with a nod and smile. He took the letter from her.

"Would you take this to Evan for me?" Miss Healy asked, also handing over a letter.

McGuire nodded and chuckled, "When this's done, I've always got me a job as postman."

He shook his head and pocketed the messages to his officers. Footsteps on the stairs distracted him from the sobering and depressing moment. He looked to see Captain Maynard setting his last belongings with the rest.

"I've everything, Sergeant. Let's be off before I make good on deserting," Joseph said, stepping into the parlor.

McGuire took his signal and stepped out of the parlor, gathering two handfuls of Joseph's belongings. Joseph turned his attention to the occupants of the room. His expression turned apologetic. Stuart approached him first, showing his pride for the boy.

"Fair journey, boy." They shook hands, "Come back soon." He struck Joseph's arm.

Surprisingly, Mrs. Conrad stepped to him next. She put her arms around him with a warm smile. She pressed her lips to his cheek and wished him luck. Stepping back, she made room for his sister.

Mary took hold of his hands, “Keep an eye on Mike, Joey. I’ll see you soon.”

Joseph took his sister into his arms, holding her to him. He felt the tears fill his eyes. He wanted to stay home and hide in the days of their youth, but he stood there a grown man with no choice. Releasing her, he ruefully smiled.

Lucretia stepped to her son next. She smiled at him, fighting the pain inside. She never wanted to let him go. She hoped he would have preferred to study at William and Mary. However, his path took another turn. Nevertheless, she was still very proud of him.

“I’ll be home soon, Mother,” Joseph said, holding her.

When his mother stepped back, Joseph’s eyes flicked to Emily. She kept her head bent and her back to him. His heart trembled, recalling the hours they spent before dawn making love. He wanted to hold her in his arms again.

“Remember my retirement and hurry back soon as you can,” his father woke him from his memories.

“I will, sir,” Joseph smiled bleakly. He shook his father’s hand, watched him nod and step back.

They all watched him. Joseph turned to the seat where Emily fought to hold back the torrent of tears building in her eyes. He took hold of her hand and led her behind him out of the parlor. He heard his father stay the others, to allow them a private farewell.

Joseph paused long enough to say good bye to Hettie and Isaiah. The closest friend to his jewel hugged him, wiping the tears from her eyes. He shook hands with her husband and told them both to watch over Emily while he stayed away. Clasping hands with Emily again, he led her out picking up his last saddlebag. He shut the door to the flat behind them.

On the steps outside the rented home, Joseph looked to Emily from a lower step. He wore that brave yet pained expression all his own. He looked as handsome as the first time they met. She eyed his uniform. Pride trickled inside her, kept at a decent pace. Two tears slid down her cheeks and she swallowed her terrified sob. Joseph's mouth opened, as if he would speak. Raising a hand he wiped away the tears with his glove.

"I'll come back. I promised. I have so much to do yet."

Not caring who watched from where or what they thought, Emily threw herself into his arms. "I love you," she cried.

Joseph pressed Emily to him. He kissed her temple and her lips. Releasing Emily, he made himself part from her no matter how he desired to do the opposite. He promised to come for her when it ended. He meant to marry her and she swore to wait. He touched the side of her head. She sniffed and blinked back her tears.

Letting go, Joseph turned his back. The door opened and McGuire joined him. Walking down the street, he coached himself not to look back. His step hesitated once, but McGuire placed a strong hand on his arm. Joseph moved forward and mounted his red horse. He looked to McGuire when the other man sat in his saddle. He saw the ruddy Irishman's stern expression. Somehow that old man's expression made him continue.

Joseph stroked the mane of the mare he bought over a year ago, barely recognizing her from the last time. Nothing felt as half as natural as sitting there, except to lay with the woman who stood back on the steps, crying for him.

Unable to prevent himself any longer, Joseph spared a last glance to the townhouse stairs. Lifting his gloved hand, he waved farewell. Emily gripped the iron railing. The tears streamed down her face, but she managed to return the gesture. Joseph turned his mount, followed by McGuire. Together they rode away.

"Hurry home," Emily whispered to his back.

The occupants of the house joined her, watching until the soldiers disappeared.

When Joseph returned to his cavalry company, he reported to a new commander, Phil Sheridan, as a major. Evan had since become the captain of the company on his return and found the brave Michael Conrad turned so many heads that he succeeded to lieutenant in his absence, as well. Further changes included demoting Meade who now took his orders from General Ulysses S. Grant.

After a joyful welcome back, Joseph settled into his new commission, knowing he would stay for the rest of the war under those circumstances. Disturbingly, the Army remained camped close to where he left to visit home. It chilled him to the bone to stand there again, afraid to face the prisons again. Such an obstacle would surely kill him this time.

Sheridan proved an exceptional leader, advancing to his rank quickly. Though he proved a younger man of less experience compared with most other leaders, Joseph still respected him. He posed a terror to the Confederate forces, foiling them again and again. Joseph was at last glad the Union finally found such a man. However, the man at the head of the entire outfit still left him to scratch his head. Joseph found it difficult to imagine taking orders from the gruff General Grant. To his relief, his orders arrived softened by Sheridan.

Sheridan took a strong liking to Joseph and kept him near. Joseph proved his ability to rally the corps around him, like a legendary knight. They followed him blindly, never questioning his orders. They trusted him and thus did Sheridan.

Joseph soon found himself in much the same relationship with General Sheridan, as he experienced under his captain at the beginning, years ago. He rarely thought of him, but now wondered if Braxton still lived. Joseph turned his attention away from such matters. Thoughts of death and loss would not help here.

Over a month since his return, Evan joined him during some free time. They saluted one another, as regulation required, and then they turned away and walked through the camp. Not much time was allowed for fraternizing, but they took it when it came.

"How have things been since your promotion?" Evan asked. "I don't get ta see you anymore."

"Fine, Captain." Joseph smiled, as he used the word, strange in his mouth when referring to his dearest friend.

"Sounds good don't it," Evan laughed. "Michael says hello. He'd a come in too, but he's been ordered on reconnaissance." He paused.

"Goddamn promotions keep me from watching that boy," Joseph cursed.

"He's no green boy, Major. He'll be fine."

"Suppose so," Joseph stopped in front of the tent where he usually took mess with Sheridan.

"Do you think Claire will appreciate my promotion?" Evan asked him.

"How is Miss Healy?"

"Very well," Evan grinned. "And little Davie shows improvement since she started to care for him."

"Your mother must be pleased," Joseph said. Evan nodded his head. "I hope you're hungry. Phil likes a good meal," Joseph said, holding his arm out to invite him in.

The dark haired and bearded man, known to them as General Sheridan sat at the table, looking at a paper and picking his teeth. He pulled the sliver of wood away and sucked at his teeth, paying no attention to the intruders. Joseph addressed and saluted him closely followed by his companion. Sheridan's head lifted and he looked at them with dark assessing eyes. He placed the paper down on the table set with dishes for the meal.

"Good evening Major, Captain," he recognized their salutes. "Have a seat," he directed them to the empty chairs around the table.

Joseph guided Evan to a place that would leave room for the higher ranking officers closer to the General. Once seated other men filtered in and filled up the other seats. Evan and Joseph kept mainly to themselves until the other men engaged them in conversation. Then they both proved the reason for being the officers they became. Sheridan smiled approvingly.

By mid June Joseph fell back into the rhythm of following orders and living as a soldier. He found them to be as deeply changed as himself. They fought in battles, but not with the heart that they showed before. They smashed themselves repeatedly against the Confederate lines late into the fall.

Men fell like chips of stone from a hammered wall. With every death the men lost the enthusiasm they held fame for, as if they were one animal that slowly fell apart. Perhaps the attitude of the North infected them all the way down there. He knew the cries for peace. He heard them while he lay in the hospital and when he lay in the townhouse getting better. He read them in his letters from home and in his sweetheart's words. *Come home and give up this fight. Let the South leave. It will cry to rejoin in a month's time. There is no fight left in us civilian's how can the soldiers keep fighting without our support.* This tone carried on until the end when it finally became satisfied.

In October, during battle, Joseph learned that Colonel Donnelly had been struck by several rifle shots to his chest. Frustrated at the unnecessary loss, Joseph reported to Sheridan as asked. He thought the man wanted him to write home to his wife, knowing Joseph's eloquence with such letters. He took enough practice.

Entering the tent of his commander, Joseph saw Sheridan sit at his desk with a grave expression. He wiped a hand over his bearded chin. Joseph saluted and stood at attention until the man noticed him. He saw him smile slightly at him and haphazardly return the salute.

"Major," he drawled. "At ease."

"Sir," Joseph nodded, falling into an ease stance.

Sheridan handed a paper to his aide and dismissed him with orders. His attention returned to Joseph. He waited in silence until the man exited. His eyes flicked back and forth.

"Colonel Donnelly's dead—he passed this morning from his wounds. Little comfort, we took more prisoners." Sheridan eyed him in silence. Joseph showed no emotion. "I've given it some thought, Major," he added, rising to his feet. "I like you. You're a good leader. A Point man." He paused, sitting on the front edge of his desk and crossing his arms. "After some consideration, I've decided to see you promoted to Colonel. You'll take over Donnelly's duties immediately. Have your tent removed to the proper place. I'll see you at mess, in proper uniform. Dismissed."

"Just like that," Joseph questioned.

"Just like that," Sheridan echoed. "I'll have them bring you the pins and patches, Joe." He paused. "Just don't get shot like Donnelly."

"I don't plan to," he said. "I've too much to do yet."

Sheridan nodded understanding. He heard Joseph talk about his woman. The picture he saw almost made him want to go to Vermont to see for himself. However, his wife would not appreciate the intention.

Joseph took leave of his commander, trembling with excitement and fear. He felt strange, celebrating the promotion and mourning the loss of his previous commander. The matter disappeared from his thoughts when he rounded up the men to move his belongings. While he stood, helping them pitch the tent, a familiar face approached him. The Corporal from his old unit walked toward him wearing a broad grin. He carried a plain paper box in his hand.

"General Sheridan sent you these," he said, saluting and passing the box. Joseph took it with a thank you and proper return. "It's good to have you back, sir."

"Thank you, Corporal. It's good to be back."

❧

An end represented something that Joseph was sure everyone desperately sought. He feared a return to prison and even more feared leaving his Emily alone in life. He prayed hard for the war to end, not for victory or glory, but an end. He wanted to be safe from the horrors that war left them. He wanted his friends and family safe from the ravages shaped by war.

By the end of 1864, his feelings turned stronger. Despite his good fortune, Joseph's mood grew dark again and more morose. No amount of glinting metal on his shoulders could change it. Wanting to throw down his rifle and put his horse in a stall somewhere, his heart gave up the fight, but his body continued forward. The days blessedly passed like leaves falling away in the wind.

When peace came in the spring of 1865, Joseph barely believed his eyes. The Confederates retreated from Richmond, leaving the city open for the Union Army to come in. They besieged the capital before, but never with such force and luck. This was the moment they worked so hard for and so many gave their lives to do.

Under the cold sun, Joseph watched the volley of shots from his position over his battalion. The American flag waved in the distance to his right. Across the field, the brazen Confederate flag defied it. Joseph woke from his concentration, hearing his name called.

"General Sheridan wants a report, sir," Sheridan's Aide said, approaching his red coated mount. He patted Aoife's neck, familiar with her.

"We've taken more prisoners—the rest are pinned down under fire," Joseph told him.

"How many?" The Aide asked.

"Twenty prisoners," he answered. "Captain Howell believes there number three hundred over the ridge, give or take."

The Aide nodded, "I've a feelin this is it."

"We've still taken casualties. Incase you missed that," Joseph said angrily. "Those are blue uniforms on the ground out there."

"Yes, sir." The man saluted and backed away, before leaving.

Joseph looked back to the field, unsure of exactly where Michael or Evan kept themselves right then. He tried not to think about it. The artillery filled his ears, exploding on both sides. He hoped the aide would prove correct in his theory.

◆

Joseph watched with a hungry gaze as Lee entered the home where Grant intended him to surrender to the Union forces. "Unlucky son of a bitch," Joseph thought with a small smile at the man's misfortune.

General Lee, commander of the Confederate States of America's Army, stood in full dress, impressive in every respect, as fit his famous image. Lee deserved more pomp and grandeur than the Union could muster for such a brave opponent. He received nothing. General Grant met him at a table where the treaty was laid out. He still wore the smeared clothes he defeated Lee in. He claimed his trunk was stuck on the back of a wagon, rutted in the mud and lost to him in the fight somewhere for now.

A bitter taste filled Joseph's mouth. His stomach roiled nervously, eager to see the matter done with. He watched the men deal with the propriety of the moment. Acid flooded his chest and the early April day felt suddenly warm. He adjusted the collar of his coat, trying to listen. His ears filled with the sounds of children laughing. He heard Emily call to him.

The moment ended. With the signatures on the paper, the war came to a close and the United States endured.

"This day will go down in history," Joseph heard one of Grant's aides say, as he exited, wearing a satisfied smile.

Not wishing to waste any more time and stand under orders to see to duties of the aftermath, Joseph searched out his tent. Inside, he sat down at his table and wrote out his resignation. From there, he folded the paper and walked to Sheridan's command post. When he entered, the General proudly greeted him. Joseph set the letter on his desk.

"I'm tendering my resignation, sir." Sheridan's smile died and he eyed the paper on his desk. He picked it up, unfolding the page. Joseph continued, "I've need to return home immediately."

Sheridan put the paper down and gave him a doubtful smile, "This Emily must be quite the gem, Colonel."

"Yes, sir. She is," Joseph smiled.

"I'll not deny you, Colonel," he said, folding his hands on his desk surface. "As far as I'm concerned, you are on temporary leave until the discharge is final. My best to you, Joseph, for a good life. I hope I've the chance to see you again, one day."

"You know where to call," Joseph smiled, touching his hat. Smiling at his new hero, he added, "Thank you, sir."

❧

Moving through the crowd of men and women, filling his home, Joseph rejoined Michael and Evan with drink for each. He smiled at them and they struck their glasses together. Tipping up the vessels containing the fine scotch, they drank. Michael grimaced and wiped his mouth. Joseph and Evan broke a smile and fell to laughter at his expression. Patting his shoulder, they harassed him for his lack of taste.

"You'd think you'd be used to that by now, boy," Evan teased.

"You forget my family," Michael said, feeling a burning gut.

"Colonel Maynard," a voice interrupted their moment.

Joseph turned to see McFadden smiling at him. He leaned on his cane and looked healthier compared with the last time they met. However, Joseph cared little. His eyes took on a dark glare.

"What exactly do you want in my home, Mr. McFadden?"

"I've come to apologize to you," McFadden said. He held out his hand.

"You nearly took my life from me," Joseph said angrily. "If I had never seen you again, it would've been a lucky day for you." He stepped toward him and the man hobbled backward. "I suggest you leave now, before I decide to remove your other foot and feed it to you. My sister and my family are no concern of yours. Don't make me escort you from the property like the last time."

McFadden hung his head with the shame of his actions. He looked to where Mary stood by her parents, enjoying herself in a good laugh. He looked back to the three angry men, ready to throw him into the street like a vagabond. What had he expected?

"I'll leave on my own," McFadden rasped. "Tell Mary I'm sorry."

"I won't tell her anything," Joseph said.

McFadden nodded and turned. He hobbled out pursued by all three Union soldiers. They made sure he left the house. When the door closed on the intruder, they turned back to the party.

"What about now?" Michael looked to Joseph desperately.

"What about now?" Joseph pretended not to know what his friend meant. Michael looked crushed.

"I gotta ask now," Michael pleaded.

"Do you think the time is right?" Joseph asked Evan.

"Now? I don't know. Shouldn't he wait? What if she says no?" He paused, grimacing. "I think she might say no."

"Forget you," Michael said swinging his hand at them. He turned away and disappeared in the crowd of revelers.

Joseph crossed his arms and watched him go. He shook his head and laughed, "I'm leaving in the morning to see Emily."

"Good," Evan said. "I wanna get home."

"We better go help him," Joseph said, stepping back into the party. "Did you accept my father's offer?"

"I want to see about Claire first," Evan said. "I may have a family to consider, Colonel."

The men smiled at each other. Together, they reached the ballroom just in time to hear Michael's speech.

"Now—I'd like to ask Mr. Maynard something very important," Michael said, putting his hand on the man's shoulder. "Would you honor me with your blessing, as I ask you for your daughter's hand in marriage?"

Smiling, John patted the younger man's shoulder, "I thought no one would ever ask. At least, no one worthy." He looked at Michael, "It would be this family's honor to see Mary as your wife, Lieutenant."

The two men shook hands. Then, Michael drew a box from his jacket pocket. Mary joined him and he bent on one knee. Looking into her face, he asked her to marry him. He slid the ring on her tiny finger and waited for her to speak. She trembled and sobbed, barely able to answer. She accepted his proposal and he stood, kissing each of her hands. He drew her close and kissed her on the mouth for the first time in front of anyone.

"Very nice," Joseph murmured. He lifted his glass and called out, "To Michael and Mary—to Blue Honor."

"Blue Honor," Evan echoed.

Michael grinned at them, standing beside Mary.

෴

The bright lavender blossoms of the lilac bushes bobbed in the wind. Emily scrapped her trowel in the soil around the oak tree. She knelt on the stone ring, meaning to plant the summer flower seeds. Her pale brow sweated from the work in the afternoon sun. She leaned back her white capped head and brushed her sleeve across her forehead. Emily drew a deep breath, feeling more tired than ever.

Emily's gloved hand dropped to her side and she looked at the shallow circles she etched there. She wondered when Joseph would come for her. A year passed since she last saw him. Her father told her weeks ago the two armies signed for peace. Perhaps Joseph never meant to come home. He sent no word since his letter a couple of weeks ago. Then, he sat in the middle of orders he saw no end to. Her eyes searched the sky a moment. Then she returned to her work.

Setting her trowel in the basket at her side, she picked up a packet of seeds. She pulled off her gloves and dropped the packet to her lap. She dropped the gloves on the garden tool in the basket. Emily sighed and picked up the seeds. She opened the top of the envelope and bent to sprinkle the small seeds in the shallow trench. Eventually, she spread all the seeds in each trench. In this method, she ignored her thoughts.

Emily turned to drop the empty packet in the basket with the others. Out of the corner of her eye, she saw someone standing near the entrance. She froze, seeing the neatly groomed beard around the familiar mouth. Her eyes lifted to the penetrating russet gaze. She felt her heart skip and her stomach flip. He wore a civilian suit. Her eyes filled with tears, knowing he stood free of the military and had finally come to bring her home.

Emily rose to her feet quickly and dashed to him with her arms out. Joseph caught her up in his hold. Closing her eyes, Emily lay against him, remembering how good it felt. Her tears sprung from her eyes and she trembled, fighting them.

"Hettie swore you'd come back," Emily told him. "I didn't think—not after the prison."

Joseph released her to look in her eyes. He held her arms gently in his hands to keep her close, "I made you a promise." Releasing her arms, Joseph dug in his pocket. "I just wanted to ask if you'd do me the honor of being my wife," Joseph said, lowering to his knee before her. He showed her the smoky blue box in his hands. "I stopped in New York on my way up. I hope you like it."

Swallowing his words and her tears, "Well—it isn't me you should ask. It'd be proper of you to ask my father."

"I want to know if you will," Joseph said. "I'll ask your daddy when I'm sure of you."

Biting her lip for her harsh words, Emily tried to stop shaking. She smiled, but the tears started again. She watched him open the box and reveal her ring. She watched the clear sapphire glint, surrounded in sparkling diamonds.

"I like weddings," Emily cried, feeling him slip the ring on her finger. "I haven't been to a wedding in ages."

Joseph looked up at her and smiled. He rose to his feet and closed his hand over hers.

"I'll ask Mr. Conrad then."

Emily smiled at him, touching his face. She placed her head against his chest and listened to his heartbeat. He kept his promise.

The End.

Historical Sources:

Cavada, Lieut.-Colonel U.S.V.F.F. Libby Life: Experiences of a Prisoner of War In Richmond V.A. 1863-1864. Philadelphia: J.B. Lippincott & Co., 1865

Commanger, Henry Steele. The New Book Of Knowledge, Vol. 11. New York: Crolier Inc., 1967

De Joinville, The Prince. The Army of The Potomac. New York: Anson D.F. Randolph, 1862

Microsoft Encarta 1997 Encyclopedia CD ROM. Microsoft, 1997

McPherson, James M. Battle Cry of Freedom: The Civil War Era. New York: Ballantine Books, 1988

Ken Burns, "Civil War Journal", PBS (Public Broadcasting System)

OPA, Dr. S. Grove, West Point Military Academy

Acknowledgements

Very special thanks to Professor Richard Kendall of the University at Albany who first took up this project with me as an independent study of the United States Civil War. I hope you enjoy the final piece! Indebted thanks to Doreen DeCrescenzo and Linda Williams for editing and your gracious eyes. Special thanks to those who kept the writer going through all the ups and downs.

Made in the USA